D13645536

FOR SURE

France Daigle

Translated by Robert Majzels

ARACHNIDE

© Éditions du Boréal, Montreal, Canada, 2011
English translation copyright © 2013 by Robert Majzels

All rights reserved. No part of this publication may be reproduced or transmitted in any form or by any means, electronic or mechanical, including photocopying, recording, or any information storage and retrieval system, without permission in writing from the publisher.

First published as *Pour sûr* in 2011 by Les Éditions du Boréal.
First published in English in 2013 by House of Anansi Press Inc.

This edition published in 2013 byy
House of Anansi Press Inc.
110 Spadina Avenue, Suite 801
Toronto, ON, M5V 2K4
Tel. 416-363-4343
Fax 416-363-1017
www.houseofanansi.com

Distributed in Canada by
HarperCollins Canada Ltd.
1995 Markham Road
Scarborough, ON, M1B 5M8
Toll free tel. 1-800-387-0117

Distributed in the United States by
Publishers Group West
1700 Fourth Street
Berkeley, CA 94710
Toll free tel. 1-800-788-3123

House of Anansi Press is committed to protecting our natural environment. As part of our efforts, the interior of this book is printed on paper that contains 100% post-consumer recycled fibres, is acid-free, and is processed chlorine-free.

17 16 15 14 13 1 2 3 4 5

Library and Archives Canada Cataloguing in Publication Data

Daigle, France
[Pour sûr. English]
For sure / France Daigle ; Robert Majzels, translator.

Translation of: Pour sûr.
Also issued in electronic format.
ISBN 978-1-77089-204-0

I. Majzels, Robert, 1950- II. Title. II. Title: Pour sûr. English.

PS8557.A423P6813 2013   C843'.54   C2012-906279-0

Library of Congress Control Number: 2012949100

Cover design: Bill Douglas
Type design and typesetting: Alysia Shewchuk

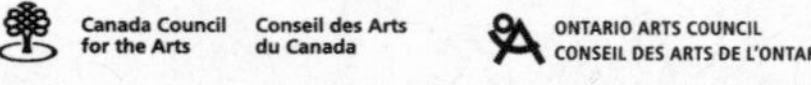

We acknowledge for their financial support of our publishing program the Canada Council for the Arts, the Ontario Arts Council, and the Government of Canada through the Canada Book Fund. We acknowledge the financial support of the Government of Canada, through the National Translation Program for Book Publishing, for our translation activities.

Printed and bound in Canada

Thanks to all who've
helped me out and that's a
lot of folks for sure

To Berthe, whom I could
never thank enough

CHAPTER 1

What he thought of as his position was, in fact, an adaptation of everything that [...] he encountered.

Daniele Del Giudice,
Atlas occidental 1.144.1
Éditions du Seuil, 1987 Epigraphs

"Dad, go on and sing dat thing you'll be doing after."

"Afterrrr..."

Terry replied absently, as he gathered up the clothes strewn about the room.

"You know! After, when we'll be sleeping."

Terry was at a loss: they'd given the boy permission to go to bed an hour later than usual, and then he'd been treated to a long and entirely new story—a story with a moral to boot!—and in spite of all that he didn't seem tired. Normally, he'd have fallen asleep four or five minutes into the story. But no, he'd listened to the story of Souricette right to the end, and now he was asking for a song! Did Terry have a momentary doubt that Étienne might be troubled or worried about something? In any case, it had been a busy day and Dad was more than ready for a bit of peace and quiet. So he wasted no time in doing what had to be done to get it.

"You mean Aragon's *Blues?*" 2.1.12

"Ya, Aragonz." Chansons

The Beaufort occurs in Scrabble when the two most valuable letters in a word both land on triple-letter-value squares. To score a little Legendre, one must place one's most valuable letter on a double-letter-value square and another letter on a double-word-value square. Same idea for the big Legendre: the word counts
3.4.11 double but the most valuable letter falls on a
Scrabble triple-letter-value square.

"Souricette got it into her head dat she wanted to be a laboratory mouse when she growed up. Well, so she went off to university and after dat she found herself a job in one of dem big companies wot make all sorts of pills. Well, on account of she was pretty sharp and scored real high on all de tests, it got so dose tests dey was givin' her got harder an' harder. Souricette was mighty proud, I can tell ya. She liked dat dey tot she was smart and all, see. Well, she was mighty proud de day de bosses decided to pick de six smartest mice — because dat meant Souricette fer sure — fer a right important test, the X-3X-X3-X test. An' you should know dat dose tests with de number tree in dem, like X-3X-X3-X, well, dose was de most dangerous.

Thinking Étienne was asleep, Terry cut off the story, but he was quickly obliged to take it up again when Étienne moved his legs, which was the boy's way of signalling that he wasn't asleep yet.

"Well alright den. On account of dey'd picked only six mice an' her name being Souricette — like French fer mouse *souris*, and *sept* being de French fer seven, see? — well, Souricette had a kind of achin' in 'er belly just tinkin' 'bout dat test. Someting was boderin' 'er alright, but she'd no idea wot. At last, comes de day of de big test. Dey took all dem six mice an' dey put 'em in a labyrinth. You remember wot labyrinth is don't ya? Course ya do. Well, dis 'ere particular labyrinth was split in two, see, wid one side all warm, and d'oder no heat at all. So tree of dem mice lands up in de heated part an' d'oder tree in de part dat's not heated. Ting is doh, dey'd gone an' put a bit of milk in de unheated part, see, but dere weren't no milk on de heated side. An' why d'you suppose dat was? On account of de company bosses was wanting to find out wot was more important to a mouse: stayin' warm, or havin' a bite to eat. Dose bosses had in der minds dat mice and wee children was more or less de same, an' what a mouse would do, a little boy or girl would do de same."

Here, Terry paused again, but he was not unhappy to see Étienne move his legs, because he himself had become engrossed in this story he was making up as he went along.

"Come two weeks, de company bosses had der answer, only 'twasn't de answer wot dey'd been expectin'. Alright, hold on now. Dey found all de mice was dead, starved to death all together on de warm side of de labyrinth. Even Souricette was dead. So…de moral of dis story is det: when a body feels sometin' deep inside of him, he's got to pay heed, see. Take Souricette: she was one of dem six mice, even doh her name had the sound of *sept* or seven in it…More dan likely she wouldn't have died if she'd paid heed to what was boderin' her. More dan likely she'd have known not to be part of dat test. She had a feelin' down in 'er belly, what some calls intuition."

4.37.7
Animal Tales

> Noise, Sex, Axing, Gaunt, Quill, Bliss, Spy, Bag,
> Drag, Zinc, Zone, Cane, Cave, Ajar, Hurrah, Fey,
> Waxing, Wig, Ozone, Debut, Hide, Puke, Feed,
> Tuft, Lodge, Yew, Tool, Mist, Puker, Morons,
> Wok, En. For a total of 320 and 205 points.

5.4.1
Scrabble

"Wot colour was Souricette, Dad?"

The tone of Terry's reply was such that it put an end to any further questions. The song was sung, the contract sealed.

"Grey."

"Awh."
6.2.2 "G'night now."
Colours "G'night, Dad."

The American architect Alfred Mosher Butts invented the game of Scrabble when he was unemployed during the Great Depression. Over a period of 20 years, he tried to commercialize his invention under different names before submitting it for patent under the name Scrabble in 1948. Since then, more than 100
7.99.3 million games of Scrabble have been sold
Names worldwide, in 35 languages.

Terry invents most of the animal tales he tells the children based on details he picks up here and there in his daily life. Sometimes he challenges himself to come up with a moral to the story, so long as the kids are still
8.37.1 awake by then. He prefers not to waste morals — which
Animal Tales are not always easy to concoct — on a sleeping child.

In her novel *1953: Chronicle of a Birth Foretold,* the Acadian author France Daigle makes no mention of the sale of 312,000 games of
9.45.3 Scrabble that year, an average of 6,000 per
Useless Details week.

"Wot ya doin', Mum?"
"Changing the time."
"On account of your not wantin' to be late?"
"No, I'll be late all the same. Only we've got to change
10.93.6 the time twice a year. Everybody does it."
Time "Awh."

Citing the novelist Maupassant as an example, the French dictionary *Le Nouveau Petit Robert* clearly recognizes the existence of the popular

pronoun *y*, *popular* referring to a word or expression the upper classes would never use. The dictionary explains that *y* was first used to replace the personal pronoun *lui* (him) before going on to supplant the pronoun *il* (he) in both the singular and plural. The *y* can be found in the works of Balzac and Anouilh. Balzac even used the interrogative *c'est-y*, as in *c'est-y vrai?* (is it true?) instead of the more proper *est-ce que c'est vrai*. In Acadia, the pronoun *y* is still widely used. The feminine *alle*, old French for *elle* (she), becomes simply *a* when it precedes
a word beginning with a consonant, as in *a* 11.30.2
chante (she sings). Chiac

"Wot was I doin' down der? Workin' a machine wot cuts puzzles is wot. Dey had me in a wee booth wid a great big screen, but sure an' 'twas like I's drivin' a lawnmower in a field. I was twistin' an' turnin' to cut around dose pieces. In the beginnin' I don't mind tellin' ya, it gave me de heebie jeebies. De design was all laid out on
de screen; I only had to follow it. Ya don't believe me? 12.130.8
Ask Tony over der. Eh, Tony?" Work

Croup [24], R(o)il [6], Don(s) [15], Crou(p)ier [12], Qu(e)en [35], (Q)uai [13], V(i)able [13], Comi(c) [22], Ja(m) [28], (B)ee [15], (O)rnate [12], Swea(t) [30], (D)ean [10], Ye(s), [24], Pe(w) [14], Hi(e) [21], (J)unta [14], (H)oeing [49], Stooge [21], (S)im [24], F(i)x [26], (E)ked [14], Y(e)t [14], (O)ld [19], Ooz(e) [13], (F)a [23], Wi(n) [6], (W)ig [9], L(a)v [8], Ga(s) [5], (o)r [2], Booz(e)d [21], T(o) [2], T(o)ld [5].
One player left with 2 points in her hand, for a 13.4.2
total of 257 and 314 points. Scrabble

It was Ludmilla who introduced Terry to the great Léo

Ferré's recording of Aragon's poems. She brought the disc to the bookstore one day, thinking it would make good background music for browsing. Terry immediately fell under its spell.

14.1.1 Chansons

"Well alright den. From now on, yer de one in charge of music."

> Beginning with Gutenberg's invention — more accurately an innovation rather than an invention — and for three centuries after that, the printing of texts using moveable type would be referred to as typography, a word that refers to both the techniques and process of printing and the style of letters and layout of texts.

15.10.2 Typography

"So dey tells me I's to follow de green dots to some place where I takes a number and waits me turn. Well, at de end of de green dots, dere was a whole lot of bodies already waitin'. So I figures I've plenty o' time to go fer me blood test 'fore they calls me name. Over at de bloodtests, most times, it's right quick. So off I goes to bloodtests, but when I gets der, tings was a whole lot slower dan usual. On account of one of der staff was sick, is wot dey tol' me. Anyhow, I could see 'twas goin' to take a whole lot longer dan I tot, so I says to meself, I'd best go back over to dem green spots, but right when I's liftin' me arse off the seat, what d'ya know dey calls me name. So in I go! All dey wanted was a wee tube full. More's de pity 'cause it were mighty fine lookin' an' a bright shiny red. Anyhow, by the time I gets meself back to de green dots, dey'd already called me name over der a couple of times. De nurses was kind doh, and dey lets me troo all de same. Only, dat didn't go down so good wid de folks sittin' der waitin' on dere turn. One of dem ups and asks me where I bin, like she knew me! I didn't say nuttin'. Anyway, 'twas written up der on de wall, TAKE A LETTER AND SIT DOWN, and dat's just wot I done, I'd taken a letter and sat me arse down."

16.15.11 Unidentified Monologues

> *L'Officiel du jeu Scrabble*®, the *Larousse* dictionary for francophone Scrabble, always capitalizes the name of the game and follows it with the registered trademark symbol ®. As for the lexigraphs of the *Robert* dictionary, the word *scrabble* refers both to a registered trademark and to a board game requiring players to make words using randomly selected letters, but in
> the *Robert*, the word is always lower case and 17.4.3
> without the ®. Scrabble

Terry handed the telephone to Ludmilla.

"It's for Mrs. Didot..."

Although Didot Books was more than four years old, there were still a few customers who thought that Didot was the name of the foreign woman with whom Terry had partnered to open the business. At first, Terry had made an effort to clear up the confusion:

"She's called Ludmilla Bellâme; dat's wot 'er parents named 'er. Didot, dat's a historical-like name fer books."

"Wouldn't dat be Diderot?"

"Naw. Diderot, dat's anudder fellow. Writer or philosopher more like. Well, really he's a bit o' boat."

"Dat's wot I tot. De *Encyclopedia* and all dat..."

"Didot, he was more a printer. Designed letters an' de spaces betwixt words an' betwixt lines, an' de like. In dose days, printing was more like an art."

"And when was dat den?"

"Around de same time as de Deportation." 18.8.2

"Ya don't say!" Didot Books

> Judging by a rapid impromptu poll taken among 102 Université de Moncton students, grey is not a particularly popular colour. The study on colour reception sought to determine if people associate specific colours to individual letters of the alphabet. The students turned

out to be eager participants — anything to get away from the official curriculum. The poll revealed that 28 subjects imagined the *a* as red, 21 saw it as yellow, 10 as white, 9 as orange, 8 as blue, 7 as green, 5 as pink, 4 as silver, and 3 as aqua. Two admitted to seeing nothing at
19.2.5 all, and the last 5 saw the *a* as beige, grey, gold,
Colours violet, and auburn respectively.

One day, when he was alone at home — Carmen having gone to see her parents with the children — Terry had launched into Aragon's *Blues*, and discovered that he knew all the words. This was a surprise since he'd made no effort to memorize them. He took pleasure then in
20.1.2 singing the song by heart, and even enjoyed belting it out
Chansons without the obstacle of a guitar in his arms.

The manuscript-like design of the earliest typographic characters can be explained by the fact that books at the time the printing press first appeared were still being copied by hand. In 1766, Fournier the younger classified typeface styles into roman, italic, bâtarde, cursive, *lettres de somme*, textura or *lettres de forme*, and Gothic Modern or *lettres tourneures*. But it was a Thibaudeau — given name Francis — who drew up what we consider today to be the first true classification of typefaces; this classification is based on the historical importance of the serif, a horizontal line of varying thickness at the base and head of a letter. Thibaudeau defined four general families of typefaces: sans-serif typefaces (Antiques family), rectangular or slab-serif typefaces (Egyptian family), triangular-serif typefaces (Roman Elzévirs family), and linear or hairline serif typefaces (Roman Didot family). Francis Thibaudeau also identified a number of sub-families. This was in 1921. 21.10.1 Typography

"Ee says ee don't take drugs, I asked him. And I believes him, I do. Doesn't seem de type. All de same, ee's fed up wid school, fed up wid baseball, don't like de girls, don't want to come up to de country, don't want to go off to Europe, don't want his licence..."

"Might be ee's got a real disease, sometin' physical."

"Dis evenin', at supper, lookin' at 'im, I couldn't help tinkin' suicide. Ruined a perfectly good stew, ee did." 22.22.10 Overheard Conversations

The 102 students, the vast majority of whom were women, were not asked to specify the shade of the colour they saw. For example, the red in question may have been nacarat, alizarin, scarlet, aniline, strawberry, crushed strawberry, raspberry, rubicond, crimson, poppy, ruby, lobster, crawfish, cardinal, dahlia, vermilion, English red, cherry, tomato, lust, ruddy, blood red, blood orange, purple, gules, peony, conclave, orangey, Tierra del Fuego, or picador, just to name a few. 23.2.6 Colours

Terry was as surprised as anyone to discover he not only had a voice, but also the ability to sing. Well, the ability to sing Léo Ferré singing Aragon, anyway. Lately he'd been amusing himself by singing some of the songs on the record for the kids when Carmen was at work. He was still far too shy about his new talent to sing in front of Carmen. 24.1.4 Chansons

Over time, printers and typographers became distinct from editors. For example, from François Didot (born in 1689) to Alfred Firmin Didot (dead in 1913), four generations of Didots laboured in various printing

related fields. Whereas François the patriarch was known to have edited all the works of the abbot Prévost, his descendants were particularly inventive in the fields of typography, printing, and paper production. In the end, with the publication of the Didot *French Commercial Directory*, they were no longer editors per se,
25.10.3 Typography
since editing is first and foremost intellectual work.

26.31.2 Questions with Answers

"Because?"
"Because, because."

Taloned 59, I(o)ta 6, (S)ize 31, (Z)en 12, Sev(e) n 16, (V)ie 10, H(a)m 15, (T)ow 17, Ble(w) 9, Re(l)at 18, Song 24, Jet(s) 28, P(e)r 15, Lai(r) 12, Jog 33, P(e)n 14, Fin(d) 18, Ra(f)t 26, Aio(l) i 5, Wef(t) 30, Qu(a) 24, L(e)g 16, Bo(a) 19, (a) xe 10, Hou(r) 25, Etc(h) 18, V(e)t 18, Tauru(s) 10, Idio(t) 10, D(i)kes 30, To(w)y 9, (G)am, 12.
27.4.4 Scrabble
One player is left with a letter worth 4 points, for a total of 326 and 269 points.

"Well take fer example: 'She gave him what for.' We say 'whatfer.' Den why don't we write *whatfer*? De way
28.88.10 Freedom
we says an' hears it? Same as we write defer and refer..."
"Sure. Why not, I'd like to know."

In the case of the letter *a*, only one of the 102 respondents named a colour the least bit out of the ordinary: auburn. All the other colours (except for the response "none," if "none" can be considered a colour) could be found in the original HTML pallet created for web site designers. Although orange, beige, and gold were not among the list of coded colours, the designers had the option to use them by typing out the name of the colour. This was not the case for auburn (not to mention "none"). 29.2.4 Colours

He was a smash hit with Étienne and Marianne. The two kids were hypnotized by their dad, who had gone from warbling while he prepared the meal to suddenly belting out a song in a voice they did not recognize and mysterious words whose meanings they could only guess thanks to Terry's gestures and facial expressions, which helped to make the meaning clear. The two children were dimly aware of witnessing something new being created before their eyes. At the end of this première presentation, Étienne stood agape, having never expected Terry to reply in such grand fashion to the simple question:

"Wot're you singin', Dad?"

With his Captain Haddock apron tied around his waist, Terry had seized the moment. He'd turned down the heat under the hamburger steak sizzling in the pan, raised the wooden spoon to capture the kids' attention, opened the floodgates and sang: *I sing to pass the time / What little of it remains to me / The way we draw on a frosted window / The way we gladden our heart*... which pleased him because these opening lines immediately invoked pleasant things like drawing, a glad heart, and skipping stones across a pond. He also liked the word *petit* at the beginning of the next verse, because it allowed him to reply more directly to his son's question. 30.1.3 Chansons

AUBURN \'c:ben, -be:n adjective. IME. Orig., of a yellowish- or brownish-white colour. Now, of a golden- or reddish-brown colour. (Used esp. of a person's hair.)

ORIGIN: Old French *albome, auborne,* from medieval Latin *albumus* whitish, from Latin *albus* white: later assoc. with *brown* by false etymology (through forms with metathesis).

31.11.4 Appropriations

MAHOGANY me;hogeni adjective. Of the colour of polished mahogany: rich reddish-brown. Origin unknown. Excerpt from *Oxford English Dictionary*.

32.8.1 Didot Books

Terry had wanted to hang a large artistic poster of various styles of type at the entrance to the bookstore, by the cash register. The poster was meant to refer to the origin of the bookstore's name: Didot.

"Wot does you tink, den? Does she come across too... intellectual? Wouldn' want folks to tink we was full o' ourselves, or de like."

"Naw, she's fine. A whole lot o' class. Folks'll like her, fer sure."

Terry knew he could trust Zed's opinion.

"I likes where de letters is all piled up in de corner down der."

Terry was particularly proud of the poster, especially the way the graphic designer—a fellow named Babin from Dieppe—had taken up his suggestions. Zed confirmed his opinion:

"Naw, I'm tellin' ya, she's right proper."

33.45.5 Useless Details

In her novel *1953: Chronicle of a Birth Foretold*, the Acadian author France Daigle makes no mention of that year's publication of the first edition of the *Dictionnaire Robert* by a small publishing house founded by Paul Robert, with an inheritance from his family, who'd owned an orange plantation.

"Wot was ee wantin' den?"

"He was askin' if we eats *chiard* every day."

"Wot fer? Are dey in de habit of eatin' potato hash every day, den?"

"Naw. Dey never even seen *chiard* 'fore now."

"I figured. Gumbo's wot dey eats."

"Every day?" 34.30.4

"Dunno, do I. Go an' ask 'em, why dontcha." Chiac

> A quick overview of the chromatic dictionary of the web site pourpre.com yielded 33 names of colours that, like auburn, begin with the letter *a*. In French, 12 percent of the 281 colours listed in that dictionary begin with the letter *a*. Only the letter *c* accounts for more: the 48 colours beginning with the third letter of the alphabet amount to 17 percent of the entries in this dictionary. By contrast, the English Wikipedia site lists 36 names of colours beginning with the letter *a*. This amounts to slightly more than 4 percent of the 869 colours listed. This number is surpassed by 9 letters including the *c* which, just as in French, accounts for the most names of colours: 91 or slightly more than 10 percent of the total.

35.2.3 Colours

"Well, if dem's useless details like she says, why does dey have to keep goin' on about 'em, I'd like to know."

"Proper question."

. . .

"Probably because, in absolute terms, useless don't exist." 36.45.9

"Now yer pullin' me leg." Useless Details

> Cited without permission from *Webster's Third New International Dictionary*©:
>
> **PLAGIARIST** *n:* (lat. plagiarus, from the gr.). one who plagiarizes: one guilty of literary or artistic theft.
>
> **PLAGIARISM** n.: an act or instance of plagiarizing.
>
> **PLAGIARIZE** v. t.: to steal and pass off as one's own (the ideas or words of another).

37.11.10 Appropriations

It was quite late by the time Terry could finally relax and review the events of his day. He wondered if Étienne's desire to put off sleep as long as possible wasn't a sign of some sort of existential anxiety. Now he regretted not having had a father's reflex to take up the issue more
38.13.1 closely and on the spot. Was he already becoming one of
Paternity those blasé parents?

> With the emergence of typography in the middle of the fifteenth century, the trades of printer, typographer, editor, bookseller, and stationer became intertwined and interelated with other vocations, such as philosopher, author, and lexicographer. Geoffroy Tory, who was born in Bourges around 1480 and died in Paris in 1533, was at once a humanist, author, professor, bookseller-editor, printer, designer, theorist of typography, and a linguist. He was a strong advocate for the use of the apostrophe and added the cedilla to the French *c* when pronounced as *s*, a distinction he found both useful and appealing. Not content with perfecting the shapes of typefaces, Geoffroy Tory also weighed in on their correct pronunciation,
> 39.10.4 thereby contributing to the standardisation of
> Typography a hitherto highly diversified French language.

"Dad, did you change yer time?"

"My time fer wot?"

"Not yer time fer sometin', just yer time."

Terry looked up from his newspaper, struck by what his son had said.

"Yer right! Naw, I never did change it, good ting yer remindin' me!"

Terry immediately started fiddling with his watch.

"Is it true den dat everybody does it?"

"Change de time? Well, I can't say if everybody in de

'ole wide world does it, but fer sure a whole lot of folks do. All the folks in Canada anyhow."

"But why? Is de time we've got no good no more?"

"Well we got to line up wid de sun, don't we. See, in summer, de sun comes up earlier, so dat's good fer de gardens. In winter, gets dark long about supper time, and dat's de time folks come in fer de night, 'cause it's too cold. Not like summer evenin's when it's nice to stay outdoors."

Étienne nodded; then he looked outside.

"Well den, today, is it winter or summer?"

40.93.7
Time

> The inventor Butts (1900–1993) decided on the value and quantity of each letter in his game based on an in-depth study of letters found on the front page of the *New York Times*.

41.7.6
Useful Details

Even though Terry does fairly well with his children, fatherhood remains something of a puzzle to him. Sure, he followed Carmen's pregnancies closely, and he was there by her side through both births, but even doing his part in all the housework, including bringing up the kids, Terry feels fatherhood is not so easily achieved.

"Lucky fer me you gives me a part to play, you make out like I's important."

"You are important!"

"I know, I knows it. Dat's not what I was meaning to say. Only it's like fer you it comes automatic like. Being yer de mudder, 'tis like magic. Whereas in my case, well..."

Carmen, uncomfortable with this apparent lack of balance, sought to encourage Terry.

"Sure it looks easier fer me. Sometimes just my being the mother seems like enough. Only kids need more dan dat, don't dey. You take 'em all sorts of places out in de world, and you explain dem all kinds of things. Me, well sometimes I can't be boddered, or I don't even think to do it."

Carmen's words went some way toward reassuring Terry.

"Well, you know how it used to be: dads just standin' there and decidin' what was good fer de family. They never did take de time to care fer each child, did dey. Nowadays things are different. An' aren't you de perfect example of how they've changed for de better?"

"We've a couple books 'bout dat at de bookstore. I've not really looked at 'em doh."

And with that, Terry slipped between the sheets, and Carmen completed her thought:

"Don't forget, really all that yer doing now'll add up
42.13.2 later on."
Paternity "So long as it adds up sometime, I suppose."

> A hodge-podge of seventeenth century and modern French, of English words pronounced in an English accent, English words pronounced in a French accent, and a syntactical mix drawn from both languages, Chiac is predominantly the lingua franca of the Acadians of southeastern New Brunswick. In spite of its echos of First Nation speech (Shediac, Kouchibougouac, Tabusintac) nothing is less certain
> 43.30.1 than the origin of the word Chiac. And still to-
> Chiac day, to speak Chiac evokes a kind of dishonour.

"You don't remember the X-3X-X3-X test?"

Marianne had to admit she had no idea what her brother was talking about.

"De story of Souricette! You knows it, *souris sept*: mouse number seven? Wid all dose mice dat died in de warm half of de labyrinth!"

Marianne wanted very much to please her brother, but she had absolutely no memory of his story.

44.133.5 "Ee told us dat story I don't know how many times! I
The Future can't believe you've gone and forgot it!"

> The letter *b* might very well blush with pride at the number of colours that begin with *b* in pourpre.com's chromatic dictionary: 26, or 9 percent, of the names of colours defined as real on the site. Together, the letters *a*, *b*, and *c* begin 107 of the 281 colours in this dictionary. Which amounts to saying that, in French, 38 percent of the colours listed in that particular dictionary begin with 12 percent of the letters of the alphabet. According to Wikipedia, *a*, *b*, and *c* are the first letters of 200 out of 869 names of colours in English, or 23 percent. Thus, in English, it appears the first three letters of the alphabet carry 15 percent less weight in introducing colours than in French. 45.3.3 Statistics

The second time Terry sang for his children happened one evening while he was scribbling something at the kitchen table, waiting for the kids' bedtime. When Étienne approached him to ask what he was doing, Louis Aragon's *Blues* sprang to mind. Hearing the first notes of the song, Marianne joined her brother, and as Terry got to the bit *We can't all be Cézanne / We'll settle for much less*, he could feel his children were as enthralled as they'd been the first time. He delivered the lines *Young man what do you fear / You'll grow old no matter what...* in the benevolent tone of a father instructing his offspring, and carried that attitude through to the end of the song.

"Youse like it when yer dad sings, don't ya?"

The two kids stood wide-eyed and waiting for more.

"Well, it's our secret, OK? A secret just fer de tree of us, right?"

And to make sure the children had understood him, he kneeled down to their height to explain again how it was their secret and that they couldn't tell anyone about how he sang for them.

"Sometime soon, I'll be singin' to surprise yer mum,

see, but in the meanwhile, it'll be our secret, right?"

Marianne signalled her agreement by hopping up and down. Étienne, for his part, did not seem to want to commit himself one way or the other. Terry leaned closer:

"It's on account of me wanting to learn a special song just for yer mum, see. One dat's not a bad bit nice..."

46.1.5 This seemed to satisfy Étienne, who allowed the secret
Chansons to take root within.

> According to the web site of the Department of Statistics and Computer Data Processing, University Institute of Technology of the Pays de l'Adour—at Pau in France—statisticians are indispendable collaborators of decision makers in any modern economy. Statisticians apply their mathematical expertise to analyze problems and propose solutions to real situations, as well as create models and digital anal-
> 47.11.2 yses of these solutions, which are then used to
> Appropriations produce reports accessible to the layman.

"Take de word *good*. Bugs me the way dey writes the Chiac for *bien* as *b-e-n*. Why don't dey spell it *b-e-i-n*? Dat's de way we says it? And dat way it'd match up wid *rein* or kidney, what sounds jus' like *ben*."

"I suppose it's on account of *ben* spelled *b-e-n* is what's in de dictionary."

"*Ben* spelled *b-e-n*: dat's in de dictionary?"

"Well, sort of. Nowadays dey calls it an old slang expression, but back in de old days *ben* was a real word. Comes from de Latin *bene* don't it, like in benefit, benevolent..."

...

"Anyways, even *rein* for kidney used to be written *r-e-*
48.33.8 *n*. Wot makes good sense, on account of de adjective's
Chiac Lesson *rénal*, isn't it?"

> Francis Thibaudeau's classification of typefaces opened the way to several other systems, including, in 1954, a classification devised by Maximilien Vox, which was adopted by the Association typographique internationale (International Typographic Association) or ATYPI. The Vox classification includes 11 categories of letters: Humanistic, Garaldic, Transitional, Didonic, Mechanistic, Lineal,
> Incised, Script, Manual, Black Letter, and 49.10.5
> Non-Latins. Typography

"Did ya see dis, Marianne? De potatoes is comin' up."

Marianne was walking hand-in-hand with her dad. A pink line encircled her smile, while the lollipop she was transfering from one side of her mouth to the other occupied all her attention.

"And o'er here in front, dose are beans."

Terry was not blind to Marianne's lack of interest.

"All along back der are de onions."

Marianne took a bite out of her lollipop.

"Over on de udder side're de animals. Let's take a look what's o'er der."

Marianne finished off her lollipop, and offered Terry the chewed up white stick.

"You wants to plant lollipops? Good idea. Go ahead, den, and plant 'em."

Marianne buried the stick among the turnips, stood and, seeing that the stick was leaning to one side, bent over again to straighten it.

"Der ya go! We'll come 'round in a couple o' weeks, an' 50.134.8
see what comes up." Marianne

> In fact, the innovation in printing we can attribute to Gutenberg was not moveable type per se — the Chinese had already invented that — but rather the lead letter melted in a mould

designed to house all letters ranging from the narrow *l* to the wide *w*. This particularity opened the door to the casting of raised metal type by melting soft metal, most commonly lead. Hence the invention of hot lead printing. Hence, also, the development of fonts or typefaces, that is, collections of melted type — letter, numerals, blanks, punctuation — all in the same style and body, assiduously distributed in the fixed order of the wooden case. Once all these elements were perfected, type-founders became distinct from printers. Eventually, cases of metal type were produced and delivered on demand to printers in a hurry to provide editors with copies of a given author's work.

51.10.7 Typography

"And like before, *cte* became *c-t-apostrophe* in front of any word what begins with a vowel or a silent *h*."

"So would ya say *cte homard-icitte* fer "dis here lobster" or c*t'homard icitte*?"

52.35.2 The Detail within the Detail

"*Cte homard-icitte*, I figure."

"Well dat sounds right fine to me."

First coincidence. The goal of the survey conducted without the slightest preparation whatsoever among students at Université de Moncton was to determine their perception of the colours of vowels, but because it wasn't properly designed, that goal was never clearly stated. The letter *a* is both the first vowel and the first letter of the alphabet. Admittedly, a weak coincidence, but a coincidence none the less.

53.17.1 Chance

"Dad, what does 'whatever'll be 'lbe' mean?"

"Will be. 'Whatever will be will be', not 'lbe.'"

"But you says 'lbe."

"Well, it maybe sounds like I'm saying 'lbe', but really I'm sayin' 'will be.' Whatever will be will be.

. . .

"Means wedder you likes it or not. No two ways 'bout it, it's gonna happen, wedder you likes it or not."

Le Petit Étienne turned toward Chico: 54.20.8

"See, din't I?[1] 'Ats what I was meaning." Language

In her novel *1953: Chronicle of a Birth Foretold,* the Acadian author France Daigle makes no mention of the classification of typefaces cre- 55.45.11
ated that year by Maximilien Vox. Useless Details

Real colours (as opposed to imaginary colours). The web site pourpre.com offers the opportunity to browse a dictionary of imaginary colours (anyone can contribute to this collection, so long as they include a brief explanation of the suggested nuance). In addition to real and imaginary colours, there are also medical colours (albugineous, purpurine), as well as some names that are not colours per se but 57.131.4
suggest colours (no examples come to mind). Parenthesi(e)s

"Had no idea what I's going to do, did I. Anyhow, I puts my C.V. about, here an' der, with de province, de université, de Radio-Canada, and l'Assomption Insurance. After a wee bit, de university called. They's lookin' fer a body to write exam questions, somebody creative, or so 58.130.12
dey tells me." Work

Still on the subject of Scrabble, a pivot is a letter that doubles or triples in value twice, first in a horizontal word and then in a vertical word. A quadruple occurs when a player succeeds

56.142.1

1. The phrase *din't I* signifies "didn't I tell you." Notes

in placing a word so that it covers two word-
counts-double squares, which quadruples the
value of the word. The same principle applies
for the nonuple, except that in this case the
59.4.10 word created falls on two word-counts-triple
Scrabble squares and is worth nine times more.

Terry's family name was widely known in Dieppe because of Thibodeau's Auto Body Shop. Proud of their achievement, Terry's father and brothers were happy to share the Thibodeau name with the children of the family's youngest and least conformist member.

"Yer sure ya don't want to name dem Després-Thibodeau or Thibodeau-Després?"

Carmen felt that giving the children the father's name was a way to evoke a paternal counterpart to the umbilical cord.

"No. Just Thibodeau's fine. It'll bind them closer to you that way. I'm their mudder, and dat's plenty."

Carmen's decision made Terry feel proud, though he tried not to show it.

"Are ya sure, den?"

"Totally."

"Cross yer heart and hope to die?"

Carmen burst out laughing, but Terry still wanted an answer:

"Wot I'd like to know fer sure, is weder you'll stick up fer me when folks go 'round sayin' I don't give a hoot fer yer name."

"Cross me heart, I'll stick up fer ya."

60.7.11 "OK. Cross me heart'll do. Anyways, I never did
Useful Details understand de hope to die part."

In the case of the two responders who claimed they could see no colour associated with the *a*, we cannot assume they saw the same no colour. Because whether we proceed by addition (in which adding the three primary colours produces white, and the black is treated as an absence of colour) or by subtraction (in which the addition of the three primary colours produces black and the absence of colour is white), both the all and the nothing can each be represented by black or by white. At least this is what was generally believed until two scientists undertook to discover the colour of the universe. Karl Glazebrook and Ivan Baldry calculated the dominant colour of more than 200,000 galaxies and concluded that the colour of the whole tends toward white. According to them, if we could enclose the universe in a box, we would see a pale yellowish ivory, a shade they baptised cosmic latte, after calling for suggestions over the Internet. The two researchers declared they chose this suggested name over all the others because it had the added appeal of reflecting their own predilection for coffee.

61.2.7
Colours

"Well, it's pretty basic, really: ya got Barbie, Hot Wheels 'n Fisher-Price."

"Is dat it den? Wot about Playstation an' all dem gadgets?

"I'm talkin' 'bout de real toys, dose dat you plays wid fer real. Computers an' de like, dat's a whole udder department."

"What've ya done wid Lego, den?"

As a matter of fact, Terry had forgotten Lego.

"Good question."

62.102.12
The Trio

The difference between a font and a typeface has become so subtle today that the two terms are almost synonymous. At one time font used to mean the characters themselves, whereas a

63.21.7
More or Less
Useful Details

> typeface was the complete set of characters in a font.

"Seems some folks way back 'round Molière's time, complained his French was too colloquial-like, not refined enough, if ya please."

"How come den, dey're always sayin' "la langue de Molière" when dey're meanin' French, like ee was de mucky-muck of de French language?"

"Most likely on account of ee became famous. Could be ee was de first French fellow to become famous."

…

…

"What else've you learned den?"

"Well, Molière was alive 'round de same time l'Acadie was startin' up. 'Tween 1600 and 1700, what we calls de seventeenth century."

"Well, ain't dat weird. I tot we was descended from dat udder fellow, Rabelais?"

"Dat's de truth. I didn't tink of it."

…

"Well, I suppose dat means I'll be goin' to the next class."

"De whole ting'd drive me round de bend. You goes to university, you tinks you've learned a ting, den some boy asks a simple question, and ya don't know anymore. De whole ting's a ripoff, ya ask me."

64.33.3
Chiac Lesson

> The little survey conducted among 102 students at the Université de Moncton also revealed that blue was the colour most associated with the vowel *e*. In fact, 44 responders selected blue — one specified a pale blue — which amounts to 43 percent of total responders. On the other hand, 18 responders declared the *e* was green — 1 described it as a shallot green — 9 described it as yellow, 7 as grey, 4 as violet.

> Orange, red, black and white were named three
> times each; brown and pink twice; and once 65.3.1
> each: amber, silver, transparent, and nothing. Statistics

A few weeks later, on a Sunday afternoon unencumbered by the slightest obligation, while Carmen was browsing a magazine and watching with pleasure as Étienne, Marianne and Terry played like kittens on the living room carpet, Étienne suddenly cried out:

"Dad! Sing!"

Marianne seconded the request by hopping up and down and repeatedly flinging her arms up in the air. Terry was quick to acquiesce.

"*Frè-re Jac-ques, frè-re Jac-…*"

"No, not like dat, Dad! De udder way!"

Terry played dumb:

"Eh sure! *Au clair de la lu-…*"

But Étienne was unrelenting:

"No, Dad! Wid yer arms an' all!"

Terry, seeing Marianne beginning to tremble with impatience, did not want to ruin the atmosphere.

"Awh! Like dat!"

Without knowing where all this was coming from, Carmen decided to play along, and began to clap her hands, drawing in the children:

"Ter-ry! Ter-ry! We want Ter-ry!"

Étienne and Marianne, imitating their mother, clapped their hands with each syllable. Marianne added a slight waddle from left to right.

"OK, OK."

Terry straightened up, his heartbeat racing. He winked at Étienne.

"Dis here's a song for you Mum."

Marianne's excitement continued for a bit, but Étienne realized that this was the moment they had been promised: the unveiling of their secret.

"Dis here's a poem Aragon wrote for his lover Elsa."

. . .

"De song's called 'Elsa.'"

. . .

"S'pposed to be Léo Ferré sings it, but dis time, well, it's me."

Terry tried to gain a few moments to slow his pulse down a bit. Étienne and Marianne had no idea what was going on, never having heard Terry introduce a song before. But their confusion quickly dissipated when Terry finally began to sing:

66.1.6 "*Is it possible you only need appear / That look that's so*
Chansons *endearing / Your hair that gesture so appealing . . .*"

> Cravat 28, (C)aging 20, Toye(r) 16, Nov(a) s 21, api(n)g 24, Ju(i)cy 34, Flin(t) 24, Mu(s) h 29, Zi(g) 26, Equ(i)ne 30, (Z)oo 24, L(o)pe 21, Dr(e)w 36, D(y)ad 13, (D)ebriefed 14, (B)it 15, Wa(f)t 20, To(w)n 14, I(s)led 15, Equine(s) 17, Debrief(s) 34, Rente(d) 8, Tom(e) 20, Ear(t) h 13, (a)xle 27, Ek(e) 14, Bo(l)a 28, O(b)it 7, O(k)ra 8, (H)ue 6. For a total of 346 (344 plus
> 67.4.5 the opponent's 2 points) and 260 (262 minus 2
> Scrabble points for the two letters remaining).

Carmen could hardly breathe, her eyes were wet with tears. Étienne and Marianne were staring at her, waiting for her real reaction. Terry, it should be said, had been especially moving. When he came to the line "like the sunlight on the window," he'd extended a hand toward the large windows of the loft without taking his eyes off Carmen, and even the children could feel how much it meant. Finally, after a long transatlantic silence that shuttled between Terry and Carmen, she ran toward Terry, flung her arms around him and, squeezing tight, buried her face in his neck. The children followed suit, wrapping themselves round two legs each, one of Dad's and one of Mum's. Tears were running down Carmen's cheeks, and

Marianne took up her swaying and chanting: 68.1.7
"Ar-gon! Ar-gon! Ar-gon!..." Chansons

> Under the title "Black A," in *Delirium II – Alchemy of the Word*, Rimbaud also mentions the colours of vowels: "I invented the colours of the vowels! — *a* black, *e* white, *i* red, *o* blue, *u* green." Easily obtainable in French on the web site rimbaudsillages.free.fr, the tone of which encourages copying and dissemination (the
> English translation can be appropriated from 69.11.12
> mag4.net/Rimbaud/poesies/Alchemy). Appropriations

"Folks'll see CHANGE CASE on der screen and dey don' know what to do wid it. Don' know what it means, do dey. Goes way back to de days of de old printing houses, lead type an' all dat. Back den, a case was dat big wooden box wid all de wee compartments where dey puts de letters. De wee letters, the teeniest, goes in de bottom of de case. Dat's why we calls dem letters lower case. Up on top, you's had de capitals, dose letters what have de accents and other stuff we don' use all that much. Some folks says 'upper case' for capital letters. Below dey put all de punctuation marks, numbers, and de blanks to make spaces betwixt de words. At first dey was lining up all de type into text by hand. Later on, der was linotype. Dey
had all dat at *L'Évangéline* when I started work der. I sure 70.15.10
would have liked to keep a set of that equipment, but den Unidentified
where would I 'ave put it, I'd like to know." Monologues

> Unlike the results for the *a* and the *e*, where a few colours dominated, perceptions of the colour of *i* were somewhat disparate. Whereas 25 responders saw yellow and 16 red, the 61 other participants voted in almost equal numbers for a dozen different colours, including white (and its derivations igloo and ivory), violet, indigo,

71.3.2 pink, purple, blue, green, grey, black, brown,
Statistics nothing, and I forget.

Camil Gaudain was a regular visitor to Didot Books, and he rarely left without buying one or two volumes. Terry had noticed that he read a bit of everything. Or he bought a bit of everything: novels, essays, biographies, philosophy, psychology, gardening, recipes, even children's literature. Terry, who very much doubted Camil had children, assumed he was buying the brightly coloured books for his nephews and nieces.

"I'd like to order Freud in the Pléiade edition."

"No problem."

When Ludmilla and he had opened the bookstore, Terry had been obliged to immerse himself rapidly in the universe of books. He had everything to learn. Thanks to Ludmilla's patience and generosity, he was managing pretty well.

"Cold enuff fer ya?"

"Funny ting is I like all sorts of wedder. Even de month o' March."

No customer had ever ordered a book from the Pléiade. This was nothing abnormal for Terry. People were always asking for authors and publishers he'd never heard of and he always managed to find them. But was Camil Gaudain in a hurry? Terry had caught him glancing at his watch twice already.

"If it's alright with you, I'll come back this afternoon. It's just that I've a meeting in twenty minutes..."

"No problem. Dat'll give me de time to do a proper search. I'd best be writing it down doh, so's not to forget."

Terry pulled out the notebook he kept under the cash register, wrote: FREUD — LAPLÉYADE. Camil Gaudain noticed the spelling.

"It's two words."

Terry did not take offence. He put a line through Lapléyade and wrote what his customer dictated:

"*La Pléiade*, capital *P-l-e* with an accent aigu *-i-a-d-e*."

Terry read the name aloud:

"*Pléiade*."

Then, to stimulate business a bit: 72.8.3

"Was der anyting else you might be wantin' me to order?" Didot Books

> On the other hand, a Blanchard is a word of little value, usually made of letters worth only a single point. For professionals, a Blanchard is a word worth less than 60 points.

73.4.7 Scrabble

Chiac is not exempt from slip-ups, which are in fact errors. For example, the sentence "Have you got enough there?" is often translated in French as "*Y en a-tu assez pour toi*?" as though we were saying: "Have you got enough for you there?" The *tu* here should be an *il* (*Y en a-t-il assez pour toi*?). The error is most likely linked to the fact that the question addresses a second person singular. If one is speaking proper Chiac, one must say: "*Y en a-t-y assez pour toi*?" just as in a particular English, one would say: "Have ya had yer fill, then?" The same applies to the exclamation "*Y en a-tu mangé* õr *whãt*!" which ought to be "*Y en a-t-y mangé* õr whãt!" in Chiac, or "*Il en a certainement mangé sa part*" in Parisian. In non-standard English, one might say, "Did he scoff his fill or wot!"

74.33.11 Chiac Lesson

> A character in Acadian France Daigle's novel *Just Fine,* Camil Gaudain, had no role to play in her two subsequent novels (*A Fine Passage* and *Life's Little Difficulties*), but this did not stop his life from continuing outside the fictional framework.

75.96.10 Characters

A few days later, Terry felt better. It may have been just fatigue that had caused him to fret over his role as a father.

"T'other night I didn't tink to say so, but I figures 'twas a right fine ting I did for de kids when I sang de Aragon for dem. 'Specially dat first time. I sure caught 'em unawares der, surprised 'em in a good way. You should 'ave seen der faces! Like dey was all admirin' me."

"For sure! I was like in shock meself."

"I know, but fer the kids, I mean 'twas like sometin went straight into der DNA, marked 'em fer real. I'm pretty sure it did. Could see it jus de way dey was lookin' up to me. Now dat's sometin' I wouldn't mind seein' more often."

"Ask me, it happens more often than you think, 'cept
76.13.3 you can't see it cause you're too close to them."

Paternity "Really?"[2]

> A parallel play occurs in Scrabble when a word is placed in parallel to another thereby creating several two-letter words. A player creates a chimney when a word is placed between two other words already on the board — or on the screen — to create several three-letter words. When a new word is formed by adding a letter at the beginning or end of a previously placed word we call it a hook, whereas creating a
> 77.4.8 word by adding a three-letter prefix is called a
> Scrabble Benjamin.

> The sign referred to by all but the initiated as a letter — and as a character by all the initiated, except for the specialists — is composed

2. There are two ways to pose this question: either the interrogative accent is placed on the second syllable, as in "realLY?" or, as is more usual, the emphasis is placed on the first syllable, thus: "REALly?!" which is a question combined with an exclamation, also known as the "Acadian interrogative" because of
78.142.2
Notes its falsely neutral tone.

> of more parts than the serif. These include the stem (vertical stroke), the bar (horizontal stroke), the bowl (a curved stroke that creates an enclosed space in the character), a stroke (oblique straight or curved line), and the ascender (the part of the lowercase letter that extends above the x-height). The serif is a line crossing the main strokes of a character, for example at the base of the stem.

79.10.8
Typography

Even Ludmilla could not believe it:

"I can't understand their logic. They published Marx after all; why not Freud? Obviously I'm missing something. Unless..."

And she plunged into a new search, navigating like Ulysses in the *Odyssey*, sailing from one site to another, as though she knew the virtual network of publishing like the back of her hand.

80.8.4
Didot Books

> In addition to typeface and size, the look of a character varies according to its value, i.e., the amount of ink, also known as its weight, its orientation—upright, slanted, italic—and its colour.

81.10.9
Typography

"Can you tell me how come I've so much trouble saying *je vais* meaning 'I'm going someplace,' instead of *je vas*, like 'I's goin' der?'"

"Well, dat's on account of the economy of language. *Vas* is shorter dan *vais*."

!!

...

"Well, I'll be! At last, an answer wot makes sense!"

82.31.5
Questions with Answers

> Lacan's matheme of "the discourse of the hysteric"

83.11.11 Appropriations

$$\frac{\not{S}}{a} \longrightarrow \frac{S_1}{S_2}$$

Discours de L'Hystérique

Carmen and Josse had wasted little time looking for a name for their bar. The Babar seemed the obvious choice. No one could come up with a good reason not to use it, although there were doubts.

"Wot if yer not supposed to use dat name? Like if someone was to call der bar Charlie Brown, don't you tink pretty soon dey'd be gettin' sued?"

"Dat may be in de States. I doubts de French'd come after us. Mostly dey doesn't even know we exist, and dem
84.104.2 Worries dat does have got lots better tings to do den bodder wid a wee bar some place out in the wilds of Canada."

> In addition to English and French, Scrabble is played in Greek, Arab, Hebrew, Spanish, Portuguese, Catalan, Italian, German, Polish, Danish, Dutch, Swedish, Finnish, Norwegian, Flemish, Czech, Hungarian, Slovak, Croatian, Slovene, Turkish, Greek Cypriot, Icelandic, Afrikaans, Russian, Anglo-Chinese, Anglo-Japanese, Malay, and Braille. Obviously, the
> 85.112.1 Languages number of tiles and the letter values vary from one language to another.

Terry learned a great deal merely from browsing La Pléiade's web site: to be published by this, arguably the most prestigious, publisher in the world, amounts to a kind of consecration (when der's a bit o' real gold on de cover, you knows dey isn't foolin' around) — few writers have gained entry to La Pléiade during their lifetimes (Gracq? in me whole life, I never heard dat name) — founded in 1931 by Jacques Schiffrin and André Gide (hurrah! at last a fellow I heard of) — bought by

Gallimard (naturally, dey owns everythin') — Volume III of Aragon's poetry goes for $130 (Jesus, how many volumes does dat boy got?). 86.8.5 Didot Books

> In French, the tiles, those small wooden squares on which Scrabble's letters are printed, are sometimes called caramels. A valuable letter is worth more than four points. A phoney is an unacceptable word. The tiles are mixed in the bag, each player draws seven, which he or she places on the rack, and then tries to make the most of by exploiting the high-value letters, occasionally ending up with a phoney. 87.4.6 Scrabble

Some time later, Josse burst into Carmen and Terry's place in a state of great excitement. She was hiding something behind her back.

"Yous'll never guess!"

Unable to contain herself any longer, she showed them the object. Carmen and Terry were enraptured.

"Well, don't that beat all!"

"Where did ya find it?!"

"Out where dey sells dem antiques on John."

Terry took the small Babar lamp from Josse, for a closer look.

"She's chipped, but der's nuttin' wrong wid dat. Goes wid de rest."

But Carmen had no desire to decorate the Babar with a bunch of secondhand junk:

"Sure an' are we gonna fill up de place wid old stuff all chipped and faded?"

"Naw. I only meant if der's a bit of old stuff, it goes wid de whole idea of de lofts, recycling an' all dat."

Carmen nodded, and took up the statuette in turn.

"Wouldn't be so bad if we could get our hands on a couple more."

Josse was bursting with pleasure:

"I found dem! Googled Babar din't I, and der dey was! On eBay! Secondhand an' bran' new! We could set a few down on de tables. Not on all of dem, just here an' der, so long as it's in keeping wid de décor. If dat's wot we want, I mean…"

88.6.1 The Babar

> Coincidence? The fact that the alphabet is sometimes referred to as the ABCs, and that these three letters, *a*, *b*, and *c*, the first three of the alphabet are together the first letters of 38 percent of the names of colours in the pourpre.com web site's dictionary and 23 percent of those of Wikipedia's List of Colours?

89.92.9 Questions without Answers

As Étienne had more or less appropriated Aragon's *Blues* and "I Sing to Pass the Time," while "Elsa" had become Carmen's song, Terry decided to learn another just for Marianne. He sang it for her one evening in her bedroom, with Étienne in attendance, since it was a première and he'd been there for the others. The song Terry had chosen was slightly more difficult than the earlier ones because it included some unusual vocal embellishments, which Terry wanted to reproduce as well as possible. He launched into "The Stranger" like a clown on a highwire, and soon had the kids laughing. At the beginning of the third verse, when Terry sang: *I took the hand of an ephemera / She followed me into my house…* Marianne imagined that this was how Terry had become her dad, and she paid even closer attention to what followed all the way to the end of the song.

90.1.8 Chansons

> The progression of the category "Useful Details" into "Interesting Details" is itself interesting. Whereas with useful details, one is justified in asking useful to whom, useful for what, in the case of interesting details, we ask ourselves interesting to whom, and why interesting. From

> an indirect object we shift into subordinated and coordinated clauses. The beginning of writing, in a sense. 91.19.1 Interesting Details

But there was no denying it: Freud's works had not been published by La Pléiade. Ludmilla seemed hurt by this omission; she disappeared into the small office at the back of the bookstore like a fox retreating into its den.

"Everyting dat Freud wrote was published in French by dis here publisher. Nuttin' of his was published by La Pléiade."

Terry handed Camil Gaudain the scrap of paper on which he'd written the address of Freud's publisher.

"You're sure?"

Camil Gaudain's surprise was comforting to Terry and, in a way, legitimized Ludmilla's dismay.

"Ya. Ludmilla was a dog's age surfin' on de Internet she couldn't believe it." 92.8.6 Didot Books

> Jean de Brunhoff's *Babar's Travels* was published by La Librairie Hachette in 1939. The original version was subsequently reprinted, notably in October 1979, in Hachette's Lutin Poche, L'école des Loisirs paperback edition. Recopied here (and translated) without permission, the first page reads as follows:

Babar the young king of the elephants
and his wife Queen Celeste
have set out in a hot air balloon
on their honeymoon.
"Au revoir! See you soon!"
the elephants shout
as the balloon floats out of sight.
Babar's little cousin Arthur
is still waving his beret.
Old Cornelius, acting chief of the elephants

93.11.8
Appropriations

whenever the king's away, thinks:
"Let's hope they don't have an accident!"

Because Acadian French is replete with old words and archaic expressions, it is perhaps the strong and often insidious presence of English that lends Chiac its particular character, and especially the clearly English pronunciation of these words. Someone from France can say they've put their car in the *parquigne* without a second thought, but an Acadian would feel like a showoff pronouncing it that way. Acadians quite naturally say "parking" exactly as they've heard it hundreds of times from the mouths of the Anglophones that surround them.

We are dealing here with a musical, rhythmic, and aesthetic rupture. Often this mix of two languages is unnoticed, but equally often it offends the ear and defies understanding. It's all a question of balance. For example, take the phrase "*je vas aouère besoin d'un troque ou d'un vãn pour haler mon botte ennewé* (Least ways, I'll be needin' me some body's truck or van to haul me boat)." Here at least the sentence seems to maintain a consistent sonic register. On the other hand, a vague menace lurks beneath the surface of the sentence: "*si que je swĩtch la lĩght bãck õn pis que la maison ẽxplode, expecte pas d'aouère ẽver ãgain d'autres outils pour Father's Day* (if I

94.30.7
Chiac

goes to switch on de light and de whole house blows up, don't you expect no more o' dem tools fer Fadder's Day)."

> Find out if there are bloodlines linking Terry Thibodeau and the Francis Thibaudeau who
>
> 95.68.1
> Projects
>
> designed the first recognized classification of typographical styles in 1921.

"To start wid, ee got aggressive like, den after a bit ee started wot dey calls panic attacks. After dat, 'twas a great big gaffer of a belly ache, so bad ee tot he'd got appendicitis. His wife drives 'im to de hospital in de middle of de night, and all. Sure, but de doctors couldn't find nuttin'. 'Til dey figured 'twas on account of 'is wife was preggies. The boy 'ad all de same side effects: worrying, belly ache, a burnin' rage to defend 'is kind, de whole kid an' kaboodle. Well, de doc asks 'im, did ee gain some weight lately, and sure enuf, ee'd took on five pounds. Dat was it den, ee had to be preggies, too. Ee was gettin' bigger jus' like 'is wife, even doh ee wasn't eatin' no more dan before. Pretty warped, eh?"

96.15.12
Unidentified
Monologues

> The word *character* when referring to a letter involves more than simply the sign. It also designates the environment of the letter, i.e., the spaces on either side and between the lines, as well as its relationship to its neighbours. The disposition on the same page of characters of different typefaces, sizes and other specifications will create, or not, depending on the typesetter's talent, a particular desired effect, which is what the art of typography is all about.

97.10.10
Typography

Terry had nevertheless taken the trouble to modify one or two of Aragon's phrases to avoid traumatising the children. His own modesty of course played a part in this. In "The Stranger," to avoid any suggestion of incest — after all, he'd dedicated the song to Marianne — he changed the words to place dragonflies on her dress and butterflies in her hair, which helped to transform the original meaning of the verse. In the phrase *Cut my throat and the peonies* in "I Love You So," he replaced his throat with roses, which somewhat attenuated the barbarism so that he could keep the line *Hurry bring me my wine my blood*, because he did not want to shelter the children from all primitive feelings nor transform Aragon's texts into innocent nursery rhymes; the kids already knew enough of those.

98.1.9
Chansons

99.98.5 Expressions

Thus the expression "read between the lines" is not purely figurative.

"Potatoes sold pretty well back den; well der weren't much to eat and not a whole lot o' choice. Dese days it's a whole udder kettle of fish. Folks're eatin' all sorts o' tings aside from potatoes. An' I'm not jus' talkin' 'bout dose dat's afeared of puttin' on a few pounds. So...fer sure, dey's gotta find some udder way to sell all dem potatoes. Like makin' bags smaller and more appealin' like, if youse catch me drift. And der's different sorts o' potatoes, 'cause it's like wine dese days, folks're startin' to know der different sorts o' potatoes. Potatoes fer makin' mashed'r no good fer boiled cod, an' potatoes ya want baked in yer oven or microwave, well dose ain't de same neither... Right, now what was I sayin'? Awh yeah! Potatoes you want fer bakin' an' dose wot you're usin' in yer fricassée, well dey ain't de same yer gonna be usin' to make fries."

100.15.6 Unidentified Monologues

Gradually a slew of terms and phrases became widespread, terms like *libido*, *oral stage*, *anal stage*, *sadism*, *narcissism*, the *unconscious*, *Oedipal complex*, *desire*, *ambivalence*, *lapsus*, *guilt*, *pleasure principle*, *reality principle*, the *ego*, the *id*, the *superego*, *aggressivity*, *death drive*, *neurosis*, *psychosis*, *anxiety*, *defense mechanism*, *conflict*, *repression*, *inhibition*, *resistance*, *overdetermination*, *transference*, *projection*; all notions that have become part of our contemporary mental toolbox.

101.39.4 Freud Circuitously

On the wall by the entrance hang a dozen or so backpacks of various sizes and colours. Those down close to the floor are smaller and livelier in colour. All together they make a pretty picture. Étienne got two new packs this September: one for the pool and one for his colouring course with Étienne Zablonski. "Course" may be exaggerating a bit, but it does dress up nicely and elevate slightly those weekly hours of babysitting Zablonski has offered Terry and Carmen. Wednesday afternoons therefore, the renowned painter Étienne Zablonski tries to teach some basic notions of visual art to the Le Petit Étienne Thibodeau.

"You don't need to bring me, Dad; I can get der on me own."

Terry quickly concealed the concern that had gripped him at the thought of letting the little one roam the hallways of the lofts on his own. Once over his initial surprise, he sought to encourage his son's resourcefulness:

"If you know how to get der, I figure yer old enough to 102.88.1
go on yer own den, fer sure." Freedom

> Cited without permission from the Gallimard catalogue concerning La Pléiade: "All the books are printed in Garamond, on bible paper, and leather bound with gold lettering. A different colour has been selected for each era: tobacco for the twentieth century, emerald green for the nineteenth, blue for the eighteenth, venetian red for the seventeenth, Corinthian brown for the sixteenth, purple for the Middle Ages,
> green for Antiquity; sacred texts are bound in 103.11.7
> grey, anthologies in China red." Appropriations

"Well, anyways, ain't de French always 'ad a revolutionary streak runnin' troo dem since de whatchamacallit de French Revolution?"

"An' what, pray tell, does dat have to do wid legal copyright?"

"On account of if der's some way dey can prove dat Babar belongs to de people, well dey'll do it fer sure, and den der could be a Babar on every street corner, no problem.
Liberté, Égalité, Fraternité, remember?" 104.82.2

"Those French're even more rimmed dan I tot." Moncton

> Acadians are often criticized — and not least by each other — for pronouncing words containing an *è* as though it were an é. *Père* (pair) and *mère* (mair) for example, are often pronounced *pére* (payr), and *mére* (mayr). Of course, this is actually the old French pronunciation. But such ways of speaking seem old fashioned in the ears of the Other, as though this inability to adapt to modern French was evidence of a failure to adapt to modern life itself.

105.33.5
Chiac Lesson

Having answered the door and greeted Le Petit Étienne, Zablonski was surprised:

"Terry's not with you?"

"No. I'm old enough."

"Yes, of course you are."

Before closing the door, the painter glanced down the hall, thinking Terry might have followed the child at some distance, just to be sure he'd arrived at his destination safely. But he saw no one. After which, he admired the candour of the little fellow who proceeded to take his usual place at the end of the room by the large windows looking out over the sun drenched city.

106.13.9
Paternity

107.138.1
The Other

> It is too soon to speak of the Other.

At first Le Grand Étienne had some difficulty imparting his knowledge to Le Petit Étienne. He thought he'd begin initially with a basic differenciation: warm colours and cold colours. Wrong. Le Petit Étienne described as warm all the colours Le Grand Étienne classified as cold and as cold all those supposedly warm. The artist came at the problem in various ways, but none seemed to work. In the end, just to avoid having to declare this first pedagogical exercise a failure, the painter declared:

"Well, really, it's not that important."

Le Petit Étienne did not disagree. The master decided

that a light snack might soften the learning curve. He fetched milk and cookies, putting on some music on the way, and came back to sit by his pupil, next to the large windows where they could watch the comings and goings in the neighbourhood. It was this pause that allowed him to break through the impasse. Le Petit Étienne had a question:

"Which colour is *vert laine*?"

Vert laine? Green wool? Étienne Zablonski tried to think where the boy had seen green wool. 108.2.9 Colours

> Freud's massive oeuvre defies simplification. Which explains the need for a roundabout approach. First impression: after several months in Paris, at age 30, Freud returns to Vienna convinced that, as the eminent Charcot had argued, the study of anatomy was complete, the era of neurosis was at hand. 109.39.1 Freud Circuitously

The small and more or less scientific survey on perceptions of the colour of vowels was taken up at the Babar, which had subscribed to *L'Acadie nouvelle* as a service to the clientele. A few lines on the survey had appeared as filler in the newspaper.

"As wot, you say?"

"Filler."

"An' wot's dat, I'd like to know."

"A short article in a newspaper. Not more than a paragraph or two usually. To fill in the space."

"Wot d'ya mean, 'fill in de space'? Wot space are we talkin' about?" 110.6.4 The Babar

> Claude Garamond created the first type foundry independent of a printer. A Parisian, Garamond (1499–1581) probably based his roman characters, which are the basis for all classical typefaces, on the type of Geoffroy

> Tory, Alde Manuce, and Francesco Griffo. The subsequent appearance of Baskerville type in England and Didot in France rendered Garamond all but invisible for more than a century, but the National French Press relaunched the style at the beginning of the twentieth century, at the time of the World's Fair. Today, publishers increasingly prefer Garamond to
> 111.10.11 Times New Roman, which was designed for
> Typography the *London Times*.

This was Marianne's second sore throat in as many months.

"Could be the same one that wasn't completely cured de first time."

"Like a relapse, you mean?"

Carmen envied Terry's use of the French word *rechute* for "relapse" rather than slipping into the English, as he might have done. His vocabulary seemed to be improving lately.

"You think she ought to see the doctor?"

Terry wasn't sure. He wasn't the type to run off to the doctor at the slightest malaise.

"T'isn't as doh she's complaining all de time. Her nose's hardly runnin' at all."

"It doesn't seem normal, a sore throat that's not a cold. Can kids that age be catchin' mono?"

Terry turned to Marianne:

"Marianne, did you go off an' kiss somebody an' not tell yer mum or dad?"

Marianne looked from her dad to her mum.

"Dad's just pullin' yer leg, me beauty. Come on over 'ere to yer mum."

Marianne did not need to be asked twice; she walked into Carmen's outstretched arms.

"Seems to me she's a whole lot quieter too, not jumpin' all over everything all de time."

Terry knew what Carmen meant.

"Anyways, one ting's fer sure, she's not havin' 'er tonsils out."

He used the English word *tonsils*.

"An' why's that?"

"Dey discovered tonsils is what processes our emotions an' memories while we's sleepin'."

Terry said *processes* in English.

"Sorry, don't know the right word fer *processes*."

This information about tonsils worried Carmen.

"Go on! Are ya serious?"

"Dat's wot I read."

Carmen fell silent. Gently caressing Marianne, she was trying to think what effect having her own tonsils out when she was six years old might have had on her.

"Well, I suppose it don't make sense tonsils would be useless after all."

"*Amygdales*!" Terry exclaimed, picking up on Carmen's use of the French for tonsils. 112.87.3

"Dat's de word I's lookin' fer." The Body

> This book is typeset in ________________.
> (This information is usually found at the end of the work.) 113.131.1 Parenthesi(e)s

Once Étienne Zablonski had understood that the *vert laine* Le Petit Étienne was talking about was not green wool, but rather Verlaine the poet, and after Zablonski had explained that *verveine* was not about green veins but rather a plant with which one makes tea, and that no, or perhaps actually, there may be a colour called *orange à mère*, though he Zablonski was not aware of it, but if there was, probably the words meant not mother's orange but rather *orange amère* or bitter orange, called in Acadian French *orange aigre*, or *haigre* — he'd also heard

it pronounced *haigue*[3] — well, once he'd understood all
114.2.10 that, the painter Étienne Zablonski went to the back of
Colours his loft to bring out a rare object from his distant past.

> At least two rumours contributed to discrediting the work of Freud: first, that he used hero-
> 115.108.8 in; and second, that he was involved in an in-
> Rumours cestuous relationship with his daughter.

> The largest consensus emerged around the letter *o*. No fewer than 61 responders associated the letter *o* with the colour orange. Ten responders declared it to be red, eight blue, seven black, six yellow, three pink, two white, two
> 117.3.4 purple, and one each green, grey and violet. No
> Statistics one answered "nothing" or "I forget."

As a rule Terry made up his own mind about which books to read. He mostly relied on his instinct to guide him. But when it came to Freud, he was stymied by the sheer number of books the founder of psychoanalysis had written, not to mention the multitude of volumes written about him and his works. Terry sought guidance from Ludmilla.

"Many authors get lost in the details of his interpretations rather than simply noting the originality of his approach for the time."

So it was something to do with a bygone era? Terry didn't feel like reading a whole lot of dusty old books.

"Are you sayin 'twould be too old, today?"

"*The Interpretation of Dreams* will give you a good idea of his work. Especially since he wrote very well. He took great care with his writing style."

---

3. As though to accentuate the sourness, Acadians add a
116.142.3 strongly aspirated *h* to the word for *bitter*. Furthermore, many
Notes do not pronounce the *r*, which makes *aigre* sound like *haigue*.

This was the first time Terry had heard of such a thing. To have a writing style. To work on your writing style. Of course. It made perfect sense. Why should it surprise him? Ludmilla added:

"*Psychopathology of Everyday Life* is also quite interesting, though a trifle long."

They were obliged to cut their conversation short 118.8.7
because a customer was waiting at the cash. Didot Books

> Here I'd like to point out that the list of authors in La Pléiade includes an Acadian. The sinologist Charles Le Blanc, a native of northern New Brunswick who, with the Frenchman Rémi Mathieu, co-edited the second volume of *Philosophes taoïstes* (*Daoist Philosophers*), and the first volume of *Philosophes confucianistes (Confucian Philosophers)*. An eminent scholar, 119.19.3 Interesting
> needless to say. Details

Le Petit Étienne stared wide-eyed at the old colour chart Le Grand Étienne laid out before him. Almost a hundred years old and designed by the famous silk manufacturers of Lyon, the chart displayed close to 500 colours in narrow silk strips, each one appropriately named and numbered. As he admired the work, Le Petit
Étienne could not restrain himself from fingering the 120.2.11
occasional strip. Colours

> Freud had the distinct impression, which he did not conceal, that he was bringing Americans the plague on his only voyage to the United States, in September 1909. Invited to receive an honorary doctorate from Clark University in Worcester, Massachussetts, Freud made the trip by boat, accompanied by Jung and Ferenczi. Though his works had won over adherents in most of Europe's great metropolises,

and even in New York, his ideas remained popular with only a minority and scandalized most everyone else. One of the happy memories Freud retained from that voyage was the fact that his steward on board happened to be reading *Psychopathology of Everyday Life*, since Freud had written that book with the express purpose of rendering his science accessible to a broader public.

121.39.2
Freud
Circuitously

The customer wanted to buy two paperbacks, *Petits malentendus sans importance* (*Little Misunderstandings of No Importance*) by Antonio Tabucchi, and *Comment je suis devenu stupide* (*How I Became Stupid*) by Martin Page, but she also asked for several other books not on the shelves. Terry happily grabbed an order form from under the register.

"The first one is *Un jour nous aurons des peintres* (*One Day We'll have Artists)* by…"

But Terry jumped:

"It's not over der wid de art books? Seemed to me…"

He walked toward the back of the bookstore, searched for a bit, but returned emptyhanded.

"No. I was sure we had a copy left. Must've sold it."

Terry returned to the order form and wrote the title and name of the author without asking the customer to repeat it. The name of Annie Cohen-Solal had stayed with him since he'd heard a discussion of her book on television.

"I'd also like *Exercises de style* (*Exercises in Style*) by Raymond Queneau. Gallimard Jeunesse recently published an illustrated version; that's the one I'm looking for."

Terry added a note in the column "Comments" on the form.

And I'd like *Poèmes épars* (*Scattered Poems*) by Gaston Miron.

"Dee Gaston Miron?"

"Yes."

"Wah, I'll be…I tot he'd published only de one book *L'homme rapaillé* (*The March to Love*)."

"Yes. This is a new one, recently published posthumously."

Terry wrote down the third title, adding:

"I suppose I'd better be orderin' more dan one den. Ever since we set up shop four years ago now, every year we're sellin' ten copies or so of *L'homme rapaillé*."

"Is that a lot?"

Terry laughed.

"'Tis plenty for us, anyway. And we're talkin' poems, mind you…"

…

"Would you be wanting me to ring you when dey come in den?"

"That would be fine, yes."

The client gave him her particulars, and Terry took the money for the two other books.

"You've a fine selection of paperbacks."

"We try."

Terry looked frankly at the woman, and smiled.

"Don't know why dat is, but I like paperbacks. I'm always hopin' a book comes out in paperback afore I get around to readin' it. Dere's plenty of good books, so I'm never in so much of a hurry I can't wait."

Surprised by Terry's pleasant manner, the customer decided he was something of a real bookseller.

"Naw, I figure I'll never be lackin' in books to read."

As he spoke, Terry raised his arms to encompass
the bookstore. The woman liked him, and returned his 122.8.8
friendly smile. Didot Books

It is in her novel *Just Fine* that the Acadian novelist France Daigle first explores the symbolism

123.12.1 Structure of the number 12, which, when multiplied by itself, is said to evoke plenitude.

"Wuchak de groundhog wasn't a bad sort. Only ting, she never knew when to stop. Say she came across a barrow full o' lettuce, well she just started in anibblin', 'till she'd ate up de whole ting. Den off she goes home in Roches-de-la-Butte, only she's so full she can hardly walk, see. An' all de while, she's burpin' an' fartin' on account of 'er tummy's churnin' so hard from havin' to digest all dat greenery."

Burps and farts were among Marianne's most favourite things.

"Well, lo and behold, one time, Wuchak goes an' finds a wagon full o' cabbage! An' if you tinks lettuce will get ya fartin', ha! Cabbage is like five times worse!"

This set Marianne off into ever greater peals of laughter. She'd heard enough storytelling to appreciate a rising dramatic action.

"Trouble was, Wuchak din't know Mrs. Bigbelly, who was in de habit of eatin' a cabbage every mornin' fer her breakfast. She'd cut it up, see, into wee bits and put 'em in one of dem big salad bowls, wid lots o' milk and some sugar, and den she eats it all up like it was corn flakes."

Marianne giggled. Meanwhile, Terry tried to think where to go from there.

"Well, does ya think Mrs. Bigbelly was goin' to sit back an' do nuttin' while her cabbages was all bein' eaten up? No sirree. Mrs. Bigbelly was no fool. You wouldn' tink so lookin' at 'er, but Mrs. Bigbelly knew a ting or two. So, when she see'd Wuchak the groundhog up on 'er hindlegs and chompin' on a big juicy cabbage, wot d'ya tink she done?"

Marianne did not want to guess. Terry pressed on with the first thing that came to mind:

"She went an' fetched her fiddle and bow, and she set herself right up close to Wuchak...On account of

Wuchak didn't mind folks watchin' 'er eat. But when she heard Mrs. Bigbelly's fiddle, well she took off like a rocket."

Marianne could not guess why.

"On account of Mrs. Bigbelly may 'ave owned a fiddle, but she weren't no fiddler. You might say she played terrible awful, you wouldn't be far off. And dere's nuttin' worse dan a fiddle badly played. So Wuchak takes off, an' right quick too. An' dat's how Mrs. Bigbelly didn't just save 'er cabbages, she saved Wuchak from a right mean swamp..."

Terry pinched his nose and concluded in a nasal tone:

"Pee-youuuu, if ya catches me drift."

Which made Marianne laugh, even though she didn't really understand what her dad meant.

Terry bent over his daughter:

"G'night, me pretty woodchuck..."

And he squeezed her tight in his arms, as though to bury the scatological edge to his story. Well it was the best he'd been able to do that night.

124.37.10
Animal Tales

> Excerpt from the novel *Just Fine* by the Acadian France Daigle, as translated by Robert Majzels, © House of Anansi Press, 1999: "Product of the three planes of space and the four cardinal points, the number 12 symbolizes both the internal complexity of the world and the celestial vault, divided into 12 sections, the 12 signs of the zodiac. We find its symbolic power in all the great civilizations, but also among lesser known peoples, the Dogons and Bambaras of Mali, for example, for whom the 3 and 4 correspond to the male and female elements, which together add up to the static number 7, and multiply to produce the dynamic number 12, representing the perpetual becoming of the individual being and the universe. Twelve

is the action number, at the same time as it represents accomplishments and the completed cycle. We find it often in the Jewish and Christian holy texts, where it symbolizes perfection. Multiplied by itself, the number 12 is said to lead to plenitude and paradise, no less.

125.11.6
Appropriations

"Price of gas gone right up again. Dese days seems like drivin's costin' me more 'n eatin'."

...

"Well, one ting, they've got that new boy workin' the pumps. I calls 'im me Gas Rookie."

...

"Dat boy's prettier dan Bill de electrician."

...

"Anyways, don't figure I've got much of a chance wid 'im."

...

"Too old I am, more's de pity."

...

"Dey's foolin' wid our nerves over at the gas station, don't ya tink?"

126.15.3
Unidentified
Monologues

The Montessuy Lyon Colour Chart is a cloth pouch that unfolds into 480 coloured binder samples. Seven panels are composed of two columns of 16 colours each; the eighth panel explains the chart along the length of a final column of 16 colours. The Chart distinguishes the colour cream (no. 1603) from the colour crème (no. 1604), the colour pink (no. 1606) from the colour rose (no. 1607) and the colour sky (no. 1614) from the colour azur (no. 1615). The many typos in the names and numbering of the colours are what lends the Chart a certain artisenal cachet.

127.21.9
More or Less
Useful Details

It's not always easy to know when one is justified in creating new old words. The French expression *quoi c'que* meaning *what is it that* for example, is a contraction of *quoi c'est que*, which is pronounced and written in simpler form in Acadia as *quoisse que* (and might be rendered in English as *wot's dat den*). However, this last version appears neither in Pascal Poirier's *Glossaire acadien* (*Acadian Glossary*), nor in Yves Cormier's *Dictionnaire du français acadien* (*Dictionary of Acadian French*). The Poirier volume does however include the words for *where*: *ousque* and *yousque* instead of *où est-ce que* and *y où est-ce que*. One might be similarly justified in including *ayousque*, which is equally common in Acadian speech and clearly derived from *à y où est-ce que*. In that case, why not *quoisque* and, for proper Sunday speech, *quesque*? The *quoisse* would continue to exist as a way to contract the *que*. Clearly, the same rule ought to apply to *qui*.

"Makes no nevermind wot you say, it's only a whole lot more rules. And who is it's goin' to make sure 't all makes sense?"

"Does we even have de right to screw around wid French like dat?" 128.30.10 Chiac

> Twelve cubed (i.e., 12^3, or 12 × 12 × 12) seems to evoke an ample and durable plenitude, more than 12 multiplied merely once by itself (12^2, or 12 × 12). The idea of 1,728 fragments, rather than 144, promises a definite breadth and strength. 129.12.2 Structure

Music played an important role in the Babar's success. Carmen and Josse had asked several talented disc jockeys and other musical connaisseurs to tape several hundred hours of music for those evenings when they had no live music. New compilations were constantly being added. Most of the DJs offered their services without charge.

"It's good practice for me. You can buy me a beer sometime."

130.6.3 The Babar "Eh! More 'n one. I'll be openin' up de opposite of a tab for you at the bar."

> The vowel *u* takes the prize when it comes to inspiring no colour: 5 of the 102 participants in the survey claimed they imagined the *u* without any colour. These respondents were nevertheless fewer than the 16 who saw it as red, 14 as yellow, 14 as green, 12 as purple, 12 as blue, 10 as orange, 9 as brown, 2 each as black, 131.3.5 Statistics white, grey, and turquoise, 1 as pink, and 1 as uranium.

"Tiddly-tiddly-tat yer pointy pointy hat!"

Marianne giggled. Terry did it again:

"Tiddly-tiddly-tat yer pointy pointy hat!"

Again Marianne giggled, and Terry did it again, this time modifiying the intonations:

"TIDdly-TIDdly-tAT yer pointy pointy hAT!"

He could have gone on like this forever. Marianne was not a difficult child, and easily amused. For this very reason, Terry and Carmen had to be careful not to neglect her, compared to Étienne who never let you forget him.

"Marianne, how'd you like to take a car ride with Dad? Eh, just Marianne 'n Dad in de car?"

"I wanna go too."

"Nope, you came along yesterday, didn't ya. Marianne's turn today."

132.134.1 Marianne Étienne, too, had to get used to the fact that Marianne occupied a place of her very own, as well.

> Second coincidence: in *Le Nouveau Petit Robert* dictionary, the definition of the word *auburn* refers us back to the word *acajou*, French for "mahogany." In the same volume,

> directly above the word *acajou* one finds the word *acadien*. And stranger still, the mascot of the Acadian Games was called Acajoux. 133.17.2
> Something to think about. Chance

For fun, two friends of the Babar who'd read the brief article in *L'Acadie nouvelle* began to interview the customers around them.

"And do you imagine the letter *a* any particular colour?"

"Yellow."

"And *e*?"

"Naw."

"How about *i*?"

"Orange like..."

"And *o*?"

"Black fer sure."

"And *u*..."

"Purple-ish..."

"And *y*..."

"White." 134.6.5

"White?! G'wan wid choo, now dat's unusual." The Babar

> Among other designers to have made their mark on the history of letter forms, we can include Fournier, William Caslon, John Baskerville, and Giambattista Bodoni. But this list is far from exhaustive. The history of the alphabet, like that of writing, belongs to civili- 135.10.12
> zations rather than individuals. Typography

"Pascal de lamb was a lamb like all de udders: he was wee an' curly an' innocent."

"Wot's innocent?"

"Means ee was nice like, not a mean bone in 'is body."

"Wot's a mean bone den?"

"Dat's just an expression. Folks been saying it so long

nobody knows where it comes from. Just means ee had no meanness in 'im."

This explanation satisfied Étienne, so Terry continued:

"An' ee was called Pascal 'cause ee's born on Easter."

"Wot's Easter, Dad?"

With this, Étienne's third question, Terry decided the story would be a short one.

"Easter's de weekend when Jesus was resurrected. You know, we all goes down to Grande-Digue an' eats Easter eggs an' Easter bunnies."

"How come den it's not a story 'bout Pascal de rabbit?"

Étienne had used the expression *How come* in English, which made Terry wince. Carmen often blamed him for the children's use of Chiac.

"On account of dis was a lamb and 'is name was Pascal."

"OK, Dad, go on den."

Terry prayed for inspiration.

"Pascal the lamb was down on 'is four knees an' bleatin' like lambs do, when ee hears a voice tellin' 'im to get up. Well, ee gets up, 'cause don't ferget, ee's innocent..."

...

"An' de voice says not to get all anxious if de earth starts atremblin' an' shakin', on account of it's just Jesus pushin' on dat rock in front of his tomb, so's ee can resurrect."

...

"So Pascal de lamb doesn't worry one bit, ee just leans down an' takes anudder moutful o' grass."

Terry paused a moment to pray again for inspiration.

"Well right den, de eart' starts atremblin'... an' shakin... an' tremblin' some more... an' Pascal de lamb, well ee jus' keeps on chompin' on dat grass, not scared one bit."

...

"An' does you know why?"

Was Étienne already asleep? Terry did not dare hope.

"Well, it's on account of ee was innocent. An' God protects de innocent, so dey say."

Terry decided to believe Étienne had truly fallen

asleep, especially since the story had reached a good place to end. He got up slowly, turned off Babar on the dresser and moved toward the door.

"Dad?"

Terry swallowed his discouragement:

"Yah?"

"Does dat mean God protects Chico?"

That took Terry's breath away.

"Yah, dat's exactly wot it means."

...

"G'night, son."

"G'night, Dad."

136.37.9 Animal Tales

> The temptation, or rather the necessity to enlarge the role of accents: for example, the acute accent on the *e* of English verbs ending in *er* — *bãnkér, clãmpér, drĩvér, flũnkér, lẽakér, mãnagér* – to indicate that these are English words the suffixes of which are pronounced as in French. In this way we make decisions, establish new rules, rethink our mistakes.

137.35.3 The Detail within the Detail

"Are ya scared to put yer finger in yer own bellybutton, den?"

"I wouldn't say I's scared. I jus' don't care fer it. Tickles me in a way I don't like."

138.137.9 Fears

> The object of facile judgments, of cartoons depicting him with a menacing look, accused of being a sexual pervert, Freud was well aware that psychoanalysis was inflicting a third narcissistic wound on humanity, the first having been dealt by Copernicus, who denied human beings their place at the centre of the universe, and the second by Darwin, who established a direct relation between the human and the monkey. Freud, for his part, like a seismic

139.39.3 Freud Circuitously tremor, had shaken the very foundations of reason.

"I'll be goin' downstairs an' do a bit o' work, catch up on some book orders, if you doesn't mind..."

Terry had said *Je vas* for "I'll go." Carmen corrected him.

"*Je vais*."

...

"No, I don' mind. I won't be late to bed, that's for sure."

How long would it take Terry to correct the *je vas* and say it properly: *je vais*? Months? Years? And did he have to make the correction at all cost, at any cost? The more often he was reminded of it, the more Terry, in spite of himself, inserted proper French in his speech, but it did not always happen. Sometimes, incompatible linguistic impulses blinked in his mind when he opened his mouth,
140.30.8 Chiac producing new errors. And so, just for peace of mind, he preferred occasionally to remain silent.

> Babar, the elephant cartoon created in 1931 by Jean de Brunhoff, is an excellent model of socialization. His story gently introduces children aged three to seven to the values of citizenship. Babar likes to dress properly, always answers when queried at school, helps others as others have helped him, and learns that each of us has an essential role to play in society. When he becomes king, Babar makes good civil and cultural choices. Under his reign, the
> 141.7.9 Useful Details elephants build schools, cultivate gardens, play music and attend the theatre.

142.15.8 Unidentified Monologues "Dey filmed lobsters underwater goin' in an' out of de traps... Turns out it don't happen de way dey always tot it did, ha ha ha!"

> In the last building to have housed the newspaper *L'Évangéline*, all the old printing material—lead ingots, cases, linotypes—lay there abandoned to dust, at the same time as the crafts quietly vanished, a language lost its footing, reality wavered, even memories gradually but steadily fading, fading also in the minds of the elders who now inhabit the place. On my computer I point and click "format," I read the instruction "change font" and a corner of the veil lifts, revealing that great extinguished body that death suddenly renders fascinating. 143.54.1 Forgotten/Recalled

"Do you know how many possible colours exist in the universe?"

Le Petit Étienne gazed at the colour chart before him as though there were already far too many to count. Zablonski continued:

"With computers, now we can create sixteen million different colours."

Étienne knew that a million was a lot. To give the number some weight, Zablonski added:

"It's almost as many as there are stars in the heavens."

The boy's eyebrows arched. The teacher sensed he was on the right track:

"But our eyes can't see all the colours. We can only distinguish around three-hundred thousand. Which is still a great many."

Le Petit Étienne considered this.

"Sometimes de sky doesn't have a whole lot of stars."

"That's true. The stars are not unlike colours: we can't see them all. Because of clouds, or because they're too far away, or because they're not in our sky, because the earth is turning."

Le Grand Étienne allowed a few moments to pass before taking up his lecture:

"What's particular about all these colours, is that very

few of them have names."

Étienne Zablonski pointed to the colour chart:

"These here, which you can see — marjoram, ondine, melancholy, picador — they're very lucky to have names, because most of the sixteen million colours are known only by numbers. Or letters. Or sometimes a combination of the two, numbers and letters."

Zablonski wondered if the child made the difference between numbers and letters, but he did not linger unnecessarily over the question:

"Which means that there are still many colours left to name."

Suddenly, Le Grand Étienne seemed struck by the idea.

"So we can very well name a colour wool green or vein green, even mother's orange, if we so desire. Nothing can stop us doing so. Nothing and no one."

Le Petit Étienne gazed at Le Grand Étienne. He felt
144.2.12 somehow the incomplete state of the universe and how
Colours much there remained to do.

CHAPTER 2

> *The stone is the friend of numerals and numbers. Nothing expresses a mathematical elegance better than a stone to which we have given well-balanced measurements.*
>
> Jean Giono, "*La pierre*" ("The Stone")
> in *Le Déserteur et autres récits* (*The*
> *Deserter and Other Stories*) 145.144.2
> Gallimard, 1973 Epigraphs

Terry called out to the customer as she was about to open the door to leave.

"An' do you know dis book over here?"

Terry grabbed hold of the large volume under the counter and moved toward the woman.

"Gaston Miron's de only Canadian dat's listed as one of de forty-nine best books of poetry in French in *La Bibliothèque idéale*."

The woman glanced at the cover of *La Bibliothèque idéale*, a work that claimed to list all the books that ought to be included in a francophone's ideal library. She did not seem to have seen it before. Terry showed her the table on pages 124 and 125.

"Eh? I don't see any udder, anyhow…"

The woman quickly scanned down the list.

"No, nor do I. But I don't know them all."

"And as doh dat weren't enuff... turns out dat was the feller's only book."

The woman nodded, going down the list again more closely.

"Maybe you'd like to borrow it? 'Tis right interestin' just to look at. A body doesn't have to read it all."

Aware that he'd switched to the less formal *tu* in addressing her, Terry offered the customer *La Bibliothèque idéale.*

"You can haul it back when yer books come in."

It was really a sales trick of his. He actually owned several copies of *La Bibliothèque idéale*, which he would lend out from time to time. When they returned it, people also tended to order a few of the books listed within. A few even ordered a copy of the reference work itself.

"Yes, I wouldn't mind."

146.8.9 Didot Books
"Like I say, it's interestin' readin' bits of it now an' den..."

> In her novel *1953: Chronicle of a Birth Foretold*, Acadian author France Daigle does not mention the creation that year of the publishing house Hachette's paperback division, Livre de Poche. Henri Filipacchi, then Secretary General of Messageries Hachette, launched three books in paperback: *Koenigsmark* by Pierre Benoît, *Les Clés du royaume* (*The Keys to the Kingdom)* by A. J. Cronin, and *Vol de nuit* (*Night Flight*) by Antoine de Saint-Exupéry. Legend has it that the idea came to Filipacchi to publish books in a smaller, cheaper format when he saw an American GI, standing in front of a Paris bookstore, tear a book in two and stuff it into his pockets. The paperback had already existed for some time in England and the United States.

147.45.2 Useless Details

"Gaw?"

"Gone?"

"Gaw?"

"Yup, de lady's gone."

Standing by the big glass door, her Tatou in her arms,
Marianne looked from side to side without spotting the 148.103.1
departing customer. Disappearances

> If the *u* seems to be the vowel that evokes the least colour, the *y* is the one that's most often forgotten. In fact, 8 of the 102 participants in the survey simply did not mention it. Although this absence is notable, it should not eclipse the fact that 39 respondants said the *y* appeared to them in yellow. For 15 others, it suggested purple. Then comes oblivion—third place, after all. Oblivion is followed by green, which was mentioned seven times; black six times; no colour four times; blue, green, and red each named three times; brown, purple, and white
> twice each; and cyan, maroon, orange, gold, 149.3.6
> turquoise, sky blue, beige, and pink. Statistics

"Only, I has de feeling she don't talk much fer her age, I mean. Like today, when she said dat, it hit me dat she don't often say real words. Don't you tink?"

"Well, might be she doesn't have a whole lot to say. There's plenty folks like that."

"I know kids don't all come up de same way, there's dem dat starts walkin' later, udders get to talkin' later, or wears nappies longer..."

"Well, sure, but 'tisn't like she doesn't understand us, is it. I don't think she's deaf or anythin'."

The ads were coming to an end, and the TV show was about to start up again. Terry made haste to get his question in: 150.94.10

"Do doctors check dat sort of ting?" Terry and

"Well, I hope so..." Carmen

In *Petites difficultés d'existence* by France Daigle (Les Éditions du Boréal, 2002), translated by Robert Majzels as *Life's Little Difficulties* (House of Anansi Press, 2004), readers learn that an arsonist completely destroyed the home of Étienne and Ludmilla Zablonski in Baltimore,
151.54.9 Forgotten/ Recalled which explains why the painter possesses so few objects from his past.

PRÉCIS

de

L'HISTOIRE MODERNE

par **M. MICHELET,**

Membre de l'Institut,
professeur d'histoire au Collège de France,
chef de la section historique aux Archives nationales

OUVRAGE ADOPTÉ
Par le Conseil de l'Université,

ET PRESCRIT POUR L'ENSEIGNEMENT
DE L'HISTOIRE MODERNE DANS LES COLLÈGES
ET DANS TOUS LES ÉTABLISSEMENTS
D'INSTRUCTION PUBLIQUE.

HUITIÈME ÉDITION.

PARIS
LIBRAIRIE CLASSIQUE ET ÉLÉMENTAIRE
DE L . HACHETTE,
LIBRAIRIE DE L'UNIVERSITÉ DE FRANCE,

Rue Pierre-Sarrazin, 12.

1850

152.84.7 History

Regarding *Petites difficultés d'existence*, the second edition of the French version of the novel is preferable to the first, because the latter contains minor errors. Luckily, these errors do not actually affect the narrative itself, but they could confuse those who take pleasure in closer readings. Mention of the second printing is included in the publications page at the end of the book. If there is no mention of a second printing, you are in possession of the version containing errors. Those in possession of the English translation, entitled *Life's Little Difficulties*, will be relieved to learn it does not contain the errors in the first edition of the French version.

153.105.10
Reserves/
Reservations

Elementary operation adding the numerals in the number 666, a number considered by some as satanic. Identical result when working from right to left, as in Arabic writing:

$6 + 6 + 6 =$	$6 + 6 + 6 =$
$(6 + 6) + 6 =$	$6 + (6 + 6) =$
$(12) + 6 =$	$6 + (12) =$
$(1 + 2) + 6 =$	$6 + (1 + 2) =$
$(3) + 6 = 9$	$6 + (3) = 9$

154.97.1
Numerals and
Numbers

Any attempt to elaborate a correct definition of desire will demonstrate to what extent people like Freud and Lacan were possessed of a kind of genius. Because there is no simple definition of desire. Similarly, the art and science of psychoanalysis is based on dense and intricate concepts, which are not easily rendered accessible to the layman. For the moment, let us limit ourselves to saying that desire is to

155.128.12 Fervours psychoanalysis what strawberries are to strawberry pie.

The addition of the numerals making up the number 1,728, the multiple of 12 supposedly representing plenitude, yields a similar result to that obtained from the presumed satanic number 666:

$1 + 7 + 2 + 8 =$
$(1 + 7) + 2 + 8 =$
$[(8) + 2] + 8 =$
$10 + 8 =$
156.97.2 Numerals and Numbers $(1 + 0) + 8 =$
$1 + 8 = 9$

$1 + 7 + 2 + 8 =$
$1 + 7 + (2 + 8) =$
$1 + 7 + (10) =$
$1 + 7 + (1 + 0) =$
$1 + [7 + (1)] =$
$1 + 8 = 9$

By the beginning of the '60s, the enormous success of the softcover cheaper format led French economists to add the paperback to their list of consumer products included in the calculation of the price index. At the same time a typically French polemic erupted around the paperback as "democratic and egalitarian illusion." None other than Jean-Paul Sartre himself signed a text in *Temps modernes* responding to the article in *Mercure de France* that had sparked the debate. Notwithstanding these arguments,
157.19.4 Interesting Details nothing seemed to slow the promised rise of the paperback, not to mention the benefits to reading, authors, and texts.

"You, yer a writer! Are you seein' colours, den?"

This had been going on for a while now. It turned out that all the residents of the lofts who were in the Babar at that moment saw the *a* as yellow and the *i* as red. All, that
158.6.6 The Babar is, 9 of the 27 residents. At 4:30 p.m. in the afternoon, on a Thursday.

> A scattered novel, then. Serenity being, after 159.12.3
> all, something that must be earned. Structure

Élizabeth is strolling in the streets of Moncton: Highfield, Winter, Portledge, North, not necessarily in that order, because all this happened some time ago. The trees along those streets are more damaged than they were back then, but they still manage to form an impressive canopy. Élizabeth is on her way to or from the hospital. She lives at
the end of one of these streets. Still lives there today. Just 160.54.4
a little bit in retreat. Élizabeth is always in retreat. Her life, Forgotten/
her work, her thoughts. In retreat, and yet, not. Recalled

> Additional results of the small impromptu survey on the perception of colours in vowels: all but 6 of the participants used loose leaf three-holed paper; 63 of these sheets were lined and bore the Hilroy insignia in the lower right-hand corner; three respondents tore loose leaf sheets from their three-ringed binders, thus tearing the holes. As for the others, 3 tore a sheet from spiral notebooks, and 1 participant used a sheet of paper that was not white, pink as a matter of fact. Also, 50 respondents used blue ink ballpoint or felt pens; 31 used pencils; 10 used black ink ballpoint or felt pens; 4 combined blue ink and grey pencil; 3 used purple ink; 2 used red ink; 1 used green, and the last
> made his or her mark by combining red and 161.3.8
> black ink. Statistics

Terry and Zed had made an appointment with a Halifax architectural firm to discuss their project and to explore the possibilities. On their way they dropped a few coins in a beggar's cap. In return the man smiled his thanks, revealing no less than a half dozen golden fillings.

162.63.12 "Well, 'tis nice to 'ave a bit of sometin' put away, like
Terry and Zed dey say."

> Boredom conceals anger and anxiety. Superstition is the anticipation of difficulties due to the projection of hostile desires. Happiness does not exist except as the realization of a childhood desire. Religion is the childhood feeling of impotence carried into adulthood and projected into culture. Paranoia is evidence of homosexuality. Groups, crowds, gangs, and families are held together by diffuse libidinal ties; disintegration and panic ensue when the erotic relation is extinguished. All dependencies are a substitute for the primary habit, masturbation. The arts are a cultural narcotic without the disadvantages that other drugs produce over time. Adult scientific curiosity is the extension of the child's search for the truth about sexual differences and the mysteries of conception and birth. Aesthetic creations, making love, war, laws, and constitutions are all means of mastering the universe, or a way to disguise the inability to master it. Fiction offers the human being a diversity of lives we require to live. Neurosis is an individual religion, religion a universal neurosis. The true founder of civization is the man who thrust an insult at
> 163.39.5 his enemy instead of a sword. Human beings are
> Freud not meant to be happy, their happiness is not
> Circuitously part of creation's plan.

"Dey went an' bought all dis stuff, den in de end dey's worse off dan when dey started. Turned out, de feller dat sold it to 'em was crookeder den a dog's hind leg, even
164.15.1 doh dey'd known him fer a dog's age, what 'appens a
Unidentified whole lot in dat business, supposedly. A real racket, or
Monologues dat's wot dey say."

In 1972, the publisher Gallimard created Folio paperbacks. *L'Étranger* (*The Stranger*) by Albert Camus became Folio's bestseller with 6 million copies sold. Hachette, meanwhile, can boast sales of 300,000 copies of novels by Mary Higgins Clark and Bernard Werber in paperback.

165.19.8
Interesting
Details

"Dad, did you see? Dat man over der trowed 'is coffee cup on de ground."

As a matter of fact, Terry could see the Tim Hortons cup rolling in a half circle on the pavement.

"Should I be goin' over der, Dad, an' tell 'im to pick it up?"

Terry thought his son was brave, though he wasn't sure this was a healthy quality in this case.

"Up to you..."

Étienne marched right over.

"Sir, yer coffee cup fell on de ground."

The paunchy worker, looking down at the small boy, made as though he hadn't understood.

"Eh? Wot's dat?"

"Yer cup fell on de ground back over der."

"Well, no matter, she's empty."

"How come den, you didn't trow her in de trashcan?"

"In de wot?"

"De trashcan..."

Étienne had used the proper French word, *poubelle*. Now he pointed to the trashcan to be sure the man had understood him.

"Awh! De dung bin."

...

"Awright den, b'y. You go on over an' fetch her, an' I'll trow her in dis 'ere bin."

"Awright."

The worker waited for Étienne to bring him the cup, and then threw it in the trashcan.

"Der ya go! Are you proud of yerself now?"

Étienne looked up at the man and nodded. As the kid didn't seem to want to go.

"Well, an' wot's de problem now?"

"Nuttin."

"So, is it awright by you, den, if I gets back to work now?

Étienne nodded."

166.130.3 "G'day."

Work "G'day."

> Fourth coincidence: the day of the small impromptu survey on the perceived colour of vowels, there were a total of 102 students in four groups who agreed to participate. There could easily have been more or fewer. Now consider that the 102 is exactly the number of letters in a game of Scrabble, both in the French and English versions. Is it possible to ignore the link between the two blank letters in
> 167.17.4 the game and the two participants who associ-
> Chance ated no colour with the letter *a*?

Carmen's position on the subject of language is not particularly easy to bear, least of all for her. As much as she would like her children to learn proper French, there are times when she can't help but smile at some particularly pretty Chiac phrase. But this is not, alas, always the case. More often than not, she feels the Chiac is a kind of laziness, a lack of curiosity, pride, or logic, especially when the proper French term is common knowledge and easy to integrate into everyday speech. In the Babar, for example, she'd like her employees to speak a slightly more elevated French naturally, without abandoning Chiac entirely. She has not yet found a way to raise the
168.20.2 issue with them; she worries she might be judged or iso-
Language lated simply by raising such a sensitive subject.

> At the beginning of the fifteenth century, when a thirst for knowledge spawned a demand for written works, an attempt was made to accelerate the production of books by engraving each page in wood and then printing copies. This process was unsatisfactory because of the problems arising from the use of wood.

169.10.6
Typography

At some point, thinking it might be useful, one of the customers in the Babar began tearing out the article about the survey on the colour of vowels.

"Hey, wot are ye at?"

The guilty party knew he'd been caught red handed:

"Well... I was tinkin' I might keep jus' de article..."

"Are you one of dose bright chuckleheads wot tears out de pages of magazines in de dentist's waitin' room? Oh me son!"

170.6.7
The Babar

> It was Demiéville who introduced Lacan to the letter toward the end of the '40s.

171.35.9
The Detail within the Detail

"How's it dey go on parkin' der? Don't dey see der blockin' everyone behind?"

Terry looked out the window, even though he already knew what he would see.

"As doh der wasn't all dat room right beside..."

Zed shook his head. Terry went to fetch another crate of books.

"I bin tinkin' on wot you said de udder day. More I tink on it, more it makes good sense."

But when he turned around, Zed realized that Terry was no longer there; he'd spoken to the wind.

172.103.8
Disappearances

> If there is a difficulty, perhaps it lies in the absence of guidelines, thus requiring each reader to figure out his or her own method to access the creative work, which simply proves that this

173.12.4 really is a creative act rather than a tried and
Structure tested method. Does it make itself understood?

Later that day, Terry thought he'd look up what status *La Bibliothèque idéale* accorded Freud. The august personality was of course included, and not just for one but for three books, which Terry found both reassuring and exciting. *Birth of Psychoanalysis: Letters to Wilheim Fliess*—most probably interesting, but Terry didn't feel in the mood to tackle an epistolary work; *The Future of an Illusion*—Terry wasn't, for the moment, particularly interested in tackling the world of religion, although he hesitated because of the notion of God as father; *The Interpretation of Dreams*[4] therefore seemed the best choice, especially since the entry also referred to *The Psychopathology of Everyday Life*, one of the titles Ludmilla had mentioned. Terry added *The Interpretation of Dreams*
174.8.10 to his order sheet, in three copies because, once he'd read
Didot Books a book, he generally found a few people to sell it to.

175.68.5 Find out who Demiéville was and to what let-
Projects ter he initiated Lacan.

Woke up with a start in the middle of the night, obsessed with the number of fragments. Got up, found a pencil and paper, drew the big cube in three dimensions, divided the surfaces into 12 by 12, counted the little cubes one by one.
177.104.5 The problem arises with the edges of the big
Worries cube. Bizarre. Start again.

"Well that's normal. With age, the gums recede, and that exposes de roots."

---

4. Recent studies of Freud's work have preferred the title *The*
176.142.4 *Interpretation of Dreaming* to *The Interpretation of Dreams*, but
Notes both are acceptable today.

Ludmilla winced.

"This 'ere's the worst of 'em, far as I can tell."

The dentist continued to explore the crowns of Ludmilla's teeth with his hooked probe, pausing on another tooth that seemed to cause her some pain, and examining it from all angles.

"This one 'ere, I might cover the base with this new product came in jus' now. Wouldn't cost you anyting, 'cause I never tried it yet, and don't know for sure if it'll do the job. S'posed to work, mind you, only sometimes what works for one body doesn't work for another. You take laser, for example. One feller told me it changed his life, but then, for others, it's like haulin' water."

The dentist returned to the tooth with the most recession.

"This one 'ere, I'll 'ave to make a real filling, as though it was a cavity. That's all a fellow can do when de root's overexposed, on account of the gum's receeded. But I won't be goin' down betwixt yer teeth. If the gum's gone down 'tween this tooth and the two either side of it, most likely it will keep right on hurtin'."

Once the examination was over, Ludmilla could finally speak again.

"Couldn't you try laser on both teeth?"

The dentist seemed reluctant. Ludmilla wanted him to say yes:

"*Allez, du courage*!" 178.87.1
The dentist smiled. Really, these French people . . . The Body

> Twelve cubed then, 1,728 fragments, in groups
> of 12 first, then in sections of 144. But can one 179.12.5
> write a novel with so many numerals? Structure

While he was at it, Terry also searched to find out who Raymond Queneau was, and discovered that he too appeared three times in *La Bibliothèque idéale*. *Odile*, a novel about love; *Exercises de style*, a book of distortions

and *Zazie dans le métro*, a novel intended to be comic but maybe not his funniest work, according to the description. Terry turned to his order sheet, pencilled in a three
180.8.11 over the one in the quantities column beside *Exercises*
Didot Books *de style*.

> Lacan, Jacques-Marie — Paris, 1901–1981. Psychiatrist and psychoanalyst, son of Alfred, a mustard merchant descended from a line of vinegar producers in Orléans. Career as a researcher, i.e., solitary, in spite of the fellowship of other major psychoanalysts. Reader-interpreter of Freud. His influence was such that many psychoanalysts declared themselves Lacanians rather than Freudians. In response, Lacan declared himself Freudian. Flirted with
> 181.34.1 symbolism, penetrated the mystery of language
> Lacan and desire, and the roots of being in speech.

The pronunciation of *quante* instead of *quand* for the French word for *when* is generalized in the Acadian language. Standard French only allows for such a pronunciation when *quand* is followed by a word beginning with a vowel or a silent *h*. As a matter of fact, there are many variations in terms relating to time in Acadian:

"*Quand c'est qu'a t'a dit ça ?*"

(When is it she tol' you dat?)

"*Ajeuve, quante que je passais en avant de chuseux.*"

(A while ago, whiles I was passin' by dat fella's house.)

"*Pis, quantaisse qu'y faut que tu donnes ta réponse ?*"

(Well den, when's it yer s'posed to give 'em yer answer?)

"*Mèque la lôde arrive. Par ce temps-là on saura si on 'n aura besoin de plusse ou pas.*"

('bout de time de load comes in. By den we'll knows wedder we needs more or we doesn't.)

"*Y as-tu dit que ça se pouvait qu'on n'aurait pas même besoin de toute une lôde?*"

(An' did you tell 'er could be, we won't be needin' a whole load?)

"*Oui. Alle a juste dit d'y dire ãs sõon qu'on pouvait.*" 182.30.11

(I did. She only said to tell her *aussitôt* we knows.) Chiac

> *P* is the only letter that can equal the letters *a*, *b*, and *c* when it comes to the number of times they appear as the first letter of a real colour in pourpre.com's chromatic dictionary. *P* is the first letter of 28 colours, 5 less than *a*, but 2 more than *b*. Together the four letters, *a*, *b*, *c*, and *p*, which constitute 15 percent of the alphabet, are the first letters of 48 percent — might as well say half — of the 281 names of colours in the above mentioned dictionary.

> Similarly, in Wikipedia's list of 869 English colours, the *c*, *p*, *d*, and *b* lead the way in the number of colours of which they are the first letter. *P* is the first letter of 90 colours, 1 less than *c*, and 15 more than *d*. Together these four letters, *c*, *p*, *d*, and *b*, which constitute 15 percent of the alphabet, are the first letters of 37.9 percent — more than a third, but less than half — of the 869 colours listed on Wikipedia.com. *A* is a
> distant tenth, being the first letter of only 36 183.3.9
> names of colours, or 4.1 percent. Statistics

One evening, while reading a passage from Alphonse Daudet's *Letters from My Windmill* to Étienne, Terry came upon the word *rouf* signifying a small cabin on a boat, which Terry imagined resembled a lobster fishing boat. The word surprised him, but he read on. Two sentences further, Étienne interrupted:

"Dad, I don't understan'."

"What is it you don' unnerstan'?"

"De words."

Terry reread the passage silently, and realized that indeed the boy could easily feel lost in this universe at once familiar and yet unknown. He started over then, adapting a bit as he read.

"Dat schooner dey called Miss Emilie, from Cap-Pelé, was old and creakin' all over when I come aboard. Der was only a wee *rouf* to keep out o' de rain and wind and waves, a wee *rouf* wid two cots an' a table. We was on our way to Cocagne. De fishermen's faces was all wet, dat rain was beatin' down so hard..."

184.20.4 Language "Ya, Dad. Dat's a whole lot better."

> Since an alphabetical count of the French chromatic dictionary at pourpre.com yields 281 names of colours, it would be logical to assume that each of the 26 letters of the alphabet would begin, on average, 11 names of colours. But on that score, aside from the letters *a, b, c,* and *p*, only the *m* and the *s* score well above the average; they are the first letter respectively for 21 and 18 names of colours. The *f* is slightly above the average, beginning 14 names of colours. The letters *e, g, i, o, t,* and *v* lead within the average, while *l, n,* and *r* are far below average with only 6 or 7 names to their credit. *D, h, j, k, q,* and *z* are the first letter in 1, 2 or 3 names of colours, whereas *u, w, x,* and *y* are completely absent from this alphabetical order.
>
> On Wikipedia's English list of 869 colours, one might expect, on average, each letter of the alphabet to begin the names of slightly more than 33 colours. Along with *c, p, d,* and *b, m, r, l, s,* and *t* also come in above the average. *A, f,* and *g* are around the average, while *o, u, e, i, v, h, w*, and *n* are first in between 25 to 11 names of colours. *J* and *y* are first in eight names, *k* in

5, and *z* in 2. *Q* and *x* are the first letter in one 185.3.10
name each. Statistics

"De udder day, ee tells me de last tree months have been sometin' of a trial."

. . .

"When ee opens up like dat, I sees just how many different me's der are in 'im, and a whole lot of different hims in me."

. . .

"Come ta tink of it, a bit of psychoanalysis might do 186.15.4
me good as well. Dese days, I'm seein' double meanings Unidentified
even in Scrabble." Monologues

187.89.1
First irritant: a novel with (too) many numbers. Irritants

La Bibliothèque idéale lay open on the counter while Terry revised his order for Raymond Queneau's *Exercises in Style*. He was suddenly curious to see what category in the book preceded "Distortions." His search led him to "Literature in Pieces," which confirmed the logic of the book. Scanning quickly down the list of texts said to be in pieces, his eye fell on the following excerpt from Emil Cioran's *Précis de décomposition* (*A Short History of Decay*): "In every man a prophet sleeps and, when he awakens, there is a little more evil in the world," a phrase that tweaked his heart and mind. He placed the thin white ribbon attached to the headband of the book on that page, with the intention of returning to it tomorrow. Then he closed up shop, because
Ludmilla, who usually did this, had taken off early to go 188.8.12
to the dentist. Didot Books

On a U.S. letter-sized sheet of white paper, a list of all the golf courses in New Brunswick. A footnote at the bottom of the page preceeded by an asterisk notes that the Atlantic provinces

> boast the highest per capita number of golf courses in Canada. This tidbit of information
> 189.57.4 Photocopies
> is clearly gratis, since there is no corresponding asterisk to be found anywhere on the page.

After the joyful distraction that the colour of vowels test had created in the Babar, Le Grand Étienne thought he'd try the exercise with his student.

"A test?"

Le Petit Étienne had not forgotten the X-3X-X3-X test and Souricette's unfortunate end.

"Oh, nothing very difficult, it's just for fun."

The boy gave a slight nod of the head.

"If I say the word *banana*, do you see a colour?"

Étienne answered with a laugh, as though the answer was obvious and the test wasn't really a test at all:

"Yellow."

Le Grand Étienne realized that this test contained traps one would do well to avoid. He took a moment to think it through and decided to stick to words referring to abstract realities.

"And if I say the word 'avatar'?"

The little one hesitated.

"Do you know what an avatar is?"

The boy did not dare reply.

"Do you see a colour, anyway?"

Le Petit Étienne was a bit confused because he was still seeing yellow, which seemed somehow suspicious. He replied with a question:

"Yellow?"

Proud of the child's perspicacity, Le Grand Étienne resolved to look for words whose meanings the child did not know.

"An avatar is someone who is not real. A kind of ghost. You understand?"

Le Petit Étienne nodded yes.

"Do you know anyone like that?"

Le Petit Étienne thought for a moment, then shook his head no. 190.14.1

"Good." Zablonski

> And why not numbers? Don't they constitute a form of thought? A kind of writing? Are they not evidence of laws as inescapable as they are recurrent? Consider the following operations, taking into account the fact that the numeral 3 represents the masculine principal and 4 the feminine:
>
> a) $1{,}728 \div 3 = 576$
> $576 \div 12 = 48$
>
> b) $1{,}728 \div 4 = 432$
> $432 \div 12 = 36$
>
> c) $48 \times 36 = 1{,}728$
>
> Elementary, I admit. But the question remains: 191.12.6
> up to what point to open up (oneself)? Structure

Le Petit Étienne was remembering Souricette, trying to feel if there was something unusual happening inside himself.

"What about the word *tumult*? Mean anything to you?"

No, nothing about this test worried him.

"No."

"And do you see a colour?"

"Blue."

Le Grand Étienne was writing it all down as they proceeded.

"And what shade of blue? Pale? Dark?"

Le Petit Étienne rocked his head back and forth.

The master got up to fetch the chart they'd been looking at earlier, and opened it up in front of his pupil.

"Do you see a blue in here that looks like the blue of tumult?"

Le Petit Étienne hesitated between Gobelin (no. 1910), China (no. 1903), old blue (no. 2012), and marjoram (no. 2052), all of which were more or less dark and edging toward purple or black. In the end he pointed to marjoram. Le Grand Étienne wrote the result down on his sheet of paper.

"Tumult means disorderly, maybe even loud. you know?"

192.14.2 Zablonski Étienne nodded yes immediately, because that was easy to understand.

> Coincidence? The fact that Firmin Didot (1764–1836), born into the long line of Didots, and responsible for the transformation of typeface engraving and casting, started out as
> 193.17.6 Chance a statistician before becoming a publisher of books containing lists.

The grand surprise finale for this family with a singing dad took place on the beach one splendid Sunday in August. Terry and Carmen had discovered this tiny but completely deserted beach — incredible! — and they went there whenever they felt the need to be alone, with or without the children. Life in the lofts offered numerous advantages, but there was also a good deal of toing and froing and brouhaha, which made the little beach a secret treasure, which they were careful not to talk about for fear of losing it. In the late afternoon, once the kids had tired themselves out running and playing, so that they were content to sit and have a bite — a slice of cheese for Marianne, a peach for Étienne — Terry suddenly announced that he'd learned a fifth Aragon song, which he was dedicating to the three of them. And without further ado, he launched into "Je t'aime tant" ("I Love You So Much"), as though he were simply completing his

sentence. Carmen, Étienne and Marianne quickly realized that the song, which was about the sea and wind and daydreams and the colour blue, suited the occasion perfectly. At the end, all three felt so united and so unique in
Terry's repeated "I love you so much" that... that... 194.1.11
"Dad! Will you always love us too much?" Chansons

> But isn't the cube the perfect incarnation of rigidity? How could life — since a novel claims to
> invoke life — flow within such a strictly defined 195.12.7
> structure, so neat and orderly, so inorganic? Structure

L'Officiel du jeu Scrabble® lists 257 French words beginning with *a* and containing at least one *y*. The list does not include the various possible forms these words can take (feminine, plural, conjugated). Here then is the list: abbaye, aboyer, aboyeur, abyme, abyssal, abysse, abyssin, abyssinien, abzyme, acétaldéhyde, acétylcellulose, acétylcholine, acétyle, acétylène, acétylénique, acétylure, achylie, acolytat, acolyte, acotylédone, acrodynie, acronyme, acrylique, acrylonitrile, actinomycète, actinomycose, actinoptérygien, acyclique, acylation, acyle, adipocyte, adipolyse, adrénolytique, adynamie, adynamique, adyton, aegyrine, aepyornis, aérodynamique, aérodynamisme, aérodyne, aglycone, aglyphe, agranulocytose, aisy, alcoylation, alcoyle, alcyne, alcyon, alcyonaire, alcyonien, aldéhyde, aldéhydique, alexithymie, alicyclique, alkylation, alkyle, allyle, alkylène, allylique, aloyau, alysse, alysson, alyssum, alyte, amarayeur, amaryllidacée, amaryllis, amblyope, amblyopie, amblyoscope, amblyrhynque, amblystome, ambystome, améthyste, amidopyrine, aminophylline, ammodyte, amphictyon, amphictyonie, amphyctyomique, amphitryon, ampholyte, amygdale, amygdalectomie, amydaline, amygdalite, amygdaloïde, amygdalotome, amylacé, amylase, amyle, amylène, amylique, amylobacter, amyloïde, amylose, amyotrophie, anacyclique, anaglyphe, anaglypte, anaglyptique, analycité, analysable, analysant, analyse, analyser, analyseur, analyste, analyticité, analytique, analytiquement, anaphylactique, anaphylaxie, anastylose, anchoyade, androgyne, androgynie, anévrysme, anévrysmal, anhydre, anhydride, anhydrite, anhydrobiose, anhypothétique, ankylosant, ankylosaure, ankylose, ankyloser, ankylostome, ankylostomiase, anonymat, anonyme, anonymement, anonymographe, antéhypophyse, anthroponyme, anthroponymie, anthyllide, anthyllis, anticyclique, anticyclonal, anticyclone, anticyclonique, antienzyme, antihygiénique, antimycosique, antimycotique, antioxydant, antipsychiatre, antipsychiatrie, antipsychotique, antipyrétique, antipyrine, antisymétrique, antisyndical, antithyroïdien, antitrypsine, antonyme, antonymie, anxiolytique, aphylle, apitoyer, apocalypse, apocalyptique, apocryphe, apocynacée, apoenzyme, apophysaire, apophyse, appuyer, appuyoir, aptérygote, aptéryx, apyre, apyrétique, apyrexie, apyrogène, aquagym, archéoptéryx, archétypal, archétype, archétypique, archichlamydée, aréostyle, argyraspide, argyrie, argyrisme, argyrol, argyromète, argyrose, arroyo, arthrogrypose, artiodactyle, aryen, arylamine, aryle, aryténoïde, aryténoïdien, arythmie, arythmique, ascomycète, asphyxiant, asphyxie, asphyxique, assyrien, assyriologie, assyriologue, astrophysicien, astrophysique, asymbolie, asymétrie, asymétrique, asymptomatique, asymptote, asymptotique, asynartète, asynchrone, asynchronisme, asyndète, asynergie, asystole, asystolie, atermoyer, athymhormie, athymie, athymique, athyroïdie, atmolyse, atractyligénine, attorney, attrayant, atypie, atypique, atypisme, auréomycine, autoanalyse, autocatalyse, autolysat, autolyse, autonettoyant, autonyme, autonymie, autonymique, aveyronnais, aveyronnaise, avoyer, axisymétrique, ay, ayant, ayatollah, aymara, ayuntamiento, azidothymidine, azothydrique, azotyle, azygos, et azyme.

The Official Scrabble Players Dictionary® or OSPD lists 314 English words (56 more than the French *L'Officiel du jeu Scrabble*®) beginning with the letter *a* and containing at least one *y*, not including the various possible forms these words can take. The list is as follows:
abasedly, abaya, abbacy, abbey, abbotcy, abeyance, abhenry, ability, abjectly, ably, abruptly, absently, aby, abyss, academy, accuracy, acerbity, acetify, acetoxyl, acetyl, achingly, achy, acidify, acidity, acidly, acidy, acolyte, acridity, acrimony, acronym, acrylate, acrylic, activity, actorly, actressy, actually, actuary, acuity, acutely, acyclic, acyl, acylate, acyloin, adamancy, addedly, additory, adenyl, adequacy, adroitly, adultery, adultly, advocacy, adynamia, adytum, aerially, aerify, aerily, aerology, aeronomy, airy, aery , affably, affinely, affinity, affray, agedly, agency, agentry, agility, agly, aglycon, agony, agouty, agrimony, agrology, agronomy, agrypnia, aguishly, ahoy, aimfully, airplay, airway, airy, aisleway, alacrity, alanyl, alary, alcayde, alchemy, aldehyde, alderfly, aleatory, alertly, algidity, algology, alienly, alimony, aliya, alkalify, alkoxy, alky, alkyd, alkyl, alkyne, allay, allegory, allergy, alley, alleyway, allogamy, allonym, allotype, alloy, ally, almighty, almondy, almonry, aloofly, alphyl, alpinely, already, alterity, always, alyssum, amatory, amazedly, ambary, amboyna, ambry, amenity, amethyst, amiably, amicably, aminity, amity, ammonify, amnesty, amplify, amygdala, amygdale, amygdule, amyl, amylase, amylene, amylogen, amyloid, amylose, amylum, anaglyph, anagogy, anality, analogy, analyze , analysis, analyte, anarchy, anatomy, ancestry, anchovy, andesyte , anergy, aneurysm, angary, angry, anility, animacy, animally, ankylose, annoy, annually, annuity, anodyne, anolyte, anomaly, anomy, anonym, anorexy, antetype, antibody, anticity, anticly, antigay, antilogy, antimony, antinomy, antipyic, antitype, antonym, antsy, anxiety, any, anybody, anyhow, anymore, anyon, anyone, anyplace, anything, anytime, anyway, anywhere, apathy, apery, apetaly, aphylly, apiary, apically, apiology,

apishly, aplenty, apocarpy, apogamy, apology, apophony, apophyge, apoplexy, apospory, apostasy, apply, apteryx, aptly, apyrase, apyretic, archery, archly, archway, ardency, ardently, areally, areaway, areology, argosy, argufy, argyle, ariary, aridity, armory, army, armyworm, aroynt, arrantly, array, arrowy, arroyo, artery, artfully, artily, artistry, artsy, aryl, arythmia, ashy, ashtray, asphyxia, assay, assembly, astheny, astony, astrally, astray, astutely, astylar, asylum, asyndeta, atalaya, ataraxy, ataxy, atemoya, athanasy, athodyd, atomy, atony, atopy, atrocity, atrophy, attorney, atypical, audacity, audibly, auditory, augustly, auntly, aunty, aurality, autarchy, autarky, autodyne, autogyro, autolyze, autonomy, autonym, autopsy, autotomy,
196.21.5 More or Less Useful Details autotype, aversely, aviary, avidity, avidly, avowedly, away, awayness, aweary, awfully, awny, awry, axiality, axillary, axiology, ay, ayah, aye, ayin, ayurveda, azygos.

197.57.1 Photocopies

> Flattened against the glass platen, pages 14 and 15 of the paperback edition of Jean-Paul Sartre's *Les Mots* (*Words*). A series of dizzying flashes (brought on especially by the punctuation) lead to my overheating. But I get a grip and, after a bit of coughing, I finally manage to expel the copy with my customary elegance.

198.104.3 Worries

"I said person, not poison."
"Awh."

199.141.6 Obsessions

> Don't the little cubes along the edges serve a double function?

The Babar did good business on Thursdays. Customers began arriving after 4 p.m., already happy to see the approaching weekend. The few elderly people who were in the habit of coming in to linger over a beer, a tea, or a coffee in the afternoons now reconnected with the reality of the working world.

"Oh sure, dey expects you to be doin' every little ting perfect, don't dey, but where are dey, I'd like to know, when de time come to pay?"

"Don't I knows it. I knows dat bunch."

The two young men who'd just come in had a lot to get off their minds.

"I says to 'im: you wants me to do dat, it's gonna cost you five hundred dollars more in labour. Well, all of a sudden he's got a face on 'im like a hen's arsehole in the norwest wind. Mine's an Alpine."

"Sleeman Cream."

"I only hopes dey doesn't call me. I got plenty udder work aside from dem. What's up, ol' man? Are ya laughin' at us again?"

The old man enjoyed a bit of attention from the young ones.

"I bin der meself. 'Twas a whole lot better den bein' old, I can tell ya dat much."

"Come along wid us to work one of dese days, I can promise you'll be rid of dem blues terrible quick. An' wot is it yer drinkin' in dat cup anyways?"

The young man leaned over and pretended to smell the contents of the cup.

"Yer not gonna try 'n tell us dat's jus' coffee in der!"

"Well, dat's betwixt me and the waitress, init."

200.6.8
The Babar

There are five types of stitches in embroidery: cross-stitches, amongst which are included the catch stitch and the chevron stitch; flat stitches, including the long and short stitches and the fishbone; line stitches, including the Romanian couching and Oriental stitches; knotted stitches, such as the bullion stitch and the French knot; and finally, daisy stitches, among which the chain and the feather stitch. The Holbein or double running stitch, for its part, is the basis of blackwork or single-colour embroidery,

> which uses a single colour of thread. In the beginning, that colour was black. Contrasts in tone are produced by using threads and patterns of different densities.

201.71.1
Intro
Embroidery

In his preface to the album *La lettre et l'image* (*Letter and Image*) by Massin, at least in the new and modified edition published by Gallimard in 1993, Raymond Queneau reminds us that there are 52 playing cards in a deck, not counting the jokers. This number, he goes on, is double 26, which is the number of letters in the French (and English, among others) alphabet. If we count the lower and upper case of each letter, there are 52 in total, the same number as there are playing cards in a deck, which is composed of four suits, each made up of 13 cards. The number 52 is therefore divisible by 13, as is 26. Here ends Queneau's observations which, unbeknownst to him, have tipped over this story of the number 12 — the dynamic of which leads eventually to plenitude — into the number 13, generally regarded in European and North American cultures as bad luck: a limit, ultimately death, or the beginning of a new cycle. And yet, 13 was the fundamental sacred number of the ancient Mexicans, equal to the number of days in the Aztec week. Hence:

$$13 \times 13 \times 13 = 2{,}197$$
$$12 \times 12 \times 12 = 1{,}728$$
$$2{,}197 - 1{,}728 = 469 = 4 + 6 + 9 = (4 + 6) + 9 =$$
$$(10) + 9 =$$
$$(1 + 0) + 9 =$$
$$(1) + 9 = 10 = (1 + 0) = 1$$

We arrive at the same result when we multiply the number 13 by the 52 cards in a deck or the number of weeks in the average tropical year.

$13 \times 52 = 676 =$
$6 + 7 + 6 =$
$(6 + 7) + 6 =$
$(13) + 6 =$
$(1 + 3) + 6 =$ 202.17.7
$(4) + 6 = 10 = (1 + 0) = 1$ Chance

> In French Canada, Germaine Guèvremont's *Le Survenant* (book one of *The Outlander* in the English translation) is the number-one best-seller with approximately 10,000 copies sold every year. This is followed by Louis Hémon's *Maria Chapdelaine* and Émile Nelligan's *Complete Poems,* which sell between 3,000 and 4,000 copies annually. *Bousille et les justes* (*Bousille and the Just Ones*) by Gratien Gélinas, *L'Homme rapaillé* (translated in part as *The March to Love*) by Gaston Miron and *Le Souffle de l'Harmattan* (remains untranslated into English) by Sylvain Trudel are also bestsellers. As I write this, of all the above authors, only Sylvain Trudel is still alive.

203.19.9 Interesting Details

When it came to the letter *e*, Le Grand Étienne stopped himself just as he was about to say the word *sévère*, thinking it might perhaps lead Le Petit Étienne too easily to the colour black. Black? Because until now, the colours his pupil had named were the same ones Zablonski himself would have chosen.

"Your grandmothers are nice, no?"

Le Petit Étienne felt like laughing. Of course they were nice.

"Aha! I bet they spoil you..."

Étienne replied in the affirmative with a big smile.

"And what's your granny's name, the one who lives in Grande-Digue?"

"Granny Després!"

"And what colour is the word *Després*?"

The boy's expression turned serious, even somewhat troubled. Le Grand Étienne guessed what was happening:

"It's not a very cheerful colour for your granny is it?"

Étienne shook his head no.

204.14.3 "You're right."

Zablonski And the painter wrote BLACK beside the *e* on his sheet.

> The need, therefore, for a degree of disorder, for imperfections, capricious forces, blurrings, that we might try to tame. The need to be human, need for events, for desires that collide and collude, even as they maintain a course toward perfection. One must forget the cube, and never forget the cube. To imagine a cube that's not a cube, to reimagine a form of per-
> 205.12.8 fection, without forgetting that perfection, by
> Structure definition, is that which does not change.

It was several days after her visit to Didot Books that Élizabeth got around to leafing through *La Bibliothèque idéale*. Opening the volume at random — she always begins this way with a book of which she knows little —
206.24.1 she landed on the "Arts through the Ages" section. And it
Élizabeth was as though the book knew her intimately.

> Numbers are not merely numbers, that is, arithmetical expressions. According to certain ancient traditions, numbers express qualities rather than quantities. Some even claim that numbers are superior to words when it comes to understanding the universe. To those who think that numbers are the product of our intelligence, the ancients argue quite the opposite, suggesting that our intelligence comes from numbers. After all don't we say "it all adds up" to mean we have reached a new understanding

or knowledge through the addition of a certain number of observations?

"Mathieu might've got de folks at Scrabble Inc. to sponsor 'im, if ee'd tawt of it."

...

"Ee phoned 'em wantin' to buy a hundred sets of letters to make his art. But dose Scrabble folks — well, Hasbro actually — dey wanted to know what ee was plannin' to do wid dem."

...

"So ee tells dem ee's an artist an' he puts dem letters in 'is art."

...

"Well, dey comes right back and says ee could be a corporate artist, so long as der lawyers decides ee ain't infringin' on copyright."

!

"Hasbro'd have to approve every work of art ee makes 'fore it comes out, to make sure it's fittin'. Sometin' to do wid der image, I figures."

...

"So ee let on like fer sure ee's interested, an ee tells 'em ee'll write 'em all about it, and den ee 'angs up[5], an' he never did nuttin' about it."

!?

"Ee wasn't takin' any chances. On account of, say dey didn't like 'is art works, den ee could be charged for copyright infringement for dose works ee'd already done. Dey'd have 'is file, now wouldn't dey."

"Dey could still catch 'im doh..."

"Sure an' dat's true, I suppose, if dey comes to get 'im.[5]

---

5. In the original Chiac, the word for hanging up is *hãng-nér up*. Further down, the Chiac term for "come get him" is *cri*. The proper spelling of these words remains undecided, awaiting revision by the GIRAFE (Grande instance

De udder way, ee's runnin' headlong and straight into proper trouble hisself."

…

…

208.22.7 Overheard Conversations

"Well den, where does ee get de Scrabble letters to make his art works, I'd like to know."

209.57.5 Photocopies

> I recognize this Folio imprint. Pages 32 and 33 of André Gide's *The Immoralist*. No overheating this time, but a sluggishness nevertheless; someone probably slipped some recycled, dogeared sheets in my paper tray again.

Zablonski was happy for the chance to really have some fun with this little exercise.

"And the word *pipi*; what colour is it for you?"

Étienne laughed for a moment, then became thoughtful, as though there was something wrong.

"It has no colour?"

Again, Le Petit Étienne wanted to laugh, twisting around on his chair before replying.

"Red! Well, would you believe that's the same colour I see?"

210.14.4 Zablonski

And Étienne Zablonski wrote RED beside the *i*.

211.12.9 Structure

> As for the order of appearance of particular subjects, it begins slowly then they all jam up at the entrance. Hard on the system. System? The system has practically no role to play here. The tentacles of the organic are on the prowl, alert to every opportunity to swallow up the cubic rigidity of the project. Does this mean we're in for a real novel? Absolutely? Questions are also part of the work.

212.142.5 Notes

rastafarienne-acadienne pour un français éventuel — Grand Institution of Rastafarian-Acadia for French Eventually).

Coincidences also elbow each other at the gates. (Although we cannot claim coincidence in the fact that the august publishing house of Gallimard is situated at 5 Sébastien-Bottin Street in Paris, given that the NRF, of which Gaston Gallimard was one of the three founders in 1911, was situated at this same location before the street was renamed — at the time, the address was 43, rue de Beaune — and that the building, which housed Sébastien Bottin's Business Almanac was nearby, end of digression.) And indeed, at the gates of the vast Gallimard headquarters, remarkable for its scope and labyrinthine design: hallways, incongrous passages, mezzanines, luxurious meeting rooms, cramped cells, sweeping, narrow, twisting, straight, metal, and wooden staircases, salons, gardens, pavilions, walls covered with mystery paperbacks or volumes from the Pléiade collection, cellars with high vaulted ceilings, all this in addition to the building's riotous exterior — extensions, acquisitions, annexes, upper storey add-ons — and the company's expansion, its bottom line, catalogue, corporate and literary shakeups. In short, a publishing house that grew into the tentacular, sometimes hallucinatory, shape of its story. 213.17.9
Exactly what a novel wants to be. Chance

"How is it dat in Chiac dey sometimes puts an apostrophe right before de *n* and udder times dey puts it right after?"

"Must be a new rule, I figures. Dat sometimes you puts it '*n* sometimes you doesn't."

"And does you tink kids should be learning dem rules, as well?"

"Eh boy, what d'ya tink! One ting fer sure, 'twould

make learnin' a whole lot easier, on account of 'twould be der real language."

"Well, how soon afore dey gets started?"

214.33.2 Chiac Lesson "Dey don't know, do dey. Dat's sometin' dey've not decided."

> In her novel *1953: Chronicle of a Birth Foretold*, France Daigle does not mention the resignation that year of Jacques Lacan as president of the Société psychanalytique de Paris (Paris Psychoanalytical Society). Lacan claimed that he was opposed to the SPA's decision to create an institute that would grant degrees in psychoanalysis, but some observers believe that the break was rather motivated by the rising popularity of Professor Lacan, whose charisma, seminars, and courses were drawing more and more students. Other psychoanalysts followed suit and resigned, among them Lagache, Dolto, and Favez.

215.45.7 Useless Details

Daniel LeBlanc of the Petitcodiac Riverkeepers was getting ready to attend a conference of the Adour-Garonne Water Agency.

"An' who're dey, I'd like to know?"

"The Adour-Garonne is a river basin of almost 350 kilometres long down in de southwest of France. It begins in the Pyrénées and ends up in the Atlantic Ocean."

...

"About half as long as the Saint-John river."

...

...

"An' how long's de Rhone, would you say?"

"About 800 kilometres, I think."

"Hun!"

...

"An' you're tellin' me dose folks is interested in de Petitcodiac?"

"The Ardour is what they call a deficient waterway, over there. Could be useful to have a look at how they do to solve their problems."

"Hope der not as slow gettin' tings done as we is out dis way."

Daniel was silent for a moment, then added:

"When I was a wee lad, my parents would listen to a song that went "*we ford across the Garonn*..." I suppose that means it's been a long while there's not been a whole lot of water in 'er."

...

"And if I've some time left over, I wouldn't mind a bit 216.22.1 Overheard Conversations
of skiing in Pau."

> 1953 was also the year Lacan proclaimed his return to Freud—when had he abandoned him?—with his manifesto-article *The Function and Field of Speech and Language in Psychoanalysis*, the subject of his first Rome
> Discourse. The second Rome Discourse, dated 217.35.12 The Detail within the Detail
> 1967, is entitled *Psychoanalysis. Reason for a Defeat*. The man was no stranger to paradox.

Le Petit Étienne was getting the hang of the test and his replies now came without hesitation. Even Zablonski had become more spontaneous in his choice of words.

"White."

"Of course! The word *bonbon* is white. And yet, bonbons are all sorts of colours, are they not?"

Le Petit Étienne nodded then added:

"My favourite's de green an' red bubblegum." 218.14.5 Zablonski

"Yes. Everyone has their favourites, of course."

> In her novel *1953: Chronicle of a Birth Foretold*, Acadian author France Daigle does not mention the fact that the pedopsychoanalyst Françoise Dolto draws a parallel between her book of

essays *Solitude* and the Adagio of Schubert's "String Quintet in C major, opus 163." And yet, the parallel is an essential structural element of *1953: Chronicle of a Birth Foretold*, a novel

219.45.12 Useless Details — which also includes a number of citations from *Solitude*. Possibly the least useful detail of all.

Various equations involving both 7 and 12:

a) $3 \times 4 = 12$
$12 \times 12 \times 12 = 1{,}728$ fragments
$1{,}728 \div 2 = 864$, which is the halfway point in the book from a structural point of view

b) $3 + 4 = 7$
$7 \times 7 \times 7 = 343$, indivisible number, with no apparent link to 1,728

And yet,

c) $1{,}728 - 343 = 1{,}385$

220.72.1 Equations — $1{,}385 - 864 = 521$
$864 - 343 = 521$

The cross-stitch is part of the larger family of counted-thread embroidery. The name signifies both the technique and one stitch pattern among others employing the technique, of which the simplest is the running stitch, also referred to as the straightforward stitch or line stitch, which happens to be the most basic

221.71.2 Intro Embroidery — stitch in hand-sewing. The cross stitch technique can be found throughout the world. It is used both in figurative and abstract patterns.

Étienne did not see why he should have to wait. "I told you, dey's goin' to change our room, see."

“But why?”

Étienne could see nothing wrong with the room they’d put them in. But Carmen did not waste time with explanations to the children when her patience was at an end and she’d already clearly stated her position.

“Because.”

Étienne would not let it go:

“It’s awful hot. I want to go swimmin’.”

Terry took up the baton:

“We’ll be goin’ real soon. We’re just waitin’ for de fellow to take us over to de udder room.”

“We’ve already been waitin’ . . .”

It was true that that the fellow in question was taking his time. Étienne threw himself onto the bed.

“I like dis room, doh.”

. . .

“I’m hot.”

. . .

“I want to go swimmin’.”

Terry summoned up his courage:

“Étienne, cut it out!”

“But why do we gotta change room?”

Terry, who happened to agree the room was fine, sighed:

“On account of women want wot’s written down on de paper.”

Carmen cast a dark glance Terry’s way, prompting him to reformulate his message.

“I mean that, when she pays fer sometin’, that’s wot a lady wants. ’Tis only right, i’nt it.”

And with that, they heard a knocking on the door.

222.133.3
The Future

The Adagio of Schubert’s “String Quintet in C major, opus 163” also enfolds Alain Corneau’s film *Nocturne indien* (*Indian Nocturn*), based on the novel by Antonio Tabucchi. Extensions are sometimes more useful or interesting than details.

223.58.7
Extensions

Various new equations in which 7 and 12 come together:

a) $3 \times 4 = 12$
$12 \times 12 = 144$
$144 \times 144 = 20{,}736$
$20{,}736 \div 2 = 10{,}368$, more or less insignificant number

b) $3 + 4 = 7$
$7 \times 7 = 49$
$49 \times 49 = 2{,}401$, the number of titles included in *La Bibliothèque idéale*[6]

c) $20{,}736 - 2{,}401 = 18{,}335$
$18{,}335 - 10{,}368 = 7{,}967$
224.72.2 $10{,}368 - 7{,}967 = 2{,}401$, the number of titles included in
Equations *La Bibliothèque idéale.*

> From Wikipedia, the Free Online Encyclopedia that anyone can edit: Pau (French pronunciation: [po]) is a commune on the northern edge of the Pyrénées, capital of the Pyrénées-Atlantiques Département in France... It forms the communauté d'agglomération of Pau-Pyrénées with 13 neighbouring communes to carry out local tasks together. The Université de Pau et des Pays de l'Adour, founded in 1972, means there is a high student population. The Boulevard des Pyrénées is 1.8 km from the Château de Pau to the Parc Beaumont, with views of the mountains... In the centre of Pau is a large castle, the Château de Pau, that

---

6. The editors of *La Bibliothèque idéale* deliberately included 49 books per category in order to give readers the pleasure of
228.142.6 completing the 49 categories with a work of their own choos-
Notes ing. Your ideal library would then contain 450 works.

> dominates that quarter of the city. It is famous for being the birthplace of the sixteenth century king of France Henry IV and was once used by Napoleon as a holiday home during his period in power. It has a small garden that was tended by Marie Antoinette when she spent her summers in the city. The château is now considered a French historical monument and contains a collection of tapestries... Pau is the home of the French military's École des troupes aéroportées, which trains and certifies military paratroops.

225.11.3
Appropriations

When he found the word *rouf* in the dictionary, Terry saw that the sole definition of the term corresponded perfectly with the description provided by Daudet, whose phrase the dictionary actually quoted as an example. The word comes from the Dutch *roef* and means the same thing. Terry then looked up *roof* in an English dictionary, and discovered that it too is derived from the Dutch *roef*, which refers to a small shelter on the bridge of a boat, but which the English also use to refer to the roof of a house, the palate of a mouth, and a mountain summit. Terry felt as though he too had attained a kind of summit:

"Acadians tink der French is bad when dey say *rouf*. Dey tink dey're saying *roof* wid a French accent."

...

"An' de sentence de dictionary uses as an example is de very same one dat got me lookin' in de dictionary in de first place! Dat's got to be de first time dat ever happened to me!"

226.19.12
Interesting
Details

> Gobelin blue derives its name from the famous French family of textile dyers based on the shores of the Bièvre river since the fifteenth century. It was also the name the French monarchy assigned to its national

> manufacturer of tapestries, which were mainly hung in edifices of the State. The Gobelin National Manufacturer workshops producing high-warp tapestries used to be situated near Les Gobelins metro station, in Paris' thirteenth arrondissement. The low-warp workshops were not far from Beauvais. In Chaillot, the
> 227.7.10 Savonnerie produced carpets with designs that
> Useful Details were original or copied from the Orient.

> Drawn or cut-thread embroidery, which is also called needlepoint lace, first appeared in the sixteenth century in Italy, the product of the *punto in aria* or "lace in air." Hardanger embroidery, which it resembles, originated in Asia
> 229.71.3 and spread throughout Persia to Italy and then
> Intro Scandinavia. Straight stitch, overcast stitch,
> Embroidery single row, or straight hemstitching.

Only the *y* remained. Zablonski searched for a common noun containing this letter, and finally came up with *lys*. But did the little one know what a *lys* was? Le Grand Étienne was no longer sure it was important whether he knew or not, but he thought it best to tell him because, in the end, he did not like to think he'd left the child in the dark.

"Lys. It's a flower. A lily. You often see it in the supermarkets at Easter."

The boy nodded, thinking Easter must also be a place one could go to.

"Red."

Taken aback, Zablonski thought of another word with a *y*.

"How about *myth*?"

Le Petit Étienne felt pretty clever:

"Red as well."

"Yes, that's what I see, too."

In truth, Zablonski saw the *y* as wine red, but since it

really sounded the same as the *i* it could very well be red too.

"And do you know what a myth is?"

Le Petit Étienne shook his head no, laughing.

"A myth is a story everyone believes, even if it's not actually true. It's a necessary story, if you like."

The little one looked at Zablonski with raised eye- 230.14.6
brows. No, he'd certainly never heard of such a thing. Zablonski

> A principle, a law, a statement. The principle: desires, when rejected by a mind that acts as an authority (and supported by culture) plunge into the subcontinent of the unconscious to achieve their ends. The law: repressed desires emerge in our dreams. The statement: the psy-
> che is governed by rigourous mechanisms that 231.39.7
> cannot prevent traces of the unconscious from Freud
> emerging everywhere. Circuitously

"Chubby chin, silver lips, knave's nose, boiled cheek, roasted cheek, tiny eye, big eye, eyebrow, eye browsy, and…knock on the noggin!"

"Hihihihihi…"

"Again?"

…

"Go on, say it: 'yes, again.'"

"G'in."

"'Yes, again'…"

"Yeth 'gin."

"Chubby chin, silver lips, knave's nose, boiled cheek, roasted cheek, tiny eye, big eye, eyebrow, eye browsy, and…knock on the noggin!"

"Hihihihihi…"

…

"…hihihihi!"

"Wasn't dere supposed to be a forked tongue in der somewhere?"

"Forked tongue? We never said dat."

"Chubby chin, forked tongue, silver lips, knave's nose, boiled cheek…"

232.98.9 "Hihihi…"

Expressions "No?"

> The Bièvre, which originates in Saint-Cyr in the Department of Yvelines, traverses the communes of Jouy-en-Josas, Bièvres, Villejuif, and Gentilly, before disappearing into the sewers of Paris. As for Dieppe, that dormitory town in New Brunswick on its way to becoming a real city, it began to expand during the 1950s, when Acadians from rural areas came to live there with the hope of finding work in nearby Moncton. Dieppe lies along the shores of the
> 233.7.12 Petitcodiac river, which eventually empties
> Useful Details into the Bay of Fundy.

The titles — accompanied by a brief description of each work — suggested by *La Bibliothèque idéale* captured Élizabeth's imagination. Élie Faure, author of *Histoire de*
234.24.2 *l'art* (*A History of Art*) in five volumes, was a doctor, like
Élizabeth her! Ha!

pic pac pic pac pic
235.55.1 driftwood lay on Cap-Pelé
Haikus drift drift drift of time

"Still!"

Josse was astonished that all the residents of the lofts who had participated in the Babar's small spontaneous survey on the colours of vowels saw the *a* as yellow and the *i* as red. The discovery had encouraged her to keep it going.

"And what, I'd like to know, does ya want me to do wid dis?"

"It's only a wee survey I'd like fer you to fill out. Won't take you long. I'll come by an' pick 'er up in a bit."

"Wha? To find out if yer customers is satisfied with yer service is it? Well, you ladies 'ave gone shocking corporate..."

But Josse had already turned to the next table:

"Can I get ya anytin' else over 'ere?" 236.6.9 The Babar

One of the methods of divination of the Yi Jing[7] requires casting 50 yarrow or bamboo stalks. One of the stalks, however, is set aside at the beginning of the procedure and plays the role of Observer or Witness:

a) $50 - 1 = 49$
$49 = 7 \times 7$
$7 = 3 + 4$

b) $49 = 48 + 1$
$48 = 4 \times 12$
$12 = 3 \times 4$ 237.72.3 Equations

Before continuing, Zablonski thought he'd better explain something of the alphabet to Le Petit Étienne.

"The sounds *a*, *e*, *i*, *o*, and *u* are vowels. They're important letters. You need at least one in every word. But there are also other letters. We call these consonants. They make sounds like *b(e)*, *p(e)*, *t(e)*, *m(m)*, *n(n)*... Understand?"

Zablonski laughed inwardly: here he was, teaching the alphabet to Terry and Carmen's son.

"Now I'd like to find out if these letters have colours for you."

---

7. The Yi Jing method of divination serves as the structural framework for France Daigle's *Life's Little Difficulties* (translated from the French by Robert Majzels, House of Anansi Press, 2004). 240.142.7 Notes

Le Petit Étienne was all ears. He felt things had suddenly become much more serious. He remembered Souricette.

"Take the *b(e)*. Do you see it in colour?"

The boy was intent on doing his best:

"Black."

"Agreed. Black. And if I say *b(a)*, instead, is it still black?"

Étienne thought hard:

"Mm… yes. Only, der's a bit of yellow too."

Zablonski looked down at his sheet, found the yellow beside the *a*. His hypothesis still held.

"And if I say *j(e)*?"

"Black."

"And *j(i)*?"

Étienne immediately saw the red of the *i* attenuate the black of the *j*.

"It's still a bit black, but wid some red."

Zablonski noted the result for the sake of form, but he had already drawn his conclusion.

"And *p(e)*…"

…

"*P(e)*…"

Le Petit Étienne shrugged. Was he beginning to tire of the game?

"Black."

Zablonski picked up the pace:

"*P(u)*?"

The boy shot back without hesitation:

"Black an' blue."

238.14.7 Zablonski was satisfied. More than satisfied.

Zablonski "That's very good. Very, very good. Are you hungry?"

> Faure's *History of Art* rubbed elbows with Klee's *Journal* and André Malraux's *Voices of Silence*. Present also were Matisse and Rodin, and an eighteenth-century Chinese work

entitled *Thoughts on the Paintings of the Bitter Gourd Monk.* 239.24.3 Élizabeth

Anyone who so desires can find the complete works of Voltaire on the web in French. Here then, without explicit permission, is an excerpt from his *Philosophical Dictionary*, as translated by Robert Majzels:

"*Tapestry (Tapisserie, s.f.)*, work done on a loom or needlework to cover the walls of a room. Loom tapestries are either high- or low-warp weaving: to make a high-warp weaving, the weaver copies the painted design placed next to him or her; but for low-warp weaving, the design is beneath the loom, and the artisan unrolls the painting as needed: both techniques employ a shuttle. Needlework tapestries are called needlepoint, because needle stitches are used. Large-stitch tapestry contains the widest spaces between stitches, and is cruder; tent-stitch or petitpoint tapestry is the opposite to large stitch. Gobelins, Flanders, and Beauvais tapestries are all high-warp weaving. In the past, gold and silk threads were used; but gold turns white, and silk becomes lusterless. Colours last longer on wool.

Needlepoint tapestries from Hungary are made of long, loose stitches of various colours; they are quite common and inexpensive. Nature tapestries may contain some small-scale figures and still be called "Verdure." Oudri initiated the fashion of animal figures in tapestries, and these are highly prized. Gobelins tapestries are copies of masterpieces by the greatest painters. Tapestries are classified as pieces, and are sold by the piece; they are measured according to their width in ells. Several pieces draped in a room are called a wall covering. They can be hung and unhung, fixed by nails, or the nails may be removed. Today, small selvages are more valued than large ones. All manner of fabrics can be used for tapestry: damask, satin, velvet, and serge (twill). Work on golden leather is also called *tapestry*. There are beautiful tapestry armchairs, splendid tapestry sofas woven in petitpoint, made either through high- or low-warp weaving.

Tapissier: m.n., is the craftsman (the tapestry weaver); he or she is known by no other name in Flanders. The appelation also refers to the worker who hangs tapestries in a residence, or upholsters furniture. There are also manservants who are *tapissiers*."

241.11.1
Appropriations

The two Étiennes sat by the large window, eating cookies and drinking milk. They were quiet, each resting and reflecting on his discoveries. Le Grand Étienne, lost in thoughts of colours and letters, ate almost automatically. The boy took the time to pry the thin wafers apart and lick the cream between the layers.

242.14.8
Zablonski

Three and four are the numbers that appear most often as the first word in the 2,401 titles of *La Bibliothèque idéale*. Three and its derivatives (trilogy, trinity, tripod, thirteen) appear in 20 titles, while four and its derivatives (forty, quartet, quatuor, *quatre-vingt,* or eighty) entitle 10. Five and six each appear in 5 titles, and two and eight in 1 each. No titles begin with the numbers seven or nine. The numeral 1, by definition indefinite, was not included in the above compilation.

243.46.2
La Bibliothèque idéale

“Doesn’t means de same ting, seems to me.”

“Wot’s dat?”

Pomme had just joined Zed and Terry at the Babar.

“Proverb I heard dat stuck in me head.”

Pomme enjoyed anything that offered a bit of resistance.

“Go on den, shoot.”

“De dogs howl, de caravan passes.”

Pomme thought hard. Terry added:

“Some folks say de dogs howl, de caravan advances.”

“Well, right der, dat don’t mean de same ting, now does it? Passes, dat means goes off someplace way over der.”

Zed jumped in:

“Or could be it passes right on troo.”

“Well, in a way. And advances, well, dat means it’s comin’ right at us, now don’t it?”

Something else occurred to Zed:

“Unless yer de one sittin’ up on de camel.”

But Terry was in a hurry to get to the punch line of his story:

“Well, in de beginning, I can tell ya, I tawt it meant dat while some folks go about whining over der lot in life, udders just go on der way and dey ends up right where dey wanted to get. In udder words, dey does what needs doin’ and udder folks can tink or say wot dey please, tanks very much.”

Pomme having agreed with his interpretation, Terry added:

“Well, now I’s wonderin’ if it mightn’t mean that dose dogs barking, means dey don’t bite. So der’s no danger passin’. Or advancin’ eider, fer dat matter. Passin’ or advancin’ don’t make no difference no how.”

Pomme found Terry’s alternate interpretation made sense, too, but suddenly he had a doubt:

“An’ how does you know dogs dat bark doesn’t bite?”

Terry had to admit: 244.100.4

“Anudder proverb.” Proverbs

245.46.3 *La Bibliothèque idéale*

> In fact, the number should be 2,405 titles rather than 2,401, because 2 of the 49 categories in *La Bibliothèque idéale* list 51 instead of 49 books. In the category of "Politics," not one but three of Jean-François Revel's books are included just as three of Molière's comedies are listed in the category "Laughter."

"Little Rock! Like de Denis Richard song!"

And the girl sang the end of the famous chorus *at the foot of a rock in Little Rock* over Johnny Haliday's hit single "Black is Black."

"What did ya say yer name was, girl?"

"Melanie Frenette!"

"And wot is it you do fer a livin'?"

"I was a social worker! I've only been in Moncton for eight months now, and I lived half my life in Edmunston. Great music, eh?"

Now the crowd was cheering a song by Moncton's Idea of North that DJ Bones usually held back until the hall was good and warmed up. After dancing:

"I was president of the August 15 Committee in Edmunston the year they decided to hold the Acadian Tintamarre parade. I spent half my time arguing you do the Tintamarre on foot, not in cars. We ended up doing it on foot. There were forty-seven of us."

...

246.22.6 Overheard Conversations

"Year after that, they did it in cars. There were twenty of them."

247.7.8 Useful Details

> At some point, it would be useful to know that *c/s* means "cans per second."

In Acadian, words ending in *o-i-r* are more often pronounced "*ouère*" or "ware" rather than "*oué*" or "way." The word *miroir*, for example, is occasionally pronounced as "*miroué*" or "meerway," but more often "*mirouère*" or “meerware.” In this context, the *w* (double *u*) could easily replace the sound “*ou.*” Many Acadian pronunciations follow neither the spelling nor the sound dictated by what is commonly referred to as standard French.

“At first, when I read *mirwère*, I ’ad no clue wot dey 248.30.3
was talkin’ about.” Chiac

> One last inference deduced from the pourpre.com site: the 13 first letters of the French alphabet introduce into language an army of colours
> twice as large as the entire second half of the 249.3.11
> alphabet, that is 189 versus 92. Statistics

“Are you one of dose dat read all de Scrabble words, 250.31.1
den?” Questions with
“Are you daft?” Answers

leeks and parsley cleave
the furrows of November 251.55.2
winter marches nie Haikus

As he munched on his cookies, Le Grand Étienne eventually found himself thinking about something other than colours. He was imagining what it might have been like for him to have a child. He thought of it as he’d never thought of it before. In other words, he was thinking about it as though he were thinking about a new 252.14.9
colour, a new texture. Zablonski

> Of Lacan’s works, *La Bibliothèque idéale* sug- 253.46.1
> gests *Four Fundamental Concepts of Psycho-* *La Bibliothèque*
> *analysis (The Seminar – Book XI).* *idéale*

“Fer example, we might be sayin’ sometin’ like de pot’s found its cover.”

“I remembers me mudder sayin’ sometin’ like dat.”

“Well, some folks even say dat different. Over in

France, dey says 'to each his cover,' wot's pretty close to the same ting."

"I suppose, only seems to me dat would be more like de cover on a mason jar."

"Dat's wot I sees, as well."

Terry had given up on using the standard French word *couvercle* for cover when he was talking with Zed and Pomme, even though he sometimes used it in front of the children.

"Well, in Turkey, dey says like de pot, like de cover, wot sounds mighty close to like fawder like son, right?"

Zed and Pomme were waiting for what Terry would come up with next.

"Den, der's de Arabs, dey says that every beard has its comb."

"Hahaha!"

"An' de Greeks, dey says that de pot finds its cover when she's rolling, wot conjures up de dish ran away wit de spoon."

. . .

254.100.2 Proverbs

. . .

"I ain't boring youse, am I? "

Two simple equations illustrate the flexibility and constance of the number 12:

a)

$$12 \times 12 \times 12 = 1{,}728$$
$$(1 + 2) \times (1 + 2) \times (1 + 2) = 1 + 7 + 2 + 8$$
$$(3) \times (3) \times (3) = (1 + 7) + 2 + 8$$
$$\{(3) \times (3)\} \times (3) = \{(8) + 2\} + 8$$
$$9 \times (3) = 10 + 8$$
$$27 = (1 + 0) + 8$$
$$2 + 7 = (1) + 8$$
$$9 = 9$$

b)

$$12 \times 144 = 1{,}728$$
$$(1 + 2) \times (1 + 4) + 4 = 1 + 7 + 2 + 8$$
$$(3) \times \{(5) + 4\} = (1 + 7) + 2 + 8$$
$$3 \times 9 = \{(8) + 2\} + 8$$
$$27 = 10 + 8$$
$$(2 + 7) = (1 + 0) + 8$$
$$9 = 1 + 8$$
$$9 = 9$$

255.72.4
Equations

Inevitably, as they went to and fro among the customers, the waitresses and waiters picked up snippets of conversation they could not resist sharing with their colleagues. This complicity was part of the social benefits of the Babar.

"He didn't!"

"I swears to God!"

"Poor ting!"

"I'm tellin' you, she looked like she'd been hauled troo a knot hole..."

"Well, I'm goin' straight home after work and warn me boyfriend right der, if ever ee's a mind to ditch me, ee better not be doin' it in a bar."

256.6.10
The Babar

> Letters as we know them are essentially what remains of figurative lines that survived the images that were rejected, forgotten or repressed. Whereas words—groupings of letters—recover, silence, dissimulate what we humans are incapable of admitting.

257.90.1
Letters

Browsing *La Bibliothèque idéale* took Élizabeth's breath away. Where did this strange and marvellous upheaval she felt come from? How did these signs laid down across the page manage to implode the void and explode everything around her?

258.24.4
Élizabeth

259.19.10 Interesting Details

> To pay her way through school and to provide for her child, a young mother had come up with the idea of tinkering with a cigarette making machine to produce a short filtered cigarette. She sold these discretely in restaurants and bars, in packages of six for two dollars, the way other women sold roses. At that price, smokers were quick to snap them up, others bought them as local artisanal products, souvenirs, oddities, or to eventually offer them as gifts.

"Ask me, I'd say Acadians have got some Belgian roots."

"An' how's dat den?"

In among all the music to which Ludmilla had introduced Terry, there were a few songs by the Belgian *chansonnier* Jacques Brel.

"Dat song where he says '*je veux qu'on rit, je veux qu'on chante, je veux qu'on s'amuse comme des fous, je veux qu'on rit, je veux qu'on danse quand c'est qu'on m'mettra dans le trou . . . — I want laughter, I want singing, I want us all to have a ball, I want laughter, I want dancing when's de time dey puts me in the ground.*' Fer sure, dat's Acadian."

"So more it was! Fer sure we's always up fer a party."

Terry added:

"Sure, dat too, only I's really talkin' 'bout de bit: '*quand c'est qu'on m'mettra dans le trou — when's de time dey puts me in de ground.*' On account of, Acadians say: *Quand c'est que tu t'en vas?* — When's de time yer off den? When's de time yer plannin' to pay me de money you owes me? When's de time youse two is gettin' hitched? Anybody round dese parts might be sayin' dat."

Ludmilla added:

"That interrogative form still exists in Belgium."

Interrogative? Terry had not considered this aspect of the form's usage. He tried but failed to come up with an Acadian example of the affirmative form of "When's de time." He was momentarily stymied, but then:

"Well, 'tain't only in questions, now is it. A body might say sometin' like "de referee calls a penalty when's de time dem players is liftin' der sticks too high."

It took a bit of explaining, but Ludmilla finally got it. Terry added:

"Carmen'd kill me sure if I'd said dat in front of Étienne an' Marianne, by de way."

. . . 260.30.12

"Jus' goes to show how deep I've got de Chiac in me." Chiac

> Modern aesthetic, aesthetic of modernity. Pictural revolution. Surprising innovation. Fundamental concepts. Art theory, artists' mentality. Colours, forms, symbols: authorial identity. Proportions. A world in turmoil. Perspective, sense of space. Perceptible forms. Magnificent. Visual order, plastic language. Savage. Evolution of ideas and styles. Sumptuous. Skittish but Herculean. Key moments in the history of art. Impressionism: epic adventure. Through and through. Critical. Evolution of taste. Systematic. Metamorphosis of printing and publishing. Splendid artistic and scientific surveys. Meeting of the writers and artists. Parallels. Deviations. Margins. Museums. Stylistic signature. Close links between the social and the visual. Tumultuous. Stupifying. Geometric theory of art. The photographer and the painter. Visual problems of history. Industrial archaeology. Science, contemplation, emblematic work. Major exhibitions. Society that engenders. Art of calligraphy. Masks, sculptures, and ritual objects. Decorator and urbanist. Patient research. Classical. Baroque. The Grotto. Verve. Regarding the influence of the physical

environment and climate. Baroque and classicism. Current affairs. Modern figure. Art brut. Art merchant. Great. Greats. Captivating. Unparalleled. Lesson in wonderment. Future function. Immense crowds jostling. The paint-
261.24.5 er of the wheat field. Drama earth garden.
Élizabeth Nuance. Light of the sky.

"An den der's de saying in English: *de pot wot calls de kettle black*. In French, we says: *le chaudron qui se moque du poêle*. In English dat would be more like: *de pot dat laughs at de pan*."

"Only you mean *la poêle*, which is a pan; *le poêle*, dat's a stove."

?

"Me granny says, *le chaudron manchure la poêle*."

"*Manchure*?"

"Must come from *amanchure — de pot handles de pan*."

"Only *amanchure*'s not right neider."

"Dat's how we says it in Acadia. De pot handles de pan."

"I suppose you could say *le poêle* instead of *la poêle*: *Le
262.100.3 chaudron amanche le poêle*, an' dat would mean de pan
Proverbs handles the stove, an' dat would make sense as well."

In total, 1,873 authors, for the most part men, are responsible for the 2,401 works in *La Bibliothèque idéale*. While the selection often includes several books by the same author, other books have several authors. Still others are anonymous or the fruit of too many authors to be named individually. The latter works can be ancient — the Sanskrit epic *The Mahabharata*, for example — or absolutely contemporary, like
263.46.4 *Paris-Berlin*, the catalogue of an exhibition at
La Bibliothèque idéale the Centre Georges-Pompidou.

"Ah? *On peuwe fioumaïye ici*?"

An Anglophone from Moncton who had begun to fraternize with the francophones at the Babar seemed to want to know if smoking was permitted.

"Dey don't mind a couple a' puffs now an' den, so long as folks control demselves and dey don't make a fuss about it. Bottom line: up to da smokers to be smart about it."

"*C'èye*... hõw dõ yõu sãy fãir en françaïye?"

"*Raisonnable.*"

"*Raïye-zônable.*"

"Well, lots of folks just say *fãir*." 264.18.7 A Place for

"*Oui. Je saïye.*" Everyone

> The rituals of obsessive neurosis are such that Freud compares this pathology to a "private religion." 265.58.1 Extensions

Élizabeth could not explain her attraction to the fine arts, an attraction that included even the words and expressions they engendered. As though art managed to infiltrate even the jargon of art. 266.24.6 Élizabeth

Convincing equation based on the number 7:

$$7 + 7 + 7 = 21$$
$$(7 + 7) + 7 = 2 + 1$$
$$(14) + 7 = 3$$
$$(1 + 4) + 7 = 3$$
$$(5) + 7 = 3$$
$$12 = 3$$
$$1 + 2 = 3$$
$$3 = 3$$

267.72.5 Equations

"Tell me, Étienne, have you a godfather?"

Le Petit Étienne looked up uncomprehending at Zablonski.

"Do you know what a godfather is?"

The boy did not appear to know.

"A godfather — or godmother — is someone who takes care of you in a special way when you're a child. It can be an uncle, or a friend of your parents. In any case, it's normally someone your parents like."

"Zed?"

"Zed is your godfather?"

Étienne could not confirm this.

"And usually, with a godfather you also have a godmother. Have you a godmother?"

268.14.10 Étienne did not know.

Zablonski "Maybe, Granny Thibodeau…"

> Materials: plain weave fabric (the same number of lateral threads in the weft as longitudinal threads in the warp), in natural or combined natural and synthetic fibres. The higher the gauge, the more threads there are per square centimetre. Aida cloth, perforated paper, Hardanger fabric, Aida cloth strip, terrytowel
> 269.71.4 with Aida band. Perforated paper is ideal for
> Intro greeting cards and Christmas tree decorations
> Embroidery because it requires no hem.

"An den der's 'Beauty is in de eye of de beholder.' I swear I don't know if dat means wotever you tink is beautiful is beautiful, or if it means de fellow or girl who sees sometin' beautiful is beautiful."

…

…

270.100.6 "Run dat by me again?"

Proverbs

> Examination for Inferential Statistics course IV (STAT 4773): the Montpellier Scrabble Club's web site informs us that the Scrabble® game is part of the plot or appears as a prop

> in 52 films. 52 is also the number of weeks in a year, and twice the number of letters in the Latin alphabet. If we divide 52 into 144 (one of the numbers on which Acadian author France Daigle's novel *For Sure* is based) we obtain the following result: 144 ÷ 52 = 2.769230. From the above, draw the maximum inferences, taking into account the intervals of confidence, the Latin squares and the degree of freedom.

271.32.1
Exam Questions

Zed asked:

"Wot about 'De straw in de eye of de shaman'?"

"Don't you mean 'The straw on de back of de camel'? Like they says: 'De straw wot broke de camel's back.'"

Pomme jumped in:

"I likes dat one, I do. I can see it wonderful clear."

"Dat's where dey gets de sayin: 'Awright, dat's de last straw…'"

"Neat!"

"In French, we's supposed to say: 'De drop that made de vase overflow.'"

"G'wan wid ya! No way!"

Pomme's incredulity made Terry laugh.

"Are you sayin' dat, in French, we've got no straw on de back of a camel?"

Pomme seemed truly offended. Terry tried to assuage him:

"Well, de water in de vase is pretty much de same idea…"

But Pomme was adamant:

"Say wot you like, de straw on de camel's back is a whole lot prettier."

272.100.5
Proverbs

New and telling equation based on the number 7:

$$7 \times 7 \times 7 = 343$$
$$(7 \times 7) \times 7 = 3 + 4 + 3$$

$$
\begin{aligned}
(49) \times 7 &= (3 + 4) + 3 \\
(4 + 9) \times 7 &= (7) + 3 \\
(13) \times 7 &= 10 \\
(1 + 3) \times 7 &= 1 + 0 \\
4 \times 7 &= 1 \\
28 &= 1 \\
2 + 8 &= 1 \\
10 &= 1 \\
1 + 0 &= 1 \\
1 &= 1
\end{aligned}
$$

273.72.6
Equations

"Not sure wot you mean. I doesn't feel like I'm part of a minority. Well, sure, I knows we's a minority an all, but troot is, I doesn't ever tink about it."

The young woman named Gerry confirmed the visiting geographer's impression.

"But that's marvellous! It proves that you're an active minority, a minority that influences the majority!"

Gerry and Bosse glanced at each other, considering the possibility. Seeing that they were not entirely convinced by his declaration, the geographer elaborated:

"It's quite possible that you're not actually in a position to feel it. These are minute and subtle modifications that take root in the minds of the majority over time. Often, one requires hindsight to notice such things. Either that or a trained eye."

"Who's up fer anudder beer over 'ere? Bosse! When did you get in?"

"Last night."

"Nice! An fer how long is ya stayin den?"

"Couple a weeks."

"Where are ya beddin' down?"

"Crashin' at Gerry's fer now. How bout you? Yer lookin' not a bad bit nice..."

The compliment pleased Lisa-M., who asked again if anyone wanted another drink.

"I wouldn't say no to another one of these."

Gerry took advantage of the Swiss showing the label on his bottle to Lisa-M. to make the introductions:

"Didier, dis ere's Lisa-M., musician, dancer an' waitress."

And to Lisa-M.:

"Didier's got in 'is head to write sometin' 'bout Moncton fer a magazine in Belgium."

"On account of de Petitcodiac river again?"

"Naw, on account of we're a minority." 274.54.10 Forgotten/

"Awh, dat's true isn't it. I never tinks about it." Recalled

> Some books are written to be read, others only to have been written. 275.12.11 Structure

Maybe she should have been a painter instead of a doctor? Not that she detests her profession. In the beginning she preferred the incurable cases. 276.24.7 Élizabeth

> To speak more proper French, when they want to say 'what,' some Acadians replace *quoisse* with *quesse*, which seems slightly more refined. 277.33.1 Chiac Lesson

There followed the usual questions.

"Are you baptised?"

Étienne didn't know.

"You go to church on Sunday sometimes?"

Étienne nodded, adding:

"Wid Granny."

"And with Terry?"

Étienne shook his head no.

"And Carmen?"

Étienne shook his head again, but then corrected himself.

"We went to see de manger at Christmas."

"So, you know what the inside of a Church looks like..."

This time, the boy nodded proudly.

"And do you say your prayers at night before you go to bed?"

Étienne hesitated. As far as knew, he did not pray, but maybe he prayed without knowing it. After all, there were so many things he didn't know.

"You've heard about Jesus?"

The child nodded, but timidly.

"Did your granny tell you about him?"

Étienne nodded with more confidence this time, but
278.14.11 Zablonski figured he had a clearer picture now.
Zablonski "Alright. Shall we get back to our colours?"

> All in all, the authors whose surnames begin with the letter *b* account for the largest number of works in *La Bibliothèque idéale*. These 190 authors, or 10 percent of the total number, wrote 253 books, or 11 percent of the recommended titles. A close second are the authors whose surnames begin with the letter *m*: there are 171 of these, and they account for 236 of the suggested books, i.e., 9 percent of the authors wrote 10 percent of the texts. Numbering 168, the authors whose surnames begin with *s* are almost as numerous as their *m* colleagues, but they have been more productive, accounting for 256 titles or 11 percent of the 2,401 books. Finally, coming in in fourth place are the authors whose surnames begin with *c*. One hundred and fifty-six of these wrote 211 works,
> 279.46.5 a ratio of 8 percent of the authors for 9 percent
> *La Bibliothèque* of the total of works cited.
> *idéale*

"How 'bout dat udder one 'bout de mote in yer eye?"

"You mean de fella dat sees de mote in anudder fella's
280.100.7 eye, but doesn't see de log in 'is own?"
Proverbs "You mean dat log is blindin' 'im?"

Grouping the authors according to the first letter of their surnames, we see that all the groups were more or less equally productive. The *a* group, for example, which represents 5 percent of the authors in *La Bibliothèque idéale*, is responsible for 5 percent of the titles. Only two groups were significantly more prolific, the *s* group, by almost 2 percent, and the *g* group by slightly more than 1 percent. As for the rest, the *e, i, j, l, o, r, t, u, w,* and *x* groups were a little lazy, whereas the *b, c, d, f, h, k, m, n, p, q, v, y,* and *z* were relatively industrious.

281.46.6
La Bibliothèque idéale

"Me, I likes de one bout bitin' de hand dat feeds you."
"Yer NOT to bite it, you mean!"
"I know. Only I likes de idea of bitin' it."

282.100.12
Proverbs

By multiplying the digits in the presumed satanic number 666, we obtain the following result:

666 = 666
666 = 6 × 6 × 6
666 = (6 × 6) × 6
666 = (3 × 6) × 6
666 = (18) × 6
666= (1 × 8) × 6
666 = 8 × 6
666 = 48
666 = 4 × 8
666 = 32
666 = 3 × 2
666 = 6

And we arrive at an identical result by applying the same operation to the number 1,728, which is supposed to symbolize plenitude:

$1{,}728 = 1{,}728$
$1{,}728 = 1 \times 7 \times 2 \times 8$
$1{,}728 = (1 \times 7) \times 2\ 8$
$1{,}728 = (7 \times 2) \times 8$
$1{,}728 = (14) \times 8$
$1{,}728 = (1 \times 4) \times 8$
$1{,}728 = 4 \times 8$
$1{,}728 = 32$
283.97.4 Numerals and Numbers
$1{,}728 = 3 \times 2$
$1{,}728 = 6$

What motivated Élizabeth to go from preferring cases that were incurable to those that are inexplicable? Is it the same inexplicability that sometimes leaves her speechless in front of the brush strokes, abrasions, cracks — and caresses, too — with which the artist responds to the canvas?

284.24.8 Élizabeth

> There is reason to believe that numbers, like letters, are primitive markings that have survived repression. Most likely, in their own way, they too silence, cover up, dissimulate the inadmissible. Nor need we examine them for long to understand that they too evoke more than merely quantitative realities.

285.90.2 Letters

One thing led to another and the two Étiennes ended their afternoon together with each one creating a freehand drawing. Both drew a person. The boy recognized a few lines of the human body in Zablonski's drawing but the whole thing seemed unfinished:

"Is it de Cripple, den?"

This made Le Grand Étienne laugh.

"No, it's Ludmilla in the bath."

Le Petit Étienne studied the drawing more closely, noting the effect of the yellow.

"And yours?"

“Dat’s Dad singin.’”

The master studied the pupil’s work. 286.14.12

“Yes, I see. It’s good. Very, very good.” Zablonski

> Why this particular structure? Probably because human beings — and writers all the more 287.12.10
> so — require many thousand lines of flight. Structure

“Wot would be de opposite of a necessity? Well, dat’s a queer question, anyway.”

…

“Alright den, how bout dose fancy hand towels women 288.31.11
put out in de batroom, even doh yer not supposed to use Questions with
dem.” Answers

CHAPTER 3

Literature remains alive only if we set ourselves immeasurable goals, far beyond all hope of achievement. Only if poets and writers set themselves tasks that no one else dares imagine will literature continue to have a function.

Italo Calvino,
Six Memos for the Next Millenium 289.144.3
Harvard University Press, (1988) Epigraphs

It had been a while since Terry had attended one of Carmen's makeup sessions in its entirety.

"Were you doin' dat before, runnin' a pencil along de line of yer cheek like dat?"

Carmen, who was being careful not to smudge her line, did not immediately reply.

"I only just bought this pencil. It cuts down the shadow."

She scooped a dab of anti-ageing cream on the tips of the fingers of her left hand and began gently tapping under her eyes.

Watching her, Terry chuckled.

"They say it's best to tap, rather than to spread it on. And you're not to tap too hard neither. Which is why it's better to use de left hand."

Terry thought that was clever.

"Is der somebody dat teaches ya all dis stuff, den, or is

it someting women're born knowin'?"

Carmen wondered if Terry was playing the innocent or truly innocent?

"Well, there are piles of magazines that talk about pretty much nothing else. I read dem over at Zone's.

Terry's memory flashed the row upon row of beauty magazines at Reid's and Chapters. Meanwhile, Carmen continued his education:

"Matter o' fact, only last week I was readin' dat now it's alright to be wearin' the same colour lipstick an' nailpolish.
290.87.2 Used to be, that was something a girl ought never to do."
The Body "Dat's right, der's the fingernails as well!"

291.54.6 Forgotten/ Recalled

> They say the entire oeuvre of a writer is already lurking in the interstices of their first book.[8]

Not all the overheard conversations were dramatic. The most ordinary surfaced after closing time at the Babar, while they were cleaning up.

"Well, I never tot dat's de way 'twas done. Wot's yer opinion?"

"I tinks he was pullin' yer leg is my opinion! Der's no way dey does it dat way."

. . .

. . .

"Still, it would be sometin' to visit one o' dem puzzle plants sometime, just to see how dey does it."

. . .

"Does you do 'em?"

"Do wot?"

"Puzzles!"

---

8. France Daigle wrote "numerous as in fibrous is love" several times in her first novel *Sans jamais parler du vent. Roman de crainte et d'espoir que la mort arrive à temps* (*Without Ever*
294.142.8 *Speaking of the Wind. A Novel of Fear and Hope that Death*
Notes *Might Arrive on Time.*)

"Lord no. I gets stomach-sick just turnin' over all de pieces right-side up afore I even gets started."

"I does 'em wid me granny when I go's to see 'er. She enjoys it. She's all de time got one on de go, on a card table in de corner of 'er room. She's in a home."

292.6.11
The Babar

> Materials continued: perle cotton, glossy silk thread, flower yarn, matte cotton embroidery yarn, wool thread, six-stranded cotton (embroidery floss), matted embroidery cotton, linen, silk and rayon floss, crochet thread, lace thread, metallic thread, sewing thread.

293.71.5
Intro
Embroidery

> Many of Lacan's discoveries are rooted in the shimmering reflections of language, language as revelatory. In fact, it was in their speech that Lacan located the mechanism troubling his analysands. In addition, he was compelled to invent many new words and to recombine locutions to reveal how and to what degree the unconscious is manifested in language.

295.34.2
Lacan

However, the symbolic numbers 666 and 1,728 produce different results in Arabic multiplication:

666 = 6 × 6 × 6	1,728 = 1 × 7 × 2 × 8
666 = 6 × (6 × 6)	1,728 = 1 × 7 × (2 × 8)
666 = 6 × (36)	1,728 = 1 × 7 × (16)
666 = 6 × (3 × 6)	1,728 = 1 × 7 × (1 × 6)
666 = 6 × (18)	1,728 = 1 × 7 × (6)
666 = 6 × (1 × 8)	1,728 = 1 × (7 × 6)
666 = 6 × 8	1,728 = 1 × (42)
666 = 48	1,728 = 1 × (4 × 2)
666 = 4 × 8	1,728 = 1 × 8
666 = 32	1,728 = 8
666 = 3 × 2	
666 = 6	

296.97.5
Numerals and
Numbers

It would be unfair not to point out the important contributions made by individual authors to their alphabetical group, particularly Balzac, Bataille, and Breton; Calvino, Canetti, Cendrars, and Cocteau; Diderot and Duby; Flaubert; Gide; Hugo; Jünger; Kafka; Malraux, Maupassant, Michelet, and Musil; Nabokov and Nietzsche; Paulhan and Proust; Sand, Sartre, and Stendhal; Verne and Voltaire; Yourcenar; and finally, Zola. At least five books by each of these authors are listed in *La Bibliothèque idéale*. Organized according to dates of birth, this list would read as follows: Voltaire (1694), Diderot (1713), Stendhal (1783), Michelet (1798), Balzac (1799), Hugo (1802), Sand (1804), Flaubert (1821), Verne (1828), Zola (1840), Nietzsche (1844), Maupassant (1850), Gide (1869), Proust (1871), Musil (1880), Kafka (1883), Paulhan (1884), Cendrars (1887), Cocteau (1889), Jünger (1895), Breton (1896), Bataille (1897), Nabokov (1899), Malraux (1901), Yourcenar (1903), Sartre (1905), Canetti (1905), Duby (1919), and Calvino (1923).

297.46.7
La Bibliothèque idéale

"Who was it again said 'hell is de udder'?"

"Nobody. Dat's a proverb, everybody says it."

"For sure, but somebody had to go and say it first, right?"

"A proverb happens when its been such a terrible long time people's been sayin' it, don't matter no more where she comes from."

"And anyhow, it's only to get people talkin'. *Pro-verb*, *pro* means 'for,' an' *verb* means 'talkin'.' 'Fer talkin'.'"

"Half de time, those sayin's don't make no sense at all."

"I tot dat one come from de Bible."

"Well, wouldn't make no sense at all comin' from de

Bible, now would it."

"Why, pray tell, not?"

"Well, who would 'ave said it?"

"Don't know, do I. You tink I knows every wag in de Bible?"

"I never heard it in Church, dat's fer sure."

"Me neider."

"Whoever 'twas, should 'ave said 'hell is de Other,' wid a capital *O*."

"When somebody's just sayin' it, folks aren't goin' to see de capitals, now are dey?"

"Right enough. De big indivisible *O*."

"Invisible, you mean..."

"I means both."

"Wot are dose two yappin' about?"

"Haven't a clue."

...

...

"Shall we haul ass out o' here den?" 298.100.1

"Awh? You don't like it 'ere?" Proverbs

> Human beings are not made to be happy? This is how Freud describes life in relation to the id, the ego, and the superego: a rider (the ego) holds a fractuous horse (the id) in check, all the while fighting off a swarm of bees (the superego). In addition to these already perilous tasks, the horseman must constantly survey the surrounding landscape, and learn from his experience as he advances. Hence Freud's idea that man does not live; he is lived by this condition.

299.39.9
Freud
Circuitously

Terry explained as best he could, and still Étienne came back with exactly the same question, and in the same words as the first time:

"How come den ee was swallowin' money?"

Terry tried again:

"On account of dat was 'is sickness: swallowin' money."

"Dat's a sickness?"

Entirely by accident, Étienne had once swallowed a dime. He'd never told anyone, because his parents had often warned him not to put coins in his mouth.

"Anytin' can be a sickness, see, if a fellow overdoes it."

Étienne was somewhat relieved, but happy nevertheless that Terry's explanation did not end there.

"See, dis fellow we's talkin' 'bout, swallowin' all dem loonies... well, fer sure dat boy 'ad a problem. On account of a normal person wouldn't do be doin' dat, now would dey."

...

"A normal fellow wouldn't even tink of such a ting. See?"

"But, how come ee was swallowin' money? How come not stones?"

"Well, wid him 'twas money he were swallowin'. Some udder fellow, might be stones, anudder might be nails. All depends on wot 'twas caused de problem in de beginnin'."

Terry slid the shepherd's pie into the oven, and glanced at Étienne; he could see his answers had not entirely satisfied the boy.

"See, a fellow might decide to swallow, I don' know, de cap off a bottle o' beer, say, just for a lark, showin' off in front of 'is pals, or some such ting. An' could be it don't even make 'im sick or nuttin'. Sure and a ting like dat could happen."

Étienne nodded.

"Right, well de next day, dat same fellow's not goin' to up and swallow anudder beer cap, now is ee? If ee do, and if ee gets to swallowin' more an' more beer caps all de time, on account of ee can't stop himself, well den, dat's startin' to be a problem. In de first place, on account of our stomach isn't built to handle metal. Could end up killin' 'im, like dat fellow who was swallowin' coins."

So far Étienne understood, but he was waiting for the rest of Terry's explanation, which didn't seem to be coming.

"An'?"

"An' wot?"

"You said in de first place. Don't dat mean der's more yet to come?"

Terry wondered if it was normal for a four-and-a-half year old child to have such a logical mind.

"Alright den. In de second place, like I says, most folks don't have a yearnin' to swallow metal and such. Most folks just wants to eat food, and food dey likes besides, food dat makes dem feel good. Take me, for example, I can't say I really likes turnip soup. Only I knows it's good for me, so I end up likin' it a wee bit anyway, on account of it's good for me body." 300.87.4

"I don't like turnip soup neider." The Body

> Among the 29 authors of whom at least five titles have been selected by *La Bibliothèque idéale*, Hugo and Voltaire share first place with eight books each; Flaubert, Gide, Nabokov, Sartre, and Stendhal are close behind with seven works each; then six each by Balzac, Calvino, Cendrars, Duby, Malraux, Paulhan, and Zola; five each by Bataille, Breton, Canetti, Cocteau, Diderot, Jünger, Kafka, Maupassant, Michelet, Musil, Nietzsche, Proust, Sand, Verne, and Yourcenar. Listed according to date of death, the list would read as follows: Voltaire (1778), Diderot (1784), Stendhal (1842), Balzac (1850), Michelet (1874), Sand (1876), Flaubert (1880), Hugo (1885), Maupassant (1893), Nietzsche (1900), Zola (1902), Verne (1905), Proust (1922), Kafka (1924), Musil (1942), Gide (1951), Cendrars (1961), Bataille (1962), Cocteau (1963), Breton (1966), Paulhan (1968),

301.46.8 *La Bibliothèque idéale*

> Malraux (1976), Nabokov (1977), Sartre 1980), Calvino (1985), Yourcenar (1987), Canetti (1994), Duby (1996), and Jünger (1998).

"De wot?"

"De Color Marketing Group, dey's de folks dat decides which colours is goin' to be in fashion from one year to da next. Once dey've made der choices — say two or tree years ahead — dey makes up wot dey calls de palette of colours fer dat year, an' dey sends 'em out to de manufacturers so dat everyting matches up."

!

302.2.1 Colours

"Wot? Were you tinkin' everytin' was matchin' up by some miracle?"

303.35.8 The Detail within the Detail

> In other words, still according to Freud, the human being is born in such an immature neurological state that it is impossible not to injure it.

"Mum! Mum! Dad wanted I should drowns meself..."

"Drown. I should drown myself."

Terry had come from the swimming pool with the children. He'd brought them in through the secret door, as he called it, to drop in for a brief moment on Carmen at the Babar.

"... an' I couldn't do it!"

Carmen could not guess the source of the child's excitement.

"I was only about showin' 'em it's not so easy to go an' drown yerself. In de end, a body doesn't want to sink."

"An' now, I'm not afeard no more of puttin' me head under water."

"Is that right? Well, that's wicked! An' how about you, me beauty? Did you swim as well?"

Marianne nodded beaming.

Terry glanced out at the bar.

"Are you busy, den?"

"Won't be long, now. Wot're you three plannin' on doing with yerselves?"

"I promised Étienne I'd make de macaroni an' sausages fer supper."

Carmen mussed her son's hair.

"Mmmm, that sounds tasty. Mum'll come up fer a bit in a while."

"To read a story?"

"If you like."

Carmen stepped behind the bar, grabbed four candied Marachino cherries by their tails, and handed two each to the kids. 304.6.2

"Wot do we say?" The Babar

> In France, they say talkie-walkie instead of walkie-talkie. 305.64.4 Opposites

Freud's father Jacob's third marriage was to a woman 20 years his junior. One of two sons from Jacob's first marriage had children, which meant that when little Sigmund was born, he was already the uncle of a child a year older than he, and who would become his favourite playmate. Also, the young Freud believed his half-brother Philipp was sharing Sigmund's mother's bed, so that he suspected Philipp was actually Sigmund's sister Anna's father. All this may shed some light on Freuds' lifelong compulsion to penetrate secrets. In addition, a nanny to whom Freud had become especially attached disappeared without explanation when he was two and a half years old, which only added more pain to a burden of confusion sufficiently heavy to justify the birth of psychoanalysis. 306.39.6 Freud Circuitously

> Sixty-one authors of *La Bibliothèque idéale* have names composed of a single word. Eight of them begin with *s*, seven with *p*, six each

with *a, c,* and *h,* and five with *e*. Once again we find the popular *a, c, p,* and *s*. The authors in question are: Abélard, Adonis, Alain, Apicius, Apulée, Aristotle, Bashô, Brassaï, Cabu, Chamfort, Cicero, Colette, Confucius, Corneille, Demosthenes, Epictetus, Erasmus, Aeschyles, Aesop, Euripides, Fenelon, Goosens, Hergé, Herodotus, Hesiod, Hitchcock, Homer, Horace, Kalidasa, Lucrecius, Menon, Molière, Novalis, Ousâma, Ovid, Parmenides, Pausanias, Pétillon, Petronius, Pindar, Plato, Plautus, Ryokan, Saki, Sallust, Sempé, Seneca, Shitao, Sophocles, Stendhal, Suetonius, Tacitus, Taillevant, Terence, Thucydides, Vercors, Virgil, Voltaire, Vuillemin, Xenophon, and Zeami. The shortest names are Cabu, author of a comic strip entitled *Le Grand Duduche*, and Saki, author of *L'Omelette byzantine*, listed in the category of "Laughter." These very short names appear all the more so in Comparison to names like Pierre-Augustin Caron de Beaumarchais; Georges Louis Leclerc, Comte de Buffon; Marie-Jean Antoine Caritat de Condorcet; José de Espronceda y Delgado; José Maria Ferreira de Castro; Bernard Le Bovier de Fontenelle; Hugues Félicité Robert de Lamennais; Félix Lope de Vega Carpio; Hippolyte Prosper Olivier Lissagaray; Oscar-Vladislas de Lubicz-Milosz; Edward Georges Bulwer Lytton; Joaquim Maria Machado de Assis; Honoré Gabriel Riqueti de Mirabeau; Francisco de Quevedo y Villegas, Nicolas Restif de la Bretonne and Giuseppe Tomasi di Lampedusa.

307.46.9
La Bibliothèque idéale

Leafing through *La Bibliothèque idéale*, Élizabeth cannot believe that the word *inexplicabilité* does not appear in any French dictionary.* 308.24.10 Élizabeth

> The doors to the psychoanalytic fraternity were opened to Lacan thanks to his theory of the mirror stage. This moment of maturation, which occurs between the ages of 6 and 18 months, when the child first encounters its image in a mirror, leads to the illusion of the self, or the ego, from which speech will emerge. Because the imaginary self corresponds to a speaking subject, the subject being that which arises from an unconscious desire as language. More or less. 309.34.6 Lacan

> In addition to Francis Thibaudeau — Terry's distant cousin? — who drew up the first real classification of typographic characters, Acadian enthusiasts of genealogy will be happy to learn that there exists a genealogy of printing characters. The founding families are the Gothic, Old Style Roman, Italic, Transitional Roman, Modern Roman, Antique, Egyptian, Calligraphic, Script, and Ornamental. 311.19.2 Interesting Details

"Der's someting about usin' a word fer de first time. 'Specially in French."

"You mean dat it's a bit tricky? On account of you can't be certain yer usin it like yer supposed to?"

"No, more like: Well, now dat's a pretty word! An' why wouldn't I use it?"

"Ya. Dream on." 312.82.1 Moncton

* In fact, it would be preferable to speak of *mystère*, a shifting, flickering word, more open and infinite than *inexplicabilité,* whose interrupted thrusts and stumbling blocks hammer away at the primitive stuttering of the universe. 310.143.9 Varia

313.138.2 The Other — It is still too soon to speak of the Other.

Demonstration based on randomly selected numbers: the 32 divisions of the Compass Rose; the 338 entries in the *Dictionnaire de la psychanalyse* (*Dictionary of Psychoanalysis*) by Roland Chemama and Bernard Vandermersch (Larousse), which includes 101 entries under the letters *a*, *b*, *c*, and *d*, or 15 percent of the letters of the alphabet accounting for 30 percent of the entries (2 of the 101 entries actually refer the reader to other entries); and finally, a factor X to be chosen in the heat of writing this:

a) 338 – 32 = 306, a more or less insignificant number;

b) 101 – 2 = 99
99 × 2 = 198, a more or less insignificant number;

However:

c) 12 × 12 × 12 = 1,728

d) 1,728 – 198 = 1,530, which might also be read as 15 and 30 percent.

And finally, selecting the five in the heat of writing, since we're now engaged in the fifth operation of our demonstration:

314.72.7 Equations — e) 1,530 ÷ 5 = 306, which brings us back to the result of our initial mathematical operation.

> A cerebral hemorrhage, or cerebral vascular accident, was the cause of death of the Italian
> 315.78.2 Accidents — author Italo Calvino in 1985. He was 62 years old.

Marianne is kind of the clown of the family. Nor does it take very much to arouse her playful nature.

"*Marianne went down to the mill, Marianne went down to the mill…*"

Immediately the child's face lit up.

"*She went down to mill her grain, She went down to mill her grain…*"

As he sang, Terry watched Marianne in his rear-view mirror.

"*She was riding on her donkey, oh my little miss Marianne…*"

Terry' decided to take a ride up by Salisbury, where someone had advertised a trailer for sale.

"*Riding on her donkey Catty, goin' down to the mill.*"

Unfortunately, he hadn't taken into account their ancient jalopy's recent minor mechanical troubles.

"*The miller saw her coming, The miller saw her coming…*"

Now here they were, waiting for the tow truck by the 316.5.1
side of the road. A Movie

> Second irritant: books with the page numbers on the inside margin. Often the page number comes close to falling into the gutter of the binding. An error in layout? This is clearly the case of the pocket dictionary *Proverbes et Dictons (Proverbs and Sayings)* published by Robert. It takes a while for one to realize that the more useful numbering in this work is that which identifies the particular saying one is searching for. A tedious process, because of the book's odd system of classification, which in the end confirms the usefulness of numbering pages, if only to facilitate replacing those pages
> when they inevitably fall out of this bizarrely 317.89.2
> designed and badly bound book. Ouroboros. Irritants

Élizabeth turns the pages. Observation, treatment.
Observation, treatment. Bodies, Spirits. Turn the page:
318.24.9 Élizabeth ways they are the same, ways they are discordant. Hector
Berlioz's *Mémoires*, Erik Satie's *Écrits*.

> Blissful blue. Sky blue, lavender blue, nattier
> blue. Periwinkle blue. Bleu d'Auvergne, *bleu
> des Causses, bleu de Bresse. Gros bleu.* Blue note.
> Blue overalls, blue boiler suit, blue jeans. Blue
> 319.83.5 Bliss and Colours Bayou. Midnight blue. Blue Blood. Bluebell.
> Blue pencil.

"*It's raining, Bergère, bring your white sheep in...*"

Marianne also liked "Bergère." She thought the song was about a particular lady named Bergère.

"*Come into my cottage, Bergère, come quick...*"

Terry looked at his watch. They'd been waiting for a half hour by now. Should he go back to the little house in the curve of the road to phone the garage again? And call Carmen, too, this time? But she'd want to know what he was doing in Salisbury.

"*I hear the rain afalling, water beating on the leaves...*"

In the rear-view mirror Terry could see Marianne was on the brink of sleep. While she slept, could he leave her alone just long enough to go and phone?

320.5.2 A Movie "*The storm is coming fast now, see the lightening
flashing."

> The infant, who does not yet know that he or
> she is a whole being, realizes that she does in-
> deed correspond to the image in the mirror.
> 321.35.7 The Detail Within the Detail This recognition allows her to anticipate the
> eventual conquest of her body, which she does
> not yet master.

In addition, the following observation:

$144 = 1 + 4 + 4 = 9$
$144 \times 2 = 288 = 2 + 8 + 8 = 18 = 1 + 8 = 9$
$144 \times 3 = 432 = 4 + 3 + 2 = 9$
$144 \times 4 = 576 = 5 + 7 + 6 = 18 = 1 + 8 = 9$
$144 \times 5 = 720 = 7 + 2 + 0 = 9$
$144 \times 6 = 864 = 8 + 6 + 4 = 18 = 1 + 8 = 9$
$144 \times 7 = 1{,}008 = 1 + 0 + 0 + 8 = 9$
$144 \times 8 = 1{,}152 = 1 + 1 + 5 + 2 = 9$
$144 \times 9 = 1{,}296 = 1 + 2 + 9 + 6 = 18 = 1 + 8 = 9$
$144 \times 10 = 1{,}440 = 1 + 4 + 4 + 0 = 9$
$144 \times 11 = 1{,}584 = 1 + 5 + 8 + 4 = 18 = 1 + 8 = 9$
$144 \times 12 = 1{,}728 = 1 + 7 + 2 + 8 = 18 = 1 + 8 = 9$

Regardless of by which number one multiplies 144, the result of the preceeding operation will always be 9.

322.72.8
Equations

Collaborative works by two authors in *La Bibliothèque idéale* are especially numerous in the "Cartoons" category. It also turns out that it often takes two, if not more, to compose music. Familial collaborations, for their part, seem to have been particularly fruitful among names beginning with the letters *g* and *s*. Among the names beginning with *g*, we should note the brothers Jacob and Wilhelm Grimm's *Fairytales*, *Cheaper by the Dozen* by the couple Ernestine and Frank Gilbreth, and the brothers Edmond and Jules de Goncourt's *Journal*. Among those beginning with *s*, are *Bolivar, Le Libertador* by Gilette and Marie-France Saurat, *The Correspondence of Clara and Robert Schumann*, and Arkady and Boris Strugatsky's *Monday Begins on Saturday*. As for the brothers Kotek (Joel and Dan), and Pebyre (Pierre-Jean and Jacques), and the Verroust couple (Jacques and Marie-Laure), they respectively tackled,

323.46.10 *La Bibliothèque idéale*

> with apparent success, the subjects of Russian agriculture, truffles, and French sweets.

"Ask me, she's gonna end up wid de tennis elbow, she keeps on readin like she does."

. . .

"Worse ting is de ideas it puts in 'er head."

"Like wot?"

"Like . . . a women shouldn't 'ave her period but twice a year, an' even den, shouldn't last but twenty-four hours. And wid none of dem cramps neider."

"Well, can't say I'd be against dat."

"Children ought to be self sufficient by de time dey's six years old."

"Well, der again, see . . ."

"I'm not sayin' dey aren't good ideas, mind you. Only der not exactly de sort of ideas'll help a body face up to

324.22.12 Overheard Conversations de real world. I mean, laird in heaven, de girl's naught but tirteen!

> The French word *bergère* means not only a shepherdess, but it is also the name in English and German, as well as French, for a relative-
> 325.21.6 More or Less Useful Details ly comfortable straight-backed enclosed armchair, with upholstered armrests and back.

Élizabeth looks up from *La Bibliothèque idéale*. Sitting on the sofa facing her large living-room window, it occurs to her that traffic on the corner of the avenue and the highway has become much denser since she moved into the apartment. The marsh has also changed: it's now populated with buildings, mostly apartments. Again, for

326.24.11 Élizabeth a moment, Élizabeth imagines herself living in one of the lofts on Church Street.

> Examination for Commercial Corporate Law Course (DROI 2215): Develop a legal

> argument for an increase in the number of *B*, *P*, and *C* tiles in the French version of Scrabble, based on the incongruity that exists between their present number in the game and their predominance as the first letter in the names of true colours on the web site pourpre.com.

327.32.2
Exam Questions

While he waited, Terry wondered which would be more useful, a cellphone or a more reliable vehicle. But did he really want to get hooked on the cellphone habit? Wasn't he rather dreaming, as his interest in that camper in Salisbury clearly demonstrated, of getting away to spend more time with Carmen and the kids?

"Sir?"

Terry jumped. He hadn't even noticed the tow truck arrive.

328.5.3
A Movie

> A study of the symbolism of the numerals 9, 6, and 8 reveals that balance is all that separates the heavens, represented by the numeral 9, from hell, represented by the numeral 6. In fact, both offer generous opportunities for abundant joy and regeneration, but only the heavens (numeral 9) are linked to the symbolism of the numeral 8, which stands for balance, meaning the infinite and all encompassing wisdom that prevents us from falling into error, which is one of the forms of evil.

329.97.7
Numerals and
Numbers

"That your daughter back there?"

The driver of the tow truck was anglophone and clearly in a jovial mood.

"She lookin' for a job?"

!

"No kiddin'. My sisternlaw's makin' a movie with a gang o' kids jest about that age. A fill'em, she calls it."

Terry wasn't sure what to make of this.

"You French?"

He did not wait for Terry to answer.

"Thought so. Wouldn't matter anyhow. All they've gotta do's play all day. The fill'em takes care o' the rest. You know, how they's behavin' 'n all that stuff."

Terry was actually beginning to believe the man.

"*And it pays, you say*?" he asked in English.

"Sure does! Couldn't believe it m'self. May be worth the trouble, seein' this hotrod you'se drivin'..."

Terry laughed. He opened the car door to extricate Marianne from her seat.

"A pack of trouble, aren't they? Can't unnerstand m'self why anybody would have 'em!"

And with that, the mechanic slid under the front of Terry's car.

"I got three. Little buggers they are."

He got out from under the car and stood up.

"Jess like their father, I guess."

"Are they in the film?"

"You kiddin' me? Can't make 'em do anythin' excep' play baseball and trade dem baseball cards."

He reached into a pocket and pulled out the shortest pencil Terry had ever seen. He searched a long time for a slip of paper, first in his pockets and then in the cab of his truck.

"I have a son too. He's a bit older..." Terry told him.

"Sure. Why not? The more the merrier, I guess."

At last the mechanic dug up an old sales receipt. He scribbled a telephone number and handed it to Terry:

"This 'ere's the number. Sandra's 'er name. You figure out the money thing with her. But I'm warnin' you, she's some tease..."

330.5.4 A Movie Terry wasn't sure what the mechanic was implying, but he was too shy to ask him to elaborate.

> Of all the titles listed in *La Bibliothèque idéale*, those beginning with the letter *c* are the most

numerous. *C* alone accounts for 250 of the selected works, which is more than 10 percent of the 2,401 suggested books. *M* also does its part with 227 titles, or just over 9 percent. *P*, with its 200 titles, represents more than 8 percent of the total, whereas the *a* comes in fourth with 173 titles, or 7 percent of the books. Together, the four letters, *a, c, m,* and *p* begin 850 titles, or 35 percent of the books included.

331.46.11
La Bibliothèque idéale

Marianne did not know that her two weeks playing in an environment specially designed for approximately 30 children would earn her parents 1,000 dollars. Nor did the filming going on around her have much of an effect on her behaviour in the big room, which had been painted in vivid colours, so that, with all the movement, noise, bumping and bouncing back and forth, it looked something like a pinball machine. The filmmaker was hoping to demonstrate that small children will naturally find a healthy equilibrium in an environment free of constraints or coercion. At the audition, worried they might not choose her, Terry had underplayed the fact that Marianne was a rather happy and easy-going child. He was afraid the director would only select turbulent children. At the same time, he felt vaguely guilty about exploiting his offspring for money.

"'Tisn't any worse dan havin' kids so dey can help out on de farm."

Terry told himself The Cripple was right.

332.5.5
A Movie

Proof that Heaven and Hell have a lot in common:

$$1{,}728 = 666$$
$$1 \times 7 \times 2 \times 8 = 6 \times 6 \times 6$$
$$(1 \times 7) \times 2 \times 8 = (6 \times 6) \times 6$$
$$\{(7) \times 2\} \times 8 = 36 \times 6$$

$$
\begin{aligned}
14 \times 8 &= (3 \times 6) \times 6 \\
(1 \times 4) \times 8 &= 18 \times 6 \\
4 \times 8 &= (1 \times 8) \times 6 \\
32 &= 8 \times 6 \\
(3 \times 2) &= 48 \\
6 &= (4 \times 8) \\
6 &= 32 \\
6 &= (3 \times 2) \\
6 &= 6
\end{aligned}
$$

333.72.9
Equations

Throughout his life, in his quest to uncover the secrets of the psyche, Freud not only treated a great number of analysands, but he also practised self-analysis. His observations led him to conclude that it is as perilous for humans to win their oedipal battles as it is to lose them. In this regard, he describes an experience undergone during his first trip to Greece: standing on the Acropolis, he had a strange feeling of derealization. Later, he concluded that he had experienced a kind of survivor guilt.
334.39.8 The voyage had given Freud the impression of having
Freud surpassed his father, whereas the oedipal, in a sense,
Circuitously interdicts one from outdoing one's parents.

> Initially signifying an incarnation or representation, the word *avatar* came to include the metamorphosis preceeding that incarnation. Its meaning later broadened to include the sense of misadventure, a meaning that also em-
> 335.76.1 braces the idea of transformation, but, in this
> Avatars case, an unfortunate transformation.

For Étienne, the script was anything but clear:

"Just play?"

"You can do wotever you like, even listen to music if that's yer fancy..."

"On account of?"

"On account of dey wants to film how children gets

along together, when dey play, an' scuffle, you know, all de stuff dat goes on between kids."

"Der's goin' to be scufflin'?"

Étienne's doubts about the proposition were only growing.

"Well, I'm not sayin' der'll be any. Only sometimes der is."

Terry tried to think of something to say to make Étienne forget the potential disagreements between children.

"You could even draw fer the whole two weeks, if dat's yer fancy."

Le Petit Étienne was silent. He was trying to figure out if two weeks was a long or short time.

"You'll see, de ladies are wonderful nice. You remember Miss Annette we met? She'd be tickled if you'd..."

"De one dat gave me a stick o' *thériaque*[9]?"

---

9. In Acadia, some say *thériaque*, others *tiriaque*. They are speaking, in fact, of licorice. Here too, we can only guess the origins of the word. There are those who believe it comes from the First Nations (*tériak*? *tiriak*?), others point out the similarity with *la tire*, or taffy, the eatable and malleable paste made of boiled molasses or maple syrup. Of the two current dictionaries of Acadian French, only Yves Cormier's *Dictionnaire du français acadien* includes the word *tiriaque*. Cormier also notes the variation *ciriaque*. Considering the well-known children's rhyme *Je te bénis/Je te consacre/Je te mets dans mon sac/Je t'emmène à Shédiac/Te faire manger du thériaque... (I praise you/ I answer you back / I put you in my sack / I take you to Shediac / I feed you thériaque*," it's surpising that the word does not appear in *Le Glossaire acadien* compiled by Pascal Poirier, who is himself a native of Shediac. And although it is not listed in *Robert's dictionnaire historique de la langue française*, the *Petit Robert* does mention that long ago *thériaque* was an antidote for snake bite. The dictionary adds that garlic was once considered to be the *thériaque* of the poor. It has not been possible to establish any link to Socrates' famed hemlock.

336.5.6 "Yes b'y! Now wasn't she nice, eh?"
A Movie It was the *thériaque* that tipped the scales.

To speak, alright. But to be heard? In 1936, Lacan attempted to present his theory of the mirror stage to the International Congress of Psychoanalysis at Marienbad. But the chair of the session rang the bell after the regulation 10 minutes, Lacan's presentation having failed to garner sufficient interest to merit granting him additional time. The reception of his presentation
337.34.5 tion of an amended version in Zurich in 1949
Lacan was scarcely better.

Perfect tripartite equation based on the numeral 7:

$7 \times 7 \times 7 = \quad 343 \quad = 3 + 4 + 3$
$(7 \times 7) \times 7 = \quad (3 + 4) + 3 \quad = (3 + 4) + 3$
$(49) \times 7 = \quad 7 + 3 \quad = 7 + 3$
$(4 + 9) \times 7 = \quad 10 \quad = 10$
$(13) \times 7 = \quad (1 + 0) \quad = (1 + 0)$
$(1 + 3) \times 7 = \quad 1 \quad = 1$
$(4) \times 7 = \quad 1 \quad = 1$
$28 = \quad 1 \quad = 1$
$(2 + 8) = \quad 1 \quad = 1$
$10 = \quad 1 \quad = 1$
339.72.10 $(1 + 0) = \quad 1 \quad = 1$
Equations $1 = \quad 1 \quad = 1$

Translator's note: On a guided tour of the Hospices in Beaune, France, founded in 1443, the translator was shown a sample of a medicinal treacle called theriac, which was apparently administered to all patients, regardless of their disease or injury. The panacea has been traced back to the Greeks in the first century C.E. The translator suspects it is mostly an opiate
338.142.9 that kills the pain and quiets the patient. Not unlike the effect
Notes of licorice sticks on children.

The first day of filming went well enough: Marianne got involved easily in all sorts of activities and Étienne found sufficient distractions throughout the day that he had little time to dwell on his doubts. The two children were in fine form when Carmen picked them up at the end of the day.

"I'm hungry, Mum."

"Sure, supper's ready. Yer dad cooked a chicken and potatoes."

Carmen thought it was a good sign that Étienne was hungry. The licorice ploy had worried her that the children would be eating all sorts of junk food during the day.

"Did you enjoy your day, den?"

Carmen felt obliged to ask the question. She would have preferred to avoid providing Étienne with an opening to grumble.

"Der was water pistols."

"Oh! You must've enjoyed that!

Étienne was a bit slow to respond.

"Yah, only mine got busted."

"Awh, that's a shame. Did they fix it for you?"

Étienne thought a bit.

"Yes."

Carmen did not pursue the subject. The money they were making from Étienne's and Marianne's participation in the project could not have come at a better time. Like Terry, she didn't like the idea of pushing the children into something merely for the sake of money but, as parents, they had agreed that two weeks of this couldn't really do any harm. They also agreed not to talk too much about it, so as to avoid the criticisms of right-minded folk.

"Are we goin' again tomorrow, den?"

Étienne's question was not without a trace of ambiguity. Carmen did her best to reply in the same spirit:

"The ladies seemed really nice, eh?" 340.5.7

And there matters stood. A Movie

> Lacan's theory of the mirror stage pointed the way to the crucial role the self-image plays in a human being's life. To begin with, the very fact of assuming the existence of a self-image turned out to be revelatory, if only because it simultaneously establishes the possibility of misrecognition, illusion, *trompe-l'oeil.* In place of Freud's description of the murky components of the human psyche as a series of problematic relations between the id, the ego and the su-
> 341.34.4 perego, Lacan proposed the structural trinity
> Lacan RSI — the real, the symbolic and the imaginary.

After three days of filming, Étienne began to grumble.

"I don't like just playin'."

. . .

"Dey want us to play all de time."

"Der's nuttin' else you could do, den? Der's no TV?"

This had to be the first time Terry had encouraged his son to watch TV. Étienne only sighed; he clearly had no intention of replying.

"Well, might be you'd be happier helpin' de ladies out?"

Terry figured he could always ask the crew to give his son something serious to do, something that could be equated with responsibility.

"Eh? Would you like to help out?"

Étienne said nothing, though he seemed to be consid-
342.5.8 ering the possibility; then he jumped up and ran off to
A Movie play with his Lego.

> Some titles from the *Bibliothèque idéale* promise a beautiful balance: *General History of the Things of New Spain* (Bernardino de Sahagún), *The Raw and the Cooked* (Claude Lévi-Strauss), *On the Motion and Immobility of Douve* (Yves Bonnefoy), *A Technical Embarrassment with Regard to Fragments* (Pascal Quignard), *The*

Journal of Montaigne's Travels in Italy by Way of Switzerland and Germany (Michel de Montaigne) and *Six Records of a Floating Life* (Shen Fu), to name a few. Others cut to the quick. For example: *A Short History of Decay* (E. M. Cioran), *Monday Begins on Saturday* (the Strugatsky brothers), *The Faculty of Useless Knowledge* (Yury Dombrovsky), *Theory of Ambition* (Hérault de Séchelles), *In Praise of Folly* (Erasmus). Still others are brilliantly concise: *Things Seen* (Victor Hugo), *Against Method* (Paul Feyerabend), *Façon de perdre* (*Ways to Lose)* (Julio Cortazar), *Paper Collage* (Georges Perros). Several authors directly address the act of writing itself, as in *Writing Degree Zero* (Roland Barthes), *The Writing of the Disaster* (Maurice Blanchot), *The Flowers of Tarbes, or Terror in Literature* (Jean Paulhan), *Monstrous Masterpiece* (Yannis Ritsos), although this last title could just as well refer to painting, much like *On Murder Considered as One of the Fine Arts* (Thomas De Quincey) and *Comments on Painting* (Shitao). Some titles take the form of puns: *Les Eaux troubles de Javel (The Troubled Waters of Javel)* (Léo Malet) and *Un coup de dé jamais n'abolira le hasard* (*A Throw of the Dice Will Never Abolish Chance)* (Stéphane Mallarmé); while others promise revelations: *Things Hidden Since the Foundation of the World* (René Girard) and *Le Supplice des week-ends (The Agony of Weekends)* (Robert Benchley); and still others seem to promise children's stories: *Joseph and His Brothers* (Thomas Mann), *The Ice Schooner* (Michael Moorcock); and finally, this title that Terry fell in love with at first sight, though he

343.46.12 *La Bibliothèque idéale*

> had no idea what it meant: *Castle to Castle* (Louis-Ferdinand Céline).

"So der's dis woman, she was havin' hard, hard times all de time. Eatin' de putty outta de windows, like we says. Den, tings got turned around, don't know why, de wind like changed direction, anyway, tings was goin' fine. An' dey only got better an' better, an' better 'n dat, until all of a sudden *slammm*! De bucket on a back-hoe up an'
344.117.1 falls on 'er head, an' she drops dead right der on de spot.
Death Her karma just couldn't take tings goin' so good."

> *Lalangue* or lalanguage, *parlêtre* or language-being, *motérialisme* or materiawordism, *jalouissance* or jealouissance are some examples of neologisms invented by Lacan to illustrate the degree to which language is rooted in the unconscious. Because Lacan considered language as we know and use it to be too general and too logical. Or as we might hear it today, "top general" and "top logical," because
> 345.20.10 the unconscious is not intimidated by linguis-
> Language tic boundaries.

"It's nice of you to have taken on landscaping our vegetable garden..."

Le grand Étienne looked up at Ludmilla, who was grinning broadly.

"But never fear, Zed, Lisa-M., and Antoinette will lend a hand."

Zablonski had been on a bender. He was a sorry sight. The aroma of the coffee Ludmilla was pouring for him and the prospect of working with Lisa M. breathed a bit of life back into the artist's otherwise dulled brain and aching temples.

"Did I do anything else I should know about?"

Ludmilla pretended to think.

"No, aside from promising Étienne you'd take him fishing."

"The kid was there?"

"No, but you went and woke him to up to say good night."

"Oh no!"

Ludmilla spread strawberry jam on Grand Étienne's toast, to his astonishment.

"I must really look bad for you to start buttering my toast..."

Ludmilla agreed, and sat down. Étienne sensed there was more.

"And?"

"Well, he seemed quite pleased."

Le Grand Étienne nodded.

"And the garden?"

"Ah, as far as the garden goes, darling, you'll just have 346.9.1
to roll up your sleeves!" The Garden

> Blissful yellow. Canary yellow, sulphur yellow,
> straw yellow. Piss yellow. Yellowish. Yellow as a
> quince, as a lemon. Yellow pages. Yellow jersey. 347.83.3
> Yellow emperor. Yellow dwarf. Yellow River. Yel- Bliss and
> low belly. Yellow with age. Yellow journalism. Colours

Terry and Carmen could tell that Étienne was making an effort to go on. Their hearts sank to see him so dispirited at the end of the first week of shooting. They decided to dedicate the entire weekend to the children, so that the latter would embark on their second week satisfied and in good humour. They pulled out all the stops, from french fries at the restaurant, bubble gum, the whole family ensconced in the sofa cushions to watch the cartoons, bread for the ducks, up to and including Terry singing Ferré singing Aragon. Everyone had a great time, so that by supper time on Sunday, things were going swell:

"Étienne, how'd you like to come downstairs and do a wee bit o' work wid your dad? I've got boxes o' books to unpack, an' papers to mail..."

348.5.9 A Movie

Étienne was more than willing. It was an honour for him to work with his dad.

349.71.6 Intro Embroidery

> Materials, final inventory: tapestry needles (blunt points and long eyes, ranging from 13 to 26, 13 being the thickest and 26 the finest), milliner needles (extra long and fine, long or darning needles), beading needles, fine wool needles, chenille needles and curved needles. Needle threader, bodkin, sewing scissors and embroidery scissors. Embroidery hoop, scroll frames and tightening frames of various sizes. Steam iron. Heat resistant long glass-headed pins. One-metre bias tape and sewing ruler, thimble, setsquare, fabric markers, magnifying glasses, masking tape or glueless, self-clinging tape (can also be glued), and woven tape (can be sewn). Clear plastic grid, tracing paper, graph paper, colour crayons, and colour chart.

350.31.9 Questions with Answers

"Does you work out all dem math problems, an' dat?"
"You mean de equations, or de real exam questions?"
"De equations."
"Yah. Dose, I tries me best to solve dem."

351.55.3 Haikus

this cloud in the sky
seawater climbs up and up
this cloud on your cheek

Perfect tripartite equation based on the number 12:

$$12 \times 12 \times 12 = 144 \times 12 = 1{,}728$$
$$(1 + 2) \times (1 + 2) \times (1 + 2) = \{(1 + 4) + 4\} \times (1 + 2)$$
$$= 1 + 7 + 2 + 8$$

$$3 \times 3 \times 3 = \{(5) + 4\} \times 3 = \{(1 + 7) + 2\} + 8$$
$$(3 \times 3) \times 3 = 9 \times 3 = \{(8) + 2\} + 8$$
$$9 \times 3 = 27 = 10 + 8$$
$$27 = (2 + 7) = (1 + 0) + 8$$
$$(2 + 7) = 9 = 1 + 8$$
$$9 = 9 = 9$$

352.72.11
Equations

> Oh, the endless and hopeless manipulations required to pierce by hand the plastic wrapper of a compact disc. As though musical works would go stale on contact with the air, when in fact the opposite is true: music needs air to be deployed and to flourish.

353.89.4
Irritants

Étienne had shelved all the books his father had indicated. Delighted with the result, Terry was about to entrust him with another task:

"Dad, do I have to go over der an' play again tomorrow?"

Before Terry could come up with a response, the child added:

"I'd radder stay 'ere an' work wid you."

Terry slipped his foot in the door barely ajar:

"You enjoy workin' don't ya? An' you do a fine job, too..."

A moment passed.

"You know, goin' anudder week on dat movie's a bit like workin', too."

Étienne did not follow.

"You an' Marianne, yer gettin' paid to do it. An' dat money'll come in mighty handy fer our whole family. Dat kind o' money's nuttin' to sneeze at."

Étienne gazed up at his father with a look of helplessness. Terry bent down to talk man-to-man:

"We were tinkin' we'd use dat money to take a trip, or maybe rent a cottage come summertime, some place we could build bonfires on de beach an' roast hot dogs an' marshmallows, look up at de stars…maybe even sleep outside, if we've a mind to."

Unsure just how much one ought to tell a child, Terry decided to be completely honest:

"So, no, youse don't have to go down der tomorrow, nor de whole week if you don't feel like it, only it'd be a big help to us if you did."

Étienne could see his father was talking seriously, and he understood what he was saying. After a moment, he threw his arms around Terry's neck:

"OK, Dad, I'll go."

Terry hugged him.

"You're a wonderful fine boy."

…

…

"I love you, Dad."

354.5.10 "I love you, too, son."

A Movie Terry was stunned: could things be that simple?

> Examination for History II (HIST 3725): Numerology allows us to approach the events of 1755, including the deportation of the Acadians, the Lisbon earthquake, and the founding of Paoli's Corsican Republic, from one of two perspectives: from the 9, derived from the sum of the numbers 1, 7, 5, and 5, or from the zero, product of the same signs. The 9 represents both an end and a beginning, in other words the completion of a cycle and its transposition onto a new plane; the zero, on the other hand, indicates above all an interval, with or without value, according to its position. For only the zero's placement can give it value. Based on the above mentioned historical events, argue whether or not there is good
> 355.32.5 cause to redefine the role of dates in our study
> Exam Questions of history.

"Would you call it illegal, den, to sell cigarettes made wid tobacco from a can? Like wid tobacco de taxes already been paid on."

"Can't see why 'twould be. Anyway, if yer talkin' 'bout de *Doucettes*, people oughts to look at dat more like it's artisenal, which it is, by de way."

356.31.6
Questions with
Answers

> In our era, paternity still retains much of the Christian concept as it existed in the Middle Ages. In the image of Joseph's role in the Holy Family, the father watches tenderly over his progeny and takes care to transmit not only a name and a resemblance, but also an education and a heritage. However, because the ecclesiastic discourse of the Middle Ages assigned more value to a spiritual paternity than to a carnal one — a Christian is first of all a son of God — there emerged the role of Godfather, a spiritual father designated at the moment of baptism and charged with transmitting his virtues to the child.

357.19.5
Interesting
Details

When Terry and Étienne came back upstairs from the bookstore, Carmen sensed that something had changed. Étienne remained cheerful throughout bath time, going so far as to bend to the whims of his sister, who kept asking for the little pink ducks that she was tossing out of the tub onto the floor.

"Mum, tomorrow I'm gonna wear my Zorro costume, OK?"

Carmen refrained from correcting Étienne's "gonna" for fear of upsetting his happy disposition.

"That's a right fine idea!"

Later, when she went to tuck him in for the night:

"Mum, does you like working?"

Carmen considered the question seriously.

"Yes, I suppose I do like it. Sometimes I get worn out

and tired, but I like to do it fer us, fer our family."

The answer could not have been more appropriate. Étienne threw his arms around his mother's neck.

358.5.11 "I love you, Mum."

A Movie "I love you too, my little man."

> Before it brcame the international symbol of American-style capitalism, Wall Street was the narrow street on which grew the sycamore, or
> 359.37.4 false-plane tree, around which breeders would
> Animal Tales gather to trade cattle.

Carmen and Terry were watching TV snuggled up together:

"'Twas a wonderful weekend, don't you tink?"

"For sure! That was a right smart idea you had for us to spend all that time with the kids."

...

"Did you say sometin' to Étienne downstairs? He was askin' if he could wear his Zorro outfit tomorrow."

"G'wan! Really?"

Étienne did not like the Zorro costume; he'd never wanted to wear it until now.

"I was only explainin' to him dat 'twould bring in a few dollars if he did de film, an' dat would give us a bit of a shove to make a trip or rent a cottage come summer, or sometin' of de sort."

"G'wan! You said that!"

From her reaction, Terry couldn't tell if Carmen was impressed or thought he was completely incompetent. He tried to attenuate what he'd said:

"Well, I told 'im he didn't have to go on wid de movie, only 'twould help us out if he did."

...

"Wah? Should I not have told 'im?"

"Don't know, really. I don't always know wot we can or can't be saying to a child."

"I wasn't sure meself. Den afterwards, I tot, wot de hell, might as well be tellin' him de way tings are fer real."

Carmen thought that was a reasonable approach, all things considered. Terry added:

"I'm tinkin' 'twas OK to tell 'im straight dat way. Gives the b'y a focus. Ee doesn't like just playin' all de time. Anyhow, you knows wot ee's like: isn't like 'im to be doin' sometin' only on account of some body tells 'im to."

"Now, I see it. That must be why he was askin' me if I liked workin.'"

"An' what did you answer?"

"That sometimes it wears me out, but I like doin' it fer the family."

"Right proper! You couldn't have said it better."

. . . 360.5.12

"Now, if he can just last troo de week..." A Movie

> Starting from three lists chosen more or less at random — the list of colours on pourpre.com, the list of authors included in *La Bibliothèque idéale* and the list of titles in that same volume — one discovers that certain letters appear more often than others at the beginning of words. In French, this is the case for *c, m, p, b, s,* and *a*. *C* dominates the field with 12 percent of the words included in this study. *M* is second with 9 percent. These proportions contrast sharply with the *l, g,* and *d*, for example, all of which place amongst the average with a score 361.48.1
> of 4 or 5 percent. Inferences

Theoretically, the fragment 72.12 represents the 864th of 1,728 fragments in this novel:

$$
\begin{aligned}
72.12 &= \quad 864 &&= 1{,}728 \\
(7+2)\times(1+2) &= 8+6+4 &&= 1+7+2+8 \\
9\times 3 &= (8+6)+4 &&= (1+7)+2+8
\end{aligned}
$$

$$
\begin{aligned}
27 &= \quad (14) + 4 &&= \{(8) + 2\} + 8 \\
2 + 7 &= (1 + 4) + 4 &&= 10 + 8 \\
9 &= \quad 5 + 4 &&= (1 + 0) + 8 \\
9 &= \quad 9 &&= 1 + 8 \\
9 &= \quad 9 &&= 9
\end{aligned}
$$

362.97.8
Numerals and
Numbers

A tireless worker, Freud recorded his thoughts and theories right up until the end. A year before his death, he began to write *An Outline of Psycho-Analysis*, a kind of scientific testament in which he did not hesitate once again to put into question fundamental concepts, in particular that of the ego. In this text, he also suggested the possibility that in the future, chemical substances capable of altering the brain's balance would render psychoanalytic treatment obsolete.

363.39.10
Freud
Circuitously

The next day, Étienne's behaviour on the movie set changed.

"What's that kid doing? He's always showing up in the background!"

Étienne's new activity consisted in cutting across the camera's field of vision disguised sometimes as Zorro, sometimes as a Ninja Turtle, and sometimes as Astérix the Gaul. It took the film crew a while before they realized that Étienne had come up with his own script and that his walk-ons were telling a parallel story.

364.26.1
The Movie

"OK, never mind. Just let him do whatever he wants."

At the moment the human infant discovers his or her "being" in the mirror, he or she also discovers, as in a negative, the Other. But how to tell from a likeness what is real, imaginary or symbolic? Any number of variables multiply the possibilities for error, as much in regard to one's self as to the other. Which demonstrates

> to what extent misunderstanding, not to say misreading, is woven into the fabric of our lives. Lacan, a freewheeling interpretation. 365.34.8 Lacan

When Élizabeth came by to pick up the books she'd ordered, and to return *La Bibliothèque idéale* to Didot Books, she asked Terry to whom she could talk about renting — maybe buying? — a loft.

"I don't tink der's anyting fer sale right now, but yer best to talk to Zed. He's de fellow wot manages de building. I'll give you his number."

Terry wrote Zed's name and number on the back of the bookstore's business bookmark.

"Nobody's sold since we opened up, must be near four years now? Has happened doh dat somebody was wantin' to sublet. Every once in a while, folks wants to get away fer a bit."

Terry turned back to the books Élizabeth had ordered:

"I read dis one here de udder day. Liked it fine. Ordered a few extra copies an' sold two already. It's a whole lot easier to sell a book you've read dan one you 'aven't. Although der's books I've read I can't go recommendin'. Dose times I just keeps me trap shut. I'm not obliged to say I didn't care fer it, eh?

Élizabeth had not expected her opinion to be solicited.

"No, I don't see why you would."

"Dat's what I tot meself."

Terry placed the books and the receipt in a bag, and handed it to the customer:

"Tanks, Élizabeth. You have a nice day, now."

Terry always remembered the names of customers who ordered books, probably because he had to write them down. But Élizabeth was surprised to hear her name, pleasantly surprised. 366.49.1

"Thank you." Élizabeth II

> Looking more closely at the titles listed in *La Bibliothèque idéale* that begin with the letter *c*, we discover that the most often used words are those that refer to literary genres of one sort or another. For example, approximately 20 titles begin respectively with the word *conte* (tale) or *correspondence.* Six to nine each begin with *confessions*, *chant* (song), *cahier* (notebook) and *chronique* (chronicle). Hence, the role of *c* as an agent of transmission of the French
> 367.48.2 language cannot be ignored, particularly as re-
> Inferences gards the written language.

"Makin' it up? An' why pray tell would she be makin' it up? De Rolling Stones did give der concert on de same hill dat de pope held mass, now didn't dey? Mick Jagger an' de pope, fer chris' sake! Who'd make up a ting like dat? OK, Salmon Rushdie, maybe. But dat's about it."

. . .

. . .

368.6.12 "Is dat yer own personal sympathy fer de devil
The Babar moment, den?

> Lacan boldy created equations, formulas, graphs, along with topological and mathematical models to explain psychoanalytical research and knowledge. His celebrated Borromean Knot — a term he borrowed from the Italian Borromeo family, whose crest consists of three intertwined rings — refers to the Real, the Symbolic and the Imaginary, intertwined such that if any one of the rings is cut, the other two are freed. Another Lacanian figure, the symptom — he adopts the ancient spelling of the word, *sinthome*, which implies "*saint homme*"
> 369.34.10 or 'saintly man' — is represented by a fourth
> Lacan ring, which links the other three.

When Carmen picked up the kids that day, the film director broke off her conversation with the cameraman to come over and greet Carmen personally.

"Your boy *muy intelligence*."

Carmen understood the Spanish word and accepted the compliment on behalf of her son and herself.

"The petite also very cute."

Carmen accepted the compliment for her daughter, and for herself, and for Terry as well after all, but she was wondering exactly from what camera angle the director had been eyeing Étienne and Marianne that day.

"*So we'll see you all tomorrow then?*" the director said in English.

Carmen couldn't think why — though she tried not to
be annoyed by it — the director would address them in 370.26.2
English. The Movie

> Numerals, it should be noted in passing, are
> characters that represent numbers. There are 371.97.10
> therefore very few numerals, but numbers are Numerals and
> varied and infinite. Numbers

The mood was upbeat on the drive home.

"An' were you dressed up like that all day long, Étienne?"

Carmen eyed her little Zorro in the rear-view mirror.

"Not de whole day."

When Carmen tried to adjust the mirror to admire Marianne's curls, which the assistant on the set had embellished with tiny coloured pearls, the metal joint squealed
and the rear-view mirror came crashing down onto the 372.26.3
dash, which the children greeted with gales of laughter. The Movie

> Freud could not imagine carrying out his psychoanalytical work without smoking a cigar. Also, during the last 15 years of his life, he suffered from cancer of the jaw. When it became clear that the pain would not end, he

> succumbed to an overdose of morphine administered at his request by a friend, according to an agreement they had struck years earlier. The week before, feeble and confined to his bed, Freud read a last book, Balzac's *The Magic Skin*. Sigmund Freud died on September 23, 1939, in London where, at his friends and relatives insistence, he had taken refuge from Hitler's regime. He had been born of Jewish parents in Freiberg on May 6, 1856.

373.39.11
Freud
Circuitously

At the supper table, Étienne hazarded a question:

"Dad, 'r we poor?"

Terry felt suddenly flushed. Was the boy's question somehow related to their conversation the day before about his participation in the movie and the money it would earn them?

"Naw, wot makes you tink dat?"

With his fingers, Étienne placed a slice of carrot on the bed of mashed potatoes he had created on his fork.

"On account of our car's so old."

Phew! Terry's cheerful mood returned.

"Lots o' folks have got an old car, doesn't necessarily mean dey's poor. You've only got to tink of Uncle Alcide."

Seeing that Étienne wasn't convinced, he added:

"Dat's just normal: we buys a car, we runs it 'till it's old, and den we buys a new one."

Étienne rejoiced at the thought that one day they'd get a brand new car, but Terry wasn't done yet.

"Well now, don't go tinkin' we's about to buy a brand-new one. We could just as well go an' buy a car wot's only half new."

This clarification did not dampen Étienne's enthusiasm; he proceeded to decorate another forkful of mashed potatoes, this time with five peas arranged in a quincunx. As he savoured this mouthful, Étienne's spirit drifted in a new direction.

"Could we go to de *circus* some time, *Dad*?"

Terry and Carmen glanced at each other. Étienne had used the English words *circus* and *Dad*!

"Where dey gots dem *bumper cars* dat crash all together an' *swings* dat turn super fast?"

Terry barely recognized his son in this travesty of language and bravado, but he restrained himself, and played the innocent:

"An' how is it yer callin' me *Dad* in English all of a sudden?"

Étienne shrugged: 374.26.4

"Lots of folks says dat…" The Movie

> According to Lacan, the idea of the father is a metaphor in the crucible of which incubates the desire of the mother. His "Name-of-the-Father" has become one of the fundamental concepts of psychoanalysis. In a late seminar, he stated, "*les Non-dupes errent*" by which he meant that, because we are all erring subjects of language, one must (strive to) to be-
> come the dupe of a discourse in order to avoid 375.34.9
> psychosis. Lacan

Without realizing it, Étienne had blown on the smoldering embers.

"When comes to the point that Étienne can see the difference…"

…

"Anyway, far as I'm concerned, it's decided. No use in waiting 'til she falls to pieces."

Carmen wasn't wrong. Terry could see the day when they would have to buy a new car, but he'd hoped they could wait a year or two.

"I tinks we might find a pretty good used one. Eh? No need fer it to be spankin' brand new?"

"Only you never know what yer in fer with a used

one, do you. We could land up with a shocking heap of misery."

Terry had expected Carmen to feel that way. He gathered up all the patience and tenderness of which he was capable:

"I'm tinkin' we can find a good used one. Der's folks dat knows cars, dey can tell how hard or not a car's been run."

Carmen did not want to be stubborn. The week had begun smoothly and she wanted things to keep on that way. Better to choose one's battles. On the other hand, Terry was far from certain he could absolutely prove his claim.

"Anyway, let's be tinkin' on it. 'Tain't sometin' we gotta decide tonight, now is it?

376.27.1 "I can think on it, sure, but I'd be mighty surprised if I
New Car change me mind..."

> In her novel *1953: Chronicle of a Birth Foretold*, the Acadian author France Daigle makes no mention of the first printing that year of the French translation of Kafka's *Letter to His Father*. It was published in the April, May, and June issues of the *Nouvelle Revue française* (*NRF*), whose first issue had appeared only several months earlier in January 1953. All indica-
> 377.45.4 tions are that Franz's letter to Hermann Kafka
> Useless Details was never delivered to its intended reader.

"Hihihi...!"

Marianne was laughing because Terry had just told Étienne he had two left feet.

"You finds dat funny, do you, two left feet?"

Marianne burst into another crescendo of laughter. Étienne, who smiled to see his sister so gleeful, jumped in:

"Two left feet, ten toes of mincemeat, one big head of concrete..."

"Hihihi . . . !"

"Alright den, dat's enough. Toto Sombrero's not gonna wait all day fer de likes of tree turtles like us, now is ee."

"Marianne Turtle, Étienne Turtle, Terry Turtle, Grandad Turtle, Granny Girdle . . ." 378.133.2

"Hihihi . . . !" The Future

> There is no apparent link between the numerals 1,728 (12^3) and 2,401 (49^2), other than that the former represents the structure of a novel 379.21.3
> and the second the structure of *La Bibliothèque* More or Less
> *idéale*. Useful Details

"Do dese 'ere bottles cost a whole lot of money?"

Terry posed the question while pretending to look for a shirt in the closet, trying for a look of cool detachment. He certainly did not want to look like he was checking on how Carmen spent her money.

"A lot o' money? Ha! More like an arm an' a leg!"

"Is dat more'n payin' troo de nose?"

"More, maybe."

Carmen's answer reassured Terry, because it opened the door to conciliation rather than confrontation.

"Well den, dat is expensive fer sure. I suppose a body could take it up as a hobby, like . . ."

Carmen found the idea comical, she'd never thought of her facial and skin care as a hobby. Terry explained himself:

"Dat's de way of hobbies, doh, isn't it? Makes you feel good, gives yer brain a bit of a rest, and always ends up costing a whole lot more'n you tot 'twould. Wedder it's golf, electric trains, paintin', bird watchin', even sewin', I figures . . ."

Carmen, for her part, saw it more as a necessity. But she had no intention of making a big deal out of it.

"I suppose you could look at it like that, if it helps to 380.107.1
swallow de cost." Necessities

> Acadians still use the verbs *sourdre*, *ressoudre*, and *ersoudre* rather than the more standard modern French *jaillir*, or *surgir de* meaning "to come up" or "arise from," for example, someone coming up out of nowhere. Citing the French novelist François Mauriac, the *Grand Robert* dictionary includes *sourdre* used in this way. As for *ressoudre*, though it is unacknowledged by the *Robert*, Acadian author and winner of the Goncourt literary prize, Antonine Maillet, taking its pronunciation into account, has spelled it *ersoudre*. All these usages might ultimately produce an Acadian version of Lacanian concepts in the following variations: for Lacan's "erring-in-discourse," "*ersoud-la-parole*" instead of "*errent-sous-la-parole*", while "the non-duped-err-in discourse" becomes "*des non-dupes-ersoud-la-parole*" instead of "*des non-dupes-errent-sous-la-parole,*" and finally
> 381.58.2 "*des Noms-du-Père sourd la parole*" for "from
> Extensions the Names-of-the-Father discourse arises."

Back home with the children at the end of the day, Carmen found a note from Terry reminding her that he was having supper at his parents' that evening.

"I'm hungry…"

Once again, Étienne's appetite was reassuring to Carmen. She was still fearful that he might get his back up and refuse once and for all to go on with the film.

"Where's Dad, Mum?"

"He's havin' supper in Dieppe, with Granny and Grandad."

Étienne looked disappointed not to be having supper in Dieppe, too.

"We'll go anudder time. It's good for Terry to be eatin' on his own with his mum and dad sometimes, just like you two're eatin' on our own with yer mum."

The prospect of "eating on their own with their mum"
did not seem to be cause for great celebration to the chil- 382.26.5
dren, but Carmen wasn't the sort to let that bother her. The Movie

> In the alphabetical listing of streets in *L'Indispensable* map of Paris, rue Sébastien-Bottin falls under *b* for Bottin. This short street in the seventh arrondissement, is an extension of what becomes the rue de Beaune south of rue de l'Université, then changes to rue de Montalembert, and merges with the rue du Bac. On a very ordinary plaque on the var-
> nished wooden door of number 5, the letters 383.56.1
> NRF are engraved in Rondes Italic. Pilgrimages

"Sure, but how's a body to know if de real is de real 384.92.3
fer real, an' not nuttin' more dan de imaginary or de Questions without
symbolic?" Answers

> In North America, *thériaque* is a candy usually sold in the form of long red twists. The black version in the form of pipes and cigars is disap-
> pearing. Other varieties in different shapes, co- 385.7.4
> lours and flavours come and go on the market. Useful Details

Carmen couldn't sleep, thinking about the morrow:

"I'm thinkin' 'twasn't such a bright idea sendin' the wee ones to make that film. You should've heard Étienne after supper. Tossin' English all over the place. *Candy* over here an' *puddles* over there, and dey put *cement* in it, and that was *awesome*, and now the boy wants a *skateboard* fer his birt'day."

Terry, too, was beginning to worry about his son's language:

"I knows it."

"The whole thing's discouraging."

"Well, jus' tell yerself der's naught but two days to go..."

“Luh! ’Tis only gettin’ started! Folks say, once they set foot inside the schoolhouse, you can ferget it, it’s over!”

Terry thought Carmen was being overly defeatist.

386.26.6 “Don’t go takin’ it so hard, girl. Is it yer period yer
The Movie expectin’ sometime soon?

> And finally, where the perfection of 7^3 meets the plenitude of 12^3:

$$
\begin{aligned}
7 \times 7 \times 7 &= 12 \times 12 \times 12 \\
343 &= 1{,}728 \\
3 \times 4 \times 3 &= 1 \times 7 \times 2 \times 8 \\
(3 \times 4) \times 3 &= (1 \times 7) \times 2 \times 8 \\
12 \times 3 &= \{(7) \times 2\} \times 8 \\
(1 \times 2) \times 3 &= 14 \times 8 \\
2 \times 3 &= (1 \times 4) \times 8 \\
6 &= 4 \times 8 \\
6 &= 32
\end{aligned}
$$

387.72.12 $6 = (3 \times 2)$
Equations $6 = 6$

“So I’m wonderin’ did ee stab ’im fer real.”

. . .

“Lucky ting me own dad was a great guy. Only me mudder had a notion to kill ’im a couple o’ times.”

“An’ why’s dat?”

“She tot ee was flirtin.”

“An was ee? Flirtin’, I mean.”

“Yaa. Turns out me mudder was right.”

388.25.5 . . .
Murder “I guess ee wasn’t nice fer nuttin.”

> Marianne isn’t quite two years old. She was
> born May-one-two, as she puts it. She enjoys
> being Étienne’s little sister, and he takes his
> 389.96.2 role of big brother seriously, making sure she
> Characters doesn’t hurt herself, and teaching her to play.

And so it was that the responsibility for transforming the rocky wasteland behind the children's playground into a vegetable garden fell to the celebrated artist Étienne Zablonski. He'd volunteered during the monthly meeting of the lofts, residents and shopkeepers. On the first Tuesday of every month a more or less official — depending on the circumstances — meeting was held at the Babar. In the absence of items requiring serious discussion, the meeting would become purely social, which was the case most times, because Zed did an excellent job as manager, and all the residents felt comfortable raising any issues with him as they came up. If things ran smoothly in the building, it was also because no one harboured unrealistic expectations. As a result, the first Tuesday of every month, a good-neighbourly evening accompanied by libations was held at the Babar, a gathering to which were also welcome friends from outside who were linked in one way or another to the dynamics of the lofts.

390.9.3
The Garden

> The science and wisdom of numbers have more to teach us than the elementary principles of arithmetic. Why, for example, is the number PHI, 1.618033989, considered to be the most beautiful numeral in the universe? And how do we get from PHI to the golden ratio, which is based on the relation between 3 and 5? And does this golden ratio really exist, or must we be content with striving toward it, as does the Fibonacci sequence?

391.97.11
Numerals and
Numbers

Later, Terry regretted having insinuated that Carmen's hormonal fluctuations had influenced her perception of Monctonian French.

"Hey der, Marianne? In French, we says *sauté*, not *jumpé*."

Marianne looked at Terry, not entirely sure what her dad was getting at.

"*Sauté*?"

"Dat's it, *sauté*."

And Marianne threw her arms up over her head and jumped:

"*Sauté*!"

"Dat's it, Marianne, *sauté*. Alright den, now we all gets in de car."

But her dad was willing to bide his time while Marianne did a bit more jumping.

"Alright, Marianne, dat's it, den. All aboard, now."

Finally, Marianne stopped jumping and let Terry strap her into her seat.

"Dad, de *trunk*'s not closed!"

"*La valise*, Étienne, we says *la valise*."

"Lots of folks says *trunk*."

"Dat may be, but we say *valise*. Get it?"

A little while later:

392.26.7 The Movie "Dad, I know we say *sauté* fer *jumpé*, so how come we say *trippé* when we wants to make someone fall down?"

> In spite of the inexhaustible variety of languages and boundless nuances that each permits, one truth remains: human beings desire clarity and simplicity. This is evidenced by the word that introduces the largest number of titles in *La Bibliothèque idéale*, the word *histoire* in French, which can refer to the stories of people or to the history of nations but, whether these histories or stories are ordinary or extraordinary, true or imaginary, that word *histoire* sets the human psyche in motion. Oddly, although the genre is promising, we cannot say the same
> 393.48.3 Inferences for historians, because only two titles in *La Bibliothèque idéale* begin with that word.

In spite of his good will, Étienne was beginning to run out of ideas to fill his work week. His collection of new words was not being well received at home. And yet it was an interesting game.

"Are you comin' over der, den?"

The other boy peppered his sentences with English words:

"We can *stamp* our feet in de *cement* an' bring de *slab* home!"

Though he hadn't quite understood what it was about, Étienne followed the boy.

"*Sure*, beats sittin' 'ere wid dis *boring puzzle*."

The fact that he could employ the same language as the other boy added the thrill of adventure to their activities. Incursion into the territory of the Other.

394.26.8 The Movie

> Even psychoanalysis has taken up the subject of numbers because, as Lacan put it, "speaking beings count and account for themselves." We can deduce from this that people suffering from neuroses (obsessional, hypochondriac) and psychoses have certain things in common when it comes to their relationship to numbers, but Lacan warns against a simplistic use of the arithmetical metaphor.

395.97.12 Numerals and Numbers

While running an errand for the bookstore, Terry noticed a van for sale parked in a vacant lot owned by the city. The vehicle looked to be in good shape, so he did a U-turn to take a closer look. He liked the van's resilient attitude, a quality that corresponded to the image he had of their little family. He took down the telephone number written on a piece of cardboard in the front windshield: 383-8383.

396.27.2 New Car

> Letters and correspondence offer humans near as much interesting material as do stories. The titles of *La Bibliothèque idéale* beginning with the words *letter* and *correspondence* are almost

as numerous as those announcing one or more stories. Entirely subjective, letters and correspondences probably function as a counterweight to the stories so painstakingly designed

397.48.4 Inferences

by authors, and to history, which historians study so assiduously.

The need for an organ of standardisation and preservation of the Acadian language is nowhere more pressing than in the case of the word for "this," *cte* pronounced "*ste*." This demonstrative article, which replaces *ce*, *cet* and *cette*, leads to the necessity of clarifying a whole battalion of deictic expressions: *sticit, sticitte, stilà, stelle-là, stelle-cit, stelle-citte, stelli-cit,* and *stiya-là* — most of which originate in the vernacular Latin — culminating in the famous *ceuses-là*.

"Dat way, dem's dat might be wantin' to say dis 'ere dis

398.30,5 Chiac

way, could go right ahead an' say: '*De cte wé-là, ceuses-là qui voudriont le dire de même pourriont itou.*'"

399.57.10 Photocopies

Recipe for carrot cake. Bof.

Despite her profound conviction, Carmen did not want to be intransigent:

"I'll wait to see it before I make up my mind."

Terry had already phoned the owner of the van and obtained some information. The owner agreed to meet them with the keys to the van in the vacant lot at six o'clock that evening.

"How is it he didn't come over 'ere with it? Would've been a whole lot simpler, seems to me."

Terry agreed with her, the best course of action under the circumstances.

"Dat's true. Shall I call 'im back, den?"

On second thought, Carmen realized that she did not want to inspect the vehicle under the noses of her neighbours, considering the touchy discussion that was likely to ensue. Nor did she relish the thought of every Tom, Dick, and Harry butting in with his opinion on the vehicle.

"Naw, never mind. Since we're goin' out, might as well stop over at the Dairy Queen with the kids. Been a long time since we did that." 400.27.3 New Car

> (Perhaps) the (supposed) opposition between Freud and Lacan stems from their different linguistic cultures. Freud, for his part, tried to describe (inscribe) as clearly as possible his research, and the ideas and conclusions that followed from it. Any yet, once these were written down (and many times rewritten), Freud still felt he had failed to do justice to the marvels of psychic nature he had witnessed. For Lacan, the unconscious is revealed first and foremost in speech. Hence the surprising gaps (traps) opened up by puns and word play (ploy) typical of Lacan's methodological choice (voice). 401.34.7 Lacan

"Like, wid dem tartan designs in Scotland, does you know if dey has to follow every, wot you call golden ratio afore dey're chosen official tartan of de clan?" 402.92.1 Questions without Answers

> Memoirs come in about halfway down the ladder of interest we can extrapolate from the titles of *La Bibliothèque idéale*. There are approximately 30 titles beginning with the word *memoirs*.[10] 403.48.5 Inferences

Carmen walked round the van again, holding Étienne by the hand. At one point, the boy pulled away to go

---

10. The French novelist André Gide claimed that memoirs are only partially sincere, highly ambiguous, and hesitate between their content and form. 406.142.10 Notes

over and kick the front tire the way he'd seen Terry do it. Carmen observed how quickly males establish a kind of authority over machines. "*Where've you been, Bergère, where've you been? Where've you been, Bergère, where've you been?...*"

Terry sang softly as he circled the van with Marianne in his arms.

"*I've been in the stable...*"

404.27.4 New Car

Meanwhile, seated behind the wheel of a muddy Grand Cherokee, with a cellphone to his ear, the owner of the van for sale was talking and looking through a stack of documents he kept unfolding, turning over, and refolding.

405.76.6 Avatars

> It would not be wrong to say that the characters in literary fiction are the avatars of their authors, that is, at once, their representations, their metamorphoses and their misfortunes.

407.54.7 Forgotten/Recalled

> The possibility considered, early on, to write one fragment for each of the six faces of 1,728 cubes. In the end, the book would have contained 10,368 fragments, or six times the number in this version. Monstrous project. No desire whatsoever to mount such a monster.

"Essentially, we eat vegetables at one of three stages of their development."

Sporting the panama hat Ludmilla had bought him for the occasion, Étienne Zablonski was explaining the rudiments of a vegetable garden to the other three, who were zigzagging with him behind the lofts building, between the children's playground and the train tracks.

"First, there's the vegetative stage, which includes the leaves and the tender roots, like lettuce, radishes, carrots and turnips."

Zablonski wondered if his approach might not be too

professorial. But since they had decided on a vegetable garden designed *à la française*, he was obliged to offer at least some explanation.

"Other vegetables, we eat at the reproductive stage. Those are the ones whose flowers we eat before they pollenate and produce seeds: broccoli, cauliflower, and artichoke, for example."

At this point Zablonski had a moment of doubt regarding the inclusion of the artichoke in the French vegetable garden. Which is understandable, because France was starting to be a long time ago by now.

"And finally there are those we eat at the post reproductive stage; in other words, vegetables whose fruits we consume. Tomatoes for example, and all the flesh that covers seeds."

"Hun!"

This initial reaction from his audience reassured Zablonski, who was beginning to worry that his assistants might not be interested in such details.

"Obviously, the vegetables we eat at the vegetative stage will be harvested long before those whose fruits we eat."

. . .

"Logically, we can plant and harvest those we eat at the vegetative stage several times — lettuce, for example — during a single cycle of the stage that produces fruit, like tomatos, squash, etc.... So it would be *handier* — as we say in these parts — to plant the lettuce with easy access, compared to the carrots, for example. That's the sort of useful detail to keep in mind when we decide where to place the planks."

"Hun!"

Lisa-M. was thrilled to learn so much basic knowledge in such a short time. Zed, for his part, knew exactly where to find the boards they would need. And rather than try to continue talking while the passenger train to Halifax clattered by, Zablonski accepted a cigarette from Antoinette.

> As for the personal “journal,” much preferred
> to literary or other kinds of “journals”, if it lacks
> the charisma of stories and correspondences,
> it comes in a close second, ahead of memoirs.
> Forty or so titles of *La Bibliothèque idéale* begin
> 409.48.6 with the word *journal.* To brush up against his-
> Inferences tory while telling one’s own experience.

When the caboose had filed past, Le Grand Étienne picked up his lecture:

“Vegetables don’t all require the same conditions to flourish. In general, those we eat at the first stage like cool weather and a bit of sun. Too much heat will exhaust them.”

. . .

“This is true for spinach, for example. We plant it in the spring and again after the dog days of summer.”

Antoinette nodded.

“Finally, the basic principle of the garden is to always have something to pick, always fresh vegetables. In France, this means all year round. But here in Canada, we’ll obviously have to adapt.”

“It’ll take a whole lot o’ work to get someting to grow in dis ’ere ground.”

The three others turned to Antoinette, who was scraping the heel of her boot against the hard, rocky soil, a movement that did little more than raise a bit of dust. Zed had anticipated the difficulty:

“I snatched up a pick in a garage sale last week. We can bust up de ground wid it.”

The Cripple’s wife was undaunted:

“Well, der’s notin’ like eatin’ radishes an’ beats an’ peas
you been watchin’ grow up from nuttin’ outside yer own
410.9.4 kitchen window. Even doh, wid dese ’ere, I’ll be lookin’ at
The Garden dem from me livin’-room window.”

> But the most surprising inference drawn from an analysis of the titles of *La Bibliothèque idéale* is the following: the number of titles beginning with the words *poem*, *poetry*, and *poetic* is equal to the number of titles beginning with the words *war* and *battle*.

411.48.7
Inferences

"So, den it's de colour you don't fancy?"

Terry was already convinced this was the perfect vehicle — and for a good price! — for their family, but he didn't want to force Carmen into liking the van. At the same time he was vaguely aware that his effort to be nice could be interpreted as a kind of manipulation. But Carmen didn't seem to notice:

"She doesn't look too old to you? No shine or anythin' . . ."

After their first discussion about replacing their car, Carmen had started to think that Terry wasn't entirely wrong, that it would probably be wiser to buy a used vehicle. But not being quite ready to say so openly, she beat a bit around the bush:

"Inside's not so bad. It's not torn up or anythin'."

Terry tried to keep from pushing too hard:

"Sure an' we'll have to get her inspected proper. Find out if she's bin driven too hard, or if she was in a crash . . . or if der's parts need replacin', stuff like dat."

He turned to his son:

"Well, den? What do you think?"*

412.27.5
New Car

* It is worth noting Terry's careful language here — "What do you think?" rather than "Wot does ya tink?" He made the effort, for example, to use the word *quesse* for "what" instead of his usual "*quoisse*" in a moment of delicate transaction with Carmen. Did he deliberately slip the more proper "*quesse*" into his question to Étienne in order to please Carmen and, in that way, perhaps influence her, or did he say it spontaneously,

In the scattered unwinding of this novel, I forgot to mention that Lisa-M., who first appeared in *Life's Little Difficulties*, had sinced moved into a loft with Pomme, who has become Zablonski's self-proclaimed impresario, not that Le Grand Étienne was looking for one, but he is amused and surprised by Pomme's tortuous and gently treacherous artistic theories.

413.7.3
Useful Details

415.39.12
Freud
Circuitously

Freud believed in the possibility of coincidence in the external world, but not in the psyche.

Étienne tried his luck:

"Me an' Uncle Étienne could paint it."

"Yi yi!"

Marianne fully supported her big brother's idea, but Étienne could not return the favour:

"Naw, Marianne, yer too little. An' you 'aven't taken de class."

Astonished by this refusal, Marianne turned to her mother, who welcomed her into her arms, while addressing Étienne:

"'Tisn't so easy to paint a car. It's not like a drawing or painting a wall..."

But Étienne was confident:

"Won't be hard fer Uncle Étienne."

Terry, too, tried to reason with his son:

"Folks have to go to college to learn how to paint cars. It's sometin' a fellow's got to study fer. Not to mention, you need all kinds of special equipment to do it."

Étienne, not daring to pursue the issue, pulled on a long stalk of grass beside him.

"Still, you can say what colour you'd like to paint 'er..."

---

which is possible though unlikely? Unless it was neither of the above, but rather that his use of "*quesse*" was simply a linguistic slippage into more proper speech.

414.143.5
Varia

Unmoved by Terry's offer, Étienne remained silent.

"Toittle!"

This from Marianne, leaping back into the fray.

"Turtle?!"

Terry chuckled as he repeated his daughter's choice of colour. But, in her innermost being, Carmen hoped the little one wasn't picking up Étienne's strange habit of constantly inventing names for colours.

"How 'bout you, den, Étienne, what colour would you paint 'er?"

The boy did not want to lose this second chance: 416.27.6

"Alizarin." New Car

> Nothing is more necessary, from time to time, than to find oneself face to face with someone absolutely out of the ordinary.

417.34.11 Lacan

"Ludmilla, have I ever said I would have liked to have a child?" 418.31.3 Questions with Answers

"No."

419.105.7 Reserves/ Reservations

> Not to always have an explanation in reserve.

The owner of the van closed his cellphone, put his papers aside and joined the young family.

"Well, den? Does she suit you?"

"Yeeesss!"

Marianne's enthusiastic response made everyone laugh, which encouraged Étienne to take advantage of the relaxed atmosphere to pronounce himself as well:

"We want to paint it!"

The owner smiled:

"I've some spray paint back home I'll trow in if yer buyin."

With a nod toward the children, Terry inferred that they could be a handful, so he'd take a raincheck on the paint.

"I can unnerstand…"

Étienne turned to Carmen and whispered:

"What's spray paint, Mum?"

420.27.8 "It's paint you *pchhhhhtt…*"

New Car "Awh! De Reo Sol can!"

> **SLANGOTHERAPIST:** n. — 2005; from *slang* and therapy ♦ Specialist in slangotherapy.
> **SLANGOTHERAPY:** n. — 2005 1. Treatment of mental problems via re-education in linguistic deviance. 2. SPECIALT secondary treatment of neuroses and psychoses of alienation.
> 421.120.6 *"Gone are the days when grammaturgs deni-*
> Fictionary *grated slangotherapy"* (Daigle).

The owner gave them the keys to the van so they could take it out for a test drive. Carmen had no trouble installing Marianne's car seat.

"Well, I suppose you might say dat's a fine start…"

Terry took the highway to Shediac. The occasional tug he gave the wheel just to check out the wheel alignment eventually prompted a reaction from Étienne:

"Wot you doin' dat fer, Dad?"

"I wants to be sure de steering wheel turns alright."

He pressed down on the gas pedal. The van accelerated slightly.

"She's not exactly yer Ferrari, but we weren't expectin' dat neider, was we?"

Carmen thought the front of the cab was well designed:

"It's comfortable, I got to say."

Once burned twice shy, she twisted the rear-view mirror in every direction to be sure it was well anchored.

Terry panicked:

"Wot'r ya doin'?!"

Carmen suddenly realized that Terry was in the passing lane, looking for a chance to get back in the right and out of the way of a fast car riding his tail.

"Oops." 422.27.9 New Car

> Other facts emerging from an analysis of the first words in the titles listed in *La Bibliothèque idéale*: the word *grandeur* appears more frequently than the word *heights*; *book* and *adventure* are neck and neck, as are *love* and *essay*; the word *child* is more common than *parent*, and the word *girl* appears more often than the word *son*. 423.48.8 Inferences

"Dad! Yer drivin' awful fast! We're gonna wind up in de *ditch!*"

"Étienne, speak properly!" Carmen said, cringing at Étienne's use of the English *ditch*.

Étienne laughed and did not correct himself. As he did a U-turn to head back to Moncton, Terry admitted to Carmen:

"Have to say, it's startin' to irritate me as well."

Carmen was happy to hear Terry was conscious of the severity of the problem:

"That's exactly what everyone says: once they're out of the house, they start pickin' up udder folks' words."

"I know it, only I never tot ee'd pick 'em up so quick..."

...

"Dat's where you see how easy 'tis fer de wee ones to learn anudder language. Seems like it goes right into der heads."

...

"She runs fine. Are ya sure you don't want to give 'er a spin?"

"Naw. I don't need to..."

Carmen was still thinking about children's speech:

"Wouldn't that mean proper French ought to be easy to learn?"

"Dat's right. Why is it harder dan de rest?"

...

"Well den, what do you think?"

"About what?"

"De vanne!"

Carmen laughed:

"Ha! I'd stopped even thinkin' 'bout it. It's like she's already ours!

424.26.9 …

The Movie "Do dey call it a *vanne* in French, as well, I wonder?"

> Lacan's pronouncements often walk a fine line between sense and nonsense, grazing difficult to grasp truths, which are at the very heart of psychoanalysis. It is therefore not surprising that so many pyschoanalysts contest his work. And if Lacan himself long resisted publishing his Seminars, it's because he suspected that to
> 425.34.12 diffuse his work might turn it into refuse, that
> Lacan publish would lead to perish.

Pomme's dream: Pomme and Lisa-M. stop for the night at a small country inn. The inn looks like a Greek or Mexican house, with whitewashed walls. Although it's surrounded by Canadian forest, the building looks like nothing Canadian. The innkeepers, an elderly couple, behave more or less normally. The woman, beautiful but taciturn, attends to the inn; the man, tall and distinguished, but rather indolent, exchanges vaguely odd banter with the few clients. In the inner courtyard, guests take the sun and fresh air around a swimming pool. One of the travellers can't seem to find her bathing suit. A shot rings out, knocking off the head of a policeman who's appeared out of nowhere. Suspicion, which falls initially on the woman who can't find her bathing suit, shifts quickly to the innkeeper. No one takes care of the policeman's headless body, which has simply been shoved against the wall. The police investigators will not come until the morrow. No one is shocked by this. While they wait, everything proceeds as usual. From time to time, the innkeeper proclaims his innocence to his wife. 426.109.8 Dreams

> One day, Le Petit Étienne asked his mother if Ludmilla and Zablonski were relations. A legitimate question, after all, since the couple was perfectly at home in the house, and neither they nor his parents were shy about lending or asking each other for a hand, or falling asleep while the others talked, or getting into arguments without that stopping them liking each other. 427.35.1 The Detail within the Detail

Carmen turned the radio on.

"Geez, it's already in French."

Terry figured the owner had probably tuned it to Radio-Canada on purpose to help the sale along.

"Well den kids? What do you tink?"

The excitement had finally won Étienne over:

"Yah! I like it!"

The boy turned to Marianne, expecting her usual enthusiastic self. Instead, he was surprised to discover his sister redfaced and straining.

"Awh, no ... Mum ..."

"What?"

"Marianne's doin' a caca. Peeyou! It stinks!"

Carmen twisted around, Terry looked in the rear-view mirror, the smell mushroomed. 428.27.10 New Car

"Dat's right, I forgot, Marianne's got the diarrhea."

> The sharp, the flat and the natural are musical accidents. 429.78.4 Accidents

Energized by the fresh air rushing into the van to flush out the oppressive odour, Carmen decided to take a turn at driving the vehicle. Terry pulled over to the side of the road and switched places with Carmen, who took her time to get familiar with the controls before setting off again.

"Do you like it, Mum?"

Étienne hoped his mother would say yes.

"Don't know yet, do I."

As she drove, Carmen glanced around outside and inside the van to get used to the driver's surroundings.

"Well, I do like the visibility."

Étienne was happy. Terry, meanwhile, tried once more to be accommodating:

"Fer sure she'll cost us more in gas."

Carmen, now comfortable behind the wheel, could think of other things:

"Well, we're not payin' all that much now..."

This was true, but Terry had something else in mind.

"We could maybe paint an ad for de Babar on one side an' de bookstore on de udder. Dat way, we could claim it on our taxes."

"Could I be painting Babar, den?"

Terry turned to Étienne:

"We'll see about dat when de time comes."

And to Carmen:

"Geez, I guess we'll have to plant a paintbrush in dat
430.27.11 boy's paw afore long."

New Car "A roller, more like."

> Aside from the better-known Acadian conjugations of the verb *to be*, such as *je sons*, *j'étions*, *y étiont*, and *alle étiont*, there are the even more surprising *que je seille* (or, in some regions, ending in *-o-n-s*), *que tu seilles*, *qu'y seille*, *qu'a seille*, *qu'on seille*, *que nous seillions*, *que vous seilliez*, *qu'y seillont*, *qu'a seillont*. Perhaps a better way to put this form in writing would be *que je sèye* (*que je sèyons*, etc.), *que tu sèyes*, *qu'y sèye*, *qu'a sèye*, *qu'on sèye*, *que nous sèyions*, *que vous sèyiez*, *qu'y sèyiont*, *qu'a sèyiont*.

How to translate these musical variations into
a non-standard English? That I are, I were, dey 431.33.9
was, she were...? Chiac Lesson

Back at the vacant lot where the owner of the van was waiting, Carmen quickly detached the baby's car seat with Marianne in it and carried it back to their old car. Terry took care of the rest:

"She's pretty much wot we's lookin' fer. Aside from de colour."

In spite of himself, the seller was intrigued:

"An' wot's wrong wid de colour, den?"

Terry didn't quite know what to say. He was sorry he'd raised the subject, because it was mostly Carmen who had a problem with the light green.

"Well, a fresh coat of paint wouldn't do 'er no harm, patch dose wee rust spots 'ere an' der."

The owner moved over for a closer look at the little scratches to which Terry was referring.

"You've got sharp eyes, I'd never seen dese." 432.27.12

The time to bargain was upon them. New Car

CHAPTER 4

Given a certain degree of reoccurrence, chance becomes no longer a coincidence, but a quality.

BENOÎTE GROULX, *La Touche étoile*
(The Star Key) 433.144.4
Grasset, 2006 Epigraphs

There were only two days of shooting left. The end was in sight, to Étienne's relief, but tinged with a touch of regret: this mixing of languages was turning out to be a lot of fun. At last, a game that was consistent and required creativity!

"Last night, I *helpé* my dad to *dédjãmmér* de *elevator*."

"Was der anybody inside?"

"Naw. Only de *pizzaman*, an' his *pouch* was empty." 434.26.10

At that very moment, the camera was on Étienne. The Movie

> *La Bibliothèque idéale* includes the titles of eight *Complete Works*. They are by Sainte Thérèse d'Avila (in the category "Spirituality and Religions"), Herodotus-Thucydides ("Antiquity and Us"), Stéphane Mallarmé ("French Poetry"), Blaise Pascal ("Philosophy"), Plautus-Terence ("Theatre"), François Rabelais ("Laughter"), Tristan Tzara ("Distorsions") and Xenophon ("Antiquity and

435.48.9 Us"). By itself this information does not really
Inferences constitute an inference.

The French word *dialyse* ("dialysis"), with the *y*—worth 10 points in the French game (only 4 in the English), placed on the letter counts double (2 × 10) and the entire word doubled (2 × 27)—hence, a little Legendre—plus a bonus of 50 points for having placed all her letters—a scrabble, already!—Antoinette opened the game with 104 points in a single stroke. Still, she hesitated, because her husband would only have to add an *R* to make *dialyser*, which would earn him 54 points, plus the value of the word he would make vertically on the *R*, which would also be worth triple. And all this not count-
436.28.1 ing the fact that he could very well produce a scrabble for
A Couple's Life 50 more points.

> With the advent of the digital age, the avatar has also come to designate entities in cyberspace. An individual can create one or several avatars to circulate in cyberspace in his or her place. BabyDy, SorrosJr, DocFarine, PickPocket, and SCrowbar, to name a few, are all avatars who, rather than concealing the fact that they are av-
> 437.76.2 atars, take pleasure in announcing themselves
> Avatars as such.

Marianne had not particularly been bitten by the language-game bug that so enthralled her brother. Happy and carefree, she flitted about, finding new little friends, handling or skipping around everything she encountered, tasting anything that was eatable, generally doing what she was told, and totally ignoring the filming.

"I'll give you half me *licorice* if you gives me half yer *chocolate bar*."

Marianne did not understand what the older girl meant.

"You doesn't want to *share half-an-half*?"

When the girl simply plucked the chocolate bar out of her hands, Marianne didn't protest in the least. Attracted by the cries of children playing in the sandbox, she took off without awaiting her due. And that's what the camera captured.

438.26.11
The Movie

> In the matter of virtue, politeness is most important because, without it, it would be difficult, if not impossible, to approach let alone accede to the other virtues. According to André Comte-Sponville's *A Short Treatise on the Great Virtues*, politeness is the first rung on the ladder. This marvellous book would undoubtedly have found a place in one of the categories of *La Bibliothèque idéale* if it had existed at the time of *La Bibliothèque*'s first printing in 1988. Nevertheless, since every reader is invited to add a book of his or her choice to each of the categories of the library, it's perfectly appropriate to add *A Small Treatise on the Great Virtues* to the "Social Sciences" section.

439.66.1
The Virtues

Suddenly, Antoinette was struck by a kind of illumination. Since *Y* is a word on its own in French, couldn't she count it as a second word, this one reading vertically, and since the *Y* would land on a word-counts-double square, wasn't it worth four times 10 points? These additional 20 points would bring her total to 124, which was not bad at all. That clinched it.

440.28.2
A Couple's Life

> The quality of inferences depends on the clarity of the message being communicated.

441.48.10
Inferences

The Cripple immediately saw the potential of the word *dialyse*. He also followed the point count, which Antoinette conducted out loud. He expected her to end at 104, and could not understand why she returned to the *Y* for more.

"*Y* is a word, isn't it. It's my vertical word. An' it counts double, so dat comes to 104 plus 20."

The Cripple had never heard anything like it.

"Vertical!?"

Antoinette repeated her explanation. The Cripple did not agree.

"Can't be a vertical word, der's nuttin above or below it!"

"Dat don't matter, 'tis vertical all de same, on account of *Y* is a word."

442.28.3
A Couple's Life

The Cripple shook his head, at a complete loss.

> André Comte-Sponville's *A Short Treatise on the Great Virtues* does appear however in the category of "Philosophy" in "La Bibliothèque idéale des sciences humaines (The Ideal Library of the Social Sciences)," a special issue in 2003 of *Sciences humaines*, a French journal of the social sciences. The other disciplines included in the Social Sciences are anthropology, psychology, psychoanalysis, education, linguistics, communications, sociology, ethology, prehistory, history, geography, political science, economy, and philosophy, according to the table of contents of this particular journal.

443.66.2
The Virtues

"I'm not riding around wid our kids in a van dat advertises Le Babar. Like it or not, children and a bar just don't go together. It seems immoral."

It was as though Terry had never heard the word.

"Immoral. You mean, like... indecent?"

But Carmen was not to be distracted.

"Not only dat, but 'twould be like we were workin' all de time. We couldn't be just our little family, out fer a picnic on a Sunday or sometin', widout everybody an' his uncle knowin' who we are. It identifies us.

...

"Are you sure we've got to put an ad on it to be deductin' it on our taxes?"

As a matter of fact, Terry wasn't sure.

"I'll check wid de accountant."

"We aren't already deductin' our car?"

"Naw, she's too old. She's not wurt enough."

...

"We can only be usin' a part of de cost o' gas. An repairs. An' dat's only if we keep de receipts. Which me brudders at de garage aren't too good at givin.'" 444.27.7 New Car

> "The Ideal Library of the Social Sciences" lists 545 books, 518 of them belonging to 14 of the disciplines named above, which it will do no harm to list once again here, still in the same order they are named in the special issue of the *Sciences humaines* journal: anthropology, psychology, psychoanalysis, education, linguistics, communications, sociology, ethology, prehistory, history, geography, political science, economy, and philosophy. To complete this list of complete works are added a number of essays dealing with related issues on life and society. This category includes 27 titles. 445.61.1 Social Sciences

The Cripple had run out of arguments. He'd never thought of the *Y* as a word in relation to Scrabble, and he'd certainly never heard of anyone counting score the way Antoinette was proposing to do.

"In dat case, we could be doin' de same ting wid de letter *a?*

Antoinette had not thought of the letter *a*:

"Dat's true! Dat gives me anudder point, makes 125."

Antoinette and The Cripple both ran through the alphabet in their heads, but found no other letter that makes a word on its own.

"Hmmm…"

It wasn't the 21 points that bothered The Cripple; it was the principle of the thing. He took the time to scan the rules of the game printed on the cover of the box, but, alas, there was nothing there to rule out counting the *Y* or the *A* as words. On the contrary, he was beginning to suspect that a strong debater would have little trouble in defending Antoinette's cause.

"Well, I just don't know. One ting's fer sure, I never did see anyting like dis 'ere before now."

In the English version of Scrabble, because *Q* and *Z* are the only letters worth 10 points, and neither is a word on its own, as is the *Y* in French, Antoinette's feat would have been impossible. On the other hand, if she were to produce the word *muzjiks* (a Russian peasant), laying the *Z* down on the letter counts double square, she would
446.28.4 score 128 points, 129 if she were allowed to count the *I* as
A Couple's Life a word in the vertical.

> Unbeknownst to her, Ludmilla had also lodged Jacques Brel in Terry's singing heart, especially the lines *But why me? Why now? Why so soon? Where to go?* that Terry would belt out from time to time when his heart filled up to overflowing. Especially since he loved the way Brel pronounced that strange line *Where to go?*
> 447.1.10 with a distinctly Acadian accent: *"Yoù aller?"*
> Chansons Clearly, Acadia had Belgian roots…

Since Lisa-M. spent many an evening at home practising her flute, Carmen and Josse knew they could always call on her in an emergency, which is what they were facing tonight, the Babar being short of arms and legs to serve the customers.

"Wot's goin' on 'ere?"

"Der's a whole lot of folks all of a sudden an' Jeannine couldn't stay. She 'ad to go an' have 'er bikini line done."

Watching Josse pop the caps on six bottles of beer at once, Lisa-M. thought how lucky the employees of the Babar were to be able to take time off for the most frivolous reasons. Dropping the bottle opener, Josse added:

"She's in such a state, it's beyond understandin'. It's her first time goin' down sowt, I didn't want to say nuttin'."

Customers were pouring into the bar. Lisa-M. rolled up her sleeves.

"Der's sometin' goin' on fer sure! I gotta find out wot."

As she spoke, Lisa-M. spotted Pierre and Antoine, and went over to make enquiries.

"What? You don't know? We're celebratin' Hektor Haché-Haché's one hundredth letter to the editor of *L'Acadie nouvelle.* Bones is comin' to play an' all!"

Lisa-M. came back to tell Josse what the fuss was about.

"Dat's wicked! When we opened up de place, dat's how we wanted tings to be! A real place fer folks." 448.18.1 A Place for Everyone

> Ethology is probably the least known of the social sciences. This discipline, which studies the behaviour of animals in their natural environment, often reveals troubling similarities between animals and humans. 449.61.2 Social Sciences

Terry had decided The Cripple was an excentric the first time he set foot in the latter's home.

"One of de walls is covered in Polaroids of Scrabble. Every skitch shows a different *game* wid different words.

"*Game*?"

Terry had used the English word *game.*

"*Jeu*," he corrected himself. "Right off I'd say der was hundreds. A body can read de words if you gets up close enough."

Carmen liked the idea.

"Ee says every... game... ee's ever played is der. Every time ee plays, he snaps a picture."

"Who, Dad?"

Ever since he'd been part of a film shoot, Étienne had taken an interest in cameras.

"De fellow who moved in down de hall. De Cripple."

Carmen jumped:

"Don't call him dat, my God!"

"He tol' me 'imself I's to call 'im dat!"

Carmen was stunned.

"Ee says dat's more like his real name den de one his folks gave 'im, Arturin LeBreton. I seen it on 'is credit card."

Étienne was beginning to want to know more.

450.16.1 "Wot does ee play at, Dad?"

The Cripple "Scrabble. It's a game wid letters."

> Love — beautifully defined as an excellence by Comte-Sponville — tops all the other virtues. Between politeness — classified by Comte-Sponville more as a value than a virtue — and love, 16 other virtues are scrutinized in order to unravel true from false, and to reveal how really difficult they are to attain. Loyalty is the
> 451.66.3 second rung on the ladder. The penultimate
> The Virtues virtue, just below love, is humour.

Lisa-M. was working hard at the Babar, but not unhappily, since the crowd was more stimulating that exhausting. The packed room was in fine spirits, thanks to the grab bag of humorous observations that Robert Melanson had gleaned from a whole gamut of human follies that Hektor Haché-Haché had taken the time and trouble to bring to the attention of the readers of *L'Évangéline* and *L'Acadie nouvelle* over the years.

"I never been dis happy to fill in dan I am tonight. I loves it when it gets shockin' crazy like dis."

Josse too was enjoying herself:

"Don't I knows it? Pete? One Alpine, two Coronas, one

Sleeman Cream an' tree Moose Dry."

Lisa-M. was waiting to give her order as well:

"Don't know 'bout yours, but mine're bending elbows like de devil."

"Dat's how it always is come pay day. An' it's early yet!"

"I'll be buyin' dat sweater I seen at Champlain Place 452.18.2 A Place for
dis afternoon." Everyone

> *La Bibliothèque idéale* lists four works each by Jean-Baptiste Poquelin, a.k.a. Molière, and William Shakespeare. From Molière the collection suggests his play *Tartuffe* in the category of "Theatre," along with *The Bourgeois Gentleman, The Learned Ladies,* and *The Imaginary Invalid* in the "Laughter" section. From Shakespeare, the book retains the *Sonnets* in "English Literature," *Midsummer Night's Dream* under the category of "The Fantastic and Marvellous", *Hamlet* in "Theatre," and *Richard III* in
> "Politics." Are the French more prone to laugh- 453.48.11
> ter than the English? Inferences

So The Cripple finally declared:

"Alright den. If dat's de way it is, den dat's de way it is."

Antoinette wrote her score down in a fresh column, on the specially designed Scrabble score sheet.

"Yer tellin' me I'm de first body to tink of it?"

The Cripple found this difficult to imagine, but:

"Looks dat way..."

He sighed deeply the way one might do after a great effort, hoping perhaps to close the surprising if minor
incident. 454.28.5
"Now, let's just see wot I can do wid dis, den." A Couple's Life

> Most of the works included in "The Ideal Library of the Social Sciences" are by single authors, but there are several collaborations.

> In addition, although the majority of authors have only one book listed, several have two, but only six have three. The six are Bloch, Freud, Habermas, Ricoeur, Sartre, and Schumpeter. Bourdieu, Braconnier, Katz, Lazerfeld, Levy, Passeron, and Sperber also have three books listed but, in each of these cases, two of the works mentioned are collaborations.

455.61.3
Social Sciences

A few days later, Terry had learned more:

"I saw De Cripple today..."

"Gawd, I can't get used to dat name."

"I asked 'im if he knew how many Polaroids ee had up on his wall."

. . .

"Der's 1,346."

"Dat's a whole bunch. Who does ee play wid, den?"

"His wife, I suppose."

. . .

"His goal is to get up to 1,728."

"On account of?"

"I don't know. I wanted to ask 'im, but ee was in de middle of explainin' sometin' and by de time ee was done I guess I forgot."

Étienne came in grumbling and wrapped himself around his mother's legs:

"When're we gonna eat, Mum? I'm hungry..."

"In a bit. Do you want a slice of apple?"

As the boy didn't reply, Carmen concluded that he didn't really know what he wanted. She held him close, stroking him tenderly, and took up the conversation.

"Wot does ee plan to do after dat? Stop playin', or just stop snappin' pictures?"

"Who? De Cripple?"

Carmen sighed to hear Étienne call him that. Terry answered his son's question:

"Right. I saw 'im again today. Ee was wantin' some books."

"Ee reads a lot, eh?"

"Looks dat way."

"I wanna be readin' too."

Terry bent down to pick Étienne up and toss him up in the air a few times.

"I believe it, you wanna read! An' you know wot? I can't wait 'till you're reading, too. On account of I wanna sell you some books. Wee books and great big ones, dem dat cost an armful and dose dat aren't so dear, an' books wid pictures, an' books wid photographs, an' books wid just words, an' big tick dictionaries in French, English, Chinese, African..."

Carmen didn't like the idea that a father would exploit his son.

"At a good price, I hope!"

"Business is business, eh, Étienne? You tell yer mudder..."

Étienne roared with laughter as he spun in the air. He'd 456.16.2
completely forgotten his hunger. The Cripple

> Between politeness and loyalty on the one hand, and humour and love on the other, Comte-Sponville explores 14 virtues in the following order: prudence, temperance, courage, justice, generosity, compassion, forgiveness, gratitude, humility, simplicity, tolerance, puri- 457.66.4
> ty, genteleness, and good will. The Virtues

Alice Léger was up in arms:

"Might as well say we's de ones dat're payin' fer de international reputation of Statistics Canada!"

"International?"

"We's pretty much de best in de world..."

"Pretty much?"

"An' on account of we's mostly women, de bosses tink we don't mind. Dey don't give a fig dat we's workin' all hours, evenin's an' weekends—on account of you doesn't do dem interviews when you please, you gots to do 'em when dey wants you to."

"An' are you dat badly paid, den?"

"Less den eleven dollars an hour."

458.22.11
Overheard
Conversations

...

"Gettin' bit by dogs an' all!"

459.66.9
The Virtues

> But what are virtues? Moral values acquired by humans over time, transmitted by culture and corresponding to a propensity to do good? More or less, yes.

Terry opened the envelope, glanced at the amount of the cheque. Satisfied, he folded the whole thing and stuffed it into the back pocket of his jeans.

"Dad!"

Marianne, who had just spotted him, came running.

"Well, if it isn't me little goose!"

In the arms of her dad, Marianne finally got to see the macaroni collages the children had been making on a large table all afternoon.

"An' where's Étienne got to, den?"

Until today, Étienne had always been first to greet him.

"Let's go an' find Étienne..."

Terry wandered from one room to another, nodding a greeting from time to time. Finally, he spotted Étienne in the backyard, playing shooter marbles with some other boys. Something about the situation reassured him. Coming closer, he overheard a bit of their conversation, spattered with English.

"My dad's a *pipefitter*."

"Mine's a *janitor*."

"Me, 'tis my mudder who's a *janitor*."

"Me, my mudder *calls* de bingo."

"How about you den?"

Étienne was ready, nonchalante.

"My dad's got a *store* o' books, an' my mudder's a *Babartender.*" 460.26.12 The Movie

Works by and other characteristics of the six writers who each authored three titles in "The Ideal Library of the Social Sciences": Marc Bloch (1886–1944), historian of medieval France, twice mentioned under history (*The Royal Touch: Monarchy and Miracles in France and England, French Rural History*), one essay (*Strange Defeat,* a memoir written in 1940); Sigmund Freud (1856–1939), Austrian, founder of psychoanalysis, twice mentioned under psychoanalysis (*The Interpretation of Dreams, Cinq psychanalyses* [Five Case Histories]), one essay (*Civilization and Its Discontents*); Jürgen Habermas (1929–), German sociologist, twice mentioned under philosophy (*The Theory of Communicative Action, Technology and Science as Ideology*), once mentioned under communication (*The Structural Transformation of the Public Sphere: an Inquiry into a Category of Bourgeois Society*); Paul Ricoeur (1913–2005), French philosopher, twice mentioned under philosophy (*Oneself as Another, Time and Narrative*), once mentioned under history (*Memory, History, and Forgetting*); Jean-Paul Sartre (1905–1980), French philosopher, writer and critic, twice mentioned under philosophy (*Existentialism is a Humanism, Being and Nothingness: An Essay in Phenomenological Ontology*), one essay (*Anti-Semite and Jew*); Joseph Schumpeter (1883–1950), Austrian economist, three times mentioned in economy (*Capitalism, Socialism and Democracy, History of Economic Analysis, Business Cycles:*

461.61.4 Social Sciences *A Theoretical, Historical and Statistical Analysis of the Capitalist Process*).

"Don't know wot's goin' on, I've a cramp in me leg all day since dis mornin'."

"If it was yer heart it'd be in yer arm you'd be hurtin'. Unless you slept crooked on it or sometin' of de sort. In dat case, you might be tinkin' 'twas yer heart, but 'twould just be on account of you slept *cramped*. Like when you goes campin'. Don' know 'bout you, but I wakes up wid a cramp somewhere's every time I goes *campin'*. *Camp cramp*, me wife says. Well, I've gotta haul ass or I'll be getting' a *call*. You takes care o' dat leg, now!"

"Ya! An' tanks fer all dat information (dat I didn't really want)."

"Anytime!"

In the above tirade, the speaker switched back and forth between the English and French pronunciations of *camp* and *cramp*. One wonders why. Was it the pervasive influence of English? A degree of embarrassment
462.35.10 The Detail within the Detail at speaking French? Just for the sake of variety? Out of nonchalance? A kind of linguistic intuition? A form of complicity?

> Comte-Sponville does not claim to have produced an exhaustive and immutable list of the virtues, but he hopes to have included the essential values associated with 30 possible virtues. As for the order in which he presents them, the philosopher explains that it is based
> 463.66.6 The Virtues more on a combination of intuition and necessity than on a desire to establish a hierarchy.

"Dad, is it true dat crows' eggs are black?"

"Der legs? Yes, sure."

"Not der legs, der eggs! Dat's wot Chico told me..."

"Well, could be. I never heard nuttin' bout crows' eggs.

To tell you true, crows aren't me all-time favourite bird. Matter o' fact, dey scares me just a bit."

"On account of?"

"Don't know, do I. Hard to tink dey's very nice wid dat croaky voice dey got. An' dey're big and black to boot. An' here you are tellin' me der eggs are black as well…"

Étienne looked with renewed interest at the three crows gathered around a partially crushed cone of french fries in the parking lot of the A&W.

"Dey don't scare me…"

"Well now, dat's a good ting. 'Tis better if we're not scared of de same tings. Dat way we can help each udder out." 464.140.4

"OK." Caraquet

> On his mother Anne-Marie Schweitzer's side, Jean-Paul Sartre was the cousin once removed of Albert Schweitzer, theologian, philosopher, musician, musicologist, medical missionary (in Gabon), winner of the Nobel Prize for Peace in 1952, and the man who swallowed an oyster, giving half the bivalve shell to each of the two individuals who were arguing over the mollusc, each claiming he had found it. A bit of trivia we were told in school.

465.65.2
Boy Cousins,
Girl Cousins

"You won't believe wot he showed me today…"

Carmen had given up any doubts she might have harboured over what Terry told her about The Cripple.

"A bucket full of screws is wot, every kind o' screw!"

!

"I'm tellin' you! A whole bucket full!"

The idea that this was a pretty poor system of classification occurred fleetingly to Carmen, but she simply said:

"Must be awful heavy."

Terry felt this was dwelling on a minor detail.

466.16.3 The Cripple “Only proves how complicated dey’ve made our lives wid all der different kinds of screws.”

> From a comparison of the titles listed in *La Bibliothèque idéale* and those in “La Bibliothèque idéale des sciences humaines,” we can identify a certain number of essential works for anyone seeking to augment his or her knowledge of the social sciences. A total of 58 titles are recommended by both reference works. For those seeking a shorter list, 14 titles not only appear in both publications, but are considered by *La Bibliothèque idéale* as one of the first books to read on the subject: in politics, *The Origins of Totalitarianism* by Hannah Arendt; in history: *The Royal Touch: Monarchy and Miracles in France and England* by Marc Bloch, *The Mediterranean and the Mediterranean World in the Age of Philip II* by Fernand Braudel, *The Age of the Cathedrals: Art and Society, 980–1420* by Georges Duby, and *The Autumn of the Middle Ages* by Johan Huizinga; in sociology: *Suicide* by Émile Durkheim and *The Civilizing Process* by Norbert Élias; in psychoanalysis: *The Interpretation of Dreams* by Sigmund Freud; in anthropology: *The Golden Bough* by James George Frazer, *A World on the Wane* and *The Savage Mind* by Claude Lévi-Strauss, *The Children of Sanchez* by Oscar Lewis, and *Coming of Age in Samoa*
> 467.61.5 Social Sciences by Margaret Mead; and, finally, the essay *The Accursed Share* by Georges Bataille.

“Saint Theresa, she’s de one lyin’ down. She was sick a lot.”

Indeed, Étienne had noticed a second woman dressed in white and carrying a bowl that resembled the one

Carmen would take out when someone looked like they might vomit.

"Did she have a bellyache, den?"

"She coughed a lot and spit up blood."

Then Granny Thibodeau added, as though by virtue of this detail, the saint had managed to have her sickness pardoned:

"But she loved roses."

Yes, Étienne had also noticed the beautiful purple roses in several of the stainglass windows. Granny Thibodeau concluded:

"Dat's de reason dey puts a wooden rosetta on all de benches."

Étienne had often let his fingers run along the edges of the rosettas without making the link between these and the roses in the windows.

"Eighth station: Jesus meets de women of Jerusalem in tears.

Étienne thought that must be the name of those long dresses they were wearing.

468.41.8
Lives of the Saints

469.117.3
Death

Agony = no end in sight. In Terry's notebook.

"Mom, are you scared of crows, den?"

Étienne and Carmen were gathering stones along the shore when a screeching crow alighted on the edge of the cliff.

"No. I don't much like 'em, but dey don't frighten me."

"You don't like de way dey croak?"

"No, I don't like wot dey eat."

Étienne was almost blown over:

"You doesn't like French fries, Mom?!"

The question took Carmen by surprise, but rather than dwelling on it, she answered quickly, hoping to cut short the unpleasant image:

"No, I don't like dead animals on de side of de road."

After that, in Étienne's eyes, crows took on a more

470.140.5 Caraquet human aspect, as meat and potato eaters.

> In his *Glossaire acadien* (*Acadian Glossary*), Pascal Poirier explains that it was graphists who preferred the word *seau* to *siau (bucket)*. Many words ending in *-eau* were pronounced *-iau* in the sixteenth century. Rabelais was somewhere in between, with *seillau*. The *Grand Robert* dictionary has conserved *seille* and its derivatives *seillée* and *seilleau*, a *seille* being a wooden bucket with ears through which to pass a rope,
> 471.33.4 Chiac Lesson similar to Évangéline's bucket at the Acadian Memorial in Grand-Pré, Nova Scotia.

Even as she waited on tables, Lisa-M. took the time to chat with friends.

"Is dat Patrick over der wid Jeannine? I tot ee was seein' someone else?"

Chantal replied bluntly:

"Dey must've changed 'is medication."

When Lisa-M. took this as a joke, Chantal insisted:

"I's serious, girl. Ee was goin' wid Jeannine last year, when dey put 'im on Zoloft. Well, after a while, the boy starts self-mutilatin' — ee's tearin' at de skin under 'is feet 'til it bleeds. — yoye! gross! — so dey switches 'im onto Effexor. Two weeks after dat, ee breaks it off with Jeannine an' starts goin' wid Nadine. But seems Effexor wasn't doin' de trick, so dey puts 'im on Paxil. Two weeks after dat, ee breaks up wid Nadine an' starts seein' Charline, off an' on like. But den, maybe two munts goes by an' ee just about freaks out on de Paxil, so dey takes 'im back to de psychiatric ward where dey cleans out 'is system an puts 'im right back on Zoloft, only tree times de dose dis time. Ee told me, 'twas a lucky ting ee was sleepin', on account of ee never would 'ave let dem. Well, turns out dat worked. So, 'ere ee is back wid Jeannine, wot makes sense."

"Poor boy!"

"Poor girls!" 472.87.8
"Poor doctors!" The Body

> Compassion, the virtue most associated with Buddhism, comes in eighth place in Comte- 473.66.5
> Sponville's scale. The Virtues

Terry was also granted a tour of his collection of watches frozen in time, with or without bracelets.

"An' where does ee get all dis stuff?"

"Don't know. Might be some folks finds 'em for 'im."

Carmen wasn't sure what to think. Was the man a little bit nuts?

"Naw, I don't tink so."

"Might be, he's just bored." 474.16.4
Terry didn't think so. The Cripple

> To the 14 works that turn out to be la *crème de la crème* of *La Bibliothèque idéale* and of the "Ideal Library of the Social Sciences" one can add 44 other highly regarded titles: *The Opium of the Intellectuals* and *Peace and War: A Theory of International Relations* by Raymond Aron; *The Formation of the Scientific Mind* by Gaston Bachelard; *Steps to an Ecology of Mind* by Gregory Bateson; *The System of Objects* by Jean Baudrillard; *The Second Sex* by Simone de Beauvoir; *Creative Evolution* by Henri Bergson; *The Empty Fortress* by Bruno Bettelheim; *The Inheritors* by Pierre Bourdieu and Jean-Claude Passeron; *The Making of Late Antiquity* by Peter Brown; *The Normal and the Pathological* by Georges Canguilhem; *Neuronal Man: The Biology of Mind* by Jean-Pierre Changeux; *Society Against the State* by Pierre Clastres; *La Peur en Occident* (*Fear in the West*) by Jean Delumeau; *The Flower of Chivalry* by Georges

Duby; *The Elementary Forms of the Religious Life* by Emile Durkheim; *Deadly Words: Witchcraft in the Bocage* by Jeanne Favret-Saada; *The Problem of Unbelief in the Sixteenth Century* by Lucien Febvre; *Against Method* by Paul Feyerabend; *The Order of Things* and *The History of Madness* by Michel Foucault; *The Presentation of Self in Everyday Life* by Erwing Goffman; *The Hidden God* by Lucien Goldmann; *The Horse of Pride* by Pierre-Jakez Hélias; *The Crisis of European Sciences and Transcendental Philosophy* by Edmund Husserl; *Pragmatism* by William James; *The General Theory of Employment, Interest and Money* by Lord John Maynard Keynes; *From the Closed World to the Infinite Universe* by Alexandre Koyré; *The Structure of Scientific Revolutions* by Thomas Kuhn; *The Language of Psycho-Analysis* by Jean Laplanche and Jean-Bertrand Pontalis; *Carnival in Romans* by Émmanuel Le Roy Ladurie; *Studies in Animal and Human Behavior* by Konrad Lorenz; *One-Dimensional Man* by Herbert Marcuse; *Understanding Media* by Marshall McLuhan; *Chance and Necessity* by Jacques Monod; *La Science chinoise et l'Occident* (1977 French edition of *Science and Civilisation in China*) by Joseph Needham; *Vichy France* by Robert O. Paxton; *The Logic of Scientific Discovery* by Karl R. Popper; *A Theory of Justice* by John Rawls; *Course in General Linguistics* by Ferdinand de Saussure; *History of Economic Analysis* by Joseph A. Schumpeter; *The Decline of the West* by Oswald Spengler; *La Droite révolutionnaire en France (1885–1914): les origines françaises du fascism* (*The Revolutionary Right in France (1885–1914): The French Origins of Fascism*) by Zeev Sternhell; and *Tractatus Logico-Philosophicus* by Ludwig Wittgenstein.

475.61.6
Social Sciences

Around eleven o'clock, seeing that the celebration was far from waning, Josse phoned Carmen:

"Wot're are you at, girl?"

"Not a whole lot. We're watchin' *Sleepless in Seattle* fer de tird time an' eatin' nachos. On account of?"

"On account of I's thinkin' you wouldn't want to miss out on de goings on over 'ere!"

"Sounds like der's a whole lot of folks, anyway!"

"A whole lot?! We's overflowin' into de street! Dey're celebratin' Hektor Haché-Haché..."

And with that Josse hung up, because her bar order was ready.

476.18.5
A Place for
Everyone

Among the scholars, are included the ethnologist, also versed in biology, anthropology and Daoism, Gregory Bateson (*Naven*, *Steps to an Ecology of Mind*) and Margaret Mead (*Coming of Age in Samoa*, *Male and Female*), who were in fact husband and wife. Their familial genograms indicate that they came from complementary situations: Margaret being the eldest of her siblings, and Gregory the youngest of his, which ought to indicate they would have a complementary relationship, one supporting the other. However, as it happens, quite the contrary was true: their conjugal life was rife with conflict and disillusion, mainly due to the difference in the way each of them tackled problems. Margaret, being the eldest of her siblings and having experienced early success, lacked neither the imagination nor the energy to overcome any problem; Gregory, on the other hand, tended to retreat when an effort was

477.65.3
Boy Cousins,
Girl Cousins

> required to resolve a difficulty, seeking instead, an understanding.

"Seems dat humans started sketchin' animals on de walls of der caves even before dey decided dat, from now on, dis or dat drawing would mean dis or dat sound. Sound, pronunciation an' de like, all dat came after."

"Not around dese parts it didn't!"

"Wot about de folks dat says, first you learns to talk, den to write? You only have to look at a baby, it's pretty obvious."

. . .

"So, de real question is dis: should we be talkin' like we write, or writin' like we talk?"

"Here's de problem: everybody knows how to talk, but not everybody can write."

"Right on!"

"Well, folks doesn't talk all dat well all de time, neither."

"Is dat right? An' who, pray tell, decides dat?"

"Ya! Wot's dat supposed to mean?"

. . .

478.22.4
Overheard
Conversations

"Hard to believe just twenty-six letters an' a couple o' accents can make such a terrible lot of trouble."

479.117.12
Death

> Leave Peace River to end one's days in Rough Waters.

Le Grand Étienne and Ludmilla also joined in the celebration.

"It reminds me of our first Christmas here. Do you remember?"

Le Grand Étienne nodded, while everyone around the table made room for Zed, who had just arrived.

"Who started all dis wrangle-gangle, den?"

"It started hours ago!"

"We're celebrating Hektor Haché-Haché! He's a hundred years old today!"

Zed did not pursue the matter, turning instead to talk to Ludmilla. 480.18.8 A Place for Everyone

> Gregory Bateson was, actually, a pioneer of the genogram, a practice that reached its zenith during the 1970s, along with family therapies and the Palo Alto school, of which Bateson remains one of the best-known founders. 481.58.6 Extensions

As a rule, folks kept quiet about the Babar's smoking policy, not to mention the source of the *Doucettes* that Jacky rolled, so as to keep this small commercial venture in the private sector and out of the hands of some anonymous corporation or the law.

"Who is doing this?" an anglophone tourist wanted to know.

His interlocutor lied:

"Some girl down in Saint-Antouène, I doesn't know her." 482.18.3 A Place for Everyone

"It is a very fine idea!"

> A genogram is a genealogical tree deployed over two or three generations that identifies biomedical, psychological, or social particularlities of an individual's family. For example, Henry Fonda's genogram reveals a reoccurrence of suicide and attempted suicide in his family. The word genogram does not appear in the 2002 edition of the *Grand Robert* dictionary. On the other hand, under the letter *g*, we do find the English words *gadget*, *gag*, *gagman* (from which is derived *gaguesque*), *gay*, *gang*, *gangster* (from which *gangstérisme*), *gap*, *garden-party*, *gasoil* (or *gas-oil*, from which *gazole*), *gentleman*, *gentleman-farmer*, *gentleman's agreement*, *géomarketing*, *G.I.*, GIFT (acronym of *Gametes Intra-Fallopian*

> *Transfer*), *gimmick*, gin-rummy, girl, glamour (from which *glamoureux*, *glamoureuse*), *glass*, *globe-trotter*, *G.M.T.* (acronym of *Greenwich Mean* — or Middle or Meridian — *Time*), *goal*, *goal-average*, *golden*, *gold point*, *golf* (and its derivatives *bunker*, *fairway*, *green*, *rough*, *drive*, *putt* and *swing*), *gore*, *Gore-Tex*, *gospel*, GPS (*Global Positionning System*), *gramophone*, *Granny Smith*, *grapefruit*, *grill*, *grill-room*, *groggy*, *groom*, *groove*, *groupie*, and *guiderope*.

483.65.6
Boy Cousins,
Girl Cousins

"An' wot would you 'ave us do wid all dose *tche* and *dje* soundin' words in Chiac? *Tchequ'un, djerre, djeule,* an' so on." Are we gonna start talkin' like dat, now?"

"We're already talkin' like dat."

"Not all of us."

. . .

484.22.5
Overheard
Conversations

. . .

"Well, oughtn't we all to talk de same way?"

> Of course it would be wrong to assume that complementary relationships automatically exist within couples both of whom are eldest siblings. A good example is Eleanor and Franklin Roosevelt, although the latter was an only child rather than an elder sibling. Their union, though difficult in many respects, became increasingly complementary because of Franklin's paralysis due to poliomyelite, after which Eleanor, a very willing elder sibling, took on a more important role in her husband's career.

485.65.4
Boy Cousins,
Girl Cousins

"Yer a writer, wot does you tink?"

"Dat would be a pinch . . . to decide once'n fer all wot our language is, wot's in and wot's out. Fer instance, would de old French words automatically be alright? An' any English words automatically bad? Some powerful smart folks would have to tink long an' hard on it, folks dat could make real sense of it all, and den explain it all so we could see the sense of it."

"Explain it! Bin twenty-five years dey been explainin' how pollution's after killing de planet. Has folks changed? Not a whole lot. Not enough anyway."

…

…

"Dey say, takes only one percent of folks to change der mind to change a trend."

"I believes dat."

"I do not."

"No way."

"I'm not sayin' everyting changes from one day to the next, but in de end tings change all de same."

"Maybe so. If yer one percent of a whole lot of folks, like one percent of a million… how much is dat? A hundred tousand?"

"Ten tousand."

"No more'n ten tousand?"

… 486.73.12

"Alright, well, maybe not den…" Shifts

> Queen Victoria reigned over Great Britain and Ireland from 1837 to 1901, marrying her cousin Albert of Saxe-Cobourg in 1840. Albert was granted the title of Prince Consort in 1857, but died four years later, leaving Victoria unconsolable and indifferent to the affairs of the realm. She only renewed her interest in governing 15 years later, when she became Empress of India. 487.65.8 Boy Cousins, Girl Cousins

"Wid me, it's de ones dat tries to talk Chiac just to be ridiculin' us. Dey're tinkin' it's easy to talk like dat, but when dey tries, dey finds out it's not so simple as dey tawt."

"An' isn't it always de same example they comes up wid: *crõssér la street.*"

"Dat an' *back*... like to say dey'r goin' back to de store: *je vas retourner bãck au magasin.*"

"You knows it! Right der, it proves dat talkin' Chiac is harder dan it looks. A fellow talkin' real Chiac wouldn't be puttin' *bãck* and *re-* in de same sentence. Ee'd say '*y vas bãck y aller*,' period. De *back* replaces de *re-*, right? Ee wouldn't even say '*y vas y aller bãck.*' On account of *bãck*, just like *re-* as a matter of fact, goes before de verb. Dat's just plain common sense. '*Je vas bãck aller au magasin.*' Or some might say '*store*' instead of '*magasin*'."

"A body has to grow up wid it, it's not sometin' you can learn in a book, or *pickér* up just like dat."

488.35.4 The Detail within the Detail

"You gots to know yer English, if yer gonna be *mêler ça* wid yer French."

"*Absolument*!"

> Exhausted from summersaulting through so many grammatical avatars, the computer spell-

489.47.3 Yielding

> check surrenders, announcing it has abandoned its task.

"Who can tell me wot dey makes vodka wid?"

Apparently no one had ever thought about it. One person in the group took a stab at it:

"Well, it's gotta be sometin' dey've got plenty of in Russia."

"Yer on de right track."

"Oatmeal!"

"Nope..."

No one had any other ideas.

"Alright den, you doesn't know. Shall I tell ya?"

The table wasn't exactly dying to solve the mystery.

"Potatoes."

490.18.9 A Place for Everyone

"Potatoes?"

"Is dat a farce or wot?"

Complicity? Between who and whom? Acadians and anglophones? Acadians and proper French speakers? Acadians and history? Acadians and the environment? Complicity marked by laziness? Ignorance? Self-sufficiency? Negligence? Or, on the contrary, by wisdom, a homeostatic response to the vagueries of history and the environment. Complicity marked by balance? Serenity?

491.35.5
The Detail within the Detail

The party in honour of Hektor Haché-Haché was in full swing.

"Matter o' fact, dose *patates* comes from South America, Bolivia, an *Perou*. De Spanish were de ones wot brought dem over to Europe."

"I tot was corn dat came from South America."

"Fer sure. Corn, as well..."

At that moment Terry came in.

"Hey, Terry! Come on o'er 'ere boy and tell Pomme to stop tellin' us all kinds of stuff we doesn't want to know."

"Speak fer yerself!"

"'Twas Parmentier — de one dey named de dish *potage Parmentier* after — who showed de French you could eat it, an' you wouldn't catch leprosy. So den, King Louis XVI decided to call 'em *pommes de terre*, on account of dat was prettier dan *patates*. Marketing, I suppose."

"An wot was dey called up until den?"

"*Batate*, or *batata*, in Spanish."

"Geez, are you fellows practicin' fer *Jeopardy* or wot?

492.18.10
A Place for Everyone

On the other hand, a certain number of authors are included in both ideal libraries, but for different titles. Among these are Theodor Adorno, Maurice Agulhon, Louis Althusser, Philippe Ariès, Sylvain Auroux, Émile Benveniste, R. Boudon, Albert Camus, Ernst Cassirer, Roger Chartier, Robert Darnton, Gilles Deleuze,

Jacques Derrida, George Devereux, Olivier Duhamel, Umberto Eco, Mircea Eliade, Moses I. Finley, François Furet, Marcel Granet, Friedrich von Hayek, Martin Heidegger, Eric J. Hobsbawn, Roman Jakobson, Carl Gustav Jung, Ernst H. Kantorowicz, Jacques Lacan, Jacques Le Goff, Emmanuel Lévinas, Bronislaw Malinowski, Marcel Mauss, Maurice Merleau-Ponty, Edgar Morin, Erwin Panofsky, Michelle Perrot, Jean Piaget, Geza Roheim, Jean-Paul Sartre, Martine Segalen, Michel Serres, Leo Strauss, Pierre Teilhard de Chardin, Arnold Toynbee, Paul Valéry, Arnold Van Gennep, Jean-Pierre Vernant, Paul Veyne, Pierre Vidal-Naquet, and Max Weber. Looking at both lists, we can say that these authors are cited for at least 2 works, but some are recommended for even more. From Sartre, for example, *La Bibliothèque idéale* recommends 7 titles, while "La Bibliothèque idéale des sciences humaines" recommends three different texts, so that all together 10 books by Sartre are listed. This process of extrapolation leads us to the conclusion that a hundred authors, men and women, have all together written 250 works judged to be of
493.61.11 Social Sciences great value, if not absolutely essential to a rudimentary knowledge of the social sciences.

494.21.2 More or Less Useful Details

"Well, I'll tell ya, she gets on me nerves, she does, wid all her useless details. First of all, who does she tink she is? An *deuxièmement*, who cares!

In her novel *1953: Chronicle of a Birth Foretold*, France Daigle does not mention the publication in French that year of *Éros et Civilisation* by Herbert Marcuse, one of the leading thinkers of the '60s generation. She does not regret

> the omission because, contrary to what is written in *La Bibliothèque idéale*, the book was actually published in 1954 and not in 1953.

495.45.8
Useless Details

Terry was listening carefully. It was the first time he'd spoken with a psychologist in the flesh — a woman psychologist, in fact, and very pretty to boot. Her name was Myriam, and she dropped in at the Babar from time to time, for a drink with her friends after their evening volleyball game.

"They've also found that the father plays an important role in the development of a child's language and intelligence. Because he will tend to use more technical terms, for instance...let me think...he'll ask for the electrical wire stripping or crimping pliers, or the combination pliers, or the needle-nose pliers, instead of just asking for the pliers."

Terry thought he'd better start improving his technical vocabulary in French. He was also wondering how come this girl — woman? — knew so much about pliers.

"Also, fathers tend to make children reformulate sentences or repeat what they asked for. This forces the child to improve his or her language, because more often than not, mothers understand their children's half-phrases, which doesn't help the children learn to explain themselves.

"Hmm...I never tawt o' that."

"Even at play. Not that mothers do a bad job at it, but fathers tend to encourage their children, to challenge them, set goals, tease them, let them find solutions themselves instead of solving the problem for them. That way, the child becomes more creative, more resourceful."

Terry found that Myriam used all the right words.

"An', it's now been shown that the affective relationship between father and child can be as strong as that between mother and child. If the father is truly involved, the child will seek comfort from him just as often as from the mother.

496.22.3 Overheard Conversations

"Geez... Well I'm sure glad I ran into you. Would you like anudder beer?"

> The Canadian philosopher, sociologist and essayist Herbert Marshall McLuhan (who—by coincidence?—follows Marcuse in the alphabetical order of the select list) gained an international reputation for his work entitled *Understanding Media*, one of the key arguments of which—that we are unaware of the medium's effect on us—is entirely consistent with Marcuse's thinking.

497.61.7 Social Sciences

"Dad, what does sexy mean?"

"Sexy? Means you tink a girl's cute, in a way dat excites you inside."

...

"Like in a way dat you want to get up close and hug her, have fun talkin' and laughin' and kissin' her."

"Like Mum?"

"Fer sure. When I met 'er, yer mudder was de most sexy girl in town."

"No, I mean like Mum now!"

498.125.1 Sexuality

> The expression *battre son plein* has two possible meanings, according to whether the word *son* is used as a noun or as a possessive adjective. If *son* refers to a sound, the expression denotes a maximum of loud and continuous noise such as might occur during a national holiday celebration, as in "the noise was deafening." If the word *son* acts as a possessive adjective modifying the noun *plein*, the expression refers rather to an action that is being accomplished with maximum strength, as in "the celebration was in full swing." This latter meaning is the one preferred by the *Petit Robert* dictionary. In

either case, the expression connotes a high degree of intensity. 499.98.1 Expressions

"I'm tellin' you, boy, when you've as many personalities as I've got, yer not a person any longer, yer a whole 500.22.2 Overheard Conversations
sect!"

"Hahaha!"

The Catholic Church forbade marriage between first cousins, that is two people having a grandfather or grandmother in common. This once removed relation implicates uncles and aunts on the one hand, and nieces and nephews on the other. The Church went so far as to forbid marriages between men and women with a familial link three times or four times removed, excluding, for example the marriage of a great-nephew with the great-great-granddaughter of a common ancestor. The rule of consanguinity also excluded marriage between a 50-year old woman, let us say, with the grandson of her first cousin. From the eighth to the twelfth century, the Church even banned marriage between persons related five, six, or even seven times removed. These interdictions diminished when it became common practice
for nobles to invoke them in contesting mar- 501.65.10 Boy Cousins, Girl Cousins
riages running counter to their interests.

"Wot're youse sayin'?"

"I'm sayin' de Americans stole America from us, and de Québécois sleeveened our *poutine*. Doesn't bodder you all dat dey took de word *poutine* to make sometin' dat's nuttin' like ours, de real *poutine?*"

"Don't dey 'ave a *poutine chomeur* den?"

"Naw, dat's der bread pudding, doh dey says it in de masculine, *un pudding chômeur.*"

…

"You ask me, dat's a clear case of rapacious cultural appropriation."

"Yes boy, dat's de truth!"

"What're you gonna do about it, den, take 'em to court?"

…

502.20.5 "You ask me, I tink *pudding* ought to be spelled
Language *poudigne*."

> The University of Toronto hosts a program that continues and expands on McLuhan's heritage, a program directed for many years by Derrick de Kerckhove, author of *The Skin of Culture*.* This unsettling work argues that human beings have become primitive again, that is they have become the primitives of a new global culture based less on rationalism, on the brain's logic — in other words, less based on the culture of writing as we know it. As a matter of fact, I
> 503.58.10 have selected this book to complete the catego-
> Extensions ry Social Sciences of *La Bibliothèque idéale*.

"Did ee say rape or rapacious?"

"Rapacious. Rapacious cultural appropriation."

"Awh, well, dat's alright den."

…

"I doesn't like it when folks toss around de word *rape* loosely."

"Awh."

504.131.3 "Doesn't bodder you?"

Parenthesi(e)s (*Shrug*)

---

* *The Skin of Culture* was published in French by the Presses de l'Université Laval as *Les nerfs de la culture*. It was also pub-
508.143.10 lished in Italian, Japanese, Dutch, Polish, and Portuguese. Mr.
Varia de Kerckhove has written several other works.

In certain regions of Acadia, when two brothers or sisters marry two brother or sisters of the other family, the children resulting from these unions are called *frérots* and *soeurettes*, something like wee brudder and wee sister.

505.65.7
Boy Cousins,
Girl Cousins

Around midnight, folks were mostly dancing to DJ Bones' smooth mixing, having left off debating the ideas put forth by Hektor Haché-Haché himself when he followed Robert Melanson up to the mic to announce he had not said his last word.

"Thank you all, and don't stop reading my column, I still have a few harrows in me quaver."

506.18.6
A Place for
Everyone

Conjugation of the verb to see in the past continuous tense of the indicative in Acadian: *je ouèyais, tu ouèyais, y ouèyait, a ouèyait, on ouèyait, vous ouèyiez, y ouèyiont*. Or *je wèyais, tu wèyais, y wèyait, a wèyait, on wèyait, vous wèyiez, y wèyiont*. Or *je oueillais, tu oueillais, y oueillait, a oueillait, on oueillait, vous oueilliez, y oueilliont*. Or *je woueillais, tu woueillais, y woueillait, a woueillait, on woueillait, vous woueilliez, y woueilliont*. Or *je weillais, tu weillais, y weillait, a weillait, on weillait, vous weilliez, y weilliont*. Or *je vouèyais, tu vouèyais, y vouèyait, a vouèyait, on vouèyait, vous vouèyiez, y vouèyiont*. How to do something similar in English? I were seein', you was seein', ee were seein', she were seein', we was seein', youse was seein', dey was seein'. Or I was after seein', you was after seein', ee was after seein', she was after seein', we was after seein', youse was after seein', dey was after seein'.

507.33.7
Chiac Lesson

509.65.9 Boy Cousins, Girl Cousins

> In Canada, there is no longer any interdiction against cousins marrying each other. The law only forbids men marrying their mothers, daughters, sisters, grandmothers or granddaughters, and women marrying their fathers, sons, brothers, grandfathers, or grandsons.

"Well, what about *je ouèyons*? Where might dat fit in, den?"

"*Je ouèyons*, dat'd replace *je ouas*. It's de verb *ouère* in de present tense. In English, you might say: *I's seein'* or *I's after seein'*."

"Well, doesn't we say it just de same in de past tense?"

"Den you gotta add an *i*: *je ouèy-i-ons*. Like, *je le ouèyons asteure ben je le ouèyions pas ajeuve.*[11] I's seein' 'im now, but I wasn't after seein' 'im back den."

"*Oueillons o-u-e-i-l-l* or *ouèyons o-u-e*—wid a grave accent—*y*?"

"Youse forgettin' de *w*."

"Naw, dat's sometin' else entirely."

"Well, youse can all say wot you will, you ask me it's terrible complicated. We'd be better off stickin' to just plain French."

"Or *L'Anglais*..."

"You mean we wouldn't be learnin' no French at all?"

510.41.12 Lives of the Saints

"If folks wants it dat way, *à cause pas*?"

"Saint-Simonaque!"

> A writer, trained as a philosopher and professor of the history of medicine, Louise L. Lambrichs published an article entitled "L'aventure de la

---

512.142.11 Notes

11. *Ajeuve*: original Acadian word, undocumented in France. Derived from the verb *achever*, to finish: *j'achève la récolte, j'achève de manger*, I finish the harvest, I finish eating: *j'achève, j'ajève, j'ajeuve. Ajeuve*: adv. a while back, back then, a while ago. *J'ai mangé ajeuve.* I ate a while ago, or I was after eatin'.

> paternité (The Adventure of Paternity)" in another special issue of the *Nouvel Observateur*, this one on the subject of fatherhood. "Above all let us not forget that, whether we like it or not, for us the question of the roll of the father is inscribed in the context of a society marked by the Freudian revolution — one of Freud's major contributions having been to put the accent on the dysfunctions of the paternal role as the origin of neuroses." Cited and translated without permission.

511.11.5
Appropriations

> (Most astonishing is the fact that) Derrick de Kerckhove stayed for a week in Shippagan at the turn of the millennium, where he lectured a group of young Acadians and other francophones on the future impact of cutting-edge technologies. (His lectures were filmed and broadcast on a regional cable channel.)

513.131.5
Parenthesi(e)s

"On de radio dis mornin', a fellow was sayin' dat de opposite of politics is fatalism."

"Wah?"

...

"Dat's wonderful odd. I'd a tawt it'd be a miracle."

...

"No?"

"Are ya sayin' dat a miracle's de opposite of politics?"

"?"

"Ya, dat makes sense, I suppose."

"Den, a ting could be de opposite of more'n one udder ting? Like, fatalism could be de opposite of a miracle and also de opposite of politics?"

"Dat're already opposites of each udder *au depart*.

"Still, dat's sometin' weird, don't ya tink?"

"Der's a whole lot of tings dat'r weird."

514.64.7
Opposites

On the other hand, the only title in "La Bibliothèque idéale des sciences humaines" to be listed in more than one discipline is *La Société contre l'État (Society Against the State)* by Pierre Clastres, who is deemed worthy of being read not only as anthropology, but also as political science. The book attempts to show
515.61.8 that the State compels humans to abandon
Social Sciences their leisure activities.

516.64.3 "De way I see's it, not only opposites attract. Constraints
Opposites attract each udder as well."

Identity amnesia is a relatively rare pathology, which occurs more frequently in men. It consists in forgetting all those references essential to an individual's ability to identify himself or to be identified. This particular form of amnesia is not accompanied by depersonalization: the individual maintains all his abilities, except that he experiences neither vertigo nor anxiety faced with this lack of any affiliation. Although the absence of anxiety is usually accompanied by an illness or disability, in some cases it takes other forms, in particular that of phobic neuroses (avoidance behaviour) or obsessional neuroses (the need to erase all traces of oneself). But identity amnesia is more a kind of
517.74.2 moral exchange between an individual and his
Hans conscience than a disease per se.

It was one in the morning by the time the crowd at the Babar began to disperse. Josse, Lisa-M., and Carmen took a deep breath.

"Josse, girl, why don't ya stay wid us tonight? We can order a pizza and play some cards. It's been a terrible long time since we done dat."

Lisa-M. chimed in:

"Why not sleep over at our place! Don't look like Pomme over der'll be goin' to bed tonight, or else, he'll be crashin' on de couch. If you don't mind sharin' me bed…"

Josse was tempted, especially since she was off for the next three days:

"Sure! Dat's a right proper idea. I was wonderin' how I's goin' to blow off dese next tree days!"

The three waitresses were re-energized somewhat by the idea of relaxing together after a long busy evening. Josse looked at her watch:

"Now, if dey could just take demselves off to de Triangle…"

Lisa-M. could not imagine working this late, night after night:

"Specially when der're just a couple o' dem left over der log-loaded…"

"Mostly we doesn't work dis late more'n twice in a week. Unless you trade shifts wid somebody. Some likes to work late on account of yer likely to get more tips."

"I tot youse divides it all up equal."

"Sure, but dose dat works right up to closin' gets a
bonus on account of dey clean up after, and dat's only
fair. Carmen figured it all out. You can tell she's good at 518.18.11 A Place for
it, on account of nobody's complainin'." Everyone

> Reread *The Skin of Culture* by de Kerckhove to 519.56.5
> see if it still holds water. Pilgrimages

Carmen was surprised by Terry's enthusiasm over what the psychologist Myriam had said about paternity.

"Well, seems to me, you already do all dat…"

"You tink? Sometimes I tawt I was bein' maybe, like, too *picky*…"

"*Exigeant*?"

Terry had used the English word *picky.*

"Dat's it. *Exigeant.* Wid Étienne especially. Maybe on account of ee's older. Or maybe on account of ee's a boy. Me boy."

"Well sure, we want him to be learnin'..."

...

...

"Do you know 'er, Myriam?"

"I know who she is. She comes by from time to time."

"She seems awful smart."

"I tink she's goin' wid Rodge. I saw de two o' dem togedder a couple o' times.

"Dat's right, ee's de one dat introduced us. Only, ee
520.13.4 never said she was 'is girl. An' it didn't feel dat way."

Paternity "Awh, well, maybe not den."

> What of Hans, who got rid of almost all his ma-
> terial possessions and who's even considering
> 521.74.1 getting rid of his identity papers? Is Hans in the
> Hans initial stages of identity amnesia?

One of the Babar's last customers would have liked to prolong the evening:

"Aw, why not come along wid us? Me an' me chum 'ere 'ave bin lookin' a long time fer some nice girls like youse..."

Josse enjoyed teasing males suffering from withdrawal:

"Naw, we've an all-girls party tonight. Too bad."

"An all-girls party? Where?"

"Well now, you're not tinkin' we'd go an' tell you dat, are you?

"Only, me pal here..."

The friend stepped forward and tugged on his pal's sleeve:

"Yer ex-pal if you keeps on like ya are. Come on wid ya. Dey got better tings to do dan listen to yer yammerin'."

"Naw, but! Look at 'em, dey's right pretty all de same, are dey not?"

His friend agreed, but he was beginning to feel embarrassed:

"Come on, den, we're off."

And with that, he draped his drunken friend's arm around his neck and dragged him toward the exit.

"You'll have to excuse 'im. Ee can be a real blabber tongue when ee's drinkin.'"

Josse sought to reassure him:

"No cause to worry on it. We seen worse!"

But, before she locked the door behind them, Josse couldn't resist extending a branch to the more sober of the two:

"Youse come back... some udder time, I mean."

The young man turned back with a gentle smile. 522.18.12 A Place for Everyone

"Fer sure."

> Obsessional neurosis and identity obsession have several points in common: in addition to a clear preference for the male psyche, they are both related to issues of morality, and are essentially a reaction to the symbolic of the father and filiation. Interesting fact, there is no trace of obsessional neurosis in texts preceding the advent of the Judeo-Christian religion, contrary to hysteria, for example, which was already well documented 2,000 years before Jesus Christ.

523.74.3 Hans

"Marianne, come 'ere, girl, and finish gettin' dressed!"

The little one was particularly mischievous that morning, and Terry did not have time to run after her.

"Marianne! I'm countin' to five..."

The children knew that their tricks were doomed once Terry began counting.

"One..."

It was early yet; Marianne knew there was still plenty of time.

"Two..."

Her room was within easy reach.

"Three..."

From Terry's tone it was clear there would be no four-and-a-half.

"Four..."

Marianne raced toward her room. Terry waited until she was almost at the door to announce the next number.

"Five!"

Watching her, Terry thought he might have a future Olympian on his hands.

"Yer a proper devil, girl, but at least you run fast. May save yer life some day. Here now, put dis on."

524.13.12 Paternity Marianne let loose a short burst of laughter; then, giggling, she pulled the underpants over her head.

> To err. A statistical analysis of the first letter of names of some 550 authors of "The Ideal Library of the Social Sciences" shows once again that the fiwst few letters of the alphABET ACCOUNT FOR THE LAgest number of au-
> 525.70.10 Errors tors, in particulqr the *b*... (writing time interrupted by reason of drowsiness).

"Dad, how come we don't pray?"

Terry was in the doorway, on his way to work.

"Pray like you do wid Granny Thibodeau, you mean?"

"Uncle Étienne asked me if I pray."

"Did 'e now?"

"Do I got a godfawder?"

"A godfawder? Well, no, you don't have a godfawder."

Terry tried to be as gentle as possible in stating this fact, which suddenly struck him as hard.

"So den, dat means I have a godmudder?"

"No, you don't have a godmudder neither."

...

...

"Do you have one?"

Terry could not deny it:

"Yeah. Me godfawder's old Arthur. You know, ee's de one from time to time fixes up old cars wid yer granddad."

Étienne knew who he was. An old, thin man who smoked a pipe.

"An' his wife Émerentienne, well she was me godmudder, only she's dead now. She was already dead when you were born."

...

"At Christmas time an' on me birthdays, dey always
gave me a present. Most times 'twas a hockey stick. One
time, dey gave me a little electric train. Boy oh boy, did I 526.129.11
play wid dat train!" Fantasies

> Unlike the obsessional neurotic, an individual experiencing identity amnesia does not attempt to hide his ploy, nor to erase his traces.
> He has simply abandoned the place assigned to
> him by his identity. The choice of the word *ex-*
> *periencing* is therefore not arbitrary, since the 527.74.4
> individual is not actually suffering. Hans

Antoinette lay down the Acadian word *zire*, meaning "disgust" or "sharooshed." It did not even occur to The Cripple to contest it.

Ten times 2, 20, 21, 22, 23, 24.

Antoinette entered the number 24 in the little box, for 528.28.6
a total of 149 in two turns. A Couple's Life

> Eventually, by virtue of dispensations, the Catholic Church ended up allowing unions between first cousins, as well as sororat and levirate marriages. Sororat marriage compelled a young woman to marry her older sister's widower. The levirate obliged a man to marry his brother's widow if there was no male

> descendant. In many countries, the Church left it to the State to legislate consanguinity in marriage. In general, laws proscribed marriage between direct relations and between brothers and sisters. The same prohibition existed against someone marrying the children of his or her wife or husband. This applies in the case of adopted children, as well as children of the same father or mother, which explains the discomfort, not to say scandal, sparked by the relationship between the filmmaker Woody
> 529.65.12 Boy Cousins, Girl Cousins Allen and Soon-Yi Previn, the adopted daughter of Mia Farrow, with whom Allen had been in a common-law marriage for many years.

"Sõ[12] I ended up recitin' de Our Fawder for 'im. I was right proud I remembered it."

Carmen approved:

"It's more down to earth dan de udders."

"Down to earth . . . I like dat."

Carmen did not worry too much over every little phase the children went through:

"Most likely, ee's just curious. I doubt very much he really wants to pray."

"Dey say dat children go troo mystic periods."

"Mystic?"

Terry wasn't sure of the exact definition of the word, so he preferred not to risk explaining it to Carmen.

"Is dat sometin' Myriam said, den?"

"Naw, it's in a book downstairs."

"Awh."

"I'm tinkin' ee'd like to 'ave a godfawder, doh[12]. 'Course,

---

12. The allongated pronunciation of the English word *so* when used in Chiac (meaning, as in English, "consequently") is dif-
534.142.12 Notes ferent from the shorter pronunciation of *do* in Chiac, which is an adaptation of the English *though*.

first we'd 'ave to baptise 'im. I suppose."

"An' you an' I'd 'ave to get married."

"Go on? Is dat obligatory?"

. . .

. . .

"Well, my mudder wouldn't mind, dat's for sure." 530.13.8

"Mine as well, even doh she won't say nuttin' about it." Paternity

> In fact, the identity amnesiac would prefer to be left entirely alone. His own name is a source of anxiety to him; he would like to rid himself of all filial constraints and obligations. He dreams of a place without conditions and, since such a place does not exist, he falls back on forgetting, which allows him to escape, to absent himself, to extricate himself completely from the field of play. 531.74.5 Hans

"Me? It's de idea of both me knees gettin' crushed betwixt two parked cars. Say de brakes was to fail or some such ting. Just tinkin' about it, I starts to hurt." 532.137.1 Fears

> The presence of a hidden defect in a novel is particularly difficult to overcome. It's the sort of ambiguity to which an author does not aspire. Because the discovery of an error in a book undermines the reading experience. The reader is indisposed, he or she balks at the thought of pursuing a less than perfect work to its end. 533.89.3 Irritants

> Blissful white. Whitewash, zinc white, silver white. White lead. White O. White meat, whiting powder. Whiter than white. So white is black and black is white? White face. Mrs. White with a lead pipe. A lot of folks named LeBlanc. Whiteout. A little white lie. 535.83.2 Bliss and Colours

Occasionally during the evening, the idea that his son might be undergoing a mystic phase occurred to Terry.

"If I'd bin on de ball, I'd shown 'im how to make de sign of de cross. I never tawt of it. 'Twould be sometin' easy to learn."

"Well, it's not too late now, is it? Wot's to stop you showin' 'im?"

536.124.1 "Dat's true enough! Jeez, it's nice to live wid somebody
Religion dat's always tinkin'..."

> The virtues that Comte-Sponville examined are consistent with the general flux of the four cardinal virtues of Christianity: courage, justice, prudence, and temperance; not to be confused
> 537.66.12 with Christianity's three theological virtues,
> The Virtues which are faith, hope, and charity.

"Are you Pomme?"

"Pomme, dat's me!"

The young man took my extended hand quite naturally. We had crossed paths from time to time.

"So, no exhibition on right now?"

"Dis 'ere's a micro-exhibition. You gotta get right up close to de wall to see it."

At first I thought he was joking; I tried briefly to decipher his statement. Then Pomme said he had to leave for 10 minutes or so.

"No problem, I'm in no hurry."

While I waited for him, I walked back and forth a bit in the room.

...

I thought I heard music, and then, nothing.

...

Then again, yes, music.

...

Something shiny on the floor in the corner caught my eye. I moved closer.

!

Up close, I saw nothing. The shining was gone. Only a bit of orange wire lay abandoned on the floor. But looking more closely, I realized the wire ran into the wall a few centimetres above the floor.

!!

The orange wire emerged a little higher up on the wall, drew an arabesque and then vanished back into the wall. I heard footsteps. Maybe Pomme returning?

…

The arabesque was a familiar form. Could it be read? I turned my head one way, then the other. Was it necessary to get down lower to really see it?

!?

In the far corner of the room lay a mass of dusty electronic equipment, one machine piled on top of the other, and all connected by miles of tangled black cable, except for one orange coloured wire. Pomme reappeared.

"Is dis wot you call an installation, den?"

"It's part of a project I's workin' on wid Zablonski."

"Zablonski's into electronics now?"

Pomme smiled, as though my question reminded him of something he wasn't about to tell. He simply said:

"Zablonski's broken troo all de media supports."

I wasn't sure what that meant, but I imagined someone larger than life, completely out of my reach. For a 538.101.1
moment I doubted my ability to interview this artist. Duos

> In general, incidents have less unpleasant con-
> sequences than accidents, except in the case of 539.78.9
> diplomatic incidents and border incidents. Accidents

Tired of waiting for some new manifestation of anxiety in his son to correct what he perceived to be his blasé attitude as a father, Terry decided to intervene.

"Étienne, you know de udder night, when you went to bed a wee bit late, an' I told you a story an' den sang a song an' after all dat, you still wasn't sleepin'..."

Fiddling with an old Transformer, Étienne nodded that he remembered that evening, and waited.

"I got de feelin' you was like a wee bit troubled. Is der sometin' bodderin' you?"

The child was listening even as he continued to undo and reshape the object in his hand. Terry waited a moment.

"Maybe you doesn't recall exactly. It's only dat if der is sometin' bodderin' you, you know you can be tellin' me an' yer mudder. Whenever sometin's troublin' you, sometimes just talkin' about it makes it not so awful bad. Turns out de ting, whatever it is, isn't so desperate a problem after all."

(*Clic clic clac clic cloc*...)

"Anwyay, you don't have to remember. I just wanted you to know dat you can be tellin' us if ever der's sometin' on yer mind."

Étienne looked up at his dad for a moment—would he say something?—but then he turned back to his Transformer without speaking.

540.13.6 "OK?"

Paternity "OK, Dad." (*Cloc*)

> In the end, it seems fastidious to apologize for every Acadian or Chiac turn of phrase in relation to standard French. Obviously, any
> 541.33.10 language will have its own many colours and
> Chiac Lesson idiosyncrasies.

"Me, it's swallowin' a piece of glass. Gets so's I can't eat some place where dey just broke a glass or dish or some such. It's always brudderin' me when I eats out anywhere."

"You just said 'brudderin' instead of 'bothering'. Maybe
542.137.3 your fear is linked to your brother?"

Fears "Me brudder Chip? Ha ha! I doubts it..."

> (Pomme was wearing a chestnut-coloured linen shirt, adorned at regular intervals with a 543.131.8
> sparkling orange thread.) Parenthesi(e)s

"Hallo, Carmen? Is Terry der?"

Usually Terry's mother took the time to chat a bit with her daughter-in-law before asking to speak to her son.

"No, ee's at de bookstore..."

"Only sometin's just happened..."

Carmen could believe it. Terry's mother was not the sort to get upset over trifles.

"I don't know 'ow to say it. Der's been a murder..."

Carmen's heart leapt.

"A murder?!"

"Is dat not 'ow you say it?"

"You mean someone killed somebody?"

"Dat's not de half of it..."

Carmen couldn't imagine what more could follow.

"Do you want me to go and fetch Terry?"

"I don't know 'ow ee'll take it..." 544.25.1

Carmen's pulse began to race. Murder

> And yet, Hans does not manifest all the symptoms associated with identity amnesia. He has not stopped talking to people, nor does he go out of his way to avoid being spoken to. He takes decisions, makes choices and, in spite of his detachment, he is considerate of others. True, he has no fixed address and his trajectory is unpredictable. However, wherever he happens to be, he is not evasive, he answers questions, neither retreating nor remaining within 545.74.6
> himself, and he seems approachable. Hans

Terry hung up the phone.

"Holy shite!"

"Wot's goin' on, fer de love...?!"

After her mother-in-law's call, Carmen had rushed down to the bookstore to tell Terry to phone his parents. She wanted to be physically by his side when he heard the news.

"Dis fellow, one of me chums when I's little — Shawn, Shawn Hébert... — last night, ee went an' killed 'is dad."

Carmen could hardly believe that Terry was somehow linked, even remotely, to a murder.

"Lord! Wot 'appened?"

"Me mom doesn't know nuttin' 'cept fer de rumours goin' round."

"Like?"

Terry did not reply. He seemed to be going in circles behind the cash.

"Been a long while since I last seen 'im, Shawn. Still..."

Carmen did not want to hurry him, but... a murder! She tried to ask her questions gently, but balancing gentleness and urgency wasn't easy.

"Ow did ee do it, den?"

"*Stabbed* 'im."

"On purpose?"

"Well! Would be kinda hard to go an' stab somebody widout noticing."

"Is it his fault? is what I mean."

Terry shrugged.

"Like if it were *legitimate defence*, you mean?"

But Terry knew very little more.

"Don't know, do I, but I'll tell you one ting, his dad was no picnic. Not dat Shawn was a saint, only his dad could be terrible mean. 'Twas abuse is wot it was, really, now dat we knows wot dat is."

"'Ow did it happen?"

Carmen was happy to have found the right tone at last, curiosity, but not without compassion.

"Dey had a fight, only I don't know over what."

"Was ee livin' wid dem?"

"Yah, I tink so. Ee'd got married, only it didn't last all

dat long. His wife ended up *takin' off* out west wid some udder fellow."

As usual, when Terry evoked his past, the English words had slid naturally into his speech. Carmen knew this was not the time to point it out. 546.25.2 Murder

> When he wants to read, Hans reads whatever is at hand. As though, in reading, the movement of the eyes were as important as the activity of the mind. It doesn't matter to Hans, what he's reading. For example, this pocket dictionary he picked up in a train station, which he reads as though it were a novel, in alphabetical order. To him, this makes perfect sense. 547.74.7 Hans

Ludmilla didn't understand how Terry could go back to reshelving books.

"But, what are you doing?"

Terry turned to her, at a loss.

"You're not just going to stay here?"

Terry finally grasped what Ludmilla meant.

"Well, I don't see wot else I can do."

He looked back and forth between Carmen and Ludmilla, as though pleading his case.

"Dese're folks I've not seen in a shocking long time. I'm not about to butt in on der business now dat tings is turned sour. I's too late now, 'tisn't my place to interfere."

And with that, Terry went back to shelving books. Carmen and Ludmilla exchanged a pitiful glance, realizing that Terry felt somewhat guilty about what had happened. Terry added:

"I'll go by me parents' at suppertime, an' see wot's wot." 548.25.3 Murder

> Blissful violet. Pale violet, dark violet, blue violet, black violet. Violet ink. Violet iodine vapour. Violet stone. Shrinking violet. White viola, blue viola, the violence of a violet bruise. 549.83.8 Bliss and Colours

No matter how he shuffled the tiles on his rack, The Cripple came up with nothing. But Antoinette knew better than to rejoice prematurely over the prolonged clacking.

“Dat fellow killed ’is dad… dat’s not someting you’d have tawt could happen in a town like Dieppe.”

The Cripple disagreed.

“Hun! Ask me, it’s a miracle it don’t happen more often.”

Over the years, Antoinette had learned that her husband’s occasionally brutal realism was rarely without foundation.

“Wot makes you say dat?”

“And even more so in old Dieppe. Well, anywhere where der’s old families, families wot ’ave been der since de beginnin’.”

“On account of?”

“On accound of, it’s like I said de udder day, everyting happens over tree generations. Dat fellow’s young, ee’s most likely part of de tird generation. An’ dat generation der is always doin’ someting in reaction against wot came before, wot de second generation done. Or didn’t
550.28.7 do, as may be. It’s as doh dey’re tryin’ to make amends.”

A Couple’s Life “An’ you talked to me about dis before?”

551.83.1 Bliss and Colours

> Where bliss is not the satisfaction of a desire
> but a place of language.

Back home that evening, Terry related the details of the patricide to Carmen, Ludmilla and Zablonski:

“Seems ee stabbed ’im tree times.”

Carmen winced:

“Tree times. Ee must ’ave ’ad a terrible lot of rage in ’im.”

Terry thought so, too.

“Like I said, I didn’t see ’im all dat often. When I knew ’im, ee sometimes came on tough, but ee never scared me. I knew ’twas just a way to cover ’imself.”

"Cover himself from wot?"

Terry didn't know exactly.

"I don't tink even ee could tell you. I mean… his dad wasn't a big man. I can't see 'ow ee'd have to kill 'im in self-defense. Mind you, you can never really know a fellow's strength."

To support Terry, in a way, Carmen wanted to give the young man the benefit of every possible doubt.

"Could 'ave been…wot dey call *mental alienation*."

Carmen used the English term. Even though she believed firmly in proper French, even she did not always have the right word on the tip of her tongue. Ludmilla blew on her smoking hot tea before speaking:

"Yes, temporary insanity is intriguing. It's so difficult to imagine, and yet, obviously it does happen."

Terry tried to imagine it:

"Fer me, it's like all de neurons in yer brain decides to change place at de same time… like a *perfect storm*."

…

… 552.25.4 Murder

"Is neuron masculine or feminine?"

> Grids and diagrams: learn to count the squares, to follow the arrows, distinguish the colours, read the annotations. Understand the pattern. 553.71.9 Intro Embroidery

Waiting for The Cripple to put a word down, Antoinette reflected on what her husband had said; she tried to imagine what the young murderer could have been trying to make amends for.

"Aha! I knew it!"

The Cripple lay all his tiles down on the board. The word *ferrures*, or "horseshoes," which combined with *dialyser* to give him 90 points.

"I figured you wasn't takin' all dat time fer nuttin'."

"I knew dey would all fit in some way, but I had to wait fer de word to come to me." 554.28.8 A Couple's Life

555.66.7
The Virtues

In the field of topology, hope is the most popular of the virtues. It is often accompanied by the adjective *good*, as in the Cape of Good Hope in South Africa. But the question remains: is there such a thing as bad hope?

Antoinette had drawn seven new letters, but she could see no word. She shuffled her tiles *R-N-Z-I-H-A-U* on her rack, hoping for a lucky accident. What she wished for above all was to double, if not triple, the value of her *Z*.

"Der's dem dat tinks Oedipus killed his fawder on account of ee was jealous dat ee was sleepin' wid his mudder. On account of Oedipus hisself was wantin' to sleep wid 'is mudder..."

...

"Freud discovered dat."

...

"Well, today, seein' as Oedipus was supposedly an adopted child... some says dat ee didn't know de man ee was killin' was his fawder, an' dat de woman ee wanted to sleep wid was 'is real mudder. He never knew dey was 'is real parents, on account of Polybus and Merope never told 'im."

Antoinette, who was only half listening, would have liked to make the word *zeux*, Chiac for "dey" but she was missing the *X*. Nor was she sure that the word was included in the Poirier or Cormier Acadian dictionaries, which also served as references since the *Officiel du jeu Scrabble®* did not include Acadian vocabulary.

"So dat de whole story of Oedipus maybe means dat children ought to know where dey comes from. Dat if dey was adopted, dey ought to be told."

Antoinette searched for a word on the board to which she could add her *Z*, but in vain.

"On account of, even if you doesn't tell 'em, dey'll sense sometin'. An' sooner or later dat's gonna blow."

Antoinette, distracted, replied:

"On account dey was adopted?"

"No. On account of family secrets end up becomin' poison." 556.28.9 A Couple's Life

557.67.6 Terry's Notebooks

> The French word for "bruise" or "wound," alone on a page: *meurtrissure*.

"Tell you troo, der's not such a terrible lot of murders, if you looks at all de problems families got."

"Wah? G'wan!"

The Cripple did not insist. His ideas often provoked such reactions. He redistributed the letters on his rack, but found nothing better to play than *myes* for 14 points.

"Wot're myes, anyways?"

"Dey're soft-shell clams." 558.28.10 A Couple's Life

"An' why is it we doesn't call 'em myes down 'ere, den?"

> Olive green, pistachio green, apple green. Celadon green. Bottle green. Green light. *Vinho Verde*. To go green. Miss the green. Greenland. Green patch. Green at the gills. Green thumb. Green rookie. Green-eyed monster. Jolly Green Giant. 559.83.4 Bliss and Colours

Preparing for bed that evening, Terry and Carmen picked up where they'd left off:

"Ee'll get a *hearing* like all de rest, den dey'll likely put 'im in *jail*. Dat's all I can figure."

Carmen had never seen Terry like this. She figured he was looking for a particle of consolation in the face of his powerlessness in the situation.

"You never know. Might be ee couldn't do udderwise but kill 'im. If his dad was like you say, it could've been provocation, don't you tink?"

"Could be. But does dat make it justified?"

The answer was obvious. Grasping for something,

Carmen fell back onto correcting Terry's use of English words.

"Well anyway, a *hearing*, dat's a trial, an' a *jail*, dat's a prison, *by de way*."

Terry didn't take it badly:

"I knows it. Just goes to show how hard 'tis when dat Dieppe Chiac runs in yer veins."

From time to time, just so as not to lose the knack, Carmen, too, let herself slip into a mixture of French and English.

"An *fer yer information*, dat's why we've a pair of *kid-*
560.25.6 *neys*, to *clean out* de blood."

Murder "Bingo!"

> Dream of an anonymous character: a few children and their parents are out for a Sunday drive at Cap-Enragé. When they arrive, the dreamer, who is one of the children, realizes that the cape is anything but enraged. Essentially, it's no more than a hairpin curve in the road at the end of which sits a small souvenir shop, more a hardware store than anything else. The family goes in, and the mother buys a few kitchen items. The possibility arises that the cape is a little further down the road, that they've not
> 561.109.3 quite arrived. The father's behaviour is difficult
> Dreams to decipher.

On her next turn, Antoinette found nothing better than to lay an *H* down on a letter-counts-triple square to produce the interjection *eh* both horizontally and vertically. She didn't like such easy solutions, even though they could sometimes be lucrative.

"Twenty-six. How low I've fallen since me 125 at the start."

"Wot's de score, den?"

"One hundred and sixty-two fer me, 104 fer you, an' it's yer turn."

Because, after all, they were not playing purely for the pleasure of making words. They also liked to bet, and to 562.28.11 win their wager. A Couple's Life

> In *L'Officiel du jeu Scrabble*®, only two words begin with an *a* and contain two *y*'s: *amblyrhynque* and *antéhypophyse*. In English, keeping in mind that the *y* in the English version is worth 4 points compared to 10 in the French, there are five words with two y's: *alchymy*, *al-* 563.110.2 *leyway*, *anybody*, *asphyxy*, and *anyway*. A Day Off

"Wot *bodders* me most is de little one... Can you imagine? Yer six years old, yer mudder *more or less* took off, *fucked off* wid anudder guy, out West of all places — I mean it's not like she was *plannin'* to come by an' see you on de *weekends*, now is it... — an yer dad's in *jail* on account of ee killed 'is own fawder, yer granddad *by de way*, who you've been living wid fer as long as you can remember, an' not just dead, but *murdered*! Dat's not just a heart attack or de like! An' by his own boy own on top of everyting, who's yer dad as well! An' you got no *favourite* uncle or aunt to *smood tings over*, let alone *adopt* you. *Anyways*, yer up de creek *eider way*, on account of obviously dose were de two men you *related most to*, weren't dey? *So*, all youse got left is yer granny, *whose* husband only just died — *murdered* by her *own* boy, don't ferget. But ee's down in *jail* now, wot isn't exactly down de road eider, I gotta say, so she don't feel so good 'bout de whole *mess*, an' now she's got a little guy six years old to care fer, not dat she don't love 'im, but der's like 70 years difference betwixt 'em, an' she's gotta *worry* ee'll end up like his dad, *who knows*? Eh? Can you imagine?"

Carmen sat in stunned silence. Terry knew he'd opened the English floodgates. 564.25.7

"Sorry, but it 'ad to come out exactly in dose words." Murder

As grammatically logical as it may be, Chiac is usually denounced as the epitome of mediocrity, a monumental deviation from normative French, a supposedly superior linguistic form (Freudian slip: ballistic form). Grin/Groan and bear it.

565.33.6
Chiac Lesson

The Cripple would have liked to make up the 58 points by which he trailed in a single turn, but his letters did not seem to be co-operating.

"Could be dat fellow never seen himself in de mirror."

. . .

The Cripple shuffled his letters as he spoke.

"Dey say dat an aggressive person probably had trouble wid der self-image when dey was little. Seems at some point a baby's got to see itself in de mirror an' dat's when they understand dat de body der seein' is demself."

(*Clic, clic, clac, clic*)

"An' wot's best is when de mudder's der to point an' tell de wee one dat der, dat's you, an de udder one alongside you, well dat's 'er. Seems dat as of dat moment de baby's all set to become a human bein'.

"Does it absolutely have to be de mudder? Won't de fawder do just as well?"

"I suppose ee would. Don't see why not."

. . .

"Anyways, wot I'm tryin' to say is dat, if it don't happen, dat's when you get de udder side of de coin, an' dat's aggressivity. If de wee one can't image-inate itself, it's as doh ee or she only sees bits of de body all separated. A body in pieces."

"Wah!"

566.28.12
A Couple's Life

. . .

"You do know it's yer turn, don't ya?"

To write a story about physical books, lost many times over, ignored, abandoned, picked

> up by strangers, then forgotten once again, and once more taken up by others. A novel of encounters, couplings between books. Humans would be no more than accessories in the life of books. 567.129.10 Fantasies

The death notice for Médric Hébert, 74 years old, from Dieppe, appeared the next day in *L'Acadie nouvelle*. The notice was brief because the man was survived by very few mourners and few close relatives had gone to the grave before him.

"Jeez, Chico's de end of de line, looks like..."

Carmen had read the notice before breakfast.

"Ya, I saw dat."

...

"Do you tink dey'll let Shawn out fer de funeral?"

Carmen raised an eyebrow. Was Terry serious?

"You tink he'd be wantin' to go?"

"Well, might be. Depends on wot actually happened, don't it."

Carmen was reading the article about the brouhaha in the house following the murder.

"Der callin' it a patricide."

...

...

"Ting is, it don't mean ee didn't love 'im, even doh ee killed 'im."

Carmen agreed:

"Probably. Even doh ee might 'ave hated 'im, somewhere deep inside, ee must 'ave loved 'im just de same."

"I don't tink ee hated 'im."

"Dat's not wot I said..."

"I know. It's only dat, on account of ee killed 'im, folks might tink ee hated 'im. Only, I don't tink so." 568.25.8 Murder

> Partial list of archaic masculine given names to have appeared in the death notices of

L'Acadie nouvelle: Abbé(e), Abdon, Abel, Abraham, Absalon, Achille, Adoria, Adorice, Aquila (Acquila, Aquila, Aquilla), Adé, Adélard, Adelbert, Adelin, Adelmar, Adelor, Adenise, Adéodat, Adeston, Adjutor, Adon, Adoris, Agapit, Agenard, Aimé(e), Ajitor, Albain, Alban, Albanie, Albé, Albéni(e), Albéo, Albini(e), Alcade, Alcida, Alcime, Aldé, Aldège, Aldéi, Aldéo, Aldéoda(t), Aldéri(e), Aldérice, Aldin, Aldonat, Aldor, Aldoria, Aldorie, Aldoris, Aldrice, Alec, Aléo, Alfareze, Alfonço, Almida(s), Almonzo, Aloysius, Alpha, Alphé(e), Alphège, Alphonce (Alfonce), Alténard, Altérice, Alvarez, Alvérie (Alvéry), Alvida, Alvin, Alyre, Alyse, Amable, Amateur, Ambroise, Amédée, Amerriau, Anaclet, Anastase, Anatole, Ancèl, Angelbert, Anicet, Anselme, Anthelme, Anthime, Antonio, Appolinaire, Arcade, Archille, Arice, Arisma(s), Arismond, Ariste, Aristide, Arizma, Armanzor, Armel, Arnel, Arnie, Arsène, Athanase, Attice, Aubert, Aubin, Audard, Auguste, Aula, Aurèle, Aurélien, Avellin, Avie, Avila, Avit, Azade, Azarias, Azarie, Baptiste, Basil(e), Bélarmin, Belone, Bélonie, Bénédict, Blaise, Boniface, Cajetan, Cajeton, Calixte (Calyxte), Carol, Cécime, Célénois, Célestin, Célime, Cérice, Césaire (Cézaire), Charlemain, Clairmont, Cléo, Cléophas, Cléophase, Cletus (Clétus), Cloric, Cloris, Clorise, Clorist, Clovain, Clovis, Côme, Condé, Crispin, Cyprien, Cyrénuce (Cyrénus), Cyriac, Cyrice, Cyril(le), Damas(se), Damien, Dassise, Dasie (Dazie), Déa, Delor (Delore, Delors), Delphin, Delphis, Désiré, Deus, Dianis, Didace, Didier, Dieudonné, Dion, Disma(s), Docithé, Dollard, Dolor(e), Dolphé, Domice, Domicien

(Domitien), Dorien, Doris, Dorismond, Dosité (Dosithé, Dosithée), Édonia, Edvard, Égide, Elderice, Éléodore, Élias, Élibé, Élide, Élie, Elieud, Élio, Éliodore, Élisée (Élisé, Élizé, Élizée), Elmo, Éloi, Elphège, Elvery, Elzé(e), Elzéar, Émédore, Emerild (Émérild), Émerie, Émerile, Émiliore, Enoïl (Enoil), Enthime, Ephrem, Épiphane, Erenel, Éthelbert, Eucher, Euclide, Eudo, Eudore, Eugène, Eugère, Euldège, Euloge, Eusèbe, Eustache, Eustazade, Eutrope, Évangéliste, Évariste, Évé, Éverend, Evremont, Exavier, Exéo, Exibé, Existe, Exite, Ézard, Fabien, Félicien, Félix, Ferain, Ferdinand, Fidèle, Fidelin, Firmin (Firmain), Flavien, Fleurant, Floribert, Florient, Florius, Fortuna(t), Freda, Freddé, Gabelus, Gabriel, Gaspard, Gédéon, Gélas, Généreux, Gernon, Gildard, Gilman, Gonzague, Guilmond, Guimond, Gustave, Hédard, Héliodore, Herménégilde, Hermile (Hermyle), Hévé, Hidola, Hilaire, Hilarion, Hilairion, Homidas, Honoré, Honorius, Horeb, Hormidas, Hurbert, Hyacinthe (Hyacinte), Hypolite (Hippolyte), Ido, Idola, Ignace, Irénée, Isaac, Isae, Isaïe, Isidore, Ismaël, Ismay, Jacob, Jadus (Jaddus, Jadusse), Jenoete, Joachim, Jonas, Jose, Josephat, Joyeux, Joyime, Jude(s), Juste, Juvénal, Ladislas, Lange, Lauradin, Lauréat, Laurentien, Laurier, Lazare (Lazard, Lazarre), Lazime, Ledwine, Léger, Lélice, Léodore, Léonel, Léonidas, Léonson, Léophane, Lévi(s), Lévite, Liboire, Liévin, Ligouri, Lionde, Lionel, Livain, Livi, Livio, Lomer, Lorenzo, Lubain, Lucas, Ludger, Ludovic, Magella, Magloire, Major, Majorique, Marcellin, Marin, Marjorique, Mathias, Mathurin, Maurel, Maxime, Maximin, Médard, Méderic (Médéric), Médias, Médor,

Médric, Melas (Mélas), Melchior, Meldric, Mélème, Mélite, Melquis, Merel, Méthode, Midas, Minto, Moïse, Montcalm, Morel, Moril, Napoléon, Narcisse, Nazaire, Nectaire, Néré(e), Néri(e), Nestor, Nidgar, Noé, Numa, Octave, Odel(le), Odias, Odilon, Odon, Odule, Offa, Ola, Olando, Olio, Oliva, Olydore, Omer, Omeril, Onésime (Onézime), Onésiphore, Onias, Onidas, Onil(e), Onisime, Onisiphore, Onizime, Oran, Origène, Oris, Orphir, Osias (Ozias), Otto, Ovide, Ovila, Ozaire, Ozana, Ozé, Ozélie, Ozius, Ozoner, Pacifique, Pamphile, Patricien, Philemon, Philias (Phillias, Philiace, Phyllias), Philibert, Philidore, Phillase, Philodo, Philomon, Philorome, Phocas, Pio, Pitre, Pitt, Pius, Placide, Polydore (Paulydore), Prémelite, Prime, Prospère, Prudent, Raduël (Raduel), Régent, Régilles, Romain, Rona, Rosaire, Rosario, Rosimond, Rubin, Rudolphe, Rufin (Ruffin), Saturnin, Sélime, Sémi, Seneville, Séraphin, Séverin (Severain, Sévérin), Sévère, Siffroi (Siffroid), Silvère, Siméon, Sixte, Sonore, Stahelin, Stanislas, Stellin, Sténio, Sylvère, Sylvéus, Sylvidore, Sylvius, Téles, Télésphore, Télex, Télexphore, Tenance, Thadée (Thaddée), Thanisphore, Théobald, Théode, Théodore, Théodule, Théophane, Théophile, Théotime, Thérence, Thiburce (Tiburce), Thimothée (Timotée), Thuribe, Tilmon(d), Toussaint, Tranquil(le), Tréflé (Trefflé), Turmel, Ubald, Uldège, Uldéric, Ulric, Ulyasse, Ulysse, Urbain, Uriel, Valdord, Valère, Valérien, Valier, Valmore, Venance, Vénard, Vérance, Vernan, Vertume, Victorien, Victorin, Vital, Vivien, Wenceslas, Wilbert, Wilbrod, Wilfred, Willard,
569.99.2 Wilmond, Xavier, Yvonnie, Zenon (Zénon),
Names Zéphir (Zéphyr), Zéphirin, Ziah, Zoël.

Carmen accompanied Terry to the funeral home. On the way, Terry told how Madame Hébert — Lauzia — had always been nice to him. And then:

"I know we're supposed to say 'my sympatees,' but seems to me, in dis case 'ere, sounds kind of light, as wishes go."

"You were closer to dem. You could say sometin' more."

"Such as?"

"Such as . . . I don't know . . . say wot you feel for real."

. . .

"Wot do you feel when you tink about all dis?"

Terry waited to complete a turn before answering.

"To be trootful, I kinda feel guilty fer having stopped being chums wid Shawn."

He thought for a moment before adding:

"Bottom line, can't help tinkin' it shouldn't 'ave happened."

"Well, dat's perfect. You tell 'er dat. She'll understand."

"Yeah, well, if I'm feeling like dat, imagine how she's feelin'!"

"Exactly, you can add dat! You can say: '. . . so I can just imagine how yer not feelin' good neider.'"

Terry thought about it, then: 570.25.9

"Don't know. Seems to me dat's pretty obvious." Murder

571.90.12

Alphabetical order is a symbolic order. Letters

There were no more than a half dozen cars in the parking lot of the funeral home.

"Der's not a whole lot of people . . ."

As they approached the entrance, Terry and Carmen agreed that they had no idea what to expect inside.

"Dis's only de second time I bin in a funeral parlour in me whole life."

"Me too. First time was for one of my uncles, when I was just a girl."

"Me, 'twas me aunt Rhéa. I remember I was afraid she'd get up, sit right up in her coffin."

Terry pointed to a large side door.

"Dat must be where dey take de bodies in an' out."

. . .

"I always wondered if dey eder do it durin' de day. We never see bodies runnin' 'round town 'cept fer funerals. How d'you suppose dey get from de hospital to 'ere?"

He opened the door for Carmen and followed her inside. To their left was a small reception room, empty.

"Well, der's nobody in de cryin' room. Dat tells you sometin'."

Terry peeked into the visitation room before entering. About a dozen people were talking quietly. Carmen took a deep breath. Terry was a little nervous, too.

"Der's only a couple I recognize..."

But he screwed up his courage, touched Carmen's elbow and escorted her toward the coffin along the back
572.25.10 Murder wall. They had taken only a few steps into the room when Shawn's mother saw them and came toward them.

> Partial list of archaic female given names to have appeared in the death notices of *L'Acadie nouvelle*: Abée, Acdée, Ada, Addie, Adée, Adélaïde, Adélia, Adelle, Adelphine, Adenise, Adora, Adrissa, Aglaé, Agnès, Ainée, Alba, Albéa, Albertine, Albina, Alcie, Alda, Aldegonde, Aldina, Aldine, Aldona, Aldorèse, Aldoria, Aldorine, Alésine, Alexcia, Alexina, Alfredgine, Alga, Alice, Alicia, Alida, Alita, Alizine (Alysine), Alma, Almaïse, Almida, Almire, Alouisia, Aloysia, Alozia, Alpha, Alphéda, Alphonsina, Alphonsine, Alta (Altha), Alva, Alvida, Alvina, Alvine, Alzina, Alzir, Amabélis, Amilda, Ammie, Amoza, Anaïsse, Anastasia, Anastasie, Anathalie, Anelle, Angeline (Angéline), Angella, Anida, Anneciade, Année, Annoncia, Annonciade (Anonciade), Anysie, Apauline (Appauline,

Apoline, Appoline, Appolines), Aqualina, Aquilina, Archange, Argentina, Argentine, Arilda, Armance, Armela, Arméline, Armenda, Armora, Arnołda, Arthance, Arthémise, Arthurenne, Arzélie, Astrid, Aubéline, Augustine (Augustina), Aula, Auna, Aureilla, Aurelda, Aurélie, Aurilda, Aurise, Azèle (Azelle), Azella, Azélie, Azilda, Babé, Barbe, Baselice (Baselisse), Basélice, Basilice (Basilisse), Béatrice, Béline, Belzémée, Belzénée, Bernardienne, Bernica, Bernise, Bertine, Beulah, Biola, Blondine, Calinda, Carmélia, Carméline, Carmélite, Cécéle, Cédée, Cédélice, Célamire, Célanire, Célénire, Céleste, Célestine, Célianne, Célina, Célistine, Cémida, Cerianne, Charlande, Claira, Clairice, Clairilda, Clairinda, Clara, Clarenda, Clarinda, Clarine, Clarisse (Clarice), Clariste, Clémentine, Cléola, Clora, Colinda, Coline, Colombe, Cordélia, Cordilia (Cordillia), Corinda, Corona, Cotilda, Cyrianne, Cyrilla, Dalila, Daphna, Déa, Decima, Delcia, Delcina, Délia, Délima, Délina, Délisca (Deliska), Deliza, Delora, Delpha, Delphine, Delta, Delvina, Démerise, Dérilda, Desanges, Desneiges, Didine, Dilia, Dina, Dionne, Docile (Docille), Dolcina, Dolorès, Doloria, Dolors, Dométilde, Domice, Domine, Domithilde, Domitile, Domitille, Donia, Doralice, Dorca (Dorka), Dorelle, Doria, Dorilda, Dorilla, Dorille, Doris (Dorice), Édesse, Édeste, Edmée, Edna, Édorine, Edwilda, Edwina, Églandine, Églantine, Elda, Éléda, Élia, Éliana, Élianne, Éliza, Elledwine, Elleminie, Elmina, Elmire, Elnora, Élodia, Élodie, Élosia, Éloudie, Élouzia, Elphégine, Elsée, Elsia, Elva, Elvine, Elwine, Élyre, Elza, Elzéa, Elzire, Émélie, Émélina,

Émelise, Emella, Emeriel, Émerique, Emerise, Émilda, Émilina, Émiliore, Émina, Emma, Émogène, Enilda, Enna, Enossé, Ernestine, Ethelda, Étiennette, Etwilda, Eudocia, Eudoxia, Eugénie, Eulalie, Eunice, Euphémie, Eusavina (Euzavina), Évangeline (Évangéline), Éveline, Exa, Exaudia (Exodia), Exéline, Exia, Exilda, Exilia, Exoré, Exza, Exzella, Ezella, Fabie, Fabiola, Fatima, Fébrinée, Fédélice, Fédora, Félécité, Felendé, Félexine, Félice, Félicité (Phélicité), Félime, Félixine, Fémina, Fidélia, Flavie, Fleurette, Florastine, Florella, Florestine, Florida, Flovila, Francelle, Franzeda, Freda, Frédonia, Froisine, Gélina, Gemma, Georgeline, Germance, Gevite, Gillette, Gilma, Glorianne, Graziella, Harmina, Hectorine, Hedwidge, Henriette, Herculine, Hermeline, Hermence, Hermina, Herminie, Hida, Hilda, Hortence, Hosanna, Hyacinthe, Icilda, Ida, Idolla, Idora, Imelda, Inède, Isella (Izella), Isèle, Isola, Itha, Jirene, Josèphat, Joséphine, Justine, Laudia, Laurina, Laurida, Laurinda, Laurine, Lausanna, Lauveina, Lauvina, Lauza, Lauzette, Lauzia, Lazarine, Lazine, Léaline, Leatitia (Laetitia, Léticia), Léda, Lédora, Lélia, Lena, Léocade, Léocadie, Léola, Léonice, Léonie, Léonile, Léonise, Léonore, Léontine, Léopoldine (Léopauldine), Léota, Léozé, Letha, Lidwine, Lina, Linova, Livina, Locade, Locadie, Lodia, Lodiane (Lodianne), Lodienne, Lonia, Lorenda, Lorette, Lorinda, Lottie, Louvina, Luce, Lucina, Lucresse, Ludivine, Ludovine, Lulia, Lumina, Macrina, Macrine, Maddie, Madelaine, Madone, Madonna, Magella (Magela, Majella), Majeline, Malvina, Mania, Mantine, Marceline, Marguerite, Marilda, Marmaie, Mathilda, Mathilde, Mécrina,

Mecthilde, Méda, Médora, Melece, Melenda, Mélie, Mélina, Mélinda, Mélindé, Mélita, Mélodia, Mélonie, Melva, Melvina, Memery, Mémie, Mercia, Mérelda, Mérilda, Mérisa (Mériza), Mérita, Métrina, Mina, Modeste, Moza, Nasarine (Nazarine), Nelda, Nélida, Néra, Noelline, Noémise, Nola, Obeline (Obéline), Oberte, Octavie, Odéa, Odélia, Odélie, Odila (Odilla), Odile, Odilette, Ola, Olésine (Olézine), Olga, Olia, Olida, Olive, Olivine, Olizine, Olympe, Omelda, Onia, Onilda, Opal, Opeline, Ora, Orilda, Orise, Osélie (Ozélie), Osithe (Ozite, Ozithe), Osithé, Oveline (Ovéline), Ovilda, Ozanna, Ozélie, Ozeline, Ozile, Palmira, Parmela, Parmélia, Paquerette, Patronile, Pélagie, Pétronille, Phebée, Phélonise, Philomène, Philonyse, Phiona, Placidie, Précille (Prescille, Préscille), Prémélia, Prémilia, Pricille (Priscille), Rébecca, Régère, Régina, Reine, Reinelde, Rélice, Rena, Renande, Rénelda, Rezeda (Rézeda), Rhéa, Rhéalda, Rina, Robéa, Ronaline, Rosalie, Rose, Rosée, Roselba, Rosia, Rosima, Rosimonde, Ruffine, Rufina, Salomé, Sara (Sarah), Saraphine, Savarine, Savie, Scholastique, Sémida, Séphrénie, Séraphie, Sérina, Séverine, Souveraine, Stella, Sylvine, Tarzile (Tharzile), Tharzille, Tassiane, Télorise, Thédora, Thelma, Théodora, Théola, Théosanne, Théotice (Théotisse), Théotise, Théotiste, Thérazile, Tilla, Tina, Trévina, Ulyasse, Una, Ursule, Valada, Valdine, Valéda, Valerie, Valida, Valma, Valtérine, Valtrude, Valzina, Vanilda, Vélama, Vélina, Velma, Veloria, Velzina, Vencela, Vénéda, Vénéranda, Vénérande, Vénérante, Venie, Venise, Venolia, Vercella, Vergine, Verginie, Verla, Verna, Vézina,

Viana (Vianna), Victoire, Victorine, Vina,
Viola, Virgine, Virginia, Virginie, Vitaline,
Vivine, Wilhelmine, Willimine, Wilma,
Winéda, Winida, Winnifred, Yvonie, Yvonisse
(Yvonnice), Yzella, Zéla, Zélande, Zelda, Zélia,
Zélica, Zélie, Zélima, Zélina, Zella, Zelma,
573.99.1 Zénaïde, Zénobie, Zéphérine, Zérilla, Zila,
Names Zita, Zonia.

Carmen had never met a woman like this! She seemed to personify the human condition all by herself—*The Human Condition*, the title of a book lying around somewhere in their house and which she had intended to read. But there was more. There was kindness in pain, joy in sadness.

"Terry?"

Without another word, the little grandmother had embraced Terry and hugged him a long time in her arms. Seeing them like this, Carmen realized Terry's deep roots in a past of which she knew very little, and felt a bit ashamed not to have made more of an effort to know that past. Then, in the space of an instant, their roles seemed to reverse and it was Terry who was carrying the little woman, who had gone from joy to tears. Then she stepped back, her wrinkled cheeks wet with tears and the tip of her nose reddened, she placed her hands on Terry's shoulders to admire him, and said simply:

"I knew you wouldn't ferget us."

Suddenly everything Terry had thought of saying vanished from his mind. He did not need to speak. Just being there was enough.

"Auntie, dis is Carmen."

Auntie took Carmen's hand in both of hers, nodding her head as she looked at her, and added only:

574.25.11 "Well, in a way, it's not a bad bit of a nice day just de
Murder same."

> And so, Hans accepts the order of the alphabet; he does not seek to change it. Who is he to question it? After all, is this order of the symbolic inferior to the register of the imaginary? Or inferior to the real? Anyway, what is the real?

575.74.8
Hans

Back in the van, Carmen suggested they go to the restaurant. This surprised Terry.

"Are you hungry, den?"

"Not so much. Only seems like I don't feel like goin' back home just yet. I don' know. I feel like us having a talk."

This worried Terry, but he didn't want to show it.

"A talk…"

"Well, a shocking lot of stuff just happened, don't you tink?"

As a matter of fact, Terry did feel that a lot had just happened, but he was surprised that Carmen had felt it, too.

"Have a talk 'bout stuff like…"

"Like der's a child back der, already wholly formed, and yet de boy's halfway alone…"

Well, that was certainly a surprise. It was the old question of a third child, which they had not succeeded in resolving.

"You want to talk about dat?!"

Terry was all the more astonished since, between the two of them, Carmen was the more reticent to enlarge their little family.

"Dat, and udder tings."

Terry was still not reassured:

"Well, can you give me like an idea of de udder tings…?"

Carmen laughed, realising that her way of presenting their talk left room for ambiguity. She stretched out her arm and caressed Terry's neck.

"*Worry pas*," she said, letting a bit of her French slide. "I just feel like us talkin', spendin' a real evening together."

"O me nerves you got me drove."

Carmen chuckled.

576.94.2 Terry and Carmen

"I know it. Don't mind me. My nerves are rubbed right raw, too."

CHAPTER 5

When I have a concept, I contemplate it with respect, I never criticize it, because if you begin to adjust a concept, it unravels, ferments, becomes corrupted, it infects all neighbouring concepts, you lose your head, say goodbye to tranquillity!

GILLES LAPOUGE, *Besoin de mirages*
(A Need for Mirages) 577.144.5
Éditions du Seuil, 1999 Epigraphs

Several weeks later, when the ground had thawed out completely, 20 people, armed with picks, shovels, wheelbarrows, and work gloves, gathered on the site of the future vegetable garden. First stage: to remove all the stones and weeds, a job requiring mainly elbow grease and dogged determination. At noon, hot dogs and hamburgers appeared, along with everything else that normally accompanies an outdoor meal.

"We'll never get 'er all done, today."

"Dey'll have to truck in a whole lot of fresh earth."

"I only hope de soil's not contaminated. Looks awful black…"

"Well, 'twas a warehouse before, wasn't it. Lord knows wot kind of horrible tings come down into de ground from der."

578.9.6
The Garden

"Dey ought to do some tests. Just to be on de safe side."

> The concept of uneven ground was introduced into the French language as *accident de terrain* (accidented terrain) at the beginning of the nineteenth century by the Swiss naturalist Henri de Saussure, father of the famous linguist Ferdinand de Saussure, son of chemist and naturalist Nicolas Théodore de Saussure, and grandson of geologist and physician Horace Benedict de Saussure, who was himself the son of agronomist Nicolas, author of several books on viniculture. Interesting that Ferdinand's fa-
> 579.78.7 ther was himself a kind of shaper of language, a
> Accidents man who crafted language to fit reality.

"Sometimes, we say we're sorry even doh we've done nuttin' wrong."

Now, Étienne thought, his father was exaggerating.

"Like, say you want to ask somebody a question, you says yer sorry on account of you might be disturbin' dem."

Thinking his father was joking, Étienne started laughing. Such behaviour struck him as ridiculous.

"An' wot're you laughin' about?"

Étienne figured Terry was still joking.

"Well geez, Dad! We don't know if we're gonna be distrubin' dem or not!"

"Dat's true enough. Only it's just in case."

Étienne stopped laughing, realizing to his surprise that Terry was actually serious.

"An', well it's a way of gettin' der attention, see. Like, you might be sayin': 'Excuse me, ma'am, I'm wonderin' if you might 'ave a BandAid, on account me finger's bleedin' an' I don't much like it..."

"Étienne could not imagine a time when he would have to ask a stranger for a BandAid.

"Or else: 'Beggin' yer pardon, sir, you oughtn't to be trowin' yer Tim Hortons cup on de ground.'"

"We're allowed to say dat?"

"An' why not, I'd like to know. De feller ought to know better. An' if ee don't like wot yer gonna tell 'im, at least, dis way, you've already said yer sorry."

. . .

"Instead of sayin': 'Hey you! Pick up dat cup you just trew on de ground.'"

. . .

"Mind ya, I'm not sayin' you ought to be goin' round tellin' folks wot to do. 'Specially not folks you don't know. Only, if you have to do it, best to say yer sorry yerself first, and say sir or ma'am, instead of 'hey you der?' Dat way dey'll know you care a wee bit, just de same. Dat's just wot we call bein' polite."

580.86.10
Apologies

. . .

581.33.12
Chiac Lesson

To die, then, or to lose (oneself). Detail?

"Read de paper dis morning?"

"No, 'aven't had the time, have I?"

"Der's an article wot explains dat children don't get irony until dey're ten years old."

"An' that surprises you, den?"

"Well, it does an' it don't. Doesn't surprise me when I tink about it. Only I wouldn't 'ave tot about it if I hadn't read it."

. . .

"Dey say up until der five years old, most kids won't get wot yer tryin' to say at all. Around de time der eight years old, dey'll understand wot it is yer sayin', only dey won't tink it's funny."

. . .

"You have to wait 'till der ten or eleven before dey can tink it's funny, de way an adult does."

. . .

"Anyway, it's good to know."

...

"Ten. Dat's about five years fer me to go wid Étienne,
582.13.10 an' seven or eight wid Marianne."
Paternity "An' you took de trouble to figure all dat out?!"

> Copied from *The Official Scrabble Players Dictionary*® by Merriam-Webster: "Scrabble® trademark. All intellectual property rights in and to the game are owned in the United States by Hasbro, Inc., in Canada by Hasbro Canada, Inc., and throughout the rest of the world by J.
> 583.11.9 W. Spear & Sons, Ltd., a subsidiary of Mattel,
> Appropriations Inc.

So, Zed had soil tests done.

"All de tests show der's no wot dey call serious contamination. Der's traces of dis an' dat, but nuttin' serious. Jus' stuff you're gonna find in de ground of any city."

Terry, the realist, wanted to prepare Zed for a more lively than usual monthly meeting.

"Some folks'll panic, jus' de same. Soon as you say dat word contamination..."

"Don't I know it. You guys, on account of de kids, does it freak you out?"

"Well, fer sure, it gives us sometin' to tink about. But, if de tests say it's safe..."

...

"Best ting would be if de folks dat did de testin' came 'round demselves and explain wot it was dey found. Dat way, folks could be askin' questions to de right people, an' you'd get a break."

584.127.11 "Now, dat's a wonderful bright idea! Aren't you the
Tactics clever boy!

> Firmin Didot's firm eventually merged with the company run by Sébastien Bottin (1764–1853),

> editor of directories and almanacs, which resulted in the publication of *l'Annuaire du commerce Didot-Bottin* (*Didot-Bottin Commercial* 585.58.5
> *Directory*) in 1882. Extensions

The relationship between Josse and Bernard — the young man with the gentle smile she'd met the night of the celebration in honour of Hektor Haché-Haché — was coming along:

"You still playin' baseball tonight?! I tot we were goin' to see a movie!"

"I know it. We should be done 'round ten o'clock. I figured you an' I could do sometin' afterwards."

"Sometin'? Like?"

"Like go down by Robichaud, make a fire by de water, look at de stars."

Josse chuckled:

"Are ya jokin', or wot?"

"Not really, no."

"An' sleep over der, you mean?"

"If you want to…"

…

…

"Alright, den."

"Fer real? Geez, dat was easier dan I tot 'twould be. I was sure you was goin' to say no." 586.43.1

"Dat's part of me strategy; to say yes from time to time." Love

> Ferdinand de Saussure's famous *Course in General Linguistics* ranks among the 10 top choices in the social sciences in *La Bibliothèque idéale*, right alongside other monumental works such as *An Inquiry into the Nature and Causes of the Wealth of Nations* by Adam Smith, *Capital* by Karl Marx, *The Interpretation* 587.54.8
> *of Dreams* by Sigmund Freud, and *Suicide* by Forgotten/
> Emile Durkheim. Recalled

All day long, Carmen had had irony on her mind.

"Well, if yer findin' it so hard bein' nice to yer kids, best not to tink of havin' anudder one."

Terry couldn't believe they were going to get into a row over this irony thing. And then, unintentionally, he poured fuel on the fire:

"I'm not findin' it hard, sometimes I makes an effort is all."

"An' how's dat any different?"

Terry tried to put it differently.

"Well, wedder you like it or not, wid kids you gotta have a bit o' patience, right?"

Carmen could not deny it.

"Well den, sometimes, instead of losin' patience, you start turnin' tings around in yer mind. And let's just say der's times dat'll put some weird ideas in yer head."

Carmen still saw no reason to disagree.

"Alright den, so wot I learned from dat paper is just dat it's not much use tellin' de kids every crazy idea dat pops up in yer head right den, on account of chances are dey won't be understandin' it, or if dey does understand, dey won't be findin' it funny. Could be, even, dey tink it's mean. Or, tird possibility, dey feel bad on account of it. Now, do you tink I wants to look mean to my kids or to go an' make dem feel bad?"

This troubled Carmen. Had she so badly misunderstood what Terry had said earlier? Had she wasted her day trying to work something out that wasn't there to begin with?

"Wot's surprisin' to me is dat you'd even have ideas dat could make dem feel bad!"

But Terry was convinced he was no worse than anyone else:

"Well, happens to all parents from time to time, don't you tink?"

588.13.7 "An' wot in heaven's name does dat mean?!"

Paternity The night promised to be a long and arduous one.

L'Officiel du jeu Scrabble® lists 237 French words beginning with the letter *a* and including at least one *x*. Two of these words each contain two *x*'s. They are *affixaux* ("affixal") and *axiaux* ("axial") — relatively simple words when compared to the two that begin with *a* and contain two *y*'s: *amblyrhynque* ("marine iguana") and *antéhypophyse* ("aterior pituitary gland").

Whereas words beginning with *a* and containing at least one *y* are far more numerous in English than in French, the opposite is true in the case of words beginning with *a* and containing an *x*. This is largely because, in French, *x* is a plural ending and many adjectives end in *–eux* or *-aux*. There are only 71 English words beginning with *a* and containing at least one *x* as listed in *The Official Scrabble Players* 589.20.5
Dictionary®. Language

"Like de worst I can imagine?"

"Go!"

"Matter of fact, I already tot about dat. An' de worst ting I could tink of is a rat runnin' around betwixt me legs while I's drivin."

"Yuck!"

"I don't know wot kind of noise a rat makes, but one ting I can tell you, if dat rat made a sound right den, well 590.137.6
boy, I'd 'a dropped dead right der." Fears

(For a long time after that, The Cripple would wonder if Antoinette had heard his play on 591.131.9
words *image-inate*.) Parenthesi(e)s

Right off the bat, Simone the biologist set the record straight: the soil was absolutely normal for an urban environment; it was not contaminated, merely impoverished by virtue of not having been able to regenerate naturally. She recommended the addition of a thick layer of fresh earth, manure, and compost. Regardless, the garden would never live up to minimal biological standards because of the railway.

"An' wot has de train got to do wid it, I'd like to know?"

"De smoke, me tinks."

"Wouldn't be no different if 'twere a road. You can't be growin' organic by a road or a street on account of de exhaust."

"An' den der's de vibrations. Train passes, boy, de eart' shakes."

"Naw, naw, now yer gettin' it mixed up wid a wine cellar. De vibrations're no good fer a wine cellar, but dat's got nuttin' to do wid organic farmin'."

"Anyway, when did we say we was wantin' an organic garden?"

"Well, we never said so, but sure we'd all have liked it."

"I would."

"I as well."

"Anyone want sometin' else over here, den?"

"A Sleeman Cream."

"Corona."

"Glass o' wine."

"Awh, what de hell… anudder Ceasar."

592.9.7 "An Alpine."

The Garden "Ginger ale."

HEBDROMEDARY: n. — 2005/2013; from *hebdomadal* and *dromedary* ♦ Weekend drunk.
593.120.1 *"The hebdromedary achieves an equilibrium on*
Fictionary *Wednesday."* (Daigle)

"In de end, dem dat wants to eat organic'll just 'ave to haul demselves down to de store and buy it. Weren't nuttin' we could do about it."

The Cripple had been too indolent to attend the

meeting. Now, listening to Antoinette's report, he regretted his laziness a little.

"An' are der a lot of folks gonna lend a hand, den?"

"We're close to twenty. Pretty much de same folks dat did de clearing. Any more an' wouldn't be wort it. We's even tinkin' of goin' bigger. I'm de one dat's in charge of makin' sure dem dat does de work gets der share before anyone else."

"Go bigger? How're youse gonna manage dat, den?"

"We'll plant down along boat sides o' de building. Not too wide, maybe one or two rows. Goin' all de way down de sides'll get us a fair bit."

The Cripple was proud to see his wife taking the project to heart.

"An' wid flowers in amongst de veggies, 'twill be a right pretty sight to see, fer sure." 594.9.8 The Garden

> Blissful red. Red meat, red cabbage, red earth. Red star. Red gold. Mercury red, lead red, pure red. Tube of rouge. Red lantern. Redneck. See red. Red blooded. In the red. Red Cross. Baton-Rouge. 595.83.7 Bliss and Colours

After Marianne was born, Terry and Carmen had pretty much decided that two children was enough. But, from to time, they found themselves imagining life with a third.

"It's terrible strange. As doh der was sometin' in me dat wants anudder one."

"It's de same ting wid me. Must be some sort of animal instinct, 'cause when I tink about it, two's plenty."

"Same wid me. I wouldn't want us to go and complicate our lives too much. I tells meself, tings are pretty good de way dey are, we ought to just keep goin' dat way."

Carmen nodded: she understood exactly what Terry meant.

"Anyway, if we decide we want anudder, we better not

wait too long. I'm older'n you are, even doh I don't look it."

As she spoke, Carmen had rolled her hips, a kind of burlesque demonstration of her powers of attraction.
596.125.6 Terry applauded:
Sexuality "Nice work, girl! Nice work!"

597.31.4 Questions with Answers

> What should a writer do when she realizes she's made a mistake? Admit to it, even though it seems incongruous to admit a mistake in a fiction.

The following Saturday, 17 people were back at it, digging, shovelling, raking, and barrowing rocks, branches, old soil, new soil, manure, mulch, and more. In the midst of all this toing and froing, wearing his panama hat, and his reading glasses perched on the end of his nose, Étienne Zablonski was drawing plans, trying to design a garden that would take into account all the various biological, aesthetic, and practical factors. Ludmilla, who was watching him work, pointed to a spot on his plan.

"And what sort of flowers will go here?"

"Nasturtiums. They'll protect the broccoli in behind."

Ludmilla had never realized that Étienne was a natural gardener.

"And here?"

"Sunflowers, behind the corn. I think there'll be sufficient space to plant three rows. Otherwise, the corncobs won't be full."

"Oh?"

"Because they have to pollinate each other. Antoinette explained it."

Ludmilla also liked her husband's generosity.

"And there?"

598.9.9 "Thyme among the cabbages. Thyme is very pretty
The Garden when it's in flower."

> Exploring *L'Officiel du jeu Scrabble*® turns out to be useful in several ways. First, because it does not include definitions of commonly used words, and only brief definitions of lesser-known words, one can easily scan all the words beginning with a given letter in an hour or two. Anyone willing to dedicate a few hours to each letter of the alphabet, could acquaint themselves with the entire vocabulary of the French language. Evidently, the French language is finite after all, contrary to the impression it gives of being a pitiless and limitless mistress.

599.20.6
Language

All this fresh ground seemed to rejuvenate the very soul of the courtyard.

"I can't wait to see all dis 'ere growin'!"

"Dat corner over der's goin' to be tropical like."

In the distance someone shouted:

"Hotdogs're ready!"

The announcement sparked a small rush toward the barbecue. Lisa-M. and a non-resident girl friend moved against the current to go over and admire the flowerbed at the rear.

"Who's dat over der den, wid de straw hat?"

"Dat's Zablonski! Sexy in't ee? His wife's shockin' beautiful, too, and real nice, to boot. Funniest ting is all de boys in de building have got a crush on 'er… but do you tink dey'd try der luck?"

"I sure wouldn't mind living 'ere, too. You're one lucky ducky!"

"Here's where dey planted dose giant flowers. It's gonna be right pretty."

A second call rang out:

"Alright den, de hamburgers're ready too!"

600.9.10
The Garden

More specifically, what should a writer do if she realizes she's made what might be a fundamental error at a relatively advanced stage of writing the book, an error, in this case, involving a false premise? First of all, remain calm, avoid a crisis of discouragement, the tempta-
601.70.2 tion to abandon the work. Then, begin to look
Errors for a solution.

"If I'd bin just a wee bit smarter, I'd 'ave gone an' fetched Chico, so ee could spend de day wid us. 'Specially wid de barbecue an' de games an' all. Ee could've even slept over if ee'd a mind to."

"Fer sure."

Terry looked truly disconsolate. Carmen sympathized, tried to comfort him:

"Well, we can't be tinkin' of everyting all de time. Dat's someting we ought to do, doh. Invite 'im over before too long, before he can't remember who we are."

"Yeah. Some time we're doin' someting dat's… wot's de word I'm lookin' fer in French?"

"Fun?"

Terry was not amused. He tried the English word.

"Sometin' like *distracting*…"

602.30.6 "Amusing? Entertaining? Diverting?"

Chiac "Diverting. Seems I can never remember dat word."

Before confirming this newly discovered and surprising finitude to the French language, it might be useful to verify the true value of language tools such as *L'Officiel du jeu Scrabble*® by comparing—why not?—the list of verbs beginning with the letter *a* in *L'Officiel*… with those in the authoritative *Bescherelle L'Art de conjuguer*, for example. The *Bescherelle* lists 528 verbs beginning with the letter *a*, including the verbs *accroire, adirer, advenir, apparoir, assavoir,* and *avenir*, although the

> conjugations of these verbs are either limited or nul. As for *L'Officiel...*, although it lists two fewer verbs than the *Bescherelle*, it does include some not in the *Bescherelle*. Together, *L'Officiel...* and the *Bescherelle* list 496 of the same verbs beginning with the letter *a*. The *Bescherelle* lists 31 that are not in *L'Officiel...*, and the latter includes 30 that are missing in the *Bescherelle*. Thus we arrive at a total of 557 French verbs beginning with the letter *a*.

> In English, one might arrive at a similar result by comparing lists of 448 verbs beginning with the letter *a* in the *Official Tournament and Club Word List* for Scrabble with a source such as the *Woxikon Free Online Dictionary*, which lists 444 verbs beginning with the letter *a*. The *Official Tournament List* contains 48 verbs that do not appear in *Woxikon*'s list, while *Woxikon* has 47 not in the *Official Tournament* list. Altogether these two sources list 397 verbs in common, which yields a total of 492 English verbs beginning with the letter *a*. 603.20.7 Language

At the end of the work day, everyone shared a big communal meal in the yard. And two particularly creative dads improvised a series of competitive games for the children.

"First, you toss de rock in the pail wid de shovel, see, den after dat, you goes an' empties your pail on the pile of rocks over der."

"Wot does we win?"

"Wot does you win?... You wins twenty-five cents. But don't go fergettin' to come back over 'ere wid yer pail. When yer done emptyin' yer pail, you gotta come over 'ere and touch de board, de board where youse started from."

"Where does we put de rock?"

"The rock's gotta land on dat big pile over der. Youse all see de pile?"

"Yes."

"Yes."

"Yes."

"Rock has to fall on de pile. If she don't touch de pile, boy, you lose right der, automatic. Understood?"

The kids nodded, they were already beginning to concentrate their attention. A question came from the attending adults:

"Wot happens if dey miss de pail?"

The other dad answered the spectators:

"If dey miss de pail a first time, dey can try a second time..."

He turned to the children to make sure they too understood:

"Understood? You miss de pail once, you can try again. An' if you miss a second time, you picks dat rock up in yer hands and put 'er in de pail, den take off wid de pail. Understood?"

To be sure they'd all understood, the first dad went through the whole explanation again, demonstrating each step along the way. In the end, the children were hopping up and down with impatience.

604.9.11 "Alright den, Roussel an' Étienne, youse two are goin'
The Garden first. Haul on over 'ere."

> Pure errors are rare. It's always possible to wring an error in order to extract an explanation, a justification, a motivation, a lesson, an
> 605.70.3 elixir, a premise, and sometimes even the pre-
> Errors text to write another book.

Then Zed filled a vat with water and tossed in seven or eight apples.

"Alright den, youse each takes a turn tryin' to bite into an apple."

The children were hopping with excitement to decide who would go first. The luck of the draw fell to Julie. She soaked her face several times before conceding defeat.

"My turn!"

"No, mine!"

"Me!"

Thomas won out. He came forward, gripped both sides of the vat and began chasing the floating apples with a wide open mouth. Finally he straightened up, his head soaked and defeated.

"Yer turn, Étienne."

Étienne understood that success was far from certain. He stood for a moment studying the apples.

"You don't want to give 'er a try?"

"Yes, I do."

He concentrated for a few more seconds and then 606.106.6 Customs
plunged.

> Since readers are invited to complete each section of *La Bibliothèque idéale* with a fiftieth book of their choice, nothing prevents us from creating a fiftieth category of books, all personal choices, in which we might include works that don't entirely belong in any of the existing categories. In this fiftieth section, I would place *Stratégies de la framboise. Aventures potagères* (*Strawberry Strategies. Adventures in* 607.95.1 Additions to *La Bibliothèque idéale*
> *the Garden*), by Dominique Louise Pélerin, published by Autrement. A pure delight.

"Deep down, isn't dat why dey do an autopsy? To prove 608.117.4 Death
wedder yer time had really come or not?"

> This fiftieth category of *La Bibliothèque idéale* could also serve to include the truly excellent books in categories that have already filled 609.58.9 Extensions
> their quota.

When night fell, to the accompaniment of applause, whistles, fatigue, and the joy that comes at the end of a long and productive day in the fields, Zed turned on all the lighting they'd installed to prettify the yard: Chinese lanterns of different sizes and colours, electric candles in the shape of red peppers and little orange pumpkins, and a few spotlights shining on the still-young trees. After a few songs, requested by both young and old, most of the residents retired to their apartments with heavy limbs
610.9.12 and sore backs, and unable to remember what life had
The Garden been like before.

The 31 verbs beginning with the letter *a* that appear only in the *Bescherelle* are: *abloquer*, *abomber*, *abricoter*, *acétyler*, *aciseler*, *(s')adire*, *(s')adoniser*, *affriter*, *agricher*, *alcaliser*, *(s')ambifier*, *aminer*, *amourer*, *analgésier*, *apatamer*, *aplomber*, *appéter*, *aquiger*, *archaïser*, *argotiser*, *argougner*, *arpigner*, *arquebuser*, *arquepincer*, *(s')arsouiller*, *artiller*, *(s')autoguider*, *(s')autosuggestionner*, *(s')autotomiser*, *aveindre*, and *azimut(h)er*. On the other hand, the 30 verbs listed in *L'Officiel du jeu Scrabble*® that do not appear in the *Bescherelle* are: *aborner*, *abréagir*, *abrier*, *abroutir*, *abuter*, *accouver*, *accréter*, *affaiter*, *agender*, *agrainer*, *aguiller*, *allotir*, *ameulonner*, *amouiller*, *anathémiser*, *anatomiser*, *anecdotiser*, *antiparasiter*, *apigeonner*, *appondre*, *aquareller*, *attraire*, *attremper*, *aubiner*, *auditer*, *(s')autodissoudre*, *(s')autogérer*, *(s')autoréguler*, *azorer*, and *azoter*.

The 48 English verbs that begin with the letter *a* that appear only in *The Official*... are: *aah*, *abduce*, *abode*, *abscess*, *abseil*, *absterge*, *abstrict*, *aby*, *abye*, *accouter*, *acierate*, *activize*, *adeem*, *adz*, *adze*, *aerify*, *affray*, *agatize*, *age*,

> *agenize, agent, agnize, ah, airproof, airth, alkalify, alkalise, alkalize, amp, anagram, anear, anele, angulate, ankle, antick, appall, argle, aroint, aroynt, astringe, atticize, attrit, autolyse, autolyze, autopsy, avianize, azotise, azotize.* The 47 verbs listed in the *Woxikon* and not in *The Official*...are: *a-bomb, about-face, about-turn, abend, achromatise, actualise, ad-lib, affranchise, air-condition, air-cool, alchemise, alkalinise, alphabetise, aluminise, Americanise, Americanize, aminate, anaesthetize, anagrammatise, analogise, anathematise, animalise annualise, anodise, antagonise, anthologise, anthropomorphise, anthropomorphize, apotheosise, arabicise, Arabicise, Arabicize, arabise Arabise, arabize, Arabize, arborise, aromatise, atom-bomb, automatise, automonitor, autorestart, autosave, autostart, autotomise, autotrace, axiomatise.* Twenty-two of the verbs above that appear in the *Woxikon* and not in *The Official*...are verbs ending in the British spelling *–ise* rather than the American *–ize.*

611.20.9
Language

"Baska de mare had bin almost her whole life deep inside a salt mine in Poland, when some folks decided dat was no life fer a horse. Baska herself never complained, on account of de miners treated 'er nice. Anyway, by den dey wasn't workin' 'er all dat hard down in de mine. In de beginnin', she was after haulin' little carts full of salt along a track but, in de end, machines were doin' dat. So dey decided to take Baska out of de mine. First ting — on account of it's dark all de time down in a mine — Baska had a whole lot of trouble gettin' used to de normal light of day. And, seemed like she couldn't get used to walkin' around in a field, on account of she'd been all dat time in de tunnels, see. Plus, anudder problem: no salt, and Baska, well, she really loved de salt. An' not just fer lickin' neither. She liked de vi-bra-tion of salt. So, dat little block of salt dey was leavin' in a corner of de field to make Baska feel at home only made 'er sickly, on account of wot can she be doin' wid a little chunk of salt? She was comin' out from a salt mine dat was 700 years old!"

Terry stopped there, because Marianne was fast asleep. He planted a kiss on her forehead and left the room. Étienne, who'd been listening from his own room, did not feel that this was a real ending for a story, but he had no right to protest since Terry had not told it in his room.

612.37.6
Animal Tales

613.95.3
Additions to
La Bibliothèque idéale

> I would complete the section "Literature in Pieces" with *Self-portrait with Radiator* by Christian Bobin.

Terry had noticed the great variety of subjects among the books The Cripple bought. He always began with a book from the series *Que sais-je? (What Do I Know?)*, which introduced readers to a particular subject. Then he would look for more specialized books on that particular subject, books Terry always had to order, since neither their covers nor their contents were of the sort to attract the average reader. Occasionally, when The Cripple ordered two books from the *Que sais-je?* series at once, Terry would amuse himself by trying to find a possible link between them. Between *Le Droit Naturel* (*Natural Law)* by Alain Sériaux and *La Sociologie du corps* (*Sociology of the Body*) by David Le Breton, for example. But today Terry could find nothing to link *Le luxe* (*Luxury*) by Jean Castarède and *Les Algorithmes* (*Algorithms*) by Patrice Hernet, although once he'd read the back cover of *Algorithmes*, the distance between the two subjects seemed to shrink by a hair or two. He went up to The Cripple's apartment to deliver the two books, along with a third.

"Dis one 'ere's only for you to browse. It's about all

kinds of collections. I tawt it might interest you. I'm not layin' on no pressure 'ere to buy it. I know I can sell it no problem in de store."

The Cripple leafed through the book, which did indeed seem to interest him.

"Dat's right nice of you. Tanks."

614.16.5
The Cripple

> The error, in this case, consists in having overestimated the value of the numeral 12 compared to the 7, of which we have retained only its statistical aspect. And yet, nothing could be more false. A closer look reveals that the symbolic value of the numeral 7 is by far more established than that of 12. Such a fundamental error shakes the very foundations of this novel, which claims to be rife with accuracy. As though accuracy were a guarantee of serenity, of plenitude.

615.70.4
Errors

Bent over a drawer in his filing cabinet, Zed is pretending to look for a file of sales and rentals, when in fact he's only looking for some way to prolong Élizabeth's presence in his office.

"We've nuttin' free just now, only could be, between now and a year from now, one or two might be comin' up fer sale. From wot I'm hearin' anyway."

"In any case, I'm in no hurry."

"I can't be promisin' you'd be de one gettin' it, neider. We've a waitin' list — dat's wot I'm lookin' for. Only de waitin' list changes. Lots of times, folks'll put der name down, an' six months later dey buy a house in some udder place, on account of dey lose hope."

Zed decides he's pretended to look long enough — he doesn't want to appear too disorganized either — and makes believe he's found the document at last.

"Ha! Der it was all along, exactly where 'twas supposed to be."

He consults the waiting list, though he already knows what he'll find there.

"See, der's seven or eight names here, only I know at least two or tree of dem're not interested any longer. De udders I'll have to check."

Élizabeth concludes that she better not get her hopes up.

"I'll see wot I can do. I'll take yer name an' phone number, just in case sometin' comes up. You never know..."

Élizabeth gives him the number.

"'Ave you bin round here long, den? You don't have to say, I's just bein' nosey is all."

Élizabeth liked his frankness

"Around ten years. Since they opened the Oncology Centre.

"Awh? You work der?

"Yes. I'm a doctor."

"Awh!"

"But I was away for a few years, then I came back."

"Awh."

Zed is silent for a moment, just looking at Élizabeth, trying to think of something elegant, something intelligent to say.

"Is there a problem? Are doctors not allowed here?"

Zed laughed:

616.43.3 Love

"No, no! Come to think of it, 'twouldn't be a bad ting at all. We got none yet."

617.21.11 More or Less Useful Details

> The comparison between verbs beginning with the letter *a* in Bescherelle's *L'Art de conjuguer* and those in *L'Officiel du jeu Scrabble*® took more time than an overview of all the words beginning with the letter *a* in *L'Officiel du jeu Scrabble*®.

"Me, I hate wastin' me time."

...

618.137.4
Fears

“I know it don’t sound like a fear, but it is.”

619.95.2
Additions to
La Bibliothèque idéale

> Complete the “Tales of Travel and Exploration” section with *The Way of the World* by Nicolas Bouvier.

“Étienne, come on over ’ere a minute…”

Whenever he accompanied Terry to the bookstore, Étienne was always quick to respond to his father’s call in the hope of receiving instructions for a task to undertake.

“I want to show you dis ’ere kind of book. See how some of de pages doesn’t open?”

Étienne watched, nodding.

“Times past der was a whole lot o’ books like dis ’ere. You were wantin’ to read it, youse had to take a knife an’ cut to separate de pages yerself.”

Terry demonstrated.

“Nowadays, books like dis are sometin’ rare. Everytin’s cut an’ trimmed at de printer’s.”

Étienne nodded again.

“An’ de paper’s more like… coarse. Go on an’ touch…”

Étienne touched the page.

“… so de paper don’t cut even. It’s more like torn.”

Étienne had already noticed the ragged edges, and thought his father was a bit clumsy.

“Der’s folks like dis ’ere kind of book better dan de udders. An’ dey’re more expensive.”

Étienne took note.

“When yer older, if ever you works in a bookstore, you’ll already know dis kind o’ book exists.”

620.113.7
Collections

“But, Dad! I already work in a bookstore!”

621.70.5
Errors

> But to be consistent, if chance does not exist, neither can error.

At first, I wasn’t sure what it was. Proof of identity, legal document, a bunch of whereas this and whereas that…

I copied it all without really paying much attention, I have to admit. Until I ran out of paper. While they were restocking me, I had time to see, flat up against my glass, a child's drawing of a sun and moon in the same sky. The colours were bright and dense, a drawing by someone who did not retreat before the thick materiality of things. At the bottom of the sheet, an adult's hand had written in quotes: "It's because of the sun that I like the moon, now. Before, the moon frightened me. It's as though the sun shines everywhere inside me. The moon only makes me think. And often I fall asleep." It wasn't the first child's drawing that had come my way, not by a long shot, but there was something special about this one, I don't know why. Something decisive, and at the same time spontaneous. A life, what! After I'd emblazed it with my light, I continued to look at it, until it went away, without knowing that I had etched it in my secret memory.

622.57.6
Photocopies

623.95.4
Additions to
La Bibliothèque idéale

> Complete the "War" section with *The Notebook* by Agota Kristof.

Because he adored potatoes, and he was often the one who cooked their meals, Terry had built up a small inventory of potato-based recipes. The whole family appreciated most of these dishes, especially his potatoes fried in bacon grease. The ingredients could not have been more basic — potatoes, bacon grease, salt, and pepper — but the trick was in getting just the right amounts, and in the cooking, because the crunchier the potatoes the more cheerful the family gathered round the table.

624.23.1
Potatoes

> If all the verbs beginning with the letter *a* in *L'Officiel du jeu Scrabble®* and in Bescherelle's *L'Art de conjuguer* are recognized as being part of the French language, a study of other dictionaries and lexicons of the French language would certainly increase the total beyond 557.

625.21.4
More or Less
Useful Details

At the grocery store, Terry would not buy just any sack of potatoes.

"No, we don't want dose in de plastic bags. Has to be in a paper bag. An' it's best if der's a little window so's we can see if de potatoes're good-lookin' or not."

Étienne gave his father a questioning look. Good-looking? Potatoes?

"Potato has to be hard, doesn't it, an' we don't want a wrinkled peel. Look, stick yer finger in de hole here..."

Étienne plunged his finger into the netting of the bag.

"Alright den, now press down on de potato. Is she soft?"

Étienne gave Terry a noncommittal shake of his head. He didn't know.

"Hold on a second."

Terry tested the potato himself.

"Not bad. We don't want nuttin' growing on de spuds neider. You know, dose white stalks dat come up sometimes?"

Étienne nodded yes.

"Dose're called sprouts. See here, der's none. Dat's good."

Terry motioned Étienne to touch the eye of a spud.

"See. Now dat's a potato eye. Dat's where de sprouts grow out of. Well, here der's none. Alright den, so dese're de ones we'll take."

626.23.2
Potatoes

> Length of thread, temporary knots and interstitches. The ideal length of thread is 45 centimetres. Temporary knots and interstitches to begin, fasten or finish a length of thread. Avoid spaces longer than 1.25 centimetres. On a frame, stitch from top to bottom. The frame and practice will ensure a uniform tautness of stitches. Various ways of holding on to lengths of thread of different colours.

627.71.7
Intro
Embroidery

Even though he expected to get her answering machine, Zed was happy to have a reason to call Élizabeth.

"Hello?"

"Élizabeth Thomas?"

"Yes..."

"It's Zed, de lofts. You came by de udder day..."

"Yes..."

"I fergot to ask you when you came... Well, der's different size lofts, an' I's wonderin' if you were lookin' fer sometin' big, or sometin' not so big..."

Zed hated the way he kept switching from the formal *vous* to the familiar *tu* when he addressed her.

"Oh, of course. Well, let me think... Are the small ones very small?"

"Dat depends, I suppose. Even de small ones' aren't all de same size."

...

"I've got one of de smallest meself, an' I like it fine. Only, I live alone, so..."

...

"All depends how a body fixes it up, I suppose."

"And the big ones?"

"On account of I tink der's one—a small one, mind you—dat could be comin' free afore too long. Most likely it'll be up fer rent at first. De boy wants to move out to Montréal, only ee's not too sure, not sure ee'll be stayin' over der. It's only my opinion, now, but I'd say de boy won't be comin' back dis way."

"Yes, I see."

"If you want to come by again, I could show you my own loft, just so's you can get an idea of de size. I can't be havin' you visit de fellow's on account of ee's not yet made up 'is mind, officially I mean."

By now the informal *tu* had prevailed.

"Yes, okay. Can I come by today?"

"Dat'd be perfect, sure. I expect I'll be around all day."

"Would this afternoon around three o'clock work?"

"Dat's just fine. I'll be in de office most likely."

"Great. I'll see you later." 628.43.9

"Alright, den. We'll see each udder dis afternoon." Love

> Prince Edward Island is number one in Canada when it comes to farming potatoes. More than 43,000 hectares of potatoes are planted there every year, compared to 31,000 in Manitoba, which is second. New Brunswick and Alberta share third place with approximately 24,000 hectares each, followed by Québec with 19,000 hectares, Ontario with 18,000 hectares, Saskatchewan with 5,000 hectares, British Columbia with less than 4,000 hectares, Nova Scotia with 2,000 hectares, and Newfoundland
> and Labrador with 255 hectares.

629.3.12 Statistics

Over time, with a word here and there, Le Grand Étienne had raised it with Ludmilla, who eventually spoke to Terry.

"You understand, it would mean a great deal to him. He'd be honoured, as would I, naturally."

Terry couldn't believe it: the great Zablonski and Ludmilla, godfather and godmother of his son!

"But we don't want Marianne to feel left out. Maybe it's too delicate..."

Terry was thinking how Marianne might take it; he wasn't sure.

"Unless you have other objections. It was just an idea, really; it may not suit you at all."

Terry sought to reassure her.

"Naw, it's a right nice idea. I'm pretty sure Étienne would be wonderful proud himself. I'll talk it over wid Carmen soon as I get de chance. Only dis evening she's workin'. "

630.44.1 Godfathers and Godmothers

"Of course."

Blissful Orange. Apples and oranges. Spanish oranges, Moroccan oranges. The House of Orange. Versailles Orangerie, Musée de l'Orangerie. "You can't eat an orange and then throw away the peel — a man is not a piece of fruit" — Arthur Miller. Halloween.

631.83.6 Bliss and Colours

"Already, no more tootpaste? Wot's goin' on in dis house? Are ya all eatin' it or wot?"

Marianne started laughing. Terry continued:

"I sure hope not, mind ya. It's not good to be swallyin' tootpaste."

"On account of?"

More and more, Étienne wanted to know the why of things.

"On account of it's no good fer us."

"But we puts it in our mouths..."

Terry understood the paradox that Étienne had grasped, especially since children were already being repeatedly warned about not putting things in their mouths.

"It's not bad for yer mout', only for yer stomach."

"Wot does it do, den?"

"Don't know fer sure, dey only tell us not to swally it."

...

"Yer stomach's made to swally food. Tootpaste, well, ya can't call dat food, now can ya?"

"Toot-pays, toot-pays..."

Marianne loved to sing her little tunes.

"It's not so bad if we swally a wee bit now an' den. I mean, when yer after brushin' yer teet', hard not to. Even if we rinses out our mout' an' all."

...

Judging by Étienne's silence, Terry suspected that the boy had not been paying a lot of attention to rinsing after brushing.

"Eh? Dat's why we rinse our mout' when we're done

brushin', instead of just swallyin' it all."

Terry followed this advice with a demonstration, took a mouthful of water, sloshed it all around in his mouth and spit it out.

"An' der she goes, dat's how."

Étienne nodded, and proceeded to brush his teeth, to rinse and spit exactly as his father had done.

"Hurrah! Dat's de way!"

Marianne's apprenticeship would take a little longer. She brushed in all directions, and she had not realized that one should spit down rather than straight ahead, but the basic idea had been grasped. 632.126.11

"Dat's good, Marianne. Yer gettin' der..." Techniques

> To confess then: since the beginning of time, the numeral 7 has, in a million different ways, symbolized plenitude, perfection, totality. What's more, the 7 is more universally symbolic in this sense than the numeral 12. There it is. I've said it. Those who are curious can consult *The Penguin Dictionary of Symbols* by Chevalier and Gheerbrant to learn how the 7 is omnipresent in almost all cultures in the world 633.70.6
> (the Chinese culture not so much). Errors

"Imagine dat, can ya? Zablonski, Étienne's godfawder?"

Carmen also found it touching, even a little bit exhilarating, that Étienne Zablonski and Ludmilla would offer themselves as godfather and mother of her and Terry's son.

"An' wot about Marianne, den? Are ya tinkin' she might be boddered?"

"We only have to find her a godfawder and mudder of her own."

"Are you tinkin' of someone in particular, den?"

"Far as I'm concerned, I wouldn't mind Zed bein' her godfawder. Godmudder, I don't know. Josse maybe?"

"Ya, Zed fer sure."

...

"Would it have to be a real baptism d'ya tink? De whole religious hulabaloo?"

Neither of them were jumping for joy at the prospect.

"Why not have a wee ceremony right 'ere? Have a bit of a soiree to make it official..."

The idea appealed to both of them as simple and sensible.

"Geez, it's like excitin'! When're we gonna tell 'em then?"

634.44.2 Godfathers and Godmothers

Terry sensed that Carmen would not be able to restrain herself for long.

635.70.7 Errors

> Since an acknowledged error has a chance of being forgiven, and every day's a new day, this book will continue to adhere to its original premise, which is not totally unfounded.

"Étienne, Marianne, come 'ere a minute!"

The two children arrived bursting with energy, almost overexcited, poking and tickling one another. Carmen wondered if this might not be the best time to raise what was a more or less serious matter.

"Sit yerselves down now, we want to explain sometin' to ya."

Étienne tickled Marianne one last time and the two children calmed down. Carmen nodded at Terry to begin.

"Carmen an' me, we tink it'd be a proper ting fer you boat to have a godfawder an' godmudder."

Immediatly Étienne leapt with joy:

"Yaay!"

Marianne, too, rejoiced, but without really knowing why. Mainly for her benefit, Terry added:

"A godfawder or godmudder is someone who cares for you in a special way."

Étienne nodded. Marianne clearly needed more.

"Well, like, from time to time, a godfawder or godmudder can take you some place special, or invite you over to der place. Sometimes, say you've a problem, der always der to help you out, or give you a present, when it's yer birthday. Tings like dat."

Étienne felt that this description corresponded more or less to his expectations. Marianne, for whom this was all new, was beginning to see the value of the idea. Carmen, for her part, impressed with the simplicity with which Terry was presenting the affair, allowed him to continue:

"Well, den, wot do you tink?"

"Yeeess! I want it!" 636.44.3

Marianne imitated her brother. Godfathers and

"Yeeess! Godmothers

> Blissful pink. Pink pom-poms, pom-pom pink. Candy pink, pink candy. Pale pink, misty pink, baby pink. Red rose, white rose, yellow rose. Rosehip tea, pale pinkish yellow. Pink flamingo, pink shrimp, pink radish. Rose tinged white. Rose jam. Rosewater. Shocking pink. When things are not so rosy, life is no bed of roses. Pink wave, salmon pink. Rosewood sweater. Pink phone. Pink male. Everything's coming 637.83.11
> up roses. See the world through rose-coloured Bliss and
> glasses. Colours

That evening, Terry was helping Marianne put on her pyjamas:

"I'm sure Josse would be tickled to be yer godmudder."

Marianne shook her head no.

"Auntie Louise, as well. Auntie Louise'd be right proud to be yer godmudder."

Again, Marianne shook her head no.

"I know! Antoinette! You know how she's all de time

sayin' she'd like to gobble you up! Dat means she loves you a whole bunch."

Terry pretended to eat Marianne's belly, which made her laugh as always, but in the end she also rejected this last suggestion.

"Really, I tink all de folks dat knows you would want to be yer godmudder!"

Marianne shook her head again.

"Alright den, when youse tawt of somebody you let us know, okay?"

638.44.4 Godfathers and Godmothers

Marianne nodded yes. Then, as though she wanted to move on to something else, she fetched Pickles, her choice of stuffed toy to take to bed that night.

> **SPIRAVALANCH:** n. — 2005/2013. 1. Violent crisis resulting from an escalation of incidents operating in a chain reaction. "Nothing was going right, he feared a spiravalanche." (Daigle/Majzels) 2. TEXTILE Splash pattern. "She never drew those spiravalanche patterned drapes from behind the panels that concealed them." (Daigle/Majzels).

639.120.9 Fictionary

"Tonight I'll be tellin' you de troo story of de deer called Zoo of Magnetic Hill. For a whole lot o' years, de government had been promisin' to widen de highway between Moncton an' Frederiction, so dat finally dey really had to do it, an' from dat day forward, life fer all de deer of New Brunswick was forever changed. On account of, do you want to know? On account of dem dat was building de highway went an' put up a wing fence on bot' sides o' de road to keep de animals from causin' accidents. Now, all de animals like to cross de highway from time to time, only when a big creature like a deer — a moose is a whole lot worse! — or a bear! Grrrrr... — wot was I sayin'? Aw yeah... — when one o' dem big creatures like a deer or a moose or a bear comes across an' right out in front of a car, well, dat can cause one terrible serious accident. Well, while dat road's gettin' built, instead of doin' like his dad an' readin' the signs to find out wot's goin' on around 'im, dat Zoo deer goes strollin' along eatin' grass and twigs in de ditch down de middle of de road, on account of ee likes de taste of salt an' dat ditch is full of de old salt from last winter. So, one time, when ee's done eatin' his supper, Zoo deer decides to take a wee bit of a walk to help wid 'is digestion an' to take in de air before ee goes back into de woods. Well, dat's when ee sees de fence. At first, Zoo didn't tink nothin' of it, ee just walked along in de trees between de two strips of highway, lookin' fer a break to get back off de road. So, der ee goes, ee's walkin' an' walkin' an' walkin' an walkin', all day long an' all night, on account of de fence just keeps on an' on an on'. Day time, ee had to be real careful, on account of der's places de trees thin out an' den it's de open field, an' dat's when anybody could spot 'im. Zoo was no different from any udder deer: ee didn't much like folks to see 'im. Only time ee didn't mind bein' seen was in de early mornin' and at supper time, in udder words, when ee's eatin'. So, sometimes, ee hides out all day in a small thicket o' trees, just waitin' till it's dark to cross over de field and keep goin' on 'is way. An' dat's how Zoo deer ended up goin' all de way up to Moncton, where some zookeepers from de Magnetic Hill Zoo caught 'im wid a big fishin' net. De moral o' dis 'ere story? Even doh yer not supposed to do it, der's times it can come in handy knowin' how to climb over a fence.

640.37.2
Animal Tales

L'Officiel du jeu Scrabble® and *Bescherelle's Art de conjuguer* open the door a crack to words coming from French-speaking countries other than France. Still limiting ourselves to verbs beginning with the letter *a*, *L'Officiel...* does make room for the Swiss French words *agender, aguiller, apigeonner, appondre,* and *azorer,*

> and for the Québécois words *abrier, achaler, aplomber,* and *(s')attriquer*. There are neither African nor Belgian French words in this group. The *Bescherelle*, on the other hand, does include the African French words *abomber, absenter* (non-reflexive form), *ambiancer, (s') ambifier, amourer,* and *apatamer*; the Belgian words *(s')adire* and *aminer*; and the Québécois
> 641.20.11 verbs *achaler* and *aplomber*, but no Swiss
> Language French terms.

Josse dreams that she's shunning her sister, who's insulted her. Convinced that her sister ought to know better than to denigrate Josse's wardrobe, Josse decides neither to listen nor to speak to her. Her sister doesn't understand what's gotten into Josse, claims she's done nothing wrong, nothing serious anyway. But Josse is determined. She'd like never to speak to that sister again,
642.109.6 and wonders what to do to make her sister no longer her
Dreams sister.

> Dine on ashes. Swallow your pride. Sell your work for peanuts. Chew the fat. Publish a lemon. Ham it up. Jam tomorrow. Walk on eggshells. Go pound salt. In a pickle. Bite your
> 643.98.1 tongue. Thinks he's a big cheese. About as use-
> Expressions ful as a chocolate teapot.

Étienne had happily accepted the Zablonski's as his godfather and godmother to be. He already knew the story of Terry and Carmen's trip to France, where they'd met Le Grand Étienne and travelled by train with him. Carmen had even shown him the diamond pin as proof.

"Real ones like in *Ali Baba*?"

Étienne had only recently been introduced to the famous "Open Sesame!" and was greatly impressed by it.

"Just like in *Ali Baba*."

The little boy studied the jewel more closely. 644.44.6 Godfathers and Godmothers

> Obviously, it would be dishonest to add a book one had not read to one's *Bibliothèque idéale*. Because a title sometimes promises more than it delivers, and because the imagined content of a book may be far more enjoyable than its actual content. 645.95.5 Additions to *La Bibliothèque idéale*

The children also enjoyed *les patates à Rose-Marie*, roasted Rosemary potatoes, with rosemary and cumin. Terry cut five or six large unpeeled potatoes into about ten pieces each, rolled these in olive oil and seasoning before roasting them in the oven. He was especially proud of having accustomed the children to eat this dish with tzatziki rather than ketchup.

"Dad, can we 'ave de white ketchup wid it?"

"De tzatziki, you mean? Der's no more."

Étienne looked totally dejected.

"We'll eat dem just as dey are, widout anyting. Der good dis way, too."

Étienne was not convinced. Terry added:

"Dat's de way you were eatin' dem before, widout anytin.'"

Étienne could not remember a before, but hearing his father refer to it like this was somehow comforting. 646.23.3 Potatoes

> For more on Terry and Carmen's first meeting with the painter Étienne Zablonski, see Daigle's *A Fine Passage* (House of Anansi, 2002). 647.54.2 Forgotten/Recalled

"Der are about sixty golf courses in New Brunswick. Dat's about one golf course fer every 12,000 people."

. . .

"In France, dey gots one fer every 120,000 people, more or less.

. . .

648.59.1 Knowledge “I’m just lettin’ you know, in case de question pops up some time.”

> Among the words beginning with the letter *a*, *L’Officiel du jeu Scrabble®* includes a handful of Swiss and Québécois French words that are not verbs, but no African French. The Québec French words are: *acéricole* (relating to the maple syrup industry), *achalant* (annoying), *adon* (a happy coincidence), *aérobique* (aerobic), *aluminerie* (aluminium factory), *aréna* (arena), *atoca* and *ataca*, *atocatier*, (cranberry and cranberry bush), *auteure* (female author), and *avionnerie* (airplane factory). Also, contrary
> 649.19.7 Interesting Details to the *Grand Robert* dictionary, for example, *L’Officiel*... does not object to the word *aréna* being masculine or feminine.

Hans ate without pausing, barely glancing up at me. Clearly he hadn’t eaten in a while. Although, admittedly, the dissection of the half-chicken on his plate required a degree of concentration.

“It’s perfectly all right to eat this sort of chicken with your fingers.”

I only said it to make his task a little easier, but he soldiered on with knife and fork, somewhat clumsily, as though he’d forgotten how to use such instruments.

“How did you manage to get into Canada?”

My question remained unanswered. I concluded that it was not yet time to talk, which I didn’t really mind since I was still trying to find a gentle way to say what I had to tell him. After a while, I simply came out with it:

“You know I can’t bring you to Moncton.”

His hands froze for a moment, then he nodded quickly and went back to dissecting the chicken in his plate. I couldn’t help thinking he looked like an idiot.

“I’m not an idiot. If I’d wanted to go to Moncton, I

would have gone to Moncton."

Briefly, I wondered if this one hadn't somehow escaped my grasp. Which would have been perfectly normal, since I had created him for precisely that purpose: to escape.

"I don't understand why you would even think I'd want to go there."

Fine. But did he realize the constant effort I had to make just to maintain a semblance of unity in my universe, and consequently, how I fretted over every lost sheep?

"And what's Élizabeth up to? How's she doing?"

I figured his hunger was perhaps abating just a little.

"Pretty well, yes."

I didn't have the heart to tell him that I'd put her aside, somewhat. Or, at least, seriously transformed her. I didn't want him to think that… Might as well admit it, I didn't want him to think at all. But he saw right through me.

"I'm not like your other characters, am I? You made me free so that you could more easily be rid of me. That's it isn't it? Don't answer that, answers are always bad on Fridays. Fridays we're on the defensive."

Was he making fun of me or did he really believe this?

"You're not going to eat your soup?"

Without giving me the time to reply, he took the bowl I'd put aside. I felt obliged to offer it to him.

"No, no. Go ahead."

He ate all my soup without pausing to say a word. Which gave me time to think. Again I was determined to be frank.

"Look, Hans, I still need you to be totally free."

He looked at me, maybe gauging my sincerity, and
then answered without rancour: 650.101.8
"Agreed." Duos

For a number of reasons, among which the desire to be entirely honest and transparent in

> attempting not to sweep the error under the rug, here are some additional considerations on the subject of the number 7: Buddha's stairway contains seven colours; that is, the six colours of the rainbow and their synthesis, white. The colours of the seven subtle forms of divine
>
> 651.70.9 Errors
>
> physiology are matte black, blue, red, white, yellow, glossy black, and green.

Marianne's reaction to the Godfather and Godmother project was more difficult to decipher than Étienne's.

"Could be I oughtn't to have mentioned it'd be de godfawder and godmudder who'd be carin' fer 'er if sometin' was to happen to us."

"No, I tink she figures it's up to 'er to choose is all."

...

...

"I just hope I didn't go an' frighten' de poor ting wid all dat."

652.44.5 Godfathers and Godmothers

And with those words, Terry got up.

"I'll take a look an' see if she's sleepin.'"

653.35.6 The Detail within the Detail

> There is also a particular way to read numerals. For example the telephone number 383-8383 is a pivoting palindromic number.

"Sounds quite lovely, no?"

"Yes..."

Of course, Brigitte can hear the hesitation at the other end of the line.

"They sound like really interesting people. I don't see what the problem is."

Élizabeth hasn't had the courage to tell her Zed's age.

"You're right. I don't know what I'm worrying about. An old reflex, I suppose."

"Listen, we should get together soon. I'll try to come over. It would give me a chance to see Acadia."

"Splendid idea! 654.49.4 Élizabeth II

> An expression he heard once that's bothered Terry ever since: the death seat, referring to the passenger's seat next to the driver, which is considered dangerous. It's especially troublesome when Carmen takes that seat. Hoping to forestall bad luck, he's decided not to mention it to her. 655.60.2 Superstitions

"Like Salmon Rushdie, who's hidin' on account of de fatwa."

"On account of wot?"

"De fat-wa. Like in fat-wot of good dat'll do me."

. . .

. . .

"Yer hung up sometin' rare on Rushdie all de same, eh?"

. . .

"I tawt 'is name was Salman like m-a-n, not Salmon like de fish."

"I knows it, only I likes de idea of salmon: Salmon-rush-die. It's like de salmon is hurryin' up de river to die." 656.88.6 Freedom

"Geez, yer a gloomy boy dis mornin'."

> Gather, over the years, all the books listed in *La Bibliothèque idéale* and open a café where it would be pleasant to sit and get to know them. 657.68.3 Projects

Terry showed the children how to suck the juice of the shrimp while you pull it out of its shell.

"If you hold de wee tail proper, de shell comes off all by 'erself. See..."

Terry demonstrated, exaggerating the technique just a bit, so the two little ones could see how it was done.

"An' den you trow de empty shell in dis 'ere bag."

Sitting at the water's edge at Pointe-Rocheuse, both

parents and children ate a while without talking. Marianne managed as well as anyone.

"So you like it, den?"

Without interrupting their labours, Étienne and
658.140.7 Caraquet Marianne nodded their heads. Terry and Carmen smiled
to see them so absorbed in the process.

> In *1953: Chronicle of a Birth Foretold*, Acadian novelist France Daigle does not mention the publication that year by the prestigious firm Éditions de Minuit of Alain Robbe-Grillet's
> 659.45.10 Useless Details novel *The Erasers*. This publication marked a
> major shift in the editorial policy of the firm.

The project quickly became an excursion for men and boys only. Terry had gone to fetch Chico the day before, just to give the boys some play time to get to know each other before being put to work.

"I'm gonna sit in de back wid Étienne an' Chico."

Pomme joined the two boys on the rear seat of the van. Étienne and Chico made room for the arms and hands dangling a pair of old torn sneakers, followed by the dishevelled hair, long body and bare feet of Pomme.

"Alright den, boys?"

Étienne and Chico acquiesced.

"Shall I get in front?"

This was Zablonski, who had arrived. Only Zed was missing, and he was not usually the type to be late.
660.40.1 Clear your Coast Checking the sun and his watch, Terry felt they were in
for a fine day.

"Stick o' gum, anyone?"

> An entrée in *Le Nouveau Petit Robert* dictio-
> 661.78.3 Accidents nary states that an accident is what is added to
> an essence.

"Do they do this every year?"

"Dey bin doin' it for a long time now, only 'twasn't official like 'tis now, wid ads in de papers an' all."

Terry and Zablonski were chatting quietly in front. Behind them, Zed was encouraging Étienne and Chico to tickle Pomme, who was sleeping, or pretending.

"It's a great idea to involve everyone this way."

"Fer sure. Der shocking organised. An' der's lots more folks comin' to help dese days, 'specially since dey added de treasure hunt at de end."

"Ah, the combination of business and pleasure, always an excellent policy."

Terry glanced in the rear-view mirror, and was reassured to see Chico happily conspiring with Étienne and Zed. 662.40.2 Clear Your Coast

> True or False: to take holy orders so as to flee
> the aleatory, precarious, disorderly

663.116.5 True or False

At the entrance to the village, a large multicoloured canopy had been erected to serve as a reception. Everyone piled out of the van to go over and see what was up. Point by point they were talked through the day's activities, and where to find the rest areas, drinks and snacks, and childcare. They were also told the plan for the big treasure hunt. Finally, they were assigned a work zone, and checked to be sure they were properly equipped for the cleanup.

"All de same, it's awful nice of dem to pay our lunch."

"I heard a lady say all de take-outs got togeder. Dat's right smart." 664.40.3 Clear Your Coast

"Wonder if we'll be gettin' some fried clams..."

> In their late fifties, Sylvia and her husband Lionel Arsenault first appeared in *Life's Little Difficulties* (Daigle, House of Anansi, 2004). A brilliant and generous businessman, Lionel Arsenault played an ingenious part in the

> success of the lofts. The childless couple owns a
> 665.54.5 Forgotten/Recalled large modern house overlooking Shediac Bay, but regularly stays over at their small loft in Moncton.

At first, the crossword puzzles were something Carmen worked on from time to time, when she had a spare moment or just to clear her head. Since she's not a slacker and appreciated by her coworkers, and also because she's a co-owner of the business, no one complained at her combining a bit of recreation with her work.

"'Tisn't like she goes an' does it under our noses when der's work to be done, now is it? Den' fer sure I'd be sayin' sometin' to 'er."

666.51.1 Crosswords "An' wot would you be sayin', I'd like to know? She's de boss, she can do wot she pleases."

> The magic password "Open Sesame!" comes from the fact that sesame seeds are enclosed
> 667.58.3 Extensions in cloves that burst open by themselves when they are ripe.

Having been assigned a field and a small copse between the road and the shore, the group of six decided to divide the area into three sections and to work in pairs. Zablonski turned quite naturally to his future godson:

"Shall we get to work?"

Even though they spent lots of time together, Le Petit Étienne was happy to team up with his godfather to be.

"How's about ya come along wid me, den?"

Zed had turned just as naturally to Chico, who was quick to step up alongside his teammate.

"Well, I suppose dat don't leave me a whole lot of choice. I'm stuck wid Pomme."

668.40.4 Clear Your Coast Since everyone knew that Terry and Pomme got along just fine, no one pitied anyone.

> A horseshoe nailed above a door points upwards so that its branches can capture celestial energy. 669.60.10 Superstitions

Zed and Chico had chosen to clean up the shoreline next to the abandoned pier without realizing the area had served as a dumping ground.

"We better keep our sneakers on so's not to get cut. Does ya tink yer granny'll mind?"

Shaking his head, Chico moved forward a few steps. The sea bed was littered with rusty cans and other undefinable detritus.

"Yuck! Good ting dey gave us gloves to wear!"

Zed had plunged his arm into the water and pulled out a torn plastic bag, which was dripping a suspicious substance back into the water. A gooey, disintegrating diaper? He quickly shoved the whole thing into the plastified mesh sack he was carrying.

"We won't be needin' to walk far to fill our sacs, dat's fer sure."

Chico silently began to pick up garbage without grimacing.

"Is dat yer baydin' suit den?"

Zed was pointing at Chico's shorts.

Chico nodded.

"Good ting! Later on when she gets hotter, we'll go in swimmin'. Der's some nice sand over dat way."

Chico smiled.

"Does ya come often to the shore?" 670.40.5 Clear Your Coast

Chico shook his head no.

> Sudden anxiety that the cube might be an old, outdated concept. 671.104.1 Worries

The thin puzzle book was kept in a specific place, in the space between the big refrigerator and the wine cupboard, on a wooden shelf too narrow to serve as anything else.

"I can't tell ya why dey put up dis 'ere shelf. I never seen a cupboard like dis anywhere."

"Must be sometin' to do wid de fridge."

The waiter, who had become more aware of such details since he'd started a course in woodwork, did not find Josse's explanation particularly helpful.

"Could be. Only 'tis still an incongruity."

"A wot?"

672.51.2 "An in-con-gru-i-ty. A *fluke*."

Crosswords "Awh."

> The 58 books the two ideal libraries have in common were written or edited by 55 authors. This difference results from the fact that two books each by Aron, Duby, Durkheim, Foucault and Lévi-Strauss were included, whereas Bourdieu and Passeron co-authored
> 673.61.10 a single book, as did Laplanche and Pontalis.
> Social Sciences Almost a useless detail.

Pomme picked up a beer bottle and tossed it gently onto the side of the road.

"Didn't tink der was still so many folks tossin' der bottles in de ditch."

...

"All dese recyclables 'ere, least ways, dey'll make a bit o' money."

...

...

...

"I'd o' known I's goin' to land up in de canal, I'd o' worn me boots."

"You knows yerself."

Pomme pulled on a wire rod, and the skeleton of an umbrella came up after it.

"Must blow sometin' fierce in dese parts..."

He picked up a piece of asphalt sheeting.

"Luh! Der's even roofin' down in 'ere."

Terry thought Pomme was talking a lot.

"Now, take a look at dis! An egg whisk! Probably flew off some tourist's car."

674.40.6
Clear Your
Coast

. . .

"Do you eat a lot o' eggs, yerself?"

> Blissful black. Jet black, ink black, coal black, black ebony. Black cat, black ant, *bête noire*. Black tie, black jacket. Black painting. Black sheep. Black hole. The Black experience, African American neighbourhood, bebop. Black and blue. Black swan. Black bread. Blackened fish, black-eyed peas, black coffee. Black mark. Black out, black eye. Black Friday. Blaggard, black mass, black magic. Blacklisted. Black market, in the black, blackjack. Blackball. Film noir. Black dog, "Paint It Black."

675.83.9
Bliss and
Colours

Zablonski and Le Petit Étienne were working the edge of the woods.

"I think there's a path in here. You see, between the trees?"

Étienne saw the pale and sinuous line his future godfather was pointing to.

"All it would take would be a bit of cleaning, cutting a few branches and to take out that old tree trunk..."

Zablonski looked around.

"That might be the best thing to do, since there isn't a great deal of garbage to pick up."

Étienne agreed.

676.40.7
Clear Your
Coast

"Here, let's begin with this one. Can you take hold of one end?"

> (Take two.) It's not without value to examine the results of a simple statistical analysis of the first letter in the names of the 550 authors

or so in “La Bibliothèque idéale des sciences humaines.” Once again, the first letters of the alphabet account for the most writers, particularly the *b, c,* and *d.* These three letters alone account for 29 percent—might as well say a third—of the authors of the recommended titles. The *l* also makes a good showing, as do the
677.61.12 *s* and *m*, but the *a* and *p* are somewhat disap-
Social Sciences pointing. A statistician’s emotion.

678.82.6 “Big wow! I mean, wer’s de wisdom in dat?”
Moncton

Lacan makes the distinction between the other, lower-case italicized *a* (for French *autre),* and the Other, upper-case *A* (for French *Autre*). The Other designates everything that does not resemble the self, everything that is constituted as different from the self. Furthermore, the Other is not strictly confined to one or more people; it is no more no less than the inaccessible *thing*, which incites desire but never satiates
679.138.3 it. And out of this unsatiated desire emerges
The Other speech.

Called away to some more urgent task, Carmen would leave the crossword she was working on for anyone to see. Either because they had nothing better to do, or out of simple curiosity, her employees would occasionally take a look. At first, when they thought they’d found the
680.51.4 right word, they would tell Carmen, who gladly filled in
Crosswords the blanks.

In the case of the the haiku, tanka, and cinquain, all short forms derived from Japanese poetic traditions, the following equations apply. First, the haiku, which contains 17 syllables divided into lines of 5, 7, and 5 syllables:

5 + 7 + 5 = 17
(5 + 7) + 5 = (1 + 7)
12 + 5 = 8
(1 + 2) + 5 = 8
3 + 5 = 8
8 = 8

The tanka, for its part, contains 31 syllables divided into lines of 5, 7, 5, 7, and 7 syllables:

5 + 7 + 5 + 7 + 7 = 31
(5 + 7) + 5 + 7 + 7 = (3 + 1)
12 + 5 + 7 + 7 = 4
(1 + 2) + 5 + 7 + 7 = 4
{(3) + 5} + 7 + 7 = 4
8 + 7 + 7 = 4
(8 + 7) + 7 = 4
15 + 7 = 4
(1 + 5) + 7 = 4
6 + 7 = 4
13 = 4
(1 + 3) = 4
4 = 4

Finally, the cinquain comprises 22 syllables divided into lines of 2, 4, 6, 8, and 2 syllables :

2 + 4 + 6 + 8 + 2 = 22
(2 + 4) + 6 + 8 + 2 = (2+2)
{(6) + 6} + 8 + 2 = (4)
12 + 8 + 2 = 4
(1 + 2) + 8 + 2 = 4
{(3) + 8} + 2 = 4
11 + 2 = 4
(1 + 1) + 2 = 4
2 + 2 = 4
4 = 4

681.97.9
Numerals and Numbers

"Hey!"

Terry expected Pomme to announce the discovery of another peculiar object in the ditch.

"I've asked Lisa to marry me!"

"'Bout time! So, tings're goin' well between de two of ya. Dat's shockin' great news!"

"Well, I tink so, anyways. An' she's me first girlfriend, so I can't really compare now can I? Tell de troot, de only folks I can be comparin' us to is you an' Carmen."

Terry was engaged in a tug of war with a long curved steel cable that refused to bend in a new direction.

"See dis 'ere ting? Der's times, wid Carmen an' me, it's pretty much de same."

"You mean tings bounce?"

. . .

"Eh? Does ya mean sometimes it bounces?"

682.40.8 Clear Your Coast

But standing now on the cable, Terry was too engrossed in trying to master it to hear Pomme's question.

683.138.4 The Other

> The Other — capital *A* for *Autre* — is therefore nothing less than the origin of speech. It is also, by that very fact, the main protagonist of literature. Hence the close relationship between psychoanalysis, literature, and writing.

Occasionally, Carmen herself would consult her colleagues. At first, they were rarely able to help, but gradually the employees began to take an interest in the puzzles. So that when, out of the blue, she called out a clue, often someone might suggest an answer.

684.51.5 Crosswords

"Nest of birds of prey...

"Plate?"

> True or false: the list (in parentheses) of names of survivors of the deceased Octave Vienneau (Arthance, Cléophas, Félendé, Hilarion, Irénée, Majella, and Vénérante) clearly

indicates that the deceased had four brothers and three sisters. 685.116.2 True or False

Zed and Chico had been working for some time now.

"Has it bin a while since you seen yer dad, den?"

Chico looked at Zed without responding, because he did not know how to measure a long time in this case.

"Like, did ya see 'im at Easter?"

Chico shook his head no.

"Awh well, dat's a good while den..."

Chico registered this as information.

"An, how are tings at school? Dey don't bodder you wid it I hope..."

"No."

"Does it bodder you me talkin' 'bout it?"

Chico replied without hesitation:

"No."

"On account of I'd understand if it did, bodder ya, I mean..."

Chico repeated his answer, but with a slight difference in tone, that fraction of a second it takes to confirm something within yourself.

"No..."

Zed picked up his sack:

"Me sacks pretty well full. Yer's too, looks like, eh?"

Chico nodded.

"Aren't you a hard worker!"

This made Chico feel like laughing:

"Dat's wot Mister Louis says, as well."

"Is dat somebody at school, den?"

"He drives de bus."

Zed looked out at the sea stretched out before them:

"I'll tell ya, I wouldn't mind drivin' out der meself some time. Do ya think ya might want to come along?"

Chico understood that Zed was talking about the place where his father was imprisoned.

"Okay."

"Does you tink yer granny would be wantin' to come as well?"

Chico didn't seem to think his grandmother would want to accompany them, but he did not explain why not. Zed let it go, let a moment pass.

686.40.9 Clear Your Coast

"How about we go in swimmin' den?"

687.95.6 Additions to *La Bibliothèque idéale*

> I'm hard pressed to think of even a dozen books to add to *La Bibliothèque idéale*. Such a sanctuary is not open to just anyone. The vast majority of the books I read will have to be content with a spot on the ordinary shelves of my library. Or those of the second-hand bookstore. Sorting.

As time passed, it happened more often that one or another employee would write the correct word in the blank space of an unfinished puzzle. So that gradually the crosswords became the collective pastime of the employees of the Babar.

"Those that prattle..."

Josse was looking over Vincent's shoulder.

"Prattlers."

Vincent entered the missing letters *p-r-a-t-e* and continued.

688.47.5 Yielding

"Aw geez, I hates dese clues, dey writes 'ch.-l. de l'arr. de...' fer *chef-lieu d'arrondissement*, an' we's supposed to know some county town in a district over in France!"

689.81.1 Titles

> First working title: *Up to the End*. In the context of a project description for a writing grant application to the New Brunswick Arts Board. Grant awarded, thank you very much.

Le Petit Étienne was happy to show his almost-godfather how hard he was willing to work.

"You're not tired? We can take a break if you like."

"No, I'm not tired."

Zablonski watched the little man toiling away for a moment. Then:

"Do you get along with Chico?"

Le petit Étienne shrugged.

"Don't know yet."

Zablonski regretted posing the question too soon, but the boy added:

"Ee's six years old."

"And you don't like the same games, is that it?"

"No. We like to play."

...

"Dis mornin' he got up afore me an' den ee went to lie down wid Mum an' Dad."

"Ohhh...that's a bit of a problem, isn't it?"

"Mum said it was on account of ee's missin' 'is dad and mum."

"Yes, that's very likely."

Le Petit Étienne shrugged his shoulders again. 690.40.10 Clear Your Coast

"All de same, ee's nice."

> The Other has no truck with the law of supply and demand. And neither does the writer. The writer does not think in terms of demand. Male or female, the writer thinks basically of survival. Writers therefore are limited to the supply side of the equation. Which may explain why, each new season, thousands of new books appear on the bookstore shelves, and that, for the most part, only a handful of these are actually sold. 691.138.5 The Other

Eventually, not just Carmen but any one of the Babar staff might take the initiative to start a puzzle. Each one wanted to see how many words they could find before calling for the others' help.

"Well! Are ya plannin' on doin' it all on yer own or wot?"

692.51.6 Crosswords "Might do. Dey appears to be gettin' easier all de time."

> Blissful brown. Brown chocolate. Brown Bear. Brown skin, chestnut-brown horse. Browning banana. Brown shirts, brown noser. Brunette.
> 693.83.10 Bliss and Colours Down a brown ale, brown-bagging. Brownie points. Do it up brown. Brown out.

The six pairs of arms Terry had recruited to participate in the "Clear Your Coast" campaign had worked tirelessly all morning.

"I'll tell ya wot I's wantin' fer lunch: I wants de fried clams an' a Pepsi."

"You got to pay de clams yerselves, der not included in de special, see. Wot's free is de hamburgers, hotdogs, and fries. An' sodas. Or juice, tea, coffee… all dat stuff."

Pomme would not surrender.

"Awh! Can't you spare just one, fer me…"

"Not up to me, is it? De headman's de one decides."

Pomme wracked his brain for something to convince the waitress.

"Last night, I asked me girl to marry me. Der's not a lot of folks dese days have de courage to go an' get married, on account of der's so many divorces."

The waitress couldn't help laughing at the young man's weak imitation of the anxious groom.

"An' all mornin', while I's workin' so hard, I's tinkin' how wonderful nice of youse to be feedin' us all, an' dose fried clams I's gonna eat fer dinner."

The waitress could see the waiting-line getting longer.

"Where's you from, den?"

"Moncton."

"Where's yer summer house, I mean…"

"Awh! We don't have a summer house. We only came to lend a hand."

The waitress eyed him, wondering if she ought to believe him.

"You don't have a summer place?"

"No, honest to god. Only, summer's we sometimes come up to swim at Caissie Cape."

The waitress looked him over again, thought he had a bit of the look of a rogue, but said quickly:

"Alright den, but mind you be sure to say you paid fer dem yerself."

Pomme agreed, thanked her and, to show his gratitude, added:

"If ever I divorce, I'll come back round 'ere lookin' fer ya."

The waitress gave him fair warning:

"Boy, I bin divorced two times, and I's not plannin' on goin' fer a tird go round. So, you enjoys dose clams and good luck to ya!"

694.40.11 Clear your Coast

> Second possible title — FD-ROM — based on a CD-ROM concept that occurred to me while on a writer's residence at the Université de Moncton. In French, we ought to call it DOC or *doc*, an acronym for "*disque optique compact*," rather than CD-ROM, which is the English acronym for "compact disc, read-only-memory," or "*cédérom*" as it's sometimes referred to. In any case, a pretentious title.

695.81.2 Titles

"In all of Canada der's maybe 2,000."

...

"Dat amounts to one course fer every 16,000 people or so. Still, compare dat to 120,000 people per course in France."

...

"Dat's near eight times more people per course. Imagine dat, if you can!"

...

"An' by now, der can't be all dat much room to be buildin' more, wot wid all de castles and vineyards an' dat over der. All de land must be taken up..."

696.59.3 Knowledge "I doesn't know do I. I never bin to France."
"Nor I. I just figure."

> Both psychoanalysis and literature rely on words in the hope of lifting the veil that masks the Other. Or veils rather, for an infinite number of veils mask the face of the Other. Faces
> 697.138.6 The Other rather, for the Other has an infinite number of faces.

Terry felt this outing offered an excellent opportunity for the boys to get to know the adult men in their lives.

"Pomme, don't take it hard, but I'm not workin' with you dis afternoon."

Pomme had no reason to doubt Terry's friendship.

"Good. I was just gonna tell ya de same ting."

Pomme's ready reply made Étienne and Chico laugh.

"Zed an' me's got a couple tings to jaw over…"

Zablonski thought it would be fine to team up with Chico and get to know him better. Pomme settled the issue by replying to Terry:

"Well den, I'm gonna work wid yer lad, an' I won't take no fer an answer. Give de boy a chance to see I'm not such a bad sort. On account of I don't know wot you tells 'im 'bout me when I'm not around."

698.40.12 Clear Your Coast Chico, busy eating his ketchup and fries, was listening to Terry and Pomme wrangling but not really.

> The Other is as evanescent and elusive as gas. And the writer, who has a good appetite and enjoys a hot meal, is constantly lighting the gas. Many writers heat with gas and some even work by gaslight. Although they are well aware of the dangers, writers will not hesitate to light the gas. Even a struggling writer doesn't need to think about it very much before lighting the gas. In fact, the struggling writer needs gas

> more than the writer in fine form. That's why neither a psychoanalyst nor a literary master would council a writer, even a struggling one, not to light the gas. The psychoanalyst and the master know that gas helps the writer navigate among the letters and phrases. On the other hand, letters and phrases sketch out the contours of the gas. Books are full of gas.

699.138.7
The Other

"Do you know where de idea of shoutin' out 'FORE' comes from?"

...

"Lots of folks tink it comes from 'forward' or 'forewarned', only de fact is, it comes from de forehead."

...

"On account of it's on der forehead most folks get whacked by de ball."

"G'wan, now yer pullin' me leg..."

"Serious! Bin proved an' all."

700.59.4
Knowledge

> White knight, black knight. White coal, black coal, blue coal. In black and white. Black chocolate, white chocolate. Black gold, green gold, red gold, white gold. Red shirts, brown shirts, black shirts. Black-jacket wasp, yellow jacket, red ant, blue bottle fly. Blond ale, blond tobacco, brown ale, brown tobacco. Red slip, pink slip, green card. Honeysuckle rose, green logo.

701.83.12
Bliss and
Colours

One day Josse arrived at the Babar excited and eager to share her discovery:

"Luh! De clues're over 'ere, in de first box, an' den you only 'ave to follow de arrow. Dat way, you doesn't have to be lookin' back 'n fort', and lookin' fer de right column. It's a whole lot more user friendly."

Josse let her co-workers examine the innovation.

"An' wer did you find dis, den?"

“At Georges-Dumont. In de wee store downstairs.”

“Who was ya goin’ to see over der?”

“Me granny had a stroke.”

“Is she gonna be alright, den?”

“Dey doesn’t know fer sure.”

702.51.8 “Hm! Dey calls dem arrow-word puzzles, *mots fléchés*
Crosswords in French!”

> Third irritant: overuse of the phrase “*la langue*
> 703.89.3 *de Molière*” in French and “the King’s English”
> Irritants in the other language.

Eventually, one of the staff brought in a crossword dictionary.

“Me aunty gave it to me. She says it’s good fer dose short bothersome words she don’t know or can’t remember.”

“Good! Dose names of towns in France is in der!”

“Dat’s ’er old copy. She didn’t know wot to do wid it.”

Carmen gladly accepted the book, but most of her
704.51.3 employees could not imagine consulting a dictionary for
Crosswords pleasure.

> The Other is understood to have existed since the word was spoken and the flesh was human. Might as well say since the beginning of time. Litterature and psychoanalysis sometimes give the impression they invented the Other, but the reverse is actually the case: the Other
> 705.138.8 spontaneously gave rise to both literature and
> The Other psychoanalysis.

Even Étienne was doing his part:

“An’ why not Monique? You like ’er hair...”

But Marianne knew the difference between a passing fancy and a life-long attachment.

“Jacinthe’d like to. She said so to Mum.”

As Marianne did not protest, Étienne took advantage

of what he felt was an opening to add:

"Dat's de troot. She said so to Mum de udder day. I 'eard 'er."

But Marianne seemed merely to be losing interest.

"Doesn't ya want to 'ave yer godmudder party?"

Oh yes, she certainly did.

"Well den, you'd best hurry up and find somebody…"

Marianne nodded yes to indicate that she was indeed hurrying.

"No, you're not hurryin' 'tall."

Marianne nodded yes again.

"No!"

…

"No!"

"Étienne, are you in de batroom? Let Marianne do 'er number two alone."

706.44.7
Godfathers and
Godmothers

> On second thought, for a book, the shelf in a second-hand bookstore is far better than the long-forgotten box in a basement, attic or shed. A book's sole reason for being is to be read; whether it's new or used is of no importance. Incidental detail.

707.128.8
Fervours

Josse's aunt's dictionary turned out to be more than useful for all sorts of words, not only those tough little ones. It quickly earned a place within easy reach under the counter, where it was later joined by a complete world atlas, a gift from Didot Books, where Babar employees had been popping in more and more often to consult it.

"An' wot is it yer lookin' for now?"

"*Arrose Romans.*"

"You mean *roman*, like a novel?"

Some time ago, Terry had learned that the word *arrose* referred to a river or waterway.

"But wid a *s* on de end."

"*Romans*. Naw, de first I ever heard de name of dat place."

The waitress Lydia was an expert at finding places in the atlas.

"*Romans-sur-Isère.* Must be it. Answer's *Isère.*"

Lydia had quickly shut the atlas and was almost at the door when Terry shouted:

"Hey! Where is dat *Isère* den?"

"In France."

Terry had suspected as much, but where in France?

"I gotta haul on out, I got no time to chat!"

"Wot? Has Carmen brought her whip out, den?"

But Lydia was already too far away to hear him, and
708.51.7 the door slammed shut on Terry's question.
Crosswords "Yoye!"

> To put it simply, the real is beyond reach. It's the bottom of a bottomless well. It's the chicken or the egg. It's the only egg we've got, and once dropped, it breaks. It lies there, a splatter on the floor, impossible to gather up. Such is the real. It escapes us, forces us to speak, to fall back on the symbolic and the imaginary. Someone lays an empty plate before us and says here, here's your egg. We have no choice but to believe it, to understand, and say thank you. Which explains why politeness is a virtue. And just as the real is the bottom of a bottomless well,
> 709.74.12 Hans is a character like the bottom of a bag
> Hans with a false bottom.

All that was missing was a good dictionary, a real one.

"Seems to me de Babar could afford it."

Carmen couldn't believe it: Josse talking about buying a dictionary!

"Was a fine idea you had, bringin' in dose crosswords."

Carmen did not want to take credit for something she didn't deserve.

"Well, I wasn't really tinkin' of it dat way…"

"Anyhow, I tink it brings us all together like, when we's workin'. Gives us sometin' to tink on aside from de job."

Jean-Pierre agreed:

"So more it was! It's like our ting. Our trademark."

"It's gotten so folks're bringin' dem in to us! Yesterday, Serge brought one in he picked up on Air France. Friggin' hard, you ask me." 710.51.9

"Awh ya? Where is it den?" Crosswords

snowflake on your cheek
a drop falls from the sky and 711.55.4
will go its own way Haikus

The integration of new employees was not always smooth.

"Me, I'd be puttin' it a wee bit higher."

"Naw, all de way up der, folks'd be bangin' der foreheads all day long."

"How about movin' er over dat way, den. Over der, she won't be in de way."

"Now we's de ones'll be slammin' into it when we'se turnin' de corner."

The carpenter had been kind enough to stop by the Babar along his way because he'd been told it was only a minor job ten minutes at most.

"I tawt you people knew wot youse wanted..."

"We know wot we wants, we just don't know where we wants it."

"I can see dat."

At last the new employees agreed on a spot to install the shelf that would henceforth hold all the reference books.

"Hey! We ought to put a couple of de crossword books up der fer de customers! It'd give folks sometin' to do while's dey's havin' a beer or a coffee. An dey can be usin' de dictionaries as well."

...

"Well, den. Wot do you tink?"

Two senior employees exchanged glances. Were they prepared to let the newcomers take over?

"Can't say really. We never done it before."

"Well... on account of why not?"

...

"Eh? Well, what do you tink?"

712.51.10 "Not sure meself. Does we have to go an' decide right
Crosswords now?"

> To leaf through a book in search of a passage that beautifully expressed something. When you first encountered it, you neglected to underline it, or scribble a note in the margin, or bend the corner of the page, so sure were you that you could never forget the source of such a brilliant thought. You can still see the exact placement of the passage on the page, you know it was the recto rather than the verso, or vice versa, and approximately where in the book the
> 713.103.6 passage is located. To search, and search, and
> Disappearances search again, but never to find it again.

A few days later, Terry and Carmen were also beginning to think that Marianne was taking an awfully long time to decide who she wanted to be her godmother.

"Really, it oughtn't it be 'er who decides. We were never de ones to choose"

"But we was just two weeks in de world, we wasn't two years old goin' on tree."

...

"An' havin' come dis far, 'twould be hard to force 'er to take someone."

714.44.8 ...
Godfathers and "Well? Wot do ya think?"
Godmothers Carmen was fast asleep.

In French, we say of a spoiled child who gets whatever he or she wants, *il fait la pluie et le beau temps*—he or she can make it rain or shine. The lexicologist Robert defines the expression more kindly as simply meaning someone who has great influence. But, as Melchior Mbonimpa explains in *Le dernier roi faiseur de pluie (The Last King to Make Rain)*, in Kibondo, Tanzania, to make rain or the sunshine is a highly important role that requires negotiating with the heavens to ensure the earth receives the rain essential for life. Once a highly important function. Until the Pink Faces stuck their noses in. 715.98.10 Expressions

In the end, Monday night became official crossword night at the Babar. Anyone could bring their reference books and participate in the contest, in which all participants were given the same puzzle to solve. Whoever completed the puzzle first won the prize, a book from Didot Books. Sometimes only five or six people showed up, other times as many as a dozen or more.

"Wot did you choose?"

"*Belle du seigneur* by Albert Cohen. Even doh, most likely, I won't be readin' it until I retire."

"An' when's dat gonna be, den?"

"In about ten years."

"Well, dat's wot's so wonderful 'bout books, wouldn't you say? Dey's made to last." 716.51.12 Crosswords

All together, among the approximately 5,000 words beginning with the letter *a* in *L'Officiel du jeu Scrabble®*, there are about 50 French words originating in Belgium, Québec, or Switzerland, and none from Africa. In the *Bescherelle*, about 10 verbs beginning with the letter *a* are identified as coming from Africa,

Belgium, or Québec, but there is no mention of
717.105.9 Reserves/Reservations any Swiss contributions. In both cases, the proportion of words emanating from elsewhere than France is approximately 1 percent.

Accompanying Élizabeth back to the door of the building, Zed tries to learn more about her. He struggles to find the right tone, not to sound like he's sticking his nose in where it doesn't belong.

"Do you live alone, den?"

"Like a big girl."

Élizabeth answers without hesitation, which encourages Zed to push on:

"You doesn't even 'ave a cat?"

Again Zed notices his inconsistent use of the informal *tu* and the formal *vous.* Élizabeth laughs. Zed tries to explain:

"I know it. Seems like I can't decide wedder to talk to ya wid de *tu* or de *vous*. One or de udder, I mean, not boat."

"No, I was laughing because cats and me..."

"Naw, me neider..."

"Most people who talk to me use *tu*."

"Most likely dey're not tryin' to make a good impression, de way I am."

718.43.11 Élizabeth turns to smile at Zed.

Love "Oh?"

The expression "*à tout bout de champ* (at every end of field)" meaning "at every opportunity" first appeared in 1636, but was preceeded by "*à chaque bout de champ* (at each end of the field)" in the fourteenth century, and by "*à chacun bout de champ* (to each a bit of the field)" in the sixteenth. Another expression, "*ainsi font les coqs à chacun bout de champ* (so go the roosters to each his bit of field)," suggests

> the introduction somewhere along the way of a confusion between the word *chant* (song), referring to the rooster's song, and the word *champ* (field), referring to the farmer's habitat, in the metaphorical process (transfer of the spatial to the temporal).

719.131.6
Parenthesi(e)s

Then, walking Élizabeth to her car:

"I know a small cove on de way to Fundy. A lovely little spot it is, where we could make a fire. I'd like to take you der."

?

"Wid udder folks, too."

. . .

"Do you know Étienne an' Ludmilla Zablonski?"

"Only by name."

"Der real interestin' people. Der loft is on de end over der."

Élizabeth looked over in the direction Zed was pointing.

"Der yer age, I'd say. An' der's Terry we met earlier, an' his wife Carmen. Terry an' Ludmilla run de Didot bookstore over der, an' Carmen owns de Babar wid a girl from Memramcook by de name of Josse. Terry an' Carmen got two kids. De little one you seen earlier, an' de little feller's called Étienne."

And then, as though he'd suddenly put two and two together, Zed added:

"Matter o' fact, I'm gonna be Marianne's godfawder!"

"Oh!"

"So, turns out, you and I could end up godfawder and godmudder together... if I'm not too far aft."

Now it was Élizabeth's turn to put two and two together. Zed shook his head:

"She's a strange one, dat girl. One ting's fer sure, she knows wot she wants."

Zed mentioned all this lightly, as though it were merely

an interesting coincidence, but the truth was the possibility thrilled him.

"We could even be cookin' ourselves a supper. In Fundy, I mean. An' I figures you could bring along somebody else, if you had a mind to…"

Zed immediately regretted the suggestion; he felt as though he'd taken one step forward and two steps back. But Élizabeth found his slightly sheepish look charming.

"No, that won't be necessary."

Zed found her reply ambiguous. Élizabeth immediately noticed his discomfort, and reassured him:

"So, you'll call me?"

720.43.12 "Fer de loft, you mean?"

Love "Or for the supper down in Fundy."

CHAPTER 6

[. . .] one more meander is the best thing a river can offer; in fact, that's what we expect of it.

NICOLAS BOUVIER, *Journal d'Aran et d'autres lieux (Journal of Aran and Other Places)* 721.144.6
Petite Bibliothèque Payot, 2001 Epigraphs

Marianne doesn't understand. She's sure she heard Terry talking to a woman a moment ago. How is it then that he's alone in the bookstore, tapping away on the computer as usual, surrounded by columns of books?

"Are ya done drawing den, Marianne?"

Holding tight to a rag of plush that once resembled a snail, Marianne is looking out the door of the store, but sees no one there either.

"Gaw?"

Busy completing an order, Terry repeats a bit mechanically:

"Gone? Who's gone den?"

"Layee gaw?"

"De lady?"

"Layee?"

"Lady? Wot lady?"

. . . 722.103.2

"Awh! De Lady! Yah, de lady's gone." Disappearances

723.116.4
True or False

True or false: the three linguistic communities of Belgium are the francophones, the Flemish, and the Deutsche gramophones.

Carmen couldn't believe it:

"But, who is she?"

"A woman dat's come in to de bookstore a couple or tree times. Her name's Élizabeth."

"Élizabeth who?"

"Élizabeth... I forget her udder name. She's tinkin' o' buying a loft."

"An' how did she put it?"

"Well, we's walkin' down de hall, an' we see Zed comin' along wid somebody. An' when we get up close, I see'd it was dat woman. An' de little one starts sayin' 'De layee? De layee?'... So, dat's when it strikes me, dat dis must be de woman she was talkin' 'bout, on account of she'd come by de bookstore afore she went to meet Zed."

Carmen, her back up against the sink, listened in wrapt silence.

"Dey comes up on us den, an' Zed does de introductions — he doesn't know I already know who she is, see — an' right den is when it happened. Just like dat. She goes right up to her, lifts her wee head to look at 'er square an' she says 'gawmer?' Den round she turns to look straight back at me an' she says de same ting: 'gawmer?'"

Carmen could imagine the scene perfectly. Her little girl had always known exactly what she wanted. For an instant, Carmen imagined herself in Élizabeth's shoes:

"And then?"

"So den I explains wot a 'gawmer' is, an' how we's lookin' fer a godmudder for de wee one. An' she starts laughin', an' bends right down to talk to 'er. She asks 'er name, an' two, tree udder questions, an' in de end she says sure, she'd be right happy to be de godmudder of a little girl like her. Like Marianne."

724.44.9
Godfathers and Godmothers

Books about love: one of the categories of *La Bibliothèque idéale* is exclusively reserved for the French romance novel, which will greatly please those fond of this nation of love. Interestingly, the word *love*, or any of its derivatives, only appears in 4 of the 49 titles of this category: *Mad Love* by André Breton, *Absolute Love* by Alfred Jarry, *L'Amoureuse initiation (Initiation into Love)* by Oscar-Vladislas de Lubicz-Milosz, and *Swann in Love* by Marcel Proust.

725.43.5
Love

"You have an appointment, you say?"

"Well, I thought I did, anyway. I may have gotten it confused..."

"Oh, it could just as easily be him. That's just the sort of thing he's likely to forget. Come in. I'll ring him."

"I can come back, if this is a bad time."

"Come in anyway. I'll phone. He's not far."

I remained by the entrance to the Zablonskis' loft while Ludmilla phoned her husband.

"Hello, darling, everything alright?"

The answer, rather a long one, made her chuckle a bit, then:

"Listen... You do know you made an appointment with France Daigle?

("Yes, why? It's tomorrow, no? Tuesday? Today is Monday isn't it?")

"Yes..."

("Oh damn! You're right. In the end I preferred Monday. I can't even remember why. Never mind, I'm on my way.")

"Right. See you soon."

Ludmilla hung up the receiver.

"He should be here in a quarter of an hour. Can you wait?"

"Dat's alright. I'm in no great hurry."

I knew Ludmilla in passing, having seen her in the Didot bookstore, but our paths did not cross often, and we'd never spoken.

"And does Moncton still suit you?"

As I said this, I was reminded of the hospital director's dialogue in *Real Life*, when he asked Élizabeth the same thing.

"Yes. We like Moncton very much."

"Is that so? Really?"

Ludmilla didn't answer. I assumed she hadn't heard my question as she had turned to go into the kitchen.

"Can I offer you something to drink?"

"I wouldn't mind a cup of tea, if you've got some…"

"Of course!"

While Ludmilla was occupied in the kitchen, I admired the disorder of the loft. She returned with a tray, saying:

726.101.2 Duos "What I find particular to this place is that it's practically impossible to take oneself seriously."

727.68.4 Projects

> To read all the words in *L'Officiel du jeu Scrabble®* not once, but twice.

Marianne couldn't understand what Carmen was asking.

"Is that why, den? On account of she was with Zed?"

The child didn't know what to say, although, yes, Zed being there, a little bit, as well. Carmen continued:

"You know, she hardly knows you. An' we don't really know her. Most times, dads an' mums like to know de godmudder…to be certain that they're nice folks who'll treat you well."

Marianne nodded, smiling. The idea of all these adults treating her well pleased her.

"Yer dad says she seems nice."

Marianne nodded again.

"An' Zed says so as well."

Marianne nodded again, adding:

"Goofer!"

"Dat's right, Zed can't wait to be yer godfawder… an' I know he'll be doin' a proper job of it!"

As she helped her daughter get into her pyjamas, Carmen momentarily abandoned finding out why Marianne had asked an almost total stranger to be her godmother.

"There, now yer all set! Shall I fetch you a teddy bear?"

728.44.10 Godfathers and Godmothers

> Is there a connection between the abundant use of the word *ça* (translated in English as "that" or, in this novel, as "dat") in Acadian speech, and Freud's *ça*, ("the id" in English)?

729.92.2 Questions without Answers

Zablonski was seated across from me, and it was time to begin the interview.

"I don't really have any particular questions."

He looked surprised, but only for a moment.

"Alright."

He lit a cigarette.

"That's strange, I never imagined you smoked."

He shrugged, laughing, as though what I imagined or didn't imagine, well…

"It's a little strange to see you in the flesh after all this time."

He forced a laugh. He could see that I found him good looking. We were quiet for a bit.

"If you have something you'd like to say, or some questions, don't be shy."

I felt unprepared. I hadn't expected to be so devoid of curiosity, without the slightest intention even. Zablonski tapped his cigarette on the edge of an ashtray. Ashes dropped. Another moment passed. Finally a question came to me:

"Do you think of Claudia sometimes?"

He looked directly at me, smiled.

"Of course."

"Often?"

"No, not so often. From time to time, she comes back to me."

. . .

"As she does to you, I imagine. No?"

He was right of course, but I didn't want him to think that everything that happened to him happened to me, too. Even if he had every right to think what he liked.

"You think everything that happens to you happens to me, too?"

Again he shrugged.

"I don't think about it that much, you know."

"Yes, I know..."

And I felt the need to add:

"...but there must be some things I don't know."

He thought about it for a moment, shrugged again:

"Maybe."

Well, the discussion seemed to be at a dead end. Was I sabotaging myself? I certainly did not want that.

"And your painting, how's it going?"

"Oh, it's really not painting anymore."

"But you enjoy it at least?"

"Let's say it's... astonishing."

"Pleasantly astonishing? Or troubling astonishing?"

Zablonski thought about it.

"A bit of both. It's new. For the moment, it's hard to say
730.101.3 Duos where it will lead."

"Yes. I understand."

> Terry's mother always gets up earlier than usual on her childrens' birthdays. She firmly believes that a mother should be the first person
> 731.60.5 Superstitions to wish her child a happy birthday, which she does by telephone, without fail.

Describing Moncton to her friend Brigitte, Élizabeth had explained that Acadians like to establish family relations right from the start, and that they're not satisfied until they've found some shared blood relation or common friend.

"I don't see any problem. Are you afraid or what?"

"Afraid of becoming a godmother?"

"Afraid to be attached, in any way whatsoever. You know, I've always felt that's why you worked with cancer patients. No?"

"There are more and more survivors now, you know." 732.49.2

"Yes, I know." Élizabeth II

733.76.8

The word *avatar* is an absolutely yellow word. Avatars

Carmen thought it was an excellent idea. Now Terry hoped everyone would be able to accept an invitation for that very evening. He telephoned Zed:

"We were tinkin' we'd have a meal fer all de little ones' future godfawders an' godmudders."

"Sure! When's dat, den?"

"Tonight."

"Tonight! Alright!"

"You knows dat lady you was wid yesterday..."

Zed felt his pulse quicken.

"She comes by de bookstore from time to time. She's not a bad bit nice, eh?"

"Uh...sure...on account of?"

"She was tellin' me she was tinkin' she might like to buy a loft. So I gave her yer phone number an dat."

Zed tried to sound neutral:

"Sure an' dat's why she come by yesterday. Looks like TomTom's goin' off to Montréal, only ee's not ready to sell just now. I suppose she might rent from 'im."

"Wouldn't be a bad ting to 'ave a doctor in de building. You never know wot can happen. I mean, I'm just sayin'."

"Naw, I knows it. I's tinkin' de same ting."

"Anyhow, do ya tink she'd come fer supper as well? I mean, would ya be alright to call 'n ask 'er? Marianne's got it into 'er head dat she's de one she wants fer a godmudder. An' den, if it looks like she's gonna be movin' in, wouldn't be half bad to get to know each udder..."

Zed could not have asked for more, but why was Terry asking him to call her? Did he suspect something? Had he guessed? Terry continued:

"Not dat 'twould bodder me to call 'er, I's just tinkin'..."

"Tinkin' wot?"

"Well since yer de one dat met 'er 'bout de lofts an' all, you knows 'er better'n me by now. We're inviting de Zablonskis as well, so we'll be a half-dozen, plus de wee ones fer a bit."

734.44.11 Godfathers and Godmothers
Zed was feeling full of beans, but he struggled to hide it. Was Terry slyly teasing him? Was the whole thing arranged? And if so, what should he say?

> Several other books about love are listed in *La Bibliothèque idéale*: *L'amour n'est pas aimé (Love is Not Loved)* by Hector Bianciotti; *Love of Perdition* by Camilo Castelo Branco; *A Love Affair* by Dino Buzzati; *The Devil in Love* by Jacques Cazotte; *Les Amours jaunes (Yellow Love Affairs)* by Tristan Corbières; *Sur le fleuve amour (On the River Love)* by Joseph Delteil; *L'Amour la fantasia* (translated as *Fantasia: An Algerian Cavalcade*) by Assia Djebar; *Le Nouveau monde amoureux (The New World in Love)* by Charles Fourier; *On Love: Aspects of a Single Theme* by José Ortega y Gasset; *Five Women Who Loved* by Saikaku Ihara; *A Love of Our Time* by Tommaso Landolfi; *The Game of Love and Chance* by Pierre de Marivaux; *L'Amour de la renarde (Love of the She-Fox)* by Ling Mengchu; *Poems of Love* by Pierre de Ronsard; *L'Amour du narcissisme (Love of*
> 735.90.10 Letters
> *Narcissism)* by Lou Andréas Salomé and *First Love* by Ivan Turgenev.

"Did you know der's only eleven punctuation marks in French? Seems like a whole lot more, don't it?"

The one partner who was hitting well enough at this point did not mind engaging in a bit of conversation.

"Well den, name dem if you can."

"De comma, period, semi-colon, colon, exclamation mark, question mark, ellipsis, parentheses, quotation marks..."

He began again, this time counting them out on his fingers:

"De comma, period, semi-colon, exclamation mark, question mark, colon, parentheses, quotation marks, ellipsis... dat makes only nine..."

...

"Awh! De dash!"

"Ten..."

...

...

"I knows de hyphen's not one of dem."

"Not? An' why not, pray tell?"

"It's more of an accent, like."

"An accent! It don't look nuttin' like an accent!"

...

...

"Well, now it's gonna bodder me all de time until I finds de one dat's missin."

"How about de apostrophe, den?"

"Naw, dat's not one eider."

...

"I sure hope dis isn't gonna ruin me game, ha ha." 736.59.5 Knowledge

Unless the expression "*à tout bout de champ*" taken literally as "at every end of a field," refers to a more or less demarcated entrances on the ends of every field, thanks to which the farmer or owner can access that section of his land

> 737.106.10 Customs with horsepower, whether motorized or the other kind, or with a camper.

Élizabeth arrived home to the phone ringing. She accepted the invitation without hesitation.

"Élizabeth, dis 'ere is Étienne and Ludmilla…"

Immediately from the start of the evening, it was as though they had all been friends for years. As a result, Terry felt comfortable explaining to Élizabeth how Marianne had come to ask her to be her godmother.

"But don't be feelin' obliged…I mean, you hardly know us, or you may not be stayin' round 'ere fer long…"

As he said this, Terry realized that he'd more or less laid down his expectations for the role of a godfather or godmother, and he was relieved that no one took up this line of conversation. Unless, Zablonski had intentionally changed the subject.

"So, Étienne, you really want Ludmilla and me to be your godmother and godfather?"

Étienne was brimming with happiness:

"Dad said you'd be takin' me fishin'?"

Zablonski was caught unawares, but quickly regained his composure:

"Of course! Obviously! Fishing, well, that's a classic!"

Zed took advantage of the moment to prompt Marianne:

"I does too, I do! An' you, Marianne? Do you take me, Zed, to be yer godfawder, fer better an' fer worse?"

Marianne thought Zed's question was funny, but she answered him without hesitation:

"Yeth!"

Élizabeth chimed in:

"And me, Marianne, you still want me to be your godmother, since it seems to please God?"

Even if she didn't quite understand it all, Marianne was enjoying the part they'd given her, and she answered gladly:

"Yeth!"

And, with Carmen's approbation, Terry concluded:

"Well den, dat's dat!"

Ludmilla and Étienne raised their glasses to mark the moment, and the others followed suit. Le Petit Étienne jumped for joy:

"Hurray! Now everyone's all fixed up!"

738.44.12
Godfathers and
Godmothers

> 7. Accidents that concern the musician (_ _ _ _ _ s).

739.51.11
Crosswords

Dream of another anonymous character: all the members of her family are busy cleaning house, throwing away things that have degraded over time, gathering together what might be sold or given away, putting away what needs to be put away. The mood is good. The house is big, the numerous children cross each other's paths often as they work. Some discover long-lost objects, others plunge back into long-forgotten moments of their lives. Little by little, the residence becomes lighter, airier. The interior structure of the building takes shape, its architectural particularities emerge in a new light. Standing in the middle of the kitchen and drying a pan, the mother watches one of her children go down into the basement: something remains buried, and will have to be dislodged.

740.109.9
Dreams

> *Virer casaque*. The word *casaque* is derived from the Turkish word *kazak* meaning "adventurer." From the occupation of the individual, the word *kazak* gradually came to designate the tabard or coat worn by the horsemen known by the Russian word for a member of the cavalry, *cossack* or *cosaque* in French. By extension, the French expression "*à la cosaque*" came to mean "brutally," whereas "*tourner casaque*" means to change allegiance or turncoat. In Acadia, "*virer*

741.98.2 Expressions

casaque" becomes more brutal and ultimately means "to become mad."

On Tuesday afternoon, as things were running smoothly, Terry dropped into the Babar to say hello to Carmen before going upstairs for a nap. But once in the bar, he couldn't refuse The Cripple's invitation to have a drink and chat a while, especially since the children were away with the Després grandparents in Grande-Digue for a few days, and Terry had more free time than usual. Once their drinks were served — a beer for Terry and a triple twelve-year-old Scotch neat for The Cripple — the quinquagenarian drew a small flask of clear water equipped with a dropper from his pocket.

"Easter water. I've an old auntie who never fails to bring me some."

The Cripple raised the flask up to the light:

"You won't be findin' purer dan dis 'ere. Der aren't too many streams left where you can find it anymore. Dis one 'ere comes from Painsec."

Terry thought it must be holy water.

"Dat's de first time I sees a body puttin' holy water in 'is Scotch."

The Cripple laughed as he continued to study the clear water:

"Holy?! Sure, directly from on high!"

The Cripple let three drops of Easter water fall into his glass and put the flask away. They talked for a bit about this and that, and then The Cripple leaned over and looked directly down into the bottom of his glass, which he hadn't touched.

"Wot is it yer expectin' to happen?"

"I don't rightly know. It's sometin' I got to sense."

Terry hesitated; he didn't want to annoy his friend:

"Sense like feel or sense like sniff sniff?"

The Cripple laughed, imagining how strange his little habits must seem to Terry. And the more he thought about it, the more he laughed. An open belly laugh, infectious as all hearty laughter is, because Terry too was laughing now, and across the room, Carmen wondered what it was the two of them found so funny. 742.16.7 The Cripple

> **INTERPROSE:** v. trans. — 2005/2013; from *inter* and *prose*. **A**. 1. To let another speak while one waits to see if one has an opinion on the subject. *"If only he'd really listened that would have been alright, but no, he was interprosing."* (Daigle) 2. To remain silent because one is unable to get what one would like to say into the conversation. *"She was talking so fast and loud that one could only interprose."* (Daigle) **B**. Fig. To savour the silences in the midst of conversation. *"She enjoyed their company because she always felt free to interprose."* (Daigle) 743.120.4 Fictionary

"On account of my age?"

"Maybe, a little, but not just that."

In the pause that followed Zed had time to worry and even to ask himself what it was that attracted him to older women (he'd not forgotten the crush he'd had on Ludmilla).

"A lot of things will surprise her, I think."

Zed kept silent, waiting.

"The way people are kind and receptive, for example."

Jus dat? Really? All things considered, he too preferred to avoid the subject, and to defer onto his people what might be wrong between the two of them.

"Is dat so? Are we really as wonderful nice as all dat den?" 744.104.9 Worries

> Examination for Advanced Research course (RES 4993): describe all the necessary stages in a research project to determine 1) to what degree Chiac is essentially a geographical

variation, an isolated language, a lalanguage; 2) if the normalisation of Chiac might threaten the existence of English, the Uralo-Altic languages, the Dravidian languages; 3) if the Polynesian languages, meridional Slav and the languages of the Oubangian sub-group are
745.32.4 Exam Questions under threat of contamination by Chiacisized English.

"Ee knows a shocking lot of stuff, ee does. A real chucklehead!"

Terry was in an expansive mood, so that Carmen did not have to prod him.

"Ee says de whole idea of morality began when a gang of brudders killed der fawder. Like, in our house we were all boys. So it's as doh de five of us boys, we get togeder an' kill our dad."

"An' why would you be doin' such a thing?"

"On account of he was standin' in de way of us sleepin' wid our mudder."

!

"Alright, so now our dad's dead, well den we get to feelin' *guilty* like."

"Well I should hope so!"

Carmen did not correct Terry's use of the English word *guilty.* Because sometimes she grew weary of being the party pooper.

"So, den, to rectify dat, we starts to *idealize* our fawder. An' dat's where de *totem poles* come from, an' even de idea of God an' all of dat."

Terry's use of the English word *idealize* confirmed Carmen's momentary resolution.

"So den... de *guilt*... how do we say dat in French again?"

"*Coupable. Se sentir coupable.*"

Carmen had replied even though the exact word, *culpabilité*, escaped her.

"Alright den. So... feelin' guilty, dat was de first ting. De second, dat was de whole ting wid incest. Not, mind you, directly de fact of a boy sleepin' wid 'is mudder. 'Twas more de fact dat de brudders are killin' each udder over who's gonna sleep wid der mudder. An' dat's when, fer der own protection, dey decides dat sleepin' wid yer mudder's against de law."

!

"Fer boys, anyway..." 746.16.8

?! The Cripple

> A moment of doubt. Go back and leaf through *Just Fine* to check on the number of Terry's brothers. Nor is this the first time I forget something from one book to the next. For the sake of clarity, I should mention here that the characters of Terry and Carmen first appeared in *Just Fine*, where they became a couple, and have never left the stage since. They reappear in *A Fine Passage* and in *Life's Little Difficulties*, a novel in which the story centres on the transformation of an old warehouse in Moncton into a small centre of cultural activity, with lofts, artists' studios and small shops for people to loiter in, like Didot Books and the Babar.

747.54.3
Forgotten/
Recalled

"What about your parents? Won't they be a little bit surprised?"

"Inside der own heads, most likely. Only der's a lot dat's changed atwixt me an' dem since I organized de lofts. Maybe dey seen more who I am really, I mean aside from bein' der boy."

...

"I never know'd me real dad. Didn't bodder me all dat much really. Only, sometimes, I didn't get along all dat well wid de one I got."

"How old were you when you met your second father?"

"Six years old."

...

"Things're better now. He's proud of me, even doh sayin' so don't come easy to him."

"That's normal. Few fathers really live up to expectations."

"Maybe so. Still, der's some dat know wot to do bedder dan udders."

"Yes, that's true."

"Awh, fer sure, it depends on a whole lot of tings. Dat's why it don't bodder me all dat much... most of de time, anyhow."

748.49.6 ...

Élizabeth II "Let's just say it's been a long while since I bawled over it."

> Which means that only 19 of 2,401 titles in *La Bibliothèque idéale* contain the word *love* or a
> 749.43.7 derivative thereof. This is less than 1 percent of
> Love the total. Someone ought to complain.

Carmen couldn't sleep.

"How was ee sayin' that, again? Without a law against incest, culture can't..."

Terry, who'd been on the edge of sleep, stepped back from the precipice and retraced The Cripple's explanation in small steps:

"Widout... de law against... incest... culture... could... not have... detached... itself... from nature. Dat's 'ow he put it: detached itself."

"An' nature, that's the animal in us, an' all that?"

"Exactly. Instinct, biology. All dose tings dat happens widout us even tinkin' 'bout it... I tink."

...

...

"That's how I feel about the Babar. If it were all the time just artists comin' in there t'wouldn't work. All those artists would end up smotherin' each other, an' the rest of us along wid 'em. It takes all sorts of folks to make it work, to keep it goin.'"

. . .

"I like the way ee says that 'bout culture, how it detaches itself from nature. It's like I can see it happenin.'"

"Dat's troo. Dey's only simple words, mind you, but it's like der made to go togedder."

"It's like a tango. An elegant tango."

. . .

. . . 750.16.9

"Elegant. Dat's right nice, too. I like dat." The Cripple

> Certain books, out of print at the time of *La Bibliothèque idéale's* publication, have been reissued since, while others are impossible to find. We sometimes discover rare books by accident, particularly in used bookstores, or on friends' bookshelves. Watch out for your copy of Gilles Lapouge's *Bruit de la neige (Noise of Snow)*, which I might be tempted to slip into my bag in order to complete my ideal library.

751.95.8
Additions to
La Bibliothèque idéale

"Me, I'm more an' more afraid I'll die before I finish my book."

"Is dat really a fear, or just a worry?"

"Mostly, I imagine a stroke, or an aneurism — don't know really, might de same ting. Either way, it'd kill me. An' for sure, I'd be a whole lot more comfortable in my grave if my book was finished.

"You mean you're not going to be incinerated?"

"(Does dat mean *cremated*?)"

"(Yes, but it makes no sense dat way. I mean, wot's more opposite dan ashes and cream?)"

752.137.12
Fears

> The frequent use of *ça* (or *dat*) amplifies the archaic resonance of Chiac. It also has the effect of infantilizing it.

753.7.5
Useful Details

The first few minutes following their departure were always vaguely turbulent, as each person found their comfort zone and signalled the parametres of their mood and territory to the others. It was also the time when the holiday spirit took hold, a permissive spirit, but not so permissive as to suspend all the usual rules.

"How come yer goin' dat way den? We'd get der a whole lot quicker goin' troo de Wheeler."

Carmen took the highway only when absolutely obliged to.

"I want the whole town to see we're goin' on vacation."

She'd even donned her slightly ridiculous straw hat for the occasion, which had made the kids laugh. Behind the wheel, the hat lent a carnival atmosphere to the entire enterprise. Terry conceded the point:

754.29.1
On the Road

"An' fer sure, it's truly a wonderful sight to see..."

> Whether they are identified as such or not, this novel's numerous anonymous characters are above all verbomotor beings, the form and content of whose speech serve to colour the background. They are the novel's equivalent to extras in a movie.

755.96.4
Personnages

The participation of Étienne and Marianne in the filming of the movie *Children By Demselves* had impressed upon Terry the importance of constantly valorizing the French language in the presence of the little ones.

"In Caraquet, everybody speaks French."

Étienne was not convinced that, by itself, this detail justified the trip.

"Wot else is over der?"

"Der's a shocking great pier, wid boats a whole lot bigger dan de ones 'round 'ere."

Carmen felt the need to add:

"We'll go fer picnics on our bikes, an bowling with de big balls..."

"An we'll cook up some wonderful tasty baked potatoes. You stick dose potatoes in aluminium foil an' trow 'em in de hot coals. By an' by, ya take dem out o' de fire, an' soon as der not too hot, you eat dem, just like dat wid yer hands, no butter, nuttin'. An' *by de time* youse finished eatin' dem yer face is all black wid soot."

Terry's *by de time* in English had not gone unnoticed.

"Dad! You went an used an English word again!"

From time to time — the result of an intuitive calculation — Terry slipped an English word or expression into his speech because, after all, this transgressive act was also part of his identity.

"Oops…"

Carmen and Terry exchanged a complicitous glance.

"Well den, 'ow do you say it in French?"

Étienne thought a bit, then:

"You gotta say 'when's.' When's yer done eatin'…"

"Dat's right. I ought to have knowed it."

Carmen caught Étienne's eye in the rear-view mirror and winked.

Terry concluded:

"An' instead of goin' off to bed when it gets dark, we'll sit ourselves 'round de fire an' look at de stars. Dat's after we's roasted a whole bag o' *marshmallows*…oops!

"*Guimauves*, Dad! *Marshmallows* is *guimauves* in French!

Étienne reflected a moment on all these pleasures to come and declared:

"It doesn't matter, Dad. I'll be der to help in Caraquet, if dey don't understand yer English words."

756.29.2
On the Road

> The Moncton Beavers, along with the Fredericton Spawn, were the stars of the first Nigadoo Ultimate Frisbee Tournament, having made up a 9–1 deficit in their semi-final against the Edmundston Mad Buckwheat Pancakes, who until then had been the only undefeated

> team in the competition. In the end, however, the Fredericton Spawn won the tournament, defeating the Québec Gravity O in the other semi-final, and then beating the Beavers in the final. The other participating teams, the
> 757.122.3 Nigadoo Acadian Skitties and the Moncton
> Sports Mud Slides, lost in the elimination round.

Zed and Élizabeth were riding in the car and talking as though everything was absolutely normal. Which may very well have been the case.

"So then, you must have known Denis?"

"Denis? You know him?"

"He was living not far from us when I's a boy. He was older'n me. His twin sister was right nice, too. Denise. I seen 'er dis past summer in Shediac. She was home for her vacations."

...

"We moved a couple times, only we always stayed in Parkton."

758.49.7 And since they were in the car:

Élizabeth II "Do you want to see? We're not far..."

> Names of the Senior Memramcook Valley Hockey League teams: the Fishermen from Cap-Pelé, the Brunswick Crane Rental from Memramcook, the Dooly's Combines from Sackville, the Gagnon Overhead Doors from Saint-Antoine, the Furniture 2000 from Richibouctou, the Maritime Doors and Windows
> 759.99.5 from Bouctouche, and the Rallye Motors Voy-
> Names agers from Dieppe.

The little family had taken its time driving up the coast: Shediac, Pont-de-Shediac, Grande-Digue and Cap-des-Caissie, then a stop to stretch their legs and eat an ice-cream at the Cap-de-Cocagne pier; from there to Saint-Marcel,

Cocagne, Saint-Thomas, Dixon's Point, Bouctouche, Fond d'la baie of Bouctouche, Saint-Édouard, then a swim and a walk on the Côte-Sainte-Anne wharf, where Terry filled his lungs with the smell of creosote.

"Geez, I love dat smell!"

Then he told them how his mother had made his brothers and him soak their feet in a mixture of water and creosote when, as kids, one of his brothers or he accidentally trod on a rusty nail.

"I suppose 'twas a kind o' disinfectant. One time, I'd climbed up de roof of de Melanson's garage to hide. Den me mudder shouts it's time fer supper. So, der I go, I jump down from de roof, an' me foot lands on an old plank of wood I hadn't seen on account of de long grass, see. A board wid a shockin' big rusty nail stickin' up out of it. Sure an' wouldn't you know it, dat rusty sparrable goes straight troo me sneaker an' right in de arch of me foot."

"Hihihi!"

Any sort of acrobatics was amusing to Marianne. The expression on Étienne's face, however, had gone from admiration to pain.

"When I raise up me foot, de nail an' de board come up wid it, de whole ting was stuck togeder. Can't say why, but it didn't hurt all dat much."

Unable to bear any more, Étienne moved away from Terry, and grabbed hold of Carmen's hand.

760.29.3
On the Road

761.136.2
The Unavowed

The Unavowable Kills.

Zed and Élizabeth drove by Zed's parents' modest little house.

"She looks smaller dan she is. Inside, it's not so small as all dat. She's well divided."

Beside the house was a vacant lot with several large trees.

"It's on account of dis 'ere lot dat dey decided to buy, on account of it gave us a place to play. All de kids from de neighbourhood were always comin' 'ere to play. Lard, we broke a lot o' windows playin' baseball! Me mudder never said a word, she liked to see us playin'.

762.49.8 Élizabeth was taking it all in as though it were a movie.
Élizabeth II "Does it bodder you when I use English words?

763.43.6
Love A priori, this novel is not a love story.

A hot sun, a feathery breeze, the blue-green sea, slate-blue sky, Bob Marley playing low in the background, Terry, his hand on Carmen's sun-warmed thigh, couldn't ask for more. Cap-Lumière, Richibouctou, Grande-Aldouane. Étienne tranquilly watched the scenery roll by. Marianne dozed.

"Dad, do dey paint de lines on de road at night?"

"De yellow an' white lines, you mean?"

Étienne saw no other lines on the road.

"Naw, dey paint dem in de day. 'Twould be too dark at night. Be too dangerous, now wouldn't it."

Étienne figured it would be even more dangerous during the day, with all the traffic. It occurred to him that he'd never actually seen anyone bent over and painting lines on the road.

"De line down de middle as well?"

Terry wondered what his son was thinking about.

"When dey come troo, dey paint all de lines at once, de yellow ones an' de white. Dey don't have time to come back too often on de same bit o' road, wot wid all de roads."

Étienne thought that made good sense.

"You ever seen any, Dad?"

"Any wot?"

"Folks dat paint de lines?"

"A couple of times. Dey do it in de spring an' summer mostly… I tink de machine does de yellow line along de edge an' at least one o' de lines down de middle at de same time."

Étienne was surprised:

"A machine does it?!"

"Well, fer sure! Would take far too many people an' too shockin' long to do all dat by hand! It's a right big truck specially made dat goes over de road."

Étienne was reduced to silence, sorry that a specially designed truck would deprive humans of such a pleasant activity. 764.29.4 On the Road

> Hence the relative importance of the confession. 765.136.3 The Unavowed

When she's with Zed, Élizabeth spends a lot of time watching him, astonished at how much in him seems to flow as easily as water from a spring.

"So den, you don't mind goin' out wid me?"

The question made Élizabeth laugh.

"So then, we're dating, is that it?"

"Well, we been to de movies, we been bowlin', you seen me parents' house, you came to Amherst wid me, an' we're goin' to Fundy."

"You forget that we're also going to be Marianne's godfather and mother."

"Even more so! We look like makin' a fine team, wouldn't you say?"

...

"To tell de troot, I left out de ting 'bout bein' godfawder and mudder on purpose."

...

"Seems like it's almost too much. I'm afraid it'll bring us bad luck." 766.49.9 Élizabeth II

> All things considered, the unavowed is the real. 767.136.1 The Unavowed

"*Marianne went down to the mill, Marianne went down to the mill...*"

Marianne had only just opened her eyes and Terry

wanted to wake her up with a song. But Étienne did not feel that this particular song's appeal was sufficient to justify its length. He preferred to follow the progress of the days of the week, of the king, his wife and his little prince.

"Dad, sing Monday morning…"

"Alright den, you start…"

Étienne was caught unawares. His father had never made such a request before. But the boy was willing. He positioned his voice properly in his larynx and sang clearly:

768.29.5 On the Road

"*Monday morning, the king, his wife an' der little prince…*"

769.21.1 More or Less Useful Details

In 2002, the government of New Brunswick bought its white and yellow road surface marking paint from the Laurentide Atlantic company of Richibouctou. The yellow paint cost $661,000 and the white $472,000.

When the vacationers saw the beach and wharf at Pointe-Sapin, they knew they'd arrived at their first destination. All the more so because the sea was full of white caps.

"*Moutons blancs* in French, like white sheep."

"White wot?"

"Sheep."

"Why do dey call 'em dat, Mum?"

"On account of it's all white an' fluffy."

Oh? Terry had never thought of it that way.

"I tawt 'twas on account of dey follows each udder, like when you counts sheep to fall asleep."

At the snack bar, Terry and Carmen drank tea, the children downed a few mouthfuls of juice and they all shared a great big oatmeal biscuit. The waitress found the little family so charming that she made a special effort to be helpful. After a quick phone call, she explained to Terry and Carmen how to get to the house of the owners who'd agreed to let them pitch their tent for the night. They set out to find it.

"And tanks a whole lot, eh, you're wonderful nice to 770.29.6
help us out." On the Road

> New Brunswick has more kilometres of road
> per inhabitant than any other Canadian prov- 771.3.7
> ince. Numberless statistic. Statistics

"Petitpoint? Do I even know wot dat is?"

Élizabeth laughed. She could understand Zed's reaction, but tried a bit of cajoling:

"It's quite engrossing once you get started..."

Zed thought about it for a moment, he liked to think he was open-minded, but he had to admit:

"Well, we'd really have to be steady on de go before I'd try dat..."

Élizabeth took his hand, raised it to her lips and kissed 772.49.10
it. Élizabeth II

> To confess to someone else or to oneself, the 773.136.4
> difficulty is the same. The Unavowed

Étienne turned out to be more helpful than Terry had anticipated when it came to putting up the tent.

"Like dis, Dad?"

"Haul some over dat way."

The boy put his back into it and the tent's nylon spread evenly.

"Dat's wicked! A fellow might tink you'd already done dis!"

Terry placed the stake and held it straight while Étienne hammered it solidly into the ground. Then, having learned the importance of planting the corner stakes in the right order, the son followed his father to the
opposite corner of the tent. 774.29.7
"Now, you haul on dis one 'ere." On the Road

> Ordinarily a jigsaw puzzle contains 15 different shapes for pieces, sometimes 16. Six of these shapes are far more numerous than the others. The pieces with two cavities and two heads are of two types: either the cavities and heads are opposed on an essentially rectangular shape, or the cavities and heads are aligned on two of the four sides of the piece. There are also pieces with three heads and one cavity or the reverse, with three cavities and one head. And finally, there are pieces with four heads and pieces with four cavities. Some, though not all, puzzles include longish pieces with two heads, placed respectively about halfway on each long side. The nine other forms that can be considered classic are far less numerous because they belong to the edges of the puzzle, and three of them belong only in the corners. The corner pieces necessarily have one cavity and one head, two cavities or two heads. The other edge pieces contain either one cavity and two heads, two cavities and one head, three cavities, or three heads. If it exists at all, a jargon specific to jigsaw puzzles is not widely known; people name the pieces as best they can — cavities, bays, blanks, heads, knobs, tabs — according to
> 775.122.2 Sports their individual imaginations. Creating a jargon is also a sport.

Brigitte is not entirely wrong, and Élizabeth knows it. And yet, this time, things are a bit different. Didn't she herself undertake steps to move into the lofts? Wasn't she attracted by this lifestyle at once communal and marginal?

"What's her name?"

"Marianne."

"Ah, that's a lovely name..."

"And she's awfully cute." 776.49.3
"And the loft, is that going to work?" Élizabeth II

> Between the unavowed and the Other there is 777.138.9
> a close link. The Other

While the men put up the tent, the women were in the field picking flowers.

"Looky, Marianne! Blueberries!"

Marianne did as Carmen did, bending over the little blue bunches, picking berries and eating them.

"Mmmm … dat's not a bad bit good."

"Mmmm …"

When Carmen moved to another bush, Marianne followed. When Carmen blew a tiny bit of stem off her tongue, the little one spluttered, as well. When Carmen smiled at the thought that she'd brought a little monkey into the world, Marianne rubbed the side of her head with the back of her hand. And when Carmen began to sing softly without realizing it the chorus of "No Woman
No Cry," Marianne rocked back and forth and sang along 778.29.8
no momen no no. On the Road

> In addition to fixing screws, there are Archimedes' screws (very useful in water pumps and grain handling), lead or translation
> screws (screw threads and ball nut drives) and 779.114.5
> worm screws (in gear systems). Inventions

"Dad, do you fall off de moon as well?"

"If I falls off de moon?"

"Yeah, when yer sleepin."

Terry thought about it for a moment.

"You mean in me dreams?"

"Yes."

…

…

"Naw, I don't tink I ever fell off de moon."
"I do."
"Is dat right! And den wot?"
"Everytin's black an' I fall an' fall..."
"How does you know it's de moon yer fallin' off?"
"Well geez, Dad! On account of I'm sittin' on it!"
"Awh..."
...
"How come you're fallin'? Has somebody pushed you off?"
"No. I fall meself."
"Wot? You let yerself fall, or you get tripped up or sometin' an' den you fall?"
"No, I don't trip. I just fall."
...
"I like it a bit, even doh it's kind o' scary. An' den I
780.137.2 wake up."
Fears "Hun!"

> **MANNOW:** n. m. — 2005/2013; diminutive of man. — by ext. immature adult male. "*They're*
> 781.120.7 *not men, they're mannows.*" (Daigle, Majzels) —
> Fictionary MAN. MINNOW.

"I like golf, too."
"Phew!"
Élizabeth chuckled. Zed continued:
"Dat's strange all de same. I wouldn't 'ave pictured you a golfer."
"Why not?"
"Don't know. It's like der's sometin' 'bout golfers, sometin' 'bout dem you can tell dey're golfers."
Élizabeth rummaged through her handbag, pulled out a photo of herself on a golf course, and showed it to Zed. She pointed to the person beside her in the picture.
"That's Brigitte."
Zed looked more closely at Brigitte.

"You two look alike. Like sisters almost."

The idea made Élizabeth smile:

"No, it's better that she's my friend rather than my sister." 782.49.11 Élizabeth II

> **MEANNOW:** n. m. — 2005/2013; lively bait fish. *"I never see'd so many meannows afore dat, a dozen schools all fightin' fer de worm."* (Daigle/Majzels) — MAR. lively minnow, ideal bait. — FIG. Particularly immature adult male. *"A mannow, you can argue it's not his fault. A meannow is so headstrong he's beyond help."* (Daigle/Majzels) 783.120.8 Fictionary

Terry, Carmen and the children had begun to spread their sleeping bags in the tent when the owner of the field came out to see them.

"De wife's cooked up a whackin' great big stew o' green beans an' salted pork fer dinner. Why don't ya come in an' eat wid us?"

Carmen and Terry looked at each other.

"Dat's awful kind of you, but just campin' out in yer field is perfect."

"Right now dis minute, de blueberry pie's cookin'."

"Booberries!"

That was Marianne, her fingers and lips stained purple, who could not restrain her enthusiasm. The large, sturdy man bent 90 degrees to address her:

"I'd say der's someone 'ere wot likes de blueberries… eh?"

Marianne nodded yes. Carmen, meanwhile was worried about the supper, and felt the need to point out that they'd promised the children to…

"'Tisn't that we wouldn't like to, only…"

"An der's a whole lot of bread an' molasses if dey don't like de stew. Bum-cheeks bread an' small rolls de wife made 'erself dis mornin'."

Terry joked:

"Did she know we was comin', den?"

The man, whose neck and arms the sun had turned to copper, left it at that:

784.29.9 "Alright den, let's say in a half-hour or so?"

On the Road "Tanks a bunch! We'll be der!"

> There are a variety of bingo games: the straight line — horizontal, vertical, or diagonal — the postage stamp in five numbers, the four corners, the hollow diamond in 14 or 15 numbers, the bonanza in 53 or 55 numbers, the gold ball, lucky ball, coverall in 50 numbers, the *X* in 18 numbers, the *B* and *O* in 14 numbers, the treasure hunt, the winner's circle, the 50/50 draw, the jackpot, coverall jackpot, and the progressive jackpot. Some games are triathlons, in which the winner must complete the hollow diamond and the treasure hunt, and hit the lucky ball. The pre-bingo is merely a warm-up period. All this requires a good understanding of the equipment and the ratios, particularly the luck/number of cards and luck/number of cards/cost per card ratios. Calculating the cost per card requires knowledge of the number of
> 785.122.5 sheets per booklet, which varies depending on
> Sports whether the booklet is small, big, or free.

"Myself, I never been golfing. Not dat I never had a chance to. I know a whole lot of people dat golf."

"I like it when you can walk, take your time. But that's increasingly rare."

Élizabeth imagined what it would be like to play golf with Zed, a beginner:

"It's a sport that's funny at first, even ridiculous. Then, with time and practise, something else settles in. A kind of complicity. Or love."

Zed had heard a great many things said on the subject of golf, but never this.

"Hun! Now golf'll give us love, you say? Well, dat would explain how come so many folks're playin' it."

With that, he turned right on the red light at MacBeath Avenue and Mountain Road, one of the city's main arter-
ies, which leads up to Magnetic Hill. 786.49.12

"You ever been to Magnetic Hill?" Élizabeth II

> Burn-beating consists in loosening and burn-
> ing the topsoil along with plants and roots, 787.126.5
> thus producing ashes, which enrich the soil. Techniques

"Eat, eat! Takes a shockin' long time to make a good stew like dis 'ere one, so you're best to eat yer fill when it comes time."

Terry did not need to be told twice; he gladly accepted a second helping piled as high as the first. Carmen only took a few more string beans because she'd already helped Marianne, who'd done her best with the generous helping Madame Gaudet had served her. Étienne, who'd eaten his entire portion without complaining, was now ready for some bread and molasses.

"You wants bread an' molasses as well! Good Laird, dis boy's hungry sometin' fierce! Do you folks not feed 'im?"

Monsieur Gaudet — Terry and Carmen had still not managed to call him Alcide, as he'd insisted several times they should — was becoming increasingly talkative.

"So den, yer off to Caraquet! I knows a couple o' fishermen out dat way. Big fisherman."

Hearing this, Étienne concluded that Alcide was
declaring his affinity for individuals as corpulent as 788.29.10
himself. On the Road

> *Noyer le poisson*: French expression, literally to drown the fish, meaning to confuse the issue

789.127.2 Tactics so as to confound the person being addressed. Comparable to the English red herring?

"I never knew me real fawder neider. Me mudder met dis 'ere fellow when I was six. So den, ee's like my fawder."

Zed and Lauzia Hébert were sitting at the kitchen table. The elderly woman had layed out tea and white cake for Zed. Chico was in school.

"I had no cocoa fer de frostin'."

Zed was revelling.

"It's perfect just as it is. Been a while since I ate a real homemade cake. It's shockin' delicious!"

Madame Hébert seemed a little sad. Zed would have liked to cheer her up:

"Yer welcome to come along wid us if you like."

"No, I don't tink I'll go. Maybe anudder time. Last time I went, it put me in a desperate state."

"Dat's understandable."

"Dey tell me I oughtn't to overtop me mind wid it..."

But the poor woman did not look convinced.

"I try, I do. 'Tain't all dat easy when 'tis yer own child. I can't very well abandon de boy."

"Fer sure."

"Fawder Cormier comes 'round from time to time. Do you know 'im?"

Zed had to admit he did not.

"Ee's a comical fellow, sometimes. Ee says 'tisn't healty
790.47.1 Yielding to be prayin' all de time."

"Awh, is dat right?"

> Wings beating, fervour soars above techniques and tactics to go to the heart of things. Fervour believes the heart of things belongs to her by right. She sees techniques and tactics as inferior processes seeking to restrain her ardour. The concept torque-clash is an excellent example of fervour. It illustrates clearly that fervour prevents

> neither errors (remarry-mule), nor pleasures (sprite-spoons), nor excesses (career-lees). 791.128.2 Fervours

That evening, as he was roasting his seventh marshmallow, Étienne learned that he was sometimes confused.

"In Moncton, sometimes, it's confusing for dem, French an' English, I mean."

"Der's some dat mix French an' English so much dey don't even realize der speakin' two different languages. Dey tink some English words is French."

"We was tinkin' to show dem places where everyone speaks only French. I meself grew up in Dieppe. Might as well say I grew up bilingual. So, I sometimes mixes up me French and English words."

Alcide Gaudet had his own personal take on things:

"I surmise it's like de lobsters. Dey wants dose chunks o' dogfish, dey'll do summersaults to get 'em, next ting dey know dey's in de trap."

Terry and Carmen agreed, laughing. For a moment, neither could think where to get a handhold on the analogy in order to continue the conversation. 792.29.11 On the Road

> Fantasy has no need to justify itself, for it exists in the absolute and exposes itself without restraint. Liberated, supposing itself above and beyond, de-posing itself. So much so, that one might say fantasy is precisely this, an excess in the economy of thought. A glove-factor. A quake-breaks. A dwarf-drench. A tears-mirror. 793.129.3 Fantasies

"Most time, I go to bed at night hopin' I won't be wakin' up in de mornin.'"

Zed was acutely conscious of the incongruity of the situation: eating a delicious cake while listening to the old woman talk of her pain.

"Der's times I's afraid fer Chico. Ee's a good lad all de same…"

"Have you no one to help you, den?"

"I've good neighbours. Dey take me to de store an' to church."

Madame Hébert poured more tea for Zed.

"I never used to be such a glawvawn, complainin' all de time. 'ere, you 'ave anudder piece o' cake, now. Der's
794.106.1 plenty more where dat come from."
Customs Zed cut himself another slice.

> The paradox being that, even to admit some-
> 795.136.5 thing to oneself, one must go through the
> The Unavowed Other.

The next morning, after generous helpings of lobster omelette, the little family went gathering stones and shells on the shore before repacking the van for their departure.

"Lucky fer us youse didn't know 'bout de campgrounds just over by de way, or we never would've met ya."

Madame Gaudet, who had rapidly fallen for the two children, took them by the hand, and spoke to them:

"When youse come back next year, we'll go out on de boat. Eh? Would you like dat?"

Monsieur Gaudet handed Carmen the bag of provisions his wife had prepared:

"Alvina boasts she grows de best cucumbers east o' Waltham. A fellow knows enough not to contradict a woman who tinks so highly of her cucumbers."

Carmen took the bag, and shook his hand warmly.

"Really, thanks a whole bunch. We'll not ferget you."

Terry, for his part, kissed Granny Alvina.

"If you don't stop spoilin' us like dis, you'll have us on your hands a whole lot longer dan you hoped for."

And Terry handed Alcide Gaudet the scrap of paper on which he'd written their address and phone number.

"If ever we can do sometin' for you in Moncton, don't be shy. An' come an' see us sometime when yer out dat way.

We'll be proud to show you round de neighbourhood."

Alvina Gaudet wiped away a tear as she watched the van go out of sight. 796.29.12 On the Road

> Backstitch, long-armed cross-stitch, Smyrna cross-stitch, reversible cross-stitch, Assisi or Holbein stitch, plaited cross-stitch, Roumanian stitch, whipstitch, straight stitch, gridded half-cross stitch, ¾ cross-stitch, star stitch, hexagonal half-stitch, point carré stitch, triangular stitch, pin stitch, stem stitch, backstitch, buttonhole stitch, isolated dove's eye stitch, fly stitch, regular row, offset row, Kloster block, eyelet, basket filling, mosaic filling, chessboard filling, drawn trellis filling, square filling, half-chevron filling, window filling, beehive filling, ribbed wheel, braided flange, picot, oblique loop, dove's eye, openwork, ladder stitch, serpentine hemstitch, knotted cluster stitch, double hemstitch, and antique hemstitch. 797.71.11 Intro Embroidery

"De udder ting people have got all muddled about..."

!

"De Bible says, 'an eye fer an eye, a toot fer a toot.' Well, you'd tink dat means de punishment ought to fit de crime, wouldn't you? Say a body kills a fellow, well dat body ought to be killed, as well, right?"

...

"Or, let's be a wee bit less extreme, an' say you go an' steal sometin', well, you gets yer hand cut off."

...

"Only 'eye fer an eye, toot' fer a toot,' dey said dat to stop folks punishin' too harsh. De very opposite of wot we's tinkin'! On account of dey were handin' out terrible harsh punishments. Like, somebody steals a loaf o' bread, well, dey gets a bit of a punishment sure, but you don't cut der arm off, fer heaven's sake."

. . .

"*Lex talionis* is wot dey call it."

798.59.12 . . .

Knowledge "Nice shot."

snow white worry-free
799.55.5 teasing a dwarf *non non non*
Haikus here comes paw-paw bear

Twice the presenter had spoken of avatars.

"Did you catch wot 'e was sayin' 'bout de avatars?"

"Naw. Der's a whole lot I didn't catch, fer dat matter."

"Same ting 'ere, but it don't bodder me. 'Twas right
800.76.9 interestin' all de same. 'Twas a kind of challenge."
Avatars

An advertisement for New Brunswick oysters
801.57.2 with photographs of the Caraquet, the Mallet,
Photocopies the Saint Simon, and the Beausoleil.

Terry was at a loss. What sort of love story was this woman looking for?

"Do you know dis one 'ere?"

Terry showed her *Belle du Seigneur* by Albert Cohen.

"Is it any good?"

"Well, I 'aven't read it, only lots of folks who 'ave tell me it's de best book dey ever read. An' it's a love story."

The woman took the book from him.

"It's awful tick..."

And the millions of tiny letters inside were irritating beyond measure.

"No. I'm not so keen on readin' wot everybody an' 'is uncle's readin'."

Terry put the book back on the shelf, and continued his search. It occurred to him that the woman might be on the edge of a kind of burnout or something of that nature.

"Well, would you be lookin' for someting more modern, den?"

"Wot do ya mean, modern?"

"Someting dat's happenin' in our time, or would ya prefer someting older?"

"Someting older, dat might do de trick."

Terry continued to look, but nothing jumped out at him. Finally he decided to gamble.

"Don't know, only I read dis 'ere book, an' I tawt it was shockin' good! An', besides meself, I don't know anyone else dat's read it."

Terry showed the customer *Zorba the Greek*. Alright, so he'd lied a little.

"Is it awful sad?"

The woman eyed the book warily, reached out and delicately took the volume from Terry's hand. The fact that Terry had read it meant that she had to treat it with some consideration.

"It's like a love story 'bout Greece."

The woman rifled the pages of the paperback, read the excerpt on the back cover, and decided to get rid of Terry:

"Looks alright. I'll tink about it, an' take anudder look
'round." 802.43.8
"No problem. If you have udder questions, don't be shy." Love

> At times, an expression can contain everything at once: techniques, tactics, fervour and fantasy. The French expression "*bouillon d'onze heures,*" for example, which means literally
> "eleven o'clock broth," and refers to a poisoned 803.138.12
> beverage. The Other

"Mum, when are we gonna 'ave our godfawder an' godmudder party?"

From the beginning, Terry and Carmen had explained to the children that they would organize a big party to celebrate the event.

"Afore too long."

"Only, afore too long when? I can't wait much longer."

804.52.1 Ceremony . . .

"All dis waitin's tirin' me out someting terrible."

Robin peck and peck
805.55.6 Haikus apple won't fall from the tree
sound branch to sup on

"Wot would be de opposite of inventin' yerself?"

"I don't know, do I. Inventin' de udder feller, I suppose."

"Hey, dat's not bad! I never tawt of dat. Most folks would've said destroyin' yerself, or some such ting, but not to go an' invent anudder fellow."

?!

. . .

"Wot is it den dat intrigues ya so 'bout opposites, anyhow?"

806.64.5 Opposites "Don't know. Only I'm drawn to it is all. Someting neutral to tink about, I suppose."

> Although the French language may be widely thought of as the language of love, the French have not been inclined to write love stories, especially not those with happy endings. It seems that love, in the French novel, serves mostly as the driving force for tales of obstacles and constraints. Perhaps the French have always known somehow that love is really a chemical affair rather than an affair of the heart, as Jean-Didier Vincent argues in his *Biologie des passions*
> 807.43.4 Love *(Biology of Passions)*, which *La Biliothèque idéale* ranks among the 49 best works in the "Sciences."

"Get married?! Holy Jesus, Joseph an', Mary! Are you serious, girl? You really want to marry me?"

Carmen couldn't understand why Terry should be so surprised.

"Geez! Does it surprise you all dat much?"

"Yes, yes... for sure I do. Only I didn't tink... I tawt maybe dat..."

Terry had never tried to put into words the vaguely confused fear lodged deep in his heart.

"Thought what...?"

"Don't know... dat, most likely, once you got to know me fer real, you'd not be likin' me so much."

Carmen frowned. Terry added:

"Well, someting like dat could happen, couldn't it?"

For a fleeting instant, Carmen saw again the Terry of their early days together, when he still lacked self-confidence. She moved closer to him:

"I suppose I don't say it to you often enough, only I can't imagine anudder life dan dis one we've got together, you and me an' de kids."

Terry received this simple declaration like a huge injection of love. He closed his eyes, embraced Carmen, who hugged him back.

"Would ya mind awfully repeatin' dat sentence you just said?"

Carmen could only laugh, Terry could be so innocent.

"An' to answer yer question, girl, der's not a hair on me 808.52.2
body dat doesn't want to marry you." Ceremony

> **WOBUBBLEY:** adj.—2005/2013; woman drunk on champagne. "She was wobubbly, the poor darling; her husband, on the other hand, was 809.120.12
> dead drunk." (Daigle/Majzels) Fictionary

"Dey say der's six million haiku poets over in Japan."

...

"Dat's one Japanese out of twenty, give or take."

...

"One out o' twenty! Dat's a terrible lot o' poets, wouldn't ya say?"

...

"Imagine dat back over 'ere. Would be a whole lot of poets at de Champlain Mall."

...

"An' on de golf courses."

810.59.11 Knowledge ...

"Fore!"

> In her novel *1953: Chronicle of a Birth Foretold*, the Acadian author France Daigle makes no mention of the publication that year of the
> 811.45.1 Useless Details bestseller *How to Play Your Best Golf All the Time* by famed champion Tommy Armour.

Terry knew very well he was repeating himself, but the situation seemed to demand it.

"Are you serious fer real, den..."

Zed nodded slowly.

"'Ave you 'ad a word wid Shawn 'bout it?"

Same nod of the head from Zed, who added:

"I told 'im ee'd always be 'is dad, all de same, an' like it or not. It's a weird ting, the boy an' me. Someting just clicked betwixt us."

Terry looked at his friend with admiration. But something else occured to him:

"An' wot about Élizabeth, den? Does dis 'ere change tings wid 'er?"

"Tell ya de troot, she's de one helped me see just how I's feelin'. In de end, she said wotever I decides, it'll be de right ting."

Terry also admired Élizabeth's cool.

"An wot did Chico say, den?"

Terry could see his friend was tearing up. Zed took a moment before answering:

"Was a wee bit weird... seemed like 'twas me askin' 'im to be adoptin' me as his dad."

This reversal made them both laugh.

"Anyhow, I finally managed to explain how I understood

it. An' when I's all done, ee looks at me an' ee says 'OK', an' dat's it."

The two friends fell silent. Zed blew his nose. Terry walked up to him and lay a hand on his shoulder.

"Dat's real good news, Zed. I can't tink of anyting better. For 'im, an' for you. An' for me as well, now dat I tinks on it. For all of us togedder, even. 'Tis like we's all gonna have anudder child."

And with that, Terry took Zed into his arms and hugged 812.52.3
him with all his might. Ceremony

> Love then would be more a biological necessity 813.107.6
> than a fervour. Necessities

Terry picked up a sweet potato, showed it to Étienne.

"Dis 'ere's a sort of potato, as well. Dey's orange inside, doh. I don't like 'em all dat much. Dey're like pastry an' sweet."

Now he picked up a Jerusalem artichoke, showed it to his son.

"Dis 'ere looks someting like a potato, only it's not is it. Dis 'ere's called a *topinambour.*"

Étienne could not restrain a smile.

"*Topinambour*. A right funny word, eh? Dey's awful good to eat raw. I'm tinkin' we should buy some all of youse can taste 'em."

Étienne nodded vigourously. Then, suddenly Terry cried out:

"Hey! Dat lady over der's wanderin' off wid our cart! Run an' fetch it!"

Étienne did as he was told, explaining to the woman. 814.23.5
Terry liked to see his son wasn't timid with strangers. Potatoes

> For golf, a five, seven, and nine iron, a five wood,
> a wedge, a light bag and balls, since it seems 815.121.9
> that's all the equipment a beginner requires. Things to Want

Carmen felt that there had to be limits, and Josse agreed with her.

"If Pierre an' Antoine 'ave a mind to get married, I got no problem wid dat. Only are we gonna be havin' a ceremony every time somebody's wantin' to make some ting or udder official."

"Exactly!"

Terry tried to explain:

"'Twould only be fer dem dat live in de buildin'. I mean, 'tisn't like we don't know dem all."

"Tell de truth, I can't say I know dem all dat well."

Josse's support for Carmen was steadfast:

"An' you don't want to be mixin' up all dem families togedder. Next ting, you'll be havin' a raising bee?"

Terry gave it one last try:

"If it were Josse an' Bernie gettin' married, wot would you be sayin' den?"

Carmen and Josse looked at each other. This was not the time to retreat. Josse quickly shot back:

"Only we's not about to be married, you can take me word on dat!"

816.52.4 "Alright, alright, den. I was only sayin'. De tawt just
Ceremony crossed me mind is all."

817.2.8 Étienne had liked the white and yellow colours
Colours of the word *roil*, meaning to disturb or stir up.

"Don't know if dis 'ere would count as one... only... when I finds a bit o' money on de ground, dat pleases me someting fierce. Even when 'tis nuttin' more dan a brown penny."

"That's sweet, but, no, I wouldn't call it an obsession."

"Even if der's times I set meself up? Like, say I's goin' out de door an' I tinks to meself, awh, I wouldn't mind findin' a bit o' money today... seems like it's been a long while since I did. An' believe it or don't, it works. One time I found me a dollar an' seventy-seven cents in loose change!"

"All in the same place?"

"Naw, but all in de same day."

"Do you dream about it at night? Is it something that's always in your mind?" 818.141.1 Obsessions

> Possible consequences of love, labial herpes, sometimes referred to as fever blister, bever blister, cold sore, coldslaw, or cankerblossom.

819.87.11 The Body

"Just as you say to somebody you pass in front of an' might be disturbin.'"

Terry maneuvered Carmen and Étienne so that they stood face to face.

"Alright den, talk..."

Étienne gazed uncomprehending at his mother. Carmen began the pretend conversation:

"Well, hallo der, Étienne! How you gettin' on, boy? Been a dog's age since I seen ya!"

Now Étienne understood they were playing a kind of game, but wondered if he should reply or not. Carmen continued:

"Are you still takin' those classes in..."

Suddenly Terry stepped between Carmen and Étienne to fetch a glass in the cupboard.

"See dat, how I got in between de two of you, an' it like disturbed yer conversation? Carmen was gettin' ready to ask you someting an' woops, I show up and bust it up. Well, when I do someting like dat, I ought to be apologizin.'"

Étienne seemed to understand.

"De best ting would 'ave been fer me to step 'round youse, so's not to break up yer conversation. Only when you got no choice but to go troo between two people, or even in front of just one person, de polite ting to do is to say 'excuse me' afore you pass, like to give 'em a *look out*."

Carmen glared at Terry, who'd used the English word. Terry corrected himself:

820.86.1 Apologies

“…to let dem know in advance* dat yer ’bout to disturb dem.”

821.71.8 Intro Embroidery

> Basic tasks: fabric preparation (washing, ironing, cutting, masking the edges, checking the balance, marking the centre) and mounting on a suitable frame (check the straight grain).

823.95.10 Additions to *La Bibliothèque idéale*

> In addition to being a world champion, the Scot Tommy Armour (1894–1968) became a renowned golf instructor. His book *How to Play Your Best Golf All the Time* sold 400,000 copies in its first printing — unsurpassed at the time — and is still considered one of the best golf instruction manuals. Perhaps it deserves to be inducted into *La Bibliothèque idéale.*

It was decided that the collective ceremony would take place at the end of August.

“Lionel and I would like you to do it at our place in Shediac. The grounds are big, especially with the beach. And we could end the evening with a campfire.”

Zed liked the idea.

“Dat’s awful nice of you, but it would mean a whole lot of folks trampin’ around yer place, don’t ya tink?”

“Not at all! We’ve done this sort of reception before, and it worked very nicely.”

Zed knew that by offering to host it, Lionel and Sylvia were intending to cover a large portion of the cost of the party.

“Honest to god, youse already done so much fer us… We could never repay you.”

Sylvia burst out laughing.

822.143.1 Varia

* An example of impoverishment of language: it would have been more economical to say “to warn them” rather than “to let ’em know in advance,” but the reflex was slow.

"Wot are you saying?! You're already repaying us!"

As she spoke, Sylvia raised her arms as though to 824.52.6
encompass the whole neighbourhood. Ceremony

polar bear bathing
tongue blackened with oil and soot 825.55.7
rotten film or pole Haikus

826.71.12
"Does we really have to start from scratch? Can't we Intro
just go out an' buy a kit? Embroidery

> A metal chinois, or China cap, is a fine strainer used in cooking. It is so called because its conical shape is reminiscent of the Asian hat popular in China's countryside. The name implies it 827.111.1
> could be made of a material other than metal. Tools

"Étienne, say yer sorry."

"Only I didn't do it on purpose."

"Doesn't matter, you ought to be sayin' yer sorry just de same."

Terry saw Étienne's expression of disbelief:

"Sometimes we don't do it on purpose, but just to be nice, we say we're sorry just de same."

"Only I didn't do anythin' wrong…"

Marianne, who was conscious of her role in the affair, redoubled her crying. Terry could see she was laying it on, but he wanted to deal with Étienne first.

"You tink she's screechin' fer nuttin' den?"

Étienne could feel the noose tightening:

"Well, I only wanted 'er to move over on account of de blocks sometimes fallin'."

"An' you didn't make dem fall wid yer foot?"

Even as she continued to cry, Marianne was banging on Étienne's shoe with a wood block.

"Maybe my foot did touch 'em, only 'twas Marianne was in de way."

Marianne had stopped crying and was hammering Étienne's foot with increasing force, as though she'd found a new game to play. Terry called her back to order:

"Marianne, don't be doin' dat."

Étienne pulled his foot out of the way. Marianne went back to crying. Terry put his book down and picked up the child.

"I'm tinkin' wee Marianne's all worn out, eh? *She's riding on her donkey, oh my little miss Marianne…*"

828.86.2 The tune lightened the mood. Étienne had escaped
Apologies having to say he was sorry.

829.136.6

The Unavowed Because the real is the Other.

Terry nodded his head up and down as he read the sheet of paper Carmen had given him, until he came up short:

"Wot's dis ting 'ere, de 'spiritual presentation'? Are ya talkin' 'bout sometin' religious for our parents an' dem?"

"Well, not only for them, for us as well. Something beautiful, that makes a body tink."

…

"Nothing complicated, mind you, just sometin' dat shows we love each udder an' dat we know what we're doin.'"

…

"You know how dey say in good times an' in bad, until death do us part. I'm thinkin' somethin' like that, only in our own words. We'd each be makin' our wee declaration."

Terry took a moment to think about it, imagined himself singing "*Is it possible you only need appear…*" but he quickly realized something like that would draw far too
830.52.5 much attention on him, and rejected the idea.
Ceremony "Alright den, I'll tink o' someting."

Although all words are fundamentally utilitarian, some are doubly so, and enter into the

> category of tools more easily than others. The French word *brelan*, which belongs in the lexicon of playing cards, is such a word. It is so much more economical than the expression "*trois du même* (three of a kind)," which also leaves some ambiguity about whether the three cards are of the same colour or same value. The *brelan*, on the other hand, specifically refers to three cards of the same value. In English, serious poker players will refer to "three of a kind" as "trips."

831.111.4
Tools

Étienne could not understand why his dad was making such a fuss over this particular field of strawberries.

"On account of der a whole lot better fer yer healt' is why. Dey don't spray dese wid chemicals to kill de insects."

"Why do dey want to kill de insects?"

"So dat dey don't eat de strawberries."

Étienne imagined a tiny brown ant trying to eat its way through a big red strawberry, and figured it was ridiculous to want to kill the ant since, clearly, it could never manage it.

"All dose chemicals, dey're no good fer us. Imagine if Carmen was pourin' a capful o' Mister Clean into de whipped cream fer de strawberries."

...

"You know, dat stuff we use to wash de toilet?"

"But, Dad! Mum would never do dat!"

"Course not, I know it. I only mean to say dat it's pretty much de same ting when dey spray dem chemicals on de strawberries. Wid dese 'ere, we'll be eatin pure strawberries, wid a whole pile of tick cream on dem. Mmmm. Feels good just tinkin' 'bout it."

"Is it still far?" 832.36.1

"Not so far." Strawberries

> Does this mean that the ego is not part of the
> real? Simplified answer: the ego is to the real
> what clothing is to the body: appearance, sur-
> 833.136.7 face. The ego covers over, protects, conceals,
> The Unavowed and the language of the ego does the same.

Under a radiant sun, the strawberries literally dropped into their hands, while a warm gentle breeze blew softly over everything and even up into the short sleeves of their T-shirts.

"Dad, would you be dyin' if you swallowed a capful of Mister Clean?"

"Ha! Well, 'twouldn't be all dat good for me I suppose, but I don't tink I'd die from it."

"How 'bout two capfuls den?"

"Not two capfuls neider, I wouldn't tink. Only, I'd have a terrible tummy ache for sure, an' most likely I'd be trowin' up."

. . .

. . .

"An' a whole glass full?"

"A whole glass?! Well, dat's not likely to happen is it? Why would I be swallowin' dat, I'd like to know. Unless somebody was makin' me, wantin' to poison me or some such ting."

. . .

"Why? You're not tinkin' of poisoning yer dad wid
834.36.2 Mister Clean, I hope?"
Strawberries Le Petit Étienne protested, laughing.

> Language hides more than it reveals. Which is
> 835.136.8 what makes confession difficult, and objectiv-
> The Unavowed ity impossible.

Zed explained to Chico that he could say a few words during the adoption ceremony, if he felt like it:

"I meself'll most likely be sayin' someting like…

tanks to me mudder an' me dad—even de one I never knowed—on account of I'm right glad to be alive after doin' dis ting 'ere today, an' I suppose I'd not be 'ere if it weren't fer dem."

Chico was all ears and eyes.

"An' tanks to yer dad Shawn, puttin' 'is trust in me, an' to Granny Lauzia an' her man Médric, who I never knowed, an' to yer mudder, even doh I don't know her, on account of widout all of dem Chico wouldn't be 'ere neider, right?"

This last twist made Chico smile.

"Tanks to Lionel an' Sylvia an' me aunty Annette, an' all de folks who believed in me, an' Terry an' Carmen, me *role model* parents... don't know how to say *role model* in French..."

As a matter of fact, Chico had noticed that the French language was often a subject of conversation in his new environment.

"An a great big tank you to you yerself, Chico, fer acceptin' me as yer new dad. I don't know how to explain it, but it's as doh I already knowed you afore I knew you. An' I promise dat I'll be doin' everyting I can so dat you have a good life."

Chico particularly liked this last part, and was eager to join in: 836.52.7

"Alright, I'll be wanting to say someting too." Ceremony

on the wooden chair
apple core sweats in the sun 837.55.8
pips will spring in time Haikus

Ludmilla sat down with her cereal bowl while her husband displayed his purchases.

"Looks fine to me."

"There were all kinds. I took the ones for trout."

Ludmilla crunched on her cereals, and listened to Le Grand Étienne's report.

"They're cork. These reels have only two ball bearings. The more expensive ones had eight."

Zablonski poured himself a coffee.

"Some had light-action reels, others medium. Some are made of graphite, more sensitive, less sensitive... a real circus!"

And then, adding sugar to his coffee:

"They even sell tiny modules called echo sounders that attach to the rod and tell you where the fish are! Can you imagine?!"

!

838.111.7 "You think they'll be happy?"

Tools Ludmilla was sure they would.

839.140.11 Étienne will forever be marked by the moving
Caraquet houses of Caraquet.

"Well, how 'bout Tide den, would Tide be poison too?"

"Holy geez, Étienne! Now yer startin' to worry me!"

But Étienne really wanted to know:

"Like, say Granny was to put de Tide in 'er strawberry pie instead o' sugar, would dat kill de whole family?"

"Well, I suppose which ever one o' us took de first bite would right away know de taste was bad, an' would spit it out or choke on it or some such ting, an' den de rest of us would hold off eatin' it. Den de police would come in to figure out wot happened, and den most likely Granny'd be hauled off to de prison, if dey could prove dat she was weary of us all and really wanted to poison de whole lot of us."

Étienne had not imagined the story could end in prison.

"But, how come de police knowed 'twas Granny?"

"Knew. We say knew."

. . .

840.36.3 "I don't know, do I. Might be de neighbours heard de
Strawberries screamin' or someting like, an' dey dialled 9-1-1."

> To arrive at a small or grand slam contract, the players must first bid in the natural manner until one of the two partners gets to a bid of four no trump. The other partner then bids five clubs if he has no aces, five diamonds if he has one, five hearts if he has two, or five spades if he has three aces. The bidder can then ask for kings in the same manner. The partner will respond with a bid of six clubs if he has no kings, six diamonds if he has a single king, six hearts if he has two, and six spades if he has three kings. Language is rife with codes.

841.127.12
Tactics

The strawberry picking was in full swing.

"Dad, is der a *jail* for kids?"

Étienne had used the English word *jail* instead of the French *prison*.

"*Prison*. Yer not allowed to say *jail*. But, dat's alright, I won't tell your mudder."

"Well, you said *ender up* in prison."

"I said dat? I never even noticed."

Terry was playing innocent, but he was conscious that he'd been increaingly lapsing into Chiac lately.

842.36.4
Strawberries

"I won't tell Mum neider."

843.122.1
Sports

> To account for.

"No, dey doesn't really have prisons fer kids. If ever a child was to do someting terrible wrong, dey'd figure it was on account of de parents didn't bring 'im up proper. An den dey sends de child to a special kind o' school where he'd be learnin' wot de parents failed to teach 'im."

Le Petit Étienne was paying close attention.

"Only dose schools're a whole lot stricter dan de schools we got 'round 'ere. Most times you 'ave to stay der a couple o' years. You sleep der an' everyting."

Terry, thinking he would like to be inside Étienne's

head to know what the boy was thinking, struggled to say more:

"Like, let's say you decide to put some of dat Tide in de sugar bowl, an' I get up one mornin' not knowing, an' I pour a whole lot of it in me Cheerios, so den I end up havin' to go to de hospital... Most likely, dey'll try to figure why you'd be wantin' to do me harm. Could be on account of I don't treat you right, or maybe der's someting inside you dat needs to hurt people, or could be you don't know de difference betwixt right an' wrong."

Le Petit Étienne had never imagined that the police made such fine distinctions.

"Chances are dey'll decide it wasn't really yer fault, on account of it's awful rare dat a child by himself is really bad. Almost always it's udder people dat made 'im de way ee is."

For a moment Étienne continued to pick strawberries, seemed satisfied.

"An' if it turned out dat I was really bad, all by meself inside me, what would happen den?"

Le Petit Étienne had used the word *quesse* or "what" instead of the more colloquial *quosse* or "wot," thereby
844.36.5 demonstrating that even he knew how to refine his lan-
Strawberries guage in a delicate situation.

> Turn the soil over with a ploughshare, fertilize it with a manure spreader, loosen it with a crop-dusting tandem or cultivator, sow with a line seeder, reap with a mower-conditioner, ted with a rake, harvest with a baler, a combine
> 845.126.1 harvester or a haywagon, and ensile with a si-
> Techniques lage blower.

Terry and his son picked in silence for a while. Only the wind in the leaves, the insects buzzing and birdsong could be heard.

"Folks dat put down de poison to kill de insects on

strawberries, do dey go to prison?"

"Not yet dey don't, but people ought to make up der minds 'bout it pretty soon. De government's still testin' to be certain all dem chemicals aren't harmin' our healt... only a fellow's gotta ask hisself how can dey not be harmful? Alright, a wee sprayin' 'ere an' dere, might not be so bad. Only now it's got so dey're puttin' it all over everyting. On de strawberries, on de potatoes, on de broccoli, on yer furniture, on yer carpets... even on children's toys!"

Le Petit Étienne figured it might be the spraying of chemicals on potatoes that was really irritating his dad.

"Take de Island — we've not taken you over der yet, but won't be long afore we do — on de island, der's fields an' fields an' fields o' potatoes. Only dey's sprayin' so much chemicals on dem dat de kids, an' even de adults, are gettin' sicker an' sicker all de time. Dey can hardly breathe over der!"

Étienne thought about it.

"I can hardly breathe meself, when I'm runnin'."

"Sure an' it's normal when yer runnin', boy. Runnin's
not easy. It's way hard on de lungs an' de legs. Dat's why 846.36.6
dey call it sport." Strawberries

> A curve has been taking shape for a while now, assuming it hasn't been there all along, and it will continue to develop for a while longer, if not forever. In fact, it's not inconceivable that we are dealing here with a circle rather than a
> cube, but it's neither necessary nor desirable to 847.73.2
> pursue this idea any further. Shifts

Terry completed his thought:

"De ting is dat nowadays dey's puttin' such a shockin' amount of chemicals everywhere, it's a whole mess of stuff dat's goin' inside us an' dat can't do udderwise dan hurt us. Der's a terrible lot of illnesses nowadays de doctors don't know what causes dem. Ask me, it's all dem chemicals."

...

It occurred to Terry he might have raised a subject that was too harsh for a child's ears.

"Sure, I don't want to put de fear in ya wid all dis talk. Only, if folks was lookin' furder dan de end o' der noses, dey wouldn't be puttin' so many o' dem chemicals all over de place. Take dis place 'ere, dey put zero chemicals an', ya see yerself, de strawberries are right fine just de same. In dose udder fields, dey's puttin' seven! Seven different chemicals!"

848.36.7 ...

Strawberries "Do you understand wot zero is?"

849.126.9
Techniques

Straight shooter.

Terry and Étienne made their way to the field's overseer's stall with their containers full of strawberries.

"By de way, which one o' yer grannies were you tinkin' might be puttin' Tide in her apple pie?"

Étienne felt a sudden hot flash.

"It doesn't matter wot you say, I's just curious is all."

Étienne loved both his grandmothers, and couldn't think what to answer.

"I bet you was tinkin' o' Granny Thibodeau."

Étienne tried to imagine his grandmother Thibodeau doing the unthinkable. It was difficult.

"Come on den, you can tell yer dad..."

Étienne neither nodded nor shook his head, although he felt it would have been easier to reply with a movement of his head than with words.

"I knew it."

Étienne wondered what it was his father knew all of a sudden.

"Don't bodder yerself about it. I'm not surprised. She's me mudder, an' I know her."

?!

"Not dat she'd do it, mind ya. Only I do believe de tawt crossed 'er mind once or twice. Don't ferget, we were five boys in dat house. An' Spinball an' Gloose were a couple o' devils when dey's young. 'Specially Spinball."

! 850.36.8

"You wouldn't tink so, eh, lookin' at 'em today?" Strawberries

Today, Friday, big job. Normally Friday is not the day they choose to overwork me. I was pressed into expectorating twice 200 copies of a multi-page questionnaire on golf. I despise being worked hard on Friday after I've stood around waiting through the entire week: the habit of work is something one loses and Friday is not a good day to regain it. In short, I took my time. I began by coughing a bit, then I crumpled* several sheets before flatly refusing to continue by simply jamming. Most likely surprised to be called upon, my most subtle mechanism — i.e., my automatic sorting tray, the equivalent to what medicine used to call the humours — refused to co-operate, triggering the paper-thickness code. Then the paper stock ran out, which was clearly not my fault, and to make matters worse, the ink supply followed suit, which normally doesn't happen every week. Result: I had company almost all afternoon. At first, I laughed to myself, but I soon tired of their clumsy fiddling, and before long I longed to be alone again to rebuild my memory and thoughts.

851.57.9
Photocopies

* The French word for crumple is *chiffonner*, but many Acadians will say *fichonner* or *fichounner* instead. The equivalent in English might be *prumcle* or *proumcle*.

854.143.2
Varia

Terry and Étienne found themselves still some distance from the small kiosk.

"Folks say dat to grow as many strawberries as dey do 'ere, a fellow's got to get inside de head of a strawberry."

"Dad! A strawberry's got no head!"

"Wot I mean, you gotta see de world troo de eyes of a strawberry. I know, I know, a strawberry's got no eyes!"

Étienne started to laugh.

"Wot dey mean to say is dat you gotta tink de way a strawberry tinks, if a strawberry could tink. Which dey very well might do, we can't know fer sure, can we?"

...

852.36.10 "Dat's de troot! Der's dem dat say plants do tink, an'
Strawberries dat sometimes dey wiggle der leaves to show it."

> Hunting moose, also called American elk, is considered a sport for several reasons: the hunter only gains the right to hunt through drawing lots, the hunting season only lasts three days per year, moose rarely move about when it's windy, calling the animal too often tends to confuse it, the hunter has to spread urine near his stand to attract the bull in heat
> 853.122.7 and, finally, because the hunter is required to
> Sports gut and dismember the carcass.

> 855.68.9 Find the video recordings of Derrick de
> Projects Kerckhove in Shippagan.

"'Ave you tawt 'bout wot yer gonna say?"

The adoption ceremony was approaching, and Zed was just a little nervous. But Chico didn't seem worried at all.

"I tink about it... only not all dat much."

In fact, Chico let his thoughts on the subject come and go, because there were so many other things in his new environment that required his attention. As a result, at the ceremony:

"Terry says me dad Shawn was good in maths in school, an' I'm good in maths in school as well."

An affectionate murmur swept through the crowd, but Chico would not be diverted.

"Now, I can't wait to find out wot I'll be good at wid Zed."

That was all it took, warm applause followed, and Zed's 856.52.8
adoption of Chico was official. Ceremony

Tried and tested, a sport not unlike settling 857.122.6
accounts Sports

Exceptionally, Zablonski was the one who spoke longest.

"I won't hide the fact that I feel I'm Étienne's natural godfather. And because the boy has talent, one might be tempted to imagine the kind of relationship between a painter and his student common in the Middle Ages. Whatever the case, in our case, I can say the master is learning as much from his student as the student from the master."

The assembled guests were touched by this display of humility from Le Grand Étienne toward the little one.

"But the real reason that I feel myself to be the natural godfather of Étienne lies in the fact that even before I knew them, I heard Carmen throwing up, and saw Terry doing his best to reassure her from our side of the door to the washroom of an airbus flying over the Atlantic. I was waiting for my turn, feeling a bit of sympathy for the poor sick girl, when Terry turned to me and said, 'She's preggies.'

Several audience members were pleasantly surprised by the accuracy of Zablonski's imitation of Terry's voice and diction.

"I was in no hurry. In fact, I was going nowhere and,

in a way, it was Terry and Carmen who, by their simple authenticity — which I continue to admire, by the way — put me back on track."

Everyone seemed to understand and to approve what Zablonski was saying about Terry and Carmen. But did he intend to go on talking for much longer?

"All this to say that Ludmilla and I find ourselves here in a place that suits us perfectly, and that Étienne is in a way the child that we never had, and that we're honoured to be accepted as his godfather and godmother."

Zablonski fell silent, but remained standing. Was he done talking? Was he too moved to continue?

"Obviously, Ludmilla and I also have a special place in our hearts for Zed and Chico. Long live Chico, long live Zed!"

"'ere! 'ere!"

"Santé!"

Everyone joined Étienne and Ludmilla in their toast to Chico and Zed, a toast that filled Chico's heart with
858.52.9 pride and joy, and that sealed forever for him his adop-
Ceremony tion pact.

859.111.2 The Y-joint with two shut-off valves allows the
Tools connection of two water hoses on a single tap.

Le Petit Étienne spoke only slightly longer than Chico:

"I wanted a godfawder on account of Dad's got one. An' me an' Dad's godfawders are old, but dat doesn't matter on account of when I'm big, I'll be de one to buy 'im presents an' take 'im out fer a stroll, on account of ee'll be too old."

Then, remembering suddenly that there was also his godmother Ludmilla, he added:

"An' I know me aunty Ludmilla likes me, on account of sometimes she smokes de pipe, but only wid me on account of it's a secret."

The laughter and applause excited Marianne, who

finally stepped out from behind Élizabeth. 860.52.10 Ceremony

> Old frames, antique mouldings. Wooden crates, packing boxes, and delivery (mandarines, Ikea furniture). Mouse traps (throw the mouse in the wet garbage bin). Pencils (lead?), old Scrabble game (Mathieu?), popsicle sticks. 861.42.5 Sorting

Now it was Élizabeth's turn:

"In my case, it's rather simple: one day, a darling little girl I'd never seen before just up and asked me to be her godmother. I hope I won't disappoint her... eh, Marianne?"

A down-to-earth statement, whose brevity was much appreciated, and which Marianne applauded along with everyone. 862.52.11 Ceremony

> Regarding the contribution and connection to the real: the book once printed has, in a sense, been sterilized, pulverised of all traces of stuttering, spontaneity, erasures, restarts, rejections, hesitations, displacements and other co-existing confusions. But loss is inevitable. It lies at the heart of all our lives, an essential dynamic. And consequently it is also the dynamic of writing. Because we will never be done with recording all those hesitations, all those glimmers of light exiled into a demi-world, all those almost somethings buried beneath the sea. Writing is an enormous attempt at recuperation. Writing is a sounding. 863.56.3 Pilgrimages

When Marianne realized that she too could address the crowd, she took Élizabeth's hand on one side and Zed's on the other and turned her shining face to the assembled guests.

...

Was she really going to say something? Carmen doubted it very much, Terry hoped she might. As for Étienne, like the other guests, he thought she looked sweet just standing there and smiling. Nor did the audience demand more; they began to applaud.

"Bravo!"

"A toast!"

"Thanks everyone, for coming…"

"A huge thank you to Sylvia and Lionel…"

864.52.12 "'ere, 'ere!"

Ceremony And with that the celebrations began for real.

CHAPTER 7

It will be achieved by the madman's meticulousness.

ELIZABETH SMART, *By Grand Central Station*
I Sat Down and Wept 865.144.7
Flamingo, HarperCollins, 1992 Epigraphs

The fire purred softly in the small stony cove bordered by Norwegian spruce.

"Fundy *driftwood*'s really a whole lot more mellow dan de *driftwood* down at Cap-Pelé."

Zed's comment made Terry laugh. But Zed was insistent:

"I tell ya troo! I noticed it more'n once. Listen close now! Dis 'ere wood hardly pops at all. All ya hears is a low whistlin'."

For a moment, everyone turned their listening attention to the fire.

"Luh! De *driftwood* down in Cap-Pelé don't stop poppin' an' spittin' sparks left an' right. Even de wood looks all twisted in pain."

Terry considered the possibility.

"Might be on account of how much salt's in de water, d'ya tink?

"Dat's wot I's tinkin'."

...

...

"How do ya say *driftwood* in French, anyway?"

Until now, Élizabeth, Ludmilla, Carmen, and Zablonski

had listened to Zed and Terry without interrupting, but the question turned the three Acadians of Acadian origin to the three Acadians of non-Acadian origin for help.

"I don't know. *Bois de mer*? *Bois flottant*?"

With "seawood" and "floating wood," Ludmilla had offered a couple of guesses. Zablonski only shrugged. Élizabeth had another idea:

"I've heard the term *bois flotté*."

Terry liked the sound of Élizabeth's "floated wood."

866.50.10 "*Bois flotté*. I like dat. On account of it's not as doh it were
Fundy floatin' still, like in *bois flottant*. *Bois flotté* gets me vote."

867.116.7
True or False True or false: there's truth in falsity.

Zed had already noticed the particularity of their little group:

"Peculiar all de same. We's tree real Acadians, I mean, born 'ere an' all dat, wid tree who can't be callin' demselves Acadians, not yet, anyway—hope I'm not insultin' anyone sayin' dat? An' de tree Acadians're all pretty young, under thirty-five let's say, an' de tree wot aren't Acadians're all over fifty, right?"

It was true. They all waited to hear the rest. But there didn't seem to be anything more. Terry wondered where Zed was going:

"An' wot does all dat mean, accordin' to you, I'd like to know."

"Don't know, do I? Only I'd say it's someting extraordinary."

Terry agreed, but could not explain it either. He turned
868.50.11 to his three elders:
Fundy "An' wot do youse tree tink about it?"

1. According to you, golf is:

a) A game.

b) A sport.

c) It doesn't matter.

d) I don't know. 869.62.1
e) I have no opinion. Survey/Men

"Hey mary, full of grace, de Lord is wid dee; blessed art dow amongst women, and blessed is de fruit of dy wound, Jesus. Holy Mary, Mother of God, pray for us sinners, now and at de hour of our death. Amen."

Étienne was mightily impressed by Chico's memorized recitation:

"Was it Granny dat tawt ya dat?"

"I already knowed it. Well, almost de whole ting."

"Does ya know any udders?"

"Our Fawder who artinheaven, hallowed be dy name, dy kingdom come, dy will be done on eart' a sitizin even. Give us dis day our daily bread, an' forgive us our trespasses as we forgive dose dat trespass against us, and lead us not into tent nation, but deliver us from evil. Amen.

Hearing this second recitation, Étienne realized that Chico was really older than him. 870.124.2

"I'll know dem, too, when I's older." Religion

> *Bédéesque*. One can argue that this French neologism meaning "cartoonish" or, to use an English neologism, *Simpsonesque*, is perfectly legitimate according to the authoritative *Besherelle, La Grammaire pour tous*. In the third volume of the *Bescherelle*, in the chapter that explains the difference between grammatical words and lexical words, it is clearly stated in article 300 that anyone, regardless of their nationality or status, can legitimately create new lexical words in response to the needs of a 871.77.1
> constantly evolving society. Grammar

Every spring, Terry cooked up a large cauldron of potatoes, lobster, and horseradish. The preparations for this meal cast a festive mood throughout their home

and an irresistible odour into the hallways of the lofts, so that friends — carrying musical instruments and wine — inevitably appeared. Terry meticulously stirred butter, buttermilk, horseradish, and other seasonings essential to the recipe into the pot before delicately depositing large chunks of lobster tails and claws. By the end of the
872.23.4 evening, the appetite of the musicians eliminated any
Potatoes chance of leftovers.

> 1. According to you, golf is:
> a) A game.
> b) A sport.
> c) Other, specify: ________________________ .
> 873.69.1 d) I don't know.
> Survey/Women e) Surveys bore me.

"Alright den, here we go..."

Terry did not simply drop the potatoes wrapped in foil into the fire. He took the time to bury each one in the embers, so that they would cook evenly. Zed turned to
874.50.3 Élizabeth:
Fundy "Terry's our potatoes expert."

> It is difficult to say exactly when a word ceases to be a neologism. Is the word *bédé*, for exam-
> 875.92.4 ple, created in 1974 from the letters *b* and *d* for
> Questions *bande dessinée* or "comic strip," still a neolo-
> without gism today?
> Answers

One might argue that hockey — an English word derived from the French *hoquet,* meaning "hiccup" — is a culinary sport. Several decades ago, an effort was made to change the name to *goret* or "piglet," but no one swallowed that, and we continue to prefer hogging the puck to hogs in a blanket. Nevertheless, listing the ingredients of a good game can be instructive. The coach, a sharp cookie, provides a recipe for victory point blank: primo, a goal tender who's cool as a cucumber, secondo, players who are ready to stir the pot. In other words, dig in, be hungrier than the opponent. Even in the locker room, we can sense this team will not settle for scraps. The players are up and off their haunches, eager to take a bite out of their opponents; they are full of beans, and they can smell victory. What's more, the coach — who has thrice tasted the champagne from the cup — knows this is his bread and butter: he must bring home the bacon. Creative and crafty, he knows how to whip up his proteges, how to use the carrot and the stick, separate the wheat from the chaff, and promise the fruits of victory. The temperature is rising: while some try to curry favour, others are warned there's no such thing as a free lunch. The goalie dons his waffle pad and prepares to deny the opponents starved for goals, especially the wingers eager to fatten their statistics by pouring shots into the net. Sometimes, though a loss will force the players to eat humble pie, it can shake up the team and show the players they need to wake up and smell the coffee. To have his lunch handed to him can give a player a taste for vengence, a willingness to pull the fat from the fire, to pepper the opposing goaltender and put some mustard on his shots. With the puck stuck to his stick, he'll dribble into the crease and beat the goalie. Even if he's slashed or speared, a player holding the blue line against two giant-sized opponents will rejoice in the prospect of whipping the cream of the crop in the quarter-finals. The fear of losing his meal ticket gives a team wings, whips them into shape, so that they get out there and dish it out. It was in a game like this that a tough bruiser — who's recently had a tendon sliced from his thigh to replace a ligament — scored the winner for his team. It must be said that a juicy victory can light a fire under the team as well or better than

an indigestible defeat: two matches* in hand will ignite the team and, rather than settle on their lees, the players want to crush their opponents and tip the cup. On the other hand, nothing is more deflating and bitter than an icing call when the other team is already living high on the hog, determined to get out of the cellar and take advantage of home ice. Nor is anything more humiliating than to have everything go pear-shaped at home, with the visitors laying it on thick and the home team slower than molasses going uphill. In the end, when the smoke clears, the head coach refuses to cry over spilt milk, and without throwing in the towel, or any hint of sour grapes, he admits the team lacked some key ingredients to pull it off. Perhaps they bit off more than they could chew and wound up with egg on their faces. They were flat and collapsed in the end. Fed up with serving up an easy victory to their opponents, and their share of the lead, the players towel off and dress, not bothering to linger or chew the fat in the locker room. Standing before the press, the head cheese admitted they'd made
876.98.6 a meal of it, but promised the next game would be a
Expressions different kettle of fish.

2. Do you enjoy smoking a cigar while you play golf?

a) Yes.

b) No.

c) I play golf in order to smoke my cigar.

877.62.2 d) A cigar is the worst encumbrance.

Survey/Men e) I like to sing while I golf.

---

* Here, the author wishes to distinguish between the French noun *match*, which is masculine and means "a game," with the feminine neologism *matche*, derived from the English "match," a bit of wood or cardboard used to light a fire. In English, the
878.143.6 two meanings share the same homonym, the origin of which,
Varia incidentally, is the old French *meche* or "lamp wick."

> 2. Do you enjoy smoking a cigar while you play golf?
> a) The cigar is an aberration.
> b) The cigar is an abomination.
> c) This survey is ridiculous.
> d) Yes. 879.69.2
> e) No. Survey/Women

Étienne lay the coin on his thumb and tried again.

"Luh! I got it!"

"Once you catch it, you gotta turn 'er upside down on yer hand, like dis 'ere."

Étienne was impressed with Chico's dexterity.

"Who was it showed ya how to do dat?"

"Shawn."

Étienne tended to forget Chico had had another dad before Zed. In a way, he envied his new friend's slightly disrupted life.

"Awh."

"Dey calls it heads or tails. On account of de head on dis side 'ere."

"Awh."

Chico sent the coin summersaulting into the air again, caught it and slapped it on the back of his hand without taking his other hand off.

"Heads or tail?"

"Tail."

Chico lifted his hand, revealing the maple leaf this time.

"Tail! You win, only it don't count. We'll be startin' fer 880.126.6
real tomorrow." Techniques

> The French expression "*but en blanc*" — "point blank" in English — means bluntly or directly. Most likely the head coach made his statement without expecting to be questioned at that moment, or on that subject. Perhaps he was about

881.25.12 Murder

to be accused of murder when the sports journalist shoved a microphone or pen under his nose to ask him what were the ingredients of a good hockey game. Journalists will do that.

"Kouchibougouac's more us, all de same."

"De fields, rivers. It's all so much calmer."

"An' ders a whole lot fewer rocks."

"Even de forest. It's more like velvety. Can ya say dat?"

"An' why not?"

"De clams, blueberries…"

882.50.1 Fundy

"Clams an' blueberries, can ya tink of anyting more Acadian dan dat, eh?"

883.98.7 Expressions

Originally, the French expression was written "*de butte en blanc*" rather than "*but en blanc*," and referred to a marksman standing on a butte or hill and shooting an arrow at the white centre of a target below. The English "point blank" has a similar origin, referring to an arrow shot from such a close distance that the white centre of the target could not be missed. On the other hand, the expression "*faire chou blanc*" means "to draw a blank," to fail. At first glance, the French expression seems richer than the English, but in the end it promises more than it delivers. A literal reading of "*faire chou blanc*" as "to make a bun white," might lead one to imagine that the expression referred to that glutton's delight, the French cream puff. Alas, no. Words will do that.

"Dey say you only have to 'it de ball once on wot dey call de sweet spot, an' yer like hooked on de game. De feelin's so wonderful good, ya can't help yerself, you gotta go back an' play again."

…

"Tell ya de troot, I wonder if I've ever 'it dat sweet spot." 884.59.8 Knowledge

> The idea has been there for some time now, lying in wait around the corner, waiting for the right moment to suddenly appear. To impose itself. 885.73.5 Shifts

Ludmilla took off her shoes to wade in the water. Terry thought he'd better warn her:

"Dat's gonna be terrible cold! Water round 'ere's always colder."

But Ludmilla, undaunted, stepped into the water without the slightest complaint.

"Well, look at dat, will you. I suppose it's not as cold as all dat."

Zed and Élizabeth took their shoes off, too. Carmen, Le Grand Étienne and Terry watched them approach the water. Zed and Élizabeth exchanged a few brief words with Ludmilla before getting their feet wet. Zed took a few steps and turned to the spectators on the shore: 886.50.2 Fundy

"Incredible! You'd tink we was in Parlee Beach!"

> The suffix *-esque*, which is strictly limited to forming adjectives out of nouns, was ideal for the word *bédéesque*, if only because of the similarity in meaning with adjectives like *clownesque, cauchemardesque, funambulesque, éléphantesque*. Although it appears sometimes in English, as in picturesque, dantesque, and grotesque, the ending *-ish* is more common: clownish, nightmarish, and childish, for example. The origin of the *-esque* is the Italian *-esco* via words such as *pittoresco* and *gigantesco*. Adjectives ending in *-esque* are qualifiers relating to appearance. 887.77.3 Grammar

Carmen and Zablonski followed, quickly grasped the

ploy, and feigned comfort. Would they succeed in drawing Terry into this basin of ice-cold water? As she walked by Élizabeth, Carmen whispered:

888.50.4 "Gives me a terrible headache like I used to get eatin'
Fundy ice cream when I was a kid."

> 3. Do you answer your cellphone or beeper during a round of golf?
> a) Yes, of course.
> b) Absolutely not. I leave all that junk in the car.
> c) I have to: I'm a paramedic.
> d) I wear a fake beeper on the course, to pretend I have a job.
> 889.62.3 e) I always phone my wife on the 17th hole, be-
> Survey/Men cause we were married on September 17.

890.79.6
Oddities "Who was it assassinated Agrippina, again?"

> 3. Do you answer your cellphone or beeper during a round of golf?
> a) Yes, absolutely.
> b) Yes, obviously.
> c) I couldn't live without my hands-free accessory and my all-inclusive music package.
> d) I tossed my cellphone in the lake at the 5th hole last week.
> 891.69.3 e) I have an assortment of fake cellphones to
> Survey/Women match each of my golf outfits.

Terry watched his friends wading in the water. He found it hard to believe the water could be that warm because, when he'd put a toe in a few weeks earlier in
892.50.5 August, it was very cold. How could it have warmed up
Fundy since then?

> On the other hand, the *Bescherelle* does not promote the invention of grammatical words,

> which are limited in number, and to which the reader is not encouraged to add. These grammatical words are the nuts and bolts of language, those tiny mechanisms that build it and make it work: non-qualifying articles and adjectives, prepositions and conjunctions. These words form a limited paradigm, i.e., they can be replaced in a particular sentence, but only by a limited number of other words. Which is to say, their inventory is closed. The words in bold in this paragraph are grammatical words. 893.77.4 Grammar

A car door slammed, then another, and yet another. Terry recognized Pomme's voice, then Sylvia's. He shouted to the five waders:

"Dey made it!"

Lisa-M., Pomme, Sylvia, and Lionel soon appeared at the peak of the cliff and began the descent along the gently sloping path that led to the creek. Terry went to meet them.

"Great! We wasn't expectin' you so soon!"

"Der was a bomb scare at de university, in de arts buildin' of all places, so dey sent us all away."

"How 'bout Lionel, did ee get back early as well, den?"

Lionel spoke for himself:

"No. Lionel never left home. I ended up doing all my business on de phone. Der's nuttin' like bein' yer own boss, eh? You ought to know." 894.50.6 Fundy

> 4. Do you spend a lot of money on golf equipment?
> a) My spending is reasonable because I know that the quality of my game does not depend on my equipment.
> b) I spend a great deal even though I know that the quality of my game does not depend on my equipment.

c) I spend a lot more for my equipment than I tell my wife.

d) I have to spend a great deal because one of my legs is shorter than the other.

e) I'm obliged to renew my equipment at my
own expense, because none of my exception-
895.62.4 ally gifted children has had the idea of offering
Survey/Men me golf equipment as a present.

"Strange how when a body uses de wrong word, folks'll say der tongue's forked. Only forks don't have tongues now do dey? Dey got teet, last time I looked, anyway."

"Most likely dey was tinkin' of a fork in de road, where she splits in two."

"An' not only dat, a fork's got more'n two teet; it's got four or six generally."

"Six? I never seen a fork had six teet."

896.106.9 "Dose're pitchforks for haulin' hay."

Customs "Awh."

897.79.8

Oddities Marianne likes her toast burned.

A cry. The kind of scream that reinvents the genre. Pomme? But where is he? Is that him over there in the water? Is he hurt? Is he drowning? No, he's swimming. But why that terrible cry? A shark? Maybe one of his feet has been torn to shreds. Or an entire leg. Both feet? Should we swim out to his rescue?

"Ee don't look like ee's havin' any trouble swimmin.'"

"Pomme? Ee swims better'n all de rest of us put togedder."

...

...

Pomme. He'd been awfully hot on the way. So terribly hot.

"Well, why didn't he say someting, den?"

Pomme. Not the kind to complain. Then, without a word, slipped away like a cat — after all, he knows the beach — up to the little cliff, knowing exactly on which

rocks to clamber up. And then he dove, divinely, into the 898.50.7
water — the ice-cold water — of the Bay of Fundy. Fundy

> Carmen's prayer: Oh Lord, watch over all those 899.124.6
> I love, and all those who love me. Amen. Religion

Pomme couldn't stop shivering. Terry threw more driftwood onto the fire, rolled the potatoes back to the edge of the pit.

"I can't believe youse all tawt I'd go in de water only 'cause you were in der. You don't know me at all."

Terry lay the marinated chicken breasts one by one on the grill.

"Have to say doh, 'twas a right cunnin' game you were playin'; I's startin' to ask meself how dat water got so warm."

Zed teased him:

"A wee bit longer an' you'd 'ave found some kind of explanation, I bet."

"Most likely!"

Terry laughed, and turned to explain to Élizabeth: 900.50.8
"'Cordin' to Zed 'ere, I's an intellectual." Fundy

> It's no coincidence that, limited in number, grammatical words are also limited in length. The *Bescherelle* establishes a direct link between the shortness of grammatical words and the fact that they are used so often, citing this as a good example of the economy of 901.77.5
> language. Grammar

"In any sport, comes a moment you gets into a good feelin', in de zone is wot dey call it."

"Only I tink dat's two different tings: de zone's a zone, and de sweet spot, well dat's a spot."

?

...

“Alright, well, whatever. One way or de udder, seems like we’ll be havin more an’ more o’ dem good feelin’s in de future, wot wid nanotechnologies an’ de like. Our bodies an’ machines ’re gonna be more joined togedder. An’ de reason dat’s gonna happen is on account of folks prefers feelin’ to tinkin.”

…

“Dat’s ’ow dey explains de fad fer tattoos an’ piercin’s an’ de like. Dat’s all about de need to feel.”

!

“An’ de whole ting wid liftin’ weights, dats more or less de idea of de human-machine.”

!!

“Same ting wid de Transformers.”

902.59.7 …

Knowledge “Wot’re ya waitin’ fer to take yer swing?”

> Once upon a time a fork had only two teeth.
> 903.111.3 Hence the name of the instrument: bident.
> Tools Bifurcation?

The fresh air, the joy and delicious smells whetted the picnickers’ appetites. Zablonski examined the two small black balls that claimed to be potatoes in his plate:

“Believe it or not, I’ve eaten completely charred potatoes like these before. In Germany, I think. They were actually quite good.”

“Dis ’ere’s de recipe dat won me a Scout’s medal in cooking.”

“Me, ’twas me sausages in salty molasses.”

“You were a Boy Scout?”

“Salty molasses?”

Élizabeth looked at each one of them in turn, found something endearing in all of them, felt totally at ease among them.

“’Ow ’bout you, Élizabeth, wot do you eat to feel like yer back in yer mudder’s womb?”

Élizabeth found the question funny, but she had a ready answer:

"A bowl of corn flakes. With lots of milk and plenty of sugar."

Élizabeth had correctly used the masculine noun *un bol.* Zed quickly corrected her in the proper Chiac:

"We say "*une bolle.*"

"An' we always say de colour of de sugar.

"White." 904.50.9

"Right. Yer kinda sweet yerself." Fundy

> 4. Do you spend a lot of money on golf equipment?
>
> a) No, because every year I wait for the sales to buy myself a complete set of new equipment.
>
> b) No, my only weakness is for the shoes.
>
> c) Does the 19th hole count as part of the equipment?
>
> d) I never spend money, I use credit cards.
>
> e) I get enormous satisfaction out of spending enormous amounts of money on pretty much 905.69.4
> anything. Survey/Women

"An' why is it yer in pain, do you tink?"

"Wot, are ya tinkin' I'm hurtin' on purpose?"

"Well, maybe not on purpose, only fer sure der's someting in you dat wants to be hurtin."

"Tell me yer jokin'..."

"Dey say dat when we hurt ourself, even doh it looks like an accident, it's not an accident."

...

"'Tisn't someting we can be admittin' to ourselves."

...

"Do you want my interpretation?"

"Do I 'ave a choice?"

"I tink it's on account of wot 'appened to Ron. You tink dat moose should've come across in front o' you instead o' 'im. Deep down, you tinks yer not worth as much as ee is."

...

...

"One ting's fer sure, I can't wait fer you to get yer degree
906.127.9 an' den open an office some place. Hopefully dat'll take
Tactics yer focus off o' me."

> 5. What's your attitude toward beginners playing ahead of you on the course?
> a) I'm a slow player myself, so I don't mind.
> b) I wait patiently, because I was a beginner once myself.
> c) Their presence is annoying, but we're obliged to tolerate them, aren't we?
> d) They get on my nerves. They ought to be compelled to learn the basics elsewhere.
> 907.62.5 e) I enjoy chatting with the young ladies in the
> Survey/Men trees beyond the rough.

Night had fallen several hours ago when the band of friends decided it was time to pack up and go. Pomme and Terry put the fire out with water and sand. Zed helped Sylvia carry an interesting piece of driftwood to the car.

"It might look good in the garden..."

Ludmilla and Élizabeth shook and folded the blankets, Lionel picked up the trash while Lisa-M. and Carmen packed the coolers.

"De vegetables'll still be good. De chicken, not so sure."

"We'll eat it."

Zablonski managed the big flashlight.

"Zab! Zap dat light o'er dis way fer a minute!"

...

"A wee red fox! Do you see it?"

"Naw. Where?"

"Down by de big rocks."

. . .

"Awh, ee's gone . . ."

. . . 908.50.12

"Alright den, Zab. We don't need it no more. Tanks." Fundy

> 5. What's your attitude toward beginners playing ahead of you on the course?
> a) Why should I have an attitude? I don't understand the question.
> b) I like to chat with them while I'm helping look for their ball.
> c) I return their ball politely when they hit it in the wrong direction.
> d) I try to get invited to play with them next time because those girls look like they're really having fun. 909.69.5
> e) All of the above. Survey/Women

"Étienne, I've some books fer The Cripple. Can you haul 'em over der fer me? I can't get away right now."

Étienne was always proud and happy to lend a hand in the bookstore.

"'Ere you go den, an' don't be fergettin' to show 'im de receipt."

Terry barely had time to slip the receipt from the cash register inside the cover of the first book before Étienne was turning around to go.

"Hang on, now! I'll ring 'im up to let 'im know yer on yer way up, an' make sure ee's der."

Étienne waited patiently, looking at the books he was getting ready to deliver. While The Cripple's phone was ringing, Terry had time to enlighten his son:

"Dis 'ere book talks about de Greek tragedies. It's teatre. You know, like at de Escaouette . . ."

Étienne nodded.

"Hello? It's Terry downstairs. I'm about to send me boy up wid yer books. Is it a good time?"

. . .

“Alright den!”

Terry hung up and quickly picked up the second book to glance at the back cover:

“Dis one ’ere’s a physics book. You’ll be learnin’ physics in school soon enough. Dis ’ere explains why a ball always ends up fallin’ down to de ground, an’ udder stuff like… what makes de colours in a soap bubble. You know, de ones we blows troo de wee round end of de stick ya dips in de bottle?”

Étienne thought that did indeed merit an explanation,
910.16.6 and what’s more, all things considered, physics seemed
The Cripple quite worthwhile.

> An avatar is a creation, a point of departure, a
> separation from our lineage, a break from the
> name of the father. A fork. The names alone
> will trigger anyone’s imagination: Joe Jello,
> 911.76.5 Paul PR, Lucky PowPow, Baby Dy, Sorros Jr,
> Avatars Doctor Flour, Pick Pocket, and S Crowbar.

Zablonski showed Marianne how to bend the onion tops down.

“See? We bend them over like this, right down to the ground.”

Marianne set to work with great enthusiasm.

“Very good. Very, very good. Now we’re going to do the whole row. You keep going here and I’ll begin at the other end. Alright?”

“Awwhite?”

Marianne watched without budging as Le Grand Étienne moved down the row.

“No? You don’t want to do it?”

Seeing that the child wasn’t moving, Zablonski came back to her.

“Would you prefer to do it together? Shall we do it together, then?”

"Awwhite?" 912.38.1 Onions

6. Do you play by the rules?
a) Depends whom I'm playing with.
b) Depends on any given day.
c) Yes, I count almost all my strokes.
d) Yes, I count all my strokes and those of my partners.
e) I stop counting after 200. 913.62.6 Survey/Men

"Normally, you've got de baby legs dat go as high as tree feet, den you got de sticks, dey can go five feet. An' de high hat — dat's just like a plate — is right practical as well. 914.111.10 Tools

6. Do you play by the rules?
a) Rules? There are rules?
b) Yes, I allow myself the right to cheat only five times.
c) The rules are an excellent guide, because no two courses are alike.
d) I hate shouting fore.
e) Not when the golf club bars women from playing. 915.69.6 Survey/Women

Zablonski advanced, pushing most of the onion stalks down, but leaving a few for Marianne who was following along behind. At one point, glancing back to make sure everything was going well, he saw that Marianne was pulling the stalks out rather than pushing them down to the ground. He watched her for a moment, chuckling to himself at her astonishment each time she discovered the brownish, whitish or wine red bulbs at the end of the stalk.

"Everything alright, Marianne?"

The child raised her head, looked at him. He decided not to interfere.

916.38.2 "Fun, isn't it?"
Onions He went back to work, and so did Marianne.

> In Numidia, in the year 354, a woman named Monica gave birth to Aurelius Augustinus, who would later become the author, philosopher, and theologian better known as Saint Augustine. When he was 18 years old, Augustine's lover gave birth to their son Adeodatus. That same year, Augustine decided
> 917.99.10 to convert to wisdom. He, in turn, gave birth to
> Names Western man.

"Take de environment. It's on account of folks feelin' so much more dat it's become such a terrible big deal."

. . .

"Same ting wid helt. Used to be, folks died an' 'twas normal. Nowadays? Folks treats it like it's an insult!"

. . .

"An' dat's how come so many people're takin' antidepressants. On account of dey focus on how dey's feeling,
918.59.9 not on wot dey's tinkin'. Wot yer tinkin's not so terrible
Knowledge important anymore. It's all about how yer feelin'."

> Another interesting section of the *Bescherelle* grammar book deals with new spelling rules: The French Academy no longer insists on the insertion of a circumflex accent above the *i* and the *u*, except in the case of verb endings (*nous rendîmes, vous crûssiez*) and of a few words where the circumflex serves to distinguish homonyms (*mur* meaning "wall" and *mûr* meaning "ripe," or *du* meaning "of" and *dû* meaning "due"). *Île, maîtresse, coût, flûte, boîte* have therefore become *ile, maitresse, cout, flute, boite*. They look naked. But the Academy has ruled that the phrase *drôle de tête*, meaning

> a “strange or funny look,” will continue to be 919.77.6
> written *drôle de tête*. Go figure. Grammar

“Dad! De light’s red!”

The day before, Chico had explained to Étienne how traffic lights work.

“You gotta wait ’til de light turns green.”

Terry explained about turning right on a red light.

“Well, ’ow long does ya ’ave to stop, den?”

“Not all dat long. So long as you stops an’ look around to see wot’s happenin’. Den’ you can go right ahead, if der’s no car crossin’ in dat direction. On account of if der’s one dat’s comin’, den I’s de one dat has to let ’im go.

“On account of?”

“On account of ee’s de one’s got de green light. Whoever’s got de green light can go right troo, no matter wot. Ee doesn’t even ’ave to stop.”

. . .

“Used to be, we weren’t allowed to do dat. Light was red? You stopped ’til she turned green. Hasn’t been all dat long now, dey changed de law so dem dat wants to turn right are allowed to go as well.”

. . .

“It’s workin’ just fine, you ask me. Doesn’t cause more accidents.”

. . .

. . . 920.73.1

“But, how come dey decided on green?” Shifts

> Occasionally, proper speech slipped in.
> Delicate combinations, correct pronunciation.
> Syllables, sometimes several in a row, alligned,
> waiting their turn to summersault along the
> banks of language’s ocean. Words, at times sev- 921.7.2
> eral in a row. Useful Details

“Fives, we’s playin’ fer fives.”

"An old maid."

. . .

"Anudder old maid."

"Luh, an ace . . . you likes aces, don't ya?"

"Der's nuttin' good fer me der. Tree Salmons an' a Jackson of clubs."

"A Jackson, now . . ."

"Tree big K-boys, real ones. Neener of diamonds."

"A neener's good. Tree neeners, an' dime-jack-queen o' spades."

"*Pfff* . . . Ocho o' hearts."

"Can't take it. Helen o' Troy."

"A deuce . . . dat's kind o' small, eh?"

"Deuce, trey, farr o' hearts."

"Dat's no big bouquet o' flowers."

"Tree farr, neener o' spades.

"An' why didn't ya put yer neener der?!"

"Sweet Mickey! I coulda been over an' out."

"She's only got a single card left? One-eyed king."

"One-eyed king, now. One, two, tree pore little deuces."

"Sax o' spades."

"A hockey stick. Are der none over der? 'Ere's anudder one. Ocho clubs."

"Trey o' diamonds."

"Tree treys. Tree wee piggies."

"Close de hockey sticks. Farr o' spades."

"No good. No good."

"*Pfff* . . ."

"A nickel an' I'm done!"

"Again!"

"Sweet Bejesus, I'm left wid a wild card!"

"Now dat's not too clever."

"I's waitin' fer someting to play 'er wid!"

"I've got 22 fer 30 cents."

"I got 17."

"Nine. Whose turn is it to deal?"

"Mine."

"Don't ferget to ante up. Seems to me, de pot's not gettin' bigger."

"I'm paid up."

"An' I."

"Fer saxes, we's playin' fer saxes." 922.122.9 Sports

> Terry does not pretend to have created avatars you might confuse with real people, as is evident from the cartoonish names he's given them: Joe Jello, Paul PR and Lucky PowPow. In any case, the point is not whether these creatures exist in the flesh. The point is to know that they exist, circulate, act, cause what may be a new kind of accident. 923.76.3 Avatars

"Take playin' golf. You walks, you stretches, you whack de ball. Everyting's green an' blue, de wedder's fine, it smells nice. Der's a light breeze, long grass, an' branches. 'Tis all physical. So wot, you say? So, all de golf courses is packed to de rafters, dat's wot."

...

"Same ting fer de extreme sports. It's like our body only just woke up. Ask me, 'tis anudder dimension of ourselves dat just woke up. A dimension dat wasn't possible afore now, fer some reason. De nano dimension." 924.59.10 Knowledge

"Luh! 'Ere she is!

> A kind of fluidity in the ordering of the fragments confirms that the story has indeed taken flight, and is now soaring on its own power, toward its conclusion. As though the goal, until now only imagined, has at last revealed itself to be possible, attainable, acheivable. Vast arrangement, slow deployment, intuition confirmed, rare emotion. 925.73.6 Shifts

"Wot's ee up to den?"

Chico had seen so many new things since he'd moved into the lofts that he was no longer entirely sure what was normal.

Étienne took up the question:

"Wot ya doin', Dad?"

"I'm measuring de toilet paper."

"On account of?"

"Just to see."

"To see wot?"

"To see if wot dey write on de package is de troot."

The two boys came closer, curious to see what this was all about. Terry decided they deserved a more complete explanation.

"Look over 'ere on de package, dey tell us de size an' number of little squares in each roll. Well, how do we know fer sure it's de troot if nobody ever takes de time to count dem?"

The two boys found this to be eminently logical and even somewhat inspiring.

"Can we be countin' some, too?"

Terry would have preferred to say no and continue his little investigation unencumbered.

"Can youse count to six?"

The two boys laughed, thinking Terry was just teasing.

"Dad! You're de one dat showed me how!"

"Me as well, me Dad showed me how."

Terry looked at Chico:

"Did I tell ya Shawn was always winning de adding, subtracting, multiplication an' division contests in school? Dat boy couldn't be beat! Der was times I's furious ee was so good."

926.53.1 Buyer Beware

Chico swelled with pride. Étienne was happy for him.

7. Do you find it important to know that a golf ball measures 4.4 centimetres in diameter and weighs 5.2 grams?

a) Yes.

b) No.

c) I don't know.

d) I have no opinion.

e) I only know measurements in inches and ounces. 927.62.7 Survey/Men

Terry set Étienne and Chico down with a roll of toilet paper and showed them how to proceed.

"An' don't go losin' count. Dis 'ere's serious!"

The two boys got down to work. Terry watched them at first.

"You hold de end, I'll do de countin.'"

"An' den after, it'll be me turn to count, okay?"

"One, two, tree, farr, five, six."

Étienne tore off the strip of six squares and laid it down on a kitchen chair. Then Chico counted six more squares, tore the second strip along the perforation and laid it down on top of the first. Terry was satisfied:

"Dat's exactly right. Now, you do de whole roll just like dat." 928.53.2 Buyer Beware

> Not forgetting that some shifts in direction can turn out to be missed opportunities. For example, the title "Robots designed to treat the injured soldiers in the heat of battle": why not forget the soldiers and send the robots directly into battle? 929.73.9 Shifts

"Win? You win?"

But Zablonsiki had not presented the taking down of the onion stalks as a contest.

"Well, alright then, you win."

Did the child expect a prize of some sort? As there was really nothing around that might serve as a gift, Zablonski resigned himself to telling the truth, at the risk of disappointing her:

"It's just that... well, I didn't think we were having a contest."

"Concon?"

"No, not a contest."

"Awwhite?"

930.38.3 "Yes, that's it. Alright."

Onions "Awwhite."

7. Do you find it important to know that a golf ball measures 4.4 centimetres in diameter and weighs 5.2 grams?

a) Yes, but I'll have forgotten in 30 seconds.

b) Yes, it's a good way to check on the accuracy of my Weight Watchers scale.

c) No, I assume they're selling me regulation balls.

d) No, I find that sort of detail exasperating.

931.69.7 e) I only know measurements in inches and

Survey/Women ounces.

"Yer dad 'as some shockin' good ideas, eh?"

Étienne could not, at the same time, nod his head and count squares of toilet paper.

"Hold on, I got muddled. I gotta start again."

Terry was wondering if the two boys would have the patience to get to the end of the roll. He also wondered why manufacturers of toilet paper sold squares measuring 9.9 centimetres by 10.1 centimetres, for a total surface of 99.99 square centimetres. Wouldn't it be simpler to adopt a standard size of 10 by 10 centimetres? What did the producer gain by this .01 centimetre of differ-

932.53.3 ence? Probably a strategy to discourage consumers from

Buyer Beware undertaking such calculations.

8. How much money do you think the golf industry generates annually in the United States (in US dollars)?

a) 5 billion.

b) 10 billion.

c) More than 15 billion.
d) Why isn't the question about the golf industry in Canada?
e) I'm no good with numbers. 933.62.8 Survey/Men

"Do you know the story of the princess who couldn't cry?"

Marianne loves stories. She nods her head and says:

"O."

"No? Would you like to hear it?"

Marianne shakes her head no and says:

"Essssss." 934.134.2 Marianne

> I am troubled, confused, perhaps even shocked—just as Ludmilla was surprised to discover the absence of Freud in *La Pléiade*—by the fact that Harper Lee's celebrated novel *To Kill a Mockingbird* is not included in the best American novels of *La Bibliothèque idéale*. Forty years after its publication, I am rereading the book to try to understand the reason for its exclusion. 935.95.7 Additions to *La Bibliothèque idéale*

Another question preoccupying Terry concerned the thickness of toilet paper: did the manufacturers count a three-ply sheet as one sheet or three sheets?

"Dad, how many squares do you use? To wipe yerself, I mean?"

Chico thought this was a good question.

"I never counted 'em, to tell de troot. I haul just enough to spin de roll a bit an' den I tear off a length."

"Awh."

...

...

"Bot I'd say five, most o' de time."

Étienne and Chico checked to see what five squares amounted to and saw it came to one square less than their strips.

"Mum takes more'n dat."

"Is dat right?"

Terry knew it, but he wanted to hear what Étienne would say.

"She rolls de paper round 'er hand a whole bunch o'
936.53.4 times, den after dat she makes like a ball wid it an' you
Buyer Beware got to wipe yerself wid dat. Dat's 'ow she showed me."

> 8. How much money do you think the golf industry generates annually in the United States (in US dollars)?
> a) 5 billion.
> b) 10 billion.
> c) More than 15 billion.
> d) Why isn't the question about the golf industry in Canada?
> 937.69.8 Survey/Women
> e) I don't know, let's say C.

"Me, every time I go to a meeting, I start colouring in de holes in de letters on de pages dey hands out. Only just de circles, mind you, like de *o* an' de *b* an' de like."

"That's most likely a fear of the void."

938.141.2 "Is dat right! An' 'ere was I tinking 'twas only a way to
Obsessions pass de time!"

> 9. The average score of a round of golf hasn't changed for 20 years. What do you think, that average score is?
> a) 87.
> b) 97.
> c) 107.
> 939.62.9 d) 117.
> Survey/Men e) 127.

Terry would have liked to explain to Étienne and Chico, since they were on the subject, that there are fundamental differences between men and women, and that the amount of toilet paper judged necessary to wipe oneself was one of them. But he did not want to be instilling fixed notions in the boys, so Terry limited himself to adding:

"If you go an' use too much, you might be blockin' de toilet."

940.53.5
Buyer Beware

> Ultimate inference: not including singular successes, the most popular authors cited in *La Bibliothèque idéale* are those whose name begins with the letter *b.* As for the works that gained the most favour, either the first word of the title begins with *c* — which includes tales (*contes*), correspondences, and notebooks (*carnets de bord*) — or the title announces a story or journal.

941.48.12
Inferences

"Also depends on the tickness o' de paper, doesn't it. Sometimes de paper's ticker. Like when Carmen does de shoppin'. Dose times, you need even less."

As one thing tends to lead to another, Étienne asked Chico:

"'Ave you ever drunk de water from de toilet?"

The idea revolted Chico.

"Naw! Yuk!"

But the question did not go unnoticed by Terry.

"'Ow 'bout you, Étienne, you ever drink it?"

"No..."

Terry detected a slight hesitation.

"Only, Antoine says you can."

Obviously, Étienne was not about to admit that he had already gotten Marianne to drink some, and that she was none the worse for wear.

"Is dat right, den? So ee's drunk some, 'as ee?"

That was a question Étienne had never asked himself; he'd assumed that Antoine was speaking from personal experience.

942.53.6
Buyer Beware “Yes.”

> The roles of the acute accent and the grave accent have also been modified. In general, the grave accent now replaces the acute. The words *céleri, sécheresse*, and *crémerie,* for example, become *cèleri, sècheresse*, and *crèmerie*. The same is true for some conjugations of verbs in the future and conditional tenses:
> 943.77.7 *je céderai* becomes *je cèderai, j’abrégerais* be-
> Grammar comes *j’abrègerais*.

“And der’s a stream, an’ dat’s kinda nice.”

944.63.11 At that moment Pomme suddenly appeared without
Terry and Zed either of them having seen him approach.

> 9. The average score of a round of golf hasn’t changed for 20 years. What do you think, that average score is?
> a) 97.
> b) 107.
> c) 117.
> 945.69.9 d) I’m perfectly happy with my score.
> Survey/Women e) I find this question indiscrete.

“Where does de toilet water go anyways? Wid de shite an’ all.”

Terry interpreted Chico’s question as a positive sign that the boy was gradually overcoming his shyness.

“Same place as de water from the sink. All de dirty water goes down to de same place. Dey call it waste water. De water from de toilet, de dish water, water from washin’ vegetables, de laundry water, yer bat’ water, all of it goes down in de same place.”

“Granny puts de water from de vegetables in her flowers.”

“Yeah, dat’s wot de smarter folks do.”

Chico felt another surge of pride, which even Étienne noticed.

"Waste water runs down in de pipes in de ground. You seen dem pipes when dey digs up de street. Well, dose pipes take de dirty water to a cleanin' factory. In a whole lot of countries, dat's how dey do it. Only all dat costs a terrible lot o' money. Dat's why dey don't want us wastin' water no more."

Now that they were on the subject, Terry decided he might as well exhaust it.

"Come over 'ere an' I'll show youse someting."

The two boys were reticent to abandon their paper-strip cutting.

"Come on den, it'll only take a minute."

Étienne and Chico got up less than enthusiastically, and followed Terry. 946.53.7 Buyer Beware

947.127.4 Tactics

Straight arrow.

Transcription (in Carmen's handwriting) on the back of a guarantee (expired) for a Sylvania vertical fan. The faded ink along the folds in the paper suggests a heavy cycle in the washing machine. The imprint (sole of an Adidas?) dates back to a recent rainy day, when, unbeknownst to Terry, the slip of paper fell as he pulled his wallet out of his back pocket to pay for gas.

Cream of Pumpkin Sauce (Ludmilla)
± 2 cups of peeled pumpkin cubes (2 cm)
1 medium-sized onion, thinly sliced
3 cups of chicken broth
1/2 cup of cold butter, in pieces
3/4 cup of cream (15 or 18 %)
1 cup of small cubes of ham
garlic croutons (2 large handfuls)
3 tbsps of olive oil
chives

salt and pepper
— sweat the onion in a thick-bottom-pan (low heat, until the onion becomes transparent) in 2 tbsps of olive oil.
— add pumpkin and sweat pumpkin (5 min.).
— add the chicken broth and salt lightly (to taste).
— allow to simmer 30 min., until the pumpkin is easy to prick.
— remove from stove and blend, adding chunks of butter.
— add cream and blend some more.
— salt and pepper (to taste).
— pour the hot sauce over ham cubes in the tureen and
948.131.7 drop croutons on top.
Parenthesi(e)s — garnish with a pinch of chives and a dash of olive oil.

> In certain regions of Acadia, a hog is a trailer hitch mount that has the advantage of reducing the weight for the pulling vehicle. The mechanism with integrated torsion is composed of a large metal bar, chains, a shaft, and various
> 949.129.8 other elements, and looks surprisingly similar
> Fantasies to a pig.

"Yes?"

"Hullo. I's volunteerin' wid de Red Cross. We's collectin' money an' household tings like furniture or dishes to help de folks in de apartment building wot burned down last week."

Élizabeth had heard about the fire.

"We leaves a sheet wid ya dat explains de details of wot you can do if you got someting to donate."

Élizabeth took the sheet, scanned it rapidly.

"Der's a phone number right der, in case you's got questions."

"Can I donate money?"

The volunteer seemed surprised by the question.

Élizabeth felt as though she had to justify herself.

"I don't really have all that many things I don't need."

The volunteer craned his neck to catch a glimpse of the apartment.

"Awh, you only just moved in, is dat it den?"

"No..." 950.49.5

"Awh no?" Élizabeth II

> 10. How much time to give yourself to find a lost ball?
> a) No more than 5 minutes.
> b) 5 to 10 minutes.
> C) 10 to 15 minutes.
> d) I never look for a lost ball. 951.62.10
> e) I never lose my balls. Survey/Men

Terry placed a chair in front of the kitchen sink.

"Alright den, get up on dat chair, boat of youse."

Chico climbed up on the chair, but Étienne remained where he was, because he'd been told many times not to play standing on the kitchen chairs.

"You as well, Étienne, go on."

Still of two minds about the situation, Étienne finally acquiesced.

"Alright den. Now, I'm gonna give you each a glass."

Terry handed each of them a glass.

"Now pour yerselves some water, as doh you'd just come in from outside an' you was terrible tirsty. Do just wot you always do when yer tirsty."

Étienne and Chico ran water from the tap to fill their glasses.

"Alright den. Now drink de water like you always do."

The boys thought the exercise was weird, but they did as they were told and drank.

"All done are we?"

Yes, they were done. Terry took back both glasses.

"Looks like Étienne only drank tree moutfulls, an' Chico maybe four. So now, normally, you'd be pourin' de rest of dis 'ere water into de sink, right?"

The two boys agreed.

“Well, dat water, clean doh it is an’ good to drink, it’ll take tree years afore it comes back in the tap.”

Étienne and Chico weren’t sure they’d understood.

“Takes tree years fer de water dat goes down dat hole to come back into our kitchen clean. Tree whole years.”

?!

“On account of even doh it’s not all dat dirty, de water’s still gotta go all de way to the purification plant to get cleaned again, just in case one o’ youse might be walkin’ around wid a cold or some such ting. After dat, I figures it has to go troo some sort o’ giant strainers to get rid of all de tons o’ scraps dat’s floatin’ around. An den de water’s gotta sit der in a big basin, perfectly still, so dat any wee bits o’ stuff de strainers missed’ll sink down to de bottom, an’ den dey check fer any bad chemicals in de water, an’ dey add der own good chemicals, an’ den dey test again to be sure dey didn’t put too much in… an’ only after all dat, dey can pour dat water back into clean pipes under de ground.”

Terry could see in the boys’ eyes that the purification process was still ongoing in their minds.

“Alright den, you can trow dat water left in yer glasses now.”

Étienne and Chico exchanged a hesitant glance.

952.53.8 Buyer Beware “Luh! ’Tisn’t all dat easy to waste de water now you knows how it all works, is it?”

10. How much time to give yourself to find a lost ball?

a) I hate to lose a ball.
b) One lost, two found!
c) I like the underbrush.
953.69.10 Survey/Women d) I hate the underbrush.
e) At least 10 minutes.

“Wid me, it’s *flossin’* me teet. Don’t know how to say

flossin' in French..."

"*Passer la soie dentaire*?"

"Dat's it, *soie dentaire.* I gots to do it tree, four times a day, or else..."

"Or else wot?"

"Or else she tinks she's gonna starve. After all, it's a meal all in *itself.*

(Laughter greets the play of homonyms)

"I don't get it."

"*Soie dentaire* is dental floss and *soi* means itself. De floss is a meal in itself!"

"Class, Class! Please!

"Sorry, Miss, I couldn't help it. Fer once, a joke makes 954.141.7
more sense in French dan it do in English." Obsessions

> Lacan thought of the human being as composed of "layers" of identity which, at one time, 955.38.4
> led him to compare the ego to an onion. Onions

Étienne and Chico had taken up their miniature cars. They would have preferred to continue cutting up strips of toilet paper, but Terry explained that it was time to move on to another far more complicated stage:

"Now I got to do some multiplication and division. 'Ave you learned how to do dat in school yet, Chico?"

"De teacher knows how."

"Does she now? An' is she keepin' it to 'erself?"

The idea that the teacher was keeping things she knew to herself made Chico laugh. Terry liked to hear Chico 956.53.9
laugh. Buyer Beware

> Examination for Electroacoustic Music course (MUSI 4302): Describe the possible organization of the 22 musical operations essential to basic self-pollination of an electroacoustic work. Do not forget to indicate the emergence of the indicator (efficiency factor) and to

> determine the speed at which the work moves
> 957.32.7 toward its own conclusion (repato, repepato,
> Exam Questions repepotato, etc.).

"Too high. I shoulda used me seven."

...

"It does smell wonderful nice, eh, right after de lawn mowin', don't it?"

...

"Did you know dat de Acadian word *harbe* isn't such a bad word for grass as all dat?"

...

"In long ago France, when dey was takin' de animals out to pasture fer grazin', dey used to say "*mettre les animaux à l'harbe.*"

...

"An' don't dat make perfect sense? Why would Acadians be startin' to say *harbe* instead o' *herbe* all of a sudden? Folks don't go changin' der ways just like dat fer
958.59.6 nutting,* now do dey?"
Knowledge "Dat's de troot."

> Shepherd's pie (mashed potatoes). Rice and spinach (rice). Soup (ham bone, beef bone, pumpkin). Spaghetti sauce. Ratatouille (frozen). Frozen parsley, basil, chives. Strawberries. Rhubarb. Lobster? Bottled mackerel (Redge's

---

* To say "fer nutting," a Chiac speaker might use the word *e-rien*, which is a deformed contraction of the phrase *un rien* meaning "a trifle." The word *e-rien* has nothing whatsoever to do with digital neologisms, such as email, e-com, Ebay, and so on, but there's no reason *e-rien* can't take advantage of these new terms to establish itself. Not unlike the way Roman Catholics
960.143.8 long ago took advantage of the Saturnalia festival to celebrate
Varia Christmas.

recipe). Black cherry coulis. Jam and muffins with sugarleaf. 959.42.7 Sorting

11. Did you know that a third of all new golf balls sold in the United States are actually old balls retrieved from water hazards and repainted?

a) Yes, I knew that.
b) Nothing surprises me anymore.
c) No, I did not know that. I'll fish out my own balls from now on.
d) Canada should close its borders to American golf balls.
e) Canadians are not any more honest than Americans. 961.62.11 Survey/Men

When his calculations were done, Terry sat the boys down to present his conclusions:

"First off, de squares are exactly de size dat's written on de package. See 'ere, wot's written under de wee kittens: 9.9 centimetres by 10.1 centimetres. Well, I measured one o' de squares out o' dis pack to see if it were true."

Terry did not merely explain; he demonstrated:

"You take de ruler like so, an' you measure just so: 9.9 centimetres by 10.1 centimetres exactly."

Étienne and Chico approved.

"An' den I did de same wid a square from de clouds pack, an' a square from the lambs pack, an' all de measurements're right."

Étienne and Chico believed him.

"Alright den. Now second ting we did was counted up de squares in a roll from each sort, an' der again, we get de same number o' squares dat's written on each packet: de wee kittens has 198 squares in a roll, an' de clouds has 187, an' de lambs, 185. Dat means wedder de paper's one, two, or tree layers tick, de number of layers don't change de number of squares in de roll. Got it?"

The two boys nodded. Terry chuckled to himself to see how seriously they were paying attention.

“De tird ting we’s wantin’ to know is which of all dese sorts is deliverin’ more fer our money. Well, to know dat we has to figure how much each roll o’ toilet paper costs. De wee kittens ’ere costs 35 cents a roll. De clouds o’er ’ere, well dey cost 41 cents a roll. An’ de little lambs cost 39 cents a roll. Only not one o’ dese brands has got de same size squares, or de same numbers o’ squares. An’ de worst ting is de tickness. Look ’ere now. Dis one ’ere has got two layers, only she’s a whole lot fluffier dan de kittens dat’s got tree . . .”

Neither Étienne nor Chico had ever imagined that the products on store shelves could contain so many nuances.

“So all dat means we gotta take de tickness of de paper into account as well. How I done dat is I weighed a roll of each sort of toilet paper, on account of it’s near impossible to measure de tickness of anyting as tin as a square o’ toilet paper. To do dat a fellow’d need precision tools, which we don’t ’ave. Only before I weighed dem, I took out de cardboard in de middle, on account of we don’t wipe ourselves wid de cardboard, now do we?”

Just as Terry expected, Étienne and Chico giggled at the idea of wiping themselves with the cardboard centre of a toilet paper roll.

“Well, all de weighin’ an’ calculatin’ ends up dat the little lambs toilet paper weighs de least. An’ on account of de little lambs squares was de smallest, an’ dey wasn’t de least expensive, I eliminated dem. An’ dat means dose little lambs’re not de ones we ought to be buyin’.”

962.53.10
Buyer Beware

Étienne and Chico seemed relieved that all their work had finally provided a concrete result.

11. Did you know that a third of all new golf balls sold in the United States are actually

old balls retrieved from water hazards and repainted?

a) No, I had no idea.

b) Someone had a clever idea.

c) I am in favour of recycling.

d) Canadians are not any more honest than Americans. 963.69.11

e) This survey is racist. Survey/Women

Always that distant past retreating further and further into history to which Élizabeth was often recalled:

"Pelletier? The Pelletiers from Madawaska?"

Acadians often questioned her about her origins.

"No, they're from Ontario."

Élizabeth could not get used to the manner in which the past here was not merely a useful concept, but rather a work in progress and a condition, a rock upon which one could gain a foothold.

"From Sudbury?"

"No, from Hearst. It's further north."

"Awh. On account of I knowed a Pelletier hailed from 964.93.12
Hearst..." Time

965.138.10
The Other is irreducible. The Other

"Now we've still got de wee kittens and de clouds — an' here's where we finds out just 'ow important 'tis to do proper testin'! — on account of de cardboard in de clouds roll weighs more dan de cardboard in de wee kittens roll. *In udder words*, if a fellow'd gone an' done de test widout removin' de carboard core, ee'd 'ave got de wrong result! *Anyhow*, dat's someting you'll most likely be learnin' in school; I'm only showin' ya now in case dey fall behind in de program an' decide to *skip o'er* dis part."

"Dad! Yer sayin' too many words in English!"

Terry was stunned. Of course, he realized he'd said "in other words," "anyhow," and "skip over" in English.

"Yer right, my son. Sometimes it just comes out like dat, an' I can't seem to help meself."

Chico couldn't see the harm in using English words. "We say English words all de time."

Terry tried to explain:

"Sure, an' we do too. Only we try to say as many French words as we can."

"On account of?"

Terry sought a simple answer.

966.53.11 "Well, on account we's French, aren't we?"

Buyer Beware "Awh."

> The Académie française's recent grammatical changes are logical. For example, to write *bonhommie* with two *m*'s rather than one makes sense since the word *homme,* from which the former is derived, contains two *m*'s; *combattivité* with two *t*'s is consistent with *combattre*; and *charriot* with two *r*'s, as in *charrette.* Similarly, the Académie has dropped the last *i* in words like *joaillier, quincaillier* since this last *i* is silent. Hence, *joailler, quincailler*, etc. Also, we may now drop the *i* in *oignon*. The result
> 967.77.8 is we have *ognon*, as the Acadians have always
> Grammar pronounced it.

"Once upon a time, a king sent word throughout his kingdom that he would give his daughter's hand in marriage to whomever managed to make her cry, because his daughter the princess had never in all her life shed a single tear."

"Hihi..."

"Well, there were many nice young men in the kingdom who wanted nothing better than to marry a princess. So many of them tried to make the princess cry, but none succeeded."

"Hihi..."

"One day a young peasant boy arrived, claiming he had a sure-fire way to make the young lady cry."

"Pessan?"

"Pessan?"

"Pessan?"

"Absolutely. A handsome young peasant."

"Hihi..."

"The king, discouraged by the failure of all those who had tried so far, was not very hopeful. But he opened the door to the young man anyway."

...

"Once inside the palace, the..."

"Pawus?"

"Yes, a great big beautiful palace."

(*Smile*)

"The young man asked to be taken to the kitchen along with the princess, where the two of them set to work peeling onions."

"Pessan?"

"That's right. The peasant and the princess pealed onions. And naturally, the lovely girl's tears began to flow. *Sniff, sniff*..."

"Hihi..."

"And so, just as the king had promised, the honest and clever young man married the princess and became a good prince."

"Hihi..."

"Isn't that wonderful?"

"Adain?"

"Again?" 968.38.9

"Adain!" Onions

969.68.7

Visit Lisbon. 1755, after all. Projects

Terry was beginning to think that this toilet paper affair had run its course.

"So den, if all me calculations're correct, de cloud toilet

roll's more expensive dan the wee kitten rolls, an' wot's more dey's also better quality. Der ticker too, an' dat means it don't take as much paper to wipe yerself, an' dat means, in de long run, yer savin'. Not only dat, but it's softer. Luh, feel it…"

The two boys reached out to touch the two samples Terry held out, and both nodded their agreement.

"Mostly women are de ones dat tinks of buyin' de soft tissue, only if ever you find yerself widout a woman
970.53.12 'round, you can remember dat it's someting wert' tinking
Buyer Beware about."

> For Arabs and Africans, the onion is a symbol
> 971.38.10 of duplicity because beneath all those layers
> Onions one upon the other there is no hard kernel.

I confess I was nervous about this meeting. I was afraid that Claudia's youth would give her a net advantage over me, the advantage of fragility, and the brute force of youth. I wondered too how she might have changed since we'd met, more than 10 years ago.

"You come here often?"

"Yes, often enough."

"I don't know this neighbourhood. So I could not have invented it."

As I'd suspected, my novelist's preoccupations left her rather indifferent.

"And your parents are well?"

"Which ones?"

!

And there you have it; clearly, it was going to go as I'd feared. The waiter brought our coffees. I took my time pouring milk into mine.

"Was there something in particular you wanted to ask me?"

She addressed me with careless familiarity. I sensed she was in a hurry to get it over with. She almost certainly had somewhere she would rather be. After all, I had neither Zablonski's nor Rodriguez's charm.

"No. I only wanted to see how you were doing."

My reply appeared to mollify her. I reminded myself that she must be fed up with being the fruit of so many writers' imaginations.

"You have a lot of...?"

She replied with a shrug before I could even finish my question. I waited a bit.

"Have you seen the pope-rabbi again?"

"Why? In your eyes, I'm just a drinking trough full of worn-out proverbs, is that it?"

!

Alright. It was worse than I'd imagined. Really, I barely recognized her. Was she really the same person I'd created? Once timid, she had become hypersensitive; once innocent, now bitter.

"Alright..."

I could think of nothing else to say. It was as though all my ideas had suddenly flown right out of my head and there was no way to recapture them. Had I infused her with my illusions back then? And was I now transferring all my disillusionment? I felt myself totally lacking in theory, and in practice. What was I trying to prove?

"But you did agree to meet me..."

She shrugged and, fingering one of her earrings, turned her head toward the large room, as she'd done several times.

"Does your earring hurt?"

"I can't hide anything from you, can I?"

I'd had enough. I was only looking for a polite way to end the conversation. I decided to simply tell the truth, and I was on the verge of doing just that when she said:

"I don't know what's wrong with me. I'm such a pain in 972.101.6
the ass lately. Do you know?" Duos

pic pac pic pac pic

driftwood down in Cap-Pelé
pic pac sss pit sss
973.75.1 Tankas driftwood down in Shippagan
shhhh sssss shhhh murmurs Fundy

When Carmen returns from shopping at Place Champlain, Étienne will barely be able to contain his excitement:

"Mum! Mum! De cloud toilet paper won."

"Awh, is dat right?"

Carmen will have no idea what her son is talking about, but she'll be disposed to listen.

974.133.4 The Future "Yes, even doh sometimes folks're buyin' de wee kittens on account of you can get dem downeasy off de shelf."

the parsley's sprightly
and how proud November's leeks
crunchy succulent
975.75.2 Tankas winter whistled in the cold
upon an ice-cracked tongue

"I remember we used to call a drawer *une tirette* instead of *un tiroir* in our house. Doh, really de way we said it sounded more like *tiroué*."

"I wonders if dat was actually de right word in old French."

"Now, we says *tiroir*, like everybody else."

"Der some folks're against dat."

"Against wot?"

"Losing our Chiac."

976.73.11 Shifts "Well, is dat right? Ask me, dey oughtta make up der mind!"

977.107.5 Necessities Books.

"Dat's a poor excuse."

Étienne didn't understand what Carmen meant, since

he had not excused himself at all; he'd merely warned her that he was going to the washroom.

"Don't I recall tellin' you not to come stompin' troo de house with yer boots full o' mud?"

Étienne retreated and removed his boots; he did not like being scolded.

"Are youse playin' in de Petitcodiac river to be gadderin' up all dat sludge?"

Sitting on the pot, Étienne managed to complete his business with a little effort.

"Der's a frog in de canal. Chico wants us to put it in a bottle."

"A frog in a bottle?"

Was Étienne about to be scolded some more?

"More likely 'tis a toad. Eider way, I don't tink a creature like dat's gonna enjoy livin' in a bottle. A box wid some kind of cover'd be a lot better, seems to me."

Étienne came out of the bathroom doubly relieved, and waited while Carmen rummaged in the storage room and returned with a crate that had contained clementines, covered with a net.

"'Ere ya go, den. If I was you boys, I'd put some hay in de bottom to block up de cracks."

Pleased and excited, Étienne put his boots on in a hurry.

"Come an' show it to me when youse caught de poor ting, so's we can tell wot it is."

"Alright, Mum!"

978.86.6
Apologies

> At the ideal moment, practitioners plant a rare seed in scientifically prepared soil; then they cosset the seedling in such a way as to favour the apparition of the gigantism syndrome. The sport as such consists in lifting and transporting this garden fruit to the site of a particular regional contest. To have a chance at winning a prize, a pumpkin must weigh at least half a ton,

> which will require impeccable lifting technique (six or seven men) and a vehicle equipped with excellent shock absorbers. Contrary to the pleasing appearance of a normal-sized healthy pumpkin, neither the pallor, nor the cellulitic skin (also called orange skin), nor the caved-in form of this giant cucurbitacea count for anything in the contest. The world record holder of pumpkins weighs approximately three-quarters of a ton.

979.122.8
Sports

"Not so easy is it, me boy?"

Étienne was struggling to grate a potato, with Terry by his side.

"Do you want me to finish 'er fer you?"

Marianne, quiet for once, watched her brother working fiercely to reduce the tubercular into hash.

"Do you wanna give it a try, Marianne?"

...

"Come over 'ere, den. You can hold on to de potato an' I'll hold de grater."

The little one stayed put.

"No? You don't wanna give 'er a try?"

Marianne shook her head no.

"Alright den. You don't have to. Yer dad'll finish up."

Actually, Terry was relieved. Things always went faster when the kids weren't in the way.

"Yeeeeeeeth!"

"Awh, Marianne does want to grate, does she? Only yer dad tawt Marianne was sayin' no she didn't."

Terry set the little one up beside him, wondering if sometimes he wasn't too kind. After all, sooner or later the children would have to learn that no meant no.

"An' now, you hold de potato like dis, an' you push."

Marianne pushed with all her might, and the tubercular dug into the grater, moving maybe a centimetre. And that was about all.

"At a girl, Marianne, dat's exactly how we do it!" 980.23.6 Potatoes

> If writing can be compared to slipping on a
> banana peel, the exultation associated with it
> corresponds to nothing more or less than the
> fraction of a second suspended between earth 981.128.3
> and sky, before crashing into the ground. Fervours

"Did you want an intermittent infusion or an intrave-
nous solution?" 982.126.2
"A solution." Techniques

> Find the school book in which is told the sto-
> ry of the princess that couldn't cry. That same
> book also tells the story of another princess,
> whose necklace falls to the bottom of the
> ocean. In this case, the young man who brings
> back the necklace wins the lady's hand. Three 983.68.6
> giants will come to his aid. Projects

"Dad, will I be growin' a beard as well?"

Étienne was watching his father spread lather on his face.

"Me boy, I knew I'd have to give ya de bad news one o' dese days: fer sure, you'll be growin' a beard."

Étienne cast a wondering look at his father. Terry explained:

"I don't know too many fellas dat enjoy shavin' every day."

"On account of?"

"On account of it's a wee bit tiresome. An' it takes up a bunch o' time."

Terry rinsed his fingers, picked up his razor and adjusted it.

"An' on account of women don't like to find yer hair all over de *sink*. 'Specially if the hair's black an' de *sink's* white."

Terry realized he'd been using the English word *sink*.

"An' by de way, a *sink* in French is *évier*.

Étienne admired the perfectly straight stroke Terry had drawn across the lather on his cheek.

"Wot colour will me beard be, Dad?"

"We don't know, do we. Most times it's de same colour as de hair, but sometimes a fella'll 'ave brown hair or black an a brown-red beard, like a brick. Dat means de boy's got a bit o' de Irish blood in 'im."

Terry rinsed his razor in the sink and got set to tackle his chin.

"Zed's got a beard mower."

"I know it. I don't like de electric razors meself."

"On account of?"

"Don't know, really. Seems like it don't shave close enough."

...

"Sure an' it's 'arder shavin' wid a razor blade like dis one 'ere. A fella's got to be careful not to cut 'imself. But after a while you *get de hang of it*."

...

"Do you understand 'get de hang,' to get de hang o' someting?"

Terry had used the English expression. Étienne
984.87.10 thought about it, and shook his head:
The Body "No. I only know '*hang up ton coat dans la closet*.'"

> There are any number of useful suggestions relating to the use, preparation, cooking, and conservation of onions. The most astonishing and possibly the least known of these suggestions is that one should not keep an onion that's already been sliced, because it will have
> 985.38.11 lost its vitamins, and the rapid oxidization can
> Onions even render it inedible.

Chico had separated hundreds of stones according to

their colours and collected them in a half dozen large metal cans.

"You doesn't see de colour like dis 'ere. Dey has to be wet."

Chico put a stone into his mouth, wet it all around, pulled it out, and showed it to Étienne.

"Luh, see?"

Étienne was impressed. No one had ever talked to him about the colour of stones before, not even Zablonski. He rummaged in one of the cans, chose a stone, wet it in his mouth so that he could appreciate its colour properly. 986.113.2 Collections

> 12. Who would you most like to meet in a copse of trees on a golf course?
> a) Warren Buffet.
> b) Queen Latifa.
> c) Tintin.
> d) The Dalai Lama.
> e) Other: ___________________. 987.62.12 Survey/Men

People talked in hushed tones — Wednesday evening's excellent and quiet musical selection was having its effect. Pomme, Zed, and Terry, who appreciated the ambience, often met for a drink at the Babar on Wednesdays.

"Me, der's nuttin' I like better dan to start de day wid brand new socks. When you's gotta tear de paper off an' all."

"Sure. Wot a treat when dey's snug on yer feet."

"I saw someting de udder day I really enjoyed."

. . .

"I never noticed dem until now."

. . .

"I mean does little bums on grape seeds." 988.102.1 The Trio

> Freudian slips don't only happen in speech. They also occur when we write, listen, and read. Here's an example of a silent reading of a

> passage from Jean-Paul Manganaro's introduction to Italo Calvino's collection *The Road to San Giovanni* (the reading slips are in parentheses): "We apprehend memory in its recovered present, in its state of purity reworded (poverty rewarded) like an inexhaustible present. In fact, the event that acts as a motor (model) is told in a manner almost distant and remote (remit), a historical event, certainly, belonging to the history of the individual and that individual's
> 989.104.7 collectivity, but not valued, at that moment of
> Worries remembering (remuneration) for what it is."

"When you tink about it, wasn't so very long ago, a fellow could've read just about all de books der was... like Diderot an' all dem boys in de 1800s. Nowadays? Just readin' all de titles'd take ya years!"

"Well den, I suppose you might say de planet's not such a global village as all dat, after all..."

"All depends. Ask me, 'tis a question o' spin."

990.102.2 "You means she's spinnin' faster dan she used to?"

The Trio "More dan dat. She's changed 'er curve."

> **TRAMPLETIME:** n. — 2005/2013; from *trample* and *time* and *trampoline*. ♦ With a great deal of irregularity, rushed ⇨ **sharooshed**. "*All of them women working on trampletime, they*
> 991.120.5 *brandished a crab in one hand and a herring in*
> Fictionary *the other.*" (Daigle/Majzels)

The first time Chico invited Étienne to come along to his grandmother's in Dieppe, the two boys looked over Chico's collections.

"Wot's dis den?"

Étienne didn't dare touch what he saw. He had an innate respect for the formalities due all collections, regardless what they were.

"Dat's sawdust."

Chico had answered nonchalantly, as though there was nothing odd about collecting sawdust in bottles.

"Awh."

. . .

"An' wot're you goin' to do wid it?"

Chico shrugged:

"It's a collection, right? You don't do nuttin' wid it."

Chico picked up one of the bottles, shook it gently and held it up to examine its contents in the light from the room's window.

"Dis 'ere was a wee bit damp when I gathered it up. 'Twas rainin' an' de folks next door was puttin' up a fence."

Étienne cast an eye over the other bottles lined up in the box, finally daring to pick one up.

"Dat one's de cupboards up in de attic. Go ahead and take a sniff, why don't ya."

Chico unscrewed the cap and placed the bottle under Étienne's nose. And yes, it did smell slightly of something. 992.113.1 Collections

> In other words, I conceal, therefore I am. 993.136.9 The Unavowed

The customers came in and out of the Babar at a regular rhythm.

"Awh, geez, not 'er."

Zed and Terry glanced discretely in the direction Pomme was looking, and saw a young woman they didn't know.

"She's after buyin' a loft. Must be fifteen times she's asked me 'bout it. She contact you yet?"

Zed wasn't sure, but he didn't think so.

"Geez, I hopes she don't see me."

Zed watched the woman make her way across the room.

"She's sittin' down wid Zipper an' dem. Where she longs at?"

Pomme spoke without enthusiasm:

"She's Okey-Dokey's sister, only just come back from some years in Montréal."

...

994.102.3 ...

The Trio "An wot about Okey-Dokey? She still in Toronto, den?"

995.136.10

The Unavowed There is no direct way.

Looking for something else in his cupboard, Chico moved a glass jug containing twisted wires.

Étienne cried out:

"Wot's dat?!"

Chico almost fell over.

"It's only some old busted guitar strings. Every time me dad busted one he'd give it to me. Ee said ee'd be famous one day."

Conflicting ideas jostled for position in Étienne's mind.

"Grandad give me de jug. Ee was usin' it fer gas fer de lawnmower."

Étienne couldn't tear his gaze away from the jug full of broken guitar strings. He'd never seen anything like it.

"Der's twenty-seven of dem. I hasn't put none in since he's in jail."

This detail brought Étienne back to reality:

"Was he breakin' dem on purpose?"

Chico laughed:

996.113.3 "Course not! Dey breaks all on der own!"

Collections "Awh."

Regarding Zed's expression "Where she longs at?," the original French "*D'yoùsqu'a d'vient*?" leaves open the question of whether Zed was asking whence she came or where she was from, or where she'd been. The author apologizes for this brief lack of vigilance. The translator, who has fallen back on the Newfoundlandese expression "Where she longs at?," has no excuse. 997.86.4 Apologies

When Chico raised the cover on the box he'd dug out of the back of the cupboard, Étienne was agreably surprised at the diversity of its contents.

"Dis 'ere's stuff I doesn't know wot to do wid."

Étienne contemplated the bric-a-brac, but was unable to identify anything.

"Why den do you keep dem?"

"Dunno."

Chico picked up an object, examining it from different angles, then put it back and did the same with another.

"Wot's dat?"

"Comes from a door knob dat me grandad took apart."

The steel square shaft threaded at each end was unquestionably attractive.

"I knows where everyting 'ere's from."

And Chico closed and replaced the box in the same place, at the very back of the cupboard. Étienne had never imagined it could be useful or interesting to know the provenance of the slightest trifle.

"I put it all de way back in 'ere, on account of Granny almost trew 'er in de trash last year." 998.113.5 Collections

Recapitulation. All things considered, the unavowable is the real. The unavowable kills. Hence the relative importance of the confession. To admit to someone or to oneself is equally difficult. The paradox is that, even to admit something to oneself, one must go through the Other. Because the real is the Other. Is that to say that the ego is not part of the real? Simple answer: The ego is to the real what clothing is to the body: appearance, surface. The ego covers, protects, hides, and the ego's language does the same. Language

999.136.11
The Unavowed

conceals more than it reveals. And this is what makes the confession so difficult, and objectivity impossible. In other words, I conceal therefore I am. There is no direct way.

"Hallo, Pomme! How's you gettin' on?"

"Awh, hallo!..."

Ginette "Okey-Dokey" LeBlanc's sister looked over the other guys at the table. Terry and Zed nodded a polite greeting. Pomme did the introductions.

"Terry... Zed... um... Sorry, I knows yer Ginette's sister, only I's fergot yer name."

"Simonne, only folks calls me Sam."

Again, Terry and Zed nodded.

"I'm Terry."

"Zed."

A slightly embarassed silence followed, and Pomme felt obliged to revive the conversation:

"Sam's tinking she'd like to be buyin' a loft 'ere."

Terry took the bait:

"Sure, dis 'ere's a fine place. Only I expect de waitin' list's awful long, eh Zed?"

Zed nodded but, as he was not partial to brutality:

"Still, sometimes folks gets tired o' waitin' an' dey buys someting else instead. So even doh de waitin' list is someting long, she's still movin.'"

Pomme added:

"'Twould be good to 'ave more buildings like dis one 'ere in Moncton."

But Sam said:

"'Tisn't only de building, doh. 'Tis de folks around as well. All de artists an dat. Me, I designs clothes. Wot I'd like is to have me own store."

Pomme's curiousity was tweaked:

"Wot sort of clothes?"

The young woman opened her coat, did a slow pirouette. The three guys agreed that her outfit was sharp:

"Dat looks alright."

She put her hand on the back of an empty chair: 1000.102.4 The Trio

"Mind if I sit meself down?"

12. Who would you most like to meet in a copse of trees on a golf course?

a) The Dalai-Lama

b) Queen Latifa

c) A rabbit

d) Nobody

e) Other: ________________ 1001.69.12 Survey/Women

"An' wot about Riopelle in all dat?"

"Well, ee was more part of de *Art Informel* dat got started in France after de war. Wasn't a real tight group. Dey had a whole lot o' different styles, wid Soulages an' a couple of udders; still dey was apart from de udders, de Italians an' de Spanish for sure, an' from de Abstract Expressionists an Cobra an' de like."

"An' what about Pollock, den?"

"Pollock, De Kooning, Rothko, Motherwell, Reinhardt...dose were de Abstract Expressionists. All dat was pretty much goin' in New York in de '40s. Dat's wot led to de Action Painting in de '50s."

"So where does Zablonski fit in all dat, I'd like to know?"

"Der's a group in France, in de late '60s, dey's called Support-Surface. De name tells ya wot was eatin' at dem. Zablonski hails from der, only now ee's gone way far beyond. Ee started by bustin' de surface, den ee busted de support."

?

!

"I don't see 'im ever comin' back from der." 1002.102.5 The Trio

!!

> Marianne is dreaming. Marianne dreams that
> she's lying on her back and Carmen is com-
> ing toward her, coming to change her diaper.
> And then it's not Carmen, but Zablonski who's
> there. He's tickling her with onion sprouts. It's
> funny. It's warm. It tickles. The tickling is com-
> 1003.38.6 ing from all sides, overflowing. Flowing over.
> Onions Warm. Everywhere. Marianne made peepee.

Carmen looked in fine form.

"Geez, you're lookin' not a bad bit nice!"

"Tanks!"

We'd agreed to meet at the Roux, the Fox Creek golf course restaurant.

"Dat was a right smart idea you 'ad to give us each a day off like dat. It's done us a world o' good."

The waitress brought the menu, asked us if we wanted a drink.

"Were you wantin' to eat?"

"I only want de fries. Dey're supposed to be good 'ere. Dey do 'em wid *yams*."

"Is dat so?"

"'Tis, and good ting Terry can't hear me sayin' *yams*. Seems I let meself go wid de English words when ee's not around."

"Well, you sometimes use English words when he's around as well."

"I knows it, and each time I'm afeared I'm just encouragin' him to do de same."

"Is ee all dat fragile? Linguistically, I mean…"

"I don't always comprehend wot's goin' on in 'is 'ead. Nor in 'is mout'. Days go by an' 'is French is just fine, den all of a sudden, it's as doh English was lyin' in wait down de road to trip 'im up."

"Lying in wait. I like that."

"Yer de one taught it to me!"

The waitress brought us our glasses. And our fries.

Carmen liked what she knew of *For Sure*; she felt as though she were collaborating in working out the plot:

"'Ave ya decided wot we'll be doin' wid de diamond yet?"

"No. I often think about the diamond thing, but never when I'm actually writing."

She seemed disconcerted by my reply. Was she disappointed?

"I've got other ideas. I don't think it's necessary to 1004.101.7
backtrack on everything." Duos

> List of post-WWII to early-1970s artistic movements: Abstract Expressionism (New York School), 1940–55; Art informel, France, 1945–60; Lettrism, France, 1946; Madi, Buenos Aires, 1946; Art Brut (called Lumpen Art in New York and rebaptized Outsider Art by Roger Cardinal in 1972); Spatialism, Italy (Milan), 1947–52; COBRA, COpenhagen, BRussels, and Amsterdam, 1948–51; Dau al Set, Barcelona, 1948–53; Subjects of the Artists, U.S.A., 1948–55; Kinetic Art, 1950; Funk Art, San Francisco Bay Area, 1950; Concrete Poetry, 1950; Sound Poetry, 1950; Happenings, U.S.A., 1950; Action Painting, U.S.A., 1951; Exat 51, Yugoslavia, 1951; Independent Group, London, 1952–57; Neo-dada, U.S.A., 1953–55; Gutai, Japan, 1955–72; Pop' Art, U.K. and U.S.A., 1955; Zero Group, Federal Republic of Germany (Dusseldorf), 1957–60; El Paso, Spain (Madrid), 1957–60; Situationist International, France, Italy, and Scandinavia, 1957–72; Hard Edge, New York, late 1950s; Gruppo T, Italy (Milan), 1959–66; Shaped Canvas, U.S.A., 1960; Minimal Art, U.S.A., 1960; Video Art, U.S.A., Europe, 1960; Computer Art, U.S.A., Europe, 1960; New Realism, France, 1960–63;

> Gruppo Enne (or N), Italy (Padua), 1960–64; G.R.A.V., France, 1960–68; New Figuration, France, 1960–79; Nul Groep, Netherlands, 1961; Fluxus, U.S.A., 1961; Panic, France, 1962; Colorfield, U.S.A., 1962; Copy Art, U.S.A., 1962; Mail Art, 1962; Eat Art, 1963; Zebra Group, Federal Republic of Germany, 1964; Body Art, 1964; Post Painterly Abstraction, U.S.A., 1964; Equipo Cronica, Spain (Valencia), 1964–81; Conceptual Art, U.S.A., Europe, 1965; Op Art, U.S.A., 1965; Mec' Art, Europe, 1965–69; Superealism, U.S.A., 1965–70; E.A.T. (Experiments in Art and Technology), USA (New York), 1966; B.M.P.T. (Buren, Mosset, Parmentier, and Toroni), France, 1966–67; Arte Povera (Poor Art), Italy, late 1960s; Sky Art, U.S.A., 1969; Mono Ha (Thing School), Japan, 1969–70; Support-Surface, France, 1969–
> 1005.99.6 72; Land Art, late 1960s in the U.S.A., early
> Names 1970s in Europe.

"Some words're spelled de way dey are purely fer technical reasons."

. . .

"Take, fer example, de word fer "oyster": *huître*. In de beginnin' it came from de Greek, den it went into de Latin, an' afterwards into French spelled *uistre*, *u-i-s-t-r-e*, wid no *h*."

. . .

"De *h* was only put der on account of folks was confusin' de *u* wid a *v*, so dat dey was reading *vistre* — which is almost *vitre* or "glass" — instead of *uitre*. Could be printing was too . . . like . . . primitive at de time, so de letters was not so clear. Anyhow, bottom line, de spelling wid an *h* was invented so folks wouldn't confuse an oyster wid a piece o' glass. Dat's wot I means by technical, wot's got nuttin' to do wid the roots of de word."

. . .

“I hope I isn’t borin’ you too much?”

. . .

. . .

“Let’s just say dat I doesn’t figure I’ll be playin’ wid you all dat often once I gets better at de game.”

“Hahaha! Dat’s wot I likes about you, a person always 1006.126.12
knows where you stand.” Techniques

> For example, possible ways to write and say the verb *to see*: *ouère, ouaire, wère, wouère, vouère, ouare, ware,* and *voir*. And for *sees* as in “he sees”: *oua, wa, woua, oueille, woueille, weille,*
> *ouèye, wouèye, wèye, voueille, vouèye, vouaille,* 1007.30.9
> and *voit*. Chiac

“Holy Jesus, Joseph, and Mary, you didn’t go an’ say dat!”

Pomme’s concern was all too real:

“Aren’t ya afraid dey’ll tink yer warped sometimes?”

“Well, you know de way it goes... when you see de words about to come out, only you can’t stop ’em in time.”

Zed put two and two together:

“Now I knows how come Chico was askin’ me if I’s afraid me parents was goin’ to die when I was a boy.”

Pomme too wanted to know:

“Well den? Were ya afraid?”

“Not really. Der was times I was almost hopin’ ’twould happen. So’s I could be a real orphan.”

“G’wan!”

Terry shared Pomme’s surprise:

“I tawt you missed yer real dad...”

Zed shrugged.

“Don’t know really. Not so much as dat, I tink. I don’t 1008.102.6
really know anymore.” The Trio

CHAPTER 8

we speak English
we speak French
we speak
all languages
fluidently

PATRICE DESBIENS,
désâmé (de-souled) 1009.144.8
Prise de parole, 2005 Epigraphs

"Yer not afeard o' turnin' 'im off?"

There he'd said it. Pomme felt that sometimes Terry was too demanding with his son.

"Well, I try to make it fun fer 'im at de same time."

"A person might tink you was wantin' to turn de boy into a jack of all trades."

"Not so much. I just want fer 'im to be curious, to like learnin' how life's workin.'"

Zed chimed in:

"I know wot yer sayin'. Dat's wot I'd like fer Chico as well."

. . .

. . .

"Well dat could be . . . As fer me, when I's a boy, I learned stuff by meself mostly. An' I haven't changed, far as dat's concerned. I gets bored wid other folks' explainin.'"

Pomme's idea did not go unappreciated.

"Eh boy! I was just de same. I liked to figure tings out meself. So, maybe I oughtn't to be all de time explainin' everyting to Étienne..."

...

"Ting is you don't always know if yer doin' de right ting or not, do ya? Yer always figurin' it out as you go."

Zed could relate to that:

"Me, I's only really learnin' a ting when I'm doin' dat ting. Den tings open up fer me."

"Me, I gotta 'ave it all in me head afore I start."

For Zed, it all made perfect sense:

"Dat's wot I been saying, yer an intellectual."

The three friends ordered another round.

"Nowadays in school, dey don't call dem problems no more. Nowadays dey're challenges. Chico shows me his lessons, an' den ee explains de challenges. I suppose it's kinda clever, when ya tink about it."

Pomme was still not used to hearing Zed talk as Chico's father.

"De word 'problem' was too *overweight* I suppose.
1010.102.7 Challenge is more *marketweight*."
The Trio "Ya mean a challenge *rattles* us less dan a problem?"

> The tilde serves to distinguish words pronounced as in English from those pronounced as in French. Hence *jãck õf ãll trãdes* and *rãttle.* It Latinizes English. As for the acute accent on the end of a verb pronounced as in English, it indicates that the end of the word should be
> 1011.7.1 pronounced as in French. Hence *tũrnér õff.*
> Useful Details This is a common form of Chiacification.

"Look, Mum, de pumpkins!"

"Wow!"

Indeed, Carmen had never seen a field so full of big, beautiful, perfectly orange pumpkins. She slowed down so that Étienne and she could admire the sight a little longer.

"Can we be puttin' up a whole family again fer Halloween?"

The previous year, Terry had worked hard to install three lit pumpkins in the window—a small one, a medium sized one, and a great big one, just like in Goldilocks and the Three Bears.

"Don't see why not."

"Dat was right nice, eh?"

Then the word had gone out to all the residents of the lofts to put a pumpkin in every one of the building's large windows, which had enhanced the stature of the building and created a festive mood throughout the neighbourhood. Families came from as far away as Dieppe and Riverview to admire the collective effort.

"Yes, 'twas beautiful!"

...

...

"Mum, could we be cuttin' our pumpkins like Madeleine did dis time?"

"Madeleine's an artist. She knows wot to do to give de pumpkin more of an expression."

"Is it troo dat she's got a special knife?"

"I don't know. Could be."

Carmen wondered what a special knife for the artistic carving of pumpkins might look like.

"Dat's wot Dad said."

Carmen felt like laughing; she imagined that Terry had probably invented the special knife to moderate Étienne's aesthetic expectations.

"Takes imagination as well, not only a special knife."

Étienne seemed to be in agreement. He watched the field of pumpkins slowly disappear: 1012.106.8

"Could someting be inventin' itself?" Customs

> The fragment 1011.7.1 on the writing of Chiac may have come too late, not to mention its limited relevance to the translation. 1013.93.9 Time

"Any other questions?"

A hand went up.

"Me, I've an idea dat runs 'round in me head a lot of de time, an' I wonders like, is it an' obsession."

"Can you tell us what it is?"

"Sure! Like dey says, 'mix a bit o' business wid pleasure,' right?'

"Absolutely."

"Well, I often tinks o' mixin' business wid pleasure."

"For example?"

"Well, in airplanes, de bags fer trowin' up in. Dey oughtta write on dem 'Address Unknown.' Dat way 'twould be sometin' we could return to sender."

"Friggin' right!"

"Awh, grõwse*!"

"Dat's not an obsession, dat's a fantasy."

1014.141.8 "Dream on."

Obsessions "Class, please! Please!"

> Third possible title: *Small Amusing Betrayals*. Referring to those minor aspects of life that come unravelled, or ravelled and escape our control. Thinking here also of Étienne, Marianne, and Chico, of all children really, of the universal child. And thinking, too, of
> 1015.81.3 words, when they betray us. But the children
> Titles in this book are not really betrayers.

> 1017.38.12 Do you know anyone who's suffered health
> Onions problems after eating a decaying onion?

A book, picked up in passing, more for its appearance than anything, a handsome antique look. On closer examination, the book's subject and author are

---

1016.143.7 * Chiac can also improve the spelling of English words that

Varia are not pronounced as they're written.

intriguing. A name we recognize, often encountered, but never read. A book to read in your spare time, or at least to leaf through. What's more, the book is pleasant to hold. How much better to be placed on a bookshelf in someone's library, modest though that library may be, than to end up in one cardboard box among many in a dusty junk closet, in a box someone fully intends to sort through some day, a day that never comes. A book, then, snatched up in passing, after decades of wandering: 1018.84.1
Michelet, *Précis de l'histoire moderne.* History

Alphabits, also…
What other kinds do you like? 1019.55.9
Those well-read primates. Haikus

Seen from behind: a classic look, not flashy, black
leather with five nerves and gold lettering. At the very 1020.84.2
bottom, slightly worn away, the numbers 1-8-5-0. History

> Jar covers, cans. Aluminum plates (and other utensils). Nails, useless screws, plumbing scraps. Metal wire. Steel wool. Old grater. Trombones. Dishes, grills, camping pots and
> pans. Broken folding chairs (aluminum). Old 1021.42.10
> toaster. Ornaments. Odds and ends. Sorting

"Do you know de tent nation?"

Le Grand Zablonski thought Étienne was perhaps alluding to tint saturation. He fetched a tube of solid red and one of white.

"Look at this bright red colour. Now I squeeze a bit of white and mix them, see how it changes to pink? We've created a lighter tint of red. Is that what you mean?"

"No, 'tisn't a colour, 'tis a place yer not supposed to go."

Étienne Zablonski thought perhaps the boy had been watching the news.

"You mean a refugee camp? Like in the news?"

Étienne shook his head.

"No, not in the news. In the prayer."

1022.124.3 Religion Zablonski really had no idea.

"No, I don't know any tent nation in a prayer."

> Not forgetting the Love Canal in New York State, the Cape of Good Hope in South Africa, Lake Constance on the borders between Switzerland and Germany, the Pacific Ocean Loyal, a small town in Wisconsin, and Lac des
> 1023.66.8 The Virtues Pises in France, since to despise is a facet of
> love rather than its opposite.

"Good evening, everyone and thank you for coming in such great numbers. I dare say the task before us is of Herculean proportion, which is why we will need all your ideas and all your linguistic talents if we are to succeed. And, let's be frank, we will also need nerves of steel, because creating a modern Acadian language on the basis of its present-day componants will be no picnic.
1024.73.4 Shifts But nothing prevents us from undertaking our task with
joyful ardour and wacky courage, since…"

> Cleaning products. Lighters. Aerosol cans. Oils (inedible), paint strippers, and varnish removers. Paints and dyes. Glue. Nail polish. Colouring (hair). Insecticides. Thermometers (mercury). Anti-flea spray. Antifreeze. Empty propane gas tanks. Wax (old candles). Pool products. Obsolete computers (diskettes?). Broken electronic games. Birthday cards containing batteries. Batteries (rechargeable and
> 1025.42.3 Sorting non-rechargeable). Old television set. Large
> appliances (toxic liquids and gases).

"We're gonna adopt anglicisms?"

"Ee said adapt, not adopt. Adapt anglicisms."

"Awh." 1026.104.4 Worries

> In the field of kitchenware, the French word
> *fusil*, which also means "rifle," is a steel knife 1027.111.9 Tools
> sharpener that resembles a sword.

"It hurts when I press 'ere, eh?"

Little Marianne looked at the woman bent over in front of her. Her name was Marie-Josée, and she'd hardly pressed at all.

"An der? Hurts a wee bit more?"

Marianne nodded yes. After all, Marie-Josée was being so nice and wouldn't stop smiling.

"Poor little darlin'! You musta had a fright when you fell, eh?"

When it happened, Marianne had felt neither fear nor much pain. All wrapped up in her Halloween onion costume, she'd tumbled down the steps of the wooden staircase, almost in slow motion and soundlessly. It was the great ree-raw that followed that had started her crying. But how was she supposed to explain all that? Carmen replied in her stead:

"Less than her mudder, I tink! I'm telling you, I go to bed at night and I see de whole scene all over again in slow motion. I can't believe she didn't suffer anything serious."

Marie-Josée was not lacking in compassion for Carmen either.

"Sure, I can imagine how you must've felt!"

"An' to think, I went all the way up dose staird wid 'er, to be sure she'd not be fallin'!"

Marie-Josée sympathized with a shake and a nod of the head.

"Fer us, 'twas when we lost our girl in Disneyworld..."

Hearing this, Carmen felt her heart and stomach tighten into knots.

"I's so afraid I can barely talk about it to this day."

Now it was Carmen's turn to sympathize as she listened to the chiropractor describe her misadventure. In the end, the two women tried to laugh off their maternal traumas and returned to Marianne's case:

"You were right to bring 'er. It's always best to be sure. If she does 'ave a problem, 'tis a whole lot easier and quicker to treat now dan later. Most people only worry 'bout the head. Dey don't tink 'bout the back bone."

"I wasn't sure if you could treat children dat young."

"Awh, sure we do, a lot. 'Specially fer de colic, ear infections... tings like dat."

"Her ears hurt, too, some o' de time."

Carmen smiled at Marianne, who allowed herself to be handled without complaining.

"Hop! Did you feel dat?"

Marianne smiled. Yes, she'd felt something, but it was mainly the contorsions that Marie-Josée was making her do that were funny.

"Nowadays, we even treat animals. Cats, dogs, horses, even rabbits! Don't be askin' me who'd bring a rabbit to a chiro."

Carmen was thinking about the horse:

"Well, must take a shockin' great chiro to crack de back of a horse."

But Marie-Josée did not reply. She was totally absorbed in feeling Marianne's neck and turning her head back and forth.

1028.87.5 The Body "Awh! Der's a wee bit o' sometin' over 'ere. I'll need me gun."

> A glass of wine = a cluster of grapes = 75 grapes. In 2006, 267 c/s of Red Bull were sold. The pit of a date is made of hardened albumen. A kilometre on foot: 12 minutes; a kilometre by bicycle: 3 minutes. Shirt cuffs begin to fray after approximatley 60 washes. There are 88 gods in a grain of rice. The useful life of a plastic

> bag is 20 minutes. The moon rises at 109 km/s. The human being learned to read a mere 3,000 years ago. 1029.42.6 Sorting

Easy to pick up, fits comfortably in the hand. The weight surprises considering how thin it is. A robust cardboard cover, a book made to last. Perhaps a schoolboy or girl's book. On the top and bottom boards a speckled medium brown dominates a paler brown background, with touches of pink. Inside the cover, a surprisingly motley flyleaf, which is perhaps suitable. The edge is smooth, sand-couloured, and subtley luminescent. The inferior endband has lost almost none of its symmetry or gilt. 1030.84.3 History

> Étienne, on the other hand, absolutely refused to dress up as a vegetable. 1031.88.4 Freedom

"Well, 'ow are we gonna do dat, den? Are we just gonna be talkin', an' whenever we runs up against an Acadian word, we stops to see wot we's gonna do wid it, or de udder way, we starts wid *A* an' we goes troo de whole of de dictionary 'till we gets to *Z*?"

"Alphabetical order would probably be best, but using which dictionary? I believe that's a valid question."

"Alphabetical order! Dat's de word I was lookin' fer…" 1032.103.7 Disappearances

> In a list in a small notebook whose pale green cover is bound by a metal spiral across the top: so what *que*, so what *si que*, how come *que*, what if *que*, whenever *que*, whatever *que*, wherever *que*, whoever *que*, *si* ever *que*, as long *que*, never mind *que*, which *que*. The last two annotations are not in the same ink as the others. 1033.67.3 Terry's Notebooks

Étienne continued his inquiries on the subject of the tent nation. He questioned Ludmilla on the subject one day as he was turning the pages of *Babar's Castle* in his godmother's office:

"Auntie, does you know wot de tent nation is?"

"Tenth nation?"

Ludmilla wondered, as her husband had previously, if her godson might have been listening to the international news.

"No, de tent nation, in prayer. Der a nation, an' dey lives in a tent. An' we don't want to go der."

Ludmilla could not think of any prayer that mentioned tents, unless it was an old Jewish prayer she didn't know.

"Is it a prayer to Moses?"

1034.92.8 Questions without Answers

"No."

Étienne did not pursue it any further; he turned another large page.

1035.66.11 The Virtues

> A principle of constance exists also in pyschoanalysis.

1036.92.5 Questions without Answers

"Are you tellin' me dat dey were mastermindin' de whole ting to make it 'appen widout anybody knowin' dat dey masterminded it?"

> The list of automatic corrections for common
> errors in Spanish (modern Spanish) is not
> 1037.112.6 Languages
> available. The component is not installed. Do
> you want to install it now? Yes. No.

Étienne had occasionally accompanied his Granny Thibodeau in her Stations of the Cross in the church at Dieppe. Most of the time, she took the trouble to explain to the boy what was happening to Jesus.

"'Ere Veronica's wipin' his face on account o' de blood dat's flowin' down. Does you see 'is blood runnin' down?"

"From 'is nose?"

"From all over, on account o' de crown o' thorns."

While his grandmother recited her prayers in a low

voice and moving her lips, Étienne looked at the imposing stain glass windows depicting the story of a nun receiving roses. He also liked to run his fingers in the crevasses of the sculpted rosettes that decorated the wooden benches.

1038.124.4
Religion

"'Ere, ee falls fer de second time."

1039.65.11
Boy Cousins,
Girl Cousins

> Just as there are propane hogs that are strictly speaking salamanders.

"Dad, how come dey kilt Jesus?"

"On account of he was too clever fer dem."

...

...

"Who was it built 'is cross, den?"

"Awh, a carpenter from around dose parts, most likely."

...

...

"Do we got crowns o' thorns 'round 'ere?"

"If we do, I never seen any."

...

...

"How come dey put a diaper on 'im?"

"Well, dey couldn't leave 'im bare naked, could dey. An', to shame 'im, I suppose."

...

...

"Was ee cold?"

"Dat's not a country where it's cold most o' de time."

...

...

"Are you afeard of de tent nation?"

"Afraid o' who?"

"De tent nation."

Terry put his newspaper down.

"Whose nation?"

"De tent nation. Granny says it in 'er prayers."

1040.124.5 “Granny says dat? Tent nation?”
Religion “Yes. An’ lead us not into tent nation.”

> Scrap paper, brand new paper. Memo pad (recycled). Newspapers, flyers, magazines. Useful cardboard, useless cardboard. Egg cartons. Tim Hortons cartons. Special little cards (drawings, birthday wishes). Wrapping paper, Christmas wrapping. Brown paper bags. Shopping bags with handles. Paper for shredding. Carbon paper. Wax paper. Post-its. Stickers. Recyclable envelopes. Notebooks. Construction paper.
> 1041.42.1 Newspaper for *papier-mâché.* Lousy books.
> Sorting Catalogues.

The cover cracks as you open it, demands attention, demands special care. The first page, the bastard title page, reads:

PRÉCIS
de
L’HISTOIRE MODERNE

And on the verso, in uneven print quality:

PARIS – IMPRIMERIE BONAVENTURE ET DUCESSOIS
1042.84.4 *55, quai des Grands-Augustins*
History

> Poor feng shui can make (reveille — reverie) difficult. The Freudian slip here involves no more than the addition of the *r* and dropping the *ll*, causing no shift in chromatic range. In French (*le réveil — le rêve*) the slip involves

> more: the erasure of the *i*, the only colour, red, differentiating the two words. Coincidence? 1043.17.5 Coincidences

"Listen to dis one: 'Life is a complicatedness; I have decided to spend my life in thinking about it.'"

Zed's curiosity was piqued. Terry elaborated:

"Ee was twenty-three years old when ee's writin' dat."

Zed seemed to think about it for a moment.

"So den . . . *complicatedness*, dat's a real word?"

Terry replied, even as he continued to leaf through the pages:

"Looks like it."

"How is it den dat, in school, *difficult* was always de proper word?" 1044.63.1 Terry and Zed

> Fourth possible title: *Point du tout* (with the double meaning of a "Point in the Whole" and "Nothing at All"). The *tout* or "the whole" refers to a plenitude, and every fragment is a point, a moment in time or a position within that whole. *Un point du tout* (*A Point in the Whole*) would no doubt be clearer, but the addition of the article *un* would obscure the current and lovely use particularly in Acadian Nova Scotia of *point* instead of *pas,* to express the negative. For example: "*ce n'était point beau* ('twasn't one bad bit nice)." The *point* is also a needle prick and a punctuation mark, a period. As is evident from the above, such a title would not have pleased the translator. 1045.47.10 Yielding

"'De human race is once an' fer all an' inherently doomed to suffering and ruin'. But dat's not de one I's lookin' fer."

Zed was in no hurry, and prepared to wait for Terry to find the passage that had struck him.

"I should've written it down."

. . .

"I could swear 'twas somewhere's 'round 'ere."

Zed leaned over to read the name of the author, saw Schopenhauer, and quickly decided not to try to pronounce it.

"Awh, 'ere she is! 'It is bad today, an' it will be worse tomorrow; an' so on till the worst of all.'"

Zed agreed that it would be difficult to imagine a bleaker outlook on life. Terry was completely bowled over.

1046.63.2 Terry and Zed

"An' to tink how many artists 'ave taken 'im as der inspiration!"

1047.95.11 Additions to *La Bibliothèque idéale*

> Try as I might, I can't seem to find other titles to add to *La Bibliothèque idéale*.

Terry was still shaking his head when he dropped the Schopenhauer book gently down on the low table.

"Fer dis fellow, de words *a happy life* was a contradiction in terms. Ee said dat life 'ad it's own idea of wot she wants an' where she wants to go, and she uses us just as she pleases to get der, an' when she's done wid us, she tosses us aside, more or less."

Zed's eyebrows arched for a long moment. When they finally descended, he simply said:

1048.63.3 Terry and Zed

"You read a whole lot dese days, don't ya?"

1049.132.4 Malapropism

> Further evidence that Freudian slips often obey the rule of colour: the life of a (décor/heros) lasts seven years. The words *décor* and *heros* are exactly identical in colour.

1050.15.2 Overheard Monologues

"You knows me. I's never gonna be a success wid dem high-dollar qualities."

> Cocteau says that beauty is always accidental, in the sense that it collides violently with our

habits. He compares it to a car accident in its tendency to transfix, to be much discussed and little understood. Reread the above.

1051.78.11
Accidents

Étienne could not believe it:

"Not like dat, Mum!"

Carmen knew this was going to take a bit of explaining:

"'Tisn't your usual kind of mirror, see."

Étienne realized the seriousness of the affair when his mother knelt down to place the mirror in the back of Marianne's closet with its reflecting surface facing the wall.

"Dis 'ere's a feng shui mirror. It's fer blocking de waves comin' out from behind de toilet."

?

"Der not good waves, an' der comin' straight at Marianne's head."

??

"De backwards mirror'll send dem back de udder way."

???

Satisfied with her installation, Carmen crept backwards on all fours out of the closet, then straightened up, took Étienne by the hand, and led him into the bathroom to show him how the drain pipe behind the toilet bowl was aimed directly at Marianne's bed.

"But Mum, der's a wall!"

"A wall's not enough. De waves can go troo walls. Only a mirror can stop dem."

Étienne only knew about one kind of wave.

"Does I got waves, Mum?"

"No, yer room's alright. It really only needs a plant, only I 'aven't found de right sort yet."

"Plants give off waves as well?"

"Fer sure! All kinds o' waves. De one we're gonna put in yer room gives off waves of good luck."

"I already got good luck."

"Do you now?"

"Well sure! On account of me rabbit's foot!"

1052.123.1 Carmen and Étienne "Dat's de troot. Only, a person can't have too much good luck, now can ya."

"Awh."

> In *Life's Little Difficulties*, Pomme imagined a hockey team called the Moncton Accidents, to commemorate the accidents particular to that city, for example, oversized trucks getting stuck under the Main Street viaduct. The team would
> 1053.54.11 Forgotten/Recalled be sponsored by an insurance company. The idea came to him during a spontaneous party that had erupted at the Zablonskis'.

The author as presented on the title page:

M. MICHELET,
Membre de l'Institut,
professeur d'histoire au Collège de France,
chef de la section historique aux Archives nationales

And as one would expect, the work carries the seal of approval of the University Council and is prescribed for courses in modern history in all colleges and public schools:

OUVRAGE ADOPTÉ
Par le Conseil de l'Université,
ET PRESCRIT POUR L'ENSEIGNEMENT
DE L'HISTOIRE MODERNE DANS LES COLLÈGES

ET DANS TOUS LES ÉTABLISSEMENTS
1054.84.5 History D'INSTRUCTION PUBLIQUE.

> Family name, team's name, Christian name, tribal name, *nom de terre* (name of land), religious name, *nom de guerre*, the war without a name. Pen name, artists' name, street name,

> brand name, what in the name of God?, ship's
> name, what's in a name? name of the father,
> name of a tool, name of a tool, not to know the 1055.99.11
> names of tools. Names

For several days, Étienne had been practising heads or tails.

"Yer gettin' der. You catch it a whole lot more often dan you did in de beginnin'."

Terry had encouraged his son to persist by generously replacing the coins that rolled out of reach during the exercise.

"Dey're not always flippin'."

"Ya have to give 'er a bigger push wid yer tumb, watch."

Terry showed Étienne how to put more into the thumb's movement and a little less in the arm's. But he missed the coin coming down, and it rolled away behind the TV.

"See dat, even I don't always get it."

"If I keeps on wid practisin', could be I'll get better'n
you, eh, Dad?" 1056.129.2

"Could be. You best keep on practisin'." Fantasies

> Another irritant: a dozen that ends up being 1057.89.10
> 10. Oranges, for example. Irritants

"I didn't know you was sellin' used books 'ere..."

As she said this, the woman lay an old copy of Izaak Walton's *The Compleat Angler* on the counter.

"From time to time, folks bring in der boxes o' books dey don't want. I keep dose I figure might sell an' send de rest to Dorchester."

"I's right happy to find dis one 'ere, aldoh 'twould be a fine book fer de prisoners..."

Terry had a feeling he knew this woman, but he couldn't quite place her.

"I already got it in English, but dis 'ere's de first one I

seen in French. After yer Bible an Chairman Mao's Little Red Book, dis 'ere book's bin reprinted more often dan any udder."

"Is dat right!"

Terry picked up the book, examined it more closely. His customer added:

"Awh yes, 'tis de fisherman's classic, written sometin' like 350 years ago."

At that moment, Terry's gaze fell on a date close to that long ago.

"Says 'ere 1653. Well, dat's old fer real."

The customer opened her handbag and handed him her credit card.

"Seems to me I seen you some place before."

Terry wondered if it might not be the credit card that had prompted him to switch from the familiar *tu* to the more formal *vous*.

"Me as well, feels like I seen you somewheres. Does you play golf?"

The question made Terry smile:

"Naw, der's no time fer golf wid two little kids."

"On account of I used to golf a whole lot. Dese days I prefers de fishin'."

"Ha! Well, dat's gotta be de first time I meets somebody dat gave up golf. Wot're you fishin' den, trout?"

Again, he found himself switching back and forth between *tu* and *vous*...

"Yup, mostly de trout. Doh I did fish a bit o' salmon a couple o' times last year. I liked dat fine. You gotta have a bit o' time on yer hands, doh."

"An' why's dat?"

The woman replied while Terry completed the sale.

"Yer trout bites on account of ee's 'ungry, see. Salmon, well, dey doesn't eat flies."

"So den, yer fly fishin'?"

"Dat's de way I learned. Dry fly fishin'. On account of der's wet flies as well, dat goes under de water."

"Awh! An' 'ere's me tinkin' dat all flies was floatin' on
de surface. Just goes to show 'ow much I knows about it." 1058.47.7
"I didn't know much meself, when I started." Yielding

> Plastic: containers with sealable lids (assorted and non-matching). Jars with screw-on tops. Freezer bags. Utensils, glasses, and disposable straws. Hangers too soft to hold up anything. Dried-up ball-point and felt pens. Greenhouse planting pots, plastic vases. Toothpaste and hair-gel tubes, deodorant applicators, pillbox-
> es. Disposable razors. Repairable toys (irrepa- 1059.42.4
> rable, A.-M. Sirois). Sorting

Wrapped in his favourite blanket and curled up alongside his mother, Étienne looked at the pages of the magazine Carmen was leafing through.

"Why're dey laughin'?"

Étienne was referring to an ad depicting a couple in their thirties who looked like they were having a fantastic time preparing vegetables in a sparkling kitchen.

"Must be on account of dey love to prepare supper togedder."

...

"Or could be one o' de two said sometin' funny."

Étienne sniffled, and studied the photograph more closely.

"Me eyes is itchin'."

Carmen put her hand on her son's forehead to check for fever.

"I'll be givin' you some more o' dat syrup afore long, an' den I'll rub yer troat wid Vicks."

Étienne knew that meant he was destined for a nap.

"Can I be lyin' down on de sofa, den? I like sleepin' in de livingroom."

"Alright, if you promise to try to sleep fer real."

Étienne nodded; he didn't have the strength to promise

out loud. He returned to the photo:

"I tink dey's laughin' on account of dey's happy."

1060.123.2 Carmen and Étienne

Happy? It was the first time Carmen had heard Étienne say that word. She laughed and hugged her son closer.

"Yer happy, too, aren't ya Mum?"

1061.120.11 Fictionary

> **PERFICTION:** n. — 2005; the illusion of perfection. *"I'm sorry to have to tell you this, but you've allowed yourself to be duped by a sublime perfiction."* (Daigle)

When he was sick, Carmen found her son especially endearing.

"I know how come I's got dis cold, Mum."

"Is dat right?"

"It's on account of you didn't put dat good-luck plant in me room yet."

This surprised Carmen, who'd forgotten all about the plant.

1062.123.3 Carmen and Étienne

"You tink?"

"Awh yeah."

1063.60.7 Superstitions

> A golfer must never ever cross the path of a shot his or her partner is preparing to take. During a round, golfers are always careful not to negatively affect the others' shots. On the green, a kind of sacred space takes shape between the ball and the hole, a space which partners are careful never to enter, even though thousands of feet have already stomped all over this unpredictable and shifting zone, and will stomp all over it again in the future. Superstition or good manners? Whichever, the point is to spare the other's nerves.

From the middle down to the bottom of the page:

HUITIÈME ÉDITION.

PARIS
LIBRAIRIE CLASSIQUE ET ÉLÉMENTAIRE
DE L . HACHETTE,
LIBRAIRIE DE L'UNIVERSITÉ DE FRANCE,
Rue Pierre-Sarrazin, 12 .

1850 1064.84.6 History

In theory, each fragment refers directly to other fragments within distinct series. This cross referencing lends a multi-dimensional aspect to the structure. Thus, each fragment is touched by and in turn bumps up against at least two others (for a total of four contacts), which creates an incalculable (by me, anyway) number of permutations. Because of this, it becomes virtually possible to read the book in any order. In other words, a reader can read the book his or her way. But these possible excursions based on the fragments are not formally identified here. Rather, they are intended to suggest a possibility that a digital version of the book would actualize. 1065.68.10 Projects

"Funny how tings change. When I's little an' I'd see an airplane cross de sky above, I tawt 'ow much fun 'twould be to pilot a plane."

...

"Nowadays, I sees de same ting, an' I says to meself, awh, anudder Chinese fellow puttin' in 'is hours." 1066.15.9 Unidentified Monologues

A poor dozen, compared to those that add up to 13, as in the illustrious baker's dozen. 1067.105.1 Reserves/Reservations

Terry and Étienne were waiting for a doctor in the small examining room of the emergency department of the hospital.

"Da_, me t_oat hur_."

"I knows it. De doctor's on de way. Ee's not far, I can hear 'im."

. . .

"Why don't you lie down on de bed 'ere?"

Seated on the floor and bent over double, Étienne did not seem to want to budge.

"Madame Léger? I'm Dr. Tremblay. I work with Dr. Cormier. What's the problem? What brings you here today?"

Terry could have covered both ears, he still would have heard Dr. Tremblay's questions clearly.

"Do you feel the blood pulsing in your head?"

. . .

"Squeeze my hand."

Terry could hear Madame Léger answering the questions, but he couldn't make out what she was saying.

"Can you squeeze my hand?"

. . .

"Squeeze my hand . . ."

"*Squēeze*! *Squēeze* yer fingers!"

The husband's voice — or that's whom Terry figured he was — carried as well and as far as the doctor's.

"Can I see your teeth?"

"Open yer mout'! Open yer mout'!"

. . .

"Can you push with your feet?"

"Yer toes! Pick up yer toes!"

. . .

"Your eyes . . ."

"Yer eyes! Open up yer eyes! Open dem!"

. . .

"Look straight ahead."

"Over der! Over der!"

The longer the examination went on, the more Terry was drawn in."

"Open it! Leave yer eye open!"

. . .

"Don't be movin' yer eye about! Yer eye! Don't move it about!"

Étienne raised his head to look at his father. Terry tried to encourage him:

"Won't be long now, ee's right next door..."

Étienne lowered his head.

"Can you feel this?"

"Does ya feels it when ee pricks ya? Does ya feel 'im prickin' der?"

Terry wondered why the constant repetitions were necessary.

"We're going to have to take a few tests, Madame Léger, to see what's going on in your head...to explain this headache."

Having made his decision, the doctor did not linger in the cubicle.

"'Ow 'bout yer glasses, does ya want dem? Does ya
want to put on yer glasses?" 1068.87.6

Étienne sniffled and swallowed painfully. The Body

> At the ninth hole, the father and son paused to 1069.128.5
> share a can of sardines. Fervours

"Madame Haché? I'm Dr. Tremblay. I work with Dr. Cormier. What's the problem here today?"

The doctor was now in the cubicle across from Étienne and Terry.

"Do you feel confused?"

. . .

"Why did you run away from your residence this morning?"

Terry wanted to laugh; he felt he was being offered a bit of entertainment."

"Why do you think they don't want to keep you?"

...

"Are you feeling depressed?"

...

"Are you afraid?"

...

"Why aren't you eating?"

...

"We're going to keep you here, Madame Haché. To run some tests to see what the problem is."

...

"No, we can't let you go. It would be too dangerous."

...

"We have no choice. We'll run some tests to see what the situation is. We have to get you to eat."

Again, the doctor was quick to leave the examining room.

"Pssst!"

Terry had wanted to attract Étienne's attention, just to offer a word of encouragement, but when he saw his son's
1070.87.7 tired and watery eyes, he couldn't bring himself to say
The Body anything, and merely squeezed the boy's shoulder.

> Deep in the ditch (vulture/culture). Again, the
> 1071.132.8 same colour (blue) for the words vulture and
> Malapropism culture.

1072.82.10 "Anudder film on The Deportation? Ferget de pop-
Moncton corn, it's chocolate we'll be needin'."

> Or *Le grand écart* (The Splits). Something in the idea of the splits must have struck me, but the halo of light seems to have faded since.
> 1073.81.7 Splitting of what from what? *Un grand écart*
> Titles (Splits) rather? Hardly better.

Which renders ultimately:

PRÉCIS

de

L'HISTOIRE MODERNE

par **M. MICHELET,**

Membre de l'Institut,
professeur d'histoire au Collège de France,
chef de la section historique aux Archives nationales

OUVRAGE ADOPTÉ

Par le Conseil de l'Université,

ET PRESCRIT POUR L'ENSEIGNEMENT
DE L'HISTOIRE MODERNE DANS LES COLLÈGES
ET DANS TOUS LES ÉTABLISSEMENTS
D'INSTRUCTION PUBLIQUE.

HUITIÈME ÉDITION.

PARIS
LIBRAIRIE CLASSIQUE ET ÉLÉMENTAIRE
DE L . HACHETTE,
LIBRAIRIE DE L'UNIVERSITÉ DE FRANCE,
Rue Pierre-Sarrazin, 12.

1850

1074.84.8
History

With all the catalogues and titles Terry had skimmed, he could have created a bank of titles containing Freudian slips, but he didn't bother to write them down. Such an unwritten list might have included Franz Kowak's *The Secreted Fool on Easter Island*, Albert Simonin's *Don't Teach the Lute*, J.D Watson's *The Double Alice*, Frantz Funck-Brentano's *The Drama of Bison*, Barbara Ketcham Wheaton's *Savouring the Paste*, Jean Montenot's *Sex Afforded to*

1075.81.6 Titles *Lucretius*, and Jean Giono's *The Harassment on the Roof.*

"Dis mornin' dey was sayin' dat de opposite of love weren't hate."

"G'wan?"

"Dat's right. Apparently, 'tis indifference."

. . .

. . .

"An' who is it said dat, den?"

"Don't know, do I. 'Twas on radio."

"In English or in French?"

"French."

. . .

1076.64.10 Opposites "Try as I might, I can't imagine de English talkin' 'bout dat."

> I'm tempted to m(f)ake a Freudian slip and write
> "we have to get you to earth" instead of "we have
> to get you to eat." Again, the words *earth* and *eat*
> 1077.132.11 Malapropism are of the same colour. But a slip can never be
> intentional. In that case, it becomes a pun.

"Alright den, but just a wee one, on account of 'tis late an' we's all worn out."

Étienne sniffled without protest.

"Der's a little bird, a wee little ting like any bird you might be spottin' 'round 'ere any day o' de week."

"De brown ones or de black?"

"More like de brown, I'd say."

. . .

"Only dis wee bird's special on account of ee's got a yellow ring on top o' 'is 'ead, see, yellow wid a bit o' orange in de middle, an' some black an' white all around. When folks seen dat decoration, dey tawt it looked sometin' like a crown, so dey took to callin' dat bird a kinglet, wot means a wee king."

Terry had no idea where he was going with this story.

"Only dis 'ere wee bird's not only special on account of 'is crown."

. . .

"Ee's special as well on account of der was a little boy who'd 'eard talk of de kinglet, only ee'd never seen one. An', ee couldn't say why, ee didn't know, but ee 'ad dis terrible need to see dat bird."

"Like Saint-Thomas?"

The question made Terry laugh.

"Good point! Only not exactly like Saint-Thomas. It was on account of ee'd read a story 'bout dat kinglet in 'is school-book an', fer some reason, the kinglet like stayed in 'is 'ead. So, stands to reason, ee'd like to be seein' one. Specially on account of de yellow'n orange crown."

"Wid de black an' white."

"Dat's right."

. . .

. . .

"An' den wot?"

Terry had been groping, but the boy's question gave him an idea for an ending.

"Den nuttin'. 'Cept dat little boy? Well, dat was meself."

Étienne opened his eyes wide, looked up at his dad as though he'd just learned something fundamentally important about him. But Terry did not give him time to speak.

"An' just today, I seen my wee kinglet."

"Where?"

"Awh, ee was just der, sittin on de floor in one of de small rooms in de hospital. An' I seen 'is crown real clear an' everytin'. . . "

Étienne smiled. Then he closed his eyes and let his head sink into the pillow, ready for sleep. Terry planted a kiss on his forehead, stood and, on his way out, turned off Babar on the dresser.

"Dad?"

"Yes…"

"Dat was a terrible lovely story.

"Tanks, me boy."

"Yer welcome, Dad."

1078.37.8 "G'night."

Animal Tales "G'night, Dad."

> 1079.118.1 Concerning Yellow
>
> *Concerning Yellow.* To run straight into the lion's den, and pick a title in spite of its tenuous link to the book. Hope that the link will emerge somehow, and that it will be luminous.

"Fer sure, language is an obsession 'round dese parts!"

"Can you explain?"

"Well, on account o' de way yer supposed to be talkin'!"

"You knows yerself! De whole ting's a right cramped mess."

…

…

"Ask me, I'd say 'tis more like a fear."

"Can you explain?"

"Naw, not really."

(*A spattering of stifled laughter)*

"All de same, 'tis an obsession."

"Would you say it's a collective obsession? A collective fear?"

"Sort of, sure. Aldoh, der's lots of folks doesn't care a rat's arse about it."

…

1080.124.9 "I'd say 'tis a religion."

Religion "A religion? Can you explain?"

> A mistake? And on the title page to boot? Is it possible? M. Michelet? Shouldn't that be Jules Michelet, the French historian recommended no less than five times in *La Bibliothèque*

idéale? Unless the "M." simply means *monsieur*? Is that possible? 1081.70.8 Errors

One of the first activities Zed and Chico shared as father and son was a bicycle ride along the Petitcodiac. The water level was at its lowest.

"Did you ever see de *mascaret*? De tidal bore?"

Chico shook his head no.

"She ought to be comin' in any time now. Do ya want to wait?"

Chico only nodded. But Zed was not discouraged; he understood that a father-son relationship was not something that blossomed overnight.

"De wave used to be a lot bigger. Taller'n me even. Nowadays we hardly sees 'er. 'Tisn't much more dan a bit o' lace dat rolls along de edge o' de shore. Not too encouragin' fer de tourists."

The image did peak Chico's curiosity slightly, but he could see that that would not be enough to satisfy the tourists.

"Wot dey doesn't see is 'ow de water in de river comes right up after. You'd tink de eart' was tiltin' over dis way an' de water was runnin' downhill."

...

"Luh, 'ere she comes!"

Zed was pointing to the bend or elbow in the river, but Chico saw nothing.

"De ripple's gonna get bigger bit by bit..."

Chico waited. Although he was hardly impressed, he tried not to show it so as not to disappoint Zed. And when the river began to swell somewhat, Zed himself admitted:

"Alright, 'twasn't de big event of de century...we'll do better next time."

Which made the boy smile. 1082.135.3 Zed and Chico

Names of (some) living languages of the world: Akan, Aleut, Algonquin, Alsatian, Amharic, Angevin, English, Anglo-Norman, Arabic, Aragonese, Aramean, Aretino this is not a language but a person, Italian who invented modern literate pornography, Assamese, Asturian, Avestic, Aymara, Azeri, Bambara, Baoulé, Basque, Béarnese, Bengali, Berrichon, Belarusian, Bizkaian, Bourbonnais, Bourguignon, Brabantian, Brazilian, Breton, Bulgarian, Calabrian, Cantonese, Carcinol, Caribbean, Castilian, Catalan, Cham, Champenois, Chinese (Mandarin), Corsican, Cornish, Croatian, Czech, Danish, Dinka, Dutch, Egyptian, Estonian, Ewe, Faroese, Finnish, Flemish, Florentine, French, Franc-Comtois, Frisian, Futunan, Galician, Gallo, Gaelic, Gascon, Gavot, Genoese, German, Greek, Greenlandic (or Kalaallisut), Gronings, Gipuzkoan, Hawai'ian, Hebrew, Hindi, Hungarian, Hottentot (or Khoekhoe), Inuktitut, Irish, Iroquoian, Icelandic, Italian, Javanese, Karelian, Kayla, Kazakh, Khmer, le Kyrgyz, Korean, Lapurdian, Lahnda, Languedocien (or Occitan), Laotian, Latvian, Leonese, Ligurian, Lillois, Limburgish, Lithuanian, Lombard, Lorrain, Luxembourgish, Macedonian, Mainiot, Malay, Malagasy, Maninka, Manchu (endangered), Man, Mande, Mansi, Manx, Maori, Marathi, Marseillais, Mongol (or Khalkha), Mozarabic, Nahuatl, Neapolitan, Nenets, Nepalese, Niçard, Nootka, Norman, Norwegian, Ostyak, Pulaar, Punjabi, Picard, Piedmontese, Pisan, Poitevin, Polish, Portuguese, Provençal, Prussian, Quechua, Rhodanien, Rouchi, Rouergat, Romani, Romanian, Russian, San, Saintongeais, Sami, Sanskrit, Selkup, Scots, Serbian, Sicilian,

Sinhala, Sienna, Slovak, Slovene, Somali, Spanish, Swedish, Tagalog, Tahitian, Tamazight, Tamil, Tatar, Telugu, Tibetan, Thai, Tuscan, Tuareg, Tourangeau, Trégorrois, Tupi, Tupi-Guarani, Turkish, Turkmen, Twents, Uyghur, Urdu, Ukranian, Uzbek, Vannetais, Venetian, Vietnamese, Wallisian, Walloon, Welsh, Wolof, Yoruba, Yupik, Zhuang and Zuberoan.

Note that the above list includes numerous French dialects, sub-dialects, and regional accents. Not included are many indigenous languages (struggling for survival), for example those spoken in Canada: Abenaki, Babine-Witsuwit'en, Beothuk, Blackfoot, Broken Slavey, Bungee, Carrier, Cayuga, Chilcotin, Chinook Jargon, Coast Tsimshian, Comox, Cree, Dene Suline, Dogrib, Gwich'in, Haida, Haisla, Halkomelem, Hän, Heiltsuk-Oowekyala, Innu-aimun, Inuinnaqtun, Inupiaq, Inuvialuktun, Kaska, Kutenai, Kwak'wala, Labrador Inuit Pidgin French, Malecite-Passamaquoddy, Michif, Mi'kmaq, Mohawk, Munsee, Naskapi, Nicola, Nitinaht, Nlaka'pamuctsin, Nuu-chah-nulth, Nuxálk, Ojibwe, Okanagan, Oneida, Onondaga, Ottawa, Potawatomi, Saanich, Sekani, Seneca, Sháshíshálh, Shuswap, Slavey, Squamish, St'at'imcets, Tagish, Tahltan, Tlingit, Tsuut'ina, Tuscarora, Tutchone, Western Abnaki, Wyandot.

Finally, note that Chiac figures in Wikipedia's list of living languages. 1083.99.12 Names

"You can moan an' sigh all ya like, time won't go by any faster. You'd best find sometin' to do."

Unforeseen circumstances had prevented Terry and

Carmen from taking the children apple picking as they'd promised. Instead of leaving in the morning, they would have to wait until late afternoon.

"An' I doesn't want to take a nap after lunch neider."

Terry had been counting on the children's nap to sneak one in himself.

"I tinks it'd do you a world o' good to have a little lie down."

"I doesn't want to lie down."

"An' why not? Dat way you won't be sittin' an' frettin' all de time."

1084.93.11
Time

"I don't mind frettin'. It's de waitin' I don't like."

1085.132.3
Malapropism

> According to Freud, even typos conceal real emotions.

1086.116.6
True or False

"Come 'ere, boy! Yer de one dat broke des 'ere tulips. True or false?

> *The March of Language*. Or *of Lalanguage? The March of Lalanguage*. Sounds too much like military music. *Concerning Lalanguage. The Misunderstanding in the Quidproquo of Lalanguage. To what quid does Lalanguage pro quo?*
>
> 1087.81.8
> Titles
>
> Now it's all beginning to sound like a bit of a joke, to be honest. *Tales of Lalanguage*?

Terry and Élizabeth were beginning to clear the table when Zed suddenly announced:

"Alright den, Chico . . . time fer yer spankin'."

None of the children had the slightest idea what he was talking about.

"Wot spankin' you say? Why his birt'day spankin'! Youse never 'eard of a birt'day spankin'?"

Zed gathered them all together on the big carpet in the middle of the room.

"When 'tis yer birtday, de udders spanks you on de

bum. Yer seven years old? We gives you seven slaps, an one so youse'll grow. We always got our spankins, didn't we now, Terry?"

Chico, wondering if Zed was pulling his leg, glanced over at Étienne to see if he knew what was up.

"Not big whackin' slaps, mind you. 'Tisn't supposed to hurt much, really. OK, Chico, are ya ready, or does we have to catch you first?"

The other children thought this new idea sounded like fun; they couldn't wait for Chico to make up his mind, since they now realized that they were going to get the chance to smack him on the bum.

"Now, don't be fergettin', Zed said dey're not to be big hard whacks!"

"One . . . two . . ."

Those first up were too gentle.

"Well, lay it on a bit harder dan dat. We gotta hear a bit of a slap . . . tree . . . four . . . dat's de spirit . . . five . . . six . . . seven . . . an' . . . one more to make you grow!"

The children were all laughing. Chico got up laughing as well, relieved to have emerged unhurt.

"Alright den, now we's can eat de cake!"

"Wait! Ee's gotta blow out de candles first!"

"Fer sure, he'll be blowin' out de candles!"

The children scrambled to sit round the table. In the
kitchen, Carmen and Élizabeth lit the candles on the cake 1088.106.2 Customs
covered in candy. Smarties, coconut, and bits of licorice.

> In his preface, Michelet states that the work was first published in 1827. He also describes what he hoped to accomplish by writing a modern history of western and southern Europe destined to be memorized by students. The preface also includes the words "*colléges*"—the acute accent was changed to a grave accent with the reform of French spelling in 1878—and "*présentassent,*" the third-person plural

imperfect subjunctive of the verb "to present," 1089.84.9 History a form of conjugation abandoned in the twentieth century.

"Wot would be de difference den betwixt a fantasy an' an obsession?"

"Can someone answer this question?"

...

"No one?"

...

"Yes?"

"I don't really know 'ow to explain it, only a fantasy seems a whole lot more fun dan de obsession."

"You said '*un obsession*' like it was masculine. Only should be '*une obsession*', on account of obsession is feminine!"

"Dat's de troot'!"

1090.141.5 Obsessions "Haha! Ha! Hahaha!..."

"Please!... Please!..."

1091.116.1 True or False In *1953: Chronicle of a Birth Foretold*, the Acadian novelist France Daigle mentions the collaboration between Firmin Didot and the editor of directories and almanacs Sébastien Bottin (1764–1853) in publishing the *Didot-Bottin Commercial Directory* of 1882.

1092.89.5 Irritants "Me, 'tis when you find yerself shakin' hands wid some fellow owes you money."

1093.118.2 Concerning Yellow Still looking for a link with yellow.

Standing on the dune, Étienne, Chico, Zed, and Terry were looking at the beached whale below:

"How come she didn't stay in de water?"

"Most likely, she didn't know she was so close to shore. Sometimes dey suffers from disorientation. 'Specially when der's a stormy sea an' de terrible big waves an' dat."

...

"Wot's dis orient?"

"Wot?"

"Yah, I wants to know as well..."

The two boys looked like a couple of hungry robin chicks, their beaks wide open. 1094.139.5 Étienne and Chico

"Say again, wot is it youse wants to know?"

"Wot's dis orient? Dis orient ocean?"

> The preface of *Précis de l'histoire moderne* is followed by an 8-page introduction, but, naturally, it is in the body of the text—some 300-pages long—that Michelet examines in depth the events that mark modern history, beginning in 1453 with the Turkish capture of Constantinople, and ending with the French Revolution in 1789. The first and last pages of this copy of the book are especially stained, the middle pages less so, except for pages 92 and 93, which are especially greasy. One might conclude that the student needed a whole lot of butter cakes to sustain the effort of 1095.84.10 History
> memorization.

The two dads launched into extensive explanations of the phenomenon of disorientation, as it relates to right and left, north, south, east, and west; and to the stars, the compass, GPS, and instinct.

"Let's say dat it's not so easy to know wair* dey ought to be goin', when yer in de middle of de ocean an' neider

---

* "*Yoù c'est, ayoù c'que*" are other ways of writing "*yoùsque.*" Yet more evidence, if it was required, of the need to regulate, standardize the Acadian language. English not being threatened, one might substitute "wair" or "whar" for "where" with- 1098.143.3 Varia
out fear of undermining the very existence of the language.

land nor any signs around … doh, sure it's not like dey can read anyhow…"

The four beached whales on the beach had attracted a crowd of curious villagers. There was no shortage of opinions:

"Der's dem dat says when a whale dies, de udder whales push 'er toward de shore."

"Why would dey be doin' dat?"

"We doesn't know fer sure. Some say 'tis a burial like."

Zed had heard a different explanation:

"A fellow over der's sayin' dey was most likely lookin' fer fish to eat when dey got pushed up on de beach by the storm winds."

"Dad! Luh! Dey's cuttin' her!"

Indeed, a fisheries worker was taking a sample of flesh from one of the cetaceans. Étienne was close to horrified.

"Dey's gotta analyze dat bit under de microscope so's dey can be findin' out if dese 'ere whales died of some disease. On account of, if dat's de case, maybe dey could keep udder whales from catchin' it."

The four watched the sampling process:

"Seems like der tryin' to cut in places whar* 'twon't show so badly."

"Could be dey're lookin' fer a special part, like de stomach or close to de gills or sometin' like dat."

…

1096.117.5 Death "Maybe dey just don't like to be wreckin' sometin' so … majestic."

> Sylvia always eats fish on Friday, a vestige of her religious education, which she originally conserved out of superstition, but that she maintains today more for health reasons and,
> 1097.60.4 Superstitions perhaps a little oddly, out of respect for her ancestors.

Touristic slip: to take the girdled tour rather 1099.132.1
than the guided tour. Malapropism

"Reminds me o' de first time you came by to take a look at de lofts building wid me, dat time we unloaded de vinyls. We was after takin' a look round de inside, an' den we's just standin' der in de middle o' de place, an' you says 'it's 'entrancing.'"

Yes, Terry remembers.

"Sure, I remember dat."

"An' den you says 'twas de first time you ever used dat word."

"Dat's de troot', I did say dat."

"Just dat wee bit — when we's standin' der, an' you says de word, an' den dat it was de first time youse ever said it — dat's sometin' I's never gonna ferget."

Terry was both touched and intrigued.

"On account of?"

"Don't know, really. 'Twas just so . . . us."

. . . 1100.63.4

. . . Terry and Zed

Vor der Kaserne
Vor dem großen Tor
Stand eine Laterne
Und steht sie noch davor
So woll'n wir uns da wieder seh'n
Bei der Laterne wollen wir steh'n
Wie einst Lili Marleen 1101.112.2
Wie einst Lili Marleen Languages

"Dad, I wants to wash me hands."

Étienne had just woken up. Terry glanced at him in the rear-view mirror.

"Wash yer hands wot fer?"

But Terry had a pretty good idea why. And since Étienne seemed to be still half asleep, his father was quite happy to let his son's request wither on the vine.

"Eh, Dad? Can I wash me hands?"

"Wot's de matter wid yer hands? I'm not about to stop fer nuttin.'"

Terry did not want to drag out their return trip, which was already sufficiently long. He dared to hope that his slightly impatient tone would convince Étienne to forget about his hands, or to go back to sleep until they got home.

"I's got whale on dem, don't I."

Terry cast a pleading look Zed's way, then dug deep within himself for all the patience he could muster:

"On account of you touched de whale, is dat it? Dat's not real dirt, ya know. It's no different dan if you'd be touchin' leather."

Zed chimed in casually:

"Leather dat's bin floatin' in salt water, to boot. Salt water doesn't make a body dirty, it cures you."

"Dat's troo. Don't ya remember when you scraped yer knee an' Granny washed it wid salt water?"

...

...

"But you said 'twere maybe sick!"

"De whale? I said she were maybe sick?"

Terry thought hard and fast:

"I only meant inside 'er belly. I's certain der weren't no sickness on 'er skin."

Étienne, both hands resting palms up on his thighs, stared helplessly at the back of the seat in front of him.

"Eh, boy? Do you believe me?"

Étienne, unsure and unwilling to abdicate completely,
1102.87.12 wiggled his fingers:
The Body "It's sticky, all de same..."

> And come to think of it, why yellow? Wouldn't any colour do just as well? *Concerning Red.*

> *Concerning Blue. Concerning Green. Concerning White.* I suppose not. 1103.118.3 Concerning Yellow

In the back seat, the two boys eventually drifted back to sleep. Their long day out in the sea air finally got the better of Étienne's hands that had touched the whale.

"Sometimes, de tings dey come out wid!"

"Don't I know it. 'Tis great!"

"You an' Chico, is it like you figured 'twould be, or better? Or worse?!"

"Up until now — touch wood — it's been smood sailin'. It's like ee was me little brudder I've known from way back."

"Great! More dan likely 'tis better dat way dan bein' a real parent."

"Ee rings up 'is granny a lot, dat's 'ow ee calls 'er, 'me granny.' I figure ee's worryin' she'll be lonesome by 'erself. When ee's on de phone wid 'er, I pretends to go to de batroom or some such ting, just so ee feels free to say wot he likes. I tries not to crowd de boy. But, when ee's done, ee tells me everytin' dey said."

"Does ee talk 'bout Shawn at all?"

"From time to time, he does."

...

"Udder day, ee tells me he dreamed dat folks wot killed der fawder or mudder weren't sent off to prison — to de *jail* is 'ow ee put it. Dat it weren't de sort of ting you get sent up to prison fer. Dat sometin' else happened, only ee couldn't say wot." 1104.109.4

"Hun! Dat's not so crazy..." Dreams

> Examination for course on Geography of the Ocean (GEOG 2831): Jonas in the belly of the whale? Really? Base your case on the fact that he boarded at Tarshish, near present-day Port Said, and that he only travelled on the Mediterranean Sea. (Bonus of five points if you

1105.32.6 draw a map of the main fish migrations in the
Exam Questions Atlantic, between the Arctic and the Antarctic).

"An' wot about Élizabeth in all dis?"

"She does a right proper job of it, she does. Gives us plenty o' time an' room. Doesn't try to be a mudder, an' dat's a good ting. An' she never tells me wot to do, unless I asks 'er."

"Geez... stop! I'm gettin' jealous!"

Zed laughed.

"Are yer wee sisters still gone head o'er heels over 'im?"

"Tell ya de troot, me parents're just as bad. Dey hauled him off to Fredericton last week — me dad had a wee job to do down der, an' next ting, dey goes an' buys de boy a brand new pair o' skates."

"Dat's wonderful nice o' dem to tink of it."

"I knows it. I figure me dad's feelin' guilty fer all de hard times ee put me troo. One o' dese days, I suppose I ought to be tellin' 'im ee doesn't 'ave to be carryin' all dat guilt."

"Might not be guilt. Might be ee just figured it out, finally!"

"Could be."

1106.63.5 ...
Terry and Zed "Yer still on de lookout fer de moose, eh?"

> The list of automatic corrections for common
> errors in German (Germany) is not available.
> 1107.112.3 The component is not installed. Do you want
> Languages to install it now? Yes. No.

"How about you, is there something in particular that frightens you?"

"Well, I'd hate to be gettin' meself killed in a car accident. De worst part'd be hearin' all dat metal gettin' mashed wid me inside it. Brrr!"

"Does this fear keep you from travelling in cars?"

“Naw. Only I’s gotta be de one drivin.”

… 1108.137.5

“You can skip me turn if you tink me fear’s too borin.’” Fears

> Reminder: check your car’s wheel nuts! Unseen defects, such as overtightening, can lead to loosening of the wheel nuts. All nuts must be checked after driving a distance of 80 km with newly installed tires. Come by your Atlantic Tire Dealers Association member sales outlet for a free checkup on wheel-nut tighteness. Your safety depends on it. This reminder is provided by the Atlantic Tire Dealers Association. 1109.78.8 Accidents

“So den, when did you start?”

Before replying to Zed’s question, Terry glanced behind him to make sure that Étienne and Chico were still asleep.

“Bin a couple o’ years now. Longer if you count de time I was lookin’ it over off and on, ’afore I made up me mind.”

…

“Didn’t want to go blabberin’ about it doh, in case I screwed up.”

…

“Now, it’s got so it’s a wee sideline. Keeps me goin.’”

…

“I did kinda want to tell Carmen, only I never did. I suppose I’s afraid she’d panic an’ tell me to stop.”

…

“Dunno really. ’Twas like ’avin’ a bit of a fling I suppose.”

… 1110.63.6

“An’ now, well…” Terry and Zed

1111.93.10 Time

> In time, all things come to rest/rust.

“It’s my first time inside a prison.”

. . .

"How are you?"

Shawn gave me a quick nod of the head. My interpretation: superfluous question. I tried to switch tracks.

"I explained in my letter why I was wantin' to talk to you. Have you any questions?"

He shrugged. My interpretation: I'm here for a momentary distraction.

"Yer not in a talkin' mood, I can see that. I can come back anudder time, if you like. Most likely some days're better than udders."

Shawn forced a quick laugh. My interpretation: good days are rare.

. . .

. . .

. . .

"'Ow's Chico doin', den?"

"Pretty well, far as I can tell. He looks like a right fine little fellow."

My answer seemed to reassure him. I added:

"Zed's takin' wonderful fine care of him."

Shawn was silent. I wondered if my mention of Zed had troubled him.

"What I mean to say is I don't think you have to be worryin' about him."

He nodded. My interpretation: no need to dwell on the subject.

. . .

"Well, den, wot was ya wantin' to know? Shoot."

I got straight to the point:

"Do you think you were treated fairly in this whole thing? I mean, do you think they were fair to ya?"

He considered it seriously.

"In a way, yes."

"An' . . . in the udder way?"

He took a moment longer to think.

"No one showed me 'ow to handle meself, how to

handle me dark side."

"When you were a boy, you mean, or since you been in 'ere?"

"When I's a boy. Once yer in 'ere 'tis too late, obviously."

It was my turn to nod.

"An' when did you realize you had a dark side?"

Shawn took the time to think about it. I could see he wasn't completely hardened.

"In a way, I always knowed it. I always felt it. Only I didn't know wot to do wid it, did I. So, I only pushed it deeper inside meself."

"An' do you feel you know more what to do with it now?"

He started to answer, but then seemed to come up against something, and tried again:

"Sometimes."

"Is there no one here that can help with that sort of thing?"

The minute that passed then seemed to go on forever. As in the previous question, something seemed to be blocking him from thinking or speaking. The muscles in his jaw contracted and I thought I saw the whites of his eyes turn red. He pretended to be distracted by something, turned his head, but it didn't help; his inner struggle continued. I was helpless, afraid he'd break. At the other end of the room, the guard was busy studying a spot he was scratching on his forearm. To my relief,
Shawn seemed to calm down. He simply said: 1112.101.12

"Help don't always come from where you tinks it will." Duos

In the convenience store adjoining the gas station, Étienne spotted a strawberry keychain he
absolutely wanted to buy as a present for his 1113.36.11
father. Strawberries

Zed felt it was his duty to warn Terry:

"Well, sooner or later youse are gonna 'ave to tell 'er..."

"Don't I know it."

Terry did not want to think about this eventuality. And yet, the longer he waited, the more he feared Carmen's reaction at having been kept in the dark.

"I tawt I might fix tings a wee bit on de sly like, widout her noticin'. 'Tisn't as doh she's checkin' up on everytin'. I's more de one dat takes care o' de family finances. She does de bar."

At the same time, Zed didn't want to be too hard on his friend:

"Well, could be a nice surprise. Der's more'n one way to look at it."

"Dat's wot I was tinkin' too, at de start, dat 'twould be a right nice surprise. Only, like you say, unfortunately, der's more'n one way to look at it."

. . .

1114.63.7 Terry and Zed "Anyhow, you keep mum. OK?"

1115.60.3 Superstitions

> Josse hasn't the least hesitation about breaking an electronic chain letter.

And then, because one confidence deserves another:

"You know, Élizabeth, she's a right fine person. Only I don't tink it'll last, de two of us."

"Awh, no?"

"No, can't explain why exactly. 'Tis more like a feeling."

. . .

"Der's nuttin' wrong really. An' I don't tink 'tis on account of 'er bein' older dan me an' all dat. 'Twouldn't be on account of dat, I don't tink."

"Der's just sometin' missin' . . ."

"Dat's it. Der's sometin' missin'."

Terry held his tongue, sensing that Zed still had something he wanted to say.

"Anyhow, I tinks she feels it as well. I suppose we ought to be talkin' 'bout it."

. . .

. . .

"Might be dat wid Chico, now . . ."

Zed had expected the addition of Chico in their lives would perhaps change something for Élizabeth and him, but Terry's way of putting it cast a different light on the matter."

"Fer sure, dat changes tings . . ."

Deep in thought, Zed did not go further. Terry thought to conclude by lightening things up a bit:

"Could be you wants Chico all fer yerself!"

"Could be!"

The idea made the two friends laugh, but Zed added:

"I's laughin' only 'tis de God's troot' all de same. It's as doh I needs Chico to feel der's somebody — one person — dat's der just fer 'im, an' dat person's meself. Only me, an' all o' me. So, in a way, yes, I wants 'im all fer meself."

Without realizing it, Terry had hit the mark.

"Might not be like dat fer all time, but has to be like dat fer a while anyhow. Chico an' me, we gotta find ourselves, gotta build a life fer ourselves. We gotta gel."

. . .

"So, deep down, could be I doesn't want Élizabeth to be der as much as all dat. An' not only dat, I don't tink she is der really. Not dat she shows it. Not a bit. Like I says, 'tis more just a feeling I's got."

Glancing in the rear-view mirror, Terry could see the two boys were fast asleep. Étienne's hands had relaxed, but they still lay open with both palms turned up.

"Does all dat make any sense at all?" 1116.63.8

"Makes sense to me." Terry and Zed

True or false: Louis Aragon met his muse Elsa 1117.140.1
Friolet in Caraquet in 1928. Caraquet

Before disappearing through the door he'd come in, Shawn turned to me and said:

"Der's a fellow comes in to see me time to time. Ee tinks ee's helpin' me out. Ee talks an' I listens. You ask me, ee needs more help dan I does."

That shook me. We weren't alone in the room. Was he allowed to shout like that? The guard didn't seem to
1118.103.5 mind. Shawn added:
Disappearances "Write dat."

> The long saga of human languages provides a terrain rich in matters for reflection. In Sudan, for example, approximately 100,000 people* speak 1 or the other of 30 languages belonging to the small Nigero-kordofanian family. Which amounts to an average of 3,300 speakers per language. Do these people have the feeling that
> 1119.112.11 their ethnic group will disappear? Are they
> Languages worried about it?

"*'Ow come* den dat Marianne's never gotta be apologizin'?"

"We don't say *how come*. We say *pourquoi*."

"*Pourquoi*, den?"

"On account of she's too young, isn't she. She doesn't understand how apologizin' works yet."

Seeing that Étienne did not look satisfied, Carmen added:

"An' on account of yer older, there's tings that Marianne'll be learnin' from you. That's why 'tis important you set a good example."

"Only, I doesn't want to give me good example to Marianne."

"An' why not, pray tell?"

"On account of she takes everytin' apart. Every time I give her sometin' she only takes it apart."

1122.143.4 * The population of metropolitan Moncton is approximately
Varia 100,000.

Carmen felt like laughing, but restrained herself.

"A good example's not something a person can take apart. 'Tis only sometin' you see and hear, an' seein' an' hearin' it often enough, you starts to figure that's the way to behave."

Étienne knew you weren't supposed to burp after drinking pop.

"Bein' de elder has its advantages as well. You can drink ginger ale, but Marianne's too young. She can only drink juice."

Carmen had been clearing the table as she spoke.

"Mum! You took me plate, only I weren't done eatin'!"

As a matter of fact, Carmen had assumed Étienne would not finish his macaroni and cheese.

"Oops!"

Carmen put back Étienne's plate:

"'Ere ya go, me big boy. I apologize."

Étienne speared a forkfull of macaronis, ate them in silence, and then concluded: 1120.86.12

"Alright den, Mum, I'll set de good example as well." Apologies

> Belated discovery: the character of Élizabeth is in fact an interpretation, an unconscious representation of another character: Lydia Towarski in Romain Gary's novel *Clair de femme* (*The Light of a Woman*). To be honest, Élizabeth and Alida, another character in *Real Life*, are both sketches of Lydia Towarski. One might deduce from this that a part of Lydia Towarski lives on 1121.96.6
> in Catherine. Catherine? Characters

no one on the beach
so many folks in me head 1123.55.11
wash dem in water Haikus

No matter how long and loud Chico shouted, Étienne did not turn around. Finally, Chico went to him at the far end of the yard.

"Yer deef as a cod!"

?

"Are ya pickin' up recyclables today?"

"OK."

Chico and Étienne never had any trouble finding recyclable drink containers in the neighbourhood, especially on the grounds of the English school next to their building. Zed had found them a small wagon for collecting.

"Wot're ya gonna do wid yer money, den?"

"Don't know. I'm savin' it."

"I's gonna buy a dustpan fer me granny's birt'day. 'Er's is old an' banged up."

Étienne liked the fact that Chico took care of his grandmother.

"I can help you pay fer it, if you like."

"Naw, I can pay fer it on me own."

...

...

"Do you buy tings fer Shawn sometimes?"

Chico shrugged.

1124.139.8 Étienne and Chico "Ee only wants a card when his birt'day comes round."

"Awh."

"Last year, I slipped a pack o' gum inside de card."

> The next day, to get a bit of perspective, I drove from Shediac along the coast to Pointe-Sapin. I stopped for an ice cream at the Cap-de-Cocagne pier, and then on for a breath of sea air and creosote on the pier at Côte Sainte-Anne, just to make sure the trip took about as long as I'd imagined.

1125.56.2 Pilgrimages

"Wot do you call it when a person's afraid of sometin' dat affects dem directly? Like a girl dat loves skiing cross-country, only she won't swim in a lake if can't see across. Or de lass dat wins de Stella Artois brewer's competition, an’ she’s right proud to be off to de national finals, only she’s dead afeard of de draft in airplanes. Is der a word fer dat, den?” 1126.92.12 Questions without Answers

> One should let a good rumour spread, because it refreshes, lightens, gives reality a bit of a push. 1127.108.11 Rumours

“You don’t know ’ow to play squares?!”

Neither Étienne nor Marianne knew what their mother was talking about.

“Well den, me children, I’m gonna show you right ’ere an’ now!”

Carmen disappeared for a moment, returning with a pink chalk. She lifted the living room carpet as though it were no heavier than a dishcloth, dropped it along the edge of the wall, and began drawing long lines on the floor. Étienne and Marianne stood watching her.

“Étienne, don’t you ’ave some bits o’ broken seashells in your things?”

“Yes…”

“Well, go an’ fetch them, we’re gonna need ’em.”

But Étienne did not move. He was unable to tear his gaze from the hopscotch that Carmen was blithely chalking on the living room floor. Did this mean that drawings of any kind would be allowed?

“You don’t want to?”

Yes, Étienne wanted to, but…

“When I’m done, I’ll tell ya wot numbers to write inside de squares.”

Étienne ran to his room to get his bottle of seashell fragments whose edges had been softened by the sea. 1128.106.5 Customs

> When she really had nothing to do, a young poet working at the Babar liked to scan the completed crosswords in search of evocative word phrases along the rows of the puzzle.

> For example, heads-shreds, shroud-earth, wandering-ps, torque-clash. She even found
> 1129.91.11 The Poet — revery-use-ere and ere-use-year. Should she conclude that dream-use-year?

"So den, you tink 'tis really wort'while?"

"Well, you gotta know wot yer doin'..."

"Is it sometin' you could be showin' me how?"

"Matter o' fact, I was tinkin' just dat. We could go in togedder, if you had a mind to. I was gonna mention it, only I's waitin' to be more sure o' meself first."

Zed agreed, adding for Terry's benefit:

"An' dat way 'twould be less of a surprise fer Carmen. She's used to me gettin' you into all kinds o' crazy schemes."

1130.63.10 Terry and Zed — "Exactly!"

> On the subject of yellow, it can connote wealth or disease: yellow gold, yellow fever; games of skill or games of chance: yellow jersey, yellow dwarf; the abstract or the concrete: yellow streak, yellow flowers; human groups or groups of humans: yellow race, yellow union;
> 1131.118.4 Concerning Yellow — the banal or the sublime: yellow pages, Van Gogh's yellow.

"Mum, can I be havin' some Smarties?"

"No, not this time."

"I's hungry."

"We'll be havin' supper in a bit."

"I want Smarties..."

"Look out, now. Let me by so's I can empty the cart."

...

"'Ere now, would you like to give me a hand?"

...

"Don't be grabbin' the bag any which way, the peas'll fall out!"

…

"Never mind den, it'll go a whole lot faster if I do it meself."

…

"How about an apple?"

"Naw."

"Der's bananas. Wouldn't you care fer a banana?"

"I want Smarties."

…

…

"*Thirty-seven sixty-four. The young feller's tired I believe.*"

"*Yes, and his Mum's just about had it as well.*"

"Wot did she say?"

"*He looks so sweet.*"

"*Yes, but he's been so stubborn today I'd gladly give him away!*"

"Wot did she say?"

"*Thanks but no thanks, I've got my own…*"

"*Well, was worth a try.*" 1132.138.11

"Wot did she say?" The Other

> Linguists currently identify 8 major language families: the Indo-European family, which includes some 1,000 languages and 3 billion speakers; the tonal languages of Asia, which are spoken by 1.5 billion people, including more than 1 billion Chinese; the 370 Afro-Asiatic (Hamito-Semitic) languages, spoken by 300 million people, including 200 million Arabic speakers; the Austronesian languages, which group together 300 million speakers and 850 languages; the Altaic language family which includes 65 languages spoken by 100 million people; 80 million people speak the 2,000 languages of Africa, 900 of which belong to the sub-group of Niger-Congo languages; the

Uralic languages counting 25 million speakers,
mainly Hungarians and Finns; and the indigenous languages of the Americas, which include 1,100 languages and 25 million speakers.
Altogether this adds up to approximately 5,300
1133.112.7 languages, but this list is neither exhaustive nor
Languages uncontested.

On the way home, Étienne could not get over Carmen's refusal to buy him some Smarties. Hence, the whining tone:

"How come we's always goin' back to de same grocery?"

"So you'll know where to find de things when yer older."

This silenced Étienne. Carmen regretted her ironic reply, and tried to soften its effect:

"And, when yer older an' drivin' de car yerself, you might be goin' to the store fer us from time to time."

Étienne thought about this eventuality, and decided,
1134.88.3 when the time came, he'd buy as many Smarties as he
Freedom liked.

Terry reads the words *haulms*, *volute*, *shingly*,
keelson, *parapet*, *cascade*, *trundle dodder*, and
1135.67.1 *nimbus* on a page of the small stapled notebook
Terry's he pulled out of his back pocket. He finds a
Notebooks pencil and adds the word *menagerie*.

1136.122.4 "'Round 'ere even language's a sport, fer chris'sake!"
Sports "Fer sure!"

And on the next page of the notebook:
Die? Meself? Really?
1137.117.10 It's about time dat sometin'
Death Leaves me friggin' cold!

Zed didn't want Chico to feel uncomfortable about not calling him Dad.

"Dat's OK dat you don't call me Dad. We know Shawn's yer real dad. Most likely, if you was still a wee ting an' you'd no memory o' Shawn, well den it'd probably come to ya natural. On account of I'd be de only dad you'd ever known."

Chico put another plate in the dish drying sink. Zed picked it up and began drying.

"I doesn't call you Dad, only in me head yer like me dad."

"Dat's right fine wid me! Wot counts is dat I help you to 'ave a proper life."

Chico agreed, but remained silent, washing a few utensils and putting them in the sink.

"Wot're ya tinkin'? Aldoh, you don't 'ave to be tellin' me. Der's times a fellow wants to keep 'is tawts to 'imself."

...

...

"Do you tink Granny's got a proper life?"

And there it was. The cat was out of the bag. For a while, Zed had suspected that Chico was carrying guilt about his grandmother. He dropped the dish rag, pulled up a chair and sat down.

"Come 'ere, boy, I wants to tell ya sometin'."

Chico came closer.

"I already told ya didn't I, dat I didn't really 'ave a real dad neider, at de start, remember?

Chico nodded.

"De ting I most likely didn't tell ya, is dat when I's yer age, I could see me mudder was 'avin' a hard time of it, see. Awh, not dat she was blearin' or anyting like dat, 'cause she's not de complainin' type. Only I could see she was workin' terrible hard to make a bit o' money to buy our food an' clothes an' a Christmas present an' all dat."

...

"Well, when she starts goin' wid Tony, I's right proud fer her. On account of ee was helpin' 'er out. An' den she marries 'im. An' der again, I's right proud fer 'er. Only, deep down, I wasn't all dat fond o' Tony. I never said a word to me mum, mind you; I didn't want to cause 'er any pain, an' I didn't want 'er gettin' discouraged."

Chico seemed to understand what Zed was telling him.

"Wot I'm tryin' to say is dat yer granny—an' I knows you love 'er a whole lot on account of she was pretty much yer mum—yer granny made de best life she could. 'Tisn't easy to understand, I knows it, but dat's de way it is. We can't go changin' de past. An' today, one ting dat'll make Granny's life better, dat's to see yer growin' up fine, wid folks dat love you an' helps you out."

...

"'Tis a fine ting you tinkin' of Granny, an' doin' stuff fer 'er, phonin' 'er, bringin' 'er strawberries an' all dat, only you mustn't be puttin' 'er life on yer shoulders. You have to live yer life too, an' you've a right to be 'appy."

Chico was almost frozen to the spot.

"Do you understand wot I's tryin' to tell ya?"

1138.135.2 Chico nodded, and Zed took him in his arms and
Zed and Chico hugged him tight.

1139.17.10 Looking everywhere for your *Bescherelle*, but
Chance not finding it. Coincidence?

Étienne spotted a second cross decorated in flowers on the other side of the ditch along the highway.

"'*Ow come* dey puts dat der, Mum?"

Carmen was torn between being happy to see her son wasn't the type to hold a grudge, and being disappointed that he'd used the English expression *how come*.

"Why do they put what?"

"Crosses wid necklaces?"

Carmen thought this was clearly not her day.

"Awh, that's to remind us that somebody was killed in a car crash right there."

Étienne twisted round in his seat to watch the little cross disappear.

"Dey want us to pray?"

"I think 'tis more a way to be tellin' us to drive careful."

. . .

"Although, I suppose there's some folks that pray as well."

. . .

"Only I wouldn't think to pray."

"On account of you didn't know dem?"

"I don't know me prayers?"

"No! De folks in de car crash!"

"Awh."

Carmen thought for a moment.

"No. 'Tis only that I wouldn't think to pray fer somebody dead." 1140.117.7

"On account of yer shy?" Death

> Misfortune is the true test of friendship. One man's misfortune is another man's gain. Every man is the architect of his own fortune. Fortune favours the brave. When in disgrace with fortune and men's eyes, I all alone beweep my outcast state. A hostage to fortune. Fortune knocks once at every man's door. The slings and arrows of outrageous fortune. It's an ill wind that blows nobody any good. It's in times of trouble that you know who your friends are. Bad luck and trouble follow you all of your days. Misery loves company. Troubles never come singly. Happiness is an agreeable sensation arising from contemplating the misery of another. Bird of ill omen. Lucky in cards unlucky in love. If I didn't have bad luck, I wouldn't have no luck at all. Some people are so fond of bad luck they run halfway to meet it. The only sure thing about luck is that it will change. Watch out when you're getting everything you want; fattening hogs ain't in luck. Bread always falls

> on the buttered side. When the gods throw, the
> 1141.60.8 Superstitions dice are loaded. At the heart of every silver lin-
> ing is a cloud.

Zed wrote a note to Chico before leaving. As he wrote, he crossed out a word, rewrote it, and crossed it out again.

"How does you write *jusqu'à temps que*? *Temps t-e-m-p-s*, or *tant t-a-n-t*?

Terry walked over to read the note.

"*T-e-m-p-s*. Meaning 'until de time dat. . . .' De udder way 'twould mean 'so long as.'"

Terry seemed very sure of himself. Zed reread the message:

"Well, dat's wot I mean, isn't it: 'so long as I's not come home.'"

"Awh. I tawt you wanted to say 'until such time as I get home,' like . . . 'while you waits fer me to get der.'"

"Well, sure, I wants to say dat as well."

Terry and Zed both leaned over the scrap of paper. Terry read aloud:

"Chico if you get home before I do, go over to the Zablonskis and stay there up until which time (*jusqu'à temps que*) I get back. Étienne will be there too."

Terry reread the note silently once more before pronouncing himself.

"Far as I'm concerned, it's *temps t-e-m-p-s*, on account of 'tis really a question of time and *temps* means 'time.'"

Zed nodded; he wanted to believe Terry.

"Makes sense, I suppose."

"You'd be writing *tant t-a-n-t* if you was saying . . . like . . . I'll take Tylenols so long as (*tant, t-a-n-t*) me headache hasn't gone.

Zed saw the difference and approved:

1142.93.4 Time "I dunno but der's times when I goes to write sometin' down, you'd tink I never went to school."

> Long ago, when Latin was the dominant lan-
> guage, French was considered a vulgar lan-
> guage, that is a language spoken by the com- 1143.112.8 Languages
> mon people.

The next day, Terry was still thinking about Zed's note to Chico. Zed's spelling question had stayed in his mind and he was no longer sure of his conclusions. He sought Ludmilla's opinion.

"Yes, people do say it that way here. '*Jusqu'à temps que*—up until the time that.' I think it's actually quite pretty. In France, they simply say '*jusqu'à ce que*—up until.' Really both expressions mean the same thing."

Ludmilla repeated the two expressions to herself, as though the words had not quite yielded up all of their secrets.

"The '*jusqu'à temps que*' is interesting because the word *temps* or 'time' seems to be beating out a rhythm: one-two-three-four-up-until-the-time-that. In '*jusqu'à ce que*', or 'up until' the '*ce*' is much weaker, though it does echo the *s* sound... '*jussssqu'à ce que*.'"

Terry wanted to remind her that it was the "*jusqu'à* tant *que*" that was the problem, but Ludmilla was on a roll:

"Parisians probably preferred '*jusqu'à ce que*' because of the alliteration. It's certainly arguable. But it would be such a shame to lose the '*jusqu'à temps que*.'"

Language as a mechanism of preferences? Terry had never thought of it that way. Ludmilla continued:

"As for '*jusqu'à tant que*'..."

Terry jumped. Ludmilla had said, "*Quant à*—As for."

"Now see! Excuse me, only, just now, you said '*quant à*—as for.' Only we woulda said de contrary. We'd 'ave said, '*tant qu'à*...'like '*tant qu'à moi*—so far as I'm concerned'; '*tant qu'à zeux*—so far as der concerned'; '*tant qu'à ça*—so far as dat.'"

"Yes, that's true... '*quant à*... *tant qu'à*...' it's a simple inversion.

Terry suspected that 'simple inversion' belonged to linguistics jargon. Ludmilla continued:

"'*Jusqu'à tant que mon mal de tête sera pas en allé* — So long as me headache isn't gone on its way.' The French would say '*jusqu'à ce que mon mal de tête s'en aille* — until my headache's gone' or '*tant que j'aurai ce mal de tête* — so long as I'll have this headache.' They probably decided to eliminate the redundancy. And the use of the negative is a trifle heavy..."

Ludmilla was not done thinking it over. For the first time, Terry was acutely conscious of the complexity of language operations. Meanwhile, Ludmilla concluded:

1144.35.11 The Detail within the Detail "But, the phrase '*en allé*' is awfully pretty: more than just 'gone,' it's like 'gone on its way,' or 'taken itself away.'" That's awfully pretty. It would be a shame to lose that, too.

1145.81.9 Titles

> Getting back to the title, *Until the End* is too closed, too definitive, almost fatalistic. Unnecessary stress.

"Look, Mum! De house is backin' up!"

Indeed, a raising and transporting company was in the process of pulling a house back from the road.

"They're someplace, looks like."

The van slowed and parked along the side of the road. Inside the entire family watched the manoeuvre.

"See the house, Marianne?"

"Could be the folks lived there felt the house was too close to de road."

...

"I never knowed a truck could haul a house."

"'Tisnt sometin' you see all that often."

1146.140.6 Caraquet "But Mum! You said! Dat's why we take trips. To see new tings."

1147.132.10 Malapropism

> On the subject of Wall Street, the beef tail in retail?

"Chico's gonna get a cat."
"Is that right?"
"Dey's fetchin' it tomorrow."
"Dey're fetchin' it tomorrow? Where?"
"At de animal shelter."
"At the animal shelter?"
"You does dat all de time!"
"What's that?"
"You says de same words I do. It's irritatin.'"
"Well, I only do it so you'll learn to say de right words."
"Only I doesn't know all de right words yet!"
"I know it. But sometimes de ones you do know are right fine. Like animal shelter. That's a wonderful nice phrase. You ought to tell it to yer dad. Could be he'll be wantin' to write it down in 'is notebook."

. . .

"What's wrong then?" 1148.123.9 Carmen and Étienne

Étienne dragged his feet.

"I'd like fer us to 'ave a dog."

> It's always pleasant, relaxing even, when coming to a fork, to go toward the right. The opposite of an irritation. 1149.54.12 Forgotten/Recalled

Zed could not have imagined it.

"I had rather grim plans for you."

He looked at me with those tender eyes I recalled.

"Wot does dat mean, den?"

I tried to think of another way to put it.

"Well, after you finished the lofts project, I thought you might be committin' suicide."

!

"No, I know, it makes no sense."

"Well, why den would I've gone an' done dat?"

"Don't know, really. 'Twould've been a kind of mystery."

. . .

"Only I know it made no sense."

Zed sat silently fiddling with a packet of sugar.

"Does it bother you?"

"Well… 'tisn't exactly comfortin' to tink you didn't 'ave any more use fer me dan dat."

I certainly understood how he felt, and tried to redeem myself.

"In any case, 'twas in an effort to try'n turn it around dat I sent Élizabeth yer way."

Zed frowned, as though it had not been the cleverest solution.

"You don't think so? Well you sure looked head o'er heals at the start."

He forced a laugh.

"I was, too."

"I know it."

"Were you really tinkin' you was gonna get me embroiderin'?"

I couldn't help but laugh at that. Then he too started laughing.

"*Phew*. I's afraid you was givin' up on me."

I'd never imagined that my characters could be conscious of my expectations of them. Did I really have expectations? The waitress arrived:

"Does you want sometin' else den?"

Zed ordered a second coffee, and I a tea.

"I don't want to say too much, only there's sometin' proper nice comin' up fer you."

1150.101.5 "Sometin' or someone?"

Duos "Awh! You'll see!

> Names of Moncton disc jockeys: DJ Bing, DJ
> Bones, DJ Bosse (fictional character), DJ Bu'da,
> DJ Cristal, DJ Cyril Sneer, DJ Leks, DJ Lukas,
> 1151.99.7 DJ Marky, DJ Pony Boy, DJ Sueshe, and DJ
> Names Textyle (or Tekstyle).

"Strange how when we wants to say 'die a slow death'

in French, we say '*mourir à petit feu,*' like 'dying by small fires, an' den we calls a dead person: '*feu,*' like '*feu* Tilmon Arsenault, fer example, meaning 'de departed.'"

...

"Are ya asleep, den?"

In lieu of a reply, Carmen merely squeezed Terry's forearm. After all these years, that was still a satisfactory answer.

1152.94.1 Terry and Carmen

CHAPTER 9

> *...[S]tories are found things, like fossils in the ground...*
>
> Stephen King *On Writing:*
> *A Memoir of the Craft* 1153.144.9
> Scribner, 2000 Epigraphs

One day, a man Terry had never seen before entered the bookstore. The customer had some difficulty opening the door, which normally posed no problem. Once the sexagenarian was in, Terry watched him getting all tangled up trying to close the door behind him.

"*Don't mind me. Some mornings I just can't manage doors.*"

The man was no less contorted as he moved toward the counter and addressed Terry:

"Françaisse, *I suppose*?"

He did not give Terry time to reply, but continued in his best attempt at French.

"It is ze fantastic town! Vary much nice!"

The man took his time removing his gloves and scarf before truly taking in the atmosphere of the shop.

"Agh! You are selling ze youzed books also?"

"Dat's right. Well, only dese shelves 'ere."

His interlocutor seemed to be waiting for further explanations, so Terry obliged.

"We only started a short time ago. Folks brings 'em in

an' we decides which ones we wants an' which we doesn't. Mostly, we don't take de ones we's sellin' in de shop."

The man was listening so attentively that Terry, unsure what more he could add, felt obliged to continue:

"We's sorta gotta 'ave a feelin' fer de book if we's to put it up on de shelf. Udderwise, if it don't sell, der we are, stuck wid sometin' we doesn't really want."

Terry shrugged, indicating that he had nothing more to add.

1154.91.1 "Zat is the good idea, a varry good idea, truly! And
The Poet why knots?"

> The standard Italian alphabet contains 21 letters, including five vowels and 16 regular consonants, all of which are also found in the French and English alphabets. Italian also contains five supplementary consonants, which are *j*, *k*, *w*, *x*, and *y*. They are used in words borrowed from foreign languages: *jeans*, *karate*, *whisky*, *xenophobia*, *yogurt*. Occasionally, the *v* and *z* will be used as regular letters (Italian can be slightly confusing). Conclusion: the *alfabeto* is made up of 21 letters, but the language is not
> 1155.90.4 adverse to using letters from other languages
> Letters when it borrows their words.

The new customer was relentless:

"Because, in truth, ze margin of profits is what is counting, is it not so?"

Terry wondered where the man had learned his French to speak it this way.

"Dat's right. An' we does sell a good number. Enough, anyway, to make it wortwhile."

The man studied Terry closely for a moment, before approving:

"Ze important for a bookstore, is zat ze peoples comes, am I not correct? Even if only to selling a book and not to buying."

And the customer leaned closer to Terry, as though to impart a confidence:

"Ze books do not leave anyone indifferent, you know. Even zose zat are not reading, zey are affected. Zis I am knowing deeply."

As he said this, the man tapped his middle finger 1156.91.2
against his chest. The Poet

> In his introduction to *Précis de l'histoire moderne*, M. Michelet sums up three and a half centuries of history in three paragraphs. Essentially, agglomerations of fiefdoms form large States, which tend to swallow up smaller entities than themselves by force or marriage. Monarchy and heredity take precedence over the republic and elected leaders, but the "System of Equilibrium" restrains their power. At the same time, commercial interests overtake religious ones, and commerce gradually supplants war as the main form of communication between different parts of the globe. Thus the great maritime powers have a clear advantage. Europeans, for their part, are unable to resist the temptation to "civilize," i.e., subdue and dominate, distant lands. The West European nations of Latin origin in particular have the means and leisure to dedicate themselves to this "civilizing" mission, the East Europeans — the Slavs — being occupied in beating back the
> "barbarians," which results in their slower po- 1157.84.11
> litical development. History

The man removed his coat and put it down on the nearest wing chair.

"I live in zen You York State, on a farm."

Terry exprienced an auditory lapsus, imagined a ring

of crosslegged Zen masters hovering over New York State.

"A mag-nific piece of land!"

The man drew a large circle with his right arm as he described his land. Then, laying his hand very gently on Terry's arm and gazing into his eyes, he repeated:

"Troully. Mag-nific."

Alright, Terry thought, I guess his land is magnificent.

"I ham vizit my daughter."

Once again the man moved closer, as though this time he was about to reveal a deep secret:

"She haz merried a kook."

Terry wasn't sure what was so special about "merrying a kook," but his customer seemed to think it was a very clever move by his daughter. So Terry laughed:

"Does she enjoy eatin' all dat much, den?"

Again the man looked very closely at Terry, smiling
1158.91.3 now and nodding.

The Poet "Yes, it iz exactly what I thought."

> True or false: Jean de LaFontaine is the author
> 1159.116.8 of the expression "A pitcher that goes to the
> True or False well too often eventually breaks."

Étienne was busy building a hangar for his mini-cars with the new slats of wood his grandfather Thibodeau had given him. Carmen was watching him work. She liked to see him play with such rudimentary objects.

"Mum, wot's me name in English?"

The question took Carmen by surprise.

"Chico says dat at school, der's a boy dey calls Antoine in class. Only in de yard ee's called Tony."

"You don't really 'ave an English name. Étienne is a French name."

"I knows it."

...

"Only, just in case somebody was wantin' to call me in English?"

"Really, I don't know any English name for Étienne. Must be the same in boat English an' French."

Carmen tried to pronounce the name Étienne in English, but any difference was barely detectable.

"See now, 'tisn't so hard to be sayin' yer name in English. You pronounce it pretty much de same."

Étienne remained sceptical, even though Carmen did not go so far as to claim that his name would flow smoothly off an English tongue.

"Well, Dad, ee's called Terry..."

Carmen could already guess what was coming.

"An' 'ow 'bout you, lot's of folks call you Carm..."

"Well sure, that's troo. Only we didn't ask fer those names, now did we. Folks just got started callin' us that a while back, an' it stuck. Now, feels like 'tis too late to change. Yer name's more French on account of dat's who we are, more French."

Étienne did not reply, momentarily preoccupied with looking for a satisfactory piece of wood to complete the roof of his hangar. Carmen took advantage of the pause to shift the conversation a bit:

"Do you like yer name?"

Étienne thought a bit, then seemed to make up his mind:

"Yes, I like it."

"*Ouf*! I'm happy."

"On account of?"

This was an easy question for Carmen:

"I wasn't all that fond o' me name when I's a wee girl. I would've liked to be called Dominique."

Étienne raised his head to look at Carmen. His mother, a Dominique?"

"I liked Martine as well."

Well, this was all news to Étienne. He stood up and walked up to Carmen to look at her more closely, trying to see his mother in these other names. Then he huddled against her for a caress, thinking of the bronze fly. 1160.123.4 Carmen and Étienne

> But where does a language begin, where does it end? When does a language become a different language? Isn't all speech an interpretation of reality, hence a kind of translation, a fleeting attempt of language, a lalanguage? And whether French is old or contemporary or standard or hybrid, isn't language, like life, nothing
> 1161.112.9 more than a long processs of uninterrupted
> Languages hybridization?

Finally the man had begun to look at the books. First at those on the tables near the counter, then those on the shelves. He would pick up a book delicately, take the time to examine the cover, then turn the work slowly round to study the spine and the back cover. He studied all these from three angles — over his glasses, through his glasses and under his glasses — and seemed to decode useful information at each stage. When he finally opened a book, apparently at random, he took the time to read a bit on each page before returning to the first pages or leafing toward those at the end. From time to time, he seemed to experience a kind of spasm. At first, Terry thought these spasms were somehow linked to the man's infirmity, but he began to suspect that that they were caused by something the man was reading. Often, the man smiled.

"Youse can sit yerself down, if you like."

1162.91.4 And the customer accepted the chair Terry had car-
The Poet ried over.

> (*Bescherelle* found.) The new rules of the Académie also simplify the plural of compound nouns: when the first word of the plural of a compound word is a verb or a preposition, the second word must now end in *s*; for example, snowdrops are *perce-neiges* and afternoons
> 1163.131.11 are *après-midis*. (In the past, the second word
> Parenthesi(e)s was invariable.)

"Hallo der. Are yer mum or yer dad around?"

"Me dad's 'ere, only ee's in de toilet."

"Awh well, let's not disturb 'im den. We's volunteers fer de Red Cross. We's collectin' money an' household tings like furniture or dishes to lend a hand to de folks whose apartment buildin' burnt down last week. I'll leave you dis 'ere flyer, wot explains de whole ting. Der's a telephone number if youse have any questions. Can you give dis 'ere to your parents, OK?"

"OK."

Once the man was gone, Chico slid the sheet under the bathroom door.

"Zed?"

"Yah?"

"Val O'Tears left dis 'ere fer you."

"Who'd ya say?"

"Val O'Tears."

" Val O'Tears? Am I supposed to know who dat is?"

"Ee came by on account of de fire." 1164.135.9

"Fire? Wot fire?" Zed and Chico

> The Académie has also decided to drop the
> hyphen in many compound nouns and allow
> them to be written as single words; for ex-
> ample, bat becomes *chauvesouris*, centipede
> *millepatte*, undertaker *croquemort*, picnic
> *piquenique*, rickshaw *poussepousse*, corkscrew
> *tirebouchon*, and purse *portemonnaie*. Perhaps
> you are thinking we could write snowdrops as
> *perceneiges* and afternoons as *aprèsmidis*? As a
> matter of fact, lexicographers are encouraged 1165.77.10
> to follow suit and practice fusion. Grammar

The man stayed for so long among the rows of shelves of Didot Books that Terry completely forgot about him, and continued to leaf through the newly arrived publishers' catalogues. It was only when the customer accidentally pushed several books onto the floor while trying to reach up to the highest shelf that Terry remembered his presence. Seeing the man in difficulty, Terry hurried over to lend a hand.

"Agh! I am zo sorry, really..."

"Believe me, youse not de first to be tumblin' de books offa dis 'ere shelf. She's too high fer most folks. We oughtta be rearrangin' tings 'ere, only we never takes de time. Which was de book you was lookin' fer?"

The customer took a book out of Terry's hands, and then another, while he was at it.

"If der's any little ting yer wantin', you only 'ave to shout."

"Yes, this I will do. Thank you."

Back behind the counter, Terry saw the man studying what appeared to the *Poems of A. O. Barnabooth*, a
1166.91.5 The Poet work that had been gathering dust on the shelf for several years now.

1167.118.8 Concerning Yellow

> A word one would expect to be yellow, but is definitely not: *lemon*.

Élizabeth stood in the doorway and cast a last look over the apartment she was preparing to abandon. The sun was lighting the room exactly as it had the first time she'd seen it. The similarity lifted her spirits. She was
1168.47.6 Yielding leaving without regrets, with a feeling that this was a fine day to turn the page.

> True or false: another initiative of the Académie Française was to agree that all compound numbers are to be written with hypens, since even the best intentioned cannot always master the writing out of a number like 251,697, or two hundred fifty-one thousand six hundred ninety-seven, which will henceforth be written in French as

deux-cent-cinquante-et-un-mille-six-cent-quatre-vingt-dix-sept. 1169.77.11 Grammar

After a few days, Carmen decided that just because he had a cold was no reason to keep her son locked up in the house.

"Wot would you say to the two of us goin' out to fetch a good-luck plant fer yer room? I thinks I know where there's some. An' after that, we can go fer a hot chocolate, if you like."

Étienne's face brightened.

"Fer sure, I want to, Mum!"

Delighted, Carmen walked over to the wall where they hung their coats.

"Now isn't this fun! It's been a dog's age since we went out, just the two of us." 1170.123.5 Carmen and Étienne

"I knows it, Mum. You work too hard sometimes."

> "The Ideal Library of the Social Sciences" does not shrink from classifying some books as essential even though they do not exist in French. Most of these works—approximately 20 of them—were written in English. Economics, Political Science and Psychology are the disciplines that have been most marked by this absence of translation. 1171.58.12 Extensions

Having located the bamboo stalks they would plant in water and stones, Carmen and Étienne found themselves in a café, blowing softly on their steaming hot chocolates. The mother discretley directed her son's attention:

"Do you see the woman with the brown coat over there, de one's gettin' up from the table?"

Étienne spotted her.

"OK, OK, now look at me!"

Étienne was taken aback by this sudden change in tone. Carmen leaned across the table to explain in a low voice:

“’Twasn’t meant to scold you, only I didn’t want you to be starin’ at ’er. On account of ’tisn’t polite to talk about a person an’ then to be lookin’ over at them. You catch me drift?”

Once Étienne had grasped this lesson in étiquette, he was granted permission to glance over at the woman again. Then Carmen told him:

“She was me teacher when I’s in grade four. Her name was Madame Rose-Marie, only we called ’er Madame Grosse-Marie behind ’er back.”

. . .

“’Twasn’t very nice, eh?”

Étienne was tempted to look over at the erstwhile
1172.123.6 Carmen and Étienne teacher again. Without moving his head, he tried to force
his eyes as far to the right as he could, but that only made
his eyes hurt.

> The grammatical corrections evoked above are
> not obligatory. The Académie has stipulated
> that old spellings remain valid, which could
> lead to some confusion and, if this isn't already
> the case, more doubts, more questions. How
> 1173.77.12 Grammar could it be otherwise? A pitcher that goes to
> the well too often eventually breaks.

After reading for a long while, Terry’s customer stood up and moved to another aisle of books, occasionally pulling volumes off the shelf, handling them all with equal care, as though they all deserved the same attention. Terry concluded that the man was the type who came to bookstores to read, but never bought anything, just as others might attend receptions purely in order to feed themselves on the snacks. He wondered if perhaps chairs were not particular conducive to sales. Because, beneath the ideal of a bookstore (to nourish the spirit) lay the commercial reality (to nourish sales), and though he loved almost everything about books,

Terry was also concerned about his bottom line. 1174.91.6 The Poet

> Since 1803, the Spanish alphabet has contained 29 letters. In addition to the 26 letters of the French or English alphabets, the Spanish includes the indivisible letters *ch* and *ll*, and the *ñ*. In alphabetical order, these follow the c, the *l* and the *n*; however, computers have problems reproducing the combined *ch* and *ll*, which has led to some confusion in Spanish dictionaries 1175.90.5 Letters
> published after 1994.

After their afternoon chocolate, as they were walking toward the van in the large parking lot of the mall, a car alarm suddenly went off at the moment Étienne was brushing past. Étienne jumped, twisting his body in a way that made Carmen laugh.

"Bit of a surprise, eh?"

...

"Must be somebody fergot where they parked der car."

Étienne's heart was still beating furiously. He only regained his speech in the van, on the way home:

"Do you 'ave a good name, Mum?"

"What do you mean, a good name?"

"De udder day, in de shop, de man said Dad had a good name."

"Awh. Ee couldn't pay, I'll bet?"

"Naw! Ee wanted to pay, only ee 'ad no money!"

Terry was in the habit of leaving the house without cash or cards, which had always irritated Carmen, but she restrained herself:

"Awh!"

"An' de man in de shop told Dad ee didn't 'ave to pay on account of 'is good name."

Carmen decided to accentuate the positive:

"Dat means yer dad's an honest fellow. The man in de shop knew ee could trust Dad to be payin' 'im later in the day, or maybe the next day. Ee could trust 'im."

Étienne nodded.

"Do you 'ave a good name as well?"

"I think so. Only most times I've the money to pay in me purse, don't I. Eidder cash or cards. Terry, well, ee walks around wid nuttin' in 'is pockets."

"Sometimes ee's got 'lastic bands."

1176.123.7 "Dat's troo, I suppose, only you can't buy nuttin' wid
Carmen and elastic bands, now can you."
Étienne Étienne knew this, but the possibility made him laugh.

> But before the novel *Clair de femme* (*The Light of a Woman*) by Romain Gary, the film by Constantin Costa-Gavras based on Gary's book, and starring Romy Schneider as Lydia and Yves Montand as Michel. The film, seen in the early '80s; the novel, read 20 years later, and steeped in memories of the film. Without a doubt the source of the characters of Alida and Rodriguez in *Real Life*. To the extent that
> 1177.58.4 an extension can stretch backwards as well as
> Extensions forwards.

"De worst progress trap I can tink of? Me girlfriend waters 'er plants wid bottled water she's buyin' at de store.
1178.128.11 Well, don't go tellin' 'er I said dis, only dat's our big dis-
Fervours agreement. Could be dat's wot'll break us up in de end."

> Partial list of yellow words in French: *ananas* (pineapple), *carnaval, patate, banane, carnage, barrage, garage, camarade, bagatelle, papaye, canard, charade, parade, glas* (knell), *sac, flash, bazar*. Obviously, words not ending in *e* are yellower than others. Another difference: in words in which the *a* is followed by an *m* or an *n*, creating the sound *an*—panda, grange (barn), estampe—yellow takes on a brownish,

orangey, or ocre tint. In a way, the sound *an* contaminates the yellow.

"Say wot you will, dey doesn't work all dat hard. Not so hard as dey'd like youse to believe, anyhow."

Anonymous #2 was fed up with certain people's artistic pretentions, and especially Pomme's and Zablonski's. I felt I was ideally placed to defend them.

"Sometimes it takes time fer these things to mature."

He or she pulled a pouty face. I'd broke the camel's back.

"You means to tell me dat you doesn't even know wot sex I am?!"

I explained that I hadn't felt the need to decide one way or the other.

"When I think of one, it works fine, an' when I think of t'other, it works just as well. Could be either one."

"An' I suppose dat's why I's got no name neidder?"

"No, not really. I could've given you a name that works with both, like Majella, Aldoria, Doris, Flavie, Wilma, Césaire, Bélonie…"

"Aren't you de hilarious one…"

…

…

"I wanted somebody neutral, somebody I see from time to time. I don't know you by name. An' yer sex, well, 'tisn't really relevant is it? Don't go takin' it personal."

"Somebody neutral. You ask me, dat's plain insultin'."

"Alright, I suppose I was insensitive."

"By de way, don't it require some kind o' permissions to be talkin' 'bout us in yer books?"

"Not if you're not clearly identified. Take you, for example, with no name an' no sex, you wouldn't have much of a legal leg to stand on…"

"Well, dat's exactly wot I's sayin'! You artists, youse tink you can bloody well do wotever you like!"

Really! I was thinking I had better things to do but, at

the same time, I was desperate to make progress in my novel. I tried another approach.

“Look, we meet a whole lot of people in this life, folks we talk to an' folks we doesn't. An' even if we talk to them, doesn't mean we know der names. Anyways, makes absolutely no difference. We can have good relations with them, even doh we don't know them by name. An' no one takes dat as an insult, now do dey?”

“Alright, dat's fine an' dandy up to a point. Once you's in a book, seems to me, you oughtta 'ave a name. Or a sex, at de very least. When you sees a person in de street, you sees der gender.”

“Dat's troo. Most of the time, anyway. Well alright, I can be givin' you one, if that's wot you want. Do you 'ave a preference?”

“No, dat's yer job, now isn't it? You's de one dat's gotta decide.”

“Alright then. 'Tis done.”

“I'll wager I's a women.”

“You win.”

“I knowed it! I knowed it!”

“How come?”

“In yer books, de men has de better parts dan de women.”

“Fer real?”

1180.101.9 “You doesn't see it, but yer borderline chauvinistic.”

Duos “Fer real?!

Terry can remember finding it strange to see the name of a character in the title of a poetry collection. Strange too that a poet would create a character who's a poet, write that character's poems and then publish the whole thing under his real name, as seemed to be the case with Larbaud's *Poems of A. O. Barnabooth*. One thing leading to another, Terry had ordered the collection, convinced that these layers of identity were bound to pique the curiosity of other poets. So far, no one had taken the bait. 1181.12.12 Structure

The plates with wide yellow borders arrived: 1182.118.9 Concerning Yellow
"I like de plates, Mum. 'Tis like eatin' bits of sun."

Along the lines of thinking the glass is half full or half empty, some people who believe they're in danger of dying are in fact in danger of living. 1183.64.6 Opposites

In the end, the man stepped up to the cash with three books. Terry was pleasantly surprised. And among them was Larbaud's *Barnabooth*.

"I am not knowing zis poet. 'Go tell Shame zat I am dying of louve for herr' . . . It iz lovely, iz it not?"

It was only with this last comment that Terry realized the man had just quoted a line from memory.

"I haven't read dis one yet. Barnabooth, dat's a weird name . . . fer a book o' poems, I mean to say."

The man seemed to agree. Then he picked up his coat and pulled out a book from the inside pocket.

"I myself alzo am a poet."

Terry was immediately wary, thinking here was another case of someone offering him a trade.

"It iz de sole one I have brought wiz me."

Terry marshalled his courage, decided to be firm, but the man did not give him time to say a word:

"I leave here it. Only for ze reading however. Not to zell."

And the man took out his wallet. Terry was dumbfounded. 1184.91.7 The Poet

Hans enjoys reading the words in the dictionary in the order in which they appear, allowing himself to be interpellated as much by the referencing as by the enigma of a koan. 1185.79.11 Oddities

Terry concluded the sale coolly, but inside he felt anxious, relieved and vaguely guilty. Then he took the time to open the poet's book, very slowly, somewhat the way the poet himself might have done, leafing through a few pages, as though he were testing the mechanism of the book. The poems were short, which pleased him. He read one, glimpsed something, reread it. What he thought he'd discovered was sketched somewhere in between the black and white of the words and letters.

"Hun!"

Here was something extraordinary. He read another, which meandered similarly in his thoughts. Now he pulled out his bag from the drawer under the cash and put the book carefully inside:

"Tanks, I tinks I'll be enjoyin' readin' dis."

The poet appreciated Terry's smile and honest face.

"It iz a genre I am invented. I calling zem *shadow poems*. I don't sure how to zay in French. *Poèmes de l'ombre*? I do not know."

"Yes, you could say it dat way."

"Yes, perhaps. Boot, zomezing iz mizzing, do you not think? A nouance?"

Terry didn't know, and didn't want to commit himself so quickly:

1186.91.8 "I'd have to be readin' a few more…"
The Poet "Yes, yes. I perfectly understanding."

1187.65.5 The family of Latin languages includes Italian,
Boy Cousins, Spanish, French, Portuguese, Rumanian, and
Girl Cousins Catalan.

"Poor fellow! 'Twas clear as day ee didn't want dat particular camera. Only you could see 'er mind was made up: dat was de exact camera she was after, an' she weren't goin' shoppin' a second longer to find anudder. She's standin' der, stiff as a board, an' not willin' to stand der more'n anudder ten seconds, waitin' on 'im to get used to de idea, an' den she twists her 'ead 'round to check up where de kids had got to, as doh any time soon dey might be knockin' o'er de displays or jackin' up de stereos. Well, der ee goes back to studyin' de tree cameras de salesman pulled out o' de locked case fer 'em. Any child could see ee's only makin' believe ee's interested in dose two udders ee doesn't want, as doh ee's showin' how fair he is, in case she's lookin' at 'im. Not dat ee'd dare to look at 'er, mind you, she's dat biniky an' wid a face like a burnt-boiled boot on 'er. So der ee is, dis fellow — totally in control — tryin' do make sometin' 'appen dat's got zero chance o' happenin', just like in a movie, right before yer bitter 'alf switches de channel.

1188.15.7
Unidentified
Monologues

> A few days later, as he was removing some long, freshly cooked crabs' legs from a bag, Terry had the sudden spontaneous idea to shake them back and forth in front of the children, while making monster noises. Marianne burst out laughing. Étienne refused to eat.

1189.140.8
Caraquet

"'Tis too big a subject, to begin wid."

"Wot do you mean by dat?"

"Der's too many angles."

"So?"

"So, 'tisn't a proper subject."

. . .

. . .

"Well isn't dat wot we're wantin'? Sometin' wid a whole lot o' potential?"

"Takes more'n dat."

"Wot else does it take?"

"A focus."

"A focus."

. . .

"A focus. I don't suppose you'd be willin' to explain dat just a wee bit?"

1190.119.1 Music

"Look, never mind. Ferget de whole ting."

1191.113.4 Collections

> There are even collectors of jargons.

The poet seemed about ready to go. Terry watched him try two or three times before managing to get inside his coat, do up a button, then another.

"De way you said de word *nuance* before...I tawt you were meanin' to say 'nuance,' only wot youse said was 'nouance'. Fer us, Acadians I mean, dat would be like tings *nouquées*, knotted togedder, sometin' like de way our shadows're tied to ourselves."

As the poet clearly didn't quite follow, Terry continued:

"I mean dat fer de *shadow poems*, 'twould be better to say *nouances* dan nuances. Dat's my way o' tinkin' anyhow."

"Nouances? Nou-ances."

And the poet repeated the word once more to get a better sense of it.

1192.91.9 The Poet

"Yes, it iz perhaps a good word I sink."

1193.68.11 Projects

> Figure out what constitutes Jules Michelet's obsessional themes.

"Mum, do you fall down off de moon when you's sleepin'?"

"In me dreams?"

Carmen took a moment to think about it.

"No, I don't remember ever fallin' down off the moon."

"I do."

"Awh, is that right? Often?"

Now it was Étienne's turn to think a moment.

"A long time."

"An' wot do you mean, a long time?"

"Well, I fall and I fall and I fall, an' den I wakes up."

"Hun! When I was a girl, I saw great thick rolls o' carpet in me dreams. Carpets with flowers that unravelled fer a long, long time, as doh they was never gonna stop unrollin', an' then all of a sudden like, oops! I's awake." 1194.123.10 Carmen and Étienne

"Mum! We're almost de same, you an' me!"

> The king is dead! Long live the king! 1195.79.9 Oddities

"Least ways we agree on one ting, 'tisn't de notes dat make de music. Right?"

"Aldoh you can't do widout dem."

"Dat's sure. Der's gotta be some notes."

. . .

"How about de length of de notes?"

?

"Wouldn't dat be a factor, like?"

"No more'n one."

"You mean to say de length's not so important as all dat neidder?"

"Well, 'tis important, in a way, I suppose. Only 'tis more a question of space."

"Space?"

"Of how you's puttin' udder notes in dat same space."

"You mean de number of udder notes?" 1196.119.2 Music

"Whatever."

> In the matter of signs and letters, Catalan is unique in its use of the interpunct (l·l) to indicate a dark l AKA consonantal sound. Otherwise, Catalan, like French, uses the entire Latin alphabet, along with several digraphs, accents and diacritical letters. 1197.90.8 Letters

When his customer was ready to go, Terry went round to open the door for him. Stepping out into the fresh air, blue sky, and blazing white snow, the poet declared:

"It iz true for ze poets as well, iz it knots? Zat books, zey are well word whale?"

Then, once he'd figured out which direction to go in,

the man took a decisive step, exclaiming:

"And many thanks... euh..."

"Terry. Terry Thibodeau!"

"Ah! Tibetoh! Yes, I knowing zis name. Tibetoh. *Au revoir*, Monsieur Tibetoh!"

Terry shook the man's extended hand and replied
1198.91.12 likewise:
The Poet "*Au revoir!*"

> The impression that speaking is the opposite of
> 1199.64.8 writing, that saying and recording are the an-
> Opposites tipodes of language.

Second yellow: the big *M* of McDonald's.

"Mum, der's a McDonald's over der."

Carmen had already glimpsed the sign that hovered over the valley, and was clearly visible from a great distance away on the highway.

"Are ya hungry then?"

"Yes."

"Terrible hungry?"

"Yes."

Carmen would have preferred to go straight home, less than an hour's drive away. But Étienne had been patient since they'd started out that morning—a return trip Moncton–Halifax—and he deserved a bit of a treat.

"Alright then. We'll stop. I's a wee bit hungry meself."

1200.118.6 Étienne was happy. But mostly he felt older and
Concerning important, because he had not had to beg to get what he
Yellow wanted.

1201.79.10
Oddities

> Another oddity: a boxing "gala."

Some evenings, Terry literally threw himself into the void:

"Alright den. Tonight's de night I tells you de story of de pheasant name of Coocoo."

Étienne let himself sink comfortably into his bed.

"You already seen a pheasant, do you remember? Out back of Grandad Després', dat big bird wid a red head an' a blue an' green neck."

"Wot does you mean a blue angry neck?"

"Green neck... de neck's blue an' green."

"Awh."

"An red on de head, right?"

Étienne was eager for the story to get going. Only he wanted to be sure he could picture CooCoo.

"Well den, does ee 'ave a face like an ant?"

Terry looked at the boy—was this word play conscious?—but quickly picked up the story:

"Naw, it's a pheasant, not a face-ant. Dose pheasants is big birds. Like chickens almost."

"Well, how come den dey calls dem Fez ants?"

At this point, Terry was pretty sure that Étienne was playing with the 'ant' sound on purpose, but how to be certain without spoiling the fun? He continued:

"Can't say, don't know. Could be on account of when de pheasant starts callin' out he can be a terrible pisant."

"Does dey call out coocoo?"

"Well, right der dat's de problem! De pheasant in me story was wantin' to be a cuckoo. Only de problem was dat... ee was too big to get in de door in de clock. So wot did ee do?"

?

"Ee bought 'imself a membership at de gym." 1202.37.11

From this point on, Terry was confidant he'd find his way. Animal Tales

> Proverb for artists: where art fails, chance succeeds. 1203.17.12
> Chance

"Well alright, wot's de basis fer music den?"

"'Tis like I said, 'tis too big a subject."

"Well, won't you try. If you had to narrow it down, wot would you say?

…

"We're in no great hurry. Just tink on it."

…

1204.119.3 …

Music …

A bell rings ding ding
"No more Shreddies on de shelf?"
"*Ass Jack, ee's out back.*"
1205.75.9 Chubby chin an' forked tongue
Tankas An' den *Pop! goes de weasel.*

"Dis 'ere's me wid me mum in Kouchibougouac."

Étienne edged closer to get a better look at the mother-daughter relation.

"Dat was me when I's a baby."

Étienne moved closer again, but the photograph was as hazy as the boy's idea of his grandmother Després in baby format.

"An' 'ere, dat's Grandad, in de arms of his own grandad."

Étienne's astonishment grew and grew. For the first time, he realized how much of a past he had in reserve.

"Ol' Nazaire. I never knowed 'im, only dey say ee was a powerful chucklehead."

Étienne leaned in, stared at the tiny yellowing photograph, trying to make out what a chucklehead looked like.

"Nazaire Després, 'is name's on dat monument next to de petit magasin."

Granny Després turned the pages quickly, skipping over most of the photographs.

"Dis 'ere's 'is wife Ursule. Yer great-great-grandmudder. Look at de collar on 'er dress. Dat were de fashion in dose days."

Étienne looked at the collar.

"Dey's awfully old pitchers, eh? Dis one 'ere almost broke in two when I's gluein' it."

The photo was of a group of men wearing felt hats and long dark coats.

"Old Nazaire again. Along side 'im, dat's de minister was in charge of de roads in dat time. Ee was visitin' the county. Dat didn't happen too often, dat one of dem Ottawa politicians came down to Kent county. I doesn't know who de udder fellers are."

Even after the album was shut and put away in the bookshelf, the black, white, yellow, and brown of the photographs continued to weigh on Étienne's eyes. 1206.105.3 Reserves/ Reservations

"Does you feel like doin' a bit o' colourin' now?"

> Then came yellow towels in a bathroom. But was that enough? 1207.118.5 Concerning Yellow

"Wow! Dis one 'ere's awful cute! I can sure see 'er in dis!"

Josse showed the multicoloured dress to Carmen, who also loved the pattern.

"Der's overalls as well!"

Carmen examined the two items:

"Der boat o' dem nice..."

"Awh, she'd be terrible cute in dat dress fer sure!"

"Problem is, she's never askin' to wear a dress."

"You lets 'er decide?"

"Well, yeah."

Carmen noticed a pair of overalls in another colour, pulled it out of the pile, but Josse preferred the first pattern.

"Awh, no, de udder colour's a whole lot prettier."

"Yeah, I like it, too. Only de straps on this one're different. You could see wot she'd be wearin' underneath a lot better.

Josse kept rummaging until she found the right model in the right colour.

"Dese, wid de straps like dis 'ere, der callin' dem overalls. Only der callin' de udder pair dungarees."

"It's gotten so 'tis as complicated as buyin' a pair o' jeans."

"Yeah, an' deys gone an' copied de price as well…"

1208.113.9 Collections "I knows it! Let's go over an' take a look at the other collections; there might be sometin' we like even more."

robin on a branch puffed puffed
eye black beak yellow leg up
tail skyward white rear
1209.75.6 Tankas red belly winter apple?
perfectly still and waiting

"Doctor Phil says a body's got to be in de mood to be cross-hecklin'. Dat if de boat o' youse aren't in de mood, der's nuttin' doin'."

1210.102.9 The Trio "An since when 'ave you been watchin' Doctor Phil, den?"

The Stations of the Cross is the extreme sport *par excellence*. First of all, one must arrange to be condemned to death for a crime falling entirely outside current criminal categories. In other words, one must confound the modern judicial system without its knowledge. Only then can all the necessary mistakes be committed to lead to the death sentence, absolute requirement in order to gain the event's main piece of equipment: the heavy wooden cross, which represents the overwhelming burden of injustice. The event itself consists of 1) collapsing a first time under the weight of the cross; 2) showing oneself to be human, i.e., showing oneself physically and spiritually broken before one's mother; 3) accepting help to carry the cross; 4) having one's face wiped in public; 5) collapsing again; 6) revealing oneself to be superhuman by consoling young women; 7) collapsing a third time; 8) being divested of one's clothes and nailed to the cross; 9) suffering

> horribly and dying in humiliation without 1211.122.12
> complaining; and 10) rising up from the dead. Sports

"Are ya dead, Dad?"

Étienne was amusing himself by tracing the long blue lines on Terry's forearms, while the latter lay on the sofa, pretending to be dead.

"Well, wot do you tink?"

"If you was really and truly dead, you wouldn't be talkin."

"Der's lots of different ways to be dead, don't you know?"

"I know dat, Dad!"

"Do ya, now?"

"Well sure! You could be dead in a car accident, or somebody could be shootin* you dead."

"Mmmmyeah . . . But you could also die laughin.' Or you might be dead tired. Or you could be wot we calls a *coq-mort*."

Étienne immediately thought of Terry's summer cauldrons of steamed clams.

"You never heard Grandad Thibodeau say *coq-mort*?"

. . .

"A *coq-mort* is de kettle fer boilin' water fer yer tea or coffee. Folks called dat a *coq-mort* back in de old days."

"How come you got blue lines all down yer arms, Dad?"

"Dose're veins, boy. Der tiny pipes dat carry de blood all over yer body. You got dem too."

---

* Just as in the word *fiïlér* from the English "to feel," the spelling of *shoötér* derived from the English "to shoot" is a case of revision by GIRAFE. There are those who claim that, in the case of *shooter,* the use of *sh* to represent the sound *ch* is sufficient indication of the word's English origin, which renders the dieresis over the *ö* redundant. Others, however, deplore
the lack of consistency with other words such as *fiïlér*, *miïtér*, 1214.143.12
and *boötér õut*. Varia

Étienne examined his forearms.

"Only yer vines are a whole lot bigger."

"Veins, not vines."

...

"Mine're bigger on account I's a dad. A dad needs a whole lot o' blood to be protectin' 'is wee children from all dem big bad wolves."

And with that, Terry transformed himself into a wolf and threw himself at his son, who laughed and yelled:

"Dad, yer ticklin' me hihihi!"

"RRRRrrrr..."

1212.117.8 "I knew you wasn't dead hihihi!"

Death "RRrrrRRRrrr..."

According to *Le Grand Robert*, there are 82 main onomatopoeias in French: *ahou, aïe, a-reu a-reu, atchoum, bé, berk, beu, bim, bing, blablabla, bof, boum, bredi-breda, broum, brrr, bzitt, bzz, cahin-caha, chut, clic-clac, cloc, cocorico, coin-coin, coquerico, cot cot codac, coucou, couic, crac, cric, cricri, crincrin, croc, cuicui, dig, ding, drelin, fla, fla-fla, flic flac, floc, flonflon, frou-frou, glouglou, gnan-gnan, gouzi-gouzi, guili-guili, guilleri, han, hi-han, miam-miam, miaou, mimi, ouah, ouille, paf, pan, patapouf, patati-patata, patatras, pif, plaf, ploc, plof, pouêt, pouf, prout, psit, rataplan, ronron, tac, tam-tam, taratata, teuf-teuf, tic-tac, tire-lire, toc-toc, tsoin-tsoin, vlan, vroum, zest, zim boum boum, zzz.*

Wiktionary lists 195 English onomatopoeias,
1213.42.11 only one that is common to both French and
Sorting English: *zzz.*

The Portuguese alphabet contained only 23 letters until 1990 when *k*, *w*, and *y* of the French

> and English alphabets were added. In the domain of language, the 10 million inhabitants of Portugal are slightly behind the 170 million Brazilians, whose official language is also Portuguese. For example, it was only in 1973 that Portugal adopted the simplified spelling
> enacted by the *Academia Brasileira de Letras* in 1215.90.6
> 1943, and ammended in 1971. Letters

. . .

. . .

. . .

. . .

? 1216.119.4

. . . Music

> **HYPOCRITIC:** n. and adj. — 2005; attitude consisting in expressing one's negative ideas and feelings to everyone except those persons who inspire them. *"Beware! The hypocritics
> recognize each other, but they walk among us."* 1217.120.10
> (Daigle) Fictionary

Even the mashed potatoes in Terry's shepherd's pie were delicious.

"Alright den, now's de time to add de secret ingredients. All of you kids close yer eyes."

Étienne, Chico, and Marianne put their hands over their eyes, while peeking through their fingers, in hopes of penetrating Terry's secret.

"When yer eighteen, I'll be tellin' you de secret, only you'll have to promise not to go tellin' it to anudder livin' soul. And 'specially, you can't be tellin' it to yer kids until der eighteen demselves. On account of dat's de way de secret of de Bourques came down to us all de way from de time of de Deportation."

Their eyes ostensibly covered, the children listened to

Terry coming and going, lifting the covers off pots, sniffing at the contents, replacing covers, occasionally dipping into one or the other. Fully aware that the children were cheating and watching his every move, he punctuated his seasoning with comic ritual gestures at which the children could not laugh at the risk of giving themselves away.

"On account of we had to keep de secret recipe from de English."

"How come?"

"On account of dis 'ere secret makes a body strong! An'
1218.23.9 we didn't want de English to be gettin' stronger dan us,
Potatoes now did we?"

> Known edible oysters (illustrated): Tallmadge, Fischer Island, Saint-Simon, Cockenoe, Belon, Cotuit, Malpèque, Moonstone, Caraquet, Hama Hama, Kumamoto, Chef's Creek, Nantucket, Mallet, Wellfleet, Trail's End and Pemaquid. A footnote specifies that the months-ending-in-er rule no longer applies to
> 1219.57.3 the freshness of oysters, because of the speed of
> Photocopies modern means of transportation.

Pomme couldn't believe it:

"You didn't go an' tell dem dat!"

"I never planned to..."

"Well, I sure hope not!"

"Only it just came out. Like de next ting you knows, der it is, and you said it."

Terry had thought about it, but he couldn't see how he might have avoided the blunder. He added:

"'Tis weird de tings you finds yerself explainin' to a kid sometimes."

Zed understood this more than ever:

"Fer sure you doesn't all de time know wot to say an' wot not to say."

Pomme tried to imagine what his own life would be like with children. Terry, the most experienced of the three in the paternal arts, added:

“An de ting is dis, no matter wot you says, der’s no way of knowin’ wot effect it’s gonna ’ave on dem. I worries when I tink wot dey’ll be comin’ out wid when dey’s twenty-five! Some ting you told ’em when dey was four years old, you never tawt would affect ’em!

And Zed added:

“One time I’s feelin’ bad on account of I tawt I’d blabbered sometin’ dat boddered ’im, so den I goes to put tings right, an’ it got terrible complicated, on account of de boy had no memory ’tall of wot I’d said in de first place.” 1220.102.8 The Trio

> Early morning Freudian slip: Herménégilde Chiasson show(er)ing in Frederiction. 1221.132.7 Malapropism

Sitting on the living-room carpet, Marianne is amusing herself taking out and replacing in her basket the eggs they had painted the day before. Terry has been watching her.

“Wot you up to, Marianne?”

Marianne does not allow herself to be distracted. Her tiny hands, also daubed in paint, continue to shuffle the eggs back and forth.

“Eh, Marianne? Wotcha doin’, girl?”

Marianne raises her head, looks at Terry, goes back to what she was doing.

“Yer puttin’ all de eggs in de basket?”

. . .

“Some folks’d say you oughtn’t to be puttin’ all yer eggs in de same basket.”

Marianne raises her head again to look at Terry.

“Does ya want me to tell ya why?”

Marianne is enjoying herself, and not asking for anything.

"No? Alright den. Some udder time, maybe."

1222.100.9 Proverbs Marianne replaces a blue egg in the basket, next to the pink and yellow egg.

> The stain-removing balls of olden times could remove everything except ink stains and rust. They were made of grated Marseille soap, pure alcohol, egg yolk, turpentine, and smectite. But in fact, there was a sort of ball that could destain almost anything: tar, wax, oil, and oil paint. This ball was made of white soap
> 1223.111.6 Tools (Marseille), pure potassium and the essential oils of juniper berries.

1224.92.10 Questions without Answers "Face it! If Acadians reads de word *c-l-o-w-n* in a French book, der not likely to be pronouncin' it '*cloune,*' now are dey. Der more likely to say 'clown,' just de way 'tis written. No?"

> Twelve idiomatic expressions in French that include the qualifier *petit* or "little": *la petite main* (little hand), an apprentice seamstress or cook, an assistant to a trained person officially possessing the know-how; *le petit mal,* an absence seizure, which simulates the epileptic seizure or fit, also known as lunatism, demonic, and the scourge of Christ; *le petit mineur*, a kind of sniggering heard preceeding a subterranean catastrophe; *le petit thé,* the name Acadians give to the gaultheria leaves or wintergreen; *le Petit Robert,* a French language dictionary contained in a single volume, as opposed to the *Grand Robert*, which is contained in six; *les petites besognes* or small tasks one might give a child to keep it close; *les petits maîtres* or minor masters, painters the encyclopedias of Art do not mention, but who have left their mark in

> a particular geographical region; *le Petit Nord*, as opposed to Canada's far north, this region is bordered to the south by Lake Superior, to the west by Lake Winnipeg, and to the North by Hudson Bay; *les petites lectures* or children's literature; *le petit mi*, the thinnest guitar string; *la petite reine*, another term for a bicycle; *la petite pilule*, a pill that miraculously relieves all
> physical discomfort, helps one to sleep, to see 1225.98.11
> life through rose-coloured glasses. Expressions

"So now 'ere dey goes, de wee boy an' de wee girl boat togedder to the henhouse wid der basket."

Terry marched his fingers across the carpet, whistling a tune, the way someone might on their way to the henhouse.

"Inside of de henhouse, dey goes lookin' troo de straw to find de eggs. Dat was wonderful fun, on account of dey'd never done it afore now. From time to time, de chickens was yappin.'"

"Naw, Dad! Chickens doesn't yap!"

"Is dat right? Well den, wot does dey do?"

"Dey pecks!"

"Naw, dey cackles!"

Étienne was impressed. This had to be the first time Chico had bested him in French.

"I'll say, dey was cacklin'! *Caaaque-quat-quat-quat-quat-caaaque*! An' in between der cacklin' dey was peckin', dat's when dey was hungry."

Marianne's gaze had wandered; clearly she was finding the story a trifle long. Terry cut to the chase:

"An' den, just as der comin' out o' de henhouse wid der basket full of eggs, *bump bump*, wouldn't ya know, de little fellow's foot trips on de door sill, an' down ee goes. An den' you hears *crack*, *crack*, *roll*, *bump*, *crack*, *roll*, *crack*, *crack*, *roll* again an' *crack-bump* again. De basket tipped o'er, an' all de eggs're broken."

The children were dismayed.

"An' dat's where folks got de idea not to put all yer eggs in de same basket. On account of if sometin' goes wrong, an' you falls o'er or some such horrible ting, well der go all yer eggs, broken. Now if dat wee boy an' girl 'ad each brung along der own basket, chances are only half der
1226.100.10 eggs would've broken, which wouldn't be near so bad."
Proverbs A conclusion that made Marianne laugh.

> Send a copy of this book with my fond remem-
> 1227.114.12 brance to Thomas Krampf, inventor of shadow
> Inventions poetry.

"Anudder example?"

Terry wanted to satisfy Chico.

"Alright den, let's say a fellow's gotta whole lot o' money. You might tell dis fellow he'd best be puttin' a parcel of dat money in de bank, an' anudder parcel in de co-operative, an' a chunk of it under 'is mattress, all like dat, only just to be certain dat if sometin' happens to one parcel in one place, ee'll still have some of 'is money in de udder places. Dat way, ee doesn't lose his shirt."

Chico seemed to be greatly interested in these financial matters.

"Losin' yer shirt, dat means you's gone bankrupt."

Chico nodded quickly, more interested in what was to follow. Terry was trying to think of financial examples
1228.100.11 that might also interest Étienne and Marianne, who were
Proverbs on the verge of fighting over the basket.

> Many more graphic signs could be used to identify words as properly Acadian or imported from English; the new letters *ã*, *ẽ*, *ĩ*, *õ*, *ũ*, and *ỹ* are the fruit of an initial and tentative reflex. Why not use the ˘ as in *Ăă* or the ˚ as in *Åå* or the ˛ as in *Ąą*, or even *Ạạ* or *Ảả* *Ẩẩ* *Ậậ* *Ắắ* *Ẵẵ* *Ặặ*...The possibilities are endless; the world

> is filled to overflowing with signs and accents. And nothing prevents us from inventing a few more. Which might be fun. Who didn't experience the thrill of discovering the cedilla and the dieresis in school? And who knows, perhaps by
> complicating French, by "signing" it ourselves, 1229.90.7
> we might make it more "significant." Heresy? Letters

"Nowadays folks doesn't only say dat fer eggs an money. Say a fawder an' mudder dat's got children are goin' on a trip, dey might not take de same plane. Dat way, if one o' de parents dies — say one o' de planes crashes or explodes or some such ting — de udder parent dat's not dead can keep on takin' care of de kids 'till der grown up."

Faced with the frozen faces of the three children, Terry
added: 1230.13.5

"Only dat don't happen all dat often..." Paternity

> Planned or spontaneous, tactics consist in taking advantage of a momentary distraction by the Other to escape a bad situation. A tactic is generally more difficult to execute than a feint.
> Its objective: in French *noyer le poisson,* to con- 1231.127.1
> fuse the issue and confound the Other. Tactics

...

...

...

"All I can tell you is dat we're not dat far along in our understanding of music. 'Tis sometin' bigger dan our intelligence."

"You don't tink dey've already studied up on all dat?"

"Dey can't but scratch de surface. Pretty quick dey come up against de black hole."

"De black hole..."

"Jumpin' dyin', dat's aggravatin' when you's repeatin' 1232.119.5
everyting I says." Music

1233.21.10 More or Less Useful Details

Terry inherited the Bourgque secret from his mother née Bourque.

"'Ow 'bout us, Mum, have we got one?"
"One wot?"
"You know, Mum, a car squawker!"
"Awh! No, we don't."
"How come?"
"On account of our car's too old."
. . .
1234.107.2 Necessities
"Anyway, 'tisn't sometin' we really need."
"Awh."

On your tongue catch it!
A single snowflake alights
moisten, melt, vanish.
1235.75.4 Tankas
To your lips thirst has risen
from the skies snow has fallen.

Granny Després has so little talent for sewing that the darning kit she'd inherited from her own mother had barely served. The basket attracted Étienne's curiosity.

"Wot's dis 'ere, Granny?"

Étienne was already removing a spool of thread, and another.

"Dose der are old spools o' thread me mudder had."

His grandmother watched Étienne remove all the spools from the basket. They made lovely little noises knocking against each other. And, since the photographs earlier had set the theme of a bygone era, she added:

"You can tell der old, on account of der made of wood. Dese days dey makes dem out o' plastic."

He aligned the spools, some according to size, and some according to colour.

"Luh, Granny, der's no yellow."

The grandmother looked up and saw the arrangement of spools on the carpet.

“Still, ’tis not a bad bit nice, eh? Makes a kind o’ rainbow...”

In her heart, she was glad to see her grandson taking
pleasure in playing with such simple things as spools of 1236.106.11
thread. Customs

Certain words fail, or barely succeed, or manage with difficulty to complement and transmit their meanings. The word *grièvement*, for example. Because it means “grievous,” it ought to impose a degree of severity. But it’s similarity to the word *brièvement* or “briefly” meaning of short duration, and hence implying lesser significance, makes *grièvement* a deceptive word. A similar argument might be made regarding the homophonic similarity between *grief* and *brief* in English. The same is true for the introductory phrase “*à l’instar de*.” The distinguished formula of the phrase, which so resembles the titles of nobility—*le duc d’Anville*—might lead us to expect what follows to be an equally distinguished subject, someone unique and set apart from the crowd. But the opposite is true. “*À l’instar de*” means very simply “like,” “just as,” “following suit.” For example, in a sentence beginning “*à l’instar des autres institutions financières, la Banque Cennes Noirs choisit de...*” we might expect that the bank in question is breaking ranks, adopting some new and different, perhaps even decent or generous policy. However, contrary to the distinct tone of the phrase, the sentence is actually stating: “Like the other financial institutions, the Brown Penny Bank has chosen to...” The Brown Penny Bank is simply following suit. What a waste! With the subtlety of a decoy, “*à l’instar de*” embellishes those who

actually lack originality, who fail to distinguish
themselves. In fact, one might conclude that
such deceptive terms are employed precisely
1237.20.12 with the intention of benefiting from their am-
Languages biguous coefficient.

Terry also made a mean potato pancake, although not necessarily the best in the lofts, because the competition around this particular dish was fierce. Zed was no slouch, and neither was Pomme, but Antoinette outdid them all. Everyone added his or her personal touch, or special ingredient, in hopes of winning the Mardi Gras prize.

"De salty onions is wot makes all de difference."

Étienne inhaled the dark herbs swimming in brine that Antoinette had placed before him before closing the jar.

"You has to add just de right amount, not too much."

...

"Not too much onion, neidder. Can't be too big. An' you has to cut 'er into wee, wee, tin pieces. You can't be seein' bits of onion in de pancake."

...

"Now den, we needs an egg. Will you go an fetch me an egg?"

1238.23.7 Étienne rose quickly. The idea of fetching something
Potatoes from a stranger's refrigerator gave him an odd feeling.

1239.128.9 Collectors are really treasure hunters, and each
Fervours object in a collection is worth its weight in gold.

"Is it me yer askin' den? On account of I couldn't tell who you was lookin' at ..."

(*Suppressed laughter*)

"Well, to be honest, I's afraid of opening me veins, slicing me wrists."

(*Holy shite!*)

“Interesting. Could be a fear of knives.”

“Tell de troot, ’twas more of a problem afore dan ’tis now.”

“Well, I suppose ’twould be harder to slit yer wrists wid a Bic razor… “

(*Laughter*) 1240.137.7

“Class, class… Please.” Fears

Balls are all you need plus a *b*. In one of Terry’s 1241.90.11
notebooks. Letters

Étienne placed the shoebox in front of Chico, and lifted the top off. Chico’s eyes opened wide.

“Holy Jesus, Joseph, and Mary! Wer djya get dat?”

Étienne was bursting with pride.

“Granny Després gave dem to me.”

Slowly Chico handled the wooden spools, removing a few from the box to better appreciate the whole. Étienne informed him: 1242.113.8

“Only der’s no yellow.” Collections

big bear eats cod fish
little bear eats tongue and cheek
seal swims nonchalant 1243.75.7
charts studies and statistics Tankas

“You means to say dat radder dan writin’ “*õverpayér*,” we’d be writin’ “**overpayer*” an’ puttin’ a star over de *o*?”

“De star’d be our accent, like? Now der’s a proper smart idea!”

“Well, one of our accents, anyhow…”

“Only ’tisn’t easy drawin’ a star, is it? Ask me, ’twould take too terrible long to be writin.”

“An’ wot would de udder accents be? Dey’d have to be matchin’ up somehow, der’s gotta be a logic to it…”

“Well, how many’re we gonna need, den?”

“Are dey fer real?”

1244.88.8 Freedom "Raise anudder sail, girl, we're flyin' high!"

1245.121.2 Things to Want Herman Melville's *Moby Dick*.

In a room that had become a holdall over the years, Chico's grandmother had been obliged to shuffle and rummage through a number of old boxes before finding what she was looking for.

"Might be in 'ere…"

Chico approached, unfolded the cardboard flaps, and discovered several wooden spools just like Étienne's. They were scattered among bits of cloth, zippers still in their wrappings and ultra-thin paper dress patterns spilling out of their envelopes.

"Hoorray! De yellow!"

"Yellow's wot you was after? Go on an' take it. I won't be missin' it. Can't recall de last time I opened dis 'ere box."

"All o' dem?"

"You wants dem all, does ya? Go on den. I's glad to be rid of dem."

Granny was happy to please Chico. She watched him searching down to the bottom of the box.

"Wot're ya tinkin' to do wid all dat, I wonder?"

Chico shrugged.

"I's showin' dem to Étienne. Ee's got some as well."

The grandmother thought that was as good a reason as any.

"Can you see anyting else in der ya might be wantin'?"

Chico examined the contents of the box, picked up a zipper, dropped it.

"Only de tread? 'Ere den, does ya want a bag to put 'em in?"

1246.105.6 Reserves/ Reservations Chico accepted the old brown paper bag his granny was offering. The spools went *ploc ploc ploc* as they fell in and knocked against each other.

> Spoiled rotten, really? In his novel *Grey Souls*, Philippe Claudel writes "rotten spoiled." A kind of opposites. 1247.64.9 Opposites

Terry found the list Myriam had sent him extremely interesting.

"Title is 'Critical Experiences of Preschool-Age-Children,' wot pretty well says it all right der."

Carmen agreed.

"Like, dey like it when you give dem a signal when to start an' when to stop doin' sometin'. Like one-two-tree-go! or sometin' like dat."

Carmen thought that went without saying.

Terry was looking through the photocopy as he spoke:

"Dis is right smart. Gives you ideas wot to do wid dem when yer at yer wit's end an' you gotta take care o' dem all de same."

Carmen wasn't sure that, at such times, she'd have the energy to drag out the list.

"Dey like to measure time an' follow der rhythms..."

...

"An' dat's why dey like us to be tellin' dem de same story again an' again. Dey like to think about wot's comin' up, dey like to remember, to go over de different bits in der 'eads."

"Dat makes proper sense."

But suddenly Terry was taken aback:

"Luh! Says 'ere dat between two an' five years old, der reaction time's up to ten seconds. So, if you ask a question, it can take up to ten seconds fer dem to answer."

Terry put the copy down.

"Ten seconds, is a long time."

"Seems to me, Étienne don't need as long as all dat."

Terry counted ten seconds in his head.

"Well, 'tis good to know. Fer Marianne, anyway." 1248.93.5

"Yes, fer Marianne, fer sure!" Time

The cachalot or sperm whale is a mammal of the cetacean order that inhabits the oceans. The genus is currently listed as vulnerable. Its distinctive shape — a very large, block-shaped head, which can be one-third of the animal's length, and a lower jaw, which is very narrow and underslung — is evocative of the whale species as a whole. Adult males measure up to 20.5 metres long and weigh up to 56 tonnes. Females measure from 11 to 15 metres long and weigh between 15 and 20 tonnes. A cachalot can consume up to one ton of squid, octo-
1249.111.12 pus, fish, seal, and shark per day. The Internet
Tools is a fantastic tool for preliminary research.

"Are ya sure you wants to be workin' on dis project? If you do, you've got to tink o' sometin'. You keep on sayin' 'tisn't possible, and can't be done."

. . .

"Could be dis just isn't yer ting . . ."

"To tell ya de troot', I only joined up fer de money. An' even den, I had to twist me own arm."

"I don't tink it'll work. Yer not really convinced."

. . .

. . .

. . .

1250.119.6 "Why don't ya take de weekend to tink it over."

Music . . .

wee girl jumps and laughs
sticky cheeks honeyed cushions
old black fly stretches
1251.75.8 drawn to a ripe apple core
Tankas winter strains to be no more

www.galaxidion.com

MICHELET (Jules) Handbook of Modern History.

Paris, L. Hachette, 1850. 8vo, contemporary half shagreen, rubbed spine, ll, ii, 307 p., foxing. Work "recommended for the instruction of modern history in schools," divided into three periods: I. 1453-1517. II. 1517-1648. III. 1648-1789.
This book is offered by the *Librairie Hatchuel.* 1252.84.12
Euro 35.00| **Order** History

Vladivostok =
ruler of the East
Vladikavkaz
Ordjonikidze (1932–1944)
(1954–1990) 1253.67.9
Dzaoudjikaou (1944–1954) Terry's
North Ossetia-Alania Notebooks

Étienne and Chico are playing with their mini-cars.

"Lucifer cut de tulips in front of de doctor's house to decorate Julie's cabin."

Lucifer was seven years old and a real devil. For the most part, those who knew him liked him in spite of everything, because his mischief was mostly motivated by good intentions.

"Dey'll trow 'im to de dogs, now."

"Are dey Julie's dogs?"

"Naw, Julie don't have no dogs."

"Are dey mean dogs?"

"Der no dogs. You doesn't need dogs to be trown to dem." 1254.117.6
"Awh." Death

Rumour is certainly related to fantasy, but it 1255.129.4
can also be related to tactics. Fantasies

1256.31.12
"Wot I mean is, 'ow long does a person look at de cover Questions with
of a book, usually? Not all dat long." Answers

1257.118.11 Concerning Yellow

Bit by bit, the thread of yellow is lost.

Without wishing to upset him, Catherine believed it was important to ask Chico a few question about his past, if only just to let him know that she was aware of what he'd gone through.

"You say that Shawn sometimes ran away... Did he stay away for long?"

Chico thought a bit before replying.

"At night, when I's gettin' into bed, I's prayin' fer 'im to come back."

...

...

"Was it your granny who showed you how to pray?"

Chico answered her questions readily.

"She taught me de 'Hail Mary.'"

Catherine allowed several seconds to pass, before continuing:

"Were you missing your mum as well?"

Chico shrugged:

"Granny showed me a picture of 'er once. Den after, she's puttin' it back in de top drawer."

Catherine guessed what Chico meant:

"You'd have liked to keep it, eh?"

Chico shrugged. Catherine concluded that it had not been easy for him to understand everything that had happened in that house.

"One night, ee shows up in a car. 'Twas near dark. I's playin' marbles in de yard. Ee'd bought me a bike, a two wheeler, brand new an' all."

Catherine was grateful for this moment of happiness to fall back on.

"You must've been mighty pleased!"

Chico nodded.

"You knows it! She were all blue an' shiny!"

...

1258.103.3 Disappearances

"Only ee didn't stay long dat time neider."

the child can't stay still
Dad, look! A flying dessert!
cloud — flash flare — cherry

1259.55.10
Haikus

"I took a chance. Bought youse a coffee widout knowin' if you'd be comin' back or not."

. . .

"'Tweren't nuttin' to it."

"Well, tanks just de same."

. . .

"I tawt: only tell me wot you wants me to be doin' an' I'll go right ahead an' do it."

"G'wan, yer pullin me leg."

. . .

"Alright den. Pick up yer guitar an' give me an *A*."

. . .

"Now an *A flat* . . ."

. . .

"An *A minor* . . ."

. . .

"An *A flat minor*. . ."

. . .

"An *A 7* . . ."

. . .

"*A flat 7* . . ."

. . .

"*A flat diminished* . . ."

". . . which is the same thing as a *G sharp diminished*, or a *D*, *B*, or *F diminished*."

"An *A diminished* . . ."

". . . Same thing as an *F sharp diminished*, an *E* or *G diminished*, or a plain *C diminished*."

"The *A flat augmented* . . ."

". . . Or the *G sharp augmented*, or an *E* or *C augmented*."

"An *A augmented* . . ."

". . . There again, same thing as a *D flat augmented*, *C sharp augmented*, or a plain *F augmented*."

"A 9…"

…

"A *flat 9…*"

…

"A *major 7…*"

…

"A *flat major 7…*"

…

"A *minor 7…*"

…

"A *flat minor 7…*“

…

"A *7* with a *diminished fifth…*"

…

"A *7* with an *augmented fifth…*"

…

"A *7 diminished to 5…*"

…

"A *flat 7 diminished to 5…*"

…

"A 6…"

…

"A *flat 6…*"

…

"A *minor 6…*"

…

"A *flat minor 6…*"

…

"OK, good enough! That's perfect!"

…

1260.119.7 …

Music "Wot, you don't want de suspended ones?"

In New Brunswick, the officials of Baker Brook are asking for the name of their village to be transformed into French. If the government agrees to their request, the village will be called

Baker-Brook, with a hyphen, instead of Baker Brook, without one. 1261.79.2 Oddities

"Put yer foot on it, den haul away wid yer hands."

Étienne did as his father instructed and the cardboard peeled off as though by magic.

"Alright, Dad! Wot do I do now?"

Wearing the carpenter's apron complete with tools that Granny and Granddad Thibodeau had made for him, Étienne was happy to be part of today's household renovations.

"Does ya see de saw someplace around der?"

"Yes, Dad. Do you want it?"

"Can't hide nuttin' from you boy..."

Étienne walked across the pieces of boards scattered on the floor to fetch the saw and bring it to Terry, who was stretched out on his back deep inside the closet.

"Now den, sit down where ya are an' point dat flashlight into de corner where I's sawing."

Terry could have managed on his own, but he wanted to give his son a chance to use his Christmas present.

"At de same time, can you push on dis 'ere board wid yer feet?"

Étienne placed both feet and pushed on the board Terry was indicating.

"Not too hard, now. Push just a wee bit...OK, now you got it. Keep dat up until I stop sawing, alright?"

Étienne nodded. Terry slipped his pencil in his mouth and went to work.

"We's workin' hard, eh, Dad?"

"You said it, boy!"

And once the board was cut:

"Der! Now can you raise yer arms as high as yer able over yer head. Dat'll tell me 'round where to put the shelf."

Étienne raised his arms and Terry put a mark on the wall.

"Alright. Now we's gotta saw two smaller bits of wood

to hold up de big board dat goes across dis way. Can you find two pieces 'bout as long as yer arm an' wide as yer hand, and tick as… "

"Like dis?"

Étienne had already found a length of wood approximatley fitting Terry's specifications.

"Dat's perfect, boy. Can you find anudder like it?"

"I'll try, Dad."

The boy finally came up with a board that a single cut would bring down to the right size. With Terry's help, he measured the desired length, drew the pencil line and sawed the board. Terry then screwed the supports into the wall, and father and son slipped the shelf into place, forcing it slightly at the end, because none of this was perfectly straight.

"Now we cleans up all around, an' den we can push de dresser back in place."

No sooner said than done, although at the end, Étienne struggled to lift his side of the small piece of furniture. Terry advised him how to go about it:

"Put yer foot under one of de legs, it'll be a whole lot easier."

Since Étienne didn't understand what his dad meant, Terry went over and placed the boy's foot under the leg in the right corner of the wardrobe.

"Now, when you takes a step, yer foot'll he helpin' lift de dresser. Won't be so hard on yer arms."

Terry went back to his side of the small furniture, placed his own foot under one of the legs to serve as a model for his son.

"Are ya ready, den? One… two… tree… go!"

The dresser moved forward a few paces in the right direction.

"Dad! It works!"

"You knows yerself, boy! Keep 'er up!"

Once the dresser was in place, Terry wanted to compliment his son:

"Lard tunderin', I tinks we'll make a real carpenter out o' you, boy…"

"Awh, no. I don't tink so, Dad."

"No? On account of?" 1262.126.3

"Dad! I never hammer any nails!" Techniques

> Romanian originally cut three letters from the
> traditional Latin alphabet *q*, *w*, and *y* and add-
> ed five that do not appear in any of the other
> main latinate languages: *ă*, *â*, *î*, *ş*, and *ţ*. One
> should not mistake these signs for accented let- 1263.88.9
> ters — they are actual, distinct letters. Freedom

"I don't like it when you make fun of religion."

I had a soft spot for Sylvia.

"On account of?"

"I don't know. Doesn't seem necessary."

"It's part of life, isn't it? Why can't it be criticized like anything else?"

"Yes, I know."

I liked her lack of stubborness.

"I know you're more of a believer…"

…

"Only, seems to me the Church can defend itself. It's not as though I were attacking some defenseless person or thing."

…

"An' anyhow, I'm not really attacking the Church or religion. I only says wot's in me head. I don't try to prove my point."

"I know."

Sylvia was twisting a bent paperclip round and round in her fingers as she spoke:

"For lots of people, that's all they've got. They have to hold on to something, so they hold on to that. I think, for those people, it's sad. It's as though you were dashing their hopes."

…

"Educated folks can probably understand what you mean. I feel like I'm speaking for the others."

"I understand."

Beyond understanding, I was moved by Sylvia's natural penchant for thinking spontaneously of those less fortunate.

"Just out of curiosity…do you consider yourself educated?"

Sylvia thought about it for a moment before replying:

"I only took a course in secretary school after high-school…but that's not really all that matters."

…

"To be honest, I've never felt that I wasn't educated. Though I don't really have any sort of proof of an education. I've no degree, no big words, nor grand ideas…"

I would have liked to dwell a while longer on those grand ideas that Sylvia associated with the idea of an education, but she had moved on:

"It's odd that we're talking about this. When the lofts opened, I really wanted one, a little one, just to be in town more often, to meet people, maybe take a class at the university. It's as though I had this need, this desire to do exactly that, to educate myself."

"Awh, is that right? Why didn't you do it then?"

"I don't really know, something else must have intervened, and it sort of passed. But recently, the idea came back to me. It still attracts me."

"You ought to do it. I think you'd enjoy it."

…

"As a matter of fact, there's a loft for sale. Someone
1264.101.11 who's moving to Montréal."
Duos "Is that right?"

But, or, then, by, against, to, of, not, and, as:
1265.68.12 conjunctions? adverbs? prepositions? Go back
Projects and reread my grammar.

"Étienne, do you hear de door?"

Terry couldn't stand the tap-taping that the front door made when it wasn't properly shut. That irregular knocking was especially unbearable when he was lying down on the sofa for a short nap.

"'Tisn't me, 'tis de wind."

Étienne's tone was very convincing, despite the fact that he had a habit of not shutting the door properly.

"De wind don't usually turn door knobs..."

Étienne did not budge. Terry counted ten seconds, then:

"Étienne...?"

"Alright. I'll do dat fer you, Dad."

Terry felt there was something amiss in the boy's reply, but gave up thinking about it when he heard the neat click that meant the door was properly shut. 1266.89.9

"Tanks, son." Irritants

> A tactic consists generally in using a technique in a new way or with an unusual aim, which has the effect of surprising and momentarily 1267.127.5
> disarming. Tactics

"Me, I knows a little fellow dat's obsessed wid poisoning folks."

"Poison...profusion, interior harm, profusion leaving me in tears in your arms.

"How old is he?"

"I'd say four of five years old." 1268.141.4

"Awh, I knows 'im, too." Obsessions

> For some reason, the character of Catherine has supplanted Élizabeth in the lives of Zed 1269.96.5
> and Chico. Characters

"You really wrote this?"

The Cripple reread the poem on the sheet of paper that

Terry had tried to hide under *L'Acadie nouvelle* newspaper, but which had slipped out and onto the floor the other side of the cash and right in front of The Cripple's armchair so that the latter only had to bend over to pick it up.

"Dat's impressive."

The Cripple seemed sincere, even slightly surprised.

"Have you written a lot?"

Terry was more than a little embarassed. He'd never shown his writing to anyone.

"Not so many as all dat. I's got a couple o' notebooks on de go, only der not full up."

The Cripple's interest encouraged Terry to explain some of the finer points of the short forms, and the rules he was conscious of violating.

"Yer supposed to be always talkin' 'bout de seasons, only not directly, an' nature, in some way or udder. Only I don't do dat. 'Tis all I can do just to be gettin' de right number of syllables, an' even den, I don't count dose dat ends in *e*."

The Cripple reread the poem again, and commented:

"'Tis sometin' all de same! You've got a powerful imagination."

Knowing The Cripple's unquenchable thirst for knowledge, Terry thought he might steer the conversation in another direction:

"Der's some fine books dat talks all about deez sorts o' poems."

The Cripple folded Terry's poem and put it in his pocket. The gesture surprised Terry, who didn't dare stop him. The Cripple explained himself:

"Take someone like Chico's dad..."

"Shawn?"

The Cripple nodded:

"Dat fellow, to go an' kill 'is fawder, I'd say 'is imagination deserted 'im. On account of I tink 'tis our imagination stops us goin' mad."

Terry, whose head had been leaning one way, now leaned it the other:

"Dat makes proper şense… " 1270.16.11
"Question is, can we be havin' too much imagination?" The Cripple

> True or false: the odrer of lertets in a wrod is umnipnortat, the olny tihng ipmrontat to raed wuthoit a porlebm is taht the frist and lsat lertets are in the rhigt pacle, baucese the haumn
> barin deos not raed erevy leettr, but rheatr the 1271.116.3
> wrod as a wolhe. True or False

"O'er 'ere, Zed?"

Zed wasn't sure.

"Gotta be snow dat's not been touched. We'll go a wee bit farder to be sure."

Chico walked ahead with a cod-salting pail in each hand, the kind of pail that's used to transport mashed potato poutine. Zed was toting a large rectangular tub and a shovel.

"I tink nobody's walked o'er 'ere 'cept maybe a bird. Does a bird count?"

Zed, torn between the thought of birds carrying all sorts of strange new viruses, and the weight of his tub full of snow, decided it was best not to go too far. He chose a spot next to the supposed bird tracks.

"Ought to be fine o'er 'ere."

But Zed was still not convinced; he continued to study the spot. Chico waited for more definitive instructions, which finally came:

"The best an' cleanest snow's gotta be under dat small outcrop o'er der. Let's go as far as dat."

Chico and Zed moved over to their right, and dug a first hole.

"She's as white as white can be. Dat's de way we wants 'er."

They set to work filling their containers with immaculate snow.

"Push down to pack 'er in proper."

Chico pressed the snow down into his containers as best he could.

"Didn't yer Granny sometimes make taffy-on-de-snow?"

"Naw. She only made mouse titties."

It had been a while since Zed had heard that name used for crow's foot greens. He burst out laughing, and Chico soon joined in.

…

1272.135.5
Zed and Chico

"Does we gotta fill de pails right to de edge?"

1273.64.1
Opposites

> The opposite of a misadventure would be a success, a triumph, a satisfaction, a pleasure.

"I've enough stuff in me pockets, I can hardly sit meself down."

As he spoke, Terry emptied the contents of his pockets on the low living-room coffee table: bits of paper; key chains; two large unmatched screws; a small golf pencil; a stone; a thin white, red, and blue ribbon; a bit of orange peel; a tiny battery; and half a wooden clothespin with the spring.

"Where did ya find all dat, Dad?"

Étienne had already grabbed hold of the stone.

"Awh, 'ere an' der, where I's been o'er de course o' de day, I suppose."

Étienne also took the little piece of wood with its metal ornament.

"Dat was at Granny's. 'Twas lying on de edge of the front porch. De udder piece was on de ground. I was tinkin' to pick it up an' put de two bits togedder, only Granny was talkin' to me an' I guess I forgot."

"Can I 'ave it?"

"You want it? She's yers!"

Terry noticed that Étienne was also holding the stone.

"An' you can 'ave dat stone, as well."

Happy, Étienne put the stone straight into his mouth. Terry panicked.

"Wot're you at, boy?!"

Étienne jumped, spit the wet stone out.

"'Tis only to see de colour. Chico was showin' me how."

Terry came over to look at the colour of the stone Étienne was showing him:

"Hmm, looks green like."

Étienne was silent. The stone lacked the brilliance of Chico's stones. He realized that Chico had not kept just any stone; rather, he'd been selective, and that was what made his stones a real collection. Étienne put the stone in his pocket, along with the more than half a clothespin, which he would examine more closely at his leisure. 1274.113.6 Collections

> Strictly speaking, it's in fact on the twelfth of February (rather than on the second—Candlemas or the Feast of the Purification of the Virgin), that one ought to observe the behaviour of the male groundhog, who pokes his head out of his den on that day in search of a female on whom to bestow his affections. According to popular belief, if the groundhog sees his shadow (because the sun happens to be shining on that day), the creature will immediately forget his desire, and draw back into his cave, thus presaging another six weeks (40 days) of bad weather (winter). However, this belief dates back to before the adoption of the modern calendar (also known as Gregorian, after Pope Gregory XIII), which shortened the year 1582 by 10 days (passing from October 5 to 15 in a single night), thus creating for ever after a 10-day lag with the date on the old calendar (named Julian, after Julius Caesar). 1275.13.12 Parenthesi(e)s

Ludmilla placed a tablemat, a knife, and a fork in front

of Étienne, and then a plate of pasta shells in cheese sauce.

"Who invented plates..."

Ludmilla had thus repeated the essence of her godson's question aloud in order to better grasp it, but in vain:

"Well, I have to say I have no idea. Why?"

"Dad says dat everytin's invented 'cept fer nature."

"Yes, I think he's absolutely right."

"Even a chocolate bar."

Étienne thought the addition of this detail might astonish Ludmilla.

"Yes, I suppose someone had to think of it."

Étienne looked at the pasta on his plate, readied his fork to spear some.

"Do you know someone who invented sometin'?

"Many things were already invented when I was born. Take plates, for example: they already existed, and I've never heard anyone I know mention who actually invented them. Probably they've been around for so long that no one worries about who's idea they were."

Étienne thought the fate of inventors was sad.

"Also, some things are invented little by little. The plate may have started out as a large shell found by the sea, or a broad rigid leaf, or a calabash. Then, with time, people got the idea to make them, in terracotta, then in porcelain, and eventually in plastic."

1276.114.6 Étienne chewed without speaking. Once he'd swallowed:
Inventions "Der's tree words I didn't understand."

> **FRICTIONARY:** n.—2005. 1. Collection of signifying units resulting from the phenomenon of friction between languages. "*The need*
> 1277.120.2 *for a frictionary in order to understand them*
> Fictionary *confirmed their exotic nature.*" (Daigle)

"Mum, who was it invented tootpaste?"

"Really, I don't know. A dentist, maybe."

The follow-up question came a little later.

“Mum, when dey was inventin’ tootpaste, did dey invent de taste first, or de tube?”

Carmen found the question rather specialized.

“Well, I suppose once dey had the paste, dey had to find a good taste fer it. Because, widout a good taste, folks would not have wanted to brush der teeth, now would dey?”

Carmen herself was impressed by her reply.

“An’ de tube?”

“Fer the tube, I have no idea. Could be dat the tube already existed, fer medicines in ointments or udder sorts of creams.”

“Well, wid wot did dey invent de taste, den?”

“Dey had spices dat give a good taste, like mint, an’ cinnamon.” 1278.114.4

“Awh.” Inventions

1279.70.1

> First, there are the typos. Errors

“Dad, will I be havin’ to play hockey as well?”

“Only if you wants to.”

. . .

“Do you?”

“Don’t know.”

It occurred to Terry that Marianne would have leapt for joy at the prospect of playing hockey.

“Chico’s gonna be startin’ to play.”

. . .

“Some folks prefers playin’ soccer. Or baseball. Depends on wot you like.”

. . .

“An’ de exercise is good fer ya.”

. . .

. . .

“I likes to swim.”

“Yes, dat’s good as well. An’ yer a shockin’ good swimmer to boot.”

"I know."

…

…

"Only bein' part of a team's fun, as well. You make a different sort of friend."

"Wot sort?"

Terry had not expected this last question.

"Well, sports friends, I suppose. Friends fer winnin'."

"Winnin' wot?"

"Well, winnin' games. Tournaments."

"Awh."

Terry felt his son's interest in hockey melting away.

"Can be travellin' friends, too, like when you has to go
1280.122.11 Sports play a game in some udder town."

"Awh."

> 1281.118.12 Concerning Yellow So that, in the end, all that was left were a few scattered pieces of the jigsaw puzzle's yellow bird.

"Dad, wot're we havin' fer supper?"

1282.82.9 Moncton "Treehump rolls wid coleslaw Deluxe."

"Hooray!"

> Numerals, equations are the mineral matter of the story, something to dig into. The system of numbering, for its part, confirms nothing less
> 1283.47.11 Yielding than the existence of a point of no return, no abandon.

"Der's times I gets de feelin' ee's got no idea wot ee's doin' whatsoever. Only I doesn't say nuttin'; I just do wot ee says."

"Well wot is it ee's askin' you to do, den?"

"To play de notes by de book."

"Just notes by demselves?"

"'Tis about as excitin' as recitin' de alphabet."

"De musical alphabet, in udder words…"
"You knows yerself."
…
"You can't be callin' dat music."
"An' does ee tink ee's gonna prove sometin' wid dat?"
"At de back of de room der's a wee black booth. Ee sits folks down in der, an' wires dem up to de brain machine dat's recordin' der reactions."
"Awh, well now… dat's not a bad bit interestin.'"
"Dat's de plan B."
"An' wot was de plan A, den?"
"I don't know, do I. I wonder if ee even 'ad one. Unless…"
?
…
"Unless wot?"
"Naw, ferget it. 'Twas only two ideas I 'ad dat crossed wires." 1284.119.8 Music

1285.105.2

Terry always kept a bit of appetite in reserve. Reserves/ Reservations

"Okey-Dokey's gonna be openin' a clothes shop in de lofts."
"Awh, an' when's dat? Did somebody close down, den?"
"Must be."
"Most likely de hemp store. I never seen a soul buy anytin' in der, ever." 1286.108.1 Rumours

swell pie in the fridge
a big scrumptious piece, two, three…
female comes, opens
temp'rary difficulty 1287.75.10
please do not adjust your set Tankas

"Marianne, come'n put on yer panties!"
Once again, the same circus.
"Marianne, come on, I told you…"

After the second call, Marianne knew her room to manoeuvre was considerably reduced. This time, she got the idea to brush her teeth.

"Awh, here you are!"

Carmen's anger melted when she saw the little one with a tube of toothpaste in one hand and her toothbrush in the other.

"You wanted to brush yer teeth? Dat's a fine idea. Mum's gonna help you."

No sooner did Carmen touch the cap of the tube than
1288.134.12 the child dropped both toothpaste and brush and ran off.
Marianne "De wee devil!"

> The question remains: if the "things to want" are sincerely wanted, since anyone who really
> 1289.121.11 and truly desires something will usually man-
> Things to Want age to get it. Nothing is out of reach.

1290.41.7
Lives of the "Dad, wot's de name of de saint wot trew de balls of
Saints paper into de fire?"

> Useful items (kitchen), decorations in good condition, puzzles. Games (Fisher-Price and others) and children's clothing. Adults' clothing. Surplus furniture. Old mattress-
> 1291.42.2 es (Nazareth House). Second-hand books.
> Sorting Archives (old photos of Dieppe).

For three long seconds, no one moved, not even Marianne. The vase lay in pieces on the floor. The vase. The archetypal vase. Beautiful, ugly. Well, unique anyway. Carmen had dug it up in a garage sale and brought it home, brandishing it like a trophy. The vase.

"Don't ya move, youse two. Understood? Youse stay exactly where youse are."

Terry was not fooling. Étienne had the presence of mind to climb up on the sofa behind him, to clear the area. He tried to convince Marianne to do likewise, but for once, Marianne did not dare move a muscle. She stood stock still and stared at Terry.

"Dat's OK, Marianne, you can sit down beside Étienne."

Marianne clambered up beside her brother on the sofa.

"Proper ting, Étienne, you got de right idea. Now, stay der until I tells you to come down. OK? Understood?"

The two children had understood so well that they hardly dared nod their heads. Satisfied, Terry went to get the broom and dustpan in the cupboard.

"Where's de broom got to?"

Étienne remembered that he'd used it to dislodge a mini-car that had gotten stuck under the dresser in his room.

"In me room, Dad!"

"Well wot's it doin' in der?"

Étienne, sensing that he had the option not to reply, chose to turn his attention to Marianne instead.

"Tap tap tap, peck peck peck, roll roll roll, in de air!"

Terry returned with the broom, the dustpan, a plastic bag and a damp cloth. Marianne allowed her brother to distract her.

"Tap tap tap, peck peck peck, roll roll roll, in de air!"

Terry, satisfied that Étienne was being helpful, concentrated on picking up the fragments of the vase.

"You boat saw wot 'appened, eh? To tell de troot, 'twas an accident. I mean to say, 'twasn't as doh we was too excited or anytin' like dat.

Was Terry trying to convince himself? In the slow sweep of the broom, the bits of glass gently clinked against each other.

"De vase dat Carmen liked so much, on top of dat..."

But which he, Terry, had always felt was ugly. He found fragments all the way under the bookshelves. The debris piled up in the dustpan. There was no way it could be glued back together.

1292.78.6 Accidents “Will we be havin’ to say we’s sorry, Dad?”
Terry pretended not to hear.

> Heart. Piece of heart muscle. One lung. Two lungs. Heart-lung block, single or double. Liver. Heart-liver block. Heart-lung-liver block. Pancreas. Heart-pancreas block. Kidney. Kidney and pancreas. Heart-lung-kidney block. Liver-pancreas-duodenum block. Intestines. Child’s digestive system (liver, pancreas, stomach, and small intestine, with or without duodenum, large intestine, kidney). Ovary. Fallopian tube. Testicles. Larynx. Eyes. Thymus.
> 1293.42.12 Sorting Cells of the adrenal gland. Cells of the human fetus. Sciatic nerve. Bacterial gene. Face.

“Me grandad says der’s all sorts of tings in de ground.”

To Chico, that was obvious. Étienne insisted:

“Even diamonds.”

“I knows dat.”

…

“Wot else, den?”

Étienne had mainly retained the diamonds; he tried to remember the other things. His gaze fell on the garden.

“Lots of food.”

Again, that was obvious to Chico. His shovel struck a rock.

“Me mum has a diamond.”

1294.139.6 Étienne and Chico To Chico, that was quite possible, since women liked jewelry. His shovel struck the same rock again.

“’Twould be fun if we was to find sometin’, eh?”

> Charles Darwin, the famous author of *The Origin of Species by Means of Natural Selection*, had married his first cousin Emma, granddaughter of Josiah Wedgwood, who was their

common grandfather and founder of the celebrated Wedgwood ceramics factory. 1295.65.1 Boy Cousins, Girl Cousins

“’Tis strange dat der’s nuttin in de dictionary about puttin’ a feather in yer cap. Seems to me dat’s a major expression.” 1296.98.4 Expressions

CHAPTER 10

To write a book is, in a way, to be rid of it.

Julien Gracq, *Entretiens* (Interviews) 1297.144.10
José Corti, 2002 Epigraphs

For the remainder of the day, Étienne waited anxiously for Carmen to get home to hear how his father would explain the disappearance of the vase.

"Will you be tellin' 'er right off when she comes in?"

"No. I tink 'twould be best to 'ave our supper first. Unless she notices on 'er own. An' youse two, mind you don't say a word. Let yer dad handle it."

Étienne watched his father come and go between the stove and the cupboard, peeling garlic cloves, dipping his fingers into a large jar to take up salt and toss it in the pan.

"Might not bodder 'er all dat much. I mean, she knows accidents can happen."

And Terry passed the jar of cumin under Étienne's nose before adding some to his mix. Étienne continued:

"Will you be apologizin' right off or at de end?"

"Well, it's no use apologizin' if yer not sincere, now is it?"

That's not how Étienne had come to understand things.

"Dat's not wot you was sayin' de udder time."

"Awh, no?"

1298.86.7 Apologies

"No..."

1299.95.12 Additions to *La Bibliothèque idéale*

> Obviously, Ann Charters' biography of Jack Kerouac, entitled *Kerouac: A Biography*, a fascinating and important work about the man and America. Published in English in 1973, and in French two years later.

Terry wasn't certain he'd heard right:

"Wot was it you said just den?"

Étienne wasn't sure from what point or what word he should start repeating.

"I told 'er to leave me alone."

"To leave you alone..."

"... fer Jesus's sake."

"Jesus's sake? An' where, pray tell, did you hear such a ting?"

"Antoinette says it a lot."

Terry was taken aback.

"Well, anyhow, dat's not sometin' we ought to be sayin.'"

"On account of?"

Étienne watched and waited for Terry's answer.

1300.124.7 Religion

"Well, on account of dat's religious, an' we's not religious, so it don't count."

1301.61.9 Social Sciences

> The social sciences aspire to make perceptible realities which are not immediately so.

•

"De cheese shop in de lofts is set to close down."

"Is dat right? On account of?

"Don't know."

"Seemed to be workin' fine. Especially since dey bin doin' de caterin.'"

"I knows it."

"Who was it told you dat den?"

"Anna, at de office. 'Er sister was in de habit of goin' der to buy a special cheese fer her girl who's allergic to sometin' or udder. Dat's de only place she could find it."

...

...

"Dat's strange, all de same, on account of dey looked terrible busy last week when I's der. Dey was even puttin' up de help wanted poster."

"Awh?"

...

"You didn't tink to apply?"

...

...

"Wouldn't 'ave done me much good, would it... seein' 1302.108.2
as dey's all set to close." Rumours

> Terry dreams that he has to fetch something he left in the apartment where he used to live with Carmen and Étienne before their little family moved to the lofts. The young couple who now occupy the old apartment receives Terry warmly. When, for some reason, Terry has to go back a second time, the couple is just as understanding. The third time however, the tenants make no effort to hide their exasperation, and turn Terry away rudely. Back in the street, Terry sees a child get run over by a vehicle. The car has no door on the front passenger's side, and the child slides quite naturally into the
> seat. The little one seems unhurt, and Terry re- 1303.109.7
> alizes that the accident is in fact a kidnapping. Dreams

"From wot I can figure, it takes someone who knows der notes perfectly..."

"Dat's why I was suggestin' ee use recordings. Only ee didn't want to. Had to be played live, an' all de time by de same person."

"On account of?"

"Ee said it could 'ave been a recordin' if 'twere a real

song, only on account of 'twas only notes by demselves, had to come from somebody playin' dem right der on de spot."

"G'wan wid you!"

1304.119.9 "An' dat's why it took somebody who wasn't about to
Music get fed up an' walk out on de job in de middle."

> Years later, Étienne admitted the disappointment he experienced that evening when
> 1305.103.4 Carmen failed to notice the disappearance of
> Disappearances the vase.

"Me, it's odd, I always like a movie dat begins wid a
1306.117.2 funeral. I mean I like dose films all de way troo to the
Death end."

> It's quite possible that very few people find opposites interesting. Judging from the way the spine cracked when I opened it, the thesis entitled *Concerning the Role of Opposites in the Genre of the Novel* had probably never left its
> 1307.64.11 place on a shelf in the Champlain Library of
> Opposites the Université de Moncton.

Étienne reconsidered the display before him.

"Did you not understand wot I meant?"

Étienne nodded, but Terry could see that something still wasn't clear.

"Well, wot's de problem den?"

Étienne couldn't believe that something as ordinary as a chocolate bar had had to be invented.

"Well, why den?"

"Why dey was inventin' it? On account of it didn't exist afore den, I suppose."

Étienne was no less mystified.

"Before who?"

"Well, before. Like way back in de olden times."

"Before Grandad an' Granny?"

"Sure, you could say dat." 1308.114.1 Inventions

Then it was Terry's turn to pay for his purchases.

> It seems that the custom of putting a feather in one's hat caused the disappearance of a number of species of birds. 1309.106.7 Customs

Even back in the van, Étienne couldn't shake the idea that someone had had to invent the chocolate bar.

"Well, wot was it dey had to invent?"

Terry lowered the volume on the radio, and looked at his son in the rear-view mirror:

"Wot?"

"Wot was it dey had to invent?"

"Well, I don't know do I? Maybe de size of de wee platters dat gives the bar its shape. An' de wee papers to wrap 'er in. An, de very idea dat somebody might be wantin' to eat a chocolate *snac*.*

Étienne couldn't imagine chocolate being eaten any other way but a little at a time.

"On account of before dat, dey was eatin' platefuls of it?"

Terry burst out laughing.

"Naw, I doesn't tink so! Most likely, dey was eatin' chocolate cakes an' cookies. I don't know if der was even boxes o' chocolates like we's got nowadays."

This seemed to satisfy Étienne. Terry turned up the volume on the radio again.

"Dad, did dey have to invent everytin' den?"

Terry turned down the volume on the radio, and looked at his son in the rear-view mirror:

"Wot was dat?"

Étienne repeated his question. Terry let his gaze sweep

---

* Gallicization of the English word *snack*. Close relative of the word *sac*. 1312.143.11 Varia

quickly over everything that existed around them before replying.

"Far as I can tell, I'd say yer right. Everytin' aside from de fields an' de trees an' de animals an' de water an' dat."

"Do you mean nature?"

"Yeah, nature, dat was de word I's lookin' fer."

Terry glanced back at Étienne again:

"You knows yerself, boy. Nature. You got all de right words."

Étienne smiled, both proud and a little embarassed.
1310.114.2 Terry would not have traded that smile for anything in
Inventions the world.

> Examination question for Literary Translation course (TRAD 2507): based on excerpts from Giono's and Jaworski's translations of Melville's *Moby-Dick*, define the approach privileged by each of the translators, and demonstrate how both these translations unnecessarily domes-
> 1311.32.8 ticate this American masterpiece for a French
> Exam Problems audience.

> 1313.132.9 Medical malapropism: what did the doctor
> Malapropism have to neigh (say) today?

Terry managed to weave through the traffic and turn left at the busy crosssroads.

"Wot was we sayin'? Awh, yeah, nature. I suppose everytin' we sees aside from nature's wot was invented."

Étienne was looking out the window. Their van was surrounded by other vehicules, stores, restaurants, merchandise of all sorts.

"Fer instance, you sees de McDonald's over der? Little by little, humans was finding in nature wot dey needed to invent bricks an' plastic an' nails an' food an' paper, all wot you'll find in de McDonald's.

Étienne understood.

"An' den some fellow had to be inventin' de very idea of McDonald's, de idea of sellin' little hamburgers, not too expensive, an' cookies wot look like animals, wid a clown an' a game room in de restaurant, so dat dey've got a place where parents don't mind bringin' der kids. Sometimes, 'tis more an idea dat dey's inventin'. Dat's wot we calls a concept.

There was still something that Étienne did not understand:

"Well den', who is it invented nature?"

Terry looked back at his son in the rear-view mirror.

"Awh, well now, dat's a terrible big question."

He stopped at yet another red light.

"Some folks'd tell you dat was God, an' de whole ting took 'im naught but a week. Udders'll say it happened all by itself, after a shockin' big explosion in de middle o' de stars an' de universe. Dey calls dat de Big Bang. An' den der's udders dat say it happened bit by bit, an' it took hundreds of millions of years."

And Terry fell silent, wondering if a child could deal with such realities.

1314.114.3
Inventions

"Well den, who was it invented chewing gum?"

1315.21.12
More or Less
Useful Details

Sylvia will not change her mind about religion.

"Wot 'appens when you makes a mistake? Must muddle 'is data sometin' fierce..."

"I don't know do I. I never makes a mistake."

"Ya, right."

...

"G'wan wid ya, yer not serious?"

...

"Well how does ya manage to be rememberin' all dose notes den?"

"'Tisn't so hard as all dat. Der's a system. Once you understands it, well..."

"Still. Der's de fingers. Yer head may know, but de

fingers, dey can fudge it, do a physical Freudian slip."

"Never happened to me..."

1316.119.10 "G'wan, yer pullin' me leg..."

Music "I swears to God."

1317.67.4 Terry's Notebooks

> (Scribbled in a hurry, seemingly.) I likes white when it's a colour. Étienne three years nine months.

That day, Chico and Étienne had been helping Zed empty the big shed in which residents accumulated all the stuff that might be useful, but no one wanted. Zed had promised them a sidetrip to the convenience store as a reward.

"Hold on der, Chico, only two tings."

Chico did not protest. He renounced the green licorice laces, returned the can of sparkling water to its place, and kept the bag of chips and the chocolate bar.

"Wot're you takin' den?"

Étienne hadn't chosen anything as yet, but he knew he wanted a chocolate bar, a can of pop and an ice-cream sandwich.

"Awh, yes! Gum!"

Chico selected a pack of multicolour gumballs, then hesitated between the chocolate and the chips. Finally, he put them both back and opted instead for a small Vachon cake coated in coconut and the gumballs.

"Alright now, 'ave youse made up yer minds?"

Zed had been following the boys' machinations with amusement.

"Étienne?"

"Yes."

In the end, Étienne placed a blue freezie and a bag of ketchup flavoured chips on the counter.

"OK, dat's it den..."

Zed paid for everything, including a chocolate bar for himself, and the three returned to the truck.

"I'll give ya a gum, if you gives me some chips."

Étienne was generally amenable to this sort of exchange. Sucking on his freezie, he handed the air filled bag to Chico, who popped it open with a single blow, and without crushing the chips.

(*Floc*)

A *tour de force*. Impressed, Zed tousled Chico's hair affectionately. 1318.135.1 Zed and Chico

> As for *Concerning Yellow*, that would lend too much importance to yellow. Any colour would have done just as well. Or almost. The impression of constant repetition. 1319.81.10 Titles

"In the beginnin', ee was workin' wid de same notes. Later on, ee started mixin' dem up."

"Was dat more like music den?"

"Let's say der was a wee bit more tension."

"Atwixt you an' 'im?"

"Naw, between de notes."

!

"I figures ee wanted it dat way so's ee could be measurin' de reactions on boat sides o' de brain."

?

"Where we've got to now, it sounds more like music. I suppose."

"Are der a lot of folks takin' de test?"

"Der two-hundred fifty."

"Dat's not a few."

"I tinks I finally come to understand wot ee's tryin' to prove. Ee wants to figure out when a person starts havin' de same reaction to de same note, or series o' notes. Dey each has to come in every second day, six times."

"Six times!"

"Only takes a half hour or so each time."

"Are dey gettin' paid?"

"Two hundred dollars fer de whole ting. 'Tisn't all dat

much, only ee had no trouble findin' people, students, folks on de dole... an' ordinary folk, half 'n half men 'n women."

"Holy Jesus, ee's got dough!"

"Awh, ee's not lackin'. Ee's on some project wid Ottawa, de National Defense."

"National Defence! Wot does dey 'ave to do wid it?"

"I doesn't know do I?"

...

"Well, actually, I does know a bit, only I's not supposed to be talkin' 'bout it."

"Anyhow, looks like ee knows wot ee's about fer sure."

"De udder day ee's after showin' me a couple o' de scans. 'Tis pretty interestin'."

"I'd go, if ever ee needs one more."

"I tinks ee's got all de folks ee needs fer now."

1320.68.8 "Figures... Only me wife's all over me back to find
Projects some work."

1321.104.11 Worries

> It's about time I finished this book; computers are up to three billion colours.

Terry took Weisner Road for the return trip to Moncton.

"Well, bin a long time since I come troo 'ere. 'Twas all forest when I was a boy. I doesn't remember all dese houses."

...

"See de bridge o'er der, an' de river? I always tawt dat's where Saint Christopher was workin'. Ee was me favorite saint. I still wears 'is medallion."

Terry pulled the chain out from under his shirt and showed Étienne the smallest of the metal charms. Étienne glanced at it and then craned his neck to get a look at the bridge and river.

"I tawt ee was livin' in a wee cabin right alongside de bridge, so dat when a kid like me came along, ee'd be helpin' 'im across. Sometimes he only took you by de hand, but a lot o' de time, ee'd carry you across on up on 'is shoulders. Dat's wot I liked best."

There were a great many things in this story that Étienne did not understand.

"Wot, was der no bridge den?"

"Sure der was, only we was always wadin' across all de same. Don't know why."

"Der was no channel?"

Terry was happy to see that Étienne knew the geology of rivers.

"Der must 'ave been one, only he was a saint, don't forget. Saints, well, dey can do a whole lot of tings de rest of us can't. Dat's how come dey's saints. Saint Christopher could be walkin' like der was no channel in de middle o' de river, an' he could swim widout runnin' short o' breath. Dat's wot dey calls miracles."

Terry slowed down as came up on the bridge. In the rear-view mirror he saw his son looking for some sort of little cabin.

"Deez days, even de cabin's gone. Ee must've moved to some udder bridge." 1322.41.1 Lives of the Saints

> True or false: the character "I" in France Daigle's novel *For Sure* is an avatar of the author, that is, a representation of France Daigle. 1323.96.7 Characters

"I was fond of Saint Bernadette, as well."

...

"She 'ad a lovely family name. Soubirous. Right pretty, eh, Soubirous?"

Yes, Étienne, too, thought it was pretty.

"Well, Bernadette, de Blessed Virgin appeared to her one day while she's in de woods to gadder up a turn o' whits. Her family was so poor dey didn't even 'ave a log to burn to keep warm. Der was a wee river — o'er 'ere we'd be callin' it a stream, really — an' on de udder side was a grotto. Saint Bernadette was gadderin' up sticks on dis side of de stream when de Blessed Virgin appeared in de grotto on de udder side. A grotto's a right pretty ting. Like a wee alcove in de side of a rocky cliff."

Terry kept glancing back at his son in the rear-view mirror while he spoke.

"De Blessed Virgin's de chief of all de saints."

"Granny says she's de mudder of de little Jesus."

"Dat too."

. . .

"Saint Bernadette was doin' all she could to help out her poor family, an' de Blessed Virgin appeared to 'er to encourage 'er an' to tell 'er a secret."

. . .

"'Er little brudders was wid 'er, only dey was playin' an' not payin' attention."

Étienne could understand that.

"Only, on account of 'twas a secret, Saint Bernadette weren't supposed to tell a living soul wot de Blessed Virgin 'ad told 'er."

. . .

"Well, folks startin' sayin' de little Soubirous girl was
1324.41.2 out of 'er mind, an' dat she'd not seen de Blessed Virgin at
Lives of the all, only she'd made it all up."

Saints Étienne could understand that, too.

> Examination question for Religion and Psychology course (SCRE 3732): devise a critical comparison between the miracles performed by Jesus and those by Mozart. Clue:
> 1325.32.9 Mozart performed his when he was in dire
> Exam Questions straits and had no other recourse.

"Der was Saint Thomas, as well. Ee didn't believe nuttin' anybody said. Ee 'ad to be seein' an' hearin' it wid 'is own eyes an' ears."

. . .

"When dey's tellin' us dat in school, I tawt dat was de reason we was always washin' our ears. So we could be hearin' Jesus."

Étienne didn't quite see the link, but he decided to withhold judgment.

"You knows 'ow Jesus died, eh? Nailed on de cross?"

"Well sure, Dad."

"An' den after, ee rose from de dead?"

...

"Well, Saint Thomas, ee didn't want to believe dat Jesus was really risen from de dead. Ee had to put his finger in de hole dat de nail'd made in Jesus' hand to be certain."

Étienne tried to imagine the size of the hole a cross's nail would make.

"Dat's why, ever since, when a fellow doesn't believe sometin', we says ee's like Saint Thomas."

"But wot was 'is miracle?"

Terry had to think.

"Hmm... Good question. I doesn't know wot Saint Thomas done aside from not believin' any old ting folks was sayin'. You'd best ask Granny." 1326.41.3 Lives of the Saints

> Other possible titles: *Write Dat, The Great Loop, Nuances, The Bronze Fly, Almost Something, Almost Something (Covered by Ocean), Small Involuntary Movements, e black i red.* 1327.81.4 Titles

"Den der's de times dey'll bite on anyting at all. 'Tis magical. Yer askin' yerself wot's goin' on, dey just keeps on bitin'.

"Hun!"

"Dose times, dey'll go after anytin' you puts on de line. Don't make de slightest difference wot fly yer usin'."

"Hun..."

"Times like dat, when you catches one, an' you cuts 'is 'ead off, it'll be full o' blood. Dat's on account of de frenzy. We calls dat miracle fishin'."

1328.129.9 Fantasies “Han!”

> Carmen doesn’t like when mirrors break. Nor does she care for shards of broken mirror. She experiences a kind of dislocation, maybe because each fragment continues to reflect anyway. Not that she believes in bad luck. The
> 1329.60.6 Superstitions difference between something we fear — a superstition — and something we don’t like.

“Den der’s Saint Louis. Hasn’t bin all dat long since I found out dat Saint Louis was a king o’ France. Ee’s de fellow ’ad de idea to create de Sorbonne, de most important university in France. You know, like de Université de Moncton?”

Étienne was beginning to grow weary of the lives of the saints.

“’Twas Saint Boniface dat decided Louis Nine ought to be a saint. Der was so terrible many fellows named Louis in dose days, dey had to give ’em numbers.”

Terry could see that his son had lost interest.

“You know Winnie-de-Pooh? ’Twas a soldier from Winnipeg invented ’im.”

Étienne’s curiosity was piqued.

“Winnipeg, dat’s a city almost smack in de mid-
1330.41.4 Lives of the Saints dle o’ Canada. An’ right next door is Saint-Boniface. Seems, even today, der’s lots o’ French people livin’ in Saint-Boniface.”

> From its Germanic origins, the *w* entered into the French language from the north and the
> 1331.90.3 Letters east, more specifically from Picardy, Wallonia, and Lorraine.

“Does dat mean dey could end up knowin’ fer sure wot combinations of notes folks’ll automatically like? Like dey could be makin’ guaranteed hits?”

"I sure hope not."

"An' why not? Musicwise, 'twould get rid of all dose bad songs..."

"One person's bad song isn't necessarily bad to anudder."

"You doesn't tink der's songs dat everyone would agree are bad?"

"Don't know. Good question, doh. Dat's why I tinks 'twould be nice to be knowin' how music's affectin' us fer real."

"You doesn't mind de job so much as you did at de start, sounds like."

"Well, I've only got a couple of weeks to go..."

"An' wot'll you be doin' after dat?" 1332.119.12

"Payin' me own coffee in de mornin's I expect." Music

> *The Ideal Library of the Social Sciences* also selected the sociological study *Travailler pour être heureux?* (Working to Be Happy?), edited by Christian Baudelot and Michel Gollac, which concludes that happiness at work is mainly the experience of those at the hierarchical summit,
> and that work is valorized mostly by those who 1333.130.2
> don't have any. Work

The door of Didot Books opened, and shut.

"Huberte Gautreau! How're ya gettin' on?"

Terry liked Huberte. He liked that she had strong opinions, and yet was capable of having a bit of fun.

"Fine! An' you folks?"

"Not a bit bad!"

Terry was not fond of this expression, which he found outdated, but there it was.

"I was passin' by, an' I thought I'd drop in an' see if de book I ordered's come in."

Huberte saw no hint of anything that might suggest the bookstore was failing.

"Came in yesterday afternoon. I was all set to call you dis mornin'!"

Huberte took her gloves off, glanced at the book Terry handed her.

"Dat's it exactly."

And as she unbuttoned the collar of her coat:

"You know wot, I tink I'll pick out a novel as well, just to reward meself fer readin' dis 'ere brick."

Terry felt generous. It was his way of showing his support for this customer's various causes.

"Don't be shy. I'll even give ya a discount!"

Huberte hadn't expected as much, but she appreciated the thought. However, very quickly the offer gave her reason to pause:

"I hope the tings I bin hearin' aren't true..."

Terry gave her a questioning look.

"... dat you're goin' to be closin'?"

"Us? De bookstore? Closing?"

Terry had no idea where such a rumour could have come from.

"Der's never bin de slightest danger. In fact, tings 'ave never bin better. We's startin' to make a bit o' profit fer our pains!"

"Dat's wot I tawt... only you never know, do you? Sometimes things seem to be goin' well and, from one day to the next, *poof*! — it all goes up in smoke."

"I knows it. Only dat's not de way tings are 'round 'ere. We've more an' more people comin' in an' buyin'. 'Tis as doh folks are gettin' less afeard o' books."

1334.108.3 Rumours

On her way home, Huberte Gautreau thought about the fear of books, and found the idea almost funny.

> Josse, on the other hand, would never think of taking down her Christmas decorations until the Epiphany, more commonly known as Twelfth Night. She believes that those who

> don't do Christmas all the way are risking a 1335.60.9 Superstitions
> year of bad luck.

"'Tis true dose panic buttons're loud. Doesn't surprise me ee jumped with fright."

Carmen savoured Terry's use of the phrase "jumped with fright" in French, like a candy he had tongued into her mouth as they kissed.

"The thing is he didn't really jump. It was more like the alarm hit him in the hips. His body more like... *curved*."

As she said the word *curved* in English, Carmen drew a graceful S in the air with the flat of her hand. Terry figured there was probably no other way to express that in French.

"In any case, let's just say dat, in a way, I saw how ee might turn out to be gay, as well. His reaction was like effeminate."

Terry thought Carmen was jumping to conclusions:

"Just because a fellow shows a bit of a feminine swing once or twice doesn't mean ee's gay. 'Tisn't dat simple, now is it."

Carmen considered this.

"That's true. Most likely not."

Satisfied, Terry was silent for a moment. Then he asked: 1336.125.2 Sexuality

"*Courbé*, isn't dat how you'd say 'curved' in French?"

> Bronze Age men perfected a solid, resistant fish hook, fashioned from materials other than fish or animal bones, pine needles or silex, but it was the Chinese who invented the fishing 1337.114.9 Inventions
> rod and line.

One day while Étienne and Chico were engaged in some urban archaeology down in the ditch at the foot of the railroad tracks:

"Me mudder does kung fu."

Chico looked so impressed that Étienne added:

"'Twas a woman showed 'er 'ow. You needs mirrors."

Chico figured that was very possible:

"One time Shawn brought me along to where Monkey was doin' some."

...

"Monkey could break wooden boards."

1338.108.6 Étienne did not want to be outdone:
Rumours "Carmen as well."

drift wood
afloat adrift
comes and goes halts and goes
1339.80.1 yielding toward a destiny
Cinquains of fire

1340.113.10 "Because, like all fisherfolk, I also collect flies. I've
Collections thirty-six of them."

1341.90.9 The letter *m* is considered the maternal letter
Letters *par excellence.*

As he bent to remove the pie from the oven, Terry called out:

"Marianne? Come 'ere fer a minute, girl; yer dad wants to show you sometin'."

Marianne came running.

"Luh 'ere, girl, at de beautiful apple pie yer dad made. No, no! Mustn't touch it, on account of it's too hot."

To be sure his daughter understood, Terry blew on the pie as though to cool it off. Marianne did likewise.

"She's not a bad bit nice, eh? See, der's none o' de juice runnin' down de sides, de edges aren't burnt, der's two lovely wee holes in de middle. An' don't she smell good. Eh? 'Ere 'ave a whiff..."

Marianne imitated Terry, sniffing over the pie.

"An' dis evenin', when we eats 'er, 'twill be like eatin' love."

"Ove?"

"Yah, dat's right, girl. Love." 1342.43.2

"Ove! Love

> Oddities and chance often have a way of crossing paths, even coming together. Take the *m*, for example: 13th of 26 letters of the alphabet, and 10th consonant of 20. Furthermore, the *m* slices the pie right down the middle when it comes to the number of vowels preceeding
> and following it in the alphabet, exactly three 1343.79.12
> and three. Oddities

"Ee did say it, but 'twas only in a manner of speakin'. On account of ee was in a rage, at dat moment."

"The accused stated that he would probably end up killing his father, and you heard him say so, true or false?"

...

"TRUE or FALSE?" 1344.116.10

"True." True or False

> Codes, pin numbers and other passwords: bonheur; CCFMNSHA; diderot; 4540130074637694; foufou9; 44419; 9951924749203; 1755; 5258634000420357 04/05-04/08; pissepotte; billyboy2; 1212; sauerkraut; 4500600097457382 06/04-06/07; blueberry; 1809; 271407394; 847492; per-
> cents; Painsec; 381653963; 927458; prairie; 1345.107.12
> Tombouctou. Necessities

Even if Élizabeth could be seen less often in the hallways of the lofts with Zed, she continued to take her role as Marianne's godmother seriously, and maintained her friendships with the residents of the lofts. For Marianne, therefore, nothing had changed. Nor did the introduction of Jean-Jacques into Élizabeth's life pose a problem.

"Would you like some cereal, Marianne?"

"Da-gon! Da-gon!"

"Dragon? Dragon cereal?"

Jean-Jacques was not yet fully informed as to the habits of Élizabeth's goddaughter, whose care he had been momentarily charged with *in extremis*. He searched in the cupboard for a cereal box with dragons on it, and found none. But, while he was searching, the defective toaster burned his toast, which triggered the fire alarm and a major brouhaha, which Marianne found highly amusing, and to which she contributed a few hollers of her own invention.

"Yes, it's very funny, eh, Marianne? Very, very funny..."

Jean-Jacques' tone was neither enthusiastic nor annoyed, but since he was climbing onto a chair to remove the alarm's battery at the same time as he spoke, Marianne assumed she was about to witness some kind of circus trick. She followed Jean-Jacques' action with great interest, but her pleasure soon turned sour when he tossed the burnt toast into the garbage.

"Marianne wants toast? No problem, we'll make some more! See? Look... we only have to put two more slices in... and pop!"

As he spoke, Jean-Jacques made two more slices of bread vanish into the slots of the toaster. This time he
1346.134.7 remained at his post next to the appliance, so as not to
Marianne forget to raise the lever when the toast was ready.

1347.113.11
Collections Angèle Arsenault collects angels.

"Alexandre wanted to be a mermaid when he grew up."

Carmen was washing the lettuce for supper.

"I'm only saying dat he probably already knew he was gay. Some people know it very early."

Carmen picked up and began rinsing a red pepper:

"Would it bodder you if one of our children turned out to be gay?"

"No. You?"

"No. Me neither."

Carmen cut the pepper in two and then in smaller pieces. Terry put the ball back into her court:

"An' wot if our kids were to have no kids o' der own, would dat be alright wid you as well?"

Carmen thought about it briefly.

"Yes, I think so. You?"

Terry had already considered it:

"I wouldn't mind 'avin' grandkids, to be der grandad an' all dat."

"Yes, I'd like that as well."

Carmen tossed the core of the pepper into the compost pail, grabbed a few small ready-to-eat carrots, and sliced them for the salad:

"In a way, 'twouldn't surprise me if Marianne was gay as well."

Carmen's declaration surprised Terry:

"Awh, yah?"

"Not you? She's pretty independant, an' she's always on the go."

"Are dose de criteria, den? Only a whole lot of children're just like dat."

Carmen savoured the word *criteria* for a moment before continuing:

"That's true, only she, I don't know… It's as doh it would suit her."

"Is dat so? Really, I doesn't see it."

"An' the fact that she wanted Élizabeth to be her godmother…"

"Are you sayin' you tink Élizabeth is a lesbian?"

"Could be. No?"

Terry leaned over to check that the children were still watching television and not listening to the conversation.
For once he was relieved to see them hypnotized by *The* 1348.125.3
Simpsons. Sexuality

> Table scraps (bury meat and fish leftovers, seafood shells, dairy products and rotten food properly to avoid attracting animals and producing foul odours). Peels (newspaper?), coffee grounds. Gardening waste. Leaves (no rhubarb leaves). Grass. Inedible apples (fallen
> 1349.42.8 from the old apple tree). Nettles (to speed up
> Sorting composting).

"Dis 'ere's de real story of de deer called Zoo from Magnetic Hill. Fer a lot o' years, de government'd been promisin' to widen de highway from Moncton to Frederiction, so dat finally dey really had to do it, an' from dat day forward, life fer de deer of New Brunswick was ferever changed. Why's dat? On account of de contractors decided to put up a fence eidder side o' de highway to stop de animals walkin' on de road an' causin' accidents. Well, animals all likes to be crossin' de road from time to time — who can blame dem, right? — an' you can bet dat a creature as big as a moose — a deer an' a bear's pretty big, too! — so, where was I, awh yah, a creature big as a moose dat runs out in front of a car, well 'tis more'n likely dat de folks in dat car are gonna get crushed, right? So, while dat road was gettin' built, instead o' doin' like 'is dad an' readin' de paper to find out wot's goin' on around de neighbourhood, Zoo deer just kept on eatin' de grass in de ditch by de road, on account of he liked a bit o' salt in 'is food, an' dey puts a whole lot o' salt along de roads in winter. Well, one night when ee's comin' out o' de bush to 'ave 'is supper by de road, Zoo seen dat ee was stuck in de wee strip of woods dat separates de road-fer-cars-goin'-one-way from de road-fer-cars-goin'-de-udder-way. On account o' de fences dey'd put up, Zoo couldn't be gettin' back into de real woods. Still, 'is dad had taught Zoo you gotta keep yer calm, so ee didn't get 'isself all into a panic. Ee just decided to walk along in de woods in de middle o' de highway, figurin' dat ee'd end up findin' a break in de fence ee could go back troo. So den dat Zoo walked, an' walked, an walked . . . on account of de fence was never endin', an' not only dat, but ee had to be walkin' in de night, so folks couldn't see 'im when he's crossin' bits of open field, on account of hunters an dem. All dis to say, it took 'im all of ten days an' nights to finally get to Moncton, where, sure, ee'd 'ave found a whole lot o' ways to escape if ee 'adn't come right up face to face wid de police from de Magnetic Hill Zoo. An' dose fellows? Well, dey's only too proud to trow der net over 'im an' put 'im in a cage in de zoo . . ."

"I's not sleepin', Dad, you can say de moral."

"Is der a moral to dis 'ere story? Fer sure der is a moral! Der's even two! Fer one, you's got to be learnin' 'ow to
read wot's goin' on around ya in de world, an second, 1350.37.5
you's gotta know 'ow to jump a fence." Animal Tales

> Not to mention, 1 person in 150 is walking around with an undiagnosed aneurism. Dixit,
> I will come like a thief in the night. Finish this 1351.104.12
> book and be quick about it. Worries

"Me, I design cardboard boxes."

"You design cardboard boxes?"

. . .

"An' where does ya do dat?"

"Right 'ere in Moncton. Well, in Dieppe, really."

"Fer which company?"

"Pack-It Design."

"An' dat's all you do?"

"Dat's it. 'Tis shockin' sophisticated dese days, neider glue nor staples nor nuttin'. All cuttin' and foldin'."

"Cuttin' an' foldin'?"

"Dat's like copy-paste, only wid us it's copy-fold."

"Awh."

"Must be a terrible long while since you's buyin' some- 1352.130.4
tin' dat came in a box, eh?" Work

1353.67.8 Terry's Notebooks

> Scribbled in the middle of a page of the small pale green notebook, the one with the spiral binding: the river('s) rising (b)road.

1354.105.5 Reserves/ Reservations

"Me, wot I'd like to know is if dey buries folks wid der gold fillings still in der mouths, or if dey pulls dem out an' keeps dem fer demselves."

1355.56.8 Pilgrimages

> Dieppe: where the racetrack used to be, where the Marsh Canteen used to be, where the first stream used to be, where the Palm Lunch used to be, where the tavern used to be, where the Five and Ten used to be, where the grey school used to be, where the Nightingale used to be, where the skating rink used to be, where Sixte Gauvin's barn used to be, where the pharmacy used to be.

"Doesn't dat hurt?"

Carmen was plucking her eyebrows.

"You get used to it."

Seeing that Carmen had several tweezers, Terry took one and pulled out a hair above his own eye.

"Ouch!"

Carmen knew that men are less tolerant to pain than women. Nevertheless:

"It's best to do a wee bit at a time. To trim them regularly. It's nicer lookin' and it hurts a whole lot less."

Terry thought that made a lot of sense.

"They've just come out with wee laser machines that don't hurt at all."

"Is dat right?"

Terry made a mental note of this novelty, as a good idea for a present for his gal who, having pencilled her eyebrows, was now brushing them first against the grain, and then with the grain.

"Like der! Why does you do it like dat?"

"On account of it spreads de colour out. So it looks more natural."

"Natural!?" 1356.64.12 Opposites

Terry felt the world had been turned on its head.

> Oddly, French dictionaries don't recognize the expression "put a feather in your cap." This expression, which originates in English, is translated in French as "*mettre un fleuron à sa couronne*," or "put a jewel in your crown." And yet, the French are certainly no strangers to the practice of adding a plume to their headgear, even to the point of entirely covering their hats with feathers. 1357.79.7 Oddities

Terry realized he was witnessing a major makeup session when Carmen knelt down to search for some product in the little cabinet under the sink.

"I'm sure I bought some more."

"Are you still alright wid yer Fridays, by de way?"

Carmen replied with her head completely in the cabinet.

"Absolutely. On account of?"

"Awh, nuttin'. Just askin'."

"You?"

"Me too. Wednesdays couldn't be better."

"That was a really swell idea you had, for us to do that."

Terry was happy to hear it. He knew it was probably silly, but sometimes he was afraid of not being entirely worthy of Carmen.

"I'd never tawt of it, if you hadn't told me 'bout all de tips yer makin' on Thursdays."

"Well den, I better not be tellin' you what I'm losing not workin' on Fridays."

Still on her knees at the foot of the sink, Carmen was pulling everything she could lay her hands on out of the cabinet.

1358.110.1 A Day Off "Wot is it yer lookin' fer, anyways?"

> Every collector ends up increasing his or her knowledge (techniques), ruses (tactics) and
> 1359.129.5 pride (fervour), but the act of collecting is
> Fantasies rooted in fantasy.

For about a year now, Carmen and Terry had each been taking a total day off every two weeks, i.e., a day off from work and from the family, to indulge their own individual small pleasures and needs.

"At first, I wasn't sure 'twould be worth it, one day every two weeks. An' I thought it might be too difficult to organize."

Carmen was speaking even while she continued to battle inside the cabinet, picking up and replacing one bottle after another.

"Sure, I wouldn't say no to a day every week. In a while, maybe…"

"Dat's it, we'll see 'ow tings go after a while."

"Der she is! I knew I had some!"

As she got to her feet, Carmen added:

"I'd forgotten the bottle looked like this. 'Twas right in front o' me nose de whole time!"

"Wot is it den?"

"It hides flaws. I've a pimple coming out."

Terry was surprised by the colour of the cream that emerged from the bottle.

1360.19.6 Interesting "Green?"

Details "I know. 'Tis weird, only it works."

> According to the eminent financier George
> 1361.57.7 Soros, the humble photocopier is responsible
> Photocopies for the fall of the Berlin Wall.

"You're serious?"

"Yes, absolutely. Try it, you'll see. I'll call you back as

soon as I can.”

Jean-Jacques gazed over his glasses at Marianne for a moment before putting a third pair of bread slices into the toaster.

“Well, Marianne! Apparently you like your toast burnt? Is that right?”

Was Marianne beginning to feel estranged with Jean-Jacques? She had fallen silent, as if in a hollow.

“Burnt to a crisp, I’m told, on a bed of embers, why not, that we’ll extinguish with a dob of butter, to make it go *pshhh pshhh…*”

That was all it took for Marianne to forget her discontentment.

“*Pshhh pshhh*, that makes you laugh does it? *Pshhh pshhh…*”

Her arms in the air, Marianne did her own version of *pshhh*.

“… and the butter and jam’ll put out the fire and it’ll go *pshhh, pshhh, pshhh…*” 1362.134.3 Marianne

And Marianne laughed.

> Avoid applying mascara to your eyelashes before powdering your face, because the resulting cloud of cosmetic powder will immediately stick to the mascara, ruining the desired contrasting effect. 1363.126.7 Techniques

“You’re probably afraid of knives as well?”

“No, not really.”

“No?”

“Wot? Now I’s gotta be ascared o’ knives as well? Lard, might as well be givin’ up de whole ting an’ end it all right now!”

“You said it, girl.”

“Me, I’s afeard o’ knives…”

“Class, please! Be serious…”

…

. . .

"Do you really think you would open your veins?"

"(She means slit 'er wrists.)"

"(Awh.)"

"... don't know, do I. 'Tis *irrational*, I suppose. How does you say dat in French? *Irrationnel*?"

"Exactly."

"Well den, dat's wot it 'tis: irrational. I doesn't tink I'd
1364.141.9 really be doin' it, only de tawt of it sticks in me 'ead. I
Obsessions suppose 'tis more an obsession, den?"

> The French word *fainéant* or "idler" is composed of the words *faire*, "to do" and *néant*,
> 1365.66.10 "nothing". To do nothing. Vice? Virtue? Reread
> The Virtues Jean Giono's *Arcadia*... *Arcadia*...

"I figures we might tink of it as a hobby o' sorts."

"What's that?"

"Dis 'ere, all wot youse do to make yerselves beautiful."

"Why would you say that? On account of how much time it takes?"

"Time, sure, an' money. Hobbies all end up takin' up loads of time an' a whole lot o' money. Golf, fishin', music, bingo, toy trains, travellin', drinkin', readin'. Even cookin'!"

Carmen had definitely never thought of her skin-and-
1366.94.3 beauty care as a hobby.
Terry and Carmen "Hmm. Well, I suppose you could see it that way..."

> Examination question for course in Spatial Organization II (ETFA 3602): 1) Describe the characteristics of the traditional Acadian hamlet through the lens of feng shui theory, and
> 1367.32.11 2) measure the tragic dimension of the Great
> Exam Questions Expulsion on the feng shui scale.

"We already played dat."

"I knows it, an' 'twas fun!"

Chico did not understand Étienne's reticence to playing the game he was proposing. And, as Étienne was sulking, Chico blurted out:

"Well, me, I doesn't like to be inventin' a new game every day!"

1368.114.7 Inventions

1369.92.6 Questions without Answers

> Isn't there a difference between "doing nothing" and "not doing anything"?

"Wot does dey put in dem creams anyhow? Some say der full of stuff like lead an' cadmium an' de like..."

Carmen knew that there was a lot of talk on the subject.

"Who knows? A body'd have to be a chemist to understand wot's written on de packets."

"That's true. De government ought to make dose companies write in a language folks can understand."

...

...

"An' you'd think de more you pay, the better quality the cream would be, not some scrap metal in disguise. Only dat's not de case."

"Awh no?"

"No."

1370.94.4 Terry and Carmen

...

"That's well put, 'scrap metal in disguise.' I like that."

> Étienne thinks that magnets have to work to stick to metal and, as a result, that they need rest to maintain their strength. It worries him to see a magnet working for nothing, like when humans leave them stuck somewhere without any reason other than simple negligence.

1371.130.6 Work

"She ate it all. Bizarre, no?"

Jean-Jacques could hardly believe it.

"That girl's quite unique."

"And what do I do now?"

"Now you find something to keep her busy."

"Yes, that's what I'm trying to do, but she doesn't sit still, you know."

Élizabeth laughed, imagining the scene.

"Yes, I know. Have you tried the scissors?"

Jean-Jacques was shocked.

"Did I hear you right? You want me to put scissors in that Young Nicolas' hands?"

Élizabeth was in a hurry; she cut to the chase:

"There's a pair of children's scissors in one of the draw-
1372.134.4 ers of the buffet. You give them to her with paper from
Marianne the recycling basket. She loves it."

1373.107.3 Closing one's eyes. So as not to see. To see bet-
Necessities ter. To sleep.

When she saw Jean-Jacques retrieving paper from the waste basket Marianne ran to the buffet, and raised her arms toward one of the drawers.

"Clearly, this little girl knows what she wants! Eh? You know what you want!"

Jean-Jacques opened the drawer, found the blunt ended scissors. Marianne ran to the middle of the living room, and let herself drop to the ground, knocking the back of her head on the floor, which fortunately was carpeted.

"Oh la la!"

But Marianne didn't even flinch.

"Lala?"

"That's right, oh la la."

Jean-Jacques settled Marianne in with paper and scissors. The child immediately set to work cutting.

"Olala?"

"Yes, oh la la."

1374.134.5 Quickly she forgot even Jean-Jacques who, amused,
Marianne watched her for a long time.

bold leeks
proud sheaths erect
no wind can bring them down
traversing hoar frost and winter
on foot 1375.80.2 Cinquains

"And do you work in the same place?"
"No. I make bar codes."
"Codes for the bar? You're a lawyer?"
"No! *Bar codes, bar codes*!"
"Awh! *Bar codes*! 'Ere in Moncton?"
"No, in Dieppe. In the industrial park. Like him."
"Awh."
...
"Yer de one installs systems, like?"
"Like. 'Tis an industry in itself now."
"I suppose so. This is the first time I meet someone who works in that field."
...
"How did you call that in French, again?"
"*Codes barres*."
"*Cas de bars, cas de bars*... like bar cases. I has to try an remember dat." 1376.130.5 Work

> Examination question for Ancient Literature course (LITT 4398): The Bible, holy text, wholly text, wooly old text. Explain. 1377.32.10 Exam Questions

"So wot're you up to today?"
Terry always liked to know how Carmen was going to spend her day off.
"I'm meeting Mimi at Winners at eleven o'clock, den we're havin' lunch together. At 1:30 I'm goin' somewhere I can't tell you about, then I think I'll go to the gym. Probably I'll come on home after dat."
Carmen had piqued Terry's curiosity on purpose.
"I know yer tinkin' I's gonna beg you to say wot you

doesn't want to tell me…"

…

"Only, I'm not gonna do it, on account of I's got me own secret I doesn't want to tell you. Well, not right dis minute, anyhow. So, fair 'nough, girl."

Carmen absorbed the shock with a straight face, and then tried to extricate herself gracefully.

"Well, in me case, 'tisn't anyting bad. You neidder, I hope…"

1378.110.3 A Day Off Terry teased:

"Is dat right! Well, I's not sayin' nuttin."

> Étienne keeps his magnets in a small wooden box that Ludmilla gave him. The fact that the
>
> 1379.89.12 Irritants magnets get stuck to each other in the little box also annoys him.

"Me, I's obsessed by de idea dat der might be cameras hidden away in de washrooms an' de fitting rooms an' all over de place."

"Well, dat's 'appened already, so I suppose it's normal to tink so dese days."

"Yah, well, on account of dat, I only goes to de toilet at home, an in a couple udder houses I trust. An' you won't be findin' me tryin' on clothes in de stores. If I can

1380.141.3 Obsessions exchange it, I takes it home an' tries it on der. If der's no exchangin', I just leaves it der. 'Tis just too bad."

> Watching Marianne cutting paper, Jean-Jacques wonders if there might be a kind of
>
> 1381.129.6 Fantasies fantasy involved, but which fantasy, he has no idea.

"Would you do me a favour some time during de day?"

Carmen who was applying her lipstick could not reply.

"You can say no, if you don't want to."

"What is it?"

"Would you stop by Home Hardware and pick up some red *tuck tape*?"

Carmen repeated it to be sure and remember:

"Red *tuck tape*."

"Dat's it, exactly."

"An' if dey don't have any, am I to buy sometin' else instead?"

"Well, dey 'ad some last week."

"Only a single roll? I imagine dey sell it in rolls..."

"One roll."

"Of red *tuck tape*."

"Of red *tuck tape*."

"I suppose I ought to be able to do that." 1382.110.4

"Atta girl! I'll be owin' ya one." A Day Off

> Envisage, steerage, assuage, presage, mirage,
> mirroir, terroir, terror, terrase, erase, enrage,
> engage, old sage, old age, bird in a cage, burn
> sage, barrage, bavardage, bad entourage, bon 1383.73.3
> voyage. Shifts

"How come yer doin' dat, Dad?"

Terry who had to concentrate on the task at hand, could not be talking during the delicate phases of the operation. Luckily, he was now at the halfway point, and could afford to pause:

"Der! Wot does you tink? How pretty is dat?"

Le Petit Étienne wasn't sure if it was pretty. Terry did not insist; he got back to work. Étienne followed every stroke of the brush. At last his father explained:

"I wants to see how long it'll be afore de colour disappears, afore de whole new nail grows out."

Étienne imagined that might be something useful to know.

"Can I does it, too, Dad?"

"Can I be doin' it. We say 'can I be doin' it.'"

Étienne corrected himself.

"Eh, can I be doin' it?"

His chin resting on his bent knee, Terry dipped the tiny brush back into the bottle of dark green polish.

"Sure an' why not?"

Pleased, Étienne began to remove his shoes and socks.

"I has to tell you doh, she's a whole lot harder dan she looks; if you goes too fast, you gets some on yer skin, an' dat's a terrible chore to get off; an' if you takes too long to lay down de second coat, she gets all gummed up and streaky."

Étienne took the time to observe his father's technique.

"Mum goes a whole lot faster'n dat."

"I knows it. She's done it a whole lot more times dan me. Dis 'ere's me first time."

1384.93.2 And Étienne thought that Chico was right: his dad did
Time have some great ideas.

> One sure advantage to putting it in the infini-
> 1385.121.12 tive is that it lends it an indeterminate quality:
> Things to Want "things to want."

"Obsessions aren't de sort of ting a person feels like blabberin' to just anyone. Seems to me, we ought'n to be obliged to be revealin' stuff like dat 'ere. Dat stuff's personal."

"You're right. And I'm not forcing anyone. I merely wanted to demonstrate how common obsessions are."

"Well, 'ow about you, den, 'ave you got obsessions?"

"Of course. Obviously."

"Come on den, let's 'ear one..."

"Alright. For example, I have a dry-skin obsession."

...

"Yes, dry skin. Mine, first of all, but also other people's."

"Dry, you mean, like it makes de *dandruff*?"

"Yes, amongst other things. Basically, all forms of dry skin."

"Wot does dat do to ya?"

"It gives me the feeling that everything is very thin, and could disappear...could be erased or fritter away simply by being rubbed, or scratched or peeled."

...

"In a book for example, I imagine a fingernail might
easily lift up the end of a sentence and remove it com- 1386.141.10
pletely. See? Exactly..." Obsessions

> In stock market language, a contrarian is an in-
> dividual who buys stocks that others abandon 1387.96.11
> for the wrong reasons. A kind of character. Characters

Catherine thought that Chico looked bored.

"You boys aren't playing in your cabin today?"

Chico shrugged and continued to run his finger along the dusty edge of the window. When he got to the end, he wiped the dust on his pants and more or less flung himself into the sofa, sighing:

"'Tis awfully hot..."

But it wasn't particularly hot. Catherine concluded that Chico just didn't know what to do with himself.

"How 'bout we go for a drive?"

"Where to?"

Catherine already had a destination in mind:

"I could show you where I used to hide when I was little and wanted to be alone."

...

"I think you'd like it..."

... 1388.115.1

... Catherine and

"OK." Chico

> One student argued that the professor was
> probably the avatar of the author, who had lift- 1389.76.7
> ed the sentence from the book. Avatars

Carmen told Mimi how Terry had beaten her at her

own game of secrets. Mimi thought this little lover's tussle was cute, and she even threw oil on the fire to drag out the pleasure.

"Now dat you mention it, de udder day I saw dem talkin', he an' Zed, an' when Terry spied me close behind 'im, ee clammed right up. I'd say der was sometin' fishy goin' on der."

Carmen took the bait:

"You want to kill me or wot?!"

But Mimi had no desire to let the lie last. Anyhow, she'd scored a direct hit:

"'Tisn't troo! I's only gettin' a rise out o' you."

Carmen tried to clear her head, but it wasn't easy. Mimi tried to reassure her:

"You knows it can't be sometin' real serious. Terry? Der isn't a fellow more sensitive an' carin' dan dat boy!"

1390.110.5 A Day Off

Still, Mimi could understand Carmen's frustration:

"If Tony tried dat on me, I'd skin 'im alive."

1391.60.1 Superstitions

There is no 13 point in typography.

Her parents had sold the family's land years ago, but Catherine had never renounced the narrow trail that led to her old refuge. She parked the car along the country road.

"See the trail beside that telephone pole over there?"

Chico finally spotted it.

"We have to walk down a bit."

Chico opened the car door without a word. Catherine gathered their things together, handed the boy a canvas bag, and the two of them walked to the head of the trail. Before starting in, Catherine said:

1392.115.2 Catherine and Chico

"See the bigger trees over there? That's where the house I grew up in was. Half of it burned down when I was thirteen. Instead of fixing it, my father and mother decided to sell the land and move into town."

The opposite of a thing to want would be some- 1393.121.4
thing fervently desired. Things to Want

"Can I help ya?"

"I'm lookin' fer some *tuck tape*."

"*Tuck tape, duck tape*, or *duct tape?*"

"Well…I'm pretty sure ee said *tuck tape*…"

"Wot's it fer?"

"I don't know. Ee didn't say."

"Well, was it fer fixin' sometin' electric, sticking on siding, tapin' a hockey stick?"

Carmen found the clerk's tone unpleasant; she took the offensive:

"I don't know, I didn't see wot ee's fiddlin' wid. Ee only asked me to pick up some *tuck tape*."

The clerk came down a notch:

"I can be showin' you wot we's got. Come along down 'ere."

Carmen followed the clerk to the end of a long aisle down to the back of the store to finally end up in front of a panel covered in a multitude of sticky ribbons destined for all kinds of uses.

"Dat's wot we got."

Carmen studied the wall, and almost immediately grabbed a packet:

"Must be this one 'ere. I just rembered ee said 'twas red."

Carmen picked up the plastic-coated packet, and read
the large lettering: 1394.22.9

"An' it's written right here, *tuck tape*! Overheard

"Awh! *Tek tape*! Why didn't ya say so, girl! Conversations

To be honest, the difference between 10 point
and 12 point in a typeface font seems smaller
than the difference between 12 point and 14 1395.79.4
point. Oddities

"Me, it's de folks who says '*quèsiment*' instead o' '*quasiment*'! It's like dey says 'practicawly" instead o' 'practically."

"An' who says dat?"

"Awh, de folks up North an' from Québec, an' dem places. Pretty much de same dat says 'Mointun' instead o' 'Moncton.' Like dey got a broomstick up der ass."

. . .

"You never 'eard somebody say '*quèsiment*'?"

"You get too worked up 'bout de language. Let folks talk as dey please, why don't ya? Wot difference is it gonna make?"

"None, most likely. Only I'm pretty sure dat dem dat
1396.82.7 Moncton says '*quèsiment*' tink dey's talkin' better dan dose of us
dat says '*quasiment*.'"

1397.92.11 Questions without Answers

> The origin of the expression "a whale of a difference"?

While she was doing her exercises at the YMCA, Carmen wondered if she ought to include Chico in the adventure. At the same time, she liked the idea of being just the four of them, the little family.

"*Are you finished here?*"

"Yes."

Carmen answered in French. She glanced at the time as she made her way over to the stationary bikes. Another 10 minutes and she'd be done. She didn't particularly enjoy pedalling on the spot. Maybe she ought to talk to Zed and Catherine? What would Terry think? *Oof*! She lowered the pace on the machine. Whoever had been using the bike before her must be training for the Tour de France. One way or another, Terry and the kids would be happy. So, when all was said and done, it was
1398.110.6 A Day Off her decision to make. Without a doubt, this pedalling
was her least favourite part.

> So that confusion about the nature of the avatar spread. And since most people only had the vaguest and more or less accurate notion, the
> avatar was left with an extremely large sphere 1399.76.10
> of activity. Avatars

"Dad? Are ya sleepin?"

Terry opened his eyes, recognized Marianne.

"How's it goin'?"

Terry blinked.

"I want to introduce you to Jacinthe."

Jacinthe approached the bed.

"She says 'er parents know you."

Jacinthe confirmed this:

"My mother grew up in Dieppe, on Gould Street. She was a Surette before she married. Mélissa Surette."

Terry's eyes seemed to smile.

"Ee understands. Go on."

"My father painted the first sign on yer bookstore. Gérard Babin."

Terry's eyes continued to smile. Jacinthe added: 1400.133.7
"That was a long while ago, eh?" The Future

> How ¡ntr¡gu¡ng, th¡s ups¡de down exclamat¡on mark that ¡sn't qu¡te an *i*, but more l¡ke an ag¡ng *i*, to be honest, w¡th bags under ¡ts eyes, but endear¡ng all the same, thanks to th¡s stretch¡ng, seen at the beg¡nn¡ng of a sentence or a word
> not so long ago—how could one not l¡ke th¡s 1401.96.8
> character? Characters

The path was overgrown in certain places but not everywhere.

"Geez, der's a whole lot o' mushrooms 'round 'ere."

"That's because it rained a lot last week. Some are good to eat, but I don't know which. Some are poisonous."

Chico began to look at the mushrooms very differently,

trying to guess which ones might be good and which were certainly bad, but eventually he became lost in conjecture, and turned his attention elsewhere.

"De wee red berries, are dey good fer eatin' den?"

"Yes. They're called bunchberries. They don't taste like much, though."

Chico bent down, picked a few, ate them. Catherine wasn't lying.

"Blueberries!"

"That's right! I forgot all about them!"

For a few moments, they abandoned themselves to picking and devouring the little round fruit.

. . .

. . .

1402.115.3 Catherine and Chico

And then Chico, who until that moment had heard only the noise of his own movements in the forest, suddenly discovered that a subtle range of sounds was riding on the breeze into his ears.

> The wind she's blowin', the leaves are fallin'
> But the larches der still a handsome green
>
> Now a fierce wind carries off de last o' de leaves
>
> 1403.112.5 Languages
>
> But de larches der still hangin' yellow
> (Der spirits keep on lurchin' back n' fort)

"Say, do you think the child might be a bit precocious?"

Élizabeth had only just arrived, and was removing her coat.

"She's cute, isn't she?"

"Cute yes, but more than that. She has a . . . I don't know how to describe it. But, well, maybe all children are like that."

"She made you one of her paper things?"

"A kind of fissured assemblage?"

"It's fun to watch her going at it, isn't it?"

"Exactly, she was putting it together almost without

paying attention but, at the same time, she knew exactly what she was doing.” 1404.134.6

“And did you see her face?” Marianne

> Considering the large number of dead or dying languages, why not recognize those who want to survive, give them a chance? Chiac for example. 1405.73.10 Heresy? Shifts

“Me, my greatest fear is to be paralyzed. I couldn’t bear it. 1406.137.11 Someone would have to kill me.” Fears

> True or false: the bits of dry skin that accumulate around the fingernails are called 1407.116.12 hankerings. True or False

“I’m not tellin’ you de whole of it in de right order or nuttin’, only I’s givin’ you a general idea of how she works.”

As he spoke, Terry kept clicking away on the mouse, opening files one on top of the other.

“De most important ting is you’s gotta be comfortable wid yer decisions. Dat way, if yer losin’ a bit o’ money, ’tisn’t all dat terrible. An’ dat way yer learnin’ wot you figured wrong. Yer learnin’ from yer own mistakes.”

Zed still had his doubts:

“Wouldn’t it be better just puttin’ de maximum in yer REER every year?”

Terry’s answer came a few clicks later.

“Better’n buying stocks you mean?”

Yes, that was exactly what Zed meant.

“De best ting is to put de maximum in yer REER, den you buys stocks wid de money you gets back from yer taxes. Dat’s de system.”

Zed was impressed:

“An’ where did you learn all dis, den?”

“Awh, readin’ ’ere an’ der…”

. . .

"Dat's funny all de same; dis mornin' I was askin' Carmen de exact same question 'bout 'er makeup. I tawt 'twas sometin' women had in dem natural. I never knew dey was readin' it in magazines."

1408.85.1
The Stock
Market

"Geez, I didn't know dat neidder."

> Work. Work hard. Put your nose to the grindstone. Do the heavy lifting, use a little elbow grease. Earn your keep, earn every penny, earn your stripes. You don't have money to burn. Spend wisely. You're not made of money. Save. Don't play the stock market. Don't throw good money after bad. Don't pour money down the drain nor spend it like it's going out of style. The noun *argent* is masculine. It doesn't grow on trees, nor will it fall from the sky.

1409.130.7
Work

They walked a while longer, Catherine leading the way, Chico following behind. The sun drew pretty patterns on the ground.

"Is she still a long way, yer cabin?"

Catherine was surprised.

"My cabin? It's just a place I went to be alone; there's no cabin."

The absence of a cabin excited Chico just a little.

"Wot is it, den? A cave?"

Chico imagined discovering a cave. He'd seen them on television, but never in reality.

1410.115.4
Catherine and
Chico

"No, it's not a cave."

1411.128.6
Fervours

> The moment of writing is one. It is the moment. All writing comes back to this moment, compression of the same into one.

"When will you be going?"

"Are some weeks cheaper dan udders?"

The agent hit a few keys on her keyboard and chatted with Carmen while she waited for the page to upload.

"System looks overloaded..."

Carmen was in no hurry, with nothing better to do. The telephone began to ring on the desk next to them.

"Telephone's been ringing off the hook since morning. You'd think everyone'd decided to go at the same time."

The agent opened a drawer, searching in it for a several moments:

"I broke me nail before comin' in to work this mornin' an' I haven't had time to file it. Rubs me nerves raw."

And then suddenly it was too much: the blank screen, the telephone ringing non-stop and the lost nail file all came together to erode what little patience the agent had left. 1412.110.7

"Lard tunderin'! Where's dat friggen file got to!" A Day Off

> In the living room, immobile, her head resting on Élizabeth's shoulder but her eyes wide open, Marianne allows herself to be rocked in the old armchair that sings cooey-pik one way and cooey-pak the other. In the kitchen, Jean-Jacques is listening to the radio while he washes the dishes. 1413.47.9 Yielding

Catherine saw the river, and wondered if Chico had spotted it, too.

"We're almost there."

But Chico was no longer thinking about how far they had to go. He was listening to their feet crackling twigs, snapping dead branches, muffling the ground where the thick roots of pine trees buckled up out of the earth like the veins on his grandfather's hands, long ago now. 1414.115.5 Catherine and Chico

> The property register was overflowing with title deeds, but not one was suitable. 1415.81.12 Titles

The weather was perfect, the surface of the river barely shimmering. Neither Chico nor Catherine felt the need to talk. From time to time, a bird's call or a squirrel's breakaway fissured the silence.

"Would you like to swim?"

Chico was more interested in exploring the edge of the shore. It was the first time he'd been on an untamed river. It was nothing like the beach. The muddy bottom was strewn with tree trunks and branches; walking through it was a real challenge.

1416.115.6 "It isn't deep. You can even walk across."

Catherine and Chico — Chico looked at the other shore. Indeed, it wasn't very far. He might very well end up going over.

> Leaf through a book looking for an expression, a phrase, a passage that struck you. This time, you underlined it, or earmarked the page. But once you find it, the passage is disappointing, seems weaker than you remembered it. Something's missing. Maybe it was the cumulative effect of the preceeding pages, the momentary flash of light, the surprise, the enthusiasm of a first reading. Confusion, sense of
> 1417.56.10 Pilgrimages loss. Perhaps every pilgrimage carries with it a sense of loss.

"... companies dat folks wouldn't tink of."

"Dat's just it! Der are a whole lot o' dose! Only, how do you decide which?"

"Well, der's a couple or tree principles: 'ow much risk yer willin' to take; companies dat're young or de more mature companies, wid or widout dividends; an' den der's de different sectors, like banks, energy, healt', consumer goods..."

Zed understood.

"Some folks say you've only gotta be buyin' in six or eight companies in tree different sectors. You buys a wee bit at a time, when de price is down. Dat means when der in a bit of a dip, like you sees right 'ere."

Terry pointed to a graph on the screen depicting a modest downturn.

"You can see 'ow, every once in a little while, she goes down a wee bit. Dat's normal. Dey says a dip o' ten percent is good. Ya see, de percentage's written 'ere."

Zed looked at the figures in the small box on the screen, found a percentage.

. . .

. . . 1418.85.3 The Stock Market

"Anyhow . . . dat's one way. Only dat's not really de way I goes about it."

> Marianne also likes to ride piggyback on Chico, especially when he rears up, whinnying, and she has to hang on, yelling and laughing at the same time. It's a little like when you have to go peepee. 1419.134.11 Marianne

Étienne had been following every one of his grandfather Thibodeau's gestures, as he worked that day to replace the veranda's supporting posts.

"How come de wood's green?"

"Dey puts sometin' on it so it don't rot."

And:

"How come you takes dem old nails, Granddad?"

"Der still good, even doh dey're a wee bit bent an' rusty. We only need to straighten dem up a bit."

And with that, the master shaper tossed another handful of old nails on the cement block and began gently hammering the shanks as he rolled the ends with his index finger.

"Luh?" 1420.126.8 Techniques

Yes, Étienne had seen.

pattern
slide the needle
take hold, oh gladsome girl
1421.80.4 these nights forever now stitched
Cinquains with stars

After a while, Catherine, ankle deep in water, stood up from the tree trunk on which she'd been sitting—a trunk jutting obliquely from the embankment where it was still anchored—and began like Chico to explore the river bottom. In the perfectly transparent water before her, she saw once more those groups of tiny fish rushing to get here and there, then suddenly turning back without any apparent reason.

"A bottle!"

Chico bent, freeing the bottle from the silt where it was
1422.115.7 buried, an old brown beer bottle, all scratched up and
Catherine and without a label, short and stout, a bottle from a bygone
Chico era. But unbroken.

> Having considered the question from all angles, Carmen was absolutely convinced that Terry was planning a surprise party for her 36th birthday. After all, 36 was the product of 3 times 12, and Terry was sensitive to such
> 1423.110.8 things. If she was right, well then her own se-
> A Day Off cret project seemed to be all the more fitting.

1424.31.10
Questions with "Would you like to walk a little further that way?"
Answers "OK."

> In the process of writing, a number of acci-
> 1425.17.8 dents occurred that confirmed the underlying
> Chance theory. That was very satisfying.

A fellow's gotta expect to be makin' a few mistakes along de way. An' you can expect de udders to screw it up as well."

"Me, I looks fer de companies dat everybody agrees on. Like, if everybody's sayin' dat de Billy Bully company's about to go up to seven dollars, 'cept fer dis one fellow who tinks she's only goin' up to four, well, den I gets real careful. On account of even de analysts're gonna fall into de trap o' wishful tinkin'. Dey doesn't do it on purpose. Dat's just de way of tings. Nobody sees one hundred percent wot's goin' on inside der own head."

. . .

"So on account of de wishful tinkin', dey comes up wid different predictions. Well, fer me, dey all has to be in de same ballpark, udderwise it's no go."

Zed was following, and agreed.

"Same time, you has to be mindful. You has to listen to de contrarians."

"De who?"

"De contrarians. Der de analysts wot's always tinkin' de exact opposite of all de udders. Dey looks fer de wee crack in de wall. On account of, wedder you likes it or not, der's bound to be one."

Zed appeared to be discouraged. 1426.85.2 The Stock Market

"Don't go gettin' all boddered. It sounds a whole lot more complicated dan it is."

> But as valuable as a theory may be, it is futile to adhere to it every day. A kind of intermittence then. A necessary intermittence, vital even. Must we absolutely grab that bull by the horns? Perhaps, but not today. No, today the bull is too much bull. Today something else calls to us. So be it. Like the movement of a pendulum. The pendulum never stops, never attains its limit. There's no relation of cause and effect here: the pendulum never stops; the pendulum repeatedly attains its limit. Who would dare argue that the pendulum retreats before the impossible? You may object that the pendulum cannot

> think in such terms because it isn't human. But who can say with certainty that we ourselves are not pendulums? Embrace the matter rather than forcing it. Become one with that which desires. Act on the manifest potential of things. And then one day, hop! The bull, both hands
> 1427.127.6 tightly gripping his horns. Intermittence. A
> Tactics technique. A tactic. A fervour. A fantasy.

They waded up to the first bend in the river, where Chico was surprised to see another splendid bend further ahead.

"She goes a long way, eh?"

"Almost all the way to Moncton."

Impressed, Chico looked once more at the river before him.

"There's a covered bridge about halfway there."

"A wot?"

"A covered bridge."

Chico still didn't understand.

"A bridge covered in wood, with a roof and windows. You've never seen a bridge like that?"

Chico shrugged, uncertain.

"We'll go by on our way, so you can see it."

They stood there in silence in the water for a while, contemplating the river's turning in the distance, before quietly turning back themselves the way they'd come.

"Did yous have a fishing rod?"

"No, only a kind of cage to catch the minnows you can see. I could catch a whole bunch in a day. I'd bring them home in a pail and put them in a big tub of water. We called it a gully in those days."

"Granny's got a gully..."

1428.115.8 "See? It's a fine word. Only in school they taught us to
Catherine and say tub, and that made us forget gully."
Chico Chico understood.

> Because I sometimes open parentheses without closing them, because I launch beginnings that lead nowhere. Because I evoke trails that evaporate. Because all this is deceptive. Readers think they've guessed a meaning, imagine a direction, a probable action, a possible resolution. Wild goose chases. Yes, open parentheses, initiatives that lead nowhere, trails that evaporate. As in life. Possibilities, ambiguities, incompletetions. In light of all of which, it becomes occasionally necessary to rethink, reinterpret, reread. Not really a theory. More like a precaution: to rule nothing out, because everything can end up being useful. Not to presume.

1429.88.12
Freedom

"Don't be takin' dis de wrong way or nuttin', only it stuns me just a wee bit to 'ear you talkin' like dis 'bout de stock market'n all."

...

"I doesn't know you dat way. Wot I mean to say, I never tawt you 'ad it in you!"

...

"I suppose it oughtn't to be surprisin' me, on account of de way you tawt of how to finance de lofts, an' den you does run yer own business..."

...

"An' Carmen wid de bar, well dat's a business as well."

...

"An you 'aven't said a word to Carmen, you little noggyhead..."

Terry was laughing.

"I can't get it in me 'ead you hid dis from 'er."

Terry, still laughing, protested:

"'Tisn't dat I wanted to be hidin' it from 'er. I only started out dat way, wid little bits. I didn't want to be tellin' her an' puttin' her on de edge of 'er nerves fer nuttin'.

She 'ad enough to tink about wid de bar startin' up an' all. Plus, she was pregnant."

Zed understood but, at the same time, it bothered him because it was as though he too was now participating in the cover-up. He'd been caught before by Carmen in this sort of misdeed, and he didn't want it to happen again.

"Well, seems to me now's de time to tell 'er."

"Matter o' fact, I almost told 'er dis mornin'. Came dat close."

"And wot?"

"Don't know. I was afraid 'twould break me luck."

"You told me luck had no part in it!"

"I know! Dat's not wot I mean."

The two guys were enjoying this arguing back and forth. Zed insisted:

"De way dese tings go, she'll most likely be tinkin' I's de one got you started."

1430.85.4 The Stock Market

Terry could see his friend's point; he even agreed with him, up to a point."

"I'll tell 'er afore long. Promise."

1431.89.11 Irritants

> Trout bite because they're hungry. Salmon, well, they don't eat flies. They bite because the fly irritates them.

"So, I'd put all the fish in the tub, and every fifteen minutes I'd go and check if they were still swimming."

...

"Dey swam for quite a while. I'd been careful to use salt water. Only I'd forgotten the cat."

Chico raised his head, looked at Catherine, who continued:

"Each time I went back, seemed to me there were fewer than I expected, only I wasn't sure. The cat was probably eating them one at a time, only I wasn't *smart* enough to see it."

Her lapse into English with the word *smart* made Chico smile.

"Over that way, there's another bridge, maybe two. Iron bridges. Then at the end, she empties into Shediac Bay, with Grande-Digue on one shore and Shediac on the other."

...

...

...

"The water level's started to come down." 1432.115.9

Then, without warning, Catherine stretched gracefully Catherine and

and slipped gently into the water. Chico

> Terry realized that he liked having a secret in reserve. 1433.105.8 Reserves/ Reservations

Toward four o'clock in the afternoon, Carmen was happy to sit down by herself, to enjoy her favourite dessert and a coffee:

"Have you got any mocha cake left?"

It wasn't the first time that, in spite of everything, her little family had been at the heart of her day off. How could it be otherwise? Mimi and she might complain about the ups and downs of their conjugal and family lives, the truth was that Terry, Étienne, and Marianne's happiness was what mattered most to her, as her visit to the travel agent amply demonstrated. In any case, Terry too did his best for them, not to mention she was now convinced that he was organizing a surprise party for her 36th birthday. Leafing through the latest issue of *Elle* magazine, Carmen had the feeling she was biding her time before going home to spend a quiet Friday evening 1434.110.12

with Terry and the kids. A Day Off

> Examination question for Ancient French (FRAN 1755): Demonstrate by means of multiple examples that Pascal Poirier is right to

> 1435.32.11 Exam Questions
>
> argue in his *Glossaire acadien* that it was, once again, the typesetters who fiddled with the word for bucket "*siau*" to make it "*seau*."

By late afternoon, Zed's introduction to the world of the stock market was transported to the Babar.

"Say a company's been around fer a hundred years... somewhere along de line, dey had to be doin' sometin' a wee bit clever to last dat long. Like, folks had to be wantin' to keep on workin' der, wot means dey's earnin' a decent wage, 'tisn't too dangerous, de bosses are nice enough, tings like dat."

Josse arrived in mid-conversation:

"Anudder beer, boys?"

Terry pushed aside the Molson he'd ordered early:

"Can you bring me sometin' dat makes sense... a Keith's."

Josse approved:

"I tawt 'twas weird you drinkin' Molson's. Aside from Québécois, I can't tink who drinks dat."

"I figured I'd test it."

But Josse was too busy to go into the details.

"How 'bout you, Zed?"

"Anudder Sleeman."

Once Josse had gone, Terry explained:

"I was after tinkin' o' buyin' some Molson's shares, only I just now changed me mind. On account of I has to like de product, I gotta be some way's proud o' wot de company's doin'."

"Me, I was tinkin' maybe Canadian Tire..."

"Now dat's a good example. Der's no reason to tink Canadian Tire's gonna be goin' out o' business anytime soon, so once you've bought in, you checks like once a week, only to be sure der's nuttin' funny goin' on. Sometimes you gets to feelin' sometin's goin' on. Like when a company's makin' big changes. Let's say, I don't know, maybe Canadian Tire decides to start buildin' churches."

Zed burst out laughing.

"Doesn't mean 'tis a bad ting, mind you, only you has 1436.85.5 The Stock Market
to ask yerself why."

> In *Don Giovanni*, Mozart more or less writes himself onto the stage by having excerpts from operas in vogue at the time, including his *The Marriage of Figaro*, played during a feast being prepared by the celebrated protagonist. In similar fashion, the character France Daigle once
> saw Carmen in a café leafing through an issue 1437.96.12 Characters
> of *Elle* magazine.

Josse returned with Terry and Zed's order:

"Where's Bernie got to dese days? Been a dog's age since I seen 'im."

"Ee's workin' in Grand Manan."

What's ee at over der?"

"Salmon tanks. A great big contract. Dey doesn't come 'ome every weekend, takes too long. Dey'd radder put in de time workin', an' finish up sooner."

And once Josse was gone:

"Well, der might still be some money in de fish busi- 1438.85.6 The Stock Market
ness after all."

> To adhere (or not to adhere) to something. To a theory, for example. The notion of adherence. Of adherences. Something that sticks, that irritates. What do I mean, exactly? I don't know. To not always know where something is going to end up, though you take pains to imagine (take pains, take pain). Yes, at times, I'm pained, the idea pains me. To save (again this notion of insufficiency, of loss) or to spare (i.e., to handle with care, caringly, with skill) time and worry, I take the gamble of agreeing with what I'll end

1439.124.8 Religion

up doing, saying, writing. I endorse in advance
what will come. A writer's religion.

It may have been the change in routine — eating supper in his pyjamas? — that made Étienne forget the shattered vase. Or was it the accident of the vase that had subliminally modifed the experience of the bath, so that before getting in, Étienne had bent over, examined his toenails carefully, and shouted out to his father in the kitchen:

1440.93.3 Time

"Takes a long time, don't it Dad?"

CHAPTER 11

> *It is because the world is not done that literature is possible.*
>
> Roland Barthes, "Kafka's Reply" 1441.144.11
> *France-Observateur,* 1960 Epigraphs

Terry didn't understand:

"Only 'tis written Tuck Tape in big black letters on de roll! Luh…"

Carmen knew it all too well, except that:

"I'm only saying, that's not what the hardware folks call it. To them, 'tis tek tape."

Examining the package more closely, Terry read the more or less readable fine print on the inside of the roll of tape.

"Aha! De company's called Canadian Technical Tape. Dat must be de reason dey's callin' it tek tape."

He showed Carmen the roll, pointed to the fine print. Carmen read it, only because it was easier to read it than not to read it, and raised her eyebrows:

"What's certain is that there's not a whole lot of logic 1442.79.1
in their system." Oddities

> Along with the fishing hook, other simple ma-
> chines include the inclined plane, the wedge, 1443.114.10
> the lever, the winch, and the wheel. Inventions

"Me, I'll quit de day someone uses the adapted English word *buyé* to tell me they bought something."

1444.47.12 Yielding "You'll never quit."

. . .

1445.67.2 Terry's Notebooks

> goatee, foldaway, topinambour, turpitude, butcher's bill, justaucorps, serpentine, parapet.

Bent over, perfectly still and quiet, Chico and Catherine scanned the river bottom, waiting.

"'Tisn't easy, but it's possible."

Chico wanted very badly to succeed.

"Hide your hand a little deeper in the sand, but without stirring it up, so the water stays clear."

The minnows came and went without the slightest hint of stopping. Great patience was required.

"Der ticklin' me toes."

"Me too. It's as though they were nibbling at me."

After another little while, Catherine gave it a try, yanking her hand suddenly up and out of the water. Chico watched the water and mud drip until there was nothing left, and no fish. They waited a few minutes for the water to clear and for the river bottom to reappear before beginning again.

"One day, I caught three."

On his first try, Chico, too, failed to catch a black sucker. Fortunately, it was such a beautiful day that they didn't mind waiting for the water to clarify, and the schools of fish to return.

"Are de wee ones easier to catch dan de big ones?"

"I don't think so."

. . .

"Most folks called them *minnows* when I was a girl, but we called them barbels."

. . .

. . .

"Me grandad used to say dat, too."

"Is that right?"

"Ee'd say: 'Haul yer ass in 'ere, ya bottom feedin' barbel!"

Chico's imitation of his grandfather amused Catherine, but the boy's past was no laughing matter.

"Hun! That doesn't sound very nice…"

Chico confirmed her impression:

"Sometimes, ee had a sharp tongue."

…

"Ee's dead now."

"I know."

A long second passed.

"'Twas me dad killed 'im."

"I know."

Catherine didn't want to say too much, preferring to let Chico tell his story his way.

"If I'd'a bin der, I might 'ave bin able to stop 'im…"

"You think so?"

Catherine had answered calmly, but she was shaken to hear Chico talk so candidly about such a shattering event.

"One time, I stopped dem. Granny was bawlin', so I startin' in yellin'."

…

"When me dad saw me, ee trew de knife down an' run off."

Catherine imagined the scene, and felt herself trapped between the awkwardness of the moment and her own emotions. But Chico did not give her time to react:

"'Ere dey come!"

1446.115.10
Catherine and
Chico

> In the U.S.A., Chapter 11 is the equivalent of a company declaring bankruptcy. Personal bankruptcies are relegated to Chapter 7.

1447.21.8
More or Less
Useful Details

"How come you's puttin' dat piece of metal in de hole o' dat udder piece o' metal, Grandad?"

"On account of dat's de way we fools nature, so de porch'll be keepin' straight."

"I knows nature."

"Awh, do ya now?"

"Yes. Nature, dat's everytin' dat we can't be inventin.'"

The old man was impressed:

"Yah, I suppose dat's one way you could be sayin' it."

And to prolong the conversation a little, the grandfather added:

"I wonders wot de bronze fly would say."

"Who's fly, Grandad?"

1448.127.7 Tactics "De bronze fly. You doesn't know de bronze fly?"

> The shards of shattered vase lie at the bottom of the pail containing broken glass, not to be
> 1449.42.9 Sorting mixed in with other recyclable trash, so as not to injure the sorters.

With lightning speed, Chico closed his hand and drew his arm out of the water. When he opened his fingers, a minnow wiggled twice and fell back into the water. Catherine was amazed.

"You got one!"

Still stunned by the surprise, Chico gazed at his open hand where the minnow had appeared and then disappeared.

"You caught one! That's so rare!"

1450.115.11 Catherine and Chico Chico liked the fact that he'd succeeded in doing something rare.

> Clumsily scribbled on a page of Terry's notebook:
>
> Yellow Breton
> 95 euros
> 19 × 32
> 1451.118.10 Concerning Yellow susanjonesart.com
> Paypal

"Houses, houses, houses. Lovely houses, ugly houses, a house where people're dyin' of AIDS, even doh dey don't look sick, another house where I's dyin' of AIDS meself an' I'm not really sick at all. Sidaware. Another house, small, all alone in a parking lot. Houses along the road. Houses you have to climb ladders to get into. Houses with cellars, houses without cellars. Houses with doors too small for me to get in. Houses, houses, houses.

"Wot do you mean by sidaware?"

"I don't know. It just seemed to fit der. Have you ever heard that word?"

"No." 1452.109.12

"Me neither. Could be I just invented it." Dreams

> Odd fact, the helical thread of screws was invented long before the screw. In fact, almost 4,000 years separate the invention of the thread 1453.79.5
> and its application to the screw. Oddities

Before heading back, Catherine suggested they pick some blueberries he could take to his granny.

"You says granny, too?"

"Sure. 'Round here, we said granny."

Leaving the path, they discovered a clearing where blueberries were large and abundant. Their harvesting went quickly.

"Are you gonna be marryin' Zed, den?"

The question made Catherine smile.

"I don't know. He's awfully nice..."

"Does you tink ee's good lookin'?"

Catherine couldn't help but laugh:

"Yes!"

...

...

... 1454.115.12

"What do you think—should I marry him?" Catherine and

"Yes." Chico

wee girl saw nothing
neither mean games nor fighting
eyes nose mouth down on the ground
1455.75.3 snowman on every side
Tankas going, gone, Patti? Patti?

"Der's sometin' goin' on wid de lofts."

"Wot're you on about?"

"Lionel an' Sylvia were in to see Zed yesterday in de afternoon. Looked right serious."

"Dat's it?"

"I don't know, I's got a queer feeling."

. . .

"Dey's sayin' ee lost a whole lot o' money in 'is companies overseas."

1456.108.5 "Been, wot, ten years folks bin sayin' dat?"
Rumours "Der's sometin' goin' on, dat's all I's sayin.'"

> In the domain of torsion, the fastener is said to be female when the thread is inside the structure, as in the common nut. The fastener is said to be male when the thread is external to the structure, for example in the basic screw. Experience leads one to conclude that our complex world would not have held together
> 1457.125.10 for 10 seconds without the sexualization of this
> Sexuality elementary machine.

"Dad, wot're you plannin' on doin' wid dose old pennies?"

"Don't know yet. Why's dat?"

Étienne shrugged his shoulders.

"Yer tinkin' you'd like to 'ave dem fer yer collections; is dat it?"

Étienne nodded.

Terry stretched out his arm, grabbed hold of the glass jar on the topmost of the corner shelves.

"Der you go. A gift."

Étienne jumped for joy.

"Now don't go wastin' dem on candies at de store. When I has a bit o' time, I'll tell you wot's special 'bout dem dat makes dem wort' keepin'. An' we'll separate out dem dat're real special from dose dat're not all dat special. So as to make sure you don't go spendin' dose dat're really wort' keepin'."

But Étienne was already in his room putting his new acquisition in his drawer of treasures.

"Did ya 'ear wot I's sayin'?" 1458.113.12

"Yes, Dad." Collections

> Examination question for Machine Design II course (GMEC 4223): design a production line in which at least one of the components is responsible for detecting any problems on said line. Also integrate mechanisms designed to remedy the different categories of problems (ref: Glassnolt scale of errors) and explain why these subtle errors must absolutely be avoided 1459.70.11
> (ref: Voltgass scale of errors). Errors

"You never eat any yourself?"

"Sometimes I bring some home, but most of the time I put them back. The hook goes in just on the corner of the lip, where the flesh is pretty resistant, so it doesn't do much damage."

...

"The most important thing is not to damage the ears, not to make them bleed. Sometimes you have to use pliers, if the hook is in too deep."

...

"To release it, you hold the trout under the water in both your hands, in the direction of the current, and wait until it recovers. When she starts to move, you know she's ready."

. . .

1460.18.4 A Place for Folks "The releasing is as moving as the catching. It's a powerful feeling to be in contact with the trout at that instant."

> On February 25, 1980, on rue des Écoles in Paris, a van struck the critic, semiologist and
> 1461.78.1 Accidents professor Roland Barthes, who died a month later of his injuries. He was 65 years old.

"Me, 'twas every time I goes to tee off. Der was all de time a tree or a shockin' big branch in me way. I had no way to take any kind o' swing, dat tree was all de time in my way."

"Me, 'tis when I goes to plant de tee! I couldn't get 'er in de ground! I's after pushin' down on 'er, over 'ere and
1462.109.2 Dreams der, and den over a ways off, only dat damn ting wouldn't go in. Can't tell ya 'ow many times I's 'avin' dat dream!"

1463.132.12 Malapropism

> At times you need a rule(r).

Terry was especially proud of his gratin Dauphinois, and its perfect crust, exactly like the one he'd eaten in Lyon.

"Hey! Me recipe's disappeared! She were right 'ere only a minute ago!"

Terry and Étienne had seen Marianne commit her larceny, but they wanted to humour her.

"Étienne, did you take me recipe, boy?"

"Wot recipe?"

"Me recipe fer gratin Dauphinois! I 'ad it right eer under me nose not ten seconds ago!

Hiding behind the cupboard and out of Terry's sight, Marianne was giggling. Étienne, who could see her plainly, could also tell that she'd soon be needing to urinate.

"Maybe it fell on de floor."

Terry shuffled a few things on the counter to pretend he was searching. Marianne was ecstatic.

"De page was right der on de corner o' de table!"

Terry pretended to look some more, opened and closed several drawers and cupboard doors.

"An' where's Marianne, I wonder?"

Étienne played innocent:

"Well, I don't know, do I, Dad."

Terry went to look for her in her bedroom.

"Marianne?"

By now she had put both plump little hands over her mouth to smother the laughter that was coming out of her eyes. 1464.23.11 Potatoes

> Simple tactic modelled on simple machines: to keep mum. 1465.127.3 Tactics

Zed asked Chico and Catherine how they'd spent the day.

"Chico had never seen a covered bridge, so I took him to see one."

"Is dat right? Where?"

"By the Weisner."

Zed was not so easily fooled:

"An' dat's wot's got de boat of you laughin'?"

Now Chico and Catherine openly flaunted their complicity.

"We're not laughing. We're just in a good mood."

"I caught a barbel wid me hands!"

"Wow!"

"Only ee fell back in de water."

"Still! Dat's terrible hard to catch a fish wid yer hands! 'Ow did you manage dat?"

Chico could tell that Zed was really impressed; he was happy to add:

"An' we picked blueberries fer Granny."

"Is dat right? Dat's right nice!"

Zed opened the fridge door: 1466.36.9 Strawberries

"Are der some fer us, den?"

Then there are errors of naming. Stag, deer, buck, elk, reindeer, moose, caribou, Alaskan elk, wapiti? The American elk is called *orignal* in French, from the Basque *oregna* meaning "stag." Just as America takes its name from Amerigo Vespucci, who was not actually its first European visitor. Columbus (1492) and Cabot (1497) had set foot on the territory before him. But — another example of the unpredictable consequences of writing — the discovery was attibuted to him because he was the first to write down, in a 32-page letter, what he'd seen and experienced during his four voyages betweeen 1497 and 1504. For it is through writing and the art of storytelling that the dis-
1467.59.2 covery of the New World spread throughout
Knowledge the old country.

"Mum, I don't understand the story of Saint Louis. Dad explained it to me, only I still doesn't understand."

Carmen had no idea what story Terry might have told.

"You know yer Dad, sometimes he says things dat you'd have to be in his head to understand."

"How come?"

"Well, ee doesn't do it on purpose, it's just the way it happens."

Étienne considered this for a moment, then:

"Wot colour is it in yer 'ead, Mum?"

To please her son, Carmen looked inside her head:

"Mmm... it's not a bad bit nice, 'tis all shades of green. Like a beautiful forest. You?"

"Me, der's times 'tis orange, den sometimes blue almost black."

"Orange is nice."

"Yes, only 'tis far. A far orange."

"Awh?"

"Yes. Only you'd 'ave to be in me 'ead."

"Hey, yer like yer dad!" 1468.41.10 Lives of the Saints

"Well, Mum, you just said de same ting I was tinkin'!"

> Fly fishing for salmon is already such an incredible experience that it takes on ecstatic proportions when the catch is made with a fly of your own fabrication. 1469.129.12 Fantasies

"Cory Melanson? I wouldn't be wastin' so much as a match on Cory Melanson."

"What about Kyle, den?"

"Kyle Richard?"

"No, Kyle Léger."

"Ti-Kyle! Him, I'd maybe give 'im a tootpick if he asked me fer one, only it'd have to be at arm's lengt'. An' don't ferget, I said maybe."

"An' Jamie?"

"Jamie Bourque? What about Jamie Bourque?"

"Well, you know..."

"You wants to know if he really went an' poured de light, sweet crude down de drain afore de cops arrived?"

...

"Well, if dat's wot you wants to know, go find yerself a plumber." 1470.103.11 Disappearances

> By means of an ingenuous combination of the wheel and the lever, the Chinese invented the wheelbarrow more than 2,000 years ago, and kept it a secret for more than 100 years. The wheelbarrow had a major impact on warfare and construction. 1471.114.8 Inventions

"Mum, do you have saints you like a whole lot like Dad has?"

"Hmm... I'd have to think about it..."

"Dad likes Saint Christopher, who lives in a cabin by de bridge."

"That's right. Ee wears his medallion."

"An' Saint Bernadette Spirou, who gaddered a turn of whits."

"Of what?"

Étienne was taken aback; he didn't think he'd used an English word.

"That's how Grandad Thibodeau says it."

"It must be an old word, say it again."

"Whits."

"No, I've never heard that word."

"Mum, yer only sayin' that!"

"No! It's true!"

"But, Mum! It's the wee branches you pick up to start the fire!"

1472.41.5 Lives of the Saints

"Well, it's a new word for me. That's normal, you know. A person can't be knowing all the words."

1473.121.10 Things to Want

A river.

"Well, come to think of it, I did like Saint Francis."

"On account of?"

"Because he loved nature. Especially birds."

As she spoke, Carmen had dug her nails into Étienne's back and scratched him slightly, instead of simply lightly grazing over his skin the way she'd been doing while they talked.

1474.123.11 Carmen and Étienne

"Awh, dat feels good, Mum."

Carmen did it again.

"'Twas better the first time."

1475.92.7 Questions without Answers

Why not the string, the ladder, and even the needle, while we're at it?

"There are a lot o' saints with de same names. Me, I like the Saint Francis dat walked barefoot."

"In de snow, as well?"

"I don't think dey had snow over there."

"Where was it den?"
"In Italy."
"Wot else was ee doin'?"
"Ee talked to the trees."
Étienne was not all that surprised.
"Wot was ee sayin'?"

"Saint Francis thought that God was everywhere, in nature, in the animals, in the plants. So, for him, it was normal to talk to trees an' animals an' plants. It was as though he was talkin' to God."

"Well, wot was ee sayin' to de tree?"

"Once he asked an almond tree — that's a tree that yields almonds — he asked the almond tree to prove that it could hear him, as doh it was 'is brudder speakin'."

Étienne raised his head to look at Carmen; this story was something out of the ordinary."

?
"An' then the almond tree flowered."
Étienne's face lit up:
"That's well said, eh Mum?" 1476.41.6 Lives of the Saints

OK
Red Riding Hood
with neither axe nor wolf
Granny's better, rises, dresses
sometimes 1477.80.5 Cinquains

"I'm afraid people'll take me fer a dumb blond."
"Dat's weird. Yer not even blond."
. . .
"An' everybody knows you knows 'ow smart you is."
"Only I'm talkin' 'bout dose dat doesn't know me."
"An' who cares wot dey're tinkin', I'd like to know?"
"I do."
"Wot difference is it gonna make?"
"I know it makes no sense, that's why it's a fear, right?" 1478.137.8 Fears

1479.107.7 Necessities

The real makes fiction necessary.

"I tink I's gaining weight."

Carmen looked Terry over to see if it was true.

"I don't think so."

"Dis mornin' I had all kinds o' trouble gettin' me hand all de way down to de bottom o' me pocket. I 'ad to suck me belly in."

As he said this, Terry studied his stomach, drawing it
1480.23.10 in and letting it out.

Potatoes "We's gonna cut back on de potatoes fer a bit."

1481.70.12 Errors

Not to mention diagnostic errors.

"Seems to me tings was a whole lot denser before."

"What do you mean by dense?"

"Thicker. It's as though I's seein' right troo everytin'."

"You mean you have the impression you see more clearly?"

"Mm yes... an' no. Der's sometin' missin'."

"Colour?"

1482.133.11 "Colour would help, sure."

The Future "Maybe you've got cataracts."

black bird
lace in her beak
she's going her own way
1483.80.6 modern method of construction
Cinquains as if

"Alright, go half 'n half. One day you invent a game, an' de next time you play a game you already know."

"Only wot happens when we forgets?"

"When you forget wot?"

"When we can't remember wot game we's playin' de time before?"

Zed found these children's problems comical, but that

didn't stop him from trying to come up with solutions:

"Well, den you do heads or tails."

He was careful to say the French phrase, "*pile ou face*"; he'd been making an effort to include more French in his vocabulary now that he had Chico.

"Wot's dat?"

Zed took a coin from his pocket:

"You take a coin, one of you says heads or tails, an' you flips de penny, an it falls..."

"Awh! *Head or tail*! I know dat."

...

"Only we doesn't always 'ave money do we."

Zed dug into his pocket, found two more pennies, and offered them to Chico.

"You can hide dem different places outside, places only de two of yous'll know where to find dem."

Chico thought that was a good idea.

"Can I go an' hide dem right away?"

"If you like." 1484.135.7

Chico took the coins and ran off. Zed and Chico

> The Basque language, spoken by less than a million people in southwest France and northeast Spain, is one of those confounding linguistic exceptions referred to as language isolates. Basque is special in that it has existed without interruption since the second millenium before the Common Era, and because it has no kinship with the romance languages that surround it, nor with any other Indo-European language. And yet, Basque includes a sizable number of dialects, including Bizkaian, Gipuzkoan, Upper Navarrese, Navarrese-Lapurdian, and 1485.112.4
> Zuberoan. Languages

Josse did not look happy.

"I just met Solange an' Bob in town. Dey was askin' me

if 'twas true de Babar's closin.'"

"That's bizarre! Last week someone thought the bookstore was all set to close."

"Is dat so! Wonder who's startin' all dese rumours."

Carmen figured it must be a misunderstanding, but Josse seemed to be speaking from experience.

"You wouldn't believe wot folks'll do just to be causin' harm."

"You think? That someone would do that on purpose? Fer wot possible reason?"

Josse wasn't sure, but:

"Still, 'tis a terrible strange coincidence, wouldn't you say?"

"Maybe, only it doesn't worry me all that much. Der's always stories goin' round that aren't true. It's as though people thrive on it."

1486.98.3 Expressions "Still. I doesn't like de feelin'. Wot's de sayin' again, when der's smoke an' no fire?"

> Even Zed was intrigued: maybe Carmen was considering the pros and cons of aesthetic surgery? But to have what done? Lift up her
> 1487.87.9 The Body breasts? Fill out her buttocks? Liposuction her tummy? The inside of her thighs?

"Me mum likes Saint Francis on account of he walked barefoot in Nitaly."

Chico liked to listen to Étienne, especially at this moment when, each one armed with a magnifying glass, they were both concentrating on burning a circle into a piece of wood.

"An' because ee spoke to the birds an' de trees."

"Wot was ee sayin' to de trees?"

. . .

"Eh, wot was ee sayin' to the trees, den?"

"Do you eat almonds?"

"Sometimes."

"Me too. Almonds grow on trees."
"Luh! Der's smoke!" 1488.139.2 Étienne and Chico

surprise!
a naked man
ha ha ha Saint Francis
the almond-shaped eyes of children 1489.80.9 Cinquains
Mueslix

"Well, I doesn't agree wid dat."

"Wot do you mean, you doesn't agree? Der's no agreein' or disagreein' wid a fact."

"Still. I tink de needle belongs absolutely in de category of simple machines. Wot could be simpler dan dat?"

"Neverdeless, she's not on me list."

"Yer list?"

"De Wikipedia list for Chris' sake. Does you tink I's invented it meself dis minute?!" 1490.89.8 Irritants

> In the domain of excuses, the alibi, the subterfuge and the pardon are considered borderline experiences. 1491.86.3 Apologies

"It bodders me just a wee bit to tink yer hidin' something from me."

"Well, it is a surprise, isn't it!"

...

...

"An' a surprise's supposed to be something good, right?"

"Mostly, yes."

"So I oughtn't to be worryin', right?"

"Normally, no."

But Terry was not entirely reassured. He was really worried because he was going to have to find a way to transform into a pleasant surprise for Carmen the fact that he was playing — he reminded himself not to use the word *playing* — the stock market.

"My surprise may not be as excitin' as yers."

"A surprise is always a wee bit exciting all the same."

"'Tis more excitin' when you doesn't know it's comin'. You don't have de time to get ideas."

"That's true."

...

...

"Well, why'd ya go an' tell me you's doin' sometin' you couldn't be tellin' me in de first place?"

"I don't know. It just came out."

...

"Anyhow, I just wanted to let you know. I find it hard keeping it to myself."

Terry's anxiety only grew because he could see how happy and excited Carmen became whenever she mentioned the surprise she was preparing.

"Anyhow, to look at ya, I's pretty sure my surprise won't be half as excitin' as yers. I mean, I wouldn't want you to get yer hopes up..."

Carmen assumed Terry was simply trying to lower her expectations, so that the surprise — the party! — would be all that much more satisfying. And yet, he did seem awfully serious, not to say worried.

"To tell the truth, I think I know your secret."

"Dat would surprise me."

Terry's reply was perfunctory, but Carmen saw this as more pretense.

"If we don't stop talking about it, we'll ruin everything."

Carmen was right, Terry could see that. He searched for an amusing way to conclude.

1492.94.5 Terry and Carmen

"Give me one guess... Yer pregnant!"

"No!"

1493.60.12 Superstitions

A superstition gains strength when it comes time.

"Thanks fer givin' Étienne 'is bath."

Normally Terry and Carmen's day off included a reduction in domestic and parental responsibilities, but this particular day Carmen had forgone that privilege.

"It's nothing. I enjoy it, an' I don't get the chance to do it all that often."

Carmen spread the blanket over Terry and cuddled closer on the sofa.

"So den, 'twasn't just a strategy..."

"Wot do you mean?"

"Well, a way to be softenin' me up fer...you knows..."

"To make you talk, you mean? Never in me whole life would I do such a thing!"

Carmen's exaggerated tone made Terry laugh, but it did not appease his curiosity.

"We ought to be givin' ourselves a time limit."

Carmen played innocent:

"A time limit for what?"

Terry played along:

"To be tellin' each udder wot we's not tellin' each udder."

The movie was about to begin. Carmen pretended she didn't want to miss anything. And, now that she was convinced Terry was preparing a surprise party, she thought she might keep her own secret a little while longer. But not without teasing Terry a wee bit more:

"You're a big boy. When yer ready to tell me what you've got to tell, I guess you'll do it."

A reply that seemed to place the ball squarely in Terry's court.

1494.94.6 Terry and Carmen

1495.107.8 Necessities

Luck.

"Does it 'ave anyting to do wid..."

But Carmen stopped him right there.

"No, you already had your question, now we change the subject."

"Alright den, alright…"

Not to leave it at that, Carmen took the lead:

"What do you tink, den, about the Queen havin' to apologize for the deportation?"

Terry burst out laughing. For a diversion, this was a hell of a big one.

"Well, what?! Dat's about all anyone's talkin' about at the bar!"

Terry acquiesced:

"Well, fer one ting, de whole story's gettin' a wee bit old, an' fer anudder, 'tisn't really Élizabeth II's fault it happened, now is it?"

"Only that doesn't matter. It's still her role to be apologizin.'"

1496.94.7 Terry and Carmen

"I knows dat, only…"

"Shh, it's starting."

1497.38.5 Onions

> German proverb: he who grows onions does not notice their odour.

At the next commercial break:

"Was yer family one o' dem wot was deported?"

"Really, I don't know. Yours?"

"Don't know fer a fact, only der's Thibodeaus down in Louisiana. Dat probably means dey was, I suppose."

…

"Me dad an' mum was never talkin' 'bout all dat when I's a boy. I doesn't tink it boddered dem all dat much. 'Tis only since folks won't stop talkin' 'bout Acadia dat dey's become Acadians, seems like."

…

"I mean, we was eatin' poutines an' chicken stew an' all dat, only 'twasn't on account of we's Acadian, 'twas just dat we liked dose tings."

"Exactly! It's on account of you were Acadians that you liked dem. If you hadn't eaten poutines when you were little, you'd have trouble eating it now. Look at de

Québécois! An remember 'ow we had to get Étienne used to eatin' it. At the start, ee was eatin' nuttin but the sugar!"

Terry did not entirely agree.

"Well, we eats Madawaska ployes, an' we was never eatin' dat before."

1498.105.4 Reserves/ Reservations

"That's different. Buckwheat pancakes are good for real."

> Catherine's dream. Catherine is lying in a quiet corridor in a hospital. The lighting is slightly bluish. Her bed is raised so that she's reading by the light of a sylized wall lamp about a half metre down from the ceiling. A childhood friend, Louise, is resting nearby, in a room in the hallway perpendicular to hers. Catherine visits her occasionally, but without leaving her bed; instead she moves the bed along on its wheels. From time to time, the two young women read together in the same bed; the bed is Catherine's, in its assigned place in the corridor. They agree to exchange books, but this seems complicated. A nurse comes to inform Catherine that the surgery she underwent was successful. However, she will require treatment for another disease, and is to be transferred to the floor above for that purpose. Louise, on the other hand, is released.

1499.109.10 Dreams

Terry poured them more coffee, and took up the conversation:

"I's tinkin' 'bout dat last night... I enjoys meetin' a real anglophone who's nice and makes an effort at speakin' French. In me head, ee's almost not an anglophone."

"Yes, I know what you mean."

"So den, wot I's wonderin' is wot're de English 'round 'ere gonna do? I mean, dem dat doesn't want to understand. Dey's de ones dat ought to be apologizin'. Or changin' der attitude, *at least*."

"*Au moins.*"

"Yes, Dad, you ought to say '*au moins*' not '*at least*.'"

"Alright, alright den, *au moins. Au moins, au moins*… I tink' I won't be fergettin' now."

Carmen looked at Étienne, and winked.

1500.127.8 "Hey, you two, are youse *gangin' up* on me now, or
Tactics wot?"

> Visit the King Cole's teahouse in Sussex and
> strike up a conversation with the owners to
> 1501.56.4 find out where Acadian's attachment to this
> Pilgrimages particular brand comes from.

"Well, if de Queen 'erself apologized, I suppose dat would get de English to tinkin' at least. She'd 'ave provided a good example."

Carmen nodded, and took up the argument:

"If you ask me my real opinion, I tink we'd like it at the time, only in de long term, I'm not so sure."

"Wot does you mean?"

"Well, now, on account of she's not apologized, we can still be sayin' dey did dis an' dat to us, stole our lands, burned our houses, shipped us out on boats, half of dem drownin'…"

Listening to Carmen, Terry felt it was perhaps the first time he'd imagined what the Great Upheaval had actually and concretely meant.

"The fact is that something really bad happened to us. If the Queen apologizes, well, that'll provide some comfort fer a while, an den afterwards, we'll have to change our story, change our attitude. Things wouldn't be the same anymore, would they?"

Terry protested:

"On account of why not? Wouldn't be erasin' de Deportation. Apologies doesn't erase de fact!"

"No? When a person apologizes, aren't we supposed to be fergettin' the harm they did us?"

Terry was not sure of the weight of a pardon. Were apologies and a pardon the same thing? But Carmen quickly added:

"In any case, wedder it erases or not, 'twould change things all de same. Once we've had der apologies, we won't be able to say, awh, all de misery we suffered, blablabla. Really, to be honest, in de end, we'd have to add: an' then dey apologized."

But Terry didn't see how an apology from the British Crown would deprive Acadians of their right to complain.

"Only, an apology dat comes like two hundred and fifty years later, dat's way too late to change anyting!"

"Exactly. Which is why der's folks dat wants money along wid de apology. So dat sometin' really changes. So dat we can catch up economically."

Carmen's reasoning reminded Terry of their first meeting on August 16th in the Parc de la Petitcodiac, when Carmen had tried to prove that the Petitcodiac River could be considered the opposite of a delta.

"Well, what do you tink?"

Terry realized that he'd drifted, and returned to the present:

"An apology wid money? Well, sure, an' why not?"

Even Carmen was not opposed to money in this case, but she knew that there's many a slip 'twixt cup and lip.

"In any case, even widout the money, if the English changed, startin' with the Queen apologizin', we'd end up seein' and understandin' things differently, too."

"You means to say we'd no longer be de real Acadians we is today?"

Yes, that's exactly what Carmen meant.

"An' would dat be a good ting, den?"

Carmen wasn't sure. Terry took a bite of his toast generously covered in jam, chewed, swallowed and, after licking a limp strawberry off his thumb where it had fallen, concluded:

1502.86.11 Apologies “No, de Acadians won’t be changin’. I can’t see dat happenin.”

> The *Robert* dictionary includes a separate entry for the *y* as the popular substitute for the third-person personal pronoun *il*, in addition
> 1503.4.9 Scrabble to the entries for the pronominal and adverbial *y*, and the algebraic *y*.

“Zed, are you gonna marry Catherine?”

Chico’s question made Zed smile.

“I’d like dat, only I don’t know if she’s willin’!”

Chico did not dare tell him he knew more.

“Me too, I’d like dat.”

“Wot? You want to marry Catherine?”

Zed’s teasing made Chico laugh.

“No! Not me! You!”

Zed put a browned minced-beef patty in Chico’s plate, beside the mashed potatoes and creamed corn.

“Most times ’tis the boy dat asks de girl if she’ll marry ’im, only der’d be nuttin’ wrong if de girl was to ask de boy.”

Chico began by tasting the potatoes, but he burned himself and spit the mouthful back into his plate. Zed pretended not to notice, and continued:

“One way or de udder, ’tis best to ask when yer close to sure dat de udder person’ll be sayin’ yes.”

“You doesn’t tink she’ll want to?”

Zed measured his words:

“Well, I tink she might, only I’s waitin’ a wee bit longer to be sure sure.”

Chico had wrapped a mouthful of meat in creamed corn, and was all set to eat it.

“I wouldn’t want ’er to be sayin’ no. ’Twould hurt me feelings, like dey say.”

His mouth full, Chico nodded to indicate he understood.

"So, you'd like it too, if Catherine came to live wid us?" 1504.135.8 Zed and Chico

> No question that we do not want to be only French. Especially if that would mean being content with a kind of bondage. Become doe 1505.58.11 rather than docile, American eland. Extensions

"Well, giving them these wasn't such a great idea."

"Wot's dat?"

Terry had replied more or less mechanically, before looking up to see the two magnifying glasses dangling from Carmen's extended arms.

"Awh, dat."

"I mean really, 'twasn't your best idea ever."

Terry took it with a smile, and tried to minimize the possible dangers.

"Well, every kid learns dat sooner or later. It whiles away de time during de long summer days. You start by burnin' a circle on a bit o' wood, den you try to burn some paper or hay."

Terry had thought it prudent to mention the latter risk, but he quickly went on before Carmen could react:

"Only nuttin' ever really catches fire, on account of 'tis too slow. A kid's only got de patience to make a few black spots 'ere an' der, an' den you sees a bit o' smoke."

Carmen tried to remember at what age she herself had learned the trick, trying to decide if she was being too severe, or if it might be reasonable to let Étienne and Chico play with magnifying glasses.

"An' anyhow, if dey really wants to make a fire, match-es're a whole lot simpler."

"Sure, only accidents happen. If they leave the glass lying about somewheres, an' de sun starts beatin' down? You know how kids are..."

Terry hadn't thought of this possibility. But did they have to be so careful all the time?

"'Tis a bit wearisome to be always tinkin' of all de pros

and cons. It breaks de *spur of de moment*."

"The spontaneity."

"Breaks de spontaneity of life, don't you tink? Our parents wasn't all de time worryin' like dat 'bout us, now were dey?"

Carmen didn't really have the strength to insist. Instead, she left Terry with the impression that she was
1506.103.12 perhaps a bit of a mother hen, and decided to simply
Disappearances make those magnifying glasses disappear.

> Ancient frescos show the Egyptians line fishing along the Nile. The Jews and the Romans are said to have fished with a line for relaxation. As
> 1507.106.3 for artificial lures, they appeared later, during
> Customs the second century BCE.

"Now what! As doh, dey was out to have fun settin' fire to every damn ting around dem!"

"Women're more likely to be worryin' 'bout tings like dat dan men are."

"You knows it."

"Still, dey says der's a terrible lot o' forest fires startin' up on account of de sun beatin' down on bits o' glass."

Terry knew this, but it didn't seem to be the same thing.

"Well den, wot're you gonna do?"

1508.13.11 Terry raised his eyebrows, thinking, then:
Paternity "I can't be obsessin' o'er it, is all."

> Irritation (superfluous?) at the disproportion between things with the same names, between a mole (on your face) and a mole (the cylindrical mammal), for example. Why? Because they
> 1509.131.2 both emerge from below the surface? (Other
> Parenthesi(e)s examples?)

"Is it a disease to be a hermit?"

...

"Eh? Did you 'ear me?"

"I'm only tinkin' on it...fer once we've a word's dat's said more easily in French dan English 'round 'ere. Hermit. A hermit. 'Tis a whole lot easier just to be sayin' *ermite*. De French was right smart to drop de *h*."

"Alright den, *fair enough*. Only is it a disease to be a 1510.82.5
nermit?" Moncton

> Often, the pronunciation of words is the only thing that differentiates Acadian from standard French. For example, Acadians may say "*ertchuler*" instead of "*reculer*" for "back up," "*aidjuille*" instead of "*aiguille*" for "needle," "*caneçon*" instead of "*caleçon*" for "under-
> pants." Also, Acadians will interchange the 1511.19.11
> "*en*" and "*ne*," and switch sentences into the Interesting
> negative without rhyme or reason. Details

"I can't find the toothpaste. Do you know where it is?"

Étienne had not prepared a lie in advance in response to this question, so he screwed up his courage and went with the truth:

"Yes."

"Well den, where?"

"Under my bed."

"Under your bed?"

"Yes."

"An' what's it doin' there?"

Étienne stood tall:

"'Twas for painting."

"For painting?"

"Yes."

Surprised as much by her son's candour as by this new use for toothpaste, Carmen hesitated a moment before deciding on how to follow up on the incident:

"Have you run out of paint, then?"

"No."

"Well, go an' fetch it, den…"

"Wot, the paint?"

"No, the toothpaste."

Étienne went to get the tube, and brought it back to his mother. Carmen squeezed some toothpaste onto her brush.

"Is your drawing done?"

"No."

Carmen gave the tube back to Étienne:

"Will you show it to me when it's finished?"

Étienne would have liked to feel triumphant, but the drawing in question wasn't turning out very well, and the idea of having to finish it left him rather cold. Nevertheless:

1512.103.9 Disappearances

"OK, Mum."

1513.107.10 Necessities

Complicity.

Entering the hardware store, Terry wasn't convinced he'd find what he was looking for.

"Hi, Terry!"

He turned round to see an old schoolmate wearing the store's regulation shirt.

"Awh, hallo Serge! I didn't know you's workin' 'ere."

"I's in de warehouse before. Dey decided to put me 'ere on de floor, so's I'd be getting' a bit of experience."

"Wot? I suppose you'll be a manager afore long?"

"Dat's de idea. Dey's doin' der best to convince me."

Terry had hit the mark. He'd alluded to the manager's job in fun really, just a way to renew acquaintance with an old school chum that he hadn't seen for years.

"Really?! Well, why not? Better you dan some udder fellow!"

"Awh, I don't know really. I'm not dat fond o' stress."

Terry could understand that:

"You was fine in de warehouse, is dat it den?"

Serge appreciated Terry’s understanding:

“Dat’s it exactly.”

“Well an’ still, ’tis nice to know dey’s tinkin’ yer smart enough to be doin’ de manager’s job.”

“Dat’s true, I suppose. Hadn’t tawt of it dat way. ’Ow ’bout you, den, wot’re you up to?”

“I belongs to Didot Books wid a partner. You know, in de lofts building on Church?”

“Sure, sure, somebody told me dat. ’Ow’s dat whole ting workin’ out?”

“Not bad at all, really.”

“An’ yer store as well?”

“Just fine. Better’n I expected, anyhow.”

“Excellent!”

“Now, if you could be givin’ me a hand wid dis ’ere...”

Terry had trouble getting his hand down to the bottom of his pocket.

“I swear I must be gainin’ weight. Dese jeans was never dis tight before.”

Finally he dug out what he was looking for, and handed it to Serge:

“Aha! A screw! An’ she’s a wee little ting, to boot!”

Serge examined the tiny metal piece.

“I’ll tell ya, I doesn’t tink we’s got one like it, only I knows where you can find dem.” 1514.7.7 Useful Details

> Contrary to what one might think, the onomatopoeia *patati-patata* is in no way related to the word “*patate*.” Rather it’s an imitation of the sound of a galloping horse’s hooves. 1515.23.12 Potatoes

A sudden cry. Had his mother injured herself?

“Étienne, come ’ere an’ take a look at dis!”

And immediately he remembered the shards of vase at the bottom of the pail of broken glass. He’d never thought Carmen would discover the misdeed at a time when Terry wasn’t home.

"What happened to my vase?"

Étienne noticed Carmen's almost neutral tone, as though since her initial cry of surprise, she'd had time to mourn her loss and to reconcile herself with life. He approached the pail, looked within:

. . .

"When did dat happen?"

"De udder day."

"What, it just fell?"

Étienne had the feeling that Carmen's questions required no reply, that his mother had simply called him to her side as a kind of witness.

"I sure liked dat vase, only things like that do break. It's to be expected."

Étienne, too, stood in contemplation of the shards at the bottom of the pail. A solemn moment passed.

"I suppose 'twas an accident, eh?"

Étienne looked up at his mother, unsure whether he ought to reply.

"Good ting der's a whole lot of nice vases. We'll find another."

As she finished her sentence, Carmen bent over, wrapped one arm around her son and plunged the other into the pail, pulled out a handful of broken shards, and admired their shapes and colour.

"They're lovely pieces, no?"

Yes, Étienne too thought they were lovely and, what's
1516.86.9 Apologies more, he figured Terry would probably not have to apologize.

1517.47.8 Yielding Abandonment could be the opposite of loss.

Having compared Terry's screw to several others he'd picked out from among the hundreds of tiny drawers aligned along the aisle, Serge concluded:

"No, we doesn't have it. Must be a machine screw. You'll find dat at Maritime Fasteners."

"Yer pullin' me leg..."

Serge understood Terry's discouragement, and tried to cheer him up:

"An' over der, if dey doesn't 'ave it, dey can 'ave it made."

Terry answered laughing:

"You mean to tell me dat, wid all de millions of screws you's got 'ere, I'll be havin' to go an 'ave one made?"

Unphased, Serge also managed a laugh:

"Yes sir, an' it'll even cost ya tree or four dollars..."

The two men took a moment to catch their breath, and for Terry to face the facts:

"An' where are dey at, den, Maritime Fasteners?"

"On Collishaw. Ask to talk to Ulysse, ee knows hard- 1518.122.10 Sports
ware inside out.

> Page 13. Understand the capitalist system thoroughly. Always remember that you are always dealing with someone trying to sell you something. Selling and reselling inevitably lead to the loss of any sense of value. The notion of 1519.57.11 Photocopies
> imperfect markets.

"Der's rumours running round dat de Babar an' Terry's bookstore're gonna be shuttin' down."

"Well, for 'eaven's sake! If der's one person who'd know if der was sometin' goin' on, 'twould be me!"

"Dat's wot I's tinkin' as well. An' I can't tink dey'd be separatin' or nuttin' like dat."

"Dose two?! No way! No, an' de wee one, isn't she de cutest ting?! I tell you, I'd swallow 'er up whole!"

"Strange, doh, de way she don't talk much, eh? Me sister's got a boy dat same age an' ee never stops comin' out wid new words."

"Children doesn't all develop de same." 1520.108.7 Rumours

"I knows it. Would you say Carm's de motherly type?" 1521.67.12 Terry's Notebooks

> Bildungsroman? Kunstleroman?

"Dat gizmo's no good at all. Won't do de job 'tall."

"Well, de water comes out. Isn't dat wot she's supposed to do?"

The worker lifted his cap, and scratched the top of his head. Was he going to abandon the job? Laugh at me?

"Ought to be comin' out like gangbusters. De way she's
1522.130.11 workin' now, we'd still be 'ere a week from Tursday."

Work "Awh."

> On the refrigerator door, a newspaper photo of Marianne and Renardi, Dieppe's mascot for the
> 1523.134.10 Canada Day celebrations. The caption states
> Marianne that she is two years old.

"Der a fellow 'ere by de name of Ulysse?"

"Ee's not in yet."

"Awh. Wot time does ee come in usually?"

"Well, ee oughtta be 'ere by now."

Terry could hear the irritation in the response. The clerk added:

"Ee 'ad to drive 'is wife to work."

Terry figured the wait would be short. But after 10 minutes, unable to endure it any longer, he thought perhaps the fellow behind the counter might be able to help him just as well. He brought his tiny screw out:

"I's lookin' fer a screw like dis' 'ere."

Busy putting away a thick and heavy catalogue, the employee glanced in Terry's direction, but did not immediately see the screw. A few seconds later, he exclaimed:

"Lard tunderin'! Dat's de tiniest screw I ever saw!"

"Dat explains how come I went an' lost one…"

"Where does she go, den?"

"On me wife's defibrillator."

"De wot?"

"You know, de razors dat tear out 'er hairs rawder dan cuttin' dem."

"Der's such a ting as dat?"

Terry's cynicism was mounting:

"You doesn't 'ave a wife o' your own to be askin' dat."

But the fellow was not lacking in nerve:

"An' wot was you tinkin' takin' apart a machine like dat, I wonder?" 1524.22.8 Overheard Conversations

All things considered, the Spanish language is yellow. 1525.112.12 Languages

"Terry thinks when he's sleeping."

There wasn't much that Étienne could say about Terry that could surprise Chico.

"Wot does ee tink about?"

. . .

"Eh? Wot's ee tinkin' about?"

"The Deportation."

"Wot's dat?"

. . . 1526.139.10 Étienne and Chico

"Eh? Wot's dat?"

Explanations. 1527.107.11 Necessities

Ulysse, who had finally showed up, proceeded more methodically:

"If I were you, I'd send the machine back to the manufacturer or to his designated repairer."

Terry was slightly surprised by the man's formal manner, and by the expression "designated repairer," although he had no trouble understanding it. He replied:

"Der's no one fixes dem 'round 'ere. I'd be sendin' it to Ontario. Dat's why I was tinkin' I'd do 'er meself, 'twould be less complicated."

Ulysse cocked an eye at Terry, thereby expressing his doubts on the ability of ordinary mortals to repair sophisticated devices. Terry wasn't going to allow himself to be overawed.

"Awh, I know I fixed 'er. Only I lost one o' de screws dat fastens de cover."

Ulysse looked squarely at Terry now, and then pulled an obese catalogue from below the counter. Terry immediately noticed that the man seemed to know exactly where to look among the hundreds of pages filled with columns of letters and numbers identifying a multitude of machines and their derivatives.

"How many are you goin' to be wantin' den?"

Terry hesitated.

"I were you, I'd take two. It's two dollars more for the second one."

"An' de first one, 'ow much is dat one?"

"Four."

Ulysse did a rapid tattoo on the keys of his calculator:

"That would come to six dollars and 86 cents in all. You'd have it in ten days at the most. We'll call you when it comes in."

Terry found that indeed Ulysse knew what he was about.

"Alright, den. Go ahead an' order dem."

Ulysse wrote a long series of letters, numbers and dashes on the order form to identify the screw in question. Terry felt confident he could trust him, but all the same:

"So den, you'll be phonin'? On account of some folks says dat, only dey never does."

Ulysse did not take it badly.

"We call as soon as we can. We don't like things to drag on. Parts can get lost."

Crossing the parking to get to his van, Terry wondered
1528.82.8 where Ulysse came from to speak such perfect French,
Moncton but without a discernible accent.

1529.97.6

Numerals and The role of the Fibonacci sequence in deter-
Numbers mining the price of gold.

"I knows yer de one startin' all dem rumours. Wot is it yer tryin' to prove anyhow?"

I was struck dumb. Josse seemed truly peeved.

"A body'd tink you was lookin' fer trouble… as doh you was wantin' sometin' bad to happen!"

Her consternation obliged me to ask myself if, indeed, I wasn't bringing bad luck down on Terry and Carmen. I decided that was not the case.

"No, I'm only tryin' to show the way people are. People like rumours. It gives them something to chew on."

Josse knew what I meant.

"Well alright den, sure, only why does you 'ave to go usin' Carmen an' Terry fer dat? Anybody else would've done just as well. I can make up stories 'bout anyone you care to name!"

"Exactly, but they're not just anyone. And that's what makes people talk."

…

I tried to reassure her:

"Anyhow, 'tisn't anything serious, now is it? A wee rumour, who cares really?"

"Well, you ask me, yer not bein' fair pickin' on dem like dat. It's on account o' dem dat folks like yer books de way dey do. Dey's de ones're makin' yer livin' fer ya!"

Clearly, Josse was forgetting that, in the first instance, I was the one giving them life, and her too, for that matter. But that was not really important.

"If I can't be writing what I like, 'twouldn't be worth writing at all."

Josse thought about that for a bit, before concluding:

"Der's times artists rub me nerves right raw. Dey tinks dey can be doin' just wot dey please, go against common sense, go against everytin'. As doh all wot dey do was so wonderful great as all dat! Well, I'll tell you sometin': dey can be burpin' hot peppers all dey like, dey don't scare me one bit."

"Did you just say burpin' hot peppers?"

"An' don't go tinkin' I's gonna help you wid dat one neider. Go find yerself some udder body to study."

She was a sight to behold. I knew she didn't mean half of what she was saying, but all the same, there was some truth to her argument.

"Artists frustrate you, is that it?"

"Don't play de shrink wid me, I's got one already an' dat's plenty."

"Awh, yeah?"

"I suppose yer gonna run home an' write dat down now? See now, dat's exactly wot I's sayin'! Youse can do whatever you please, you always gets de last word. Dat's wot rubs me raw."

"How come you're seein' a psychologist?"

"Yer' pullin' me leg, I hope..."

I still hoped I could win her over, give her back her good humour:

"The main reason you'd have to see a psychologist would be on account of you're too quick to say what you think, right?"

"You oughtta know."

"I bet you make 'im laugh..."

Josse recovered a bit of her good mood:

"You knows it, girl. De way tings are goin' now, dey's de ones ought to be payin' me."

"Dey? Wot, yer seein' more'n one?"

"G'wan wich ya! Don't go pretendin' you doesn't know!

I thought I'd press her just a wee bit more:

"So den? 'Ow's Bernie?"

"You wants to know if we's still in love?"

Of course, that was exactly what I wanted to know. She blushed a little in answering:

"'Tisn't easy to love one boy atta time. Me, seems like it takes two to make one."

"You won't be tinkin' dat when yer pregnant."

1530.101.10 "Oh Jesus, don't tell me yer gonna do dat to me!"

Duos "Not me. Him."

Notice in a building under renovation in Moncton (translated both ways):

We apologize for
any inconvenience.

(Nous regrettons
tout inconvénient.)

* * *

Nous faisons des excuses
pour n'importe quel
dérangement.

(We make excuses
for any disturbances
whatsoever.)

1531.17.11
Chance

Terry had the advantage of experience; he knew exactly what he was looking for. Standing behind him, Zed had to be content with watching lists, graphs, and tables of all sorts leap on and off the screen.

"Dey's mullin.'"

"Dey wot?"

"Dey's mullin' it over. Means dey're tinkin', waitin' to see wot 'appens."

"Awh, dey're ponderin.'"

...

...

"I tink der'll be a late mornin' turnaround."

Zed decided not to annoy his friend by asking him to explain every bit of the jargon.

"So den, 'ave you told Carmen wot yer up to 'ere?"

"Sort of."

Terry clicked a couple more times before adding:

"Turns out she's got sometin' she's not tellin' me neider."

Zed noted the irony of the situation.

"Like, you boat know dat de udder one's got sometin' der not tellin', only you doesn't know wot dat is?"

"Dat's it, on de nose."

"Geez, dat's kinda funny."

"Yeah, you knows it."

"Well, 'twere me, I'd be curious sometin' awful."

"I is curious sometin' awful."

. . .

"Only now de whole ting's turned into a wee bit of a game. A couple's bit of a game."

"Is dat a good ting, den? Fer de couple, I mean."

Terry didn't have to think about it for long:

"Yah, kind of..."

1532.85.7 The Stock Market

Zed realized that Terry had thought it out, and decided not to pester him about it.

"Well den, are we makin' money or not?"

> Open work stitching, which draws the fabric's threads together to create a lacy see-through effect, eventually became the specialty of the women of Dresden. These women, excluded from the all-male Guild of Master Embroiderers, produced embroideries as fine
> 1533.71.10 Intro Embroidery
> as the silk and gold works of the so-called masters, but for a far lower price. Do open-work embroidery for one's hope chest.

And then, pointblank:

"Mum, wot would you like to be gettin' as a great big present right now?"

Aha! At last the cat was out of the bag. If Carmen had not already been 100 percent certain what it was that Terry was hiding from her, Étienne's question absolutely confirmed her suspicions.

"How big? Like if it was in a box as big as a chair, you mean?"

Étienne looked at a chair, then a different one, but wasn't sure what to think. Carmen tried to help:

"Or do you mean that it could be something a wee bit expensive, only it wasn't all that big, like a pretty necklace, or a pair of shoes…"

This time, Étienne's hesitation surprised Carmen, but she shrugged it off quickly, intent on showing her son that she was taking his question seriously:

"Gee, dat's a proper question. Let me think on it a wee bit."

While Carmen was thinking, Étienne had an idea for the appropriate size of the present.

"I tink the old stew pot would be a good size."

Carmen wondered if Étienne was suggesting she ask for a pot as a gift.

"Hmm…that's pretty big. I guess I'll have to think on 1534.121.1
it a while longer." Things to Want

> My meetings with my avatars were becoming
> increasingly dangerous, letting self-criticism 1535.76.11
> show through. Avatars

"Take a gock at dis one 'ere hahaha!"

"Hey! I remember that day. 'Twas at Grand-Pré. Mum had a new camera an' she didn't know how to work it."

"Dad looks fed up."

"Well, sure! We'd been der fer upwards on fifteen minutes waitin' on Mum to press de button." 1536.133.10
"Who's de fellow beside dem?" The Future

1537.31.8
> What is money, if not a sort of permission to Questions with
> continue? Answers

"Me, I's afraid of havin' bin brainwashed."

"About what?"

"About French."

"Alright. And what does this fear make you feel?"

"Rage."

"Can you explain?"

"De udder day, I's searchin' fer the word *snoro* in the Acadian dictionaries, only 'twasn't there. So den I thought to look in de *Robert* dictionary, in case it turned out to be a real French word. On page 2099 of dat dictionary, where the word *snoro* would have been if it were a real word, der were forty udder words. An guess wot. Half o' dose words was English! Let me list dem fer you, OK?"

!

"*Slip* (plus der was *string* in bold in de definition), *slogan*, *slow*, *smart*, *smash* (an' *smasher*), *smithsonite* (wasn't sure 'bout dat one), *smocks*, *smog*, *smoking*, *smolt*, *smurf*, *snack* (an' *snack-bar*, wid *fast-food* in bold in de definition), *sniff* (an' *sniffer*), *sniper*, *snob*, *snober*, *snobinard* an' *snobisme*, *snowboard*, *snow-boot* an' *soap-opéra*. Exactly half de words on de page came from English. Not to mention der were a few words dat came from Arab an' Italian, and from Denmark an' Holland, an' udder places like dat. All in all, der was maybe five words you could say come from French. Dat's five outta forty."

. . . ?!

! . . . ?? . . . !

? . . . !! . . . ?

!?

. . .

1538.137.10 Fears

"Well, so den I closed de dictionary, I's half afeared to check de udder pages."

1539.121.7 Things to Want

Ludmilla's quiet elegance with language.

"You sure do measure a whole lot of tings, eh, Dad?"

"Sometimes, dat's de only way you can understand someting."

Terry and Étienne had been comparing by sight their now partly coloured toenails: relatively speaking, the growth had been approximately equal, except for two nails on both their right feet.

"You've got two dat grew back faster than de udders, as well. And, not only dat, but dey're de same two as mine!"

Étienne was happy to share the same particularities with his father, who was now applying the ruler to his big toe.

"From wot I can see, 'twill most likely take a year before de whole nail on de big toe grows all de way out."

Terry then measured the polished and unpolished parts of the nails on the four other toes of the same foot.

"Hun! Looks like 'twill only take six months fer dese udders to grow completely out."

The difference seemed to astonish Terry, whereas Étienne thought it was perfectly normal.

"Well sure, Dad! They're smaller!"

Terry nodded, but his expression showed that he didn't understand.

"You don't understand, Dad?"

"Well, shouldn't all de toes take de same time to grow out der whole length, wedder der big or small?"

Étienne did not reply, absorbed in the realization that for the first time he understood something his father did not.

"Do you see wot I's sayin'?"

Étienne did not dare answer.

"If de nail's smaller, don't dat mean der's less strength fer growin'? An' dat would mean, logically, ee oughtta take about as long to grow from A to Z as de big one."

Étienne didn't see what A to Z had to do with it.

"De way it looks 'ere, de nail on de big toe's takin' twice as long to grow."

To Étienne it was obvious:

"Well, it's because it's twice as big!"

Terry could see that, but he couldn't make sense of it. He turned frankly to Étienne:

"Well, boy, you understand it better'n I do..."

Étienne wasn't altogether sure he was ready to assume

his suddenly massive intelligence:

1540.73.8 Shifts "It doesn't matter, Dad, even if I's startin' to be smarter'n you. On account of I'm not smarter dan Mum, yet."

> All things considered, in spite of his identity amnesia, Hans has not fared badly as Acadian author France Daigle's avatar. You only need to compare his lot to the woman statue in her *Histoire de la maison qui brûle* (*Story of the House That's Burning*), or the man who drowns
> 1541.76.12 in *La Beauté de l'affaire* (*The Beauty of the*
> Avatars *Thing*), to name but two.

"Do you sometimes think about the possibility that Chico might have similar problems to Shawn's? I mean, that it could be in his genes?"

"Sometimes. I suppose I tawt more about it at de start."

Catherine had been wary about raising the question with Zed; she didn't want to start him thinking about something that might weigh on him unnecessarily. But Zed's reply was untroubled, and so Catherine added:

1542.104.10 "I think about it, too, sometimes. Maybe I shouldn't."

Worries "'Tisn't possible not to tink about it."

daddy
gazes outside
bites an apple, ponders
1543.80.8 his son admires him, taste yourself
Cinquains and see

"She's workin'..."

"How does you know, den?"

"By dis 'ere little light dat's blinkin'. When she's green, dat means she's ready. An' red means she's gone out."

Chico waited, but nothing seemed to be happening.

"At school, she doesn't take dis long at all. You press on de button and she starts right away."

Zed, too, thought the printer was taking a long time to get going.

"Could be on account of she's new, on account of dis 'ere's de first time we turn 'er on."

Zed opened the accompanying instructions again, reread the steps, sighed. Chico worried that Zed might be getting ready to quit. Then suddenly, while both their noses were buried in the manual crammed with diagrams, numerals, and arrows, something started up, the printer gave a little shake, and several little lights — yellow and orange ones, along with the green and red — began to flash one after the other, until finally the word "*Prête*" appeared on the small, discrete screen. 1544.135.10

"Hun! She's already in French. Dat's right nice." Zed and Chico

> She reflected on the departure of the French for the New World in the seventeenth century. How could one not expect their language to undergo the countershocks of such a radical displacement? What are a few so-called abnormal language configurations in the face of an ocean's distance and 400 years of history on a different continent? Invert the language rather than reverse the crossing. Why should the Parisians in their finery, who love the sound of *s* words, take precedence over the pioneers shot through with the beating of tam-tams? Why fret over a redundancy when the word itself contains two *d*s? 1545.128.7 Fervours

"I only asked 'er how she was; I wasn't askin' fer her blog." 1546.82.3 Moncton

> RCH, SKR, NOA, MNB, TKO, HEO, SEI, PSR, CRY, BWC, MDZ.A, NEM, AVL. 1547.67.10 Terry's Notebooks

"I fails to see why we couldn't write *swĩng* the way we

actually pronounce it in French: *swigne*."

"Which would lead to the verb *swigner. Je swigne, tu swignes, il* or *elle swigne, on swigne, nous swignons, vous swignez, ils* and *elles swignont*."

"I fear that that might lead to confusion with "to heal" or *soigner*: *je swigne, je soigne*... You see the problem?"

"As far as I'm concerned, there's sufficient difference between the two. Especially since we pronounce *soigne* as *souègne*."

"You may very well be right, my dear lady. And, in any case, let's admit it, no language is ever entirely safe from the occasional misunderstanding."

"But would that apply, then, to all verbs containing *-ing*? I'm thinking of *rĩng, strĩng*..."

"We ought to begin by deciding which English verbs we accept; then, we can discuss which conjugation *fits*."

"*Fĩt*! Der's one we ought to talk *ābout*!"

"Personally, I'm afraid that if we admit *rigne* for *rĩng*, referring to either doorbells or other sorts of bells, before you know it, people will be saying things like '*j'ai rigné la dõorbell*.' I completely disapprove of opening the door to *dõorbell*."

"Perhaps we might simply create a verb *drigne* for *drĩng* the doorbell, and reserve *rigne* for the boxing arena. What do you think?"

"And I suppose we'd accept, if the need arises, that people *strignent* their Christmas decorations as of December 10, as suggested by Energuide, and that they *strignent* themselves to show off on the beach?

"I believe you mean, that they *strigniont* themselves."

"That doesn't solve the pronunciation of the *r*. Are they
1548.133.8 going to *strigner* themselves like the French, or *strĩgnér*
The Future themselves like the Americans?

Hans got back up, brushed off his trousers. The bus had skidded, knocking him down in the aisle. Luckily, the vehicle had not overturned,

> but had merely slid awkwardly onto the shoulder of the highway. No panic, no blood. Hans wondered if it might be a sign that he shouldn't be going to Moncton. But an accident can happen anywhere, after all. Whatever the case, he concluded that there would certainly be a few 1549.78.12
> rough patches. Accidents

"Dad, wot does deportation mean?"

Terry was busy serving two customers at the same time.

"Eh, Dad?"

"Look, Dad's serving de ladies right now. I'll explain it to you later, OK?"

Étienne looked at the customers. Both had turned radiant smiles on him. Intimidated, the boy took refuge 1550.130.10
in Ludmilla's office. Work

1551.56.12

> Any sort of explanation is a kind of pilgrimage. Pilgrimages

Marianne ran after the rolling carrot slice, caught up and picked it up, and popped it in her mouth.

"Wait, Marianne! Come 'ere, Dad's gonna show you sometin."

Marianne turned, not daring to clamp her jaws down completely.

"When sometin' to eat falls on de ground, it gets dirty, even doh it might not show, so we oughtn't to be eatin' it."

Terry got down to Marianne's height to be sure she'd understand.

"De slice of carrot you picked up off de ground, well, 'twas probably a wee bit dirty, or could be it picked up some germs, so we'd best wash it before we eats it, or if 'twere too dirty, we'd be trowin' it in de garbage. Understand?"

Marianne took the slice dripping with saliva out of her mouth, and handed it to Terry, who went to rinse it off before giving it back.

"Alright den, now you can go ahead an' eat it."

The little one ran off, and Terry went back to slicing carrots, adding for the benefit of Étienne, who was cutting the tails off string beans on the table:

"If de ting dat falls on de ground is dry, you could just blow on it, and den eat it, only Marianne's too small to make de difference, so I's just tellin' you."

Étienne acquiesced, proud that his father recognized in him a greater degree of judgment than in his little sister, who was almost still a baby. At the same time, he regretted the unblemished square of Chicklet's gum he'd spotted that very morning on the ground in the parking lot of the convenience store.

1552.134.9
Marianne

MIDDAYCATION: n. — 2005; from *midday* and *medication* ♦ 1. medicine to be taken with midday meal. *"I'm going to prescribe a middaycation for you."* (Daigle) 2. laughable, useless medicine (FIG.) *"It's nothing, he forgot his middaycation."* (Daigle)

1553.120.3
Fictionary

Zed pressed on the accelerator and made a quick left turn, rapidly cutting across the two lanes of the avenue where traffic was usually constant and fast.

"I hates to do dat, only dey almost doesn't give us a choice."

Once they were in the parking lot of the clinic:

"It may take some time..."

"There's no rush. Anyhow, I've got a book."

Without being one of those people of whom we say they've always got their nose in a book, Catherine usually carried a book in her handbag. Always a book; never a magazine. Magazines can't hold Catherine's attention; they make her feel like a chicken running around with its head cut off. Whereas books take her by the hand and lead her down paths across open fields.

"Is dat de book Terry was wantin' you to read?"

"No, I finished that one."

"Already? Was it good, den?"

Catherine was rarely categorical about books.

"There were some good bits, only I think Terry liked it more than I did."

Nor was she the type to get lost in interminable discussions of her books. 1554.73.7

"I've never been a big fan of legends." Shifts

> French that flows naturally. Without embellishments, but without serious blunders either. Subtle, polished accents. You emerge refreshed, as from a playful, sun-filled wave. Fervour? 1555.128.1
> Fantasy? Fervours

Étienne had been astonished to learn that a person could simply be expelled from their home.

"That's not nice, eh Dad?"

Terry, who had naturally simplified the history of the Deportation a bit, was happy to see that Étienne had grasped the essential.

"No, 'tisn't nice, fer sure. 'Tis even mean."

"How come de police didn't stop them doing that?"

"Well, in a way, dose dat did dat, dey was de police demselves."

Étienne had never imagined the police could be cruel.

"They were fearsome police?"

"Hey, boy! Fearsome police. Dat's well said. I like dat."

"Granny Gaudet says dat word. She says 'er cat's fearsome."

Étienne seemed to enjoy saying the word.

"Dat's good, dat's a fine word. Yes, dey were fearsome police."

Étienne had deduced from his father's explanations that even he, Terry, would have been powerless in the face of the British soldiers.

"Mum wouldn't 'ave been afeard."

The phrase made Terry smile.

"Awh, no? Well, maybe not. Wot does you tink she'd 'ave done, den?"

Étienne thought about it:

"She'd 'ave put poison in de pizza an' she'd 'ave fed it to de police an' after supper de polices would've all died."

Terry noted the recurrence of his son's predilection for poisoning.

"An' me, I'd be hidin' in de closet wid Marianne an' after Mum would've come to fetch us."

As a father, Terry didn't like being kept out of the dramas that might have struck their little family.

"An me, where would I 'ave bin, den? Wot would I be doin'?"

Étienne began by shrugging, then finally:

1556.23.8 "You'd 'ave put the suitcases in the car. The suitcases
Potatoes an' a whole lot o' potatoes, so we'd 'ave sometin' to eat."

1557.77.2 *Dequoi*, sometin'. *Desfois*, der's times dat.
Grammar *Commensque*, 'ow're.

"Wot's de difference betwixt a straight shooter an' a straight arrow. Ask me, der de same."

"Straight shooter tells you straight wot's wot. He doesn't miss de mark."

"Well don't a straight arrow do de same?"

1558.82.11 "Only if yer an Indian. Udderwise straight shooter's a
Moncton lot quicker."

looks at
her crackled bowl
broken yet not broken
1559.80.3 lifts her eyes asks for permission
Cinquains to eat

"Over there's a whole lot of trucks, eh Mum?"

Carmen had explained to Étienne that, on the road,

it was always best to stop in restaurants frequented by truckers, because they knew the good places to eat.

"See the thickness of the cream on the lemon pie? Now, that proves that we're in a real truckers' restaurant."

The boy had concluded that truckers were clearly peo- 1560.106.4
ple with a great deal of power. Customs

message in a bottle
worn smooth by the sea and time
words within like wine
asleep, almost forgotten 1561.75.11
this floating passage that breathes Tankas

"I've got it! I knew there was sometin'! A camera! I'd like to be takin' a whole lot of beautiful pictures of you an' our family."

Étienne gave the impression he approved and, as
though satisfied with the outcome, asked no further 1562.121.6
questions. Things to Want

1563.132.5
Political malapropism: the bull is in their court. Malapropism

"Have you ever seen the bronze fly?"

Chico shrugged, as if to say he'd seen a great many flies, but whether among all those flies, he'd seen that particular one, well...

"My grandad, says you have to please the bronze fly."

Chico thought about it before replying:

"An' 'ow does we do dat, den?"

Étienne shrugged in turn.

"Wot does bronze mean?"

Chico explained everything he knew about bronze.

"Dat's an Olympic medal. 'Tis de tird medal, only dey gives it first. Dat's wot de teacher said."

Étienne was not in the habit of questioning what the teacher said.

"Can you ask de teacher if she's ever seen de bronze fly?"

1564.139.9 Étienne and Chico "OK."

> 1565.67.11 Terry's Notebooks And on another page of the same notebook: ALS, ALZ, ONC, SRD, PEI, BVX, NTC, and PZZ.

Daigle admitted, in the course of the interview, that she had to get up very early in the morning to try and understand Lacan, so as not to misrepresent his arguments.

1566.34.3 Lacan "After 10 a.m., I was no longer sure I understood him, so it might be a good idea for readers to read those passages early in the morning, as well."

> 1567.129.1 Fantasies The French expression "*treize à la douzaine*" or "thirteen to the dozen," is translated in English as "a baker's dozen." How not to imagine a baker, chubby, cheerful, and covered in flour, with a love for life and those around him, and unable to resist putting one more, rather than one less, in his dozen biscuits or bread rolls?

"Zed wants a dog."

Chico said it without enthusiasm, as though he himself was indifferent.

"Wot about you, don't you want one as well?"

"Yes. Me as well."

Étienne thought about it, then:

"I'd like one, too."

Chico added:

"Well, 'tis more Zed dan me dat wants one."

1568.139.7 Étienne and Chico Étienne acquiesced, but there was something odd in that detail.

> 1569.58.8 Extensions Balzac's *The Magic Skin* appears in the section entitled "The Fantastic and the Marvellous" of *La Bibliothèque idéale*.

You could hear it when Étienne returned from a day or two with Chico at Granny Gaudet's house in Dieppe. "*Tiroir*" or "drawer" became "*tirette*," or "pull out" as in:

"Mum, de scissors aren't in de pull out."

…

"*Dévisser*" or "unscrew" became "*désavisser*" or "unenscrew," as in:

"Dad, can you unenscrew dis?"

…

"*Contrarié*" or "frustrated" became "*connetrairée*" or "crousty," as in:

"Wot's de madder wid you, Marianne? Yer lookin' terrible crousty."

…

And, undressing to take his bath, "*un fils décousu*" or "loose thread" became "*une défaisure*" or "ravel," as in: 1570.20.1
"Luh, Mum, I've a ravel in me sock." Language

Even the word *hasard* has its origins in Arabic.
The English *hazard* meaning both "danger" 1571.17.3
and "chance" comes later from the French. Chance

Seated at the big three-sided table, with access to most of his various occupations, The Cripple was deep in thought. Before him, lay a sheet on which were written a few words in the form of a poem.

raisin dust
my computer washes up
the sevens tempt me

Antoinette, who had never seen her husband so perplexed, wanted to rescue him from his impasse: 1572.16.12
"Ask Terry. He's the one who knows this stuff." The Cripple

1573.121.3
Depth. Things to Want

“I used to see Canada as a great big country where a fellow could roam. Nowadays, I sees it wid Caterpillar machinery everywhere an’ holes all o’er de place.”

…

“’Tisn’t wot’s on dis earth dat counts any longer, ’tis wots underneat.’”

…

“An’ before, I’d get terrible vexed wid de banks makin’ all dat money. Now, I can’t say I mind.”

…

“It’s got so I’s even readin’ de stickers on car licences.”

…

“Speakin’ o’ cars, we ought to be takin’ a ride down
1574.85.11 The Stock Market by Sisson Brook some time. Der’s supposed to be a new tungsten an’ moly mine openin’ up down der.”

> Before running to his mother, Étienne had
> 1575.103.10 Disappearances quickly shoved both the drawing and the tube of toothpaste as far as possible under his bed.

“Do you have books from la Pléiade collection here?”

“We’ve a couple second hand. Unless you’s lookin’ fer dose by Charles Le Blanc on de old Chinese philosophers?”

“As a matter of fact, I’m looking for the second one, on the Confucian philosophers.”

“Yer in luck, we’ve got one left. An’ she’s signed, to boot.”

1576.130.1 Work “Wicked! I’ll take it.”

> No mention of the death of the Russian composer Sergei Prokofiev the same day as Stalin,
> 1577.119.11 Music March 5, 1953, in Daigle’s *1953: Chronicle of a Birth Foretold.*

Without intending to, Carmen had planted the seeds of doubt in Terry’s mind concerning the eventual sexual orientation of their children. And like any good forward-looking father, especially in the case of Étienne, who was growing up at an alarming rate, Terry had begun to look for an opportunity to raise the subject of homosexuality with his son.

"Well, den? Was de party alright?"

"Yes! We played kick-the-can an' hide'n-go-seek!"

"Wow! We played dat as well, when I's a boy..."

"I kicked de can twice!"

"Twice! You musta bin pretty clever hidin', eh?"

"Yes, an' I was runnin' fast."

His mouth stained with orangeade, Étienne began to rummage through his bag of surprises.

"Was der a lot o' people?"

The boy nodded while he reached down to the bottom of his bag.

"Was der girls der, or mostly boys?"

"Der was a whole lot of folks, and uncles an' aunties."

Terry continued to probe for an opening:

"An' girl cousins?"

Étienne didn't know. Terry looked for another way in:

"Wot've you got in yer bag, den?"

Étienne pulled out candy, a mini-car and a skipping rope.

"A skippin' rope! In my day, 'twas de girls wot played wid skipping ropes."

Étienne registered the remark as information, and began to unwrap a giant pink bubble gum:

"Kick-de-can's de best kind of game." 1578.125.4

"Yes, I liked it as well..." Sexuality

> To obtain a straight edge, line up the paper to a full line (metric measurements) or a dotted line (American measurement). Place the paper to be cut against the ruler at the top of the tray and against the paper guide to the left. To cut an oblique of 30, 45, or 60 degrees, place

> the paper along the corresponding diagonals. Paper cutting requires caution: do not place your fingers too close to the blade while you are doing precision cutting. If the blade creases the paper instead of cutting it, tighten the screw at the head of the pivot rod located under the carriage. Beware! Do not put your fingers past the finger guard. Keep the handle down and the blade latch locked when the guillotine paper cutter is not in use, or when transporting. Do not grease the blade. Do not remove the blade guard. Do not put your hand or fingers under the blade to hold the paper cutter when transporting. Keep away from children.
> 1579.111.8 The 10-year limited warranty does not cover a
> Tools product damaged by misuse or overuse.

Terry stopped in front of the veteran to buy some plastic poppies. He explained to Étienne:

"This man 'ere was in de war. See 'is medals? Dat's on account of ee was brave an' ee fought fer us."

Proud that a young man would take the time to explain such a thing to a child, the veteran, wanting to do his part, pinned the poppy on Étienne's jacket himself.

"There! Now you'll be a little soldier for us old-timers."

Étienne couldn't see how the poppy made of him a soldier, and didn't think to say thank you. Terry reminded him:

"Aren't you gonna say thank you?"

"Thank you."

"Yer welcome. That's a right fine jacket you've got. Is it fer yer baseball team?"

Étienne had not chosen the jacket he was wearing. Carmen had pulled it out of the cupboard one day and he'd simply put it on without protesting.

. . .

"Ee's not in a mood fer talkin' today..."

Terry was about to agree with the veteran when Étienne's tongue suddenly loosened:

"War wid real guns?"

"Real, fer sure!"

"On account of?"

"On account of? Because 'twas necessary. Der was some bad people an' we had to be rid o' dem. War's not nice, only we had to defend our freedom."

Étienne retained the word *freedom*, and asked no further questions. 1580.88.5 Freedom

1581.116.11 True or False

True or false: Diamonds like the cold.

Terry had the feeling the day would never end. Nevertheless, he launched into the story of Pépée.

"Dis 'ere story happened in France in de days of de hippies. I already told you 'bout de hippies, do you remember?"

Étienne drew his hand out from under his pillow and flashed the peace sign, which made Terry laugh.

"Exactly! So, der was dis couple—dey were a fellow and 'is wife—who was strollin' along when, all of sudden out o' de blue, dey come upon a man who had dese wee monkeys, like five or six wee monkeys playin' togedder, an' seems dey was a pretty sight to see, an' comical as well. When de woman saw dem, well, right off she wants one. Well, seems de man, ee didn't really care for dem. Only de woman, 'twas like she couldn't go on livin' if she didn't 'ave one o' dose little monkeys. So, in de end, de man says alright, on account of he loved 'is wife an' all..."

Étienne smiled, as though he already had a vast experience in love.

"So den dey hauled one o' de little monkeys home wid dem. At de start, ee was cute an' comical an' everytin' was fine. Only de monkey, ee started growin' and getting' big, an' den ee wasn't a wee little monkey anymore at all! Ee turned out to be a shockin' big, tall monkey, an' terrible strong as well. Well, de woman in particular, but de man a wee bit too, livin' wid de monkey all dat time, dey got used to 'im, same as if he were a cat or a dog. An' you knows 'ow easy 'tis to spoil a creature you loves... So de big, tall monkey became terrible spoiled, an' wrangle-gangle: ee's climbin' over everytin', jumpin' an' doin' flips anytime an' anyplace ee felt de urge. An' wid his hands almost like ours, ee's grabbin' hold o' tings and pullin' dem off, or ee drags 'is arm off de tablecloth an' brings de whole supper down on de floor... all tings like dat."

The situation as Étienne imagined it made him laugh, but at the same time he knew this story wasn't going to be all rosy.

"Well den, dat monkey got to be a terrible misery. Ee was wantin' der attention all de time, an' doin' anytin' to get it. Especially when de couple was havin' guests over. Fer instance, radder dan shakin' der hand like yer supposed to, ee'd grab hold of de visitor's hand an' give it an awful twist. An' ee'd drash de chair out from under dem, ee'd eat right out o' der plate, slobber all o'er dem, walk on de table, climb de lamps, trow tings, wotever you can tink of, dat monkey was doin' it."

Étienne was beginning to look stressed.

"An' it kept on like dat fer years. Let's say five or six years. De fellow kept on sayin' dey ought to be getting' rid o' dat monkey, only de wife wouldn't hear of it, or else it got to be de reverse, I doesn't recall fer certain. Whichever, one ting's fer sure, der got to be some terrible bickerin' in dat house. Most likely dey had udder reasons to be bickerin', only Pépée wasn't helpin, dat's fer sure. Oh, dat's true, I 'aven't told you de monkey's name yet, 'ave I? Pépée. Wid an extra *e* on de end. Dat's wot dey called 'im, on account of de monkey was a female monkey, actually."

Étienne nodded, understanding.

"Well den, Pépée got so crazy dat nobody was wantin'

to visit wid dose folks. De whole house was a reeraw. Pépée was even takin' apart de roof, so dat sometimes 'twas rainin' in de house. I suppose de roofs in dat country're easier to take apart dan dey are 'round 'ere, only I can't say fer a fact. Anyhow, it only goes to show how strong Pépée was."

Again Étienne nodded.

"By den, de man was pretty much fed up wid all o' Pépée's mess. Sometimes he was out walkin', he didn't want to be comin' 'ome, imagine dat! Some folks was even sayin' dat ee was startin' to tink 'is wife was as daft as de monkey. One time, ee stayed away fer two whole weeks, on account of ee couldn't stand it no longer."

"Where did ee go, den?"

"Well, same place you or I'd go. A friend's place. 'Is best pal's. Right?"

Étienne smiled. Terry continued:

"De wife was phonin' an' cryin' fer 'im to come on home, only ee didn't want to, did ee. So, to make 'im come home, she told 'im dat if ee didn't come 'ome, she's gonna murder Pépée."

!

"Ask me, she ought to 'ave said de opposite: dat she'd kill Pépée if he was agreein' to come home. Well, like I's sayin', she was startin' to get a wee bit rimmed 'erself by den, I figure. Anyhow, de fellow didn't believe 'er, an' ee didn't go back 'ome. So de wife, she asked de neighbour to come over an' kill Pépée, an' a couple udder creatures while der at it, a pig an' a dog, I tink. On account of dey had udder animals as well."

Rather than letting his son languish in suspense, Terry answered the question written all over the boy's face.

"So, yes, de neighbour comes round wid a rifle an' *bang, bang, bang*, ee kills Pépée, ee kills de pig, an' ee kills de udder creature, probably a dog. Well, when de husband of de woman heard dat — somebody rang 'im up it seems — ee almost went roary-eyed 'imself. Ee couldn't believe it! So off ee goes. Ee gets 'ome right de same time dey's gettin' ready to muck 'is wife off to a sort of hospital. Ee buries Pépée an' de two udder creatures, an' seems ee took it hard, even doh all dat time, 'twas as doh ee didn't care all dat much fer Pépée."

Étienne was at a loss.

"Well, in de end, can you guess wot ee did wid all dat?"

?

"Ee made a song. A song dat's called Pépée. Just dat. Pépée."

"Have you ever heard it?"

"Awh yes. We has it 'ere. We can listen to it tomorrow, if you like."

Yes, Étienne wanted to hear it. His eyelids heavy in spite of the slightly sordid nature of the story, he turned in his bed while Terry tucked him in.

"G'night, boy."

"G'night, Pépée."

Terry was stunned for a moment, unsure if the boy
1582.37.12 had said it on purpose or if it was a slip of the tongue,
Animal Tales from Papa to Pépée. He would probably never know.

1583.104.6 Not to have gone far enough in modifying the
Worries language.

"Der's some who say you ought to wait until dey bring it up demselves. Dat's 'ow you know der ready."

"I only wanted to tell 'im it's OK, so ee doesn't worry 'bout it, if ever."

"Yes, I understand. Now ee'll know... if ee didn't already."

...

...

...

"Regardless, sometimes I ask meself if you can really call it normal."

"Wot? Being gay?"

Terry changed the channel, stopped on images of Asia.

"I don't think *normal* is the right word."

"Wot would be de right one den? Not *preference*, I hope."

Terry surfed past a few more channels. No, Carmen did not particularly like the word *preference* to describe homosexuality:

"No. *Preference* sounds as though dey 'ave a choice, only dey keep tellin' us dat dey didn't choose to be that way themselves."

"Exactly."

Carmen cuddled closer to Terry's bare chest.

"I love you, you know dat. Yer not a bad bit smart…"

Terry felt flattered but decided, for once, to feign detachment.

"Whatever."

Carmen found him irresistable, grabbed the remote, 1584.125.7
made the world disappear, and slid beneath her man. Sexuality

CHAPTER 12

We write because we do not know what we want to say. Writing reveals it to us.

J. M. Coetzee, (interview) 1585.144.12
LIRE, May 2007 Epigraphs

"So do you, like know all dat's gonna 'appen wid us?"

It had been a long time since I'd sat down with Terry to have a bit of a chat.

"Not really."

"G'wan! You must know..."

In fact, I really didn't have anything in particular in mind. It played out day by day. But his curiosity was comforting.

"I heard dat somewhere, writers sayin' dat der characters ends up takin' over de story, only I find dat awful hard to believe. I mean, de story doesn't fall from de sky, somebody's gotta be tinkin' it up. On account of, wedder ya like it or not, der's still gotta be a mind behind all dis. No?"

"Yes. That's true. Only, I couldn't tell you how the whole thing works, really."

"We's avatars of you, is dat it den?"

He wasn't entirely wrong.

"Yes, in a way. Except that you're better than I am."

"Dat's on account of you embellish us, wot's kind o'

nice on yer part, by de way."

I had to think about that. Was I really embellishing them?

"I think I'm just a filter. I'm doing me job as a filter."

Terry seemed to like the image, although:

"All de same, you must know wot's gonna be happenin' to us, eh?"

"What is it yer wantin' to know exactly?"

"Am I gonna be in hot water wid Carmen on account of de stock-market ting?"

I couldn't help smiling at his concern. I decided to give him a bit of a respite:

"No, not really…"

A wave of relief washed over Terry.

"Only don't take too long before you tell 'er, and don't go forgettin' her birthday."

Terry forced a smile.

"An' I'm wonderin' if you might be tellin' me wot 'tis she's hidin' from me…"

No sooner were the words out of his mouth than he retracted:

"No, no. Ferget dat question. 'Twouldn't be fair, I knows it. Only she's terrible hard to sweet talk, dat one."

I recognized Terry's good sense. Then I glanced at the time, and realized I was late.

"Yer leavin' already? You only just sat down!"

"I've got to go to the optometrist. I was only stopping by to buy some coffee."

He looked sincerely sorry to see me go. It broke my
1586.101.4 heart a little. As I went on my way, I wondered if it was
Duos normal to prefer characters to real people.

In any case, since the French dictionary now
includes *djebel*, *djihad*, *djellaba* and *djinn*,
1587.77.9 amongst others, why not also include *djob*,
Grammar *djeule*, *djaque*, and *djoke*, amongst others.

"All dose English words... my question is: how come 1588.88.7
dey can be doin' dat, and we can't?" Freedom

> On the reverse side, excerpts photocopied from Umberto Eco's *The Open Work*. Rereading the underlined passages, I realize the important
> role this book played in the very conception of 1589.57.12
> *For Sure*. Photocopies

Chico and Étienne could see that the needle was moving, trembling.

"Dat's on account of de needle's like a *magnet*, an' a *magnet* is always drawn to de north."

Zed thought that Chico would be able to appreciate the particularity of the phenomenon, but he wasn't sure Étienne would understand.

"See? De four directions — nort', sout', east, west?"

Zed had pointed to each direction as he named them, and Chico had nodded. Étienne, on the other hand, seemed to be expecting a magic trick, as though each of the cardinal points would make something appear in Zed's hand.

"In de old days — before we had de GPS — dat's 'ow folks found der way in de woods. Dey found de nort', an' den dey was guided by dat wid dis 'ere wee machine."

Zed would have been hard put to explain how it actually worked, but he thought it important that the boys be aware of the existence of the device.

"In French we calls it a *compas*, even doh on de package
'twas written *boussole*. Dat means boat words are 1590.102.10
OK." The Trio

> Minor mystery to clear up: find out what
> Gallimard did, or did not do, with Jan Potocki's 1591.68.2
> *The Manuscript Found in Saragossa*. Projects

"Which does you tink is harder? Winnin' de Masters

in tennis or singin' soloist in an opera?"

"Wot, are you tellin' me dey's really an' truly measured dat?"

...

"Alright, I'd say winnin' de Masters."

"No. Singin' soloist."

...

"On account of dey already knows de *score*."

...

1592.86.8 Apologies "Don't mind me. I's only tryin' to be creative wid me Chiac."

1593.132.2 Malapropism

> Internet malapropism: sinbox.

In spite of everything, Terry had difficulty believing it.

"So, yer not even a wee bit vexed?"

"An' why would I be vexed?"

"Well, usually you prefers fer us to be decidin' tings togedder."

Carmen knew what Terry meant. At the same time, she herself had taken her own initiative without consulting Terry.

"Seems to me, in dis case, 'tisn't quite de same thing."

"Awh, no?"

"No. We both of us need a bit o' freedom, as well. Small things we can be decidin' an' organizin' on our own."

"Exactly. Dat's well put. Dat's wot I tink as well."

"An' anyhow, I've confidence in you. I know you'll not be doin' anyting crazy."

Terry knew very well that Carmen believed in him, but it was nice to hear her say so.

"Seems to me, when we was startin' to go out togedder, you wasn't so sure o' me as all dat."

"Well, I didn't know you all that well den, did I?"

Terry thought that made sense.

"Dat's troo. I suppose I could say de same meself."

Terry took the vegetarian shepherd's pie out of the

oven, placed it in the middle of the table, and cleared his
throat: 1594.88.11
"So den, does dat mean I can keep goin' wid it?" Freedom

> What's more, *hardes* or "clothing," and *barda,* or "domestic chores," two undeniably old Acadian words, come to the French directly from Arabic, as do *truchement* (with the aid of), *raquette* (racket or snowshoe), *gerboise* (jerboa), *estragon* (tarragon), *chiffre* (numeral), *satin*, *chasser* (to hunt), *jupe* (skirt), *sirop*
> (syrup), *artichaut* (artichoke), *mesquin* (petty), 1595.56.6
> *goudron* (tar), *nuque* (nape), and *calibre.* Pilgrimages

"'Tisn't an exact science; that's why you have to develop tactics."

...

"You have to read the river, identify the insects flying in the area. The more of them there are, the better."

...

"It also helps to know when the tides come in and out. You have to gauge the light, the shadows, the currents, the wind, the leaves, how much room you've got for your casts. You have to have some idea where the fish are hiding to decide where to place yourself. You might decide to use an attractive fly rather than an imitative fly."

?

"Of course, in spite of all that, and even in the best conditions, you may not catch anything. Some things we just don't know. Some days they're biting, some days they're not. You never really know why. So, from one time to the next, you come up with tactics to attract the fish, to outsmart it. Because you know he's there, he's
swimming down below the surface, he sees your fly, but 1596.126.4
he's not biting." Techniques

bottle
a note within
who finds it will reply
1597.80.11 ruining the silence for oceans
Cinquains of years

"*Give up*, den?"

Étienne wasn't ready to yield so quickly.

"Well? Does you *give up*?"

But making Chico wait wasn't easy either, especially
1598.47.4 since he had no idea.

Yielding "OK, I *gives up*…"

> The important thing is not having a huge va-
> 1599.105.12 riety of flies at your disposal. More important
> Reserves/ Reservations is to have all the sizes in a few select varieties.

"'Tisn't an exact science; that's why you have to develop tactics.

…

"Over 'ere, you has all de stocks on de TSE."

Terry continued to work the keyboard.

"Well see, dat's it right der! I wouldn't be comfortable wid any old company. Like, I'd have a hard time investin' in some company dat's clear cuttin'. Or a uranium company, even doh I suppose we needs dem. An' not de banks neidder, I doesn't feel like helpin' dem any more dan we has to."

"Fer sure, 'tis a proper ting to know de companies yer investin' in."

"Alright den, how does we know der really honest? Dey can say anytin' dey like, fer all we knows…"

"Der's people been studyin' dat for a right long time. Dat's de idea behind de list of fifty companies I's showin' you. All dose have got a proper track record."

Zed looked once more at the list in his hand.

"Or you can go fer de real fair-trade companies,

companies dat wants to make a profit by bein' fair wid 1600.85.8
people an' wid nature. Der's more an' more of dose." The Stock
"Alright, sure, only are dey makin' any money?" Market

> Periphairy. The nonexistence of certain words
> is so astonishing that it's with great joy that we 1601.107.4
> bring them into the whirled. Necessities

"Josse doesn't tink de lofts're so great as all dat."

"Awh, no?"

"I's hearin' her talkin' to Simon, who was tinkin' o' movin' in der, I suppose."

"Simon? Wid Nadine?"

"I couldn't make out wid who."

"Well who's movin' out, den?"

"You doesn't know? Alain found hisself a dot-com in
Montréal." 1602.108. 9
"Alain?! I tawt der was sometin' fishy goin' on!" Rumours

> Irritation on the subject of the subtitle
> *Unidentified Monologues*. It ought to be under- 1603.15.5
> stood as monologues from anonymous sourc- Unidentified
> es, generic, or unattributed monologues. Monologues

Terry had been so relieved that Carmen wasn't angry with him for his stock-market activity that, for several days, he forgot that she too had a secret to reveal to him.

"So, when does I find out wot you's hidin' from me, den?"

Carmen was burning with impatience to show him her surprise; nevertheless, she managed to hold off a few moments longer:

"Are you sure yer ready?"

"Well, I can't say I'll ever be as ready as I'd like to be..."

But that was her limit. Unable to bear it any longer, Carmen pretended to change the subject. She bent over:

"Seems like der's something caught under the cushion

yer sittin' on."

Terry looked around, saw nothing, and did nothing more."

"Looks like Marianne's giraffe... take a look an' see."

Terry got up, lifted the cushion, but rather than a
giraffe, what he found was a light blue plastic pocket
1604.94.8 Terry and Carmen folder on which, among others, were the words *sun* and
vacation.

"Wot de..."

> Standing with his hands on his hips, the man
> studied the ground, taking a few steps in one
> direction, turning around, looking. It was rare
> to see anyone at all in this small wood. Then
> 1605.78.5 Accidents the policeman signalled for her to advance and
> Josse advanced.

As they did most Thursday nights once the kids were in bed, Terry had been expecting Carmen and he to watch a film and munch on a few snacks. He was certainly not expecting to find four airline tickets under one of the sofa's cushions.

"Are you pullin' me leg or wot?!"

But Terry was already imagining his little family disguised in tropical duds, dragging their suitcases through an airport. He lifted the flap on the plastic case, searched a bit to discover their destination.

"Holy Jesus, Joseph'n Mary!"

Carmen was gleefully watching Terry's every move.

"How did you manage dis?!"

Carmen laughed with joy. Terry shook his head slowly back and forth as he read the details of their itinerary. Carmen thought she could detect a thin veil of moisture in his eyes.

"Geeze... I never been in de sout' in me whole life. De furdest I ever been in dat direction was Bangor."

"I've been saving my tips for two years fer this. Do you

think 'twas a good idea?"

"I can't believe it! 'Tis glorious! Totally glorious!"

Carmen was proud of herself.

"Well, dat's a surprise alright! I'd never 'ave tawt 'twas anytin' like dis, sometin' so shockin' big, I mean."

Terry embraced Carmen, squeezing her tight, then tenderly, and tight again. It was a kind of thank you.

"I can't wait. 'Tis like I can see us..."

"Me too, I can already see us!"

...

"I loves you, girl..."

"I love you, too. Shall we watch de film now?"

1606.94.9 Terry and Carmen

> Render unto Caesar that which belongs to Caesar. *The Open Work* read in the context of a writer's residency at the Université de Moncton (1997), where I was trying to imagine how the novel could draw inspiration from digital technology.

1607.128.10 Fervours

"Have a gock at wot me dad gave me."

"Wot is it?"

"'Tis writin' fer folks dat can't be readin' wid der eyes."

?

"Dey only 'ave to touch de wee bumps wid der fingers an' dey can understand."

Chico asked for the cardboard sheet, examined it more closely.

"Hun!"

Étienne was happy whenever Chico hadn't already learned something at school.

1608.139.11 Étienne and Chico

> I'd photocopied those excerpts from *The Open Work* because the book was out of print. It has since been reprinted, and I've bought it (Harvard University Press). Appropriations are

1609.121.8 Things to Want — not an end in themselves; they necessarily lead to something else.

“Me, I’m afraid of a shovel comin’ down on me foot and slicin’ off me toes.”

“That’s a tangible fear, easy to circumscribe and to surmount.”

1610.82.12 Moncton — “*Tangible*, *circumscribe*, *surmount*, wot do all dose big words mean?”

thriller
bears seals codfish
inspect prosecute net
1611.80.7 Cinquains — police and troubled fisherfolk
fish fry

“When I’s older I’s gonna pilot helicopters.”

Chico’s declaration seemed to come out of the blue. Zed was as surprised as he was moved. And he also noted the boy’s use of the proper French word *piloter* rather than something like... *drĩvér*?

“Well, dat’s a right smart idea! What made you tink of it?”

As a consequence, and without thinking, he’d used *quesse* for “what” instead of his usual *quoisse*.

“Did you hear talk ’bout helicopters in school, den?”

“No. I was just tinkin.’”

Zed decided not to push the matter any further. The fact that the boy was imagining any sort of future seemed already sufficient victory.

“Well, I wouldn’t be afraid to go up in a helicopter wid
1612.135.4 Zed and Chico — you. I know you’d know exactly wot to do.”

Chico looked pleased.

Hans will end up staying quite a while in Fredericton, where he’ll find enough work to buy himself a new pair of pants, shoes, and several shirts. He's in no great hurry to come to Moncton, taking his time, putting aside a little money. Does he realize that he won't see Moncton in this book, with this author? No. He's convinced he'll make it to Moncton in this book.

1613.31.7
Questions with Answers

"Hallo Serge!"

"Terry!"

"'Ave you got a minute?"

"Sure!"

Terry pulled out the roll of tape from the pocket of his jacket.

"Wot does you call dis 'ere sort o' tape?"

"Tek tape. How come?"

"Well, on account of dey's written 'tuck tape' all over it. Tuck t-u-c-k."

Serge shook his head sadly, as though to say things were never that simple:

"Do you want the whole story, from de very beginning?"

Terry explained himself:

"Well, it's only dat it don't make no sense!"

"In dis 'ere business, there's a whole lot of things that don't make no sense, let me tell you."

Serge took the roll from Terry's hands and began:

"When dis 'ere tape was first introduced on de market, some twenty years ago, we called it tek tape or Tyvek tape, because dey was usin' it to tape up Tyvek joints. It was a tape specially approved for dat in de building code. The name 'tuck tape' wasn't written on it in those days."

Terry nodded: this was exactly the sort of explanation he was looking for.

"The name 'tuck tape' isn't commonly used dese days. Dey tend to say 'sheathing tape,' 'tek tape,' or simply 'red tape.' The problem with 'tuck tape' is that folks get it mixed up wid 'duct tape.'"

Terry was amazed: that was exactly what had happened to him.

“In de last ten years, duct tape — you know, dat’s de grey tape — has more or less caused a revolution, on account of it’s become de best tape to fix all sorts o’ tings: furniture, broken windows, ripped car seats, bed covers, cable … pretty much anyting.”

Terry nodded again. He could see why the owners of the hardware wanted Serge to run the store. Serge continued:

“Me, if I was sendin’ someone to de store to fetch a roll of tuck tape, I’d take de trouble to add, dat’s ‘tuck’ wid a *t*, like in Telesphorus, an’ I’d even add more, I’d tell dem it’s de red tape dat costs around ten dollars a roll. If I was wantin’ anudder sort, I’d tell dem to buy de grey duct tape — an’ dat’s ‘duct’ wid a *d* as in Donald de duck.”

Terry noticed that, in addition to being clear, Serge’s explanations were quite pleasant to listen to. Serge now returned to the roll he was holding:

“I’m pretty sure that dis ’ere company — Canadian Technical Tape — sells a whole lot o’ different tapes, like masking tape, hockey tape, electric tape, an dat dey is de ones dat called der red tape ‘tuck tape.’ An’ dat can’t have been too long ago. Only folks call it ‘tek tape’ so as not to be confusin’ it wid de original red tape, made by 3M, dat is, if I isn’t mistaken.”

Serge had come to the end of his explanations.

“Is dat wot you was askin’?”

“Alright, I tink I got it. Der must be times de whole ting drives you round de bend.”

Serge laughed, and added:

1614.76.4 Avatars “Most likely widin a couple o’ years, dey’ll change de colour, an’ it’ll only cause a whole lot more red tape.”

1615.116.9 True or False

> True or false: gossip and rumour are forms of sociology.

“Are you afraid he won’t make something of himself?”

“Well, wid de life ee’s had an’ all dat, I might ’ave tawt maybe …”

"Could be, he sensed that."

"Still, day by day, me entire focus goes on makin' sure de boy's alright."

"Of course. Only things like that are communicated somehow."

...

"Probably he told you that so you wouldn't worry."

"So den, 'tisn't true ee wants to pilot helicopters?"

"Maybe it will be true. But more likely he felt the need to say it to you, probably to reassure you."

Zed didn't particularly like to think of Chico having to make such calculations.

"It isn't conscious. I know, it's hard to believe, only that's how it is: one unconscious speaks to another."

"Dat gives me de shivers down me spine. Are you sure?" 1616.60.11 Superstitions

death
like some big X
in the curve of his back
the railway lines in the palm of
his hand 1617.80.12 Cinquains

"Me, I'd say yer fear of yer toes gettin' sliced off by a shovel is more a worry dan a fear. I mean, there's not much chance of it happening, now is der?"

"An how can you be so sure?"

"Well, dat shovel'd 'ave to be sharp as razor, or else you'd be dealin' wid some wild muscleman. Tink 'ow much strengt' 'twould take."

... 1618.104.8 Worries

"No?"

Forty years or so later, Umberto Eco wrote *How to Travel with a Salmon.* 1619.133.6 The Future

"Mum, luh at dat building over der!"

"That's the old convent. All dat's left are de walls because de insides went up in flames. Everyting was made o' wood in dose days."

1620.140.3 Caraquet Étienne imagined the insides of a wooden building wrapped in flames and rising up high over the roof.

1621.130.9 Work In Fredericton, Hans washed dishes in The Palate restaurant for several months.

"Hahaha. Dese're tiny strawberries, eh, Dad?"

Étienne wasn't used to strawberries so small that they had to be kept in a proportionally small jar. Terry tried to attenuate the boy's comment in front of their hostess:

"Wee field strawberries! Dat's rare! I remember gatherin' dem when I was a boy."

Madame Dugas, the innkeeper added:

"I've put in twenty-three bottles dis year, dat's four more dan last year. Ask me, 'twon't happen again. De blueberries're invadin' us."

Étienne looked at his father, his mother. Invading? Terry explained:

"Dat means der everywhere, more an' more o' dem."

And he added, for the benefit of his hostess:

"Dat's a shame, on account of dese wee bottled strawberries're not a bad bit nice!"

"But, Dad! I tawt you only liked de big fat strawberries widout chemicals!"

"Sure, only dat's aside from de wee strawberries from Caraquet. Tink of 'ow long it takes just to be fillin' a wee bottle. Dat's 'ow you can tell der worth a whole lot."

"Like gold?"

Carmen choked — in a manner of speaking — on her mouthful of coffee. Terry threw her a look. Quietly, he'd begun to introduce his son to natural resources. Madame Dugas, however, was not the type to be outdone:

"'Round 'ere we'd say 'tis rare as a pope's shit."

Étienne found it strange that anyone would compare

something as good to eat as strawberries with excrement; 1622.140.2
he endeavoured to forget the analogy. Caraquet

> There is also a kind of tape called "duck tape," that has the image of a happy little yellow duck on the package. This particular tape, apparently the same width as those called "tek," "tuck," and "duct," is available in several colours, in- 1623.127.10
> cluding green, red, blue, and yellow. Tactics

For several days following his conversation with Myriam the psychologist, Zed continued to wonder to what extent Chico had been conscious or not of seeking to reassure him by declaring his intention to become a helicopter pilot. He tried to figure out a subtle way to find out.

"'Ow'd you like to go out an' hit some balls?"

Chico enjoyed whacking tennis balls back and forth with his new father. Neither he nor Zed was especially good at it, but it gave them pleasure, and felt good, all the same.

"You can ask Étienne to come, if you like."

Chico appeared to hesitate, looked up at Zed.

"I'm only sayin' if you wants to, yer not obliged. A fellow doesn't always feel like it."

Chico seemed to agree.

"Alright den, are we ready?"

Chico nodded.

"Let's go, den!"

As they walked down the hallway to the exit, Chico
slipped his hand in Zed's. The need to figure anything out 1624.135.6
exploded like fireworks. Zed and Chico

> Carmen's dream: on Mother's Day, Terry, Carmen, and the two kids spend the weekend at Carmen's parents in Grande-Digue. On Sunday morning, while preparing for mass, Carmen

offers to pin a red rose on Étienne's sweater, but the boy doesn't want the red flower; he wants a white one. Try as she might to explain why he must wear a red one, Étienne refuses. It seems to Carmen that she's never seen him so obstinate. Terry intervenes. He, too, explains to his son the reason for the red rose. Étienne calms down, but continues to refuse the red rose, and to demand a white one. Terry suggests to Carmen to drop it, and tells Étienne he'll wear a red rose or nothing at all. Étienne chooses to wear nothing at all. His grandparents don't understand Étienne's behaviour either, but they don't make a fuss. Obviously, Carmen tries not
1625.109.11 to worry too much about it, but she can't help
Dreams wondering if she is dead in her son's eyes.

"Hallo. Somebody told me you've got the whole first series of *Acadieman* for sale?"

1626.133.1 "Down in de corner, behind de yellow chair."

The Future "Great..."

Pour sûr. Does the expression come solely from the English "for sure"? Too bad. The gradation from *Pas pire* to *Pour sûr* suits me *just fine*, not to mention that "*pour sûr*" thumbs its nose at the redundant cliché "*sûr et certain,*" which I place in the same category as "*la langue de Molière*"
1627.81.5 and "*la langue de Shakespeare.*" Have I men-
Titles tioned my love-hate relationship with language?

The cartoon showed a couple of small pigs — one male wearing a cap, and a female wearing an apron — gardening in the yard of their little house.

"Funny de way dey is always showin' a man an' a woman in de cartoons..."

...

…

"Sometimes dey shows fish."

"I mean when it's parents, 'tis always a dad an' a mum togedder, never two dads or two mums."

"Sometimes dey show kids."

…

"I likes *Snow What an' de Satinwarves.*"

Terry decided to throw caution to the wind.

"Did you know der's some children dat's got two dads or two mums, instead of one dad and one mum?"

"That doesn't matter, Dad."

"Well, alright, we agree on dat. Dat…"

The cartoon had just taken a new direction: the farmer pig had planted a seed that immediately began to grow straight up into the heavens. Terry didn't want to tear his son away from the story, so he put off the discussion he wanted to have with the boy until another time. 1628.125.8 Sexuality

> The real Élizabeth exists. I've just met her. Her name is Mireille Savoie. 1629.99.9 Names

"Where's Lisa-M. at? It's bin a shockin' long time since I seen 'er."

"You didn't hear? She got de carpal tunnel in 'er wrist from playin' de flute. Dey's gonna have to operate."

"Awh, is dat so?"

"So she can't be liftin' trays an' dat."

"I'd never 'ave tawt you could get dat just from playin' flute."

"In de beginnin' some folks was sayin' 'twas a tumour, only dat was just anudder rumour." 1630.108.10 Rumours

at last twas open
merge yield merge yield were blinking
the old man smiled
the offramp called out to him 1631.75.12
to quit life without regret Tankas

“Wot sort of animal would you be, if you was one?”

Chico had already thought about it:

“A squirrel.”

Zed was quite fond of squirrels.

“Awh, yeah? On account of?”

Chico shrugged:

“I likes wot dey can do: run fast, climb in de trees an’ jump in de branches, hold right still widout movin’, eatin’ peanuts…”

“Yes. An’ dey’s right comical when der runnin’ one after de udder.”

…

…

“I likes de little brown ones wid de black line. I seen a grey one once, only ee wasn’t so nice.”

“We was callin’ de brown ones wid de black line little chipmunks. I doesn’t know if dat’s der real name.”

“You, wot animal would you be?”

Zed, too, had thought about it.

“A bear. A big black bear.”

…

“Wid two or tree little ones around. A big bear wot cares fer de wee ones.”

1632.135.11 Zed and Chico The image made Chico smile; then he stood up to toss a stone into the water.

1633.43.10 Love

> Correction: maybe this novel is a love story after all.

“Me, wot I likes are all de wee *bips* in me body, all de little *twitches* you doesn’t have the least bit o’ control over. Sometimes I lies down still, just to be feelin’ dem.”

!

…

“Dat’s life, I suppose. A bunch o’ wee *twitches* you doesn’t have no control over.”

…

…

"Did I say *twitch* in de masculin?"

"Seems to me you did…"

"Hmm…"

"Well, I wouldn't sit me arse down on top o' de stove about it."

"Dat's some strange, on account of in me head de word *twitch* is feminine. *Une twitch.*"

…

"Der's times I tinks French gets inside us an' we doesn't 1634.82.4
even know it." Moncton

> Proverb in the Babar: the glasses're breakin' 1635.100.8
> like water. Proverbs

There was no lack of choices.

"You can 'ave more'n one if you like. Dat way, one saint won't be doin' all de work by demself."

Étienne looked at his father. Terry seeing that his son had not grasped the irony, chose to distract rather than to explain, and pointed to one of the medallions:

"Dat one der's right nice."

Étienne had thought a good way to begin might be to choose his father's favourite saints.

"I wants de same ones as you."

"Yi yi!"

Marianne didn't understand much of what all these medallions were about, but obviously she wanted the same ones as Étienne. Chico — thank heavens! — seemed to want to make up his own mind.

"Saint Peter? That's a good choice. A person couldn't go wrong wid Saint Peter. You can each have tree. OK?"

"Yi yi!"

"Yes, Marianne. You can have tree, as well."

Chico bent over to examine other medallions without touching them, unlike Étienne, who was handling them all.

"Étienne, be careful, boy! Yer puttin' dem back in de wrong boxes."

Then, catching a shadow in the corner of his eye, Terry corrected himself:

"Alright, Étienne. Don't be touchin' dem no more. De man's gonna be takin' dem out fer us."

The man in question was standing at rigid attention before the little band. Terry tried to show he had his brood under control:

"Two Saint Christophers fer sure. An' one Saint Bernadette..."

Étienne was suddenly worried:

"I wants a Saint Bernadette de Spirou, too!"

"Shhhh... not so loud, Étienne. Alright den, you each get a Saint Christopher an' a Saint Bernadette. Does you want any o' dem, as well, Chico?"

Chico having agreed, the clerk took six medallions from two different compartments and let them drop one by one into a small bag, as though he were counting them. Even Terry was momentarily hypnotized by the gesture.

"Alright, dat makes two, tree fer Chico wid 'is Saint Peter. Are ya alright wid dat, Chico?"

Chico nodded.

"You doesn't want one fer Granny? A special one, maybe, a wee bit bigger, like dis 'ere of de Virgin Mary?"

While Chico chose a medallion for his grandmother, Terry tried to settle Étienne's and Marianne's choices.

"Are der any of Saint Thomas, Dad?"

Not for the first time, Terry noted his son's excellent memory.

"Why not Saint Louis?"

"No, I want Saint Thomas."

"Saint Louis was a whole lot nicer dan Saint Thomas, you ask me."

"No, I want Saint Thomas!"

"Alright, alright... An wot about you, Marianne? How

would you like Saint Teresa? Eh? A little Saint Teresa fer Marianne?"

Marianne twisted an wiggled in her father's arms before answering at last:

"Yeyessa!"

"Right! Saint Teresa!"

Terry looked at the clerk and, seeing the man had lost none of his earlier rigidity, poured a little oil on the fire:

"Well, I guess she wants Saint Teresa."

The clerk complied, relieved at last to have something else to do but stand there enduring the childrens' antics.

"Dad, can we buy one fer Granny, as well?"

"No, just Chico."

"Why not?"

Terry reconsidered.

"OK den, you can pick one out fer Granny Thibodeau, she'll like dat."

"Hooray!"

As he was paying for everything, Terry couldn't resist
one last jab at the clerk: 1636.124.10
"Youse wouldn't 'ave some safety pins, by chance?" Religion

> Postal malapropism: Here, you carry the mail, 1637.125.5
> I'll carry the female. Sexuality

"An den, just as we was goin', dey started seein' all de udder stuff: de rosaries, statues, de lucky charms, lampions. An den de pictures, Saint Joseph, Saint Anthony, Saint Benedict, *la bonne* Saint Anne, mountains of pictures, which Marianne knocked all over de floor, of course, reachin' fer a first communion crown. A real dollar store of religion, dat place!

Carmen was relieved not to have been in Terry's shoes, nor those of the clerk.

"The salesman must have been happy to see you go." 1638.124.11
"Ee held de door fer us an' all." Religion

1639.38.8 Onions

Arab proverb: an onion offered with love is worth a whole sheep.

"So den, you didn't know yer man was writin' poems!"

"Awh, ee doesn't tell me everyting he's doin'!"

The Cripple was astonished nevertheless. Was Terry hiding some part of himself? And, if so, why? And had he, The Cripple, revealed his secret?

"I don't tell 'im everytin I do, neidder. A girl's gotta keep a few cards up 'er sleeve."

Carmen was thinking mainly about the little secrets that led to pleasant surprises for the Other. Not to mention, she couldn't imagine Terry plotting something bad behind her back.

"'Tis only a bit o' fun, so that life doesn't become too dull, too repetitive from one week to de next."

The Cripple couldn't recall the last time he'd prepared a nice surprise for Antoinette, who did so much for him and never complained.

1640.16.10 The Cripple

"You know wot, yer makin' me tink…"

"Well, dat's wot we're here fer. Anudder Scotch?"

1641.24.12 Élizabeth

In fact, Élizabeth had not really enjoyed *How I Became Stupid* by Martin Page.

"Mum, does you tink inventin' a new game every day is too much?"

Carmen had no idea what Étienne was getting at. He added:

"Chico, well, ee doesn't like it."

Carmen was putting on her coat on her way out.

"Well, der's times we like to do tings we know. 'Tis like listenin' to a song or a story we already know. Must be de same ting wid a game. Der's some we like a whole lot, an' we want to play often. An' we don't really know if we're gonna like de new game quite as much as de games we know and like."

The explanation was clear. Étienne turned, looking a little disappointed. 1642.114.11 Inventions

> On a page, the words: *contusion*, *Venetian Ceruse*, *penumbra*, *sliced pan*, *cluster*, *bocage*, *shamelessly*, *bindlestiff*, *shock of hair*, *lambrequin*. 1643.67.7 Terry's Notebooks

"Hey! I already dreamed dis!"

…

"You was doin' exactly dat. Grabbed de book, opened de tap…an' 'twas right before supper, just like now."

"Enjoy it, while it lasts."

"Awh, it's already done an' gone. Would be fun if it was to last a wee bit longer."

"Dey calls it a déjà-vu."

"I know."

"Der's some dat says 'tis a wee vein in yer brain dat busts, an' dat makes a gap atwixt wot yer seein' an' de time you takes to figure out wot's happenin'. So, really, it's biological, an' nuttin' whatsoever to do wid yer dreams."

"G'wan! Is dat right?"

"Well, sometin' like dat."

…

…

"You oughtn't to have told me dat. I liked it a whole lot better de udder way." 1644.109.5 Dreams

> Teaching or teething? Agriculture or ogriculture? Monetary or monastery? Sprain your ankle or sprain your angle? Say goodnight or flay goodnight? The Woori Bank or the Worry Bank? A weekend or a weak end? Nevertheless or never the leash? Checkmate or chuckmeat? 1645.141.12 Obsessions

"The fly has to look as much like the real insect as possible, that means at the exact stage of that particular insect's development on that day."

!

"In other words, you have to select the fly of the hour."

?!

"Take the May fly, for example: that insect has thirteen stages of development. And even then, a May fly on the Kouchibougouac River doesn't look exactly the same as the Notre Dame River May fly, which means your fly also has to correspond to that specific location's insect."

!!

"Otherwise, the trout will know it's an artificial fly. In the jargon, we call that the bronze fly."

...

"The trout will swim around it, but it won't bite. A big trout, twelve or thirteen years old, has seen its fill of insects, and fisherfolks! She can tell the difference between a natural fly and our flies. Lucky for us, once in a while, she makes a mistake!"

?

1646.37.3 "Same thing for the way the fly lands and lifts off the
Animal Tales water. A trout can tell if that movement is natural or not."

> Carmen had insisted they take their trip to
> Grand-Pré after her birthday, because she
> 1647.56.9 wanted to be sure to have her new camera on
> Pilgrimages hand to record everything.

"Ah! Now I knows where 'twas I saw you! You was pickin' strawberries last week in Anita's field, wasn't you?"

Terry immediately recognized the woman:

"Dat's right! You was in de row next to us!"

...

"Yer brudder-in-law rubs yer nerves raw; dat's de impression I got anyhow..."

The woman laughed, adding:

1648.36.12 "The nice thing is that, when I'm fishing, I forget all
Strawberries that!"

Remember that now, thanks to the revised spelling rules, the French word for "onion," *oignon* may be written without the *i*. We might follow the French example and spell "onion" the way it sounds, "unyun," so that, while the French mind their own business, as in "*se mêler* 1649.38.7
de ses ognons," we would "know our unyuns." Onions

"Probably ee's still too young. That stuff doesn't interest him."

Terry had more or less come to the same conclusion.

"No, I knows it. Only I tawt I'd just let 'im know matter o' fact, dat it exists."

Carmen began applying her second night cream:

"Speakin' of dat, I think Marianne's missin' Élizabeth."

"Wot, you tink 'er big crush 'as got 'er pinin' away?"

Carmen laughed, and shot back:

"Well, in a way, yes."

"Not dat I wants to be discouragin' you, only I don't tink Marianne's got any o' dat in 'er 'ead. You ask me, de girl's as bad or worse dan Étienne."

Carmen screwed the top back onto her jar of cream. Terry added, laughing:

"Der's times I asks meself if you mightn't be de one wid dat in yer head."

Carmen took it with a laugh.

"Wot, that I've got a crush on Élizabeth?"

"Well, maybe not on Élizabeth in particular, but on udder women…"

Carmen rinsed her fingers and put away her jars:

"You really think that?"

But Terry didn't want to reveal the extent to which he 1650.125.9
might or might not be serious. Sexuality

Timeout, unless unconsciouses are speaking to 1651.93.8
one another. Time

Étienne did not want to contradict Carmen, but he had his own opinion all the same:

"But, Mum, Chico knows frogs better dan you do."

A reply that left his mother speechless, and that Josse
1652.64.2 later found highly amusing when Carmen recounted the
Opposites incident.

> Following along the lines of *e black i red... a*
> 1653.81.11 *yellow e black* and *a yellow i red* would do just
> Titles as well.

"If I'm not mistaken, it's like dodgems."

"Like wot?"

"*Bumper cars*."

"Awh."

"Or like a game of flippers."

"*Pinball*, you mean?"

"Dat's it."

...

"Well, to each 'is English, I suppose."

1654.4.12 "Englishes, you mean."

Scrabble "We gotta keep de lingo, boy."

pizza
wife arrives
beer or a glass of wine
1655.80.10 a long hard day but it ends well
Cinquains slog on

"But Dad! You promised!"

"I know I promised, only Ludmilla's ill. I just can't go."

"You promised yesterday, an' you promised de day before dat!"

"I'm sorry, Étienne, it's just not possible. We'll go tomorrow."

Étienne would have liked to sulk, but Terry had apologized, which raised a doubt in his mind.

"You know I keep me promises usually."

That was true, Étienne could not deny it.

"Der's times tings happen, an' you has to change yer plans. Eh?"

Terry was right, Étienne knew it. But did that mean he had to give in so easily?

"Only, I was wantin' to go…"

"We'll go tomorrow. It'll be just as much fun tomorrow."

That evening, as he was going to sleep, before Terry left the room, Étienne asked:

"Dad, are apologies stronger dan promises?"

Phew. Tough question. Terry suddenly had the feeling he was walking on eggshells but, still, he did not retreat.

"Sometimes one is, sometimes de udder. Depends."

Would this reply satisfy his son?"

…

"G'night, son."

"G'night, Dad." 1656.86.5

(*Phew*!) Apologies

> Examination question for Evolution and Industrialization course (SOCI 2736): contextualize the appearance of the crowbar in relation to monkeys' nails, and explain how its uses ended up qualifying it as an instrument rather than as a tool. 1657.32.5 Exam Questions

"Wot does you mean, you have to read de numerals as well?"

"Seems der's twelve o' dem dat are radars, an' der's like a secret code in dose twelve sections."

"Wot's a radar, I'd like to know?"

"A number dat's de same, no matter wot way you reads it. Like 113.131.1. De word *radar* is de same ting: *r-a-d-a-r* or *r-a-d-a-r*, 'tis de same ting bot' ways."

"Awh! A palindrome!" 1658.108.12

"A wot?" Rumours

> The French word *carotte* also refers to a tubular core sample a mining exploration extracts from the earth, a game played with a knife, and
> 1659.9.5 in tennis, a ball with spin on it that foils the
> The Garden opponent.

"Terry?"

"Julien!"

Even though they hardly knew each other, Terry and Julien always greeted each other warmly, since they were both in the book business.

"You're on vacation?"

"Dat's right, we tawt we'd spend a few days in Caraquet. I don't remember if you's met me wife, Carmen?"

Julien and Carmen greeted each other with a nod.

"Yes, at the Babar, once…"

"An' dis one 'ere's Marianne, an' dis is Étienne…"

"You ought to call yourselves the Mustachio family…"

Looking to his mother for some explanation of the man's comment, then glancing at Terry, and Marianne of course, Étienne realized that yes, all four of them were sporting whipped cream mustaches.

"Are you going to stay for the Tintamarre?"

"That's de idea. An' you, de new bookstore's doing well?"

"Yes, we're happy."

"We can't complain neidder. Come to tink of it, I's got sometin' I's wantin' to show you, seein' as you know more about old books dan I does. 'Ave you got a minute to
1660.140.9 spare, I'll fetch it from de car?"
Caraquet "Sure!"

1661.112.10
Languages *Hecho en China.*

"No! I don't want to be all decorated."

"An' why not? Everyone dresses up, dat's wot we do for de Tintamarre."

…

“Come ’ere, Marianne, Dad’s gonna tie yer flag so you doesn’t get yer feet all tangled up in it.”

“Ag?”

“Dat’s right, a flag. Do you want de bell or de whistle?”

Marianne wanted both.

“No, one or de udder. If you take de bell, Dad’s gonna have de whistle.”

Terry gave her time to make up her mind.

“De whistle? Alright den. Dad’s gonna take de bell.”

Terry clanged the bell a few times, and Marianne changed her mind.

“’Ow about you den, Étienne, do you want de whistle?”

“No, I want the bell.”

“Marianne’s got de bell. Der’s de whistle an’ de trumpet left.”

“The trumpet.”

“Maybe Marianne will let you borrow de bell later. Eh,
Marianne?” 1662.140.12
“I wanted the drum.” Caraquet

> Josse was still smiling over the frog story when she went to serve a customer who had to rummage through all his pockets to find enough money to pay for his beer. She was about to offer him the beer on the house when the man hand-
> ed her a 20 dollar bill. Something in the strang- 1663.74.9
> er’s gesture had a tiny but strange effect on her. Hans

“I sure am happy you likes baloney, too.”

Zed was preparing the snack they would take with them to Kouchibougouac Park the next day. As a parent, he always lent a hand during extra-curricular school activities or when they needed someone to accompany the children on class trips.

“Which Vachon cake do you want? De caramel or de strawberry?”

“Caramel.”

Chico was rinsing the apples under the tap.

“De teacher says we might be goin’ canoein’ if der’s enough *life jackets*.”

Chico corrected himself, laughing:

“Well, really she said “*brassière de sauvetage*.”

1664.135.12 “A rescue *brassière*!”
Zed and Chico Zed, too, was laughing.

1665.131.10 (Marianne’s mustache could have gone without
Parenthesi(e)s saying.)

1666.133.9
The Future “Granny! Talk Chiac!”

> In the end, I will not have managed to avoid a
> kind of entropy of the text, that is a condensa-
1667.89.7 tion of meaning, an organizational structuring
Irritants of the story that I experience as an irritant.

“You tell me, was it really necessary to invent all des ’ere different kinds o’ screws, den? Ask me, der was no need to make it so shockin’ complicated...”

Zed, however, recognized a number of basic principles:

“Der’s a whole lot o’ tings dat need considerin’, like de tread, de torque, de lengt’, de colour. An wedder yer dealin’ wid wood, cement, or gyproc...”

“Wot about de heads, den? How come der’s all dese different drive types? Dese days, takes tree *screwdrivers* just to take apart de smallest thingamabob! Is it all just one big money racket, or wot?!”

Zed was surprised that Terry had used the English word *screwdriver* when even he, Zed, would have said “*tournevis*.”

“Do you tink all de countries’ll ever come togedder an’ agree on one system, de way dey done wid degrees in temperature an’ for metres an’ feet? If dey only boiled ’er down to just two systems, dat’d already be a whole lot better dan de way 'tis now."

Zed doubted very much that the universalization of screw heads would happen in his lifetime. Then Terry changed the subject.

1668.63.9
Terry and Zed

1669.79.3
Oddities

Yupik is a language?!

"Wot were you up to in de bedroom?"

"I'd written de title of a book on a piece of paper dat I can't find. I's searchin' in me udder jeans to see if I'd left it in one o' de pockets."

Carmen didn't believe him for a minute. She was certain Terry had been rummaging around for something — more than likely her birthday present. She'd heard the sound of plastic bags.

"Wot, your jeans were in a bag?"

With a sardonic smile on her lips, Carmen was pressing on purpose, just to see how Terry would manage to extricate himself. Terry played innocent:

"Wot do you mean?"

"I could hear plastic bags..."

"Awh. Dat's de big bag full o' clothes we doesn't wear no more. We ought to get rid of it, takes up space fer nuttin'."

As a matter of fact, Carmen had forgotten about the bag. And yet...

"So, you're gettin' rid of yer jeans, den?"

"No, I's just lookin' all around de bag, in case de paper'd fallen der. An' wot's all dese questions about, all of a sudden?"

"Nothing. Only I didn't understand wot you were doin' out der, that's all."

Terry could see that Carmen suspected something. That was not necessarily a bad thing.

"Étienne told me you wanted a camera fer yer birt'day, by de way."

"Awh, so ee did tell you, did ee?"

1670.94.11 Terry and Carmen

"Just so you doesn't go getting' ideas, dat's not wot yer gonna be gettin.'"

"Awh no?"

1671.136.12 The Unavowed

> I write because I don't trust words/others. One way or another, a Freudian slip?

"'Bout time you got 'ere! Were ya lost!?"

Terry, who had been forewarned about the fellow's gruff manner, was still busy unstrapping Marianne from her car seat.

"Had to drop off some books wid a fellow in Lakeburn. 'Twasn't meant to take long, only you know 'ow some folks won't let you go."

The man decided Terry — who was stuck dragging a child along, to boot! — had to be the sort of fellow people pushed around.

"Generally, I'm not late. Sorry."

The man looked at his watch.

"Well anyhow, I hasn't got all day. Come on den, she's over dis way."

Terry lifted Marianne onto his shoulders and followed the man, who was making great strides toward the field of long grass.

"Starts o'er where de fence is, den it goes up into de trees."

"It ends over by de trees?"

Terry was unfamiliar with large rural surfaces.

"No! She goes way back in der. Ya see on de udder side, de wee green sign? Dat's de udder line. So you've got de whole field, plus, I'd say, a quarter mile into de woods."

"So de stream's in de woods?"

"Halfway in, I'd say."

Terry gave up going that far that day, with Marianne and the hill to climb.

"About how wide is it?"

"Well, a stream's a stream isn't it, 'tisn't a river. I dunno, maybe seven, eight feet."

Terry looked at the size of the field, tried to imagine the depth of the forest.

"Are der big trees in der?"

"Der's some. You can go take a look fer yerself, if you like, I doesn't 'ave de time."

"No, I won't go today. Would it be alright if I came by some udder time wid anudder fellow?"

"Be my guest! If you wants to go all de way 'round,
follow de trees marked wid red paint. Dat way you'll see 1672.110.9
all de way back. An' de stream." A Day Off

> Singing is like writing by hand. When I die, 1673.91.10
> bury me in a piano, or a guitar. The Poet

Antoine and Pierre had barely left the bookstore before Terry called Étienne over.

"You seen de two fellows dat just left?"

Étienne looked outside and saw two young men exchanging a furtive kiss:

"Antoine an' Pierre?"

"Awh, I didn't know you knew dem…"

"Well sure, Dad…"

Terry pretended to look for a pencil but, in fact, he was trying to find a way to continue.

"Did you know dat sometimes a man can love anudder man radder dan lovin' a woman?"

Étienne wondered where his father was going with such an obvious statement.

"An' a woman as well…she might be lovin' anudder woman radder dan a man."

Étienne wasn't sure if he ought to show agreement with such platitudes or bide his time.

"Wot I mean, even doh most of de time, a man's gonna fall in love wid a woman an' a woman's mostly gonna fall in love wid a man, right?"

"Well, Dad, I know that."

"Wot I means to say, 'tis alright fer a man to be in love

wid anudder man, radder dan wid a woman. An' de same goes fer women. Dey can just as well love a woman as a man."

Étienne opted for patience.

"De problem is dat der's some folks dat tinks 'tisn't alright to be doin' dat, an' sometimes der mean about it."

. . .

"Only Carmen an' I, an' a whole lot of folks we know, we tink it's fine. Dey loves each other, right? An' dat's wot's important."

. . .

"So den, if ever it happens to you to love anudder boy more dan anybody else, dat's just fine. An' you oughtn't to be tinkin' it shouldn't be dat way, on account of sometimes dat's just de way it is."

. . .

"Anyhow, dat's just sometin' I was wanted to let you know."

"OK, Dad."

In retrospect, Terry felt he'd been slightly abrupt in his
1674.125.12 Sexuality way of handling the subject, but he was satisfied that boy
seemed to have grasped the essential.

1675.105.11 Reserves/Reservations

Ah ≠ ha. Ah ah ≠ ha ha.

Étienne and Chico were playing quietly at digging a quarry.

"Me, I's gonna pilot helicopters when I's older."

Chico's declaration seriously impressed Étienne. Suddenly he saw Chico as an older brother, much older than he, and from whom he would learn a great deal
1676.139.3 Étienne and Chico about life.

"An' how're you gonna do dat?"

Chico shrugged: he hadn't gotten to that point, yet.

1677.67.5 Terry's Notebooks

Wonky — in the dictionary!

"Wot does she tink? Dat we'll like 'er fer free'?" 1678.96.1 Characters

> Language as a tool for seduction. 1679.126.10 Techniques

"An' den wot?"

Pomme had just joined his two comrades at the Babar. He'd taken the time to hang his coat on the back of his chair before intervening.

"Eh? An' wot?"

Terry and Zed knew very well they'd end up explaining everything to Pomme in time, but neither figured the time was quite now.

"An' nuttin'. We's just talkin', dat's all."

Pomme studied them slowly each in turn.

"Alright, den. How about dis: Lisa's pregnant." 1680.102.11 The Trio

And time to celebrate.

> Eventually, in spite of the ban on marriages between cousins seven times removed, the Catholic Church decided it could grant dispensations up to cousins thrice removed, in order to protect inheritances and all that relates to heritage. Protecting one's heritage, saving one's heritage: an essential preoccupation of Acadians. From the beginning of time, defending one's village, cattle, lands, church, and ultimately one's language. From the beginning of time, and most likely until the end. 1681.106.12 Customs

"I can't be goin' troo, if you puts yer *dump truck* der..."

"Yes, you can."

"No! On account of I has to *plow* dis 'ere side of de butte."

"Only afterwards, when I goes to *dump* me rocks, I won't be able to slew around properly. Luh..."

The two boys studied the whole of the work site, and Chico made a proposal:

"You could be movin' de rocks wid de *crane*..."

Étienne considered it.

"Alright."

...

1682.139.4 Étienne and Chico

...

"Hey! Where's de *cement truck* got to?!"

> For several months, every two or three days, an envelope would arrive for Chico, not very big, white with a pale blue design inside, and containing only a small drawing, a bit of color,
> 1683.96.9 Characters
> a few stick characters without heads. Then nothing more.

"Dad?"

"Wot?"

"You remember de time we went strawberry pickin', just you an' me?"

"Last summer, you mean?"

This reference disoriented Étienne, who did not yet have a clear sense of time. Terry brought him back:

"De strawberries wid no chemicals in dem?"

Étienne nodded.

"Alright... an' den?"

"Well, I didn't really tink dat Granny Thibodeau would've put Mister Clean in de pie, because dat wouldn't be nice."

Terry was impressed:

"Yer still thinkin' 'bout dat? Well, yer absolutely right, me boy, Granny would never do a ting like dat."

This surprised Étienne.

"But, dat's wot you said."

"Me, I said dat? Well, maybe so. Only, I don't really tink she'd do such a ting; 'twas only in a manner of speakin'."

Étienne found it troubling that there could be more than one manner of speaking. Terry added:

"Granny Després wouldn't do such a ting neidder, far

as dat goes. To tell de troot', der's not many folks would. Der's not dat many folks're dat mean."

As he spoke Terry remembered that he had indeed tried to get Étienne to say which of his two grandmothers he was thinking of when he raised the possibility of poisoning.

"Boat yer grandmudders wouldn't hurt a fly. Now, dat's a manner of speakin', as well. On account of dey do kill some flies, from time to time. It only means dat dey wouldn't be hurtin' people."

Étienne looked content, relieved.

"Dat's wot you was wantin' to tell me?"

Étienne nodded:

"I tawt you were tinkin' I didn't like Granny Thibodeau."

"Granny Déspres, you mean."

"No, Granny Thibodeau!"

Now Terry was completely confused about the details of the imagined poisoning, but he concluded that the result was the same, one way or the other.

"Well anyhow, you're doin' de proper ting tellin' me when der's sometin' worryin' you. 'Tisn't a good idea to keep tings like dat bottled up inside. Alright?" 1684.132.6 Malapropism

"I know, Dad. You already told me that."

> Chico doesn't like things being put away under his bed, thereby preventing the dust from going where it will. It makes him feel like he's suffocating. 1685.88.2 Freedom

"Can we go back to wot we was sayin' before?"

"Of course."

"Colourin' de spaces inside letters, wouldn't dat be like puttin' de golf ball in de hole? Wot I mean, 'as no one ever said der could be some sort o' link atwixt playin' golf an' fear of de void?"

"Interesting question..."

"(Friggin' right!)"

"I am not aware of such a link ever having been made. It certainly merits looking up. If not, it would be an excellent topic for study."

. . .

"Just in passing, the hole on the green in golf is called '*une oubliette*,' or 'forgotten place,' a dungeon accessible only through a hole in the ceiling."

"G'wan wid ya!"

"Yer pullin' our leg!"

"No way!"

"Well, right der, see! De word *oubliette* tells you der's
1686.141.11 sometin' to be fergotten. Dat could be de void dat fright-
Obsessions ens, right?"

> 1687.45.6 Essentially, "useless details" are useless because
> Useless Details they come too late.

Zed and Terry were once more alone on the road in Zed's truck. They enjoyed moments like these.

"It's got so anybody at all can be bisexual dese days. Even Carmen says 'twouldn't bodder 'er to be sleepin' wid anudder woman."

Zed pulled his tumbler of hot coffee quickly away from his lips. Oblivious, Terry continued:

"Not dat I's sayin' Carmen is just anybody at all. I'm only saying dat even she's talkin' like dat."

Zed thought for a moment, but could see nothing alarming in it:

"Most likely, der's not dat many folks nowadays dat's all one or all de udder."

Terry went even further:

"Sometimes, I tries to imagine how much farder tings could go."

Zed tried for a moment to imagine a future society,
1688.125.11 but unable to conjure up much, went back to imagining
Sexuality Carmen in the arms of a woman.

Names and places of origin of the first French colonists to settle in the colony that came to be known as Acadia.

1689.57.8
Photocopies

Étienne couldn't quite describe what he'd seen.

"Roads? What sort of roads?"

"Lots of roads."

Terry tried to help him out:

"Like a whole lot o' roads all tangled up togedder?"

"No. Dey weren't tangled."

...

...

"An' wot about you, where was you?"

Étienne took a mouthful of his peanut butter and jam covered toast.

"Were you in a car or was you walkin'?"

Étienne shrugged.

"Were you alone, den?"

Étienne didn't know.

"Were you feelin' alright?"

Étienne nodded, adding:

"It was never the same road."

Terry was almost tired of the guessing game, and thought he might bring the discussion to a close with some kind of general conclusion about dreams, but Étienne wasn't quite done:

"One time, it was like in a field, we were comin' down a hill. Der were trees."

"Was it a field or trees? I don't understand..."

Étienne nodded.

"Den after, der was no more hill, only sky. Only 'twas a road all de same."

Considering the general confusion, Terry decided to deliver his general conclusion:

"Sometimes we can understand our dreams, an' udder times we can't. You just have to leave dem be in yer head. An' sometimes we forget dem, udder times dey erase demselves, an udder dreams replace dem."

1690.109.1 Étienne nodded.

Dreams "I know."

> 1691.124.12 Where economy and religion meet: he who
> Religion sings prays twice (dixit Saint Augustine).

"Mum, wot's neck's ear?"

"Wot?"

"Neck's ear. (*Cloc*)"

Carmen thought for a moment, but nothing came to mind.

"Who is it said that?"

"*Cloc clac cloc*..."

Carmen insisted:

1692.123.8 "Was it someone on de television?"

Carmen and Étienne "Yes. Ask for yours and see the difference neck's ear."

> And again, thanks to the *Visual* dictionary, a
> 1693.111.5 gift from Zed: dump truck – *camion benne*,
> Tools crane – *grue*, cement truck – *bétonnière*.

Terry realized in just how fine a form he was that day, when he saw Alphonse Lemaître, aka LeSage(!) open the door to the bookstore. Needless to say, the retired professor was not one to invite familiarity, and—of this Terry was convinced—he was always asking for books he knew were not on the shelves.

"Is der sometin' I can do fer you today?"

Terry had no trouble accepting the occasional criticism from clients, but he was wary of people who never had anything nice or even polite to say. What's more, he had some experience with this particular pretentious client—Alphonse Lemaître aka LeSage(!!)—who was always careful to pronounce every word perfectly, as though he hailed from Versailles rather than Shediac.

"No, I'm not looking for anything in particular, I

simply wanted to look over your new arrivals."

Terry looked for the dig, but held off jumping to conclusions. Still, he was happy he'd restocked his shelves the day before. At the same time, he had something entirely different in mind for the elderly gentleman.

"I've got sometin' 'ere might interest you…"

It was the first time Terry had ventured onto Alphonse Lemaître aka LeSage's territory.

"Ah, do you, now?"

Terry took note of the professor emeritus' ambiguous tone, even thought he detected a kind of malicious pleasure.

"Somebody was tellin' me you used to teach Baudelaire at the university…"

"Yes…"

Lemaître aka LeSage seemed unhappy to learn people were talking about him in his absence.

"I found dis 'ere old copy of de *Flowers of Evil*. Doesn't look to me like sometin' all dat easy to get hold of…"

Terry showed the book to the professor, who took it with a mixture of hesitation and haste that betrayed his interest and his surprise.

"Came from a fellow brought me a couple of boxes of old books ee didn't want."

"Ah, did he?"

Alphonse Lemaître aka LeSage examined the volume's every stitch, and was obliged to admit:

"So, you're on the lookout for rare books, then…"

It was the first time the old professor had shown any interest at all in Terry.

"I'm startin…"

But Alphonse Lemaître aka LeSage quickly interrupted the last syllable of the second word Terry had uttered, as though he was suddenly afraid that…

"Yes, of course, I'll take it."

Terry didn't move, which seemed to destabilize Lemaître aka LeSage.

"It is for sale, I presume."

"Well, dat's just it. I hadn't made up me mind wot I's gonna do wid it."

"Ah, is that right?"

"An when you tink wot it's wort', well..."

"You know it's value?"

"I've a pretty good idea. Wid de Internet nowadays..."

Alphonse Lemaître aka LeSage gave him a little twisted
1694.99.8 grin; he suddenly knew, this time he would not come out
Names on top.

> Zed doesn't like to lose the drawings that
> 1695.128.4 Shawn sends Chico. He recovers them quietly,
> Fervours and shows them to Zablonski.

"An' by de way, I started dis whole ting all on me own dis time. I'm tellin' you on account of I wouldn't want you to go blamin' Zed."

Carmen had long ago accepted the fact that Terry and Zed were in some way inseparable, spiritual brothers.

"No, I've known for a while that you're perfectly capable of having your own hare-brained ideas."

As she spoke, Carmen drew Terry to her for a hug.

1696.94.12 He hugged her tenderly.

Terry and "Hare-brained, eh? Hmmm..."

Carmen Carmen laughed. To Terry, that was a good sign.

> For Zablonski, Shawn's drawings complete the squaring of the circle. The artist who, in spite of himself, served as the inspiration for the Prizon Art movement, now discovers, purely by chance, the drawings of an unknown prisoner who is groping in the world of the sign. Zablonski notices that the figures are always
> 1697.56.11 composed of five strokes, but he doesn't notice
> Pilgrimages that they are all headless.

"Dad, do computers tink?"

Terry looked at his son in the rear-view mirror:

"No, not yet. Far as I know, anyhow."

"Well den, wot do dey do?"

"Dey makes connections. Dey can be puttin' millions an' millions of wee scraps togedder, only we has to be de one's tellin' dem wot to do. On der own, dey wouldn't be doin' it."

Terry thought his explanation sounded plausible; he continued, conscious that he was enjoying listening to himself talk:

"Like, a computer can only be tinkin' wot somebody programmed it to tink. We human bein's, we tinks fer ourselves."

At that moment, Terry glanced at his son in the rear-view mirror to see if he was listening. The boy was looking at him, too.

"Do you understand wot I mean?"

The child nodded yes, and added:

"Me, I like to think. Only der's times I don't know how."

"Dat's on account of yer still young. You'll learn, don't you worry. Dat's part o' growin' up."

Le Petit Étienne agreed and turned his gaze toward the exterior. 1698.110.10 A Day Off

> Well, I'll be darned: I've reread *To Kill a Mockingbird* by the American Harper Lee, and I admit I can't decide if I would include the book in my additions to the *La Bibliothèque idéale*. I suppose I'll have to read it a third time. I can't believe it.

1699.95.9 Additions to *La Bibliothèque idéale*

"Luh, Dad, looks like der's somebody campin' o'er der."

Terry answered absent-mindedly:

"Where's dat?"

"Der! In de trees!"

Étienne's vaguely overexcited tone woke Terry from his

reverie; he looked over toward his right. After a moment of observation:

"You know wot, boy, I tink yer right."

On the shore of the Hall stream, at the mouth of the Petitcodiac, someone had built themselves a discrete shelter in the brush between the pine trees.

"Mostly likely, 'tis a body hasn't got a house."

Another few seconds of observing passed.

"Or else somebody on de road."

"Is he gonna be building hisself a fire?"

"Awh, might be. Only chances are de police'll be movin' 'im out o' der."

"On account of?"

"Well, dey doesn't want folks settlin' in anywhere dey please."

1700.110.11 "On account of?"

A Day Off . . .

> All of a sudden the absolute certitude that I should be writing "*pélerinages*" rather than "*pèlerinages*." Is it merely a question of the ac-
> 1701.56.7 cent? A sudden feeling of not knowing where
> Pilgrimages one stands.

"Dad, are we's gonna sleep in de tent in Caraquet?"

"Are we gonna be sleepin'. Are we gonna be sleepin' in de tent in Caraquet..."

"Well? Are we gonna?"

"No. We're gonna be sleepin' in a house where they'll be makin' our breakfast. Dat's a whole lot o' fun as well, you'll see."

Étienne had never imagined that breakfast...

"Dad!"

Terry jumped, thinking there'd been an accident.

"You made me tink dat breakfast!"

Terry regained his composure, adding:

"You can be sayin' it that way. When you says dat, you

have to add sometin' on the end of it. Like, you made me tink dat breatkfast...is good in de mornin'. Or, dat breakfast, someone has to make it..."

...

"You see wot I'm sayin'?"

"Yes. Only I just want to say dat breakfast..." 1702.78.10

Terry let it go. Two corrections the same day was a lot. Accidents

> It is considered impolite to divulge one's gains on the stock market. The same goes for one's losses.

1703.85.9 The Stock Market

"Carmen'll never agree."

"On account of?"

"On account of de stream. She'll be afeard fer de kids."

"You tink? She's not dat much of a mudder hen as all dat." 1704.117.11

"I'm tellin' you. It'll rub her nerves raw." Death

little pink piggy
draw her dad draw her for me
corkscrew of a tail
vest and handkerchief in plaid
wolf eyes on the horizon

1705.75.5 Tankas

"Lakeville."

"Lakeville Painsec or Lakeville Saint-Philippe?"

"Lakeville Painsec."

Lisa-M. felt something bursting open.

"Ought to be called just plain Painsec. Like 'twas in de old days."

Lisa-M. was already throwing herself completely into the idea of a return to the land:

"Wid a stream on top of everytin'! 'Tis like a dream!"

Pomme had never seen her so enthusiastic, including when he'd asked her to marry him:

"Lard, girl, I didn't know you 'ad all of dat in you."

Lisa-M. would not budge:

"Dat's where tings is goin'. We has to learn to be relyin' on ourselves."

!

"I can't wait! When does we find out?"

"Afore long. An' don't ferget, now, yer not to tell a soul!"

1706.129.7 Fantasies

"I knows it. Only 'tisn't gonna be easy!"

> Hans did not usually drink alcohol. But that day he'd gained some awareness of the size of the universe, and thought to himself, why not. ("Infinite to the naked eye, our galaxy, the Milky Way, is located on the periphery of a cluster of galaxies, that is of a group of at least a thousand galaxies. Scientists have recorded 86 clusters, which suggests the existence of at least 86,000 galaxies.")

1707.74.10 Hans

"Mum, can we be inventin' words ourselves?"

Carmen took the time to think about it, then began:

"Yes... only you can't force other people to use them."

Étienne took his own time to reflect. Drifted away. Only to come back to it the next day:

1708.123.12 Carmen and Étienne

"Mum, is der anytin' you can force udder people to do?"

1709.111.11 Tools

> In the end, the six-pronged fork turned out to be very handy.

"Gold is uncertain."

1710.85.10 The Stock Market

...

"It'll probably be a *dead cat bounce*."

> In 43, after condemning (Saint) James the Great to death, King Herod had (Saint) Peter imprisoned, ordering that he be chained in a cell. An

> angel rescued him, breaking his chains. Hence the name Saint-Peter-in-Chains. 1711.41.11 Lives of the Saints

Carmen was stunned:
"A stream?!"
"Well, way over at the end of de land. An' 'tisn't deep."
Terry held his breath.
"How far an' how deep?" 1712.117.9 Death
"Well..."

> There was a time, not so long ago, when it was quite common to see a boy pull a penknife out of his pocket and use it skillfully — to whittle a stick, cut a rope, open a clam, repair a flat bicycle tire. 1713.93.1 Time

"Hans? Hans?"

Élizabeth had come be the Babar by chance, thinking she might take Marianne to the Magnetic Hill Zoo.

"Hans!"

Hans opened his eyes. The people gathered around the body stretched out on the floor could appreciate Élizabeth's skills in action. She kept one hand on his pulse and the other on his forehead.

"Élizabeth? Is that you?"

Comically, someone thought of Gabriel being reunited with Évangeline. 1714.74.11 Hans

an X in the hand
or a sharp knife in the back 1715.55.12 Haikus
death will sign its folk

"I heard Terry an' Zed made a killin' on de stock market."

!

"Seems dey had shares in a wee company dat just got bought up by General Electric fer sometin' like twenty times de price dey paid."

"Good fer dem!"

"Dey's tinkin' o' buyin' land in Lakeside..."

1716.108.4 Rumours "Wot fer?"

"I don't know, do I. An investment, I suppose."

1717.121.5 Things to Want Luck.

"Does you like drawin'?"

Chico shrugged. No, it wasn't generally something he did of his own volition. But maybe he ought to try? Only Étienne didn't pursue it.

"Do you want to read?"

Chico shrugged again. Drawing, reading, on what strange planet had he landed?

"Do you want to make a boat?"

Now, Chico's face became a question mark. Étienne opened two doors near the floor that concealed a small workbench for making things with wood. Chico put his hand on the real hammer. Étienne showed him the nails.

1718.139.1 Étienne and Chico "I never hammered nails before, only now I knows how."

1719.96.3 Characters

> The character of the photocopier could have been more developed.

"I heard Terry an' Zed lost der shirt in de stock market."

?!

"Seems dey put all der money in a wee company dat went bankrupt."

"Dat surprises me. Seems to me, der not so stun'd as dat."

"Dey bought an ol' house fer next to nuttin' behind Lakeside, I suppose dey'll be movin' out der."

1720.85.12 The Stock Market ...

"Der wives aren't all dat suited..."

To go on, in spite of everything. We can't al-
ways wait for clarifications, or retrace our steps. 1721.107.9
Allow real life to operate within the work. Necessities

"Fer Bas-Caraquet, you's gotta turn right when you gets across from de hospital."

Étienne interrupted them:

"But, Dad, der's no hospital!"

Terry was happy to see that the boy was attentive to conversation around him.

"Well, troot is der is one. It's only dat 'tisn't near as big as it used to be. Dey closed down some of de sections."

Étienne wondered at what age one began to understand things properly. Then he thought of the sky-blue windows of the old eviscerated convent, drifted off. And
came back. 1722.140.10
"Mum, do you tink birds are lucky?" Caraquet

Names of Acadian dogs: Prince, Brownie, Ginger, Rex, Sabre, Prince II, Vagabond, Coco, Bijou, Kayle, Keisha, Maggie, Corneille, Fido, Bailey, Tootsie, Baldor, Sandy, Rosie, Zack, Niki, Louis, Chopper, Popotte, Milou, Ti-Lou,
Pépé Cool, Maxi, Pooh, Choco, Pitou, and 1723.99.4
Moka. Names

"Saint Cecilia painted a church in Caraquet."

"Wot colour?"

"A whole lot o' colours."

…

"Only der all de same." 1724.139.12

… Étienne and

"Blue." Chico

The perfect sentence on the art of becoming
cheese, read somewhere, and never found 1725.47.2
again. Yielding

"Terry?... Terry?..."

...

"Terry!"

And Terry opened his eyes. It worked every time. Zed had learned the trick a long time ago, watching Élizabeth pull Hans out of a slumber that seemed like it might last forever."

"De foal's born. She's a filly. Perfect healt."

Even paralyzed and mute, Terry remained Zed's best friend, and the latter came by to see him almost daily.

"Chico's youngest wants to call 'er Nadine. Can you imagine dat? Der tryin' to convince 'er to call it Dina—Nadine, Dina, 'tis almost de same ting. Don't know if dey'll succeed doh, she's one hard case, dat one."

...

1726.133.12 The Future "An' how 'bout you, den! Are dey gonna get you up today?"

1727.98.8 Expressions

> To be the object of ridicule, but to put on a good show.

1728.41.9 Lives of the Saints

"Eh, Dad? Wot's de name of de saint wot trew de paper balls into de fire?"

INDEX

7. Useful Details

41.7.6
60.7.11
141.7.9
227.7.10
233.7.12
247.7.8
385.7.4
413.7.3
753.7.5
921.7.2
1011.7.1
1514.7.7

8. Didot Books

18.8.2
32.8.1
72.8.3
80.8.4
86.8.5
92.8.6
118.8.7
122.8.8
146.8.9
174.8.10
180.8.11
188.8.12

9. The Garden

346.9.1
390.9.3
408.9.2
410.9.4
578.9.6
592.9.7
594.9.8
598.9.9
600.9.10
604.9.11
610.9.12
1659.9.5

10. Typography

15.10.2
21.10.1
25.10.3
39.10.4
49.10.5
51.10.7
79.10.8
81.10.9
97.10.10
111.10.11
135.10.12
169.10.6

11. Appropriations

31.11.4
37.11.10
47.11.2
69.11.12
83.11.11
93.11.8
103.11.7
125.11.6
225.11.3
241.11.1
511.11.5
583.11.9

12. Structure

123.12.1
129.12.2
159.12.3
173.12.4
179.12.5
191.12.6
195.12.7
205.12.8
211.12.9
275.12.11
287.12.10
1181.12.12

13. Paternity

38.13.1
42.13.2
76.13.3
106.13.9
520.13.4
524.13.12
530.13.8
540.13.6
582.13.10
588.13.7
1230.13.5
1508.13.11

14. Zablonski

190.14.1
192.14.2
204.14.3
210.14.4
218.14.5
230.14.6
238.14.7
242.14.8
252.14.9
268.14.10
278.14.11
286.14.12

15. Unidentified Monologues

16.15.11
70.15.10
96.15.12
100.15.6
126.15.3
142.15.8
164.15.1
186.15.4
1050.15.2
1066.15.9
1188.15.7
1603.15.5

16. The Cripple

450.16.1
456.16.2
466.16.3
474.16.4
614.16.5
742.16.7
746.16.8
750.16.9
910.16.6
1270.16.11
1572.16.12
1640.16.10

17. Chance

53.17.1
133.17.2
167.17.4
193.17.6
202.17.7
213.17.9
1043.17.5
1139.17.10
1203.17.12
1425.17.8
1531.17.11
1571.17.3

18. A Place for Everyone

264.18.7
448.18.1
452.18.2
476.18.5
480.18.8
482.18.3
490.18.9
492.18.10
506.18.6
518.18.11
522.18.12
1460.18.4

19. Interesting Details

91.19.1
119.19.3
157.19.4
165.19.8
203.19.9
226.19.12
259.19.10
311.19.2
357.19.5
649.19.7
1360.19.6
1511.19.11

20. Language

54.20.8
168.20.2
184.20.4
345.20.10
502.20.5
589.20.3
599.20.6
603.20.7
611.20.9
641.20.11
1237.20.12
1570.20.1

21. More or Less Useful Details

63.21.7
127.21.9
196.21.5
325.21.6
379.21.3
494.21.2
617.21.11
625.21.4
769.21.1
1233.21.10
1315.21.12
1447.21.8

22. Overheard Conversations

22.22.10
208.22.7
216.22.1
246.22.6
324.22.12
458.22.11
478.22.4
484.22.5
496.22.3
500.22.2
1394.22.9
1524.22.8

23. Potatoes

624.23.1
626.23.2
646.23.3
814.23.5
872.23.4
980.23.6
1218.23.9
1238.23.7
1464.23.11
1480.23.10
1515.23.12
1556.23.8

24. Élizabeth

206.24.1
234.24.2
239.24.3
258.24.4
261.24.5
266.24.6
276.24.7
284.24.8
308.24.10
318.24.9
326.24.11
1641.24.12

25. Murder

388.25.5
544.25.1
546.25.2
548.25.3
552.25.4
560.25.6
564.25.7
568.25.8
570.25.9
572.25.10
574.25.11
881.25.12

26. The Movie

364.26.1
370.26.2
372.26.3
374.26.4
382.26.5
386.26.6
392.26.7
394.26.8
424.26.9
434.26.10
438.26.11
460.26.12

27. New Car

376.27.1
396.27.2
400.27.3
404.27.4
412.27.5
416.27.6
420.27.8
422.27.9
428.27.10
430.27.11
432.27.12
444.27.7

28. A Couple's Life

436.28.1
440.28.2
442.28.3
446.28.4
454.28.5
528.28.6
550.28.7
554.28.8
556.28.9
558.28.10
562.28.11
566.28.12

29. On the Road

754.29.1
756.29.2
760.29.3
764.29.4
768.29.5
770.29.6
774.29.7
778.29.8
784.29.9
788.29.10
792.29.11
796.29.12

30. Chiac

11.30.2
34.30.4
43.30.1
94.30.7
128.30.10
140.30.8
182.30.11
248.30.3
260.30.12
398.30.5
602.30.6
1007.30.9

31. Questions with Answers

26.31.2
82.31.5
250.31.1
288.31.11
350.31.9
356.31.6
418.31.3
597.31.4
1256.31.12
1424.31.10
1537.31.8
1613.31.7

32. Exam Questions

271.32.1
327.32.2
355.32.5
745.32.4
957.32.7
1105.32.6
1311.32.8
1325.32.9
1367.32.12
1377.32.10
1435.32.11
1657.32.3

33. Chiac Lesson

48.33.8
64.33.3
74.33.11
105.33.5
214.33.2
277.33.1
431.33.9
471.33.4
507.33.7
541.33.10
565.33.6
581.33.12

34. Lacan

181.34.1
295.34.2
309.34.6
337.34.5
341.34.4
365.34.8
369.34.10
375.34.9
401.34.7
417.34.11
425.34.12
1566.34.3

35. The Detail within the Detail

52.35.2
137.35.3
171.35.9
217.35.12
303.35.8
321.35.7
427.35.1
462.35.10
488.35.4
491.35.5
653.35.6
1144.35.11

36. Strawberries

832.36.1
834.36.2
840.36.3
842.36.4
844.36.5
846.36.6
848.36.7
850.36.8
852.36.10
1113.36.11
1466.36.9
1648.36.12

37. Animal Tales

4.37.7
8.37.1
124.37.10
136.37.9
359.37.4
612.37.6
640.37.2
1078.37.8
1202.37.11
1350.37.5
1582.37.12
1646.37.3

38. Onions

912.38.1
916.38.2
930.38.3
955.38.4
968.38.9
971.38.10
985.38.11
1003.38.6
1017.38.12
1497.38.5
1639.38.8
1649.38.7

39. Freud Circuitously

101.39.4
109.39.1
121.39.2
139.39.3
163.39.5
231.39.7
299.39.9
306.39.6
334.39.8
363.39.10
373.39.11
415.39.12

40. Clear Your Coast

660.40.1
662.40.2
664.40.3
668.40.4
670.40.5
674.40.6
676.40.7
682.40.8
686.40.9
690.40.10
694.40.11
698.40.12

41. Lives of the Saints

468.41.8
510.41.12
1290.41.7
1322.41.1
1324.41.2
1326.41.3
1330.41.4
1468.41.10
1472.41.5
1476.41.6
1711.41.11
1728.41.9

42. Sorting

861.42.5
959.42.7
1021.42.10
1025.42.3
1029.42.6
1041.42.1
1059.42.4
1213.42.11
1291.42.2
1293.42.12
1349.42.8
1449.42.9

43. Love

586.43.1
616.43.3
628.43.9
718.43.11
720.43.12
725.43.5
749.43.7
763.43.6
802.43.8
807.43.4
1342.43.2
1633.43.10

44. Godfathers and Godmothers

630.44.1
634.44.2
636.44.3
638.44.4
644.44.6
652.44.5
706.44.7
714.44.8
724.44.9
728.44.10
734.44.11
738.44.12

45. Useless Details

9.45.3
33.45.5
36.45.9
55.45.11
147.45.2
215.45.7
219.45.12
377.45.4
495.45.8
659.45.10
811.45.1
1687.45.6

46. *La Bibliothèque idéale*

243.46.2
245.46.3
253.46.1
263.46.4
279.46.5
281.46.6
297.46.7
301.46.8
307.46.9
323.46.10
331.46.11
343.46.12

47. Yielding

489.47.3
688.47.5
790.47.1
1045.47.10
1058.47.7
1168.47.6
1283.47.11
1413.47.9
1444.47.12
1517.47.8
1598.47.4
1725.47.2

48. Inferences

361.48.1
367.48.2
393.48.3
397.48.4
403.48.5
409.48.6
411.48.7
423.48.8
435.48.9
441.48.10
453.48.11
941.48.12

49. Élizabeth II

366.49.1
654.49.4
732.49.2
748.49.6
758.49.7
762.49.8
766.49.9
772.49.10
776.49.3
782.49.11
786.49.12
950.49.5

50. Fundy

866.50.10
868.50.11
874.50.3
882.50.1
886.50.2
888.50.4
892.50.5
894.50.6
898.50.7
900.50.8
904.50.9
908.50.12

51. Crosswords

666.51.1
672.51.2
680.51.4
684.51.5
692.51.6
702.51.8
704.51.3
708.51.7
710.51.9
712.51.10
716.51.12
739.51.11

52. Ceremony

804.52.1
808.52.2
812.52.3
816.52.4
824.52.6
830.52.5
836.52.7
856.52.8
858.52.9
860.52.10
862.52.11
864.52.12

53. Buyer Beware

926.53.1
928.53.2
932.53.3
936.53.4
940.53.5
942.53.6
946.53.7
952.53.8
956.53.9
962.53.10
966.53.11
970.53.12

54. Forgotten/Recalled

143.54.1
151.54.9
160.54.4
274.54.10
291.54.6
407.54.7
587.54.8
647.54.2
665.54.5
747.54.3
1053.54.11
1149.54.12

55. Haikus

235.55.1
251.55.2
351.55.3
711.55.4
799.55.5
805.55.6
825.55.7
837.55.8
1019.55.9
1123.55.11
1259.55.10
1715.55.12

56. Pilgrimages

383.56.1
519.56.5
863.56.3
1125.56.2
1355.56.8
1417.56.10
1501.56.4
1551.56.12
1595.56.6
1647.56.9
1697.56.11
1701.56.7

57. Photocopies

189.57.4
197.57.1
209.57.5
399.57.10
622.57.6
801.57.2
851.57.9
1219.57.3
1361.57.7
1519.57.11
1589.57.12
1689.57.8

58. Extensions

223.58.7
265.58.1
381.58.2
481.58.6
503.58.10
585.58.5
609.58.9
667.58.3
1171.58.12
1177.58.4
1505.58.11
1569.58.8

59. Knowledge

648.59.1
696.59.3
700.59.4
736.59.5
798.59.12
810.59.11
884.59.8
902.59.7
918.59.9
924.59.10
958.59.6
1467.59.2

60. Superstitions

655.60.2
669.60.10
731.60.5
1063.60.7
1097.60.4
1115.60.3
1141.60.8
1329.60.6
1335.60.9
1391.60.1
1493.60.12
1616.60.11

61. Social Sciences

445.61.1
449.61.2
455.61.3
461.61.4
467.61.5
475.61.6
493.61.11
497.61.7
515.61.8
673.61.10
677.61.12
1301.61.9

62. Survey/Men

869.62.1
877.62.2
889.62.3
895.62.4
907.62.5
913.62.6
927.62.7
933.62.8
939.62.9
951.62.10
961.62.11
987.62.12

63. Terry and Zed

162.63.12
944.63.11
1044.63.1
1046.63.2
1048.63.3
1100.63.4
1106.63.5
1110.63.6
1114.63.7
1116.63.8
1130.63.10
1668.63.9

64. Opposites

305.64.4
514.64.7
516.64.3
806.64.5
1076.64.10
1183.64.6
1199.64.8
1247.64.9
1273.64.1
1307.64.11
1356.64.12
1652.64.2

65. Boy Cousins, Girl Cousins

465.65.2
477.65.3
483.65.6
485.65.4
487.65.8
501.65.10
505.65.7
509.65.9
529.65.12
1039.65.11
1187.65.5
1295.65.1

66. The Virtues

439.66.1
443.66.2
451.66.3
457.66.4
459.66.9
463.66.6
473.66.5
537.66.12
555.66.7
1023.66.8
1035.66.11
1365.66.10

67. Terry's Notebooks

557.67.6
1033.67.3
1135.67.1
1253.67.9
1317.67.4
1353.67.8
1445.67.2
1521.67.12
1547.67.10
1565.67.11
1643.67.7
1677.67.5

68. Projects

95.68.1
175.68.5
657.68.3
727.68.4
855.68.9
969.68.7
983.68.6
1065.68.10
1193.68.11
1265.68.12
1320.68.8
1591.68.2

69. Survey/Women

873.69.1
879.69.2
891.69.3
905.69.4
909.69.5
915.69.6
931.69.7
937.69.8
945.69.9
953.69.10
963.69.11
1001.69.12

70. Errors

525.70.10
601.70.2
605.70.3
615.70.4
621.70.5
633.70.6
635.70.7
651.70.9
1081.70.8
1279.70.1
1459.70.11
1481.70.12

71. Intro Embroidery

201.71.1
221.71.2
229.71.3
269.71.4
293.71.5
349.71.6
553.71.9
627.71.7
797.71.11
821.71.8
826.71.12
1533.71.10

72. Equations

220.72.1
224.72.2
237.72.3
255.72.4
267.72.5
273.72.6
314.72.7
322.72.8
333.72.9
339.72.10
352.72.11
387.72.12

73. Shifts

486.73.12
847.73.2
885.73.5
920.73.1
925.73.6
929.73.9
976.73.11
1024.73.4
1383.73.3
1405.73.10
1540.73.8
1554.73.7

74. Hans

517.74.2
521.74.1
523.74.3
527.74.4
531.74.5
545.74.6
547.74.7
575.74.8
709.74.12
1663.74.9
1707.74.10
1714.74.11

75. Tankas

973.75.1
975.75.2
1205.75.9
1209.75.6
1235.75.4
1243.75.7
1251.75.8
1287.75.10
1455.75.3
1561.75.11
1631.75.12
1705.75.5

76. Avatars

335.76.1
405.76.6
437.76.2
733.76.8
800.76.9
911.76.5
923.76.3
1389.76.7
1399.76.10
1535.76.11
1541.76.12
1614.76.4

77. Grammar

871.77.1
887.77.3
893.77.4
901.77.5
919.77.6
943.77.7
967.77.8
1165.77.10
1169.77.11
1173.77.12
1557.77.2
1587.77.9

78. Accidents

315.78.2
429.78.4
539.78.9
579.78.7
661.78.3
1051.78.11
1109.78.8
1292.78.6
1461.78.1
1549.78.12
1605.78.5
1702.78.10

79. Oddities

890.79.6
897.79.8
1185.79.11
1195.79.9
1201.79.10
1261.79.2
1343.79.12
1357.79.7
1395.79.4
1442.79.1
1453.79.5
1669.79.3

80. Cinquains

1339.80.1
1375.80.2
1421.80.4
1477.80.5
1483.80.6
1489.80.9
1543.80.8
1559.80.3
1597.80.11
1611.80.7
1617.80.12
1655.80.10

81. Titles

689.81.1
695.81.2
1015.81.3
1073.81.7
1075.81.6
1087.81.8
1145.81.9
1319.81.10
1327.81.4
1415.81.12
1627.81.5
1653.81.11

82. Moncton

104.82.2
312.82.1
678.82.6
1072.82.10
1282.82.9
1396.82.7
1510.82.5
1528.82.8
1546.82.3
1558.82.11
1610.82.12
1634.82.4

83. Bliss and Colours

319.83.5
347.83.3
535.83.2
549.83.8
551.83.1
559.83.4
595.83.7
631.83.6
637.83.11
675.83.9
693.83.10
701.83.12

84. History

152.84.7
1018.84.1
1020.84.2
1030.84.3
1042.84.4
1054.84.5
1064.84.6
1074.84.8
1089.84.9
1095.84.10
1157.84.11
1252.84.12

85. The Stock Market

1408.85.1
1418.85.3
1426.85.2
1430.85.4
1436.85.5
1438.85.6
1532.85.7
1574.85.11
1600.85.8
1703.85.9
1710.85.10
1720.85.12

86. Apologies

580.86.10
820.86.1
828.86.2
978.86.6
997.86.4
1120.86.12
1298.86.7
1491.86.3
1502.86.11
1516.86.9
1592.86.8
1656.86.5

87. The Body

112.87.3
178.87.1
290.87.2
300.87.4
472.87.8
819.87.11
984.87.10
1028.87.5
1068.87.6
1070.87.7
1102.87.12
1487.87.9

88. Freedom

28.88.10
102.88.1
656.88.6
1031.88.4
1134.88.3
1244.88.8
1263.88.9
1429.88.12
1580.88.5
1588.88.7
1594.88.11
1685.88.2

89. Irritants

187.89.1
317.89.2
353.89.4
533.89.3
703.89.6
1057.89.10
1092.89.5
1266.89.9
1379.89.12
1431.89.11
1490.89.8
1667.89.7

90. Letters

257.90.1
285.90.2
571.90.12
735.90.10
1155.90.4
1175.90.5
1197.90.8
1215.90.6
1229.90.7
1241.90.11
1331.90.3
1341.90.9

91. The Poet

1129.91.11
1154.91.1
1156.91.2
1158.91.3
1162.91.4
1166.91.5
1174.91.6
1184.91.7
1186.91.8
1192.91.9
1198.91.12
1673.91.10

92. Questions Without Answers

89.92.9
384.92.3
402.92.1
729.92.2
875.92.4
1034.92.8
1036.92.5
1126.92.12
1224.92.10
1369.92.6
1397.92.11
1475.92.7

93. Time

10.93.6
40.93.7
964.93.12
1013.93.9
1084.93.11
1111.93.10
1142.93.4
1248.93.5
1384.93.2
1440.93.3
1651.93.8
1713.93.1

94. Terry and Carmen

150.94.10
576.94.2
1152.94.1
1366.94.3
1370.94.4
1492.94.5
1494.94.6
1496.94.7
1604.94.8
1606.94.9
1670.94.11
1696.94.12

95. Additions to *La Bibliothèque idéale*

607.95.1
613.95.3
619.95.2
623.95.4
645.95.5
687.95.6
751.95.8
823.95.10
935.95.7
1047.95.11
1299.95.12
1699.95.9

96. Characters

75.96.10
389.96.2
755.96.4
1121.96.6
1269.96.5
1323.96.7
1387.96.11
1401.96.8
1437.96.12
1678.96.1
1683.96.9
1719.96.3

97. Numerals and Numbers

154.97.1
156.97.2
207.97.3
283.97.4
296.97.5
329.97.7
362.97.8
371.97.10
391.97.11
395.97.12
681.97.9
1529.97.6

98. Expressions

99.98.5
232.98.9
499.98.12
643.98.1
715.98.10
741.98.2
876.98.6
883.98.7
1225.98.11
1296.98.4
1486.98.3
1727.98.8

99. Names

7.99.3
569.99.2
573.99.1
759.99.5
917.99.10
1005.99.6
1055.99.11
1083.99.12
1151.99.7
1629.99.9
1694.99.8
1723.99.4

100. Proverbs

244.100.4
254.100.2
262.100.3
270.100.6
272.100.5
280.100.7
282.100.12
298.100.1
1222.100.9
1226.100.10
1228.100.11
1635.100.8

101. Duos

538.101.1
650.101.8
726.101.2
730.101.3
972.101.6
1004.101.7
1112.101.12
1150.101.5
1180.101.9
1264.101.11
1530.101.10
1586.101.4

102. The Trio

62.102.12
988.102.1
990.102.2
994.102.3
1000.102.4
1002.102.5
1008.102.6
1010.102.7
1210.102.9
1220.102.8
1590.102.10
1680.102.11

103. Disappearances

148.103.1
172.103.8
713.103.6
722.103.2
1032.103.7
1118.103.5
1258.103.3
1305.103.4
1470.103.11
1506.103.12
1512.103.9
1575.103.10

104. Worries

84.104.2
177.104.5
198.104.3
671.104.1
744.104.9
989.104.7
1026.104.4
1321.104.11
1351.104.12
1542.104.10
1583.104.6
1618.104.8

105. Reserves/ Reservations

153.105.10
419.105.7
717.105.9
1067.105.1
1206.105.3
1246.105.6
1285.105.2
1354.105.5
1433.105.8
1498.105.4
1599.105.12
1675.105.11

106. Customs

606.106.6
737.106.10
794.106.1
896.106.9
1012.106.8
1088.106.2
1128.106.5
1236.106.11
1309.106.7
1507.106.3
1560.106.4
1681.106.12

107. Necessities

380.107.1
813.107.6
977.107.5
1234.107.2
1345.107.12
1373.107.3
1479.107.7
1495.107.8
1513.107.10
1527.107.11
1601.107.4
1721.107.9

108. Rumours

115.108.8
1127.108.11
1286.108.1
1302.108.2
1334.108.3
1338.108.6
1456.108.5
1520.108.7
1602.108.9
1630.108.10
1658.108.12
1716.108.4

109. Dreams

426.109.8
561.109.3
642.109.6
740.109.9
1104.109.4
1303.109.7
1452.109.12
1462.109.2
1499.109.10
1625.109.11
1644.109.5
1690.109.1

110. A Day Off

563.110.2
1358.110.1
1378.110.3
1382.110.4
1390.110.5
1398.110.6
1412.110.7
1423.110.8
1434.110.12
1672.110.9
1698.110.10
1700.110.11

111. Tools

827.111.1
831.111.4
838.111.7
859.111.2
903.111.3
914.111.10
1027.111.9
1223.111.6
1249.111.12
1579.111.8
1693.111.5
1709.111.11

112. Languages

85.112.1
1037.112.6
1101.112.2
1107.112.3
1119.112.11
1133.112.7
1143.112.8
1161.112.9
1403.112.5
1485.112.4
1525.112.12
1661.112.10

113. Collections

620.113.7
986.113.2
992.113.1
996.113.3
998.113.5
1191.113.4
1208.113.9
1242.113.8
1274.113.6
1340.113.10
1347.113.11
1458.113.12

114. Inventions

779.114.5
1227.114.12
1276.114.6
1278.114.4
1308.114.1
1310.114.2
1314.114.3
1337.114.9
1368.114.7
1443.114.10
1471.114.8
1642.114.11

115. Catherine and Chico

1388.115.1
1392.115.2
1402.115.3
1410.115.4
1414.115.5
1416.115.6
1422.115.7
1428.115.8
1432.115.9
1446.115.10
1450.115.11
1454.115.12

116. True or False

663.116.5
685.116.2
723.116.4
867.116.7
1086.116.6
1091.116.1
1159.116.8
1271.116.3
1344.116.10
1407.116.12
1581.116.11
1615.116.9

117. Death

344.117.1
469.117.3
479.117.12
608.117.4
1096.117.5
1137.117.10
1140.117.7
1212.117.8
1254.117.6
1306.117.2
1704.117.11
1712.117.9

118. Concerning Yellow

1079.118.1
1093.118.2
1103.118.3
1131.118.4
1167.118.8
1179.118.7
1182.118.9
1200.118.6
1207.118.5
1257.118.11
1281.118.12
1451.118.10

119. Music

1190.119.1
1196.119.2
1204.119.3
1216.119.4
1232.119.5
1250.119.6
1260.119.7
1284.119.8
1304.119.9
1316.119.10
1332.119.12
1577.119.11

120. Fictionary

421.120.6
593.120.1
639.120.9
743.120.4
781.120.7
783.120.8
809.120.12
991.120.5
1061.120.11
1217.120.10
1277.120.2
1553.120.3

121. Things to Want

815.121.9
1245.121.2
1289.121.11
1385.121.12
1393.121.4
1473.121.10
1534.121.1
1539.121.7
1562.121.6
1573.121.3
1609.121.8
1717.121.5

122. Sports

757.122.3
775.122.2
785.122.5
843.122.1
853.122.7
857.122.6
922.122.9
979.122.8
1136.122.4
1211.122.12
1280.122.11
1518.122.10

123. Carmen and Étienne

1052.123.1
1060.123.2
1062.123.3
1148.123.9
1160.123.4
1170.123.5
1172.123.6
1176.123.7
1194.123.10
1474.123.11
1692.123.8
1708.123.12

124. Religion

536.124.1
870.124.2
899.124.6
1022.124.3
1038.124.4
1040.124.5
1080.124.9
1300.124.7
1439.124.8
1636.124.10
1638.124.11
1691.124.12

125. Sexuality

498.125.1
596.125.6
1336.125.2
1348.125.3
1457.125.10
1578.125.4
1584.125.7
1628.125.8
1637.125.5
1650.125.9
1674.125.12
1688.125.11

126. Techniques

632.126.11
787.126.5
845.126.1
849.126.9
880.126.6
982.126.2
1006.126.12
1262.126.3
1363.126.7
1420.126.8
1596.126.4
1679.126.10

127. Tactics

584.127.11
789.127.2
841.127.12
906.127.9
947.127.4
1231.127.1
1267.127.5
1427.127.6
1448.127.7
1465.127.3
1500.127.8
1623.127.10

128. Fervours

155.128.12
707.128.8
791.128.2
981.128.3
1069.128.5
1178.128.11
1239.128.9
1411.128.6
1545.128.7
1555.128.1
1607.128.10
1695.128.4

129. Fantasies

526.129.11
567.129.10
793.129.3
949.129.8
1056.129.2
1255.129.4
1328.129.9
1359.129.5
1381.129.6
1469.129.12
1567.129.1
1706.129.7

130. Work

12.130.8
58.130.12
166.130.3
1333.130.2
1352.130.4
1371.130.6
1376.130.5
1409.130.7
1522.130.11
1550.130.10
1576.130.1
1621.130.9

131. Parenthesi(e)s

57.131.4
113.131.1
504.131.3
513.131.5
543.131.8
591.131.9
719.131.6
948.131.7
1163.131.11
1275.131.12
1509.131.2
1665.131.10

132. Malapropism

1049.132.4
1071.132.8
1077.132.11
1085.132.3
1099.132.1
1147.132.10
1221.132.7
1313.132.9
1463.132.12
1563.132.5
1593.132.2
1684.132.6

133. The Future

44.133.5
222.133.3
378.133.2
974.133.4
1400.133.7
1482.133.11
1536.133.10
1548.133.8
1619.133.6
1626.133.1
1666.133.9
1726.133.12

134. Marianne

50.134.8
132.134.1
934.134.2
1288.134.12
1346.134.7
1362.134.3
1372.134.4
1374.134.5
1404.134.6
1419.134.11
1523.134.10
1552.134.9

135. Zed and Chico

1082.135.3
1138.135.2
1164.135.9
1272.135.5
1318.135.1
1484.135.7
1504.135.8
1544.135.10
1612.135.4
1624.135.6
1632.135.11
1664.135.12

136. The Unavowed

761.136.2
765.136.3
767.136.1
773.136.4
795.136.5
829.136.6
833.136.7
835.136.8
993.136.9
995.136.10
999.136.11
1671.136.12

137. Fears

138.137.9
532.137.1
542.137.3
590.137.6
618.137.4
752.137.12
780.137.2
1108.137.5
1240.137.7
1406.137.11
1478.137.8
1538.137.10

138. The Other

107.138.1
313.138.2
679.138.3
683.138.4
691.138.5
697.138.6
699.138.7
705.138.8
777.138.9
803.138.12
965.138.10
1132.138.11

139. Étienne and Chico

1094.139.5
1124.139.8
1294.139.6
1488.139.2
1526.139.10
1564.139.9
1568.139.7
1608.139.11
1676.139.3
1682.139.4
1718.139.1
1724.139.12

140. Caraquet

464.140.4
470.140.5
658.140.7
839.140.11
1117.140.1
1146.140.6
1189.140.8
1620.140.3
1622.140.2
1660.140.9
1662.140.12
1722.140.10

141. Obsessions

199.141.6
818.141.1
938.141.2
954.141.7
1014.141.8
1090.141.5
1268.141.4
1364.141.9
1380.141.3
1386.141.10
1645.141.12
1686.141.11